Sunshine, Sex & Easy Money

Sunshine, Sex
&
Easy Money

Diary of a Call Girl

Maria van Daarten

Maria van Daarten
c/o AutorenService.de
König-Konrad-Str. 22
36039 Fulda
maria.van.daarten@freenet.de

Translated by: buchuebersetzer.webs.com

ISBN: 978-1-54-9732133
ISBN-13: 978-1549732133

Dedicated to Violet

1

As a teenager, I planned to leave the country village I grew up in someday. At the age of 19, I married a German soldier and we moved to a nearby small town. – Although this was the first step, I always dreamed about living in a place others go for vacation. Years later, I found myself single again and quite dissatisfied with my present life. So, I have decided to take responsibility for my future even if it means giving up certain securities and accepting risks. My goal is this: I want to live in the sun and by the sea. I want to work less, schedule my own hours, and yet still make a good living. But above all, I no longer want to keep my profession secret, considering this is what I have been doing. For many years, I have been working as a part-time prostitute. And a working girl does not just come out and profess to her family she is a prostitute. Even friends and acquaintances are kept in the dark. Who would want a prostitute as a daughter, sister, partner, or friend?

I do not know anyone! – Through the years, this part-time job has filled my wallet so I could afford things and, moreover, set money aside. I belong to those people who need financial security in order to enjoy spending money. And so, I pursue my goal of establishing myself as a self-employed female escort. Given the fact that the rural area where I live is unsuitable and since I am uncertain I can keep my work secret in major German cities, I pack two suitcases and fly to Athens. The city is far enough away from my former surroundings that it allows me to work in this profession without being recognized – not to mention, it is near the sea!

Initially, I rent a room in a small, relatively inexpensive hotel in Athens' Piraeus district. In order to obtain local information about my profession, I buy the English weekly newspaper, *Athens World*, and find what I am looking for in the classifieds: In the 'Escort' section, women advertise sexual pleasures for sale. Carefully, I read all the ads and decide to call a woman who goes by the name 'Lovely English Lady'. Unlike many others, she does not advertise she is young or a model, thus, I hope she might be a bit older because I am too. I am 42, in essence, considered past my prime — although it did not hamper my professional success in recent years. After all, I sell myself as a 35-year-old. It is an extremely attractive age. Many young men crave sex with women in their mid-thirties and a large number of older men lust after those other than young girls. Therefore, in principle, I am the perfect age to establish myself as a self-employed prostitute who earns good money. I consider myself good-looking with long blonde hair, blue eyes, a slim figure, groomed appearance, charm, and I am always well dressed. Plus, I can be quite sexy and flirtatious when I want. – I rarely encounter problems passing myself off as thirty-some years old.

I dial 'Lovely English Lady's' cell number and she picks up with a friendly:

"Hello!"

"Hello! My name is Anika. I'm new to Athens and I would love to work here as a call girl. I wanted to ask if you could provide me with information on local rates, hotels, and so on."

"Oh!" A brief pause. "What's your nationality?"

"I'm German."

"Are you here by yourself?"

"Yes."

"How old are you?"

"Forty-two."

"And you've already worked in this trade?"

"Yes, for many years, but only part-time. Any chance we can meet in person? Perhaps at a café, that way we can have coffee while we chat?"

Another brief pause. "I need to think about it. Call me back early tomorrow morning. Bye!"

The line goes dead. I understand her cautiousness. She does not know if I am the person I make myself out to be. I could be the wife of a client who discovered her phone number on the husband's cell phone. – There are numerous possibilities. Therefore, I do not mind waiting while she makes up her mind. I see another interesting ad about an escort service posted in *Athens World*. Perhaps I could learn some vital information about my future profession if I call and pretend I am applying for a position. I dial the listed number and a woman's voice answers in Greek.

"Excuse me, do you speak English?" I ask politely.

"Yes, of course! This is *Seven Heaven* escort service. How may I help you?"

"Hello. My name is Gaby. I'm German, 35, and interested in joining your escort service."

"Have you ever done something like this before? Do you have any experience as a prostitute?"

"Yes, more than 10 years."

"Where are you right now?"

"In Athens."

"Uh, hold on a second. — Would you be willing to meet me? I would have to see you in person before I can reveal details. You said you're 35... that's no longer young!"

"I know, but perhaps once you meet me my age will be less important. I can meet you at any time."

"Great. Our office is located in the city center. Could you be at the Café Rena in two hours? It's catty-corner from the Akropoli Subway Station."

"Yes, I can be there around 4 p.m."

"Great. See you later, Gaby. Your name is Gaby, correct?"

"Yes, and what is your name?"

"Oh, sorry, I'm Elena! Okay, see you in a couple hours!"

"Okay, Elena, I'm looking forward to meeting you!"

I look at the clock and realize there is no time to waste. I have to doll myself up. I decide on a red, sleeveless, knee-length sheath dress. It is chic and emphasizes my figure. Even though I do not want to work for the escort service, I want to make a good impression so I can get as much information as possible. It will come in handy for my own business. As it is one of those days again where my hair has a mind of its own, I bend over and brush it vigorously. Returning upright, I comb it out, leaving a lot of volume while styling it into a lion's mane and applying hairspray for good measure. I apply makeup so my blue eyes pop, but omit lipstick. All that is missing is a spritz of my favorite perfume, *Must de Cartier*. Checking myself from all angles in the mirror, I know I have done my best. I slip into my red pumps, grab my little gold purse, and leave the hotel.

I hail a cab and the surly driver drops me off near the Akropoli station, demanding 19 euros for the fare. Glancing at my watch, I realize I have plenty of time. First, I locate the café where I am to meet Elena and then stroll around the area. This is the Plaka, Athens' old town, with narrow streets, shops, and restaurants. I make sure to remain on the shady side of the road because the sun is unbearably hot. At 2:50 p.m. I enter Café Rena and sit at one of the small round tables.

Considering the scorching outside temperature, it is pleasant inside the air-conditioned room. The waitress comes and l order a Diet Coke. Never beverages with sugar! They only go to the hips. A small woman with short, black hair enters the café and looks around. Seeing me, she nods and I nod back. It must be Elena. She approaches the table and greets me with a handshake.

"Hello, I'm Elena."

"I'm Gaby, nice to meet you, Elena. Thank you for taking the time to meet with me."

"Of course. Our escort service is always interested in a new face. So, you live in Athens?"

"Not at the moment. I'm only here for a week to check out the area. I'm thinking of moving here for good this fall — sometime in September."

"Okay! Well, you certainly are pretty and have a good figure. You obviously take care of yourself, but then there's your age. You're already 35. I mean, you are 35 or are you older?"

"I'm actually 38, but I advertise myself as 35, which I have no problem getting away with."

Elena laughs.

"Well, it's not like it's uncommon in our industry. We all lie about our age. Most of the women working for us are actually much younger than you. You would be the oldest on the team. It doesn't matter though, it's not like you work together. Okay, let's say I take photos of you and add them to our catalog. In return, we expect our ladies to work full-time and be reachable at all hours. – At times, you might be expected somewhere within one hour after a client's call. How you manage that with your family is your business. Let's say you get a call from us and we give you the client's address, telephone number, and time of the appointment. How you get there at the appropriate time, either by taxi, public transportation, or with your own car, is entirely up to you. Just make sure you're on time. It's extremely important. An appointment is usually 45 minutes to one hour. We provide safe sex in all possible positions, as well as oral sex without a condom."

The waitress arrives at the table and Elena orders a coffee frappe with lots of sugar and milk. Then she continues:

"The customer pays you the price we've agreed on, usually 200 euros an hour. Anal is extra. These details aren't important right now. In any case, you take the money home. The next day, at the latest, you give us half. – We can arrange a meeting by phone or we can send a messenger to your home. – That's entirely up to you. Remember, half the money is ours! Naturally, any tips you receive from clients are yours to keep. If a client happens to asks for anal intercourse or an additional hour of service without prior arrangement with us, you must add on the extra charges. However, once again, half of that money is ours. Trying to keep extra services secret will do you no good because we always confer with our clients to ensure they're satisfied with our service!"

Elena sips her coffee and lights a cigarette.

"Okay, so far so good. I'm accustomed to such working conditions from Germany. What other services does *Seven Heaven* offer their clientele?"

"Quite a few. We try to cover any possible wishes a client might ask for, – but obviously, no pedophilia or any other criminal sexual practices. That brings me to my next questions. So, what do you do? What can you do? What languages do you speak?"

"I speak German, English, Dutch, and a little French. I've worked as a dominatrix among other things and can role-play. How much do you charge for domination? Or for role playing?"

"Now and then we have a client who likes to be dominated, but it's uncommon for Greek men. They prefer to be in charge. They're all macho guys. You never know what a client might ask for and we'd be happy to use another lady who can take care of such services. We charge 400 euros for a domination session and 300 for any role-playing games. In each case, you keep half the fee!"

"Okay. I have another question, Elena. Am I reimbursed for travel expenses?"

"No, you pay that cost. We pay for all advertisements, some of which are in English newspapers, others in Greek, and on the Internet. We'll schedule appointments and provide you with steady work. You simply do your job and earn a good income without having to do much else. Easy money!"

"Sounds good, Elena. I guess now it depends on whether you, well, actually the escort service you work for, would hire me, come September."

"Gaby! I don't think it will be a problem. Make sure you don't let yourself go. Always be well groomed and do everything the client asks of you. The client is king! This is important to us. Stick to what we agreed to with the client by phone. No rejections! You must accept every client even if he's fat, ugly, repulsive, or stinks. Since starting this business, we've been trying over the years to build up a clientele list of pleasant and friendly men. And I think we've succeeded. The well-being of our employees is of great importance to us. We do not tolerate any mistreatment of our women! Well, I guess we can talk about the other formalities in September. What do you say?"

Since I've received all the information I want, I reply:

"Great! It sounds like a plan. I'll call you when I'm back for good in September. Thank you so much for seeing me, Elena!"

"My pleasure. Your Coke is on me!" she says while reaching into her purse.

"Thank you!" I reply and grab my handbag. Elena places a few bills on the table. We stand and leave the café together. Out on the sidewalk, we exchange a last glance and go our separate ways.

The next morning, I give 'Lovely English Lady' another call. She is friendly and tells me she has decided to meet me. I note the suggested café's address and agree to a time. That afternoon I take a bus to Glyfada, a southern area of Athens located directly on the coast. Since I am not familiar with the place, I hail a taxi and give the driver the address. On the phone, we discussed how we would recognize each other and she said, 'I have long blonde hair'. 'Me too', I replied.

At a table on the café patio, I do not have to wait long before a medium-size blonde flits around the tables, her handbag dangling from one hand, her eyes searching. When her gaze falls on me, I make a small hand gesture. She walks slowly toward me, her eyes looking me up and down.

"Hi, darling!" She greets me warmly. "I'm Violet."

"Hi, I'm Anika. My real name is Ilona. Thank you for seeing me!"

"Let's call each other by our aliases. That'll be fine!"

She sits and looks around suspiciously. I quickly assure her I am who I say I am and that I came alone. I estimate she is about my age, perhaps even a few years older. She orders black tea and starts asking all kinds of questions: Where I live, how long I plan on staying, do I have a family, etc. — Since lying never accomplishes anything, nor do I have reason to, I answer truthfully. Granted, when it comes to our profession, it is different, because who reveals their real name, their actual age, or true origin? Furthermore, I want information from her; possibly, even make a friend among colleagues. Such objectives require honesty, even among prostitutes. We like each other right from the get-go. She tells me she has been working in Athens for more than 15 years and has established a large customer base while only advertising in *Athens World*. At times, she does business in hotels but prefers working in her home. Her usual rate is 150-euros per hour. She only practices safe sex, no anal. The majority of her clients are Greeks. However, she is frequently contacted by businessmen from around the world when they are in town. She typically meets them at their hotel. Those she is already better acquainted with can come to her home. Her cell phone rings once. She looks around nervously, gets up, answers, and starts pacing while talking to the other party. I only hear: "Hi, darling, how are you?" When she returns to the table, she nonchalantly says:

"I just made an appointment for Monday morning with Christo, one of my regulars. I've known him for many years. He always sees me on a Monday or Thursday, but he can only afford 60 euros. Considering you'll be new here, you might want to be flexible now and then. Not every Greek can pay 150 euros. Not in this crisis! Make sure you do not to give tourists or businessmen you meet in upper-class hotels a break. The cheap Bulgarian and Russian whores you find loitering in the streets or the drug addicts sell themselves for way less. For as little as 30 euros, I've heard. Moreover, they practice all sorts of unprotected sex. Disgusting!"

Violet tells me all about the no-tell hotels in Athens where I can conduct my business and arrange to meet my clients. She also reveals that although in Greece prostitution is illegal when independently exercised, it is still commonly practiced and tolerated. Granted, there is still a need to avoid the police. So far, she has been fortunate. She tells me about her earlier years when she frequently went to upper-class hotel bars to find clients. Reminiscing must have put her in the mood because she asks me if I want to go fishing with her one evening.

"Together, we'll be more successful. Let's say there's a man who wants both of us. We each charge 100 instead of 150 euros. That's still good money for us."

She cannot stop talking. I am flattered by her frankness. I have never done anything like fishing before. So far, I've only worked in a bar and various clubs. At one time, I had a well-paid relationship. I met the respectable man in a hotel and now and then, he took me out for the evening. I am excited Violet has invited me to go fishing and that we will do something together. We chat for quite a while longer and before we say goodbye, we agree to meet the next evening at 8 p.m. in the town square in Glyfada.

Meeting Violet made me extremely happy. Now I know enough to establish myself as a self-employed call girl in Athens!

2

The following afternoon, I lay out the clothes I want to wear for my evening out with Violet. I choose a short, figure-accentuating, black summer dress and matching black, high heels. In addition to the usual stuff I keep in my little handbag, I pack four condoms, a small vial of massage oil, and a second pair of panties. It should suffice for this evening. At 7 p.m., I leave for the bus station. It is mid-June and quite hot. I feel I am in great shape for my first fishing expedition! The bus stops directly at the town square in Glyfada. I get out and cross the street to a square adorned with tall pine trees, flowerbeds, and park benches in various spots. At the other side of the town square, directly in front of me, are fashion boutiques, cafés, a Greek electronic shop, and a large department store. Looking around, it does not take me long to find Violet. She is wearing a light red dress that, although it is longer than mine, accentuates her figure. For her age, she looks quite sexy with her long, blonde hair and matching red lipstick. Men who notice her turn around and stare at her. We greet each other with pecks on the cheeks and since it is still too early to go fishing, we stroll down Metaxa Street with its many fashion boutiques. Violet has already planned the evening for us and wants to take me to a prestigious hotel where she cast her net in the past. She says it is not only frequented by tourists but businessmen also. The hotel barman, Michalis, knows her profession and looks the other way because on previous occasions she always tipped him when she went with a hotel guest to his room.

Since I do not know Glyfada or the hotels businessmen stay at, I unquestioningly place myself in Violet's hands and agree to go later with her to the Ammas Hotel. I feel elated and free as we stroll down the street window-shopping and gabbing. Relishing that I have left the small town out in the countryside where I spent most of my life, I am convinced I can handle whatever occupational and private challenges this strange land might have in store for me.

The Ammas Hotel is a good 500 meters away from the Glyfada town square. Around 9 p.m., we slowly head for the hotel while exchanging all kinds of information from our professional and private lives. Violet also left her home because she had been afraid of not being able to keep her work as a prostitute secret. Once she was far from home, she felt secure working as a call girl because her unfamiliarity of the place provided her with a certain distance to her social environment.

As we enter the hotel foyer, I marvel at its luxurious furnishings. No hotel back home out in the country comes even close. Most are small, family operated businesses whose clientele mainly consists of relatives or friends of the farmers living in the surrounding area, not wealthy businessmen. And, I have never stayed in such a luxurious hotel during any of my previous vacations. — We take the elevator to the top floor of the Ammas Hotel and step out onto a rooftop terrace featuring a bar, tables and chairs, and a swimming pool. I am taken aback seeing a swimming pool built into the roof of the hotel! Violet laughs at me and my apparent naiveté at my age. We head for the bar where two middle-aged men sit enjoying their drinks watching a sports program on the TV set on one of the bar's back shelves.

Here and there, tables are occupied by couples and families. No singles. Michalis, the bartender, immediately recognizes Violet and greets her warmly. She introduces me as her German girlfriend and asks if the hotel is busy. Michalis confirms this and tells her they have businessmen as well as vacationers from America, South Africa, and England.

Since the bar is L shaped and the two men are sitting along the long leg, we sit at the short one so they have a good view of us. Obviously, this is Violet's idea. We each order a freshly squeezed orange juice and then Violet clues me in:

"I've chosen these seats not only so those two men notice us, but anyone who uses the facilities. See, the bathrooms are right around the corner!"

I admire Violet for her shrewd tactics. The two men have already looked at us with apparent interest. Violet and I converse quietly and giggle every now and then. I am quite curious how the evening will un-fold. Are we going to approach the two men or do we wait for them to make a move? As Violet is experienced in fishing, I patiently wait instead of bugging her with needless questions. Besides, it is not the end of the world if we do not lure a catch into our net. For me, it is a great practice run. – Violet and I are getting to know each other a bit better, which is fine with me for our first evening out. From time to time, Violet looks over at the men and gives whoever makes eye con-tact a lovely, charming smile. From the men's perspective, they might think Violet is interested. It gives them hope. For conversation? A flirtation? Sex? In the places where I previously worked, it was perfectly clear what was what, but this current situation makes me insecure. However, I say to myself, this is merely a different playing field. This game might start differently, but it ends the same way — getting paid for sex. So, Ilona, stay calm and don't panic! I might not sit here in sexy lingerie and openly advertise myself, but my chic little summer dress also makes me look sexy and flirtatious. Over an hour passes during which nothing happens. Michalis turns off the TV that captured the two gentlemen's attention. The older of the two men gets up and as he passes us on his way to the bathroom, he greets us warmly in English, inclines his head, and smiles. Another guest steps onto the rooftop terrace and strolls up to the bar. He looks to be in his mid-fifties and is tall, muscular, with short dark hair, and a cleanly shaven face. He orders a drink from Michalis and starts up a conversation. That is when Michalis looks over at us and the new guest follows his gaze. As he smiles at us, Violet whispers to me:

"He could be a candidate. We could share him if it doesn't work out with those other two." She leans in even closer and whispers in my ear: "If he goes for it, we'll each ask for 100 euros, but we won't give him lesbian hanky-panky. I'm not into that!"

"Fine with me."

When the gray-haired man returns from the bathroom, he smiles at us again and quickly continues to his buddy where they end up in a deep conversation.

Meanwhile, Violet has set her eyes on the new guest. Every now and then, I find the courage to look over at him and smile shyly. Just then, he picks up his drink and walks over to us.

"Hi! I'm Jack. May I join you?"

"Certainly," I answer much too quickly.

Violet offers him her hand and says:

"I'm Violet and this is my friend Anika."

Jack also shakes my hand and says:

"Pleased to meet you!"

Pulling a barstool closer at an equal distance between Violet and me, he sits down. – Crossing my legs, my dress rides up and effectively exposes the lower half of one of my tanned thighs. My gesture is immediately rewarded with a smile.

"May I buy you ladies a drink?" asks Jack. He orders our requested vodkas that we mix into our orange juice.

"Here's to you, my lovelies!" he says and we clink glasses. It seems we have a fish in our net! My instinct tells me this man does not merely want idle chitchat at the bar, he also wants sex. It is simply a question of whether he knows he will have to pay for it. I have no idea if Michalis implied something when he ordered his drink. Jack asks what we are doing in Athens and if we are on vacation.

"No, we live and work here," replies Violet without hesitation.

Naturally, he now asks what we do for a living, but before I have a chance to voice something inappropriate, Violet beats me to it:

"Anika dances and I give massages!"

As she says this, she moves her hands in a slightly rotating way with the fingers spread and looks enticingly at Jack. Wow! That was quite obvious. I am stunned by her courage to be so up-front with a stranger without even blushing. Instead, Jack seems to be momentarily embarrassed and at a loss for words. Hesitantly, he replies:

"Oh, how interesting!"

Not surprising Violet does not leave it at that and breathes in a seductive voice:

"It's our day off – but we're always up for a little dancing or massaging."

She starts moving to the music playing quietly from the rooftop speakers while still sitting on the barstool.

"Isn't that right?" she asks me.

"Absolutely," I reply while attempting a coquettish smile.

"Well, here's to your evening off!" says Jack and raises his tumbler with whiskey again. I still cannot get over how casually Violet proposed a little dance and massage to him.

"So, what're you doing in Athens?" I ask out of sheer embarrassment.

"I'm a traveling salesman. The company I work for manufactures nautical radar systems that I sell here in Greece. — But let's not talk about my work, I came here to forget about work!"

"I'm sure we can help you with that," replies Violet quickly, and once again, I'm amazed at her boldness. I cannot wait to see how Violet talks him into taking us up to his room for a little remuneration. I myself cannot think of anything, not to mention, I do not want to say something stupid and spoil everything. Violet nonchalantly steers the conversation to trivial things, from the summer in Athens to Athens' Plaka, to the restaurants in the Plaka, to the prices they ask, and, finally, to the current ongoing crisis. During all of this, we order another round of drinks and maintain a laid-back atmosphere. Obviously, the vodka helps. It tastes great and relaxes me. My self-confidence is back. The fish is snared with no way to escape! Now it is a question of how much it will bring in. Violet nudges one of my knees to let me know it is time for a bathroom break. I grab my bag from the hook under the bar counter and we excuse ourselves. Once inside the bathroom, Violet touches up her lips and says:

"Now we have to find a way of getting into his room. It's best if we don't waste any more time. – I mean, we don't want to get too drunk."

"Sounds good. But I leave the reeling in of the fish to you. I'm sure you've noticed I haven't contributed much."

"Yes I have, but it doesn't matter. You'll learn! Don't worry about it, — let's go!"

She nudges me slightly with her elbow while giggling like a little girl. I quickly inspect my eye makeup before we return to the bar. Jack is speaking with Michalis. As we sit back down on our barstools, Violet asks:

"Jack, darling, are you staying in this hotel?"

"Yes," he replies, "I am. Why do you ask?"

"Maybe you're in the mood for a little party, just the three of us?"

A brief pause. — Jack takes another sip of his whiskey.

"I sure am..." he says slowly while looking questioningly at Violet with raised eyebrows. Oh God, I am so glad Violet is in charge and I do not have to speak. I could never talk with a stranger about this subject in such a direct manner! Violet leans forward, softly places her right hand on Jack's thigh, gives him an enchanting smile, and then whispers:

"That's great, darling, now we only wish for you to be generous. – What do you say?"

Jack places his hand on hers and briefly looks over at me and asks:

"How generous would I have to be?"

"As it's our day off, we can be generous too. Say 200 euros for the both of us."

I cannot believe her confidence, right to the point without a fuss! Jack scratches his head and makes a face, one I do not like, — but then his eyebrows shoot up again and he looks content:

"It's a deal! I deserve a treat every now and then. I'll order us another round and then we can go up to my room."

"Great, darling, thank you!" replies Violet.

Instead of looking triumphant, she continues in her youthful, charming, and cheerful way and talks about Greek music. Before I know it, she has us engaged in lighthearted conversation again as if nothing happened.

Now that the deal is sealed, I regain my confidence. The unfamiliar part, the part about fishing, is over. Now the party girl in me can come out and get to work. As I get ready to re-cross my legs, I purposefully spread my thighs slowly before lifting a leg over so Jack gets a good look. A little, up-front treat for him. Our drink order arrives and Michalis serves them without letting on that he is aware of Jack's and our business. We clink glasses again and then Violet leans close to Jack and whispers in his ear:

"Tell us your room number. Then, finish your drink and say goodbye to us so the other guests think you're leaving alone. We'll leave five to ten minutes after you. — In the meantime, freshen up so we can spoil you properly."

She winks at him.

"I'm in room 617," replies Jack, "it's on the sixth floor, next to the elevator."

Visibly excited, he downs his drink and asks for the bill. Once he pays, he gets up, nods at us, and with one last look at my exposed thigh, he finally says goodbye. Violet glances at her watch and pays the bathroom another visit. We wait five minutes before paying for our orange juice and Michalis wishes us a nice evening. Violet hands him a ten-euro tip that he takes with a smile and a thankful nod.

3

As we enter the elevator, I say to Violet:

"You really handled this magnificently. Wow! I hope I haven't come across as too inept."

"No, everything's fine. I was only that courageous because you were with me! My God, more than twenty years ago, when I first came to Greece, something like this was merely a game that brought in easy money. You wouldn't believe how crazy Greek men were about blondes and everyone had money to take one to bed. I was here on vacation with a friend and we were quite naughty girls. We did it wherever, in an olive orchard, at the beach, in the car. — We took more money home than we came with. The men we met paid for our drinks, food, and lodging – not one of them were stingy as long as they could flirt, kiss, touch us, or perhaps even have a little tumble."

The elevator reaches the sixth floor. We get out and Violet whispers to me:

"Remember! No lesbian games, only safe sex. No anal for me, but if you want to accommodate him go right ahead, that's your business."

"I remember! And just so you know, I'm also not into anal sex."

It has been quite a while since Violet serviced a client with another woman. She has been working alone for many years and prefers it that way, regardless of the fact that two women have it easier since the man wears out faster. We knock on door 617. Jack opens it wearing only underpants. A strong, muscular man stands in front of us.

"Come on in, ladies!" he says. We follow him into the room and I ask him to put on music.

"Whatever you like," he replies. He flips through the TV channels until he finds a station playing slow, melodic music. Violet has slipped out of her dress and is wearing only a red lace bra with matching panties. Moving behind Jack, she places her hands on his shoulders and starts massaging them gently.

The three of us stand in the only open space between the bed and bathroom with not a lot of room to spare. We can all see each other in the large wall mirror in front of us. I try to find the right rhythm to the 70s music that is playing and put on a little striptease.

Once I am wearing only my black satin panties and matching high heels, I approach Jack and snuggle up to him. One of his hands immediately grabs one of my breasts while the other reaches into my panties. He angles his head to kiss me. Although kissing a customer is not one of my usual services, I let him have his way because his breath does not smell and because we caught him. Violet remains pressed up behind Jack, but is now massaging his back down to his buttocks and ending up between his thighs. The cock in his underpants is already rock hard. I stop kissing him and glide my tongue slowly down over his chest, stomach, hip, and then finally take his member deep into my mouth. Jack groans. I pull off his underpants and lick, alternating between his balls and cock.

"Oh my God!" he whispers. "You're driving me crazy!"

A few minutes later, I make eye contact with Violet and we silently communicate that it is time to steer Jack onto the bed. I remove my panties and say:

"Now it's our turn to have some fun, darling, — lie down!"

As soon as he is on his back, we crawl up to him from opposite sides and work his pole with our tongues. He is so aroused he squirms a-round on the sheets. That is the way I like men. They lose their minds and only think with their little brain. A while later, I move away from his cock and position myself over his head so my pussy hovers over his face. Urgently, he pulls me down further and starts licking me. I hold onto the headboard for support and pretend I am really enjoying his wild licking. Nevertheless, I will not go ahead and fake an orgasm. I would rather wait and see if he even needs me to. Most people assume a whore always fakes orgasms, which is why I am stingy with such a performance. When I deceive a regular client I have known for some time into thinking I like sex with him, he feels incredibly flattered. That is the reason I try to avoid faking sexual climax. I keep my moans and movements to a minimum with Jack. I turn around and notice Violet has stopped licking his cock. Presently, she is unrolling a condom over it. She gives me a sign, we change places, and I slide my wet-licked pussy onto Jacks protected cock and say:

"Ah, yeah, that feels great, baby. God, you're big. It feels so good!"

Violet kneels with her legs spread apart next to us within Jack's reach. He does not know where to look or what to touch first. As I ride him, he grabs one of my boobs with one hand and with the other, grabs Violet's breast. I am sure he would also love to fool around with her pussy. Oh well, it is his decision what to do with his two hands... Jack is horny and insatiable. He will not have a problem dishing out the agreed upon money. I am positive! I fuck him slowly and rhythmically. When he is about to explode, I get off his proud member and roll the used rubber off and replace it with a fresh one that is lying on the nightstand. I give Violet a sign and she removes Jack's hands from her tits. She then mounts and rides him, moaning urgently straightaway.

Silently, we agree it is time for him to finish. I assume the doggy-style position with my knees spread far apart so Jack can get a good look at my pussy as well as stick in his finger. He is absolutely randy and gives his best to handle both us girls. Violet fucks him faster and faster and then what must happen happens: He comes! Jack arches his back and moans aloud, his face contorted with pain. He grabs Violet's

14

hips and thrusts forcefully upward. With eyes closed, he finally slumps onto the sheets and breathes heavily, yet blissfully.

"Oh my, ladies, that was absolutely fabulous," he whispers.

We lie down, sandwiching him between us and listen to his wheezing breath. Jack wraps his arms around us and gives each of us a kiss on the forehead. Although he is exhausted, he looks happy. That is what I absolutely love: in addition to making money, I also provide somebody with real happiness! Violet offers Jack a little massage before bedtime, but he declines and says:

"It's time to throw you two out. Otherwise, I'm afraid I won't get any sleep. And I have to get up early to catch my flight to Amsterdam."

I get up and ask if I can use the bathroom. Jack nods. I slip into the shower, quickly wash, and then thoroughly rinse my mouth with antiseptic mouthwash. After wrapping myself in a bath towel, I return to the main room.

Now it is Violet's turn to disappear into the bathroom. I chat with Jack as I dress, who gets up and places two 100-euro bills on the desk. When Violet returns, he points to the money and says:

"This is for you two lovely ladies. Thank you, Anika and Violet! This was really an exciting experience for me. Can I have your phone numbers? I'm sure I'll be returning to Athens and I'd certainly like a repeat performance."

Since I am not established yet, I nod at Violet. She scribbles her cell phone number on a piece of paper with our names and a heart next to them. We thank him for his generosity and give him little pecks on the cheeks, wishing him a good night. Once we are out of the room, Violet's face turns into an expression of satisfaction. I am also satisfied, quite satisfied! After all, I have just earned my first money in Athens.

I am still amazed we caught a fish on our first evening out. –Moreover, I am greatly pleased to have met such a delightful and amiable colleague. – Exiting the Ammas Hotel, we step outside into the mild, warm evening air of Athens. We hug conspiratorially for a brief moment on the sidewalk out front before heading toward the town square in Glyfada. It is almost midnight and I have no idea if the buses still run to Piraeus at this time. Granted, I could spring for a taxi, but I am too stingy for that. Naturally, if there is no bus service, I must catch a cab. I pull a five-euro note out of my wallet and hand it to Violet, my share of Michalis' tip. Violet thanks me and says:

"That's the best way to do it, always go Dutch. To reciprocate constantly each time is plain stupid. This has nothing to do with friendship."

We chat as we walk, re-examining the night and our successful fishing trip. Violet says:

"My God, tonight I feel 20 years younger! Like when I went on vacation to the Greek islands."

I reply:

"I'm so happy I've met you. Thank you for everything, Violet!"

"Oh, think nothing of it. And don't thank me! Worry about placing an ad in *Athens World*. Believe me, if you're crafty, you can make lots of money here."

We reach the town square in Glyfada and I inspect the bus stop shedule. I am in luck; I have not missed the last bus. We quickly hug and exchange kisses. – I get in and watch Violet stroll away, swinging her little handbag. Tired, I lean my head against the back of the seat and enjoy the rocking ride back to Piraeus.

4

The little hotel I am staying at in Piraeus is located on a hill behind the Zea Marina. Standing on my balcony, looking over the houses in front, I see the circular-shaped marina with its variety of berthed boats and the vast sea beyond. Although my room is small, it features a fridge, air-conditioning, a TV, and Internet access. It is all I need for the moment.

The room rate is 35 euros per day without breakfast. Considering I want to set up shop in Athens until sometime in September, I do not want to spend more than 5000 euros in the next two months. That should leave me enough for the start-up phase. Obviously, I still need to budget my money. If I come across a cheaper hotel in a good location, I will probably move even though I am quite happy with my current accommodations. In front of the hotel is a taxi stand and a bit down the road at the Piraeus town square, a bus station servicing all areas of Athens.

This morning I have something important to do: I need to prepare my ad for *Athens World*. I go into my bathroom to get ready for my outing. Once my hair is nicely combed, my makeup decently applied, and my entire body rubbed with suntan lotion giving my skin a velvety-look, I slip into some summer clothes. I love wearing light airy clothes! It is not like there is a guarantee I can do so in Germany during the summer.

I hand in my room key at the reception desk, leave the Lilo Hotel, and walk toward the town square. Once there, I treat myself to breakfast, a Nescafé with milk and a puff pastry. Everything is so different compared to Germany, the coffee, the pastries, the heat, the hustle and bustle, and all the noisy people — simply everything. I am delighted at how great the pastry tastes that I have chosen for today's breakfast. It is called bougatsa and so I do not forget, I write it down in my notebook the way it sounds. I really must learn the Greek language and its weird alphabet so I can read words spelled out only in Greek. For example, on menus or bus stop schedules. I already learned the Greek number system on a previous vacation here. Back then, they had the drachma and it was important to me to understand the Greeks when I asked the price of whatever interested me. — It is surprising how well I retained it. I can still count to one hundred.

Finding a nice shady place under a sycamore tree, I get comfortable, take out my notebook, and try to come up with the right phrasing for the ad I want to place in *Athens World*. It is Tuesday and if I want to see my ad in this week's Friday edition, I have to submit and pay for it at the editorial office by Wednesday afternoon. I definitely do not want to

miss this week's deadline! I think about the wording and write down in my notebook:
Charming Lady from Germany would like to meet nice gentlemen ... cell phone number. — I am not happy with it and try again:
Attractive Lady from Northern Europe would like to meet nice, outgoing gentlemen who like to have fun... cell phone number. — No, that will not do either. Playing around with it in my head, I come up with this:
Incredibly attractive lady from Germany would like to meet a generous gentleman... cell phone number. — Yes, that is better. I like it. I read and reread the sentence until something even better pops into my head!
Very attractive and charming lady from Germany would like to meet a generous gentleman... cell phone number. — There, that sounds much better! I am extremely satisfied.

Paying for my breakfast, I use the opportunity to ask the waitress where I can find a cell phone service provider close by. The pretty, young Greek woman points down the road and tells me there is store not far away. In reality, I end up walking at least a kilometer before I discover the store.

I look at the SIM cards and available numbers. I have almost 20 to choose from and go with the number 69978 69 22 69. It is the easiest to remember. I pick a smartphone in the lower price range that has all the features I need for my work as a call girl, and inquire about an extra battery in case the one in the phone goes dead when I am on the road with no way to recharge. My entire purchase comes to 388 euros. Now I have the most important device a call girl requires: A cell phone!

Next on my agenda is the *Athens World* editorial office, which is located downtown in Omonoia Square. Violet told me where the newspaper's offices are, but she also advised me not to explore the area after my business is concluded because it is supposedly swarming with drug addicts, dealers, pimps, illegal immigrants, and all kinds of crooks. – I look at my tourist map for bus and subway stations, but regrettably, I cannot find one in my immediate vicinity. The closest one is at the Port of Piraeus, which, from my present location, is quite far off. Considering I have to budget my money and I am new to the city, in the beginning, I plan to avoid taking cabs and instead use public transportation to meet clients. Violet may discourage me from doing so because it may take too long to get wherever my destination is — but at least I want to try. Right now, it is important for me to acquaint myself with the available public transportation so I get to a hotel or a client's private address as quickly as possible.

I get out at Omonoia Square and walk up the stairs instead of taking the escalator. At least this time! It keeps me and my figure in shape. Once topside, I refer to my tourist map on which I had marked the location of the *Athens World* editorial offices. It is ahead around a few corners. I follow the route and enter the building. The small room is separated by a long counter, clientele on one side, on the other, two desks, one of which is manned by a lady who I address:

"Good morning. I would like to place an ad in the next edition of *Athens World.*"

She briefly looks at me, nods, and continues typing. Eventually, she gets up and walks over to me.

"What category do you want to place your ad?"

I place my prewritten note with my newly added cell phone number in front of her and say:

"Under *Escort*, please."

She looks as if she is judging me. Does she think I am too old or not pretty enough? I do not know. Who cares! At least she reads my text thoroughly. Then she looks at me again and asks:

"How many weeks do you want your ad to run?"

"Four weeks, please."

"That comes to 44 euros. That is 11 euros per week."

I hand her a 50-euro bill. She takes it and walks back to her desk, opens a drawer, reaches in, and returns with my change. There is also a receipt book and she writes me an invoice for 44 euros.

"Thank you!" I say.

She does not acknowledge me, simply turns around, and returns to her desk with the receipt book. Oh well, I have completed my mission! As of Friday, my ad will be in *Athens World*! I am happy about my accomplishment and think about what I can do with the rest of the day.

Omonoia Square does not look like the terrible place Violet made it out to be. Three lanes of traffic with noisy cars, scooters, taxis, and buses go around the square. Also, it is the middle of the day, what could happen? I do not see any harm in exploring the area a little. All over Omonoia Square are peripteros, Greek kiosks, where a person can buy all kinds of things: baseball hats, reading glasses, T-shirts, magazines, porn magazines, cigarettes, toys, drinks. While walking, I pass a large Greek department store, a hotel, boutiques, shoe stores, a small shop that sharpens knives, a cell phone store, fast-food restaurants, an old, seemingly traditional coffee house, and many subway entrances. Street vendors offer fashion jewelry and sunglasses. I see beggars, tourists, in addition to well and poorly dressed people from various countries. I pass a tiny sex shop where I sneak a quick peek, but do not see any-thing interesting. – As I reach a main thoroughfare running along Omonoia Square, I take out my map again. I see it is Stadiou Street and it runs from Omonoia Square to Syntagma Square. Relishing the chaotic hustle and bustle on the street as well as on the sidewalk, I stroll slowly down it. Moped riders park wherever they can. Numerous times, I circumvent obstacles such as chairs, tables, and boxes of delivered goods. Many men look Pakistani or Hindu. Some men stare, some try to chat with me. Then I discover on the third floor of a commercial building a display window of a sex shop. I could use a well-equipped sex shop in my line of work. Entering the store, I see I am the only customer. The shop is run by a sinister-looking man in his 50s and a dolled up woman of the same age who seems to have let herself go. I ask in English if I can browse. Apparently bored, both merely nod. I not only see toys, movies, and books, but also a large collection of sexy lingerie. I love it! What do I look through first? The leather clothes, the vinyl clothes, or the great outfits made from mesh, satin, and lace?

I decide to rummage through a stuffed basket of discounted panties. Some have no bottom; others have strings of bead where fabric should be. Although I already have a fantastic collection of this type of underwear, I admit I like them and cannot have enough. Examining the mesh clothes, I discover a red bodysuit edged in vinyl and held in place only at the neck, back, and instep. Trés sexy! I must try it on. I grab the hanger and drape the bodysuit over my arm. I hope it fits. Together with my red strapless fishnet stockings and red patent leather high heels that I only wear for work and never on the road, it would make an awesome ensemble. Most men adore red sexy lingerie. Me too. Most of my undergarments are either black or red. Although, during the summer when I am nicely tanned, I also like wearing brightly colored underwear, like orange, yellow, gold, acid green, and pink. Just not purple or blue! I search a bit longer and among the leather items, I find an exceptionally nice set. The mini skirt's front and back panels are only connected by simple silver metal rings. The top is held in place with a Velcro strap around the neck and back. It is tailored so that the breasts are pushed upward and the nipples remain exposed. I am truly mad about this outfit and pile it on top of the red, fishnet bodysuit. That is enough. I ask the saleswoman where the changing room is.

Not exactly the same, but they have something akin to what I am used to, a little nook separated by a curtain where customers can try on revealing clothes behind it. It comes with a stool and a large wall mirror. I look around for a hook to hang my selection on, but no luck. I end up hanging the clothes on the rod from which the curtain hangs and remove all my clothes except my panties. Wow! The red fishnet bodysuit fits like a glove and looks damn sexy on me! The price tag says 59 euros. Well, items like these are always expensive in sex shops. I take it off and carefully place it back on the hanger. Looking at the leather outfit's price tag, I see it costs even more — 149 euros. I try it on anyway. Viewing myself in the large wall mirror, I conclude I simply look spectacular. My nipples protrude magnificently above the push-up bra's cup. I play with them and they immediately harden. When I look at myself in the mirror while wearing such sexy outfits, I sometimes cannot help but get turned on, which I take as a sure sign men will feel the same. God, – it is a hell of a sexy leather outfit! – With my black leather thigh boots, whip, and handcuffs, I would make an extremely provocative dominatrix. I tug on my nipples again and briefly rub a finger over my clit simply to see if I can stimulate it. Delighted, it pulses. Too bad I am currently in a sex shop or I would pleasure myself. However, I can always do that later back in my hotel room. Now it is time to dress and exit the store. I hope the items I like will not sell quickly, so I can come back later. Once I make a good chunk of money, I will upgrade my work wardrobe to include black leather and red mesh clothes!

5

Back in my room at the Lilo Hotel, I plug my new cell phone into an outlet to charge the battery while I play around with it. I enter Violet's cell and home phone numbers into the address book. Then, I choose a background picture, check out the preinstalled apps, and try the camera. I also make sure I have access to the Internet and a search engine, which is crucial.

Other than those, I am not interested in any other extras. Next, I place the half-unpacked suitcase on the bed, sort the rest of my clothes, and stow them in the closet. Now I am set in case I receive a phone call from a prospective customer on Friday. Once all my clothes are neatly put away, I pack a small toiletry case: condoms in two different sizes, lube gel, a small bottle of massage oil, and a small black vibrator. From now on, I will always carry the case in my handbag. In another bag, a slightly larger one, which I will also take from now on, I pack a matching sexy black lingerie set and a pair of strapless stockings. These are what I will wear with my next client. In a large shoulder bag, I pack a short black vinyl dress, matching black vinyl gloves, thigh boots, a whip, a spanking paddle, a pair of hand-cuffs, and a long blonde ponytail hairpiece. Next, I add another dildo — slightly bigger, nipple clamps, as well as two, one meter, black soft ropes and place the pre-packed bag in the closet. It feels great to be ready in the event someone calls who is interested in domination. Now that I am finished, I call Violet.

"Hello, Violet! It's me, Anika. How are you? Did you make it home all right? The number displayed is my new work cell phone. That's the one I'll be calling you with from now on, so you might as well save it in your directory!"

"Hi, darling. It's good to hear your voice! I'm glad you took care of business. Yeah, I arrived home safely. I've had a busy day so far. Janis called at 10:00 a.m. and came over at 11:00 a.m. Then I went shopping and Jack called me. Not our Jack, mind you. My Jack! So I had to rush to get back home by 2:00 p.m. because he couldn't make it a half hour later! — God, he was his usual awful self again. Just imagine, he walks in, puts a 100-euro note and a box of chocolates on the table, then grabs me and kisses me so hard, my lips almost started bleeding. He then drags me into my bedroom and fucks my pussy sore! Ha, but I was lucky because it didn't take him all that long, fucking me so hard. Haha! — Until six months ago, he always paid 150, but since his wife left him, he only springs for 100 and always adds a box of pralines or a bouquet of flowers! What do you think? I really don't know what to do with that man. I mean, I've known him for twelve years, but he cannot seriously think I'd go out regularly with him. Lately, after each sexual encounter, he asks me out on a date. He wants a relationship with me, but I always say: *No Jack! I have work to do. I can't spend an entire evening with you!* — I hate the situation. It's not like I want to lose his business, he sees me weekly. Oh well, c'est la vie! I'll be at the Hilton Hotel this evening. Jerry, he's from Aegina, is flying to London tomorrow for a month and he wants to see me before leaving for so long. I'm glad business is so good, but sometimes I simply want to watch my favorite TV shows. — Anyway, enough about me. How are you, darling? We had fun last night, didn't we? We should do it again. Summer is always better for fishing than winter. It allows us to dress in flimsier clothing that shows more of our assets. — So, what are you doing now? Have you spoken to the manager of the Lilo Hotel to see if you can get a better rate for a long-term rental?"

Violet takes a deep breath and I use the opportunity to answer: "No, I haven't talked to him yet. – Maybe I'll get to it later today, otherwise tomorrow morning. Let's see when the mood strikes me... Anyway, I'm doing fine! – I placed my ad in *Athens World* and I can't wait to see what'll happen on Friday. I've completely unpacked my suitcases and everything is in its place. Tomorrow morning I'm planning to go back to the inner city to get better acquainted with it. — Hey, you want me to read you my ad?"

"Yes, I'm curious, darling! You know, I haven't changed my ad in years. I believe every man in Athens knows it by now."

I read my ad to Violet:

"'Very attractive and charming lady from Germany would like to meet a generous gentleman... cell phone No. 69978 69 22 69' — what do you think, you like it?"

"Fantastic, darling! Trés appealing. And it suits you! You could have easily used the word sexy because you are, once you let go of your inhibition. Yesterday evening, after we struck the deal with Jack, you really let loose. – And then in Jack's room, you were anything but awkward or shy. You merely have to learn how to come on to guys out in the open. But you will! It's useful!"

"Yes, I believe I'll have to watch you for a while longer. I admired how easily you always steered the conversation back to the topic. Simply marvelous! – So, Violet, I hope you have a nice day and I'll call you when I have something new to report. Take care!"

"Yes, do that, darling! Kisses!"

It is 6:00 p.m. and still hot outside. My stomach growls and I realize I have not eaten anything since breakfast this morning. I grab my handbag and stroll down to Zea Marina. On the promenade, I discover a large supermarket that also offers household products. I am glad I found a store like that nearby because I plan to buy a kettle and a toaster so I can make breakfast in my room. It is cheaper than going out to eat, not to mention, – I do not care much for Nescafé. Except for bougatsa, there are not many pastries I like. I long for a real German breakfast! I see a Greek burger joint and go in. Although it offers sidewalk tables, I prefer to sit inside because it is too noisy for me outside with the vehicles zipping by. I ask for a Diet Coke and a menu and sit down at an empty table near the front window. From here, I can entertain myself by watching the crowds passing by. When all is said and done, I leave the restaurant a bit disappointed and dispense with making a note about its food in my book. I stroll around the marina and look at the boats. God, it is so incredible to be near the sea and smell it. To be in a foreign country where the temperature is balmy, where I can run around in a mini skirt without worrying about being recognized and talked about behind my back — it feels so good!

I love the anonymity. Completely free. Back in the clubs where I used to work as a prostitute, I was always afraid a man might walk up to me that knew me. Or, perhaps an older man who knew my father. Or, even a friend of someone. — Every time I was called into the screening room by a new customer, I was anxious and approached him hesitantly while my heart pounded fiercely. Only when I was close enough to be sure I had never met the guy did I finally calm down.

Luckily, I never ran into a customer who knew me during those years. I believe it was also due to the fact that most of the clientele did not live in the surrounding area. However, some of our regulars were locals. They liked to stop by on their way home from work for a quickie before watching the daily evening news on TV and dinner with the family. I guess for some men it is a part of relaxing after work. But that was the past! – Now I am in a place where I can enjoy my work without the worry of being recognized hanging over me. Moreover, I am extremely happy to be self-employed so I do not have to share half my money!

Along the marina promenade is one sidewalk café after another. Most tables are occupied by people in lively conversations. The only person I have to talk to right now is Violet. – Maybe I should give my father a call. I promised I would so he knows I arrived safely in Athens. – What am I going to tell him? My family and friends assume I went to Athens to get a summer job in the tourist industry. Like taking a little adventure without knowing the outcome. Most of them considered such an undertaking as courageous and wished me good luck. None of them has the slightest idea about my real purpose. That is just as well. As a teenager, I had taken an apprenticeship as an office assistant.

Later on, when I married Manfred and we lived in that small town, I had worked at an engineering office. Even back then I had occasionally worked as a prostitute, first in a bar and then in various clubs when Manfred went on a business trip, which had been often. He had no idea about my part-time job and it was not the reason we broke it off. After our divorce, I moved back into my father's house that he owns and where I grew up. After thirteen years, my childhood room still looked the same. On one hand, moving in with my father provided me with a limited social life, but on the other, with a sense I was not stuck there. I knew I still had my life, a new beginning, to look forward to whenever I was ready. In the neighboring village, I worked as a part-time office assistant for a local construction company and three to four nights a week I worked at a club. My father and all those who knew me believed I was babysitting. Three weeks ago, I quit my part-time office job and started packing my bags. Thirst pulls me out of my reminiscing and back to the present. I sit down at the next sidewalk cafe and order a glass of white wine. The waiter returns with my drink and a bowl of assorted nuts, which I do not touch. — Too many calories and I do not want to get fat. I pull out my private phone with the German number and scan the online papers. After looking at all the photos I took during the last few days here in Athens, I finally add the Greek number of my new work phone to my address book. The name of my new contact is: Anika!

6

When I wake up the next morning and look at the clock, it is 7:30 a.m. Although I know I will not be able to fall back asleep, I snuggle in and think about what needs to be taken care of today. I need to find a nail salon and a tanning studio. Friday is only a couple of days away and I want to look my best by the time my ad appears in *Athens World*. Among other things, an overall tan and nicely painted toe and fingernails are a part of it. Also, I must talk to the Lilo Hotel manager about the possibility of a better room rate for a long-term rental, otherwise, I must search for cheaper accommodations elsewhere. Once out of the way, I will take my tourist map and go to Syntagma Square in the inner city. Violet revealed there are many hotels frequented by businessmen. I need to look at these to familiarize myself with my new work area. I swing my legs over the edge of the bed and make my way to the bathroom. Once dressed and ready to go, I look one final time in the mirror. The reflection I see pleases me. Downstairs in the hotel lobby, I tell Spiros the receptionist I need to see the manager. He informs me he is not on the premises, but will return in a half hour.

I use the time to go eat breakfast. While enjoying my second cup of coffee, I save some of my most important phone numbers and addresses from my private cell phone to my new, work cell phone. Back at the Lilo Hotel, George the manager is waiting for me.

"*Kalimera*, Kiria Ilona," he says and invites me into his office adjacent to the reception desk. Naturally, he addresses me by the name in my passport. I follow him and take a seat in front of his desk.

"I hope there isn't a problem with your room?" he asks and offers me a cup of coffee.

"No, I like my room just fine. I'm here because I plan to stay in Athens a bit longer. As I told you, I expected to stay for only a week or two, but my plans have changed. I'm staying for at least two months. I like your hotel, but I cannot afford to stay here at the current room rate. I want to ask if it's possible to receive a discount."

George sits in his chair with his legs crossed and listens. He scratches his chin.

"Two months?" he parrots.

"Yes. At least."

"Right now we're talking about up to mid-August, right?"

"Yes, until mid-August."

"Well, here's what we could do. — On the fourth floor, we have a few rooms with balconies and sea views. One of them is even a little bigger than your current room. Since we have no elevator and most of our guests do not want to climb that many stairs, we rarely rent out the rooms. So, Ilona, if you don't mind moving up to the fourth floor, you can have the room at a rate of 23 euros per day."

Although my heart joyfully skips a beat, my outward composure remains unchanged.

"Can I see the room, George?"

"Of course. Let's go, Ilona. I'll show it you!"

At the reception, George asks Spiros for the room key and we start climbing the stairs to the fourth floor. Yes, the room is definitely bigger than the one downstairs.

I walk over to the balcony door, pull the curtains aside, and surprised, notice the better view from up here. Although I am thrilled, I will not let George know. I inspect the bathroom and say:

"Yes, walking up all those stairs — I can see how you might have a problem renting out the rooms."

I pause as I look around the room again and then continue:

"But since I like your offer we have a deal! I'll move into this room for the next two months."

Like me, George's expression remains cool, although, I am convinced he is happy to have rented out this room for so long. Now he nods with obvious satisfaction, smiles, and asks:

"So, Ilona, do you want to move in today or tomorrow?"

I briefly consider it and decide to move in today. Tomorrow will be Thursday and my ad in *Athens World* appears in Friday's edition, by which time everything has to be ready.

"I would like to move in as soon as possible. When could you have the room ready?" George looks at his watch.

"Let's say an hour. I'll send for Sophie right now and she'll give it a once over."

Fine! I go back to my room, neatly refold and repack my clothes into my two suitcases. Shortly thereafter, there is a knock at the door. It is Sophie the maid coming to tell me my new room is ready to move into. Now, room 42 has fresh towels, a bath mat, shower gel, the bed is made, the refrigerator hums, the TV is plugged in, and the airconditioning is running.

It is a relief knowing I do not have to search for new lodging! — Now it is time to unpack again. The closet, which is also a wardrobe, has a somewhat different setup and I am short hangers. I run downstairs to the lobby and ask Spiros for more. He disappears into a storeroom and returns with a handful of hangers. I grab them and run back up to my new room. Yippee! — Now I am in a larger room with an even better view and pay a lower rate than I was actually willing to spend!

It is 2:30 p.m. by the time I am finished moving into my new room. I push Violet's stored number but she does not answer. Presumably, she is with a client. I will try her again later. Walking swiftly, I leave the hotel and head for the Port of Piraeus. As I arrive on the subway station platform, I am in luck and immediately board the waiting train bound for Syntagma Square. I arrive at the station and climb five flights of stairs to get back above ground. As I already have done enough exercise today, climbing up and down staircases, I use the escalator for the last flight of stairs!

Exploring Syntagma Square and a few neighboring streets, I see plenty of large luxury hotels. Today I am wearing black and white checkered hot pants with a snug fitting black top. In this outfit, together with my high, black summer pumps and blonde hair, I attract more attention than I like... Other female tourists are not dress snazzily or sexy. Be that as it may, I muster up the courage and enter the famous luxurious hotels. In the lobby, I see a small table with brochures and magazines for guests. I pocket a copy of the June/July edition of the Athens Guide. This little glossy brochure lists numerous hotels, ads for shops and restaurants, and provides information on upcoming events. It might come in handy. Dressed in hot pants, I attract many glances. I leave the beautiful hotel, thinking I will return some other time when I am more suitably dressed. Quickly, I peek into two other classy hotels and then stroll around Syntagma Square. The indispensable Greek peripteros occupy each corner and in the middle stands a huge water fountain. Park benches are situated in the shady areas provided by the trees. I sit down on one with a particularly nice view of part of the square and try Violet's number again. This time she answers on the third ring.

"Hi, darling, this is Anika! How are you? Are you busy or do you have time to answer a question?"

"Oh, hi sweetie! It's nice to hear from you. – How are you? I've already been shopping this morning. I ran out of butter, bread, and water. Gosh, I hate schlepping all those water bottles! But, I need it at home for my customers. I mean, don't ask me why they drink water when they're at my place, they don't do that when I meet them in a hotel. I really don't get it. In any case, I have no choice but to lug all those bottles home. You know I have to walk 200 meters to the closest mini market. – And, a six-pack of bottled water weighs nine kilos! I guess my customers seem to forget that little fact. Anyway, I don't want to give them tap water, it tastes horrible, especially during the summer. Maybe I shouldn't set out an entire bottle and a glass, and instead, only offer a glass? Perhaps I should toss in a few ice cubes too, then I wouldn't use as much bottled water! What do you think? Does it seem rude? I mean, it's not about the cost. My main concern is all that schlepping! — So, tell me, darling, what have you been up to? Have you spoken to the hotel manager? I'm so excited for you. Today is Wednesday and come Friday your phone may ring and you'll have your first customer! Aren't you excited? Thinking back when I started, damn, girl, it was an incredibly electrifying time!"

"Yes, I agree, it's exciting. – By the way, I have good news; I'm staying at the Lilo Hotel. – George the manager gave me a room on the fourth floor for only 23 euros a day. Isn't that fabulous! I immediately agreed. My new room is even slightly larger and since I'm on the fourth floor, I have a much better view! I've already settled in. What do you think about that?"

"Wonderful! Congratulations, darling, I'm happy for you! Considering you have all the amenities and internet, 23 euros a day is a good rate. You really have no reason to complain. – Renting an apartment would cost more. Okay, an apartment would be bigger and provide more comfort, but it's not like you need that now. — Anyway, darling, I have another appointment. I have to go to the 6 X Hotel in Glyfada. I'm meeting a new client there. But you know I don't service new clients in my apartment. Let's see what kind of man he is. Perhaps he'll never call me back, who knows. Anyway, I have to get going soon. What are you up to right now?"

"At the moment, I'm in Syntagma Square looking for a place to eat. I'm starving. Perhaps you can help me out. Where do you go to get your nails done? Can you recommend a place that's not too expensive but still does a great job?"

"Darling, I always go to Maria. She has a small studio on Metaxa Street in Glyfada. It's easy to find. Hold on; let me give you her phone number. It's better to make an appointment with her!"

"Violet, any chance you can text me the number? That way it's already stored on my phone."

"Of course, darling. I'm sending it now. Say hi to Maria for me! She knows me as Violet."

"Okay, good to know! I'll talk to you later. Have a great day. And good luck with your new client!"

"Thanks, darling. Hugs and kisses. Don't forget to call me!"

Great! That is taken care of. I will call Maria as soon as I get the text. Maybe I can make an appointment for late tomorrow morning. I no longer see the man who was watching me when I was on the phone with Violet. At the nearest periptero, I check out available magazines.

As I flip through a German magazine, the man who was watching me appears out of nowhere and stands directly next to me. The vendor and the man exchange a few Greek words and then both look at me. Since I do not speak Greek, I have no idea what passed between. The man standing next to me addresses me in English. He is about one meter ninety with gray hair. I estimate he is around 60 years old and is wearing tan trousers and a short-sleeved beige shirt. Although he is quite tall and muscular, he blends in.

"What's your name?" he inquires.

Oh! What do we have here? Is he coming on to me? A thousand thoughts cross my mind because all I see is a fish I could catch.

"My name is Anika. What's your name?"

"I'm Richard. I'm from Canada."

His face has an odd expression as he speaks. The periptero vendor laughs and makes a remark that obviously amuses both men. Are they laughing at me?

"Everyone here knows me," states Richard.

"This vendor here and the periptero vendor over there. – I live here. Everybody knows me as Richard from Canada!"

I am not sure if he is telling me this simply to gain my trust. The reason does not matter because I cannot think of an answer. I am sure he is only talking to me because I am in hot pants and I look like I..., what, like I want to attract attention? Well, I guess in my case it is true. Let me see how this plays out. I will use Richard for a bit of fishing practice!

"Nice to meet you, Richard!" I say and smile at him. I hold out my hand, which he shakes.

"What are you doing here?" he asks me.

I take a few steps so we are out of earshot of the vendor. Naturally, Richard follows me.

"I work in Athens," I reply.

"Doing what?"

I take a deep breath, muster all my courage, and say:

"I provide sex for money."

Phew! That was not easy. Standing in my high-heel pumps, I feel my knees tremble.

"Oh," says Richard, "would you do it with me?"

"Certainly."

"Great! Do you want to go to my place? I live right over there."

"Okay. But just to verify, you understand, I'm not having sex with you without payment, right?"

"Obviously, I'm not stupid. I guess I should know how much you charge."

"150 euros."

"That's too much. I'll give you half, deal?"

"No! My rate is 150 euros for an hour!"

"I won't need an hour, 30 minutes is plenty. Come on, let's go!"

God, what am I supposed to do now? Seventy-five is good money for a quickie. — Why not! I never made that much at the club I used to work at and that was for a 40-minute session. So, Ilona, do not let pride get in the way now! Richard didn't call about the ad in *Athens World*. It is merely a chance encounter.

"Okay, I'll play along. Where exactly do you live?"

"Right over there." He points.

We leave Syntagma Square and make a right turn, followed by a left. Richard walks toward a large glass-paned entrance and opens the door.

Once we are in the elevator, he pushes the button for the fifth and seemingly top floor. – On the ride up, he gives my body a once over, smiles, and says:

"You are gorgeous."

"Thank you," I reply. Suddenly, my stomach feels a bit queasy.

We climb a staircase up to another level before arriving at an apartment door after exiting the elevator on the fifth floor. Richard unlocks it and we entered the penthouse apartment. He says:

"Feel free to look around. Oh, and make sure to go outside. The view from up here is fantastic."

Two sides of the apartment are entirely floor to ceiling glass panels. The large, built-in sliding doors are open wide and I step out onto a huge terrace partially covered by a pergola. Wow! From up here, I can even see the Acropolis. As I walk along the railing and take in the scenery, I call to Richard:

"The view from your terrace is incredible!"

Richard finally joins me and tells me he bought the apartment many years ago. Before that, he lived in Canada and was a professional boxer.

"Come on!" he says, "let me show you some pictures of me."

And what do you know, the walls in his office are full of pictures of him from former boxing events. Different shots taken during matches, after a win with his arms stretched up high, holding a wide championship belt. Richard says:

"I was a champion a few times. – But 15 years ago, I had a stroke. What you see is all that's left of the former champion."

For some reason, I think he may have also received a few too many punches to the head. I immediately hate myself because it is unkind. It does, however, explain why Richard looked and sounded so strange when he first approached me at the periptero.

"Where do you want us to get comfortable?" I ask, wanting to get business out of the way as quickly as possible.

"Nowhere. Undress yourself. I want to fuck you right here."

"What, right here at the desk?"

"Why not? — You don't mind, do you?"

"No, it's fine."

I take off my shirt and drape it over the desk chair. I undo my bra and slip it off, then place it neatly on my top. Richard watches me. Hoping the show turns him on, I peel off my hot pants, turn around slowly, and set it on top my other items. Then I remove my panties.

When I turn back around to face him, I am wearing only my high-heel pumps. Lecherously, Richard appraises me. I saunter slowly up to him and feel his crotch. Good, I have his attention! I unfasten his belt and zipper and Richard pulls down his pants along with his big tighty-whities. His member is rock hard and I wrap the fingers of one hand around it. Having already laid out a condom from my small toiletry bag, I reach for it with my other hand and open the wrapper with my teeth. With the rubber in my free hand, I move my body against Richard and slide down until I end up on the ground on one knee. I roll the rubber over his dick and immediately put it deep into my mouth. Throwing his head back, Richard moans loudly. Gently, he grabs hold of the back of my head and starts slowly moving his hips back and forth. In the next instant, he pulls his penis out of my mouth and asks me to turn around and brace myself against the desk. As he moves into position behind my spread legs, I wet the fingers of my right hand and run them through my crotch so I am moist, making it easier for him to slide in his cock.

As soon as I am done, I feel him penetrate me violently. His cock is big and I feel it deep inside me. Momentarily painful, I immediately relax and let him fuck in his rhythm until he comes. The moment of his orgasm, he grabs my hips with both hands and roughly thrusts his pelvis against my butt.

So that is how a former boxing champion fucks. I patiently wait until he finishes climaxing and remain silent until he pulls out. I immediately turn around to make sure the rubber is still in place. Everything is fine. I smile at him and stroke his shoulders and upper arms.

"Damn, those are quite some biceps! What a strong man you are," I say softly, receiving a smile for my flattery.

"May I use your bathroom?" I ask.

"Naturally! I take it you know the way?"

"Yes, thank you. I saw it earlier."

I remove my clothes from the chair, place my toiletry case in my shoulder bag, and carry everything into the bathroom. Where are the clean towels? – I open the closet doors and find a stack of fresh towels. Once dressed, I leave the bathroom and find Richard sitting outside at the patio table.

"Okay, Richard, darling, I'll be on my way. It was nice meeting you. Would you like my phone number?"

"Yes, hold on, you can write it down for me!"

He gets up and goes back to the desk where he fucked me. He hands me a pen and a piece of paper. I am happy I memorized my new phone number. I write: Anika — 69978 69 22 69. Richard reaches for the wallet in his back pocket and pulls out a 50 and a 20-euro note. — Crap! We agreed on 75! I look at him questioningly.

"I don't have a fiver," he says. "It's not the end of the world. We could go have a coffee somewhere and then I'll have change."

"No, I'll let it pass this time, Richard. Have a nice day and call me should you get the hots for me!"

I stand on my tiptoes, kiss him goodbye on the cheek, and leave. That went off without a hitch! I look at my watch.

All in all, I only spent 35 minutes in Richard's apartment and made enough money to buy a toaster and a kettle. The rest of the afternoon, I spend strolling through the inner city, thrilled I caught my own first fish in Athens!

7

It is still early morning as I sit with a fresh, self-brewed cup of coffee on the small balcony of my room on the fourth floor of the Lilo Hotel. Since last night, I am the proud owner of a toaster, a kettle, a glass French press, and everything else I need for an enjoyable breakfast. This is the first time I have prepared breakfast in my room. Toast with cheese and one with orange marmalade. Basking in the morning sun and gazing out over the sparkling sea, I feel like I am on vacation. I have never enjoyed a nice breakfast as much as this. At 11:00 a.m., I prepare to go out. I made an appointment for a manicure and pedicure with Maria in Glyfada.

In front of the open wardrobe, I opt for a white, sleeveless stretch dress. The way it is cut and arranged at the seams gives it a nautical flair. Since I do not know how much walking I will do today, I once again slip on my solid, cork-soled, gold high-heels that allow me to run around for hours without my feet getting sore. Checking my purse, I exchange the black satin lingerie set for one in red lace. Today, red is better. As is my habit before leaving my room, I examine myself in the mirror: Yes, I look great! I spend two hours at Maria's modern cosmetic salon in Glyfada. When she finishes, I have beautiful, red lacquered finger and toenails. I call Violet to thank her for the recommendation and to tell her about yesterday's fishing encounter.

"Congratulations, Anika! You did well with Richard! Don't worry about the money. I told you the situation is different when you pick up men on the street versus when a man contacts you through your ad. Many of my initial customers have remained faithful to me over the years because I haven't upped my rate much. It all depends on what they can afford. Like Dimitri, he only pays 50 euros! That's been his rate for fourteen years. – Back then, he paid me the equivalent in drachmas. Several times, I tried to make him understand that living costs constantly increase and that he should correspondingly dole out more obols. — However, I know he can't afford to pay more and so I let him come for that amount. Let him come! Ha, ha, ha! — Don't forget that I've been seeing him almost every week for more than 14 years! Looking at it from an annual perspective, it totals a good amount of money. And Dimitri doesn't demand much. I guess he simply needs to have regular sex from time to time with a woman he can grope a little so it's not only him jerking himself off. I only have to touch him and his little weenie pops up! Then I rub it a little and he comes! He can come on whatever he wants, my tits, my stomach, my butt — but not in my face! I've never used a condom with him in all these years and I have never had his cock in my mouth. You can certainly not complain about making 70 euros from a guy like Richard who doesn't need long and is undemanding. That's how you create regulars. – It won't happen if you say NO to every guy not wanting to pay your regular rate."

"I get it now. – And Richard literally threw himself at me! It all happened so effortlessly, I still hardly believe it myself. God, I was proud of myself once I was out of there. — So, what are you up to today?"

"Socrates is coming over this evening. He always brings a bottle of red wine and we first have a nice time chitchatting and drinking wine. When he's ready, we retire to the bedroom. He always stays at least two hours. We've never talked about the price for an evening because he's exceedingly generous. I leave it up to him how much he wants to pay. He's tactful and usually puts 400 - 600 euros on my nightstand when I'm in the bathroom. At Christmas and on my birthday, I get flowers plus an extra hundred. He's a real gentleman. He's my only appointment for the evening. I'm going to make a crab salad now and eat it watching my favorite TV show while I wait for Socrates to show up."

"Well, have lots of fun then, Violet! — I'll get back in touch. Maybe we can go out together again, perhaps some evening next week?"

"Yes, we'll do that! In the middle of the week, we can search hotels for bored businessmen and during the weekend, we can try our luck in a bar. I know of one frequented by lots of Englishmen in Glyfada. I went there often many years ago looking for customers. Anyway, we'll see... bye, darling, and don't forget to call me!"

After my phone conversation with Violet, I stroll along Metaxa Street and window shop. It is time to eat, but I am not in the mood for fast food again. Maybe I should have a sundae and in the early evening, a nice warm Greek meal. The Ammas Hotel, where I went with Violet, is not far away. I could go there for ice cream and at the same time check out the roof terrace and swimming pool in daylight. Maybe it is a place to spend a summer afternoon while waiting for work! I should see how it is during the day.

I cross Glyfada's town square and walk toward the Ammas Hotel along Poseidonos Street. It is a major three-lane thoroughfare that runs from Glyfada to Piraeus. Traffic is heavy. The narrow sidewalk I am on is more like an extra lane for speeding cars to avoid sideswiping each other. Some motorists blow their horns and yell something at me through already rolled-down windows.

About 200 meters away from the Ammas Hotel, a black Jeep pulls up next to me and the passenger window opens. The driver is a handsome, slender man with dark blond hair no more than 50 years old. When he looks over at me, he removes his sunglasses and asks me nicely in English:

"Can I give you a lift?"

In a situation like this in Germany, I would never reply to a stranger, let alone get in his car. It is different here though, I think to myself: He did not stop to offer an unknown woman a ride so she would not have to walk on the badly paved sidewalk. This man saw me walking down the road in my white snug-fitting summer dress, my blonde hair blowing in the breeze, and was attracted to me. That is the reason he pulled up next to me. And since he asked me to get in, he obviously finds me attractive.

He likes to flirt. But I am ready for even more! He could be my next fish, which is why I cast my net. Smiling politely, yet still hesitant, I answer:

"No, thank you! It's not necessary. I'm almost at my destination." I point ahead to the Ammas Hotel, which is already within view.

"Oh, come on, get in! I'll drop you off in front!" The driver of the Jeep is insistent. I see no harm, open the passenger door, and get in.

"Hi!" I say. "I'm Anika."

Climbing onto the passenger seat sends my dress riding up my thighs to just below my panties. Amused, the driver gazes at my bare legs.

"Hi! I'm Adonis. Nice to meet you!" he says.

He glances in the rearview mirror and merges into traffic. I adjust my dress a little and look at him from out of the corner of my eyes. Adonis is wearing dark blue trousers, a white short-sleeved shirt, a Rolex, and a wedding ring. His clothes look expensive like his car with its tinted windows, leather seats, air-conditioning, and built-in dashboard navigation system.

"That hotel over there?"

"That's the one. The Ammas Hotel. You can drop me off there."

"Do you live there? Are you on vacation?"

"No — I go there for drinks and ice cream. The hotel has a rooftop terrace with a swimming pool and fabulous views."

"Oh! I didn't know and I drive by it every day. May I join you? Now I'm curious to see the rooftop terrace. — Of course, the drinks and ice creams are on me!"

"Oh... Okay, why not," I reply somewhat hesitantly. "I don't mind."

In fact, I am quite pleased how quickly and effortlessly he swims into my net. Adonis pulls into the parking lot adjacent to the Ammas Hotel. We get out and walk together through the lobby to the elevator. Once we are inside, I push the button next to the sign — Roof Garden. The elevator is cramped, forcing us to stand close to each other. Smiling cheerfully, Adonis looks at me, giving me the feeling he is looking for the price tag. Or, am I imagining it because it is exactly what I want? – Whatever the case, I am presented with another opportunity to practice my fishing. The best views from the roof terrace are to the south over the sea and north to the distant green hills behind Glyfada. Here and there around the pool are benches and lounges with pullout side tables and umbrellas. The pool area looks incredibly inviting. Nevertheless, I do not waste time thinking about when I might use it. I am focused on catching a fish. So far, I have no clue how to get Adonis to become a paying customer. We sit down at a large round wooden table in the shade of an umbrella and Adonis speaks to the waiter. Michalis must only work evenings. Adonis turns toward me and says:

"They have an assorted ice cream, *Fantasy*, mixed ice cream with fruit salad, – ice cream with hot raspberries, a chocolate cup, and naturally, whip cream, if you like. So, which ice cream would you like? And what would you like to drink?"

"I'll have ice cream with hot raspberries and a Nescafé with milk."

"Would you like your Nescafé hot or iced, a so-called frappe?"

"Hot, please."

Adonis translates my order for the waiter who then disappears. I have no clue what Adonis ordered. Uncertainty spreads within me. It is time to strike up a conversation. What do I talk about? Maybe I should ask a few questions about him. But what? Have you finished work? Are you on your way home? Where did you come from? Where were you going before you met me and became sidetracked? Why do you have time to invite a woman you do not know for ice cream?

"So, Anika! Tell me, what are you doing in Athens?"

"Funny, I was about to ask you the same thing!" I reply quickly.

"Yes, of course, forgive my rudeness. I work at a shipping company in Glyfada but live in Piraeus. I got off a half hour ago and was on my way home when I saw you. Well, as is obvious, I enjoy talking to pretty ladies I see on the roadside and offer them a ride. Or, like in your case, invite them for a drink."

I am sure Violet would have come up with an apt reply, – but his macho remark only reinforces my insecurity. How am I supposed to respond? I silently pray my ice cream and coffee is served shortly, giving me something to do. – Adonis must sense my insecurity. He breaks the awkward silence:

"Okay, tell me about yourself. Where are you from? Listening to your accent, I'd guess Germany. Are you in Athens on vacation or for some other reason?"

I take a deep breath before answering his questions:

"You're correct. I'm from Germany. And no, I'm not here on vacation. I'm in the process of starting my own business."

"What line of work are you in, if I may ask? Are you working for one of the German companies here?"

"No. — I'm a call girl," I manage to say. Not surprisingly, being the coward I am, I cannot look at Adonis as it comes out of my mouth. There is no better way of saying it. Fortunately, the waiter arrives and I focus my attention on him. I wait for him to serve my ice cream and coffee. Once he walks away from our table, I look over at Adonis. His expression is unfazed when he says:

"Enjoy your ice cream!"

I wonder if he even heard what I said. I take a spoonful of ice cream with a dab of hot raspberries and let it melt on my tongue while my mind goes into overdrive. Why do I believe Adonis actually works for a shipping company? Because he said so? He could just as well be a cop. Perhaps even undercover.

How can I be sure he is not from vice out catching prostitutes? How can I be so dumb to come right out to a complete stranger and reveal that I am a call girl? Violet would never have jumped the gun! I am positive. She would have asked him more questions first. I feel like an idiot and eat my ice cream without really enjoying it. — Calm down, Ilona! Do not panic! — I try to calm down by telling myself I am overreacting, that he is not a cop. I mean, what undercover cop drives a Jeep Cherokee? And a cop would not invite an alleged prostitute out for coffee and ice cream. No. This is a normal man who wants you. Eat the ice cream, calm down, and see what happens!

"This is delicious!" says Adonis.

"Yes, mine too," I reply, but I am still afraid to make eye contact.

"So, you want to work as a call girl. For an agency or freelance?"

It seems Adonis heard what I said. He simply needed time to come up with a response. He managed to turn my embarrassing revelation into normal conversation. Grateful for his openness, I reply:

"A self - employed call girl. I placed an ad in tomorrow's edition of *Athens World*. It's a weekly English magazine published in Greece. I'll go to hotels and make home visits. At least that's my plan."

I let the ice cream melt on my tongue. It truly is delicious, so smooth and creamy. Slowly, I regain my self-confidence.

"Did you work in the escort business in Germany?"

"No, I worked there as a prostitute in several clubs, not as a call girl. — So what about you? Are you married?"

"Yes, of course. I am a husband and father." He chuckles.

"And as you might have already guessed, I'm in the mood for an extramarital adventure. So, since there's no more need for beating around the bush, how about it? Do you have time to drive to another hotel with me?"

"Oh! – Yes, I have the time for that. But you have to pay me, you understand that, right?"

"Naturally. So, what deal can I get! How much do you charge as a call girl?"

"150 euros an hour."

"Ouch. That's pretty steep! I'm sorry, but I really can't pay that much. However, I'm curious about you, so I'm willing to pay half. How about it? Do we have a deal?"

"Come on, at least make it 80. It's a nice round number!"

"*Panajia mou!* Okay, 80 it is. – You're lucky I'm so turned on by you. But for that price, I want to fuck you real good!"

"Sure, darling, you can do that!"

I am so proud of myself, I take another tasty spoonful of ice cream covered in hot raspberries and let it melt on my tongue. When we finish our ice cream, Adonis says:

"There's a hotel further down Poseidonos Street, toward Piraeus. Is it okay if we go there? Or, tell me, where do you live?"

"Yes, that's okay. Let's go to the hotel. – I also live nearby in Piraeus, but it's a small, family run place that doesn't allow male visitors," I reply, trying to smile slyly.

We sip our coffees, Adonis lights up a cigarette, and we chitchat about German virtues, which apparently are especially interesting to Adonis. Finally, he signals the waiter for the bill and we leave. We reach the other hotel after a ten-minute drive. The large illuminated sign above the entrance door reads: 6 X Hotel. – Violet mentioned this place. Did she not say it was in Glyfada though? I ask Adonis about it and he explains that the 6 X Hotel is a hotel chain where couples can rent rooms hourly for sex. Once Adonis parks the car in an inconspicuous spot behind the hotel, we get out. He quickly grabs a briefcase from the backseat of his jeep and winks at me. I look at him questioningly, yet he keeps me in suspense:

"You'll see soon enough. It's a little surprise!"

8

After receiving a key for a room on the third floor, we enter a tiny elevator.

"Oh my God, the two of us barely fit in here!" I say and snuggle provocatively up against Adonis' back. Looking into the mirror affixed to one of the elevator's walls, I see his amused smile. My behavior encourages him to push my dress up and touch my crotch. The elevator stops on our floor and we walk down the dimly lit corridor to room 31. Painted in pink tones, the room has many mirrors, a round bed, and plush wall-to-wall carpeting. I am familiar with such rooms from the clubs I worked at in Germany. When it comes to work, I prefer partly kitschy, overly erotic décor and dim lighting over conventional hotel rooms.

"Give me a moment to freshen up in the bathroom, baby," I say to Adonis as he places his briefcase on the bed. Inside the small bathroom, I remove my dress and white underwear and slip into my red lingerie set that pushes my breasts up and leaves my nipples and the upper half of my breasts exposed. As I look into the mirror, I am turned on by my reflection.

When I see myself dressed in sexy lingerie and become aroused, it is definitely time to pleasure myself. Since I find myself incredibly sexy just now, I walk back into the room full of confidence. Adonis is lying on the big round bed, wearing only a skimpy pair of white underpants. His briefcase is open. Even from my point of view, I see it is filled with sex toys. All types of dildos lie neatly arranged next to each other.

"Wow!" he says as I slowly sashay toward him while running my hands over my breasts.

"Damn, you look sexy, baby! — Wait, let me freshen up too."

He disappears into the bathroom. Curious, I lean over the open briefcase to look closer at the selection. Everything is there that would pleasure a woman. In addition to the usual dildos and vibrators, I see plugs, anal beads, love eggs, pussy pumps, and nipple clamps.

Returning from the bathroom, Adonis says, "Pick something I can use to pleasure you with before I fuck you." My fingers glide over his treasures and I grab a big purple silicone vibrator and switch it on. It is a rabbit vibrator with a penis-like top where sex gel can be inserted and it can be electrically controlled to rotate or reciprocate. Further down, it also has a little silicone finger sticking out at an angle, a so-called clitoral stimulator, the one feature that scares me! I switch it off again and put it back. I am sure I can do without that one! The club, Rosis Angel, where I worked, had one of these monster dildos. – Fortunately,

I always talked customers out of using it on me. Next, I reach for a flexible, approximately 15-centimeter long dildo with a head that resembles the tip of a penis plus a shaft with strongly pronounced ridges. I like this one much better. Moreover, I do not believe Adonis will hurt me with it.

"Hey!" I say, "I like this one! This is the one you can pleasure me with."

I take a rubber out of my small bag and roll it over the dildo. Standing in front of the bed, I take the tip in my mouth and use my tongue on it. I use one hand to move my panties aside and stroke my pussy. Adonis watches, obviously aroused. His underpants cover the already large bulge. I crawl up next to him on the bed and lightly slide the already lubed dildo over his hairy chest down to his undies. His cock is rock hard and spasms when I touch it. I assume the doggy position so Adonis has a great view of my ass and pussy. I spread my legs, hand him the dildo, and say:

"Okay, darling, put it inside me and fuck me with it!"

Slowly and gently, Adonis pushes it into my pussy. It is much too slow for me because in my current state it turns me on.

"Damn, Anika, your pussy looks great. I can't wait to fuck it. First, I want to see how turned on you get. I want you really horny!"

Sticking the dildo deep in my pussy, Adonis slowly rotates it back and forth. I allow myself to be stimulated by it. If I wanted to, I could reach climax at any given moment. The last time I pleasured myself was more than two weeks ago when I was still in Germany. And the last time I had sex with a man who was not a client was more than half a year ago. Maybe I should have an orgasm before he fucks me. Then he will be satisfied and it will be over sooner.

"Give me the dildo!" I say after a while in order to take over control. "I really want to suck your cock now. — Lie down, darling."

Adonis lies on his back and I study his upright member closely. It looks clean and healthy. Considering Adonis is married, I think he would make sure he does not contract an STD. Therefore, I am fine with taking it into my mouth condom-free. Before I start the blowjob, I push the dildo deep into my pussy and leave it there. It feels incredibly good. Taking Adonis' dick in my mouth, I work it vigorously. Feeling his growing arousal, I release his cock and say emphatically:

"Don't come in my mouth!"

"I won't, I promise! I still want to fuck you!"

With Adonis no longer in my mouth, I pull the dildo out of my pussy, lie down on a pile of pillows, and urge him:

"Now, baby, why don't you watch as I pleasure myself! You said you wanted me really horny!"

Adonis kneels next to me, takes his wet cock in his hand, and slowly strokes it. I rub the dildo's pronounced ridges over my clitoris and I am immediately fully aroused. – Unbelievable! – I am no longer paying Adonis any attention. I am solely focused on me and my increasing desire. If I were at home alone, I would take my time and delay my orgasm for a while. However, this is not the time. This is work. I have to come quickly. I have to come now! Blood rushes to my head and I implode. Sweet contractions drive me wild. I move in sync to the rhythmical waves of my orgasm and ride it out as expected without trying to reach an even higher climax. Naturally, Adonis watches the entire time and asks:

"That was for real, right?"

"Oh yes!" I moan happily. "It was absolutely real! Now it's your turn! Come and fuck me, baby"

I roll a condom onto his erection and pull his hips down to my wide spread legs. His hard cock enters me and I let him fuck me hard. It does not take all that long before I feel he is about to come. His movements slow and his thrusts become deeper, more urgent when he groans aloud and slumps together. It is over. He came! Once both of us are finished showering in the bathroom and dressed, he pays me and we exchange phone numbers.

"You might want to save my number. That way you'll know it's me. — I'll definitely call you, Anika! You really are one hot broad. I knew it the first time I spotted you walking along the sidewalk." He winks at me.

Adonis gives me a ride to Piraeus where I ask him to let me out at the Dimotiko Theatro. – We kiss each other on both cheeks and then he brazenly grabs my crotch and grins. Now it is late afternoon and I am extremely satisfied. I cross the street in front of the theater and stroll across the town square, looking for a place to eat moussaka and drink a glass of wine.

9

It is Friday morning. Today my ad appears in *Athens World* for the first time. Although I know better than to expect too much, I cannot help being excited. After an extensive breakfast, I start packing my bag for work. In addition to the regular items I carry around in my handbag every day, I also pack my black lace bra and panty set, a striped sexy bodysuit whose light fabric barely covers my breasts and pubic area, and black strapless stockings that complement both outfits. In a small transparent toiletry bag, I put five normal and five extra-large condoms, a small bottle of massage oil, lube gel, a small black vibrator, and a flexible medium-size silicone dildo. After looking longer than usual through my wardrobe, I finally choose a red cotton pencil skirt, a black top with spaghetti straps, and black high heels. Although attired in this manner will probably attract attention, it also allows me to make hotel and home visits without rubbing my profession in everyone's face. Taking one last glance in the mirror, I leave my hotel room satisfied.

I stop by the front desk and ask Spiros if there is a laundromat nearby. He tells me arrangements can be made through the hotel to have my clothes laundered. – Once in Piraeus' town square, I head to one of the peripteros to buy a copy of *Athens World*. At the next sidewalk café, I sit down at a small round metal table and order a Diet Coke. – Even though I am anxious to read my ad, I scan each page of the newspaper until I arrive at the 'Escort' classified section. What do you know, there it is! My ad that will allow me to create a new life for myself:

'Very attractive and charming lady from Germany would like to meet a generous gentleman. Tel. No.: 69978 69 22 69'

Quickly scanning the column, I discover my ad listed last in the section. That, I believe, is beneficial because the first and last ones are the most prominent. All ads are numbered and in alphabetical order. Taking the time to read each of the thirty-two ads thoroughly, I conclude that I did quite well with the way I phrased mine!

Satisfied, I contemplate about what to do with the rest of the day. Finding a suntan studio is not necessary yet. It can wait another couple of days. One possibility would be to go back to my hotel room and wait for the phone to ring. —Or, I could take the subway to the city center and window-shop in the shade department stores and shops provide. If someone calls for an appointment, I would be centrally located, able to reach any one of Athens' suburbs in the same amount of time. Therefore, the city center seems to be the best place to spend the afternoon.

In case my phone does ring, I have already thought of what I am going to say about myself and the services I provide: I am 35, blonde with blue eyes. I make hotel or home visits. I charge 150 euros for one hour, 250 for two hours. Anal sex costs an extra 50. – For the entire evening,

I charge 600. As long as my phone rings, I am available. My general working hours start at 6 a.m. until 3 a.m. I only practice safe sex. I only agree to oral sex without a condom after inspecting the specimen. I decide if kissing is permitted. It all depends on his appearance and odor. — Although I have a rough outline in my head, I also know I will be confronted with wishes I have not thought of yet. Regardless, I know my preferences and boundaries. As I play out possible conversations in my head, my phone rings. Both nervous and excited, I look around to make sure I am out of earshot of other guests in the café. Since no one is in my immediate vicinity, I answer the call. It registers as an unknown number.

"Hello?"

"Anika?"

"Yes. Who's this?"

"It's Richard. Can you come over today?"

"Oh, hi, Richard darling. How are you? Of course I can come over. Are you at home?"

"Yes, but I'll meet you downstairs in the café. Are you coming now?"

"Richard, I need about an hour to get to Syntagma Square. Which café are you going to be at?"

"The one to the right of my building's front door. You'll see me. See you soon. Kisses, sweetie."

"Okay, until then, kisses, darling!"

How nice of Richard to actually call! I am happy — a fantastic surprise! I neatly fold my copy of *Athens World* and shove it into my large handbag. I glance at my wristwatch to get an idea of what time it will be once I arrive at Syntagma Square. It takes about 15 minutes to walk to the harbor. The subway ride takes another 20-30 minutes including switching trains. So, there is no need to rush. It is important to be relaxed and look my best when I join Richard!

After reaching the inner city, I walk to his apartment building and notice he is standing at the café counter next door waving at me. I gesture for him to come outside. We greet each other with fleeting kisses on the cheeks and he insists we first have a drink. I am really not up for it, but I cannot think of anything to dissuade him. With no other appointments or in a hurry, I relent and indulge him. We go inside and Richard introduces me to the woman behind the counter:

"This is Anika, my girlfriend from Germany!" he brags and puts his arm around my shoulders.

I am angry at myself for playing along with his stupid game; however, I do not want to cause a scene. Richard asks what I want to drink.

"A Greek coffee, please," I say.

By the time Richard lights up a second cigarette, I try to talk him into leaving the café.

"Richard!" I whisper in his ear, "drink up and let's go. – I want you to fuck me, baby!"

"Oh, yes! I'm hot for you, Anika! Just a minute longer, then we'll go."

I hope he is serious. I try to relax. Richard chats with the waitress in Greek. Naturally, I cannot understand a word of their conversation. Another reminder of how important it is for me to learn Greek. I cannot expect every Greek man who calls to speak passable English. Therefore, I have lots to do! In this profession, money does not simply land in your lap. I take another sip of my Greek coffee and lightly nudge Richard. He finishes his frappe and pays. Finally! From now on, I must have more patience, regardless if he only pays me 70 euros. Now I have to pretend I have all the time in the world. After entering his penthouse apartment, I walk straight out onto the sizeable rooftop terrace and marvel at the view. Richard follows and stands beside me.

"Do you want to get fucked now?" he asks bluntly.

"Yes," I reply and turn toward him. I touch his strong upper arms and assume they must have been even bigger back when he was training:

"You're such a handsome, strong man, Richard. Come on, let's go to your office."

Richard follows and asks:

"Do you like me, Anika?"

"Yes, Richard. I regret I never saw you in the ring. I'm quite flattered to be fucked by a former boxing champion."

While speaking, I remove my top and place it on the desk chair like before. Richard stands in front of me, intimately watching as I shimmy out of my skirt. Dressed only in a skimpy black bra and thong, I walk over to the couch in front of the wall.

"Come and sit over here, baby."

"Yes, Anika. I'll do whatever you want. God, you're so beautiful. Just looking at you makes me wanna come."

Secretly, I smile. Richard is like a big kid. I do not know if it is due to the stroke he suffered, the numerous blows to the head, or if he has always acted in this manner. As he sits on the couch, he opens the zipper of his pants and pushes them down in one swift movement until the waistband catches on his knees. I take off my bra and straddle him. Tentatively, he touches and caresses my breasts. I steady myself with one hand on one of his broad shoulders while the other reaches behind to grab his proud member. Yes, his little weenie is already hard. While rubbing and lightly squeezing it, I feel him attaining a higher state of arousal. In order to maintain this level of sexual tension for a while longer, I get up, remove my panties, and set them aside. I help Richard remove his pants and underwear. With my legs slightly apart, I sit sideways on one of Richard's thighs and place one arm around his shoulders.

As he seems clueless, I guide one of his big hands to my crotch. He is visibly surprised at the invitation to touch me there and cannot stop staring at my pussy. One of his thick fingers gently probes. Becoming bolder, he unsuccessfully tries to insert a finger into my slit. He is simply too clumsy. I get up, grab a condom, and roll it over his boner. Clueless, he does not know what to do with his hands. I straddle him again, but this time I slide further down so his erection enters my pussy and I start fucking him. I move up and down slowly. Since his hands still lie limply next to his body, I grab and place them on my breasts. He gently caresses them and starts wheezing. I take it as a sign to speed up my movements and start riding him faster. I feel his cock twitching in my pussy. Not long now and he will come. Instead of holding him back, I ride him even faster. Abruptly, the moment arrives. While coming in the rubber, he thrusts his pelvis upward and at the same time lifts me. He was lightning quick again! Once he is finished, my right hand reaches between my legs to ensure the condom is still in place. Everything is fine! Grabbing hold of both of his cock and rubber, I slowly dismount the softening champion. With his eyes closed, Richard relaxes against the back of the couch. I get up and kiss him on the forehead.

"That was extraordinary, Richard — you're an incredibly strong man and your cock is magnificent!" I flatter him. I see he enjoys my compliment and believes me. Gently, I roll off the condom and take it with me to the bathroom for disposal. By the time I shower and return, Richard has put his pants back on. As I dress, he asks:

"Do you feel like going out to eat with me, Anika?"

"Oh, darling! That's sweet of you to invite me to dinner, but I have other plans. Maybe next time, okay?"

"All right, we'll do it another time. Maybe next time I call you?"

"Yes, we might do that, providing I have time!"

He gets up, fishes for his wallet in the back pocket of his pants, and pulls out a 50 and a 20-euro bill.

"Your present," he says, handing me the bills. I refrain from reminding him about the five euros he owes me from the first time. I do not want to come across as being petty. – I pocket the money and say: "Thank you, Richard!" and give him a goodbye kiss on the cheek.

"Enjoy the rest of the day, darling, see you soon!"

He accompanies me to the apartment door. I walk down the stairs and turn around one last time. He throws me a kiss.

10

Since I am currently in the city center, I look around for the tourist office. I am in luck and find it near Syntagma Square. I relish the air-conditioning. The air in the city is oppressive as the outside temperature has already climbed above 36 degrees Celsius. Several women and men dressed in dark blue uniforms stand behind desks advising tourists. Looking around, I see beautiful posters featuring the Greek Islands, the sea, beaches, mountains, and Greek villages. When it is my turn, I ask for two city maps and inquire about brochures listing bus and railway services within Athens. The friendly German-speaking lady hands me five folding maps with all the bus, subway, and tram lines in the relevant districts drawn in. I also ask about hotels and the lady supplies me with a small glossy brochure containing a large number of three – five-star hotels with their address and telephone numbers.

Back outside in Athens' menacing heat, I check my cell phone. So far, no calls. However, it is only noon. Seeing a small café under the shade of a few large trees in front of the Grand Bretagne Hotel, I walk over, sit at one of the tables, and call Violet. She answers:

"Hello?"

"Hi, Violet, it's Anika! How are you?"

"Oh, Anika, hi, darling! I'm great. How about you? I've been wondering what you might be up to. Your ad is in today's paper, right? You know, I no longer buy *Athens World* regularly. I learn everything from the radio and television. Why would I waste money buying a paper every week just to check if my ad is in it? I can tell it is published by the calls I receive. – Okay, I haven't received a call, but that's not unusual because most prospective customers call in the afternoon once they are off work. Obviously that doesn't apply to regular clients. Are you excited?"

I reply affirmatively and relate the details about my encounter with Adonis.

"Darling, you can't jump into a stranger's car! It's far too dangerous. He could've kidnapped and raped you. Oh, my God, you were quite reckless!"

"But, Violet, he was driving a Jeep Cherokee and dressed in expensive trousers and an ironed short-sleeved shirt. He didn't look like a criminal, more like a gentleman. That's why I got into his car. We chatted amicably for half an hour on the rooftop terrace of the Ammas Hotel before driving to a no-tell hotel. He was very accommodating. Everything worked out fine, except for the fact that he only paid me 80 euros, which will probably be his regular rate now... Then again, Richard only pays me 70! – By the way, I just came from Richard. He called me this morning! Once again, he was fast. Easy money. So, what do you say to that?"

"That's great! You should make sure to keep him on your good side, darling! I'm sure he'll call you regularly and, nowadays, 70 euros isn't chump change. Remember the crisis Greeks are currently experiencing! Considering what you told me about Adonis, I'm sure he'll call you again. But, darling, you should know that a well-dressed man driving an expensive car is no guarantee he is a good character! You were rather careless. I'd be too scared to jump into a stranger's car. But enough of that! – What do you say we get together on Monday, providing of course we don't have appointments that evening? It would be nice to see each other and chat a little. I don't have anyone else to talk to about work. Do you have someone? Are there any women in Germany you talk with over the phone? Have you revealed your profession to a friend or acquaintance? — I haven't told a soul!"

"Same here. I wouldn't even tell my best friends. In Germany, the only people I talked to about work were co-workers and the club owners. Although those conversations can't compare to ours, which is why I'm so glad we met! — So yes, if nothing comes up, I would enjoy getting together Monday evening. Do you have any appointments for today or tomorrow?"

"No, not yet. My new customer, the one I met at the 6 X Hotel in Glyfada, won't be back in Athens for another two weeks. His name is Ben. I think he is around 60 years old. He is a nice, simple man who takes care of himself. First, he wanted oral sex and then took me from behind. None of that pesky groping! My God, when I think about everything young men demand! If Ben calls again, I've even considered letting him come to my apartment. I actually prefer older men coming to my home because they appear respectable and don't stand out. Should one of my neighbors see me in the hallway with a client they might think he's a friend or a relative. Okay, some might be curious why I have so many male acquaintances, but it's not like there's a parade going on. I don't think my neighbors have the slightest idea what goes on within my four walls. — You should come visit me at home one day! Okay?"

"Yes, I'm sure I will. Thanks for the invite! God, I'm so anxious right now. I can't wait to see if I get a call from a prospective customer today. Anyway, everything I need for the job is in my bag. I'm ready to go to a hotel or make a house call. I'll call you as soon as something happens. Goodbye, sweetie, and wish me luck!"

"Yes, I do. Kisses!"

I unfold and place the map of Athens on the table and use my phone to Google the exact addresses of some of the hotels listed in the brochure and mark their location on my map.

Now I have an overview of the entire city of Athens. It is much better than looking only at displayed sections of the city on the small screen of my cell phone. I also mark Richard's home and the hotels I frequent; the Ammas Hotel and the 6 X Hotel in Alimos. This overview will help me get my bearings faster and provides me with a better idea of commuting time. In a small notebook, I write:

Jack: Ammas hotel, Poseidonos Street, Glyfada, €100
Richard: Voula Street, City Center, €70
Adonis: 6 X Hotel, Poseidonos Street, Alimos, €80
Richard: Voula Street, City Center, €70

Naturally, I have already tallied it up: So far, I have earned 320 euros. Delighted, I note my earnings. I am a collector. I most passionately collect money, shoes, and lingerie. Since I am on the subject of collecting, I recall the well-equipped sex shop near Omonoia Square is only one subway stop away. – Now I can afford the red mesh bodysuit with vinyl trim. It is also an investment in my business and it will satisfy my passion for lingerie, at least for a while. — Although I already have lots of alluring underthings, in my business you can never have enough and looking at it as an investment allows for a clear conscience! I pay for my Diet Coke and walk to the subway station.

At that moment, in the middle of Syntagma Square and surrounded by crowds, my phone rings. No need to panic, Ilona! Removing my phone from my handbag, I glance at the display. Unknown number. Not dwelling on it, I answer the call.

"Hello?"

"Hi! My name is Pete. – Am I speaking with the very attractive and charming lady from Germany?"

My heart skips a beat. I take a deep breath and say:

"Yes, that's me, Pete. My name is Anika."

"Can you tell me something about yourself and your rates?"

"Of course! I am 35, slim with blonde hair and blue eyes. My rate is 150 euros an hour."

What do you know, easy peasy!

"Okay, sounds good. Where do you live? Can I come to your home or do you go to hotels?"

"I don't have my own work place — I am only available for out calls. Basically, I go to hotels or make home visits. If you want, I can meet you at one of the hourly hotels."

"Yeah, that'll be fine. What days and hours do you work?"

"Every day as long as my phone is on. Generally, from early morning until late at night. If you want to see me, you must give me at least an hour to get there."

"Unquestionably. Athens is a big city with heavy traffic. Okay, Anika, thanks for the information. I'll get back to you."

"Bye, Pete. Thanks for calling."

"Bye, Anika."

Phew! My heart is racing. — Did I do it right? I have no idea! My mind is in overdrive, re- and replaying the conversation from start to finish. Did I leave anything out? No. I still feel unsure. I lost track of my rehearsed spiel. — Then again, it was my first call. All I have to do is proceed according to the motto, 'practice makes perfect' and I will gain experience and confidence!

Only now do I slowly calm down and become aware of the people, cars, and mopeds around me. – I was in my own little world during the call. – I hop on the subway to Omonoia Square. Topside seems to be teeming with foreign street hawkers. It is noisy and hot. Rushing to the sex shop, I find the red mesh body suit where I left it. Since it is a one of a kind, I do not need to try it on again. Not searching for anything else, I pay and leave the shop. Rolled together, the bodysuit is only as big as a banana and lighter than my smartphone. It is the ideal reserve outfit to carry around daily. Standing outside again in the Greek sun's merciless heat, I realize it is time to buy a sun hat to prevent my brain from liquefying. Examining what the street vendors around Omonoia Square have to offer, I only find caps and simple, small hats that do not match my wardrobe. My phone rings again. This time it is a Greek cell phone number. I step into the next entryway to block out the street noise.

"Hello?"

"Yes, hello! This is George. Did you place an ad in *Athens World*?"

"Yes, I did. My name is Anika."

"Hi, Anika!" What do you charge for an hour? Oh, and how old are you?"

"I'm 35 and I charge 150 euros an hour."

"Wow! That's a lot. Can you make me a better deal?"

"No, sorry, darling."

"Okay, thank you."

He hangs up. Just like that. Well, I guess I am too expensive for him. Although it is not the end of the world, I am irritated. I step into the subway station to catch a train back to my hotel. After all, I cannot walk around the city all day in this impossible heat. I need to rest a bit in a cool room. Closing my eyes while listening to the gentle clatter of the train, I replay the last few days in my mind. All in all, they were successful. I should not feel down simply because a man who could not afford me hung up. After reaching the last station in Piraeus, I still need to walk a good 15-20 minutes to my hotel. I make the journey in the shade of the houses along my route. Today is the first day I have a little difficulty walking. It is definitely hotter than yesterday. I need to ac-climatize to such high temperatures.

Once in my hotel room, I close the balcony door and crank the air conditioner, setting it to 22 degrees Celsius. Exhausted, I completely undress and stretch out on my bed. I have placed the cell phone on the nightstand next to me. Intending to rest my eyes only for a few minutes, I immediately fall asleep. Eventually, my ringing phone wakes me. Startled and still half-asleep, I grab it. It is another Greek cell phone number.

"Hello?"

"Bonjour. My name is Anton. To whom am I speaking?"

"My name is Anika."

"Hello, Anika, I saw your ad in *Athens World's* escort section. It is yours, correct?"

"Yes, you have the right number. What can I do for you, Anton?"

"I would like to know how old you are, if you make house calls or work from home, and how much your hourly rate is."

I answer all of Anton's questions and also tell him I only practice safe sex and that I need at least an hour to make it to an appointment.

"Okay. Do you know the Lipsy Hotel near the Syngrou Fix Station?"

"No, I'm sorry, I don't know the place. If you text me the address and phone number of the hotel, I'll know how to get there."

"Yes, I'll do that. Are you already booked for tomorrow afternoon? Can we meet at 2:00 p.m.?"

"2:00 p.m. works for me. Please tell me your full name and room number. Once you've texted me the information I'll call you back."

"Anika, it's a no-tell hotel! That's not a problem for you, is it?"

"Oh, I didn't know! — Okay, it's not a problem. Go ahead and text me the address of the hotel. Tomorrow, when you're at the hotel, call me. — I'll be in the vicinity and can be in your room in a few minutes. Does that work for you?"

"Yes, that's fine!"

"Good, until tomorrow then, Anton!"

"See you tomorrow, Anika!"

That went smoothly. I have an appointment for tomorrow afternoon — yippee! He did not even comment on the rate. I felt more confident this time giving out my information. At once, I am wide-awake and excited. I immediately call Violet.

"Hey, sweetie! I have an appointment at the Lipsy Hotel tomorrow afternoon with a man named Anton. Ever hear of him? He sounds like a Frenchman."

"Anika, that's fantastic! Unfortunately, I don't know the Lipsy Hotel and I've never heard of a guy named Anton. You say he's a Frenchman? — No, the name doesn't ring a bell. What's your impression of him?"

"He was polite and didn't quibble about the price. I'm still waiting for him to text me the address of the hotel. Tomorrow, he'll call me as soon as he has the room number. Everything will go smoothly, don't you think?"

"Yes, it will! I hope he's a nice guy!"

"He certainly sounded like it, but you never know simply by talking on the phone. But don't worry, I'll give you a detailed report!"

"Yes, you do that. — Oh, I'm sorry Anika, but my phone is ringing. I have to go! Talk to you soon, darling. Don't forget to call me!"

In the meantime, I have received Anton's text message. I open my laptop and Google the hotel. I scroll through the displayed page without finding a hotel with that name. Maybe it does not have a website. Anton also confirmed our appointment: Saturday afternoon at 2 p.m. Searching Google maps, I find the address of the hotel and mark the location on my city map with the other marked the hotel locations. I spend the rest of the day learning Greek words, eating out, peeking at my phone repeatedly, and taking an evening stroll around my hotel block. Finally, as I fall tired and disappointed into bed, I realize my hoped-for appointments did not transpire. Although my phone rings five more times before 1 a.m., each caller only asks for information. Okay, three men sounded as if they were interested. – Oh well, we shall see!

11

The next morning after breakfast, I use the hotel telephone in my room to call my father.

"Vertongen," he answers with his last name in the good old-fashioned manner. He always complains when I answer my phone with 'hello'.

"Hi, Dad! It's Ilona. How are you?"

"Oh, hello, child! I'm glad to hear from you! I was thinking about you, hoping everything was all right there. I can't believe you're in Greece. Tell me, how are you doing? What are you doing? Do you already have a lead on a job? Or will you be coming back home soon?"

"Dad, I already found a job. I start tomorrow. Imagine, so far everything has worked out wonderfully. I'm sharing an apartment with two other women, — one a Swede, the other a Brit. I'm waitressing in a bar until the end of August. It is downtown, so it gets lots of tourists. It's okay. I'm getting by with the little Greek I know, but I make sure I learn a few words every day!"

"That's great. So, tomorrow you start your new job, you say?"

"Yes, tomorrow. I'll work six days a week. I'm really happy about it. Nevertheless, before the end of August, I'll have to figure something else out. Who knows what doors might open up for me by then. — In any case, you don't need to worry about me. I'm doing great!"

"I'm glad to hear it. I feel much better now. How is the weather in Athens? It's raining here again. Thankfully it's not cold."

We exchange a few more compulsory sentiments before saying goodbye.

As soon as I hang up, I take a deep breath. It seems my father believes every word I said. Next time I am in the city center, I should look for a bar and take a picture of my alleged work place. That way I will have a few photos to back up my story, should it become necessary. I treat myself to a third cup of coffee and slowly sip it while reading a newspaper on my phone. Today might be the day I have my first customer thanks to my ad in the paper, but I am not all that excited. Perhaps it is because I have already had engagements with different clients this week in hotel rooms. Standing in front of my open closet, it takes a while before I opt for a yellow-flowered, knee-length dress. It makes me look très chic. Not really sexy or striking, just chic. 'Attractive and Charming' — just as my ad says. I select a handbag that complements the floral pattern of my dress. After packing light blue lace underwear for my visit with Anton, I get on my way.

At a 1:15 p.m., I emerge from the Syngrou Fix Station near the Lipsy Hotel. Once again, it is maddening hot.

I search for shade, but the sun is too high in the sky for the buildings to cast any shadow except for a narrow band on the sidewalk along the facades. I wish I had found a sun hat. I really have to find one! The Lipsy Hotel is located on a street parallel to Syngrou Avenue. Examining the front, it does not look very inviting. Although most buildings are old, this one is gray, dusty, and neglected. Its shutters are also closed. Looking through the glass entrance door, I see a small lobby, an old sofa, and stained gray elevator doors. What else did I expect from a dive? All I care about is that the room is at least clean! Nearby, I discover a small pedestrian zone with several cafés. I walk to the nearest one, sit down at an umbrella table, and order a Diet Coke. At 1:48 p.m., my cell phone hums. A text from Anton. He is in room 46. I text back: *I'm on my way!* I place change on the table for the Coke and walk back to the hotel. I am meeting my first customer that contacted me through my ad in *Athens World*. Phew! The older gentleman at reception greets me without really looking at me and immediately turns his attention back to the television on the desk. The elevator appears ancient. It creaks and squeals as it slowly rises to the fourth floor. Now that I am about to knock on number 46, I suddenly feel quite anxious because I do not know who is waiting for me! I realize what a huge difference it is when I enter a hotel room with a customer I have already spoken to in person, compared to speaking to him on the phone and coming to the hotel room alone! I briefly hesitate, give myself a quick pep talk, and knock on the door. That is the way it is in the female escort profession! Anton opens the door wearing only a pair of blue and white checkered boxer shorts. It seems he has already freshened up, which I like. I take another deep breath and concentrate solely on my work.

"Hi, darling! I'm here," I say charmingly, and although I do not feel it, I exude self-confidence.

"Hello, Anika!" Anton greets me in a French accent while looking at me somewhat strangely. Immediately unsure again, I wonder if he does not like me. Can he perhaps tell my real age? Something is not quite right here. — At once, I am extremely uneasy.

"Is everything all right, Anton?" I ask suspiciously.

"Um — yes! Damn, you look good! I didn't expect that. It's common for ladies to exaggerate in their ads. I'm pleasantly surprised, Anika, that's all! I apologize for staring!"

A huge weight is lifted from my shoulders! Relieved, I answer:

"Thank you, darling! Let me freshen up and change, then I'll be right with you!" Phew! — He is pleasantly surprised! And here my initial impression was that he was disappointed and about to send me on my way. Damn, this is so exciting! Violet was right! It is a common hotel room, not big, but everything looks spick and span.

With the thick blue window drapes securely shut, the few small wall lamps illuminate the room in a pleasant, subdued light. The tiny bathroom has a stool where I can place my handbag. I hang my dress over the towel rod affixed to one wall and change out of my yellow satin underwear into my lacy light blue lingerie. For now, I continue wearing my silver high heels. I change the ringer on my cell phone to vibrate. Grabbing my little cosmetic bag containing the condoms from my handbag, I return to the room. Anton lies on the bed with his with arms crossed behind his head. I estimate he is in his early 60s. He is around 1.80 meters tall, slender, short gray hair, and wears glasses. Now that I have returned, he removes his glasses and places them on the nightstand. – His skin is white as snow and his chest nearly void of hair. Glancing at his armpits, I feel a bit disgusted because he has powdered them. Yuck! Who does that? Obviously, I do not let on that I am repulsed by the powder and give him a charming smile.

"God, Anika, you're gorgeous!"

"Thank you, Anton. May I give you a massage?"

"Oh, that would be nice! You know how to do that?"

"Well, I'm not a masseuse, but I can manage a short relaxing massage. Why don't you turn around and lie on your stomach, darling!"

Anton does as I ask and I see his back for the first time. It is full of large, dark liver spots. Perhaps that is the reason he does not go out in the sun and is so pale.

"May I remove your underwear, Anton?"

"No, please wait. I don't want them off yet, but you can pull them down a little."

"That's okay. — So, you're French, right, darling?"

"Half French. My mother was Greek. She passed away a long time ago. She left me her house here in Athens, so from time to time I live here."

I squeeze oil onto my palms and start massaging his back, running my hands up and down in slight circular motions. When I reach his shoulders, I knead them with a bit more pressure and he groans.

"Am I hurting you, Anton?"

"No, not at all! On the contrary, it feels great. Please continue, Anika. Your hands are magical!"

I still cannot get the powdered armpits out of my head! I only hope he does not powder his pubic hairs too. – I really do not know how I would react. Unable to get over my disgust, I hope I can continue hiding it. Other than that, Anton's manner is that of a gentleman. I focus on the massage and run my hands in ever changing circular motions, applying light pressure up and down each side of the spine. Every time I reach his shoulders, I knead them a little harder before running my hands back down to his buttocks.

This time, however, my right hand continues further down until it reaches between continues further down until it reaches between his thighs. Anton jerks violently yet remains silent. I slide my hand a little further underneath his wide-cut boxer shorts and briefly touch his balls before withdrawing my hand again. It is obvious he enjoyed the little interlude. I pour a few more drops of oil onto my right palm and move it back underneath his boxer shorts. Immediately he groans aloud. Aha! Are you about to come, baby?

"May I remove your shorts now, darling?"

"No, not yet please, Anika. I'd like to turn around and hold you in my arms for a while."

Hold me in his arms, with powdered armpits? Oh my God, does this have to happen? Well yes — it is part of the job and I simply have to manage somehow. Maybe he uses powder as a deodorant substitute because of his sensitive skin. Maybe he is allergic to regular deodorants. Maybe his powder even smells good. Nevertheless, no matter what I tell myself, I cannot override my disgust! Anton turns around and lies on his back, stretching out his right arm invitingly.

"Wait a second, Anton. I want to slip out of my clothes."

I quickly strip out of my beautiful light blue underwear and toss it onto the armchair holding my cosmetic bag. I do not want my unmentionables exposed to the powder! Right now, they are clean and I want to keep them that way so I can wear them for the next customer. Tense and uncomfortable, I lie down in his arm, but not before arranging my hair so it falls over his upper arm and does not touch his armpit. Now Anton's left hand starts stroking me. I gather he cannot see well without glasses. His touch is soft and gentle. Caressing one of my breasts, he touches the nipple. Since he pulled his underwear back up, there is no way to tell if there is any movement. When I start stroking his chest, he immediately asks me to stop. I am simply to lie still and do nothing. Inactivity makes me uncomfortable. After a while, he pulls his arm out from under me and kneels beside me. I raise my upper body and support it with a couple of pillows so I will not miss a thing. I believe I see a small bulge in his boxer shorts. It would be strange if by now nothing has begun to stir. I seductively wriggle around on top of the white cotton sheets. Anton slightly spreads my legs. He leans down and studies my pussy up close. The distance between his face and my clit is no more than 10 centimeters. I guess without glasses he needs to be adjacent to see what he is looking at. And, it seems he wants to see every little detail of my pussy!

"I like this, nicely clean-shaven, Anika," he says as he gently brushes a hand over my Venus mound. I remain quiet, continue to lie still, and merely observe. Apparently, he is doing what he dreamed about and seems quite content. Nevertheless, I am not satisfied. I cannot help wondering why I have not seen his cock yet.

Why will he not pull it out? Is something wrong with it? Did he powder his pubic hair? Does it have a rash? Is he sick? Can I catch it? I really need to know!

"Darling, I'd also like to play a bit with you," I say lovingly, pretending to want his cock.

"Later, Anika, later."

Inconspicuously, I look at my watch. Twenty minutes have already passed. Okay — it is still within the normal time range. He did after all book an hour. Although in my profession, like school classes, one hour is only 45 minutes. All I need to do is be patient! After what seems like an eternity, he finally asks me to flip over. Oh no, what is he up to now? Naturally, I abide by his wish and turn over on my belly. Now I am in no position to watch what he is doing, something I do not care for at all! I hear my cell phone humming in my handbag. Anton seems unaware of it. If he is, he simply ignores the intrusion and starts caressing my legs. He grabs my foot and massages it gently.

"Anika, you have a beautiful body! Your skin is so smooth and soft. I like your even tan! You really are a rare sight to behold."

Considering my age, his compliments thrill and flatter me. I leave him alone, believing he will eventually orgasm! I try to relax by thinking about the easy money I make by doing exactly what I want. I have had numerous experiences that were by far less pleasant. Anton is a simple man who is happy showing tenderness while enjoying looking at a beautiful woman's body. The powder is nothing more than deodorant. My phone hums again and although I cannot answer, I am delighted someone is trying to reach me. Anton stops caressing me and actually speaks:

"Now you can roll the condom on, Anika."

Nothing would please me more! I lie on my back again and watch as he removes his boxer shorts. A medium-size, normal-looking penis. It has no red spots, no rash! His dangling scrotum also looks quite normal. It is slightly hairy, basically, the way balls are. The best thing, his pubic hair is not powdered! Relieved, I grab a regular-size rubber out of my cosmetic bag and gently roll it over his penis. It seems Anton is quite aroused. His cock is hard and not far from reaching climax. Should I suck on it or does he want to fuck me right away? Since I have no idea, I lean forward, making it clear I am going to take his cock in my mouth next. Anton restrains me.

"No, Anika. Please turn around again. I'd like to look at your back while I fuck you. I'm enormously turned on by your backside."

"Sure, darling, whatever you want!"

With moistened fingers, I part my pussy and guide his cock to the opening, making it easier for him to slide in his penis. Gently, he starts fucking me. Although his rhythm is slow, his thrusts are deep.

I try not to disturb his movements and just lie there, moaning now and then so he believes I am enjoying it. He continues the steady paced movements until he suddenly thrusts hard and deep and groans out loud with a long sigh. He came. – Still not moving, I give him time to settle down before one of my hands checks whether the condom is still on his cock. Everything is as it should be. Holding his softening cock, I move a bit forward until it slides out of my pussy. Turning around, I find Anton still kneeling in the same spot with his eyes closed and breathing heavily. I fluff up two pillows and make myself comfortable. This worked out great! Anton opens his eyes and gives me a glorious smile.

"Wow. That was fantastic! I really needed that. — Damn, Anika, you're a class act."

Here I think: What did I do except lay motionless? Nevertheless, his praises please me. It reassures me that I can be satisfied with myself and my services.

"Thank you, darling, I'm happy to hear it. I truly enjoyed your tenderness." I tell a little lie. Anton pulls off the rubber, knots it, and discards it in the ashtray on the bedside table. He puts his glasses back on and stretches out on the bed. To avoid lying back down in his arms, I quickly turn on my side and prop myself up on one elbow. We can make eye contact and talk for a few more minutes. Anton does not seem to be in a chatty mood, so I ask:

"How about it, Anton, may I use your bathroom to freshen up while you lie here and rest?"

"Yes, go right ahead, Anika. I'm rather pressed for time as well. My family is expecting me. You know how it is. I always have to be sneaky about it. Now it's time to get out of here. Go ahead, use the bathroom."

I get up, take the condom from the ashtray with one hand, grab my cosmetic bag and my lacy lingerie with the other, and disappear into the bathroom. Shower, towel off, dress, brush hair. I touch up my lipstick and glance at my phone. Two missed calls, both from the same number. Completely dressed, I reenter the room. Anton has dressed while I was in the bathroom. He picks up two bills from the nightstand and hands me 150 euros.

"This is your present, Anika. Thank you!"

"No, thank you, darling! I hope you have a nice weekend!"

"I wish you the same, Anika. Would it be okay if I call you again?"

"Of course, Anton! I'd be delighted!"

Being the gentleman he is, he walks me to the door, opens it for me, and gives me a peck on each cheek before I exit, beaming joyfully.

12

Walking out of the no-tell hotel, I am immediately assaulted by the Greek summer heat. Fortunately, all hotel rooms are equipped with air-conditioning! I cannot imagine how someone would survive a summer in this city without it. I head for the subway. This afternoon I plan to explore the Monastiraki. It is the part of the old town that is famous for its many small shops, bars, cafés, restaurants, and, in particular, daily flea market. It is also where I will search for a bar where I will alleged-ly work for the next two months. Reaching my destination, Monastiraki Square is already swarming with tourists. Making my way through the crowds, my cell phone starts ringing. Glancing at the display, I see it is the same person who tried to reach me twice before.

"Hello?"

"Hi! I'm calling in regards to your ad. Are you available now?"

"Yes, I'm available. Who am I speaking with?"

"My name is George. And you are?"

"I'm Anika."

"Okay, Anika, could you come to my home?"

"Yes, I can."

"Great, let me give you my address."

"Hold on a second, don't you want to know a bit about me?"

"Oh, yeah, I guess. How much do you charge?"

"150 euros an hour."

"Okay, that's reasonable. I live in Glyfada."

"That's no problem, George. Give me your full name, home address, and your landline number."

"I live in Glyfada at 340 Eleftherios Street. Your phone shows my cell number, right?"

"Yes, I have that, but I need your landline number, George."

"Why?"

"Simply because I need to call that number to make sure you're actu-ally home."

"But I don't have a landline. I swear!"

"I'm sorry, George, but if that's the case I can't come to your home. If you like, we can meet in Glyfada at a hotel."

"No, I want you to come to my home!"

"As I said, I only do home visits if I have a customer's landline num-ber. I don't think I can accommodate you."

"So, you're not coming to Glyfada?"

"You're correct. In any case, I hope you have a nice weekend. Per-haps you'll find another lady willing to come to your home. Bye, Geor-ge!"

I hang up. I am not willing to entertain such a risk, especially after Violet warned me not to make house visits without a landline phone number, thus ensuring he actually lives at that address. Apparently, there are men who get a kick out of summoning a call girl somewhere without intending to go through with the arrangement. Some like to hang out in the vicinity and take photographs of the prostitute as she attempts to identify the customer. Violet told me she experienced this. Definitely something I can do without. The fact he did not ask any questions immediately made me suspicious. Maybe he is a young man who thinks this is an entertaining weekend game. In any case, I save the number under: 'Caution - George'. If he calls again, I will immediately know who it is.

Luckily, the pedestrian walkways in the Monastiraki are narrow and shady. Exploring the small, narrow, and at times tube-like shops, I see knick-knacks, souvenirs, white cotton robes, leather sandals, handbags and backpacks, carpets, woven blankets, ceramic wares, and olive oil products.

Each time I walk out of a shop and onto the sweltering, crowded walkway, I keep an eye out for a suitable bar I can sell as my new place of employment to my father and my German friends. At one point, I am pulled along by the crowds. I end up on a wide cobblestone path that coils around the Acropolis. I have to be careful where I step so as not to ruin my silver high heels. Along my new route, I encounter one café or bar after another. That is how it is in Athens, restaurants, bars, and cafés are abundant in clusters, unlike Germany, where establishments are divided between shops, stores, and houses. Here it seems they are all concentrated in certain areas. One small restaurant catches my eye with its colorful, cheerful decorations. Directly in front of the building, large rectangular umbrellas line up close together, providing a nice shady area for the small round tables underneath. Every single one is occupied. On the other side of the walkway, directly across from the bar, is a large, gravel square with several shady trees here and there with tables and chairs belonging to the bar, most of which are empty. I walk over to one and sit down. The waitress approaches. I order a Diet Coke and a club sandwich because my stomach is growling. My phone rings again. A Greek cell number. Looking around, I see the people sitting nearest me are far enough away that they will not be able to overhear my conversation. I answer the call.

"Hello?"

"Kalimera! Do you speak Greek?"

"No, unfortunately I do not. Let's talk in English. I'm Anika by the way."

"Hello, Anika, I'm Jason. It's all right if you don't speak Greek, English is fine. So, tell me, are you actually from Germany? How old are you, if you don't mind me asking?"

"Yes, I am German and I'm 35. Would you like more information?"

"Please!"

After telling him about my services and rates, he says:

"That sounds good. Are you free this evening? I'd like you to come to my house at 11 p.m. I live in Kifissia. Is that possible?"

"Kifissia? Where is that?"

"Kifissia is located in the northern district of Athens. I can text you the address. How about it? Can you come over at 11 p.m.?"

"Yes, I can, however, I need your landline phone number. Are you home now?"

"I am. I can call you from my landline and then you'll have my home number. Would that be okay?"

"That's fine, but you also need to text me your address."

"Yeah, sure, I'll do that. First, let me call you back from my landline. Talk to you in a minute."

Jason hangs up. I stare at my phone, anticipating his return call. In a minute, it rings.

"Jason?"

"Yes, it's me. Okay, now you have my home number. See you tonight, Anika!"

"Yes, see you tonight, Jason!"

He hangs up and I save both numbers: 'Jason - Kifissia'. Shortly thereafter, my phone announces an incoming text:

Avrou 178, Kifissia, Jason.

I text back:

Thank you, we're all set!

Fantastic! Now I have to look up the exact location in Kifissia. Typing it into Google maps, I find it in the northern area of Athens, just as Jason said. As the waitress serves my club sandwich my phone rings again.

"Hello?"

"Hi! My name is George. Did you place an ad in *Athens World*?"

"Yes, I did. My name is Anika."

"Hi, Anika. Okay, how much do you charge for an hour? What do you look like? And what services do you provide?"

"I'm 35, blonde with blue eyes, and a slim body. — For an hour of normal, safe sex my rate is 150 euros."

"What, no anal?"

"Yes, but that costs 50 extra."

"Oh, okay... Is there anything you specialize in?"

"I can role play. If you'd like me to be a dominatrix, then you called the right number. But those services are a bit more expensive."

"Okay. How much for an hour of domination? You're actually experienced, right?"

"Yes, I am. In Germany, I worked in a BDSM club for quite a while. For that service, the rate is 250 euros an hour, 400 for two. Role playing, such as a secretary, maid, school girl, etc., is 200 an hour."

"I take it you have a dominatrix outfit and all the toys such as handcuffs, whips, and whatnot?"

"I sure do. Are you interested in that service?"

"Yes, most definitely, but I'm inexperienced! Let me think. — I find the rate a bit steep. Considering this is a new experience for me, could you knock the price down to 200?"

"Darling, please! I have set rates and I don't like to haggle. Here's my proposal: You pay the full 250 euros and if you enjoy being dominated, I'll extend the session for an extra half hour. How do you like that offer?"

"Let me think ... Let's say I don't like being dominated, could we switch over and continue with normal sex and anal intercourse is included in the price?"

"All right, I can live with that. So, when and where do you want to meet?"

"Can you meet me at 5 p.m. in Glyfada?"

"George, that doesn't work for me. – I require at least an hour notice for appointments so I can get there on time. Right now, it is 4 p.m. — I'm currently in the city center. I would have to go home to Piraeus to get my dominatrix outfit and accessories and then catch a ride to Glyfada. I don't think I can make it before 6:30 p.m. Does that work for you? Or perhaps later?"

"Hm, I guess an hour will work. I could meet you at a hotel closer to where you live."

"Okay. Do you know one in Piraeus?"

"Yes, I know the X-Dream Hotel in Piraeus. I can meet you there. Could you then meet me at 6 p.m.?"

"Yes, that's possible. However, I don't know the hotel. Text me the address so I can show it to the taxi driver."

"I'll do that, Anika! Can I trust that you'll actually show up? I don't want to sit and wait in the room in vain!"

"Don't worry, darling, I'll be there. Believe me! I will see you later, George. I have to hurry now so I won't be late for our rendezvous!"

"Fantastic! See you later, my mistress!"

Hanging up, I cannot help giggling when I hear him call me *my mistress*. I wolf down a few bites of my club sandwich. Unfortunately, I cannot finish a whole sandwich when rushed, which is a shame because it tastes so damn good and I am still so hungry. Regardless, work takes priority over everything else. I signal the waitress and pay my bill. I hurry to the nearest subway station.

When I arrive in Piraeus, it is 4:53 p.m. I hail a cab and it drops me off in front of the Lilo Hotel seven minutes later. Taking the steps two at a time, I hurry to my room on the fourth floor. From the closet, I grab the already packed large shoulder bag containing a black vinyl dress and other items a dominatrix needs. I take out the long blonde, clip-on ponytail because I want to wear it later to extend my natural hair. The bag is stuffed like a jam-packed gym bag, exactly the way it should be. I swiftly undress and hop into the shower. While toweling off, my cell phone announces an incoming text. It might be a text from George. It is. It reads:

Piraeus, X-Dream Hotel, Notios Street 34, room 17.

Okay, I'm on my way! I reply. I scribble the hotel address on a note-pad and tear it off to show to the cab driver. Now I am faced with the difficult decision of what to wear. For visiting George, the yellow floral dress is too conservative. The red pencil skirt with a black top and my black high heels would be more appropriate. I comb my hair back, fasten it into a ponytail, and clip on the hair extension. God, it looks fantastic! Pulling the hair back gives me a stern look, suitable for a dominatrix. I outline my eyes with black eyeliner, paint my lips a bright red, dab on perfume, and, voila, the dominatrix is ready! 5:36 p.m. Inhale deeply! I think I made good time, but now I am fired up. I tell myself to take it down a notch. I need to be calm to prepare for my upcoming role as a dominatrix. That requires withdrawing into myself, getting into the role. If I want to give a good performance, I must be convincing, seductive, stern, and sexy. — I cannot think of a scenario for a beginner like George. I will have to wait and see. I will use my past experiences to gauge what turns George on. Do I have everything I need? Yes. It looks that way. — Off to work I go!

13

Outside on the street, I wave to the first cab I see. He stops and asks me where I need to go even though someone is already sitting in the back seat. I show the taxi driver the piece of paper with the address of the X-Dream Hotel on it. Without a word, he hastily rolls up the front passenger window and speeds off. The next cab driver reacts similarly. The one after that already has two passengers in the back, but he stops anyway and asks me something I do not understand. I tell him the name of the hotel in Piraeus. He briefly raises his head, rolls up the window, and drives off. Thankfully, the next taxi that pulls up is empty. I get in and then hand the driver the piece of paper with the address. Looking at it, he makes a face, grumbles something in Greek, and drives off. Relieved, I sit back and relax.

Since there was no time to Google the hotel's exact address, I do not have the slightest idea where it is located in Piraeus. As we drive down the road behind the theater, the cab driver turns toward the harbor. A short while later, he pulls into a narrow one-way street and reduces his speed. I failed to pay attention to the street's name. After about 200 meters, the taxi driver stops and points to the hotel's illuminated neon sign. It is 5:54 p.m. I made it in time!

From the outside, the X-Dream Hotel looks good. Stepping into the large, modernly furnished hotel lobby, the young man at the front desk addresses me:

"Good evening. Can I help you?"

"Yes, thank you. How do I get to room 17?"

"Take the elevator to the first floor and take a left."

"Thank you!"

"You're welcome!"

The elevator is equipped with a large tinted wall mirror. I remove my black sunglasses and inspect my reflection. I do not see anything someone would complain about. Breathing deeply, I step out of the elevator. After a few steps down the hallway, I arrive in front of room 17.

Once again, I do not know who is expecting me. Suddenly, I am nervous again. What difference does it make! I simply have to get accustomed to meeting clients in hotel rooms or in their apartments for the first time. I knock on the door. Muffled footsteps approach and George opens the door.

"Hello, Anika! Come on in." — Hey, you look delicious!"

"Thank you."

I offer him a cheek and he blows a little kiss on it. George has already shed all his clothes except for tight, black undies. I hope he used the bathroom to freshen up. He looks to be in his early to mid-thirties.

He is tall, slender, with a mane of black thick hair, and quite the hairy body. His face is cleanly shaven, giving him a laid-back appearance. I doubt he is the type who likes to play *slave*. The room is adequately decorated but in the typical brothel style, all red tones, illuminated by soft, subdued light. The wall opposite the bed is covered in gold-framed Baroque mirrors in a variety of sizes and shapes. The bed itself is king size. On top are numerous heart-shaped pillows. A large round mirror is attached to the ceiling directly above the bed, perfect for watching you and your partner during sex. The room is also furnished with two upholstered red velvet armchairs to the right and left side of a long, narrow Baroque table. A big screen TV stands on a low chest of drawers that effectively complements the rest of the ornate furnishings.

"Do you have any particular fantasies? A special request? Or do you want to leave it up to me?" I ask.

"Anika! I have no idea. Do what you want! I merely want to experience serving a dominatrix."

"Okay, then I suggest you be my sex slave. You must obey me from now on. Does that suit you?"

"Yes, Anika, that's fine!"

"You will address me as Lady Anika!"

"Oh, yes, of course, Lady Anika!" he replies, grinning. He really needs to stop grinning.

"And if you, for whatever reason, want to end our game, you must have a safe word. How about: Armageddon? As soon as you say Armageddon, I'll stop the domination game. Does that word work for you?"

"Yes. Armageddon, I get it. As soon as I speak that word you'll stop the game!"

"That's right. However, we also need a safe phrase in case you cannot or don't want to experience any more pain. When it becomes intolerable, you could say, for example: World pain. How about it? Can you remember that phrase?"

He grins again.

"Yes, that's fine. I say world pain if I can't stand the torture. Got it!"

"Okay, we shall begin momentarily. Um, — anything else you want to know beforehand?"

"No, Lady Anika! You can begin!"

He is still grinning. — Not for long though! He seems to enjoy addressing me as 'Lady'. I am standing in front of him with my two bags hanging off each shoulder. I still have not put them down.

"Get down on your knees and only look me in the eyes when I explicitly permit you to do so."

George kneels down, his eyes directed at the floor. I hold out my handbag and say:

"Take my bag and set it over there on the table."

George gets up, which I anticipated, so I slowly and sternly say:

"Get back down on your knees! — You will not stand or walk upright unless I permit it or order you to do so. Get on your knees, crawl over to the table, place my bag on it, and crawl back to me, now!"

Kneeling in front of me in his tight undies, his grin immediately disappears. He now bears an expression of incredulity. Much better. I am curious if he will endure the entire domination game. It is obvious he has no clue what it means to obey his mistress. Hastily, he crawls on his knees to the table, places my handbag on it, and hurries back to me.

"Well done. Now crawl over to the armchair and wait until I return from the bathroom to give you further instructions. You better be still kneeling! Keep your eyes directed at the floor and your arms crossed behind your back. — Understand?"

Without replying, George scoots over to the chair and assumes the ordered position. Good boy! Still, I have to reprimand him. I walk over, grab a tuft of his long black hair, and pull his head back so he has to look at me. Sternly, I ask:

"How're you supposed to respond?"

He seems clueless. I take a deep breath and say:

"Whenever I order you to do something you will politely respond by saying: 'Yes, Lady Anika!' Is that clear?"

"Uh, yes, Lady Anika!"

"What do I want to hear?"

"Um, yes, Lady Anika!"

"I don't want to hear 'uh' or 'um'!"

Still holding his hair, I gently place my right foot on his gender. He seems irritated. He absolutely does not enjoy the pain on his scalp, yet he might enjoy the slight pressure on his privates.

"I'm sorry. I mean, yes, Lady Anika!"

"That's better! – Yet you still lack proper manners. Don't worry though,

I'll make sure you learn some! It might be painful for you if you act clumsy or stupid."

I remove my foot from his genitals and release his hair. Pushing his head down, I make him stare once more at the floor. I disappear into the bathroom. Now I can take my sweet time dressing. No need to hurry. It will be good for George to be alone on his knees. It will teach him humility. Although the bathroom is quite large, there is no stool. Crap! Where am I going to put my other bag or hang my clothes? Looking around, I notice a shelf above the towel rod that is full of clean towels with nowhere else to place them. Ha! What do I have a slave for! Opening the bathroom door, I see a disobedient George. He has made himself comfortable, resting his buttocks on his heels and looking around the room. And here I thought he would practice being humble!

"Hey! What do you think you're doing? I didn't tell you to get comfortable! You better get back on your knees and crawl over here this instant, you imbecile!" I admonish him. I am still not certain if he likes my domination game. I have to figure out if he likes obeying me and being humiliated. – How much pain can he tolerate and still stay aroused? I have to play my role just right. How sternly do I have to act? Some slaves like being insulted and spit on, others like being beaten or urinated on. Other guys like me to be polite and look down on them whereas some prefer I yell at them while calling them vulgar names. Some can endure lots of pain for their mistress and others cry like a baby with every little slap. I prefer a client who already knows what he likes so I have an idea how to proceed. With George, I am left entirely to my own imagination. Nevertheless, once we are done, I will ask him what specifically turned him on during my introductory game of domination. Who knows, maybe he has gotten a taste for something I have done to him?

"Yes, uh... yes, Lady Anika!"

George crawls on his knees over to me. When he is next to me, I grab one of his ears.

"That's for saying, 'yes, uh', — and because you made yourself comfortable and looked around the room, you get this!" I drill the heel of one of my shoes into the front of his underwear, squarely on his cock. Nothing is moving yet in his undies. I am not surprised though. I do not believe an average macho man like he is, gets a hard on when a pretty woman orders him to crawl around on his knees and reprimands him by yanking one of his ears. In his place, I would not be turned on either.

"Watch what you say and follow my orders or else you'll regret it!"

"Yes, Lady Anika!"

I take the stacked towels off the shelf, hold them out to him, and order:

"Take these towels and place them on the table over there next to my handbag. — Hurry up!"

"Yes, Lady Anika!"

George obeys, quickly grabbing the towels and crawling away. Satisfied, I watch him and firmly say:

"Now crawl back to your place and assume the correct position. – Don't even think about looking around the room, grinning like an idiot!"

"Yes, Lady Anika," George replies like an eager student.

Shutting the bathroom door behind me, I undress. I neatly fold my clothes and place them on the newly empty shelf. From my large shoulder bag that hangs on the doorknob, I withdraw my black boots and black vinyl dress. The sleeveless mini dress with collar laces down the front to below the navel.

I remain braless so that my cleavage pushes brazenly against the lacing. As the final touch, I don long black vinyl gloves. I am ready for my first performance in Athens as a dominatrix. Satisfied with my image, I open the bathroom door and remain standing in the opening for a moment. I want to see what my slave does. How will he react? As soon as George sees me, he lowers his head. The only sound in the room is the soft even humming of the air conditioner. It is almost hypnotic. Sure enough, George remains silent while obediently kneeling beside the armchair. I approach him slowly, trying to tempt him into raising his head for a look. He only sees a part of my seductive dominatrix outfit from underneath his eyebrows.

"So, little one, I want to take a close look at what kind of toy I have here. Let's see if you have what it takes to satisfy me. I hope you understand that's what is expected of you!"

"Yes, Lady Anika," he replies like a good little boy.

"Stand up and turn around!"

"Yes, Lady Anika!"

George has a difficult time rising. His legs must be numb from kneeling for such a long time. Not even trying to throw a curious glance at me, he immediately faces the wall.

Now able to see in the wall mirror, he catches sight of me behind him, which is exactly what I want. As long as he does not look me directly in the eyes, he has to have the opportunity to see something desirable. If he does, I must punish him.

"Listen to me so you don't slip-up. Otherwise, you'll regret it! — Take off your underwear and place it on the armchair!"

"Yes, Lady Anika!"

"Then, stand there with your legs slightly spread."

"Yes, Lady Anika!"

George does exactly as I order and stands with his legs spread slightly apart. One of my gloved hands reaches between his legs and grabs his balls. It seems he likes the feel of vinyl material touching his balls for I feel his pride twitching slightly. Good, it seems I am making progress. My other gloved hand reaches around his waist and I run my fingers over his flaccid member. I snuggle close and rub my breasts against his back, driving him a little crazy. Seemingly aroused, George cannot stop staring in the mirror.

"I hope you and your little friend are able to satisfy me," I say and lightly slap his cock. I release George and go over to open my bag containing my domination equipment. I remove my black leather spanking paddle and a thick black leather covered dildo with tassels on one end. Armed for the next round of my introductory domination game, I sit down on the empty, red velvet armchair. George remains motionless. He tries to remain a good, obedient slave. I spread my legs. My dress rides up, exposing my clean-shaven pussy.

"Come here!" I say firmly. "Now! Stand directly in front of me and do not look me in the eyes. Only look at my pussy! That's what it's all about. You understand?"

George does as I order. Standing in front of me, he says:

"Yes, Lady Anika!" followed by a brief peek into my eyes, then down to my breasts where again, he becomes sidetracked before actually looking at my pussy. I stretch provocatively and lustfully slide my gloved hands over my pussy and inner thighs. Adopting a gentle voice, I say:

"Come here, I want to touch your cock and have my way with it!"

His member quickly grows to a respectable size. With one hand, I firmly grip his penis so the tip sticks out. To moisten the head, I briefly stick it in my mouth. Taking the leather-covered dildo, I slowly run the tassels over the tip before wrapping the thin leather strands around it. His proud member seems to like this new stimulation. Satisfied with the way things are progressing, I use my stern voice again and say:

"I have a job for you: Assume the doggie position between my legs and lick my pussy!"

Enthusiastic, he promptly gets down on his hands and knees. He is quite tall and I am sitting in a low armchair, so he must crouch in order to reach my pussy with his tongue.

"I can't hear you!" As a warning, I smack his butt with the paddle.

"Uh... yes, Lady Anika!" he immediately replies.

"What was that? Another 'uh'? Are you supposed to say that?"

I give him another smack on the butt.

"No, excuse me, Lady Anika!"

"So get to work!"

As he moves his head between my legs, I squeeze my thighs together so only his tongue can touch my pussy.

"Lick it properly!" I order him. He really has to stretch his tongue to get the tip between my lips. Once he touches my clitoris, I quickly grab his hair and pull his head back.

"Only my pussy, stay away from my clitoris! — Got it? If you touch it again, I'll really smack your ass. — Now, pay attention to what you're doing!"

I loosen my thigh pressure to allow him more room to maneuver. He immediately endeavors to lick only my pussy. To keep the game exciting, I deliberately move my hips so his tongue — inadvertently — touches my clit. At once, I swing the paddle, smacking him on the butt. He winces and immediately stops licking me. His face betrays his dislike for pain. I will have to handle him differently before he uses the safe word.

"You're not good at it! You use your tongue clumsily, spoiling my pleasure. Stop licking me! — Here, take this leather cock and stick it in my pussy!"

George takes the dildo and handles it awkwardly. Eventually he succeeds in sticking it into my slit. He is probably afraid of doing something wrong. Acting impatient, I seize the dildo and cruelly state:

"You really are quite inept. Give it a rest now! Back up a bit and get back down on your knees. Watch how it's done. Maybe you'll learn something."

Using my right index and middle finger, I spread my labia, giving George an unobstructed view into my pink vagina. I know the picture he sees all too well. Oftentimes, I watch as I pleasure myself and seeing the erotic play of my opening and closing lips drives me over the edge. Every single time. George watches every movement intently with great fascination. Provocatively, I wriggle around in the armchair while my two fingers keep the entrance of my pussy spread wide open. Since I believe George has enough time to become stimulated by the view, I slowly let the dildo disappear between my labia. George's cock is rock hard and sticks out at an angle from his body. Just the way it should be! I unhurriedly push the sex toy deeper into me and then back out until only its penis-like tip remains inside me.

"Now get back over here and do it exactly as I've shown you!"

George scoots over and takes control of the leather cock.

"I can't hear you!" I say firmly.

"Yes, Lady Anika!"

While he is focused on pushing the dildo deep inside me and back out again, I strip off my gloves and loosen the laces of my dress enough so that my nipples poke out. Using both middle fingers and thumbs, I start twisting and pulling on my nipples. George repeatedly looks fleetingly between my breasts and the enticing fondling of my hard nipples and the dildo he is using slowly to gently fuck my pussy.

"Stick the dildo deep inside me and leave it. Make sure it doesn't slip out. I want you to suck my nipples now!"

As I order him, I sit upright so my breasts are directly in his face. – George seems confused. Apparently, he is clueless how to manage both. I say:

"Hold the dildo with one hand and make sure it stays in place while using the other to grab my breasts and stick my nipples into your mouth. Don't tell me it's too much for you to handle."

"No, Lady Anika, I'm sorry."

"Now focus on what you're supposed to be doing before I get turned off again!"

He does as he is told and switches between grabbing my right and left breast, sucking on each nipple enthusiastically so that they remain hard. If this were a personal interlude, I would be really turned on, but since this is work, I do not let it get to me and remain focused on my role.

70

I cannot let him get control of the situation. It is important I keep making the rules of the game. I get comfortable with my upper arms resting on the chair's arms as I play my role as dominatrix and have my slave pleasure me sexually.

No longer wearing gloves, I can look inconspicuously at my watch. Almost an hour has elapsed since I entered the room. That gives me another half an hour to end my introductory domination game. George is currently doing his best to follow my orders. I do not even have to punish and hurt him. He seems to be enjoying the game much more. This is good. Perhaps he likes the little taste he got and will call me again. Perhaps not! Or, he might seek out the services of another dominatrix. Who can say? Most often, in the beginning, new customers are totally fascinated by me and want to see me often, but over time, their interest usually wanes until such time they do not call me at all. At least, that was what happened in the German clubs. The same goes for other women who worked there. They also had numerous lusty admirers, but only a few remained loyal over the years. Anyway, that is the way it is in my profession. Men are programmed that way. Then again, loyalty is not required in our industry. Nevertheless, it is nice and it makes us happy when a customer turns into a regular.

"Okay, that's enough licking. Now it's time for your cock to see action and do its thing. Come on, get up!"

We both rise. Taking him by the hand, I lead him to the mirrored wall. I position us so we both can watch in one of the big, gold-framed mirrors. Thankfully, the pause does not affect his boner. I lace up and hide most of my breasts again. Slowly circling him, I touch his naked body wherever I want. My hands run over his buttocks, thighs, cock, balls, hairy chest, chin, face, neck, and shoulders.

"Spit in your right palm!" I order, for which I receive a look of irritation, yet he does as he is told.

"Spit in it again and make sure no spittle runs off your palm! I want the spit in your hand, not on the floor or wherever. Do you hear me?"

"Yes, Lady Anika." I see he is trying to create more saliva in his mouth. As he spits again, I say:

"Okay, that's enough. Now rub the spittle over your cock. I want it nice and shiny. Then, masturbate for me!"

Carefully, so as not to lose one drop, George rubs the gooey substance all over his cock and starts masturbating.

"Yes, that's what I want to see. Get your cock nice and hard and then, and only then, will you be allowed to fuck me with it."

I walk over to the table where my handbag is and take out two extra-large condoms. As I open one packaging, I glance at George. Like a good boy, he waits in front of the mirror and instead of watching himself play with his cock, he uses the mirror to watch every move I make.

I am perfectly fine with that. – The important thing is that he stays aroused. — Hm... how and where do I want to fuck him? On the bed? Then I could tie his hands and feet. That would be good. It will not hurt, yet I can immobilize his movements, causing him a little discomfort by not being able to touch me. Yes, that is what I am going to do. I take out my hand and ankle cuffs before walking back over to him.

"I like the way you stroke your cock, baby. You know what you are doing, don't you?"

"Yes, Lady Anika."

"Now it's time your cock had a bit of fun. Lie down on the bed on your back. Cross your arms over your head and keep your feet tightly together!"

George releases his boner and does as he is told. Obediently, he stretches his arms above the head. There is a sparkle in his eyes and for the first time, I actually receive a smile, not a grin. I kneel beside him and place both rubbers on the bed above his head.

Joining his two wrists, I handcuff them. They are heavy-duty handcuffs given to me years ago by a German police officer who was a customer. They are much heavier than ones available in a sex shop. The ones I am using are covered in black velvet. Men like the plushy feel on their skin. And velvet looks classy, not kinky. My ankle cuffs are made of two round flexible black plastic rings connected by a short chain. Although they are a carnival accessory, they suit my work. I wrestle the elastic rings over each foot and, voila, his feet are tied. Lying there, restricted in his movements, I squat over George's hips so my crotch is directly above his erection. This makes him grin again, which I do not like. He should not be grinning while playing this game. Even now. Without warning, I slap his face with my right hand and say angrily:

"You better stop grinning immediately or there won't be any fucking! Understand?"

"Yes, Lady Anika!" he replies, startled. He is as horny as he can get. His cock is rock hard and throbbing. Now it is time to roll a condom on it and invite him to fuck me. As he slowly sticks his member into me, I can tell it is a bit longer and thicker than my black dildo. And that thing is quite big. George groans. He no longer has time to grin. He is too obsessed with fucking me. Then again, I want him to exert himself! I slightly raise my hips to provide a better angle for his pelvic thrusts.

I command him:

"Come on, fuck me! Get a nice even rhythm going and fuck me hard! I want to feel your thrusts in my brain! You understand? Nice, steady, and hard!"

"Yes, Lady Anika!"

He enthusiastically thrusts his pelvis upward and forcefully rams his cock deep into my pussy. I can tell he likes the challenge. Everything is going according to plan and I let my mind drift. – Is he married? Why else would he ask for the service of a prostitute?

A colleague of mine once told me that except for a few, most Greek men cheat. And mostly with prostitutes. We call them whoremongers. Is George one of them? – I should help him reach climax. Changing position, I place my full weight on him. Loosening the lacing, I once again expose my breasts. They bounce rhythmically with his thrusts.

"Come on, make me come. Let me see what you can do!" I say encouragingly.

George is in his element and my goading has the desired effect. He is giving it his best. I pretend to be on the verge of an orgasm and as I feel he is about to ejaculate, I moan and groan aloud and then quiver as if I came. Over time, I have learned several variants. With him, I knew I had to explode. He erupts. I hope the condom does not break!

As a precaution, I take the pill so I cannot get pregnant, although there is always the risk of contracting AIDS. I cannot protect myself against that. George's after-orgasm panting ends, so I allow him to grin. I check if the rubber is still intact on his cock. It is.

I rise slowly up so his cock slides out of my pussy without the condom coming off. I am relieved to see the little receptacle on top is full of George's cum. — When I return from the bathroom, George is sitting on the bed smoking.

"So, baby, tell me how you feel about being my sex slave?"

I put on my bra and panties and sit down next to him on the bed. George offers me his pack of smokes, which I decline with a gracious gesture.

"Well... I didn't really enjoy being pulled by the hair and ears. However, being allowed to look into your spread pussy — wow! No woman has ever shown her pussy to me like that before. That was the best experience ever. And seeing you in that black vinyl outfit drove me absolutely crazy! Damn, that outfit is incredibly sexy on you. When you came out of the bathroom and walked toward me, right then I wanted to take you and have my way with you, — maybe even spank your ass a little..." He laughs mischievously and takes a long drag from his cigarette. "But then I thought, domination requires patience before I get rewarded. — Anyway, I definitely want to see you again. But next time I want to fuck you normally and also have a say in what we're going to do."

He takes another drag and grins apologetically.

"Of course, we can do that," I reply. "In any case, you have gained another experience. Now you know you're not into pain or being humiliated. And you also know you're not a guy who likes to only follow orders when it comes to sex. — Tell me, are you married? I mean, you don't have to answer if you don't want, I'm merely curious."

"No, that's okay! I have no reason to keep secrets from you. No, I'm not married yet, merely engaged. – We've known each other for five years. But we're not living together, at least not yet. She's still studying, whereas I work in the computer industry. — I still live with my parents. I don't know why, but our relationship isn't as exciting as it was in the beginning and that is probably why we got engaged. I know, stupid move. Anyway, I think she would love it if we didn't have sex anymore. I mean, she doesn't show any interest or enthusiasm in bed. You should see her, she's so beautiful, always dressed smartly — such a desirable young woman... Something stands in the way of us really having fun in bed."

"It's quite normal for a couple's sex life to mellow over the years. In a relationship, other things take precedence."

"It sure seems so," he replies.

Given the fact he is a young, handsome man, I do not understand why he would hook up with a prostitute. – I am sure if those two marry, they eventually will have children and the normal life of a Greek family. His wife will blossom in her role as wife and mother while George will most likely continue using the services of prostitutes. In any case, it is an arrangement that may satisfy both parties. George finishes his smoke and stubs the cigarette out in the ashtray. He stands up and extracts his wallet from the back pocket of his folded jeans.

"I owe you 250, right?"

"That's correct."

He counts off 50-euro bills and makes a fan before handing them over to me. I pocket the money and say:

"Thank you, darling! — I'll dress now and leave you to your own devices."

George glances at his Rolex and nods.

"Yes, I also have to get going soon. I wouldn't want to be late meeting my fiancé!"

He grins mischievously. – I go into the bathroom and grab a quick shower before dressing. After packing up all my stuff, I put my black sunglasses on above my forehead. George kisses me on both cheeks and with a 'bye, darling' I walk out.

Leaving the X-Dream Hotel, I am in a great mood because I am 250 euros richer.

14

My business is running like clockwork today. – I am absolutely thrilled! As I cross the street, my stomach rumbles. No wonder, the last thing I ate was a few bites of my club sandwich at lunch. Definitely not enough nourishment to sate my appetite for the entire day.

It seems my new profession as a call girl will deny me a regular meal schedule. That is okay, – as long as I eat good meals and only revert to surviving on junk food when business calls and I am pressed for time. I should keep an eye out for restaurants serving wholesome dishes such as salads, pasta, fish, and vegetables.

The taxi I treat myself to stops in front of my hotel. – As I enter the lobby, Spiros calls out to me from the small storeroom behind the reception counter. Stepping up to the desk, he emerges with a white bag that he proudly hands to me.

"This is your laundry bag, Kiria Ilona! You can drop it off here with me. Three kilos of laundry costs 15 euros. Dresses and blouses needing ironing are billed separately. How does that sound to you?" – Spiros grins.

"Spiros, I love it. Thank you very much!"

"Not at all. It's my pleasure to do you a favor, Kiria Ilona! Have a wonderful evening!"

"Thank you, Spiros. Same to you!"

When I enter my room, the first thing I do as is turn on the AC. My room is hot and stuffy. Although it is counterproductive with the air conditioner running, I open the balcony door for some badly needed fresh air. I discard my bags on the bed and strip down to my underwear. Stepping out onto the balcony, I sit under the awning in the shade. A few minutes later, I close the balcony door except for a crack so the room has a chance to cool down. Since I am now a bit accustomed to Athens' weather, I remain outside a while longer.

It is shortly before 8 p.m. and it is another three hours until my next appointment with Jason. Closing my eyes for a few minutes, I listen to the early-evening traffic. Every now and then, someone honks. The loudest noise comes from mopeds zipping through traffic. Apparently, they run faster without a muffler. Feeling inner peace as well as reenergized, I re-enter my room, shut the balcony door, and down a big glass of water. Walking over to the bed, I empty my bags onto it. Grabbing the vinyl gloves, I wash them with soap under hot running water in the bathroom. Examining my dress, I decide it only needs airing out and place it on a hanger. I stuff the small socks I wore with the thigh high boots into the laundry bag. After cleaning and sorting my domination equipment, I remove the clip-on hairpiece and brush it thoroughly. I unbind my hair and brush it into the usual lion mane.

Once my black eye liner is eliminated, I apply discreet makeup. – I search my closet. Although I arrived with two large stuffed suitcases, I cannot help feeling that I did not bring enough clothes. My wardrobe is extensive, lots of chic dresses and costumes for when I go to restaurants or bars. I have a long dress for the theater and there are even a few conservative, plain summer dresses for home visits. And, unquestionably, short, sexy dresses and skirts with matching tops. After some initial indecisiveness, I finally choose the short-sleeved, knee-length dark blue sheath dress for visiting Jason at his home. It is elegant and I am presentable if I accidentally ring the wrong doorbell. While thinking about food and my upcoming journey to Kifissia, my phone rings.

"Hello!"

"Hi! I'm Lucio," a gentle voice whispers.

"Hello, Lucio. I'm Anika. – Are you calling in regard to my ad in *Athens World*?"

"Yes, I am. Anika, what a beautiful name you have! Is that German?"

"I don't think it's actually German in origin. I was told it's Scandinavian. So, what can I do for you? Do you want more information about me and my services?"

"That'd be great, Anika!"

I tell Lucio the pertinent information.

"Wow! 150 euros... that's a lot!"

"No, it isn't, Lucio. The price is justified considering the services I provide."

"So you say, but I still think it's a lot of money. – At least for me it is. I'm a yoga teacher, so I don't make much. Do you do yoga, Anika? – Maybe we can come to some arrangement where I compensate you with free yoga classes..."

Oh my god! I have to put an end to this!

"Lucio, darling! I am only paid in cash. I don't accept any other arrangements. Perhaps try your luck with a colleague of mine. As for me, I have to say no, it definitely doesn't work for me."

"Wait, Anika! Please don't hang up! Let me make you another offer: I'll pay you 100 euros to come to my house and I don't even want to fuck you. I simply need someone to talk with. Naturally, I'd like to get to know you too. – Please! – Your voice sounds so sweet, even when you're upset. You know, I really like that. – What do you say, Anika? Pretty please!"

Breathing heavily, I am about to hang up when I change my mind. Why not go to his place and make an easy 100 euros for just talking! — Now I am actually curious to meet the man.

"So, let me get this straight, Lucio, you don't want to fuck me? — Okay then, I'll accept your offer of 100 euros. When and where would you like to see me? Today is out of the question."

"You agree? I'm delighted! Thanks, Anika! Well, Monday through Saturday I'm busy giving yoga lessons, so that leaves Sunday, but it has to be after dark. I don't want my neighbors seeing who's visiting me. You understand, please be discreet, Anika! — How about tomorrow evening at 10:00 p.m.? Does that work for you?"

"Yes, that's fine, but I need your full name, home address, and landline phone number."

"Of course. – Let me give it to you. Do you have a pen and paper ready, Anika?"

"Okay, hold on a moment so I can get something to write on. I'll be right back. – Okay, let me have it!"

"My name is Lucio Fabris. I live in Alimos, on Agios Antonios Street No. 5. My landline number is 210 899833126. Do I need to repeat it, Anika?"

"No, I got it! Once we hang up, I'm going to call you at that number to verify it's actually yours, which I'm sure it is. Then we're on for tomorrow evening. Okay?"

"Yes! But please, don't come directly to my house. — Call me shortly before you get here, perhaps when you are at the periptero at the beginning of my road — that's where I'll meet you. My neighbors can hear my doorbell and they don't need to know I am entertaining that late. The house is badly insulated, so discretion is in order, Anika! — Oh, wait, I have another question. Are you afraid of dogs?"

"No, I'm not, as long as he's not aggressive."

"Oh no, Anika! He is a she and she's very sweet. Once you're in the apartment, I'm sure she'll want to sniff your hand to get your scent. Then she'll be happy and I'll put her in the kitchen for the time being. Don't worry, she won't stay with us!"

"That's fine with me. Okay, it seems we've discussed everything. — I'll call you right back on your landline. Talk to you shortly, Lucio!"

I hang up and save his cell phone under, 'Lucio - Yoga', than I dial his number and he answers after the first ring.

I record the appointment in my notebook along with Lucio's phone numbers and address. It is now time to get ready for my appointment with Jason. — All of a sudden, I seem to be starving! — On the other hand, I need to dress. I use the perfume decanter and pack my big handbag with all the necessary items. After one last glimpse in the mirror, I switch off the AC and out the door I go!

I am in luck. I catch an approaching taxi to the subway station at the Port of Piraeus. Fortunately, the ride saves time for I need to grab a bite at one the small establishments around the harbor. I opt for a typical Greek restaurant and order a Salata Choriatiko, which comes with tomatoes, cucumbers, peppers, onions, feta cheese, and olives. The table is set with a paper tablecloth, a small carafe of water, and a basket of bread that also contains silverware wrapped in a napkin.

A salad is just what I need. It does not take long to be served and I dig in. Breaking off a hunk of bread, I dunk it into the salad bowl to suck up the healthy olive oil. Come to think of it, a shot of ouzo would go nicely with my meal. Then again, I do not usually drink during working hours and I want to keep it that way. After finishing half the salad, I feel properly nourished for the rest of the evening. The subway ride north to Kifissia takes a good 45 minutes. It is also the end of the line.

15

In Kifissia, I walk along a large tree-lined avenue until arriving at this district's town square. Compare to Piraeus, it is not as hot, but rather a delightful summer evening. Now would be a pleasant time to stroll hand-in-hand with a friend window shopping, maybe grabbing a bite to eat somewhere, and perhaps afterward a drink wherever... Oh well, at times, I dream of such things. — But I am alone and I already ate. Besides, I am on a mission. Looking down one of the side streets, I see many bars and cafés with chairs and tables on the sidewalk and almost all of them are occupied. Some establishments have a large flat screen TV hanging on their walls and each one is broadcasting some soccer game. All I see are locals, not one single tourist. The patronage seems to range from 20-40 years old. All are in loud and lively conversation. The majority are smoking and drinking a cold coffee drink called a frappé that is popular especially in summer. I recall tasting it on a previous vacation to Greece and ending up with a stomachache. I am not a fan. A small bistro table is being vacated. Quickly grabbing a seat on one of the stools, I order a diet Coke. While waiting, I watch the hordes of passersby strolling down the road in both directions in front of me. Having seen enough, I take my phone and read today's news. Looking at the sports section, I read the Greek and Russian soccer teams face each other in a European championship that is being broadcasted live. That explains the crowd of locals. Jason must not be a soccer fan, otherwise, I am sure he would have asked me to come later. Nearby is a taxi stand. At 10:40 p.m., having already finished and paid for my drink, I head over to the stand and talk to a cab driver. Showing him the note with Jason's address, he says, "Okay, let's go," and I hop into the back of his yellow cab. This evening's appointment will be my first actual home visit. I am not counting Richard because the first time we went to his apartment together. The situation awaiting me is entirely different. Thinking about it curdles my stomach again. I promptly try to calm down. Shortly before 11 p.m., the taxi slows and pulls into a dark, quiet residential street.

The big houses lining the road are hidden behind high hedges or fences with their own plot. From most of the houses, dim light shines through the windows. Arriving at a two-story red brick building, the cab driver stops and points to the plaque next to the front door — number 178.

"Thank you! Please pull a little forward and I'll get out," I say and hand the driver a 5-euro note. The taxi driver obliges me and thanks me for the tip. I walk back to house 178 and stop in front of the garden gate, looking in vain for a doorbell. Unsure, I grab my phone and call Jason. He picks up immediately and I whisper:

"Jason, it's Anika, I'm in front of your garden gate and I don't see a bell."

"Oh, sorry, Anika! I forgot to tell you, the doorbell is by the front door. Open the garden gate, it isn't locked and come to the door. I'll be right there."

I step through the garden gate as the front door opens. Jason greets and beckons me. He is average height, most likely in his mid-fifties, with thick, dark blond hair, blue eyes, and a gut. We enter a large hallway. Jason opens the first door on the right and we step into his living room. The sturdy furnishings are dark mahogany and the lighting is pleasantly dim. A glass of red wine and a burning cigarette resting in a heavy glass ashtray sit on the coffee table in front of the couch.

"Please, Anika, sit down. You are a lovely lady!" says Jason, pointing to the couch. "Can I offer you a drink? A glass of wine or champagne?"

Since it is impolite to decline, I say as I sit:

"Yes, please. A glass of red wine would be nice."

To pace myself I'll sip it. Jason goes to the living room cupboard and pulls out another wine glass. Grabbing the open bottle of red wine off a side table, he first fills my glass before topping off his own.

"Cheers, Anika! Here's to meeting you!"

"Cheers, Jason! I'm also pleased to meet you!"

Clinking glasses, followed by sips, I suddenly feel self-conscious in front of Jason. Thankfully, he strikes up a conversation.

"So, where exactly in Germany are you from, Anika?"

"I'm from the Rhineland, close to Cologne."

"Cologne. No, I've never been to Cologne. I've been to Hamburg and Munich, and Berlin, of course. – So, how long have you been in Greece?"

"About a week. I rent a room in Piraeus."

"Ah, Piraeus. – I have my office there. My family is in the shipping business. We own oil tankers."

Jason pauses, – lights a new cigarette, exhales, takes a gulp of red wine, and continues:

"My work requires a lot of traveling. Mostly to New York and London, but I'm the happiest when I'm on my farm. It's my passion."

"Your farm?" I inquire, intrigued.

"Yes! — I have a large tract of land near Nemea, which is in the northeastern part of the Peloponnese. I bought an old farm many years ago. I've renovated it and now it's back in operation. I have employees growing lettuce, potatoes, strawberries, cabbage, and many other vegetables. There are over a hundred olive trees and I don't know how many orange and lemon trees on my land. I also have rabbit and chicken coops. While there, I enjoy caring for the sheep, goats, and donkey."

Again, he takes another big swig of red wine.

"Yes, Anika, I also have one donkey. God, I love that beast!"

Full of enthusiasm, Jason tells me all this and when I sneak a peek at the clock, it is already 11:15 p.m. I guess it is time to get down to business. That is why he called me after all. However, he takes much delight in his story and continues his narrative while drinking wine like it was water. I must think of something to stop him or we will be sitting here for who knows how long.

"Oh, I, of course, have dogs. A German Shepherd and two Labradors. God, they're great animals. Do you like dogs, Anika?"

"Yes, darling, I like dogs very much. Actually, I'm fond of all animals. I can sympathize. After living in the city, it must feel great being out in the country from time to time."

Quickly, so he does not take my remark as an invitation to continue his story, I add:

"Jason, darling, you're sitting so far from me. Don't you want to scoot closer or perhaps we can go into another room? — And, darling, where would I find the bathroom? I'd love to freshen up."

"Yes, of course, Anika. Come on, I'll show you where the bathroom is." Taking another quick drag, he places his cigarette in the ashtray and we walk into the hallway. A few doors down, he opens the bathroom door, reveals where the freshly laundered towels are kept, and walks out again, closing the door behind him. After ensuring it is properly shut, I admire the big beautiful precious marble tub, gold-plated faucets and fixtures, and big tinted mirror. I slip out of my clothes and change into the light blue lacy lingerie I protected from Anton's powdered armpits this afternoon. I am sure Jason will love it. I disable my phone's ringer, grab the little bag containing my work equipment from my large handbag, and exit the bathroom. Dressed in only the sexy lingerie, I walk back into the living room in my silver high heels and notice Jason has refilled his glass and is smoking a new cigarette. He looks at me and smiles.

"Damn, you're gorgeous!"

Since I do not want him to become preoccupied with another story, I approach him and sit down on his lap.

"Wait!" he says and puts out his cigarette.

He places his arm around me, giving me the impression he is a bit shy. Maybe because we do not know each other yet. Some clients need to feel a certain familiarity before they lose their inhibitions. Therefore, I make the first move and start caressing him. Oh-so gently, I blow little kisses on his forehead, cheeks, and neck. As my lips wander further down, I kneel between his legs while simultaneously unbuttoning his checkered shirt. He does not utter as much as a word. As I run my fingers through his hairy chest, I brush my lips all over it. Embarrassed, he smiles. I am positive he enjoys the performance. My other hand cups the zipper of his jeans and I can immediately tell he is hard. Given the fact he remains quiet and I am not sure whether he wants to do it here on the sofa, I ask:

"So, darling, are we staying here or are we going into another room to get cozy?"

"Yes, you're right. Let's go into the bedroom. Follow me."

I get up, grab my small bag, and follow him into a huge bedroom. Framed photos of young people are in the place of honor on the night-stand bedside the double bed. His children? There is also one of an attractive woman. His wife? – Possibly. Jason undresses and hangs his clothes on a valet stand. I fold back the light bed cover all the way to the foot of the bed and lie on the side I assume is his. As I stretch and wriggle around seductively, he surprises me by literally pouncing on me. Quickly, I spread my legs for Jason to lie down between. Enthusiastically, he showers my neck with kisses while frantically moving my bra aside. He eagerly moves his mouth to my breasts. After a while, he begins kissing me down along my belly and ends up at my thighs. — He is frantic, reminding me of a wild animal. I glimpse his cock and see it is medium sized and hard. Grabbing a condom, I open it, and say:

"Come on, darling, let me touch your cock," I whisper and adjust my position so I can hold of his penis. He does not hold me back. After rolling the rubber properly on, I lean further down and take his penis in my mouth. He groans.

"Stop, wait!" he says, "I want to fuck you!"

Lying on my back with my legs spread far apart, I move the flimsy material covering my crotch aside to make room for his cock. Breathing heavily, Jason lies on me with his full weight and shoves his erection into my pussy. I can barely move. I did not expect him to weigh so much. Like a man possessed, he rapidly thrusts his cock in and out my pussy. After a while, he heaves his body off me and lies down on his back, panting heavily. "Come on! Sit on me!" he manages to say between gasps.

Removing my askew bra, I toss it at the head of the bed. I lower myself onto him. His cock is still hard. The condom looks intact and does not need replacing. Since he is all the way in me, I lean back and use my hands to support myself to keep from falling backward. Jason now has a clear view of his penis moving in and out of my pussy. It is obvious he likes this arrangement. I stay in this position and slowly ride him in a rhythmic motion. It does not take long before I sense he is about to ejaculate. To help him along, I hasten my movements and he shoots off his load abruptly. Jason rears up one final time and then collapses on the bed. With eyes closed, he moans:

"Oh, my God! — Oh, my God!"

He was quick! I hope I satisfied him. – I mean, I did not do all that much before it was over. I slowly dismount his softening penis and inspect the condom. Everything is as it should be. As I lie down next to him, he pulls me into his arms and says:

"That was fantastic, Anika. Tremendous. I really like you. Hopefully, you'll stay in Athens for a while longer and come see me again."

"I'd love to, darling. – I'll be here until the end of August, if not longer. — So, whenever you're in the mood for my company, all you have to do is call. I like you too. You're a real gentleman — and quite a wild one in bed."

"Ah, Anika, you should have seen me in the prime of my life. I used to have much more stamina, but nowadays I quickly run out of breath."

Not wanting to say the obvious, I sit up and ask:

"Do you want to enjoy another smoke before I leave?"

"Yes, that's a great idea — and you still haven't finished your glass of wine. Come on; let's go back into the living room."

Just as I intended. I grab my stuff and slip into my high heels. In the bathroom, I quickly shower, dry off with fluffy and probably expensive bath towels, then brush my hair, and use a little hair spray to get it just right. After touching up most of my makeup, the only thing left is lipstick, but I skip it because I do not want to smudge his wine glass. Finished, I walk back into the living room. It is 11:45 p.m. A quick fuck, just the way I like it. I take my previous seat and cross my legs.

"Cheers!" Jason holds up his full glass toward me.

"Cheers, darling!" I raise mine in response.

"Jason, I have a favor to ask. Can you call me a cab or tell where I might find one quickly? It seems you live in a secluded area and I don't think many taxis can be found here at this time of night."

"Yes, you're right. You won't find a cab at this hour. I'll drive you to the subway station. There's always a taxi available there. — Or take the subway, it'll be cheaper than taking a cab to Piraeus."

"Yes, I thought about taking the train back home, but the last one leaves at midnight. It's too late for that, so I have no choice, I have to take a cab."

"Oh! Oh, I'm sorry. I didn't think of that when I asked you to come at 11:00 p.m. — For what it's worth, I'll drive you to the station and make sure you get safe and sound into a taxi!"

Considering all the glasses of wine he had just in my presence, I am not sure it is such a good idea. Then again, he does not seem to be drunk. I guess I can trust him to get me there in one piece. I pick up my glass and take another sip of the deliciously red wine. As soon as Jason stubs out his cigarette in the ashtray, I get up before he lights another one. After all, I only meant to keep him company for one cigarette! Jason, who threw on bathrobe after we had sex, stands up and says:

"Give me two minutes, Anika. I'll be right back."

While waiting, I meander through the room and look around. I find more family photos on a sideboard. One is Jason as a soldier and another one when he was a groom. Although I do not know what his wife looks like today – perhaps she is already deceased – but looking at the pictures of her, I can say she was a true Greek beauty. While I'm looking at their wedding picture, Jason walks back into the living room and says:

"That's our wedding photo, taken 28 years ago. We married young. She's a fantastic woman and mother. But nowadays she lives in New York for most of the year. She only comes to Greece over the Easter holidays. She's still as beautiful as she was back then. I love her!"

"I believe you. She is strikingly beautiful! How many children do you have, if you don't mind me asking?"

"Three. Two boys and a girl. I took our eldest under my wing and taught him how to run the company. The younger boy left three years ago to study in London. Our daughter studies art history in New York. — They're great kids. They're good hearted and intelligent."

Jason walks over to me and asks:

"How do we do it, Anika? Is it okay if I just hand you the money?"

"Yes, that's fine, darling!"

He hands me two green bills.

"Take it, Anika, the taxi ride will be expensive. The night tariff goes into effect after midnight, double the usual fare."

I am more than happy and thank him for his generosity. A customer like him needs to be treasured! Jason leads the way down the hallway and grabs his car keys out of a bowl sitting on a cupboard next to the front door. We continue into the two-car garage. Both parked cars are Mercedes; one is an SUV, the other an S class. He opens the passenger door of the SUV and assists me inside. Yes, regardless that he looks like a Canadian lumberjack, he is a true gentleman. After a ten-minute drive, we reach the subway station in Kifissia. Five cabs stand in line waiting for fares. Lowering the driver side window, Jason talks with the taxi driver first in line and then turns to me:

"Okay, Anika, he'll drive you to Piraeus. That's your destination, right?"

"Yes, it is."

"Okay, then good night, Anika. I'll call you!"

"Good night, Jason, — and thanks for everything. Have a great weekend!"

I exit the air-conditioned SUV and climb into the air-conditioned taxi.

Tired and satisfied, I lean back and relax. Showing the driver my note with the name and address of the Lilo Hotel, he nods and drives off. While watching the lights of Athens zip by for 50 minutes, I reminisce about past evenings spent in clubs, vacationing on a Greek island…

Suddenly, I think about what the future has in store for me. Looking at my phone, I notice I have not received any calls. However, considering the hour, that is fine with me. Although happy, I am also quite tired and merely want to go to bed and sleep.

16

I wake up in the middle of the night and go outside on my balcony. Loud music radiates from the bars in the surrounding area, but the hellish noise from cars and mopeds zipping around is even worse, at least to my ears.

That is how it is in Athens; quiet nights are unprecedented. Most Greeks do not become active until late evening, long after the sun has already set. They drive their cars, mopeds, or motorcycles around, or go out to dinner, music bars, or nightclubs, amusing themselves into the wee morning hours. This is unfamiliar to me as it is unheard of where I come from. There, after eight in the evenings, sidewalks are empty and families sit at home in front of the TV. Stark naked, I grab a bath towel, spread it over the white plastic chair, and settle in. I am thrilled I can sit outside unclothed without being cold! In Germany, this would only be possible on a few summer nights.

Thinking about the previous day, the day my ad appeared in *Athens World* for the first time, considering I made 450 euros, I am extremely pleased. I am not used to that either. The clubs I worked at, my payment was 30 euros, half the fee the customers paid. Each evening, I had to satisfy quite a few customers so I could also go home happy. Granted, if I provided special services I made more money. For anal intercourse, I received an extra 20 euros on top of the regular 30. As a dominatrix, I earned as much as 100 euros. Earning more money with that service was the reason I developed an interest in that type of work early on. When I was 26, the first club I worked at as a prostitute clarified it for me: A dominatrix or mistress plays the dominant role by giving orders and at times, acting sadistically — the man plays the submissive — obedient or subservient, or as we in the profession refer to it, the slave or the degraded.

The club also had a torture chamber in the basement. The room measured four by six meters and the floor was gray tiles covered in different sized, dark-red Persian carpets. Affixed to one of the chalk-white walls hung a man-size, red-lacquered diagonal cross with soft leather straps on all four legs for tying and holding a man captive. On the opposing wall hung a large mirror where the bound man could watch. In the middle of the room stood a piece of decommissioned sports equipment. The height-adjustable pommel horse had its handles or blocks removed, but, if necessary, they could be quickly re-attached. A dominatrix would command the man to bend over this horse in order to whip him — and this room only saw men — or to lie on his back or belly on it so as to tie him up in an uncomfortable position to inflict further pain. – It all depended on which abuse the customer enjoyed more. In one corner was a badly built prison cell. It consisted of round iron bars embedded in a wooden frame on the ground as well as on the ceiling with welded crossbars to the longitudinal pipes.

The door contained the same iron bars inside a wooden frame. Inside, there was nothing but gray tiled flooring and a metal bucket. Once, I witnessed a prisoner pee in the bucket and then bring it to his mouth to drink his own urine. Two metal-screened ceiling lamps provided sparse lighting. There was also a moveable spotlight on a telescopic stand used for interrogation. This allowed a dominatrix to shine the light on whatever part of the man's body she deemed necessary. A sturdy, large wooden dining table and matching chairs stood against one wall and, at times, depending on the game, came into play. The shelves of a simply constructed cabinet, approximately three meters in length by two meters high, held a selection of masks, whips, hand and foot cuffs, dildos, crucifixes, tin cups, chains, and various other items for creating a sinister atmosphere.

The torture chamber also contained a black lacquered throne upholstered in dark red velvet for the dominatrix. It stood three steps up on a dais against one wall. The elevated platform was also covered in red velvet. It was large enough for the subject to lie down or kneel in front of his dominatrix in order to kiss her boots, to worship her, or to jerk off in a bowl for her.

Even though the club had an elaborate torture chamber, it did not employ a full-time dominatrix. – She was only by special request and always arrived in a white Mercedes with Belgian license plates. With a suitcase full of equipment, she immediately entered the basement's torture chamber to meet her customer. However, she also played the submissive, which earned more money than the role of a dominatrix. My boss told me being a customer's slave was lucrative, making anywhere between 400 and 1000 euros per session. After such sessions, I saw welts on her body or red skin from being beaten at times. She always applied ointments and tinctures to these to speed up recovery.

I asked my boss if I could assist the dominatrix during the next session free of charge. I wanted to learn the skills. The dominatrix agreed, providing the customer had no objections. From then on, I was the dominatrix's assistant. I was allowed to hand her whips and cuff the customers. Oftentimes, I merely stood there with a glass of champagne or some kind of torture device, never uttering a word. My role was to play my mistress' servant and to obey her every command. Some customers found it erotic to be in the presence of a young, completely naked woman who also had to follow the directives of the mistress. It definitely made the dominatrix appear more authoritative.

I found those S&M sessions mysterious and I never discovered anything personal about the dominatrix. Even though I was allowed to assist her in the torture chamber most of the time, she was always reserved toward me. Depending on my role and the duration of the session, she gave me a tip because she knew I could not service customers and make money as her assistant. She never spoke to any of the other women who worked for the club either. With my boss, she only talked business and only when absolutely necessary.

Other than that, she did her job, – collected her fee, and disappeared in her white Mercedes as quickly as she had shown up. I believe she wore a wig. – Whenever I saw her outside the torture chamber, she always wore large, dark sunglasses. I admired that woman, but mainly because of all that money she made with her services.

Later on, while working at other clubs, I offered to play the role of a dominatrix and simply copied my teacher's performance. So far, I have never offered to play the role of slave, mainly because I am afraid of the pain I might experience. As all this goes through my mind, I stretch in my chair again and look out at the illuminated houses of Piraeus with the dark sea in the background. Damn, I am doing great! Just the fact that I no longer have to worry about being recognized at work is a huge relief. Back in Germany, constantly coming up with excuses and sneaking around bothered me. I always lived with the fear that my family or friends might discover my part-time job. Now without this concern, I am actually aware of how much it had weighed me down.

The employees at the Lilo Hotel assume I am writing an article for a German magazine about 'Germans Living in Mediterranean Countries'. I wonder if George the manager or Spiros the front desk clerk bought my story. Nevertheless, I do not care.

I finish my glass of water and go back to bed in my air-conditioned room. I really do not like the way beds are made up in Greece. On top of the fitted sheet, there is only a sheet and a blanket. I miss a proper duvet with a nice, soft cotton cover. Maybe I should buy my own bedding and, perhaps, a new suitcase or a sizeable handbag for all my new acquisitions, in case I move out of my current residence.

The next morning, I realize I forgot to recharge my cell phone overnight. It is dead. I slept so soundly not even the beeping of the low battery warning woke me. Then again, I was actually able to sleep in. It is already 9:30 a.m. when I get out of bed. Momentarily groggy, I snap out of it and plug in my phone.

A couple seconds later, I hear it beeping. I missed three calls, each one from an unknown number. So what, no big deal. Nonetheless, I must make it a habit of plugging my phone in before I go to bed and switching the ringtone to low so I can still hear it but it will not wake up any of the other hotel guests if it rings in the middle of the night. I walk out onto the balcony. Although the traffic noise is no quieter than last night, it is daytime and a part of it, thus I do not perceive it as disturbing. This morning's breakfast is toast with butter and honey, Nutella and Tilsiter cheese, as well as a banana and a small bowl of yogurt. I like starting my day this way. On my cell phone, I check out the latest news. Greece won last night's soccer match against Russia, one to zero. I am pleased to read this as it will guarantee cheerful, happy customers. Men can get so upset when their team loses, so much so that they are not even interested in sex.

This evening, I have an appointment with that weird yoga teacher. Cannot wait to see what type of man he turns out to be. Until then I have to figure out how to spend the day. A swim in the sea? – That is wishful thinking because if I receive a call, there is no way I can meet a customer with unmade hair, salty skin, and my massive beach bag. Going for a dip in the big pool has to wait for the time being. I am going to do that when I take a day off and can fully enjoy it.

At the moment, I can live without knowing when that day will occur. Getting my business established takes priority. Nevertheless, I should definitely do something to maintain my tan. The last time I visited a tanning studio was in Germany. Therefore, that is on today's agenda!

After I lay out a floral, turquoise short stretch dress that emphasizes my curves, I grab my big silver handbag with everything I need for work. Impulsively, I consider packing and taking along my laptop bag with clothes and equipment needed for playing a dominatrix. If I had that bag with me yesterday, I could have taken my time with the club sandwich and gone directly to George instead of rushing back to my hotel first. — What would I need? A dominatrix should have thigh-high boots, black strapless fishnet stockings, and a pair of black patent leather stiletto heels. Also, a matching vinyl bra and panty set with a zipper along the crotch. All these items are not heavy and do not take up much space and therefore, not a burden to carry around. I also pack elbow-length mesh gloves without fingertips so my red polished nails are exposed and a belt. The belt consists of two chains attached to a leather piece and a buckle. If need be, I can use the belt as a punishment or restraint device. Naturally, I also pack my black leather, 2.3-meter long bullwhip. After one final look around to make sure I have everything I need, I close my laptop bag satisfied.

The bag looks conservative and reveals nothing. It is more suitable for hotel visits. Having made my bed and tidied the room, I shower, shave, and lotion my body head to toe. Using a hairdryer and a round brush, I style my hair into its usual lion's mane. Today, I have decided on turquoise eye shadow to go with my everyday eyelash lengthening, waterproof black mascara. I tint my lips with a touch of pink. Now I wear discreetly applied makeup and look attractive, not overdone. Appropriate for a summer day. One final touch, a dash of my favorite perfume and I am done.

With two stuffed bags, I leave and walk toward the town square. While searching for a tanning studio, I also examine the upper floors of buildings because I have noticed they are often rented out to businesses such as cosmetics, nail and hair salons, and medical practices. Shortly before the town square, I find what I am hunting for on the second floor of a commercial building. After climbing the stairs and searching the hallway, I see the small reception area of the tanning studio through a thick glass door.

A bell tinkles as I push the door open. A young, dolled-up woman rattles off something in Greek and looks at me, obviously annoyed at having her idleness disturbed.

"I'm sorry, I speak very little Greek. Do you speak English?"

"*Ne*," she replies in Greek. *Ne means yes.* I inquire in English about prices, the type of sunbeds, and if there are any available right now. In appalling English, she answers my questions and points to a sign. It lists the prices for eight, ten, twelve, fifteen, twenty-minute sessions for a strawberry sunbed or a kiwi sunbed, which is the cheaper one.

Unfamiliar with the differences, I ask. She explains that the more expensive model provides a quicker tan. Okay, makes sense. Interrupting her busy schedule again, I ask which tanning bed and length she would recommend considering my current tan. She merely replies: "Strawberry, twelve minutes."

Next, she opens a drawer, pulls out a flyer, and hands it to me. What do you know, a brochure with all the information in English! I buy a card for 80 minutes. It is cheaper than paying for individual sessions. Considering I am going to be here for at least another two months, it is a good investment. While chewing gum unabashedly, the young woman shows me to the strawberry sunbed booth. It is bathed in red light in accordance with the strawberry theme. I hope I do not end up looking like one. Even though I do not really trust the recommendation of the seemingly disinterested young woman, I know a 12-minute session will not do any harm. After stripping out of my clothes, I lie on the sunbed. In Germany, I really enjoyed going to a tanning studio especially in winter. It made me feel so much better. Outside it was freezing and I was inside naked exposed to intense heat. Having received my artificial yet intensive sunbath, I leave the studio with a slightly red tone to my skin, although I know within a few hours the slight redness will have turned tan.

Checking my cell phone, I see there are no missed calls… I could explore the area where my appointment with Lucio is tonight. Alimos is not far away from Piraeus. I find it unbearably hot again. It must be around 38 degrees Celsius. Standing in the shadow at a bus stop, I wait for one with A1 on the front. After what seems like an eternity, the bus finally pulls up and opens its doors. I quickly squeeze my way in and validate my ticket at a machine, immediately regretting having boarded this bus. All seats are taken. Making my way through the crowded aisle, I stop at an open window and grasp the bus' handrail tightly with one hand. I must hold both bags with the other hand, making me regret having taken my laptop bag. Both bags in one hand is too heavy and cumbersome. The bus departs Piraeus and bounces down the road. Every time it slows down, swerves, or accelerates, I really have to hold on tight to the rail and balance myself and the bags so I do not slam into the other passengers. As we cruise down along the coastal road, the equal amount of passengers disembarking is replaced with those boarding. I still have not snagged a seat. Standing there, shifting my weight from one foot to the other, I enjoy the fresh air flowing through the open window, but at times, it also becomes quite breezy. This is anything but a smooth ride. Why did I do this? I could have as easily made myself comfortable on my balcony while listening for possible calls. If someone called, I would only have to dress, grab my bags, and hop into a taxi in front of the hotel. I would actually be relaxed. Oh well, now it is too late! Therefore, I enjoy the scenery on both sides of the bus. One is a six story high-rise building with shops, cafés, and restaurants on the ground floor. The floors above are rented or condominiums. On the other side of the road, I see parallel-running train tracks. Next to them, along the sea, is a palm-lined promenade packed with people. However, it is not unusual considering today is a Sunday. Countless colorful umbrellas occupy the beach and young and old people enjoy frolicking in the sea. One of the next stops should be Kalamaki or Alimos. For a better view of the upcoming bus stop signs, I move while making sure no other passenger touches my laptop or handbag. The entire trip is absolutely stressful! After another five minutes, the bus finally stops at the station in Alimos.

Pulled along with the throng of disembarking passengers, I am glad to be outside again and, although it is hot, breathing fresh air. Okay, so where am I right now? I set the laptop bag on a bus bench and consult my cell phone. Ah, — I see, I am not far from where Lucio lives. Looking around, I see a park directly next to a marina with many berthed sailing boats a bit further up the road. If it were not so hellishly hot, I would not mind exploring that area. – However, it is now the hottest time of the day and simply impossible. Perhaps I will find a café or restaurant in the park to sit down at and wait for a business call.

I am dragging my feet by the time I reach the recreation area. Thankfully, I discover a place and find a free table inside. Yes, inside where it is nice and cool thanks to the air-conditioning. It is essential I cool off!

From here, I see the beach and sea. Sunday is definitely family day. Once the waiter serves my Diet Coke, I call Violet. She picks up after a couple of rings:

"Hi, darling! How are you?"

"Hello, Violet. I'm okay. The heat is getting to me today. It's so much different here than in Northern Europe! How are you doing?"

"I'm all right. I am sitting comfortably on the sofa, doing my nails, and watching an English TV show on animals that have been dropped off at a shelter and are now in need of a new home. They're such cute cats and dogs! I'd love to have a dog, a couple of cats, and, of course, live out in the country. Regrettably, I live in Glyfada. At least I feed and give the stray cats in the neighborhood a little attention. But I won't let them in my apartment. I can't. What would my clients say? You know cats are unteachable. Who knows what they might do when customers show up. Just imagine if one of my customers was allergic to cat hair. — It's sad, but it won't work. No matter how much it breaks my heart the cats simply have to stay outside. — So, how's business? Were you successful yesterday?

I tell Violet about the calls I received in regard to my ad and the appointment I have in Alimos this evening with Lucio.

"Oh, I know Lucio! – I've been to his place. He's a crazy guy, but completely harmless. It's simply that he doesn't have much money. How could he, he's a yoga teacher. — Nothing to be afraid of. It has been a few years, but if my recollections are correct, he likes role-playing. – Yes, I'm sure. – He wanted to play student and teacher or something along those lines. Anyway, you'll find out tonight. Strangely enough, he never fucked me. That I remember. I believe he played with himself. Yes, that was it."

"Well, it's good to know he's harmless. I might have been skeptical, but curiosity got the better of me. — What does your schedule look like? Can we get together tomorrow or are you busy working?"

"Oh God, darling, I almost forgot. I'm meeting Bob at the Hilton. Let's get together another day. How about next Saturday? Business is usually slow on Saturdays, at least in the evenings. Most businessmen go home for the weekend and the majority of Greek men spend time with their wives, girlfriends, or buddies. You were lucky with Jason! Okay, Kifissia might be far away and the taxi ride expensive, but he also paid handsomely. I know it's frustrating if the entire tip goes to the cab drivers, leaving us with nothing extra our wallets. In our business, we have quite a few unavoidable expenses. But what can I say?"

"Yes, that's the way is. — Okay, so we are on for next Saturday."

"Yes, let's go to the bar I told you about. Is that okay? — It'll be nice to have a girls' night out again for a change. Unfortunately, all I do is shop and visit hotels. Other than that, I'm alone at home. I keep busy by cleaning my apartment and watching TV while waiting for the phone to ring. Apart from that, every now and then I take a customer into my bedroom. That's my usual routine! A little change will do me good. What do you think?"

"Most definitely. And I would love to see you again! — Yes, our profession may make us rich, but it also gets lonely... but that's only because it has a bad reputation. In actuality, we're not doing anything

bad! Anyway, that's the way it is. Sadly, we can't change that... —
Okay then, let's meet next Saturday in Glyfada."

"Yes, it's a date! But call me again, darling. One of these days, I have
to show you where I live! You'd come and visit me, right?"

"I most certainly would. Just let me know when. Okay, Violet, talk to
you soon, take care!"

"You too, Anika! Don't forget to call to let me how it went with
Lucio!"

"I will! Bye, darling!"

The rest of the day I spend on the coast at Alimos reading and
walking barefoot along the beach, while the waiter keeps an eye on my
bags and shoes. I also eat a proper meal — a salad with chicken meat.
Considering the heat, it was perfect. Regrettably, my phone never rang
once.

17

The street where Lucio lives is in a quiet residential area not far from the coastal road. Since there is plenty of time, I decide to walk to his home. On Agios Antonios Street, I turn around and return to the corner where I saw a periptero. From there I call Lucio.

"Hi, Lucio, it's Anika. I'm down the road at the periptero at the intersection. You said you wanted to pick me up."

"Yes, Anika, I'll be right there! Do you mind if I bring my dog Sahira along for the walk? It would also give her time to get to know you."

"That's fine as long as she doesn't jump up or drool on me. Please keep her on a leash."

"Yes, I will. Okay, see you in a minute."

A minute later, I see a man of average build and a small white dog walking toward me. He is wearing a colorful shirt and shorts. His dog does not pull on the leash, obviously trained. Come to think of it, I mistakenly agreed to meet Lucio on the street. I might stand out to people who know Lucio. And that is something I like to avoid. I walk a few meters farther so it does not look like I am waiting for someone. When Lucio catches up to me, he asks:

"Anika, right?"

The periptero vendor looks over at us. I wonder what he is thinking. I am uncomfortable and quietly say:

"Yes, I'm Anika. You must be Lucio."

"That's right, my sweet!"

To make matters worse, Lucio steps up to give me a hug. At the last second, I avoid his embrace by quickly bending down and petting his dog behind the ear. Obviously interested in my shoes, she sniffs them for a while and waggles her tail. All is well; she has accepted me.

"Lucio, it's time to go! The vendor is staring at us. I really don't like this."

"Don't worry, Anika! I know him. He's a nice guy. — Anyway, let's go."

I am tense as we walk to his apartment. Not one word is exchanged. Arriving at his building, Lucio opens the garden gate. It screeches horribly. We climb a few stairs through the narrow front yard and step up to a slightly open lime green wooden front door. Lucio unclips Sahira's leash and the dog slips into the apartment. He opens the door all the way and beckons me inside. As promised, he places Sahira in the kitchen. Lucio might be Italian, not only because of his name, but like many southerners, his skin is slightly darker compared to North Europeans. He is bald and terribly skinny. In the hallway, he asks:

"Would you like some tea, Anika?"

"No, thank you, Lucio. Where are we going to get comfortable?"

"Let's go to my yoga room. It's cozy."

Obviously, our opinions differ when it comes to what is cozy. That is okay, to each his own. – The well-ventilated room looks clean. The walls are decorated with cotton batik and cheap posters sporting Hindu motifs. Several colorful foam mats lie on the floor and one wall has shelves stuffed with knick-knacks, books, CDs, and a stereo system. Lucio pushes a few yoga mats out of the way, grabs one of the stacked wooden stools from next to the shelf, and places it in the middle of the room. I am standing there and do not know what to do.

"Lucio, where can I put my bags and where can I sit down?"

"Oh, wait! Let me get a stool for your bags. Any chance you want to sit with me on the floor?"

"Better not. Can I sit on one of those stools?"

"Yes, of course. Wait, let me get a stool and then I'll find a seat for you!"

Swiftly, he slips out the door and returns with a typical Greek wooden chair with a woven reed seat. Lucio has removed his sandals and is running around barefoot. After setting up the chair in a corner of the room, he looks at me and gestures to it.

"There you go, for your bags and clothes! A lady valet, so to speak."

I have to smile. A lady valet! – So, he wants me to undress. We will see. I have not decided yet. First, I want to know what is expected. Lucio takes another stool and places it next to the one in the middle of the room. Seemingly unsure, he stares off into space. Abruptly, he grabs another stool and places it with the other two.

"Ready!" He beams and gestures with a sweeping hand for me to take a seat. Placing my bags on the chair in the corner, I go back and sit opposite Lucio. Lucio sits and immediately jumps up. He rushes over to the stereo system. I can already guess what kind of music he is going to play. Sure enough, it is meditation music with harps and bells.

"Cute," I lie as I smile at him. "What can I do for the young, friendly man?"

"Tell me, Anika, where are you from! I'd like to get to know you."

Inconspicuously, I glance at the clock. 10:05 p.m. By 11:00 p.m., at the latest, I want this appointment to be finished.

"Wouldn't you rather tell me about you and your passion? I can tell it's yoga, right? Do you also teach Tantra yoga?"

"No, not at the moment. The Greeks are too shy to learn Tantra Yoga. If you're interested, I can teach you. My offer still stands. I'll give you yoga classes instead of paying for your time with euros. Of course, Tantra Yoga too."

"No thanks, Lucio! Okay, let me tell you a bit about me. I'm from Germany, taught sports, and worked as a prostitute. I'm here in Athens for the summer. I haven't decided if I am going to stay longer or return to Germany in the autumn. Now it's your turn. You're Italian, right?"

"Half Italian, half British. My father is Italian, my mother English. I was born and raised in England. In Kent. When I was a young man, I went to explore Italy. From there I took a little trip to Greece and the rest is history. I stayed. — Excuse me, Anika, but why did you bring your laptop? Do you always carry it around or just today? Don't tell me, you have movies or photos on it for customers?"

"No, the laptop bag holds work related items. Not a laptop or notebook. It's an undercover bag, so to speak."

"Aren't you a sly one, Anika! May I see inside? I'm curious! I want to learn as much as possible about you. Could you please undress while we talk? Please, Anika!"

I do not mind taking my dress off for 100 euros nor do I mind him looking in the bag. After I slip out of my dress, I drape it over the so-called lady valet. Remembering the way he said it makes me smile again. In only my sexy white satin lingerie and high heels, I return to the stool with my laptop bag and set it on my thighs. Lucio stares at me wide-eyed and whistles through his teeth.

"You're much prettier than I had hoped! You have a terrific figure, Anika. Are you aware of that? Yoga would be perfect for you and your body! And I'm not just saying that, I know."

Lucio is amazed by the bags' contents.

"Oh, Anika! My, my, my!"

He shakes a raised index finger admonishingly as if to say my stuff is unseemly.

"My God, Anika! What's that, a whip? — Anika!"

"Yes, that's my whip."

Removing it, I unroll it with a quick flick of my wrist. It is my braided leather bullwhip. It is the first whip I bought and my oldest companion. – With room, I can unleash it and make it snap. I have practiced, but never actually had use for it during domination. Placing my laptop bag on the free stool next to us, I stand up. Gripping the handle of the unfurled whip over my head, I seductively turn in place, its long tail skillfully slinking around my body. Lucio stands up and watches in fascination. Liking my own performance, I look around for a mirror. Unfortunately, there is no mirror in his yoga room. As I come to a stop facing him, I grab the whip's tail with my other hand and stretch it between my outstretched arms and ask:

"You liked that, didn't you?"

"Oh, yes, Anika. You have no idea! May I hold the whip?"

"Only if you're a good boy!"

Violet mentioned Lucio was into role-playing. All I need to do is steer him in the right direction. I certainly do not know what else I can talk to him about. Usually, I charge more for role-playing. So what! We already agreed on the price over the phone, but because he will not get to fuck me, I can make an exception. Although, for a 100 euros I will not get completely naked nor is he allowed to touch me. There must be limits. I did not catch him. He contacted me through my ad in *Athens World*.

"I will be a good boy, Anika! Tell me what to do! Should I brush your hair or kiss your feet?"

Aha! He is that type of guy.

"First, take off your clothes in front of me. I want to see you naked!"

"Oh, Anika! – I feel so ashamed!" he says primly. "But I'll do as commanded!"

I watch him remove his shirt, shorts, and underpants, all of which he nicely folds and places behind him on one of the yoga mats. As he stands naked in front of me, it is obvious he is not inhibited. The yoga teacher stares at me in obvious delight! His body has a seamless tan. I do not picture him using a tanning bed and wonder where he got such a nice tan. Is there a nude beach somewhere along Athens' coastline? I sit on the stool, cross my legs, and order him:

"Take off my right shoe and kiss the heel. Really put it in your mouth and suck on it as if it was a real cock. Otherwise, you can forget about holding the whip!"

Lucio kneels before me and pulls off my right shoe. Enthusiastically, he sticks the heel in his mouth. Next, he uses his tongue to lick it up and down, and then, – almost passionately, showers it with kisses. I wonder if he is bisexual. Or, perhaps, he can assume a yoga pose that allows him to blow himself? Whatever the case, it is apparent he enjoys my game. That is fine with me because it is such easy work.

"Great, Lucio! I like it when my pumps shine. Now lick the entire shoe."

Wordlessly, he slides his tongue all over my shoe. He caresses it lustfully and for the most part, keeps his eyes locked on me.

"You have nice, delicate feet, Anika! They look healthy. May I kiss them?"

"No!"

"Oh, that's a shame!"

I believe Lucio is familiar with my type of game. I wonder if he has a girlfriend. Does he have affairs with his yoga students? – That is a distinct possibility. As their teacher, the seduction would not be a problem. The room is softly lit with aromatic incense permeating the air and meditative music plays in the background as they have tea. Then, he slinks around while teaching them stimulating yoga poses. Once aware of his peculiar predilections, they break it off. Yes, I easily imagine him with such a love life. Since he wants to act out his fantasies, every now and then he hires a prostitute. I assume he has called many women who advertise in *Athens World*. I am sure Violet and I are not the only ones who have seen him in his home. Deciding the licking has gone on long enough, I order him to place the right shoe back on my foot and perform the same act with the left one. Without complaining, he does as I say. Once again, he mainly keeps his eyes glued on me. I guess it turns him on to look at my body. Or, is it licking my shoe? I have no idea. At least his little pecker is bouncing around in his lap.

"Enough of that!" I say after a while. "Put the shoe back on my foot. Make sure you remain squatting and close your eyes! You'll feel the whip soon enough."

As soon as he is finished, I get up and position myself behind the still squatting Lucio. I snake the whip several times around his naked upper body including his limp arms. Grabbing the tail of the whip with my other hand, I pull it taut. With eyes closed, Lucio rolls his head back and whispers:

"Anika! The leather feels so erotic. Please, pull it a bit tighter. I love that feeling!"

I like it this way. He makes it easy by telling me what he wants! As I increase the tension on his body, I step closer to him so that my lower abdomen touches the back of his bald head.

"How does it feel, baby?"

"Just look at my willy and you'll know, Anika!"

His manhood grew into a boner. Not a big one, but it is proportionate to his physique. Recalling Violet's words regarding Lucio's preference, I ask him:

"Lucio, tell me, were you a good boy when you went to school? Did you pay attention in class instead of looking at girls?"

"No, Anika, I wasn't a good boy. Although I paid attention, I always tried to look up my teacher's skirt when she sat on her desk."

"Did your teacher ever notice you trying to sneak a peek?"

"Yes, she noticed, though she never scolded me. Occasionally, she deliberately spread them a little wider. I believe she liked me looking at her bush. She never wore panties, Anika! It wasn't my fault; I was just a curious little boy."

"You were a naughty little boy! I'm sure you were aware it was inappropriate when you looked under your teacher's skirt, right? – I mean, you knew she was your teacher! Did you also masturbate in class?"

"No, Anika, not during class. I wouldn't have dared. The students sitting next to me would have seen it. However, every day after school, I masturbated at home. It was always the picture of my teacher's bush in front me, Anika! I wasn't interested in the young girls at school. All I wanted was to kneel between my teacher's legs and get a close look at her thick bush while taking in her infatuating scent. It's what I've dreamed of when masturbating. I've always wished for it, Anika!"

"And nowadays, do you still wish for it?"

"Oh, yes! Just thinking about it gets me going. — Also, I wanted to slide her skirt up and rub my willy against her bush. I didn't want to stick it in, Anika! Only rub it against her bush, just once, against that thick, strong scented bush of hers. Is that so reprehensible? — Anika, do you think I could rub my willy against your pussy? Only rubbing, I won't stick it in!"

"No way! That is a crazy idea you have! — However, I would like to see you masturbate. Stay put. I'm going to loosen the whip so you can remove the hand you use to jerk off with. Then you can show me what you do when you think about your teacher's bush!"

I loosen the whip. Lucio immediately pulls out his right arm and his hand reaches for his twitching boner. I pull the whip tightly around him again, grab both ends with my left hand, and step nearer. Lucio has his rod in his hand and starts masturbating. Although my pussy has no bush, it does have its scent. I stick my free middle finger deep inside and then wave it in front of Lucio's face. Greedily, he leans forward and tries to lick my finger. Should I allow it? No! Definitely not!

"Keep your tongue in your mouth or I'll pull my hand away this instance! Be glad I'm even letting you smell my pussy!"

To give him a good whiff of my pussy, I place my hand over his face so my moist finger is directly under his nose. Lucio moans with desire.

"Yes, that's a good boy. Now show me how you masturbate when you think about your teacher. I want to see you squirt all over!"

I am fine with him coming soon. For the 100 euros he is paying, he has certainly received more than enough. I can end my hour on time. He is yanking on his peter like there is no tomorrow. Then, his whole body spasms and he ejaculates onto his thighs. Not a single drop lands on a yoga mat. Slowly, Lucio sinks down and moans softly until his climax spasms subside. I loosen the whip and slowly uncurl it from his upper body.

"Now that was a good boy. Once you've showered you can hold the whip!"

"Yes, Anika, the whip! I completely forgot about it. I'm going to hop into the bathroom. I'll be right back!"

Lucio promptly leaves the studio. When he returns, the scent of soap follows him. Holding out the whip, he absentmindedly grabs it and runs his fingers over the soft leather:

"Thank you, Anika. I liked the feel of your whip on my skin!"

"Would you really like to feel it at another time?"

"Oh yes! I might like that. But only on my butt! Like the teacher would have done if she had caught me masturbating in class. I would have had to stay after class and once we were alone, she would have punished me right there on her desk!"

"Well, we can arrange for that to happen. But not today. Today's class is over, don't you agree?"

"Yes, of course... But you could stay for a while longer, Anika. I can brew tea and we can listen to some music and chat."

"No, thank you, Lucio! It's time for me to go. Is there somewhere I can wash my hands and freshen up?" I ask. Lucio leads me to the bathroom. By the time I return, he has fully dressed again. I quickly put my clothes on, place the rolled up bullwhip in my laptop bag, and close it. In the end, it was good I schlepped the bag around. Granted, it was not much fun, but the sight of the whip exposed Lucio's proclivities and saved me from having to come up with something. He made the job easy. Lucio pulls a hundred euro note from his pocket and says:

"For you, Anika."

"Thank you, darling! – I can find my way out. You don't have to accompany me."

"Oh, come on! I'll walk with you for a bit. Wait, let me get Sahira. She'll be happy for another little walk."

"No, Lucio! I don't want to be seen with you in public. Who knows who we might run into and I really don't want to be stared at again. It made me uncomfortable. So, please, let me leave by myself. You can always walk your dog after I'm gone."

"But it would be nice if Sahira and I accompanied you, Anika!"

"Why is that? Do you do the same thing with all the prostitutes you hire?"

"Yes, of course!"

And there you have it! No wonder the vendor stared at us. He knew what was going on! Who knows, maybe Lucio brags to him about his female company!

"I see. — Regrettably, you won't be picking me up anymore. Understand, Lucio?"

"Yes, Anika, that's fine, since it means so much to you, — but please don't be angry with me!"

"I'm not mad at you. Don't worry, we're okay. It's a rule of mine not to be seen in public with clients. That's all. — Okay then, thank you, Lucio, and take care of yourself," I say in a conciliatory tone.

As quietly as possible, I walk through the wooden house door and the squeaky garden gate. Why does he not oil the hinges if he does not want his neighbors knowing when someone enters or leaves? Unless... he wants his neighbors to hear!

On Poseidonos Street, I head for the nearest bus stop. The wait is not long before the A1 bus pulls up. There are plenty of seats to choose from for my ride back to Piraeus. I did not earn much today and my phone never rang. I am a bit perturbed, although there is no need to worry. Tomorrow is a new day.

18

It is 2 a.m. when the humming of my cell phone wakes me from a sound sleep. I turn on the bedside lamp while reaching for the phone.

"Hello?"

"Hi! Where do you work?"

"I don't have my own place, I only meet in hotels or come to private residences. Where are you right now?"

"I'm in my car and in the mood for a good fuck."

"Too bad. I don't do it in a car. Try someone else. Good night!"

I lie back down and take a deep breath. The shock of being torn from a sound sleep is disconcerting. My God, who the heck was that? Mulling the short conversation, my phone rings again. Since I did not pay attention to the previous caller's number, I have no idea if it is the same guy or someone else. I pick up anyway.

"Hello?"

"Yes! I said I'm in the mood for a good fuck! You placed an ad in *Athens World*. You're the German whore, right?"

"Yes, I am. However, I don't work at this late hour. You should try your luck elsewhere. Good night and thanks for calling!"

It's always good to be polite, I think to myself. I hang up and save his number under 'Night-driver'. He sounded drunk, so I would not put it past him to call me a third time. I turn off my cell phone. I need more sleep! As I try to fall asleep, I start questioning if I should keep my phone off all night long...

Right now, while I am attempting to establish myself through my ad in *Athens World*, perhaps I should keep it on 24-7. If a businessman staying at a luxury hotel returns to his room at this time of night desiring company and sex, he would not be able to get in touch with me! If I leave it on and speak with him, there is a good chance he will want me to come to his hotel. Someone calling in the middle of the night for sexual favors wants them soon and they are usually not picky. Torn between fatigue and a sense of work duty, I finally sit up and turn my phone back on. During that short interval, Night-driver relentlessly tried to reach me five more times. Hopefully, the message was clear and he will not call again. That would be nice! Turning on my side with a clear conscience of having done the right thing, I soon fall back asleep.

The next morning is the hottest since my arrival in Athens. To help my acclimation along, I keep the AC off as long as possible. Sitting in a bikini on my balcony, I eat breakfast, read the newspaper, and learn Greek words while waiting for my phone to ring. Around noon, I dial Violet's number but she does not pick up. – At 1:40 p.m. my phone finally rings for the first time. I enter my room and close the balcony door before answering.

"Hello!"

"Hi! Are you the woman with the ad in *Athens World*?"

"Yes, I am. My name is Anika."

"Hello, Anika, I'm Michael. I have a few questions, if that's okay?"

"Certainly, what would you like to know?"

"Do you have beautiful feet?"

"Yes, or so I've been told, just yesterday as a matter of fact. I think so too. Why?"

"Well, I'm crazy about beautiful feet, but only when they're really beautiful. I see women walking around with no socks or pantyhose, but not everyone has nice feet. — I mean, are your feet nicely shaped, free of corns, crooked toes, callused skin, and the like?"

"Yes, they are. My feet are nicely shaped and well maintained. My toenails are painted red."

"Did you or someone else do it?"

"This past Thursday, I was at a nail salon. I believe my nails still look fine."

"Ah, I like that you didn't do them yourself. There's a difference, you know. Perfection demands someone else do it. — So, Anika, how much do you charge for an hour? As you might have guessed by now, I have a foot fetish."

"I charge 150 euros an hour."

"Wow, that's a lot. – Any chance you can give me a break? I'm a student."

"No, darling, I don't give discounts. 150 euros is a reasonable rate for all the pleasures I provide."

"Okay. Can you at least come to my home? I can't afford to rent a hotel room."

"Yes, I can do that. Where do you live?"

"In Kallithea."

"I'm drawing a blank as to where Kallithea is right now. I haven't been in Athens long. Where is it? How far away is it from Piraeus?"

"It's close to Piraeus. If you head south, it's before the town of Phaleron. I live on Spartacus Street. – It's a small side street off Dimosthenous Street."

"Okay. I've never heard of those streets, but I'm sure I'll find your place. Do you want to make an appointment now, Michael?"

"Of course!"

"When?"

"Right now, I mean, as soon as you can get here."

"Okay. I can make it there in an hour. I need you to text me your full name, home address, and landline number. Can you send me that info?

I'll call you back on your home phone to reconfirm and then I'll be on my way."

"No problem, Anika, I'll do that. Talk to you soon, okay?"

"Okay."

As soon as Michael hangs up, I grab my cup of coffee from the balcony and place it on the dressing table I use as a desk. Thinking about what I should wear, considering it is a home visit, I decide on something conservative. Maybe I will wear the yellow floral dress again, but this time with gold high heels. I am sure a man with a foot fetish appreciates nice shoes. So my heels do not develop scratches, I stick them in my bag on top of the other things I already have packed and wear my cork heel shoes for the commute. My cell phone beeps, announcing Michael's incoming text. He lives at 23 Spartacus Street. I save his two phone numbers under 'Michael-Foot'. Next, I call him back on his landline number and then I quickly go to the bathroom and get ready. I write his address down to show the taxi driver.

Outside the hotel, I do not have to wait long before I see a cab. I show the driver Michael's address, he nods and drives off. As luck would have it, the taxi has air-conditioning.

Since I am being chauffeured, I look up Michael's address on my cell phone. It really is not far from Piraeus. That is good because it keeps my expenses down. At that moment, the driver pulls over, rolls the passenger window down, and asks a passerby if they know Spartacus Street. Considering the day and age we live in, I really do not understand why every cab in Athens is not equipped with a navigation device. How can they do their job properly without staying up-to-date? Thankfully, the pedestrian gave the taxi driver proper directions because a few minutes later he pulls into the little side road where Michael's apartment building is located. I pay the 6-euro fare and get out. Today's sun is excessively hot. I do not think I would have survived a bus ride. Walking up to the building's door, I call Michael. He picks up immediately and I hear the door buzzer.

"Push the door open and come up to the third floor," he politely reminds me.

The elevator is already on the ground floor. I get in and quickly change into my other shoes and check my appearance in my compact. I am satisfied with my reflection. Michael never bothered to inquire about my looks or age. His only interest was my feet. That is why I did not volunteer anything. I hope he is not upset when he sees I am not a spring chicken.

The elevator stops and I step into a dimly lit corridor that runs in both directions. The closest apartment door to my right is ajar and I see the head of a young man. Michael beckons and I walk toward him. He opens the door all the way and I quickly step inside. By the looks of him, he really could be a student with his shoulder-length, wavy brown hair, and clean-shaven face. He stands in front of me wrapped only in a terry cloth robe.

"Hi, Anika. Did anybody see you? Was anyone else with you in the elevator?"

"No one saw me and I was alone in the elevator."

"Good, you see, I live here with my parents. – They're currently spending a few days at the beach. Right now, I have a bachelor pad, so to speak." He smiles at me, looking a bit nervous.

"Well, come on!" he says and I follow him into his room. It looks like a typical adolescent room. The bed is placed along one long wall. The sheets and pillow are crumpled. Across the room on the opposite wall under a window is a large table full of computer monitors, hard drives, keyboards, speakers, headphones, booklets, books, and pens. Poster images of basketball players and motorcycle plaster the walls except for one of a bikini-clad blonde beauty lounging on the deck of a boat. I find her pumps quite alluring. I wonder how old Michael is. Studying him, I get the impression he is 23, 25 at the most. However, I will not ask because he might inquire about my age. Coming across as 35 on the phone is no problem, but standing in front of such a young man, I might start blushing.

"May I close the curtains? It makes it cozier," I ask, as he pulls a chair in front of his bed.

"Sure, go ahead!" he replies.

The truth is I want the curtains closed because bright sunlight does not make me look younger. Glancing around the room, I ask:

"Is it okay to put my bag on the desk chair?"

"Yes, of course! And please, Anika, sit here!"

Michael points to the chair placed in front of his bed. As I sit down, I make sure my dress rides, exposing my tanned thighs as much as possible. Michael sits down on the bed facing me and gives me a once-over. His gaze lingers on my feet and he starts rubbing his hands together.

"May I?" he asks, nodding at my feet.

"Be my guest! They're all yours. At least for the next hour," I reply.

We laugh and his eyes visibly change from an initial expression of restraint to that of lust. Michael tenderly takes my left foot in his hands and looks at it. He caresses my shin and calf. Sliding my gold pump off, he carefully places it on the ground.

"Yes, you really do have nice feet. I'm ecstatic. After our phone call, I was suddenly afraid I might not like your feet, that they wouldn't be beautiful enough — then what would I have done with you?"

He looks at me and laughs from embarrassment. There is no need for him to feel that way. I am quite pleased he is pleased with me. Curious, I wonder what fascinates Michael the most about my feet and how I can satisfy him. Not every foot fetish is the same. As he loosens the belt of his robe, it falls open, exposing his naked body. He wears no underwear, is nicely tanned, and has black body hair. Michael pulls my foot toward his nose and sniffs the sole. After a big whiff, he rubs my foot against his forehead, brushes it across his cheek, and then kisses my toes. He is solely focused on my foot. When he places the foot against his manhood, I try to keep my leg as relaxed as possible. Applying light pressure, he gently uses my foot to massage his slowly hardening cock.

"Give me the other bare foot, Anika!"

I slip the shoe off and stretch my foot out. He grasps it and places the foot with the other next to his manhood.

"Ah, that feels fantastic!" he says, his eyes on my feet. "The soles of your feet are so velvety."

He moves my feet slightly apart so that his brown cock pops up between them, then he angles my soles inward and presses both feet against it. Looking at me, he says:

"Hold my boner like that! I want to enjoy this for a while."

He releases my feet and leans back on his unmade bed with his arms crossed behind his head. Slowly, he starts moving his hips.

I do my best to keep his cock between the soles of my feet while moving harmoniously with his movements. I really have to concentrate to keep up. I am trying to sense what feels good to Michael. My skillful feet strive to hold his erection, but I am unsure how long I can maintain this uncomfortable position. Basically, it is a balancing act with my legs stretched out with my soles turned inward while steadying myself with my hands behind me on the chair back.

The pose reminds me of advanced yoga. Michael has no idea how strenuous this is. He is too busy enjoying the soles of my feet caressing his cock. Before I end up with a charley horse, I move my calves by using the toes of my left foot to grab his shriveled ball sack while my right foot pushes his penis flat against his abdomen. I happily notice he likes the change. This makes my work a bit easier and I can take part. Carefully, I run my toes gently over the tip of his penis while making certain it is not too uncomfortable for him. The toes of my other foot are still fondling his balls. Despite playing sports regularly, I feel my abdomen twitching. As I contemplate this, Michael sits up and places my feet beside him on the bed. What a relief! Without a word, he lies down on his right side directly in front of my feet and tenderly pushes them against his chest. He rolls onto his back, moves my feet toward his face, and covers the soles with kisses. Thankfully, it does not tickle! Even though my feet are still in Michael's hands, I bear most of the weight of my legs.

"Can you please remove your dress?" he asks after setting my feet on the bed and sitting up.

"Of course!"

I rise, unzip my dress, and let it slide down my body. After picking it up, I drape it over the back of the desk chair. Thinking for a moment, I conclude there will not be a need for a condom. Perhaps some oil? I ask Michael:

"Should I cream my feet so they're even smoother?"

"Oh, yes! That's a great idea. Do you have oil or should I get some?"

"I have some, darling."

"Let me have it! I want to cream your feet."

I take my little bottle of baby oil and hand it to Michael. He smells it. Stunned, he says:

"This isn't olive oil!"

"No, it's baby oil."

"Okay. You know olive oil is good for the skin, right?"

"Yes, I know. However, it's heavier and not everyone appreciates the smell. You don't like this oil?"

"No, it smells nice. I'll use it."

Once again, back in the chair dressed only in champagne-colored lingerie, I swing my feet back into his hands. Sitting directly across from me, he places one on his right thigh and the other on his left. He looks at me and says:

"You have a great figure for your age, Anika. Good for you!"

Thank God, I think. I feel so much lighter. So, he did notice I am considerably older. Perhaps it was why he was a little anxious when he asked me to take my dress off. Did he expect a nasty surprise? Anyway, I am relieved he said something positive about me and my age!

"Thank you!" I answer chirpily as I adjust my position to emphasize my figure. Many times, the right posture makes all the difference. Michael dribbles oil onto in his palm, rubs his hands together, and takes his time massaging my feet. When he finishes, he leans back on his elbows, spreads his legs wide, and presents his cock. With my creamed soles, I spoil him in a fashion similar to earlier. Now, since I do not have to worry about my dry feet chafing his cock, I exert more pressure. Michael repeatedly pushes his hips against my feet. His boner is rock hard. Looking at his facial expression, I know he is fast approaching climax. Out of nowhere, he straightens up and frantically reaches for my right foot. He presses it firmly against his hairy chest. Next, he pushes my left foot under his balls, retracts his hand, and starts masturbating. I believe he is about to explode because he abruptly presses my foot against his face. Struggling to keep from toppling over, I hold on to the chair for dear life. The position of my legs, which I am sure he does not even think about, makes staying upright down right awkward. Although it is strenuous, I manage. — It is imperative I stay in this position! Any wrong move could ruin his orgasm and that would be a damn shame. – Especially for me because then I would have to start all over to get him there again. – I am overjoyed when I feel him twitching and see his cum squirt in a high arc. He positions his rod so the majority of cum lands on my shin. The rest drips onto the floor. Eyes half-closed, Michael moans with an expression of pain on his face. Well done, boy! Finally, I can get comfortable and relax. Once Michael recovers from his orgasm, he reaches for a box of tissues and hands it to me so I can wipe the sperm from my shin. He also offers me the use of the bathroom. The apartment building he lives in could have been built in the 60s, as the shower, toilet, and sink are the same moss green as the bathroom fixtures in my father's house. I rinse only my legs off in the shower because Michael has not touched me anywhere else. Back in his room, I slip into my dress. Michael offers me a glass of water and invites me to sit again. This time I choose the desk chair. Unobtrusively, I look around to see if he has already laid out my fee. There is no money in plain sight. Michael, once again wrapped in his terry cloth robe, stands next to the shelves and fiddles with the stereo, turning the radio to a Greek music station. The water is refreshing. I hope Michael will not make me wait long before opening his wallet and dismissing me. However, he also pours himself a glass of water and sits down on a chair facing me. Apparently, he is not in a hurry to pay me and say goodbye. He better have the money. Or have I been conned by a student?

"That was great! Thank you, Anika."

"Please, I simply performed my job," I reply with a smile, hoping he catches the hint that he needs to pay me for my service. It is obvious Michael has all the time in the world. After all, his parents are gone for a few days and he has the house to himself, so he is not worried about being caught with a strange woman. Should I chat with him for a few minutes? What about? Should I ask about his major? Better not. I just hinted I finished the job. He could say something now, but he is simply looking at me, sipping his water, and nodding.

"Darling, thank you for the water, it hit the spot, but it's time for me to go. It was nice meeting you. And I'm glad you liked my feet. — If there's nothing else, I have to leave now."

"Yes, of course, Anika. Feel free to leave at any time. But ... I can also refill your glass and we can sit and talk while you rest. I have nothing else planned for today. You're not intruding."

What am I going to do now? Do not tell me I have to beg to be paid. I would truly hate that. However, I could do with another glass of water. I am terribly thirsty. So, I try to humor him and say:

"Yes, I would like another glass of water. That's sweet of you. Thank you!"

Michael picks up the water bottle from the floor and fills my glass. I take a big swig and drink half of it.

"I find it quite hot today, but being born here, I'm sure you're used to it. Or do you also think it is hotter than the last few days?" I ask.

"Yes, of course. It's definitely much hotter than yesterday. On the radio, they said the temperatures would get up to 43 degrees Celsius. I think we're already there, but it's not so unusual to have a heat wave now and then. I know this from my childhood. For me, it's not so bad. The air conditioner in the hallway keeps my room cool. — On a day like this, I'm not going to the beach; it's too hot to play with my friends and a beach ball. We definitely don't do that during a heat wave. You become dehydrated too quickly and tire easily."

"I can imagine. I still have to adjust to the heat. On my way home, I should stop in the city to buy a sun hat. — Yes, I'm going to do that right now. — Okay darling, thanks for the water! I'll be going now!"

I set the empty glass on the desk, grab my handbag, and stand up. Michael also gets up. Questioningly, I look straight into his hazel eyes. I guess I must have succeeded because Michael pulls three 50s out of his terry cloth robe, hands them to me, and says:

"I still owe you something, Anika!"

"Yes, you do! Thank you, darling! Have a great day!"

Quickly I pocket the three bills. I walk into the hallway relieved that I did not have to bring up my payment. Michael follows and opens the door he secured with the chain and a second safety lock. He gives me a peck on the cheek, touches my arm, and says:

"Adiós, Anika. – It was a real pleasure. Maybe I'll call you again sometime."

19

I am leaving Michael's apartment in an exceptionally good mood. Inside the elevator, I switch into my cork-soled shoes. The appointment went smoothly.

I have seen to a young customer's happiness. Considering my profession, this small achievement boosts my self-confidence and increases my happiness. I walk along the partially shaded roadside until I find a bus stop. Even though it is incredibly hot — I am not looking forward to the bus ride — I refrain from taking a cab to save money. It is not like I am in a hurry to meet my next client. The only thing I plan on doing is to purchase a sun hat in the city center. That expense is practical. I do not mind parting with money for things like that, but unnecessary taxi rides do not fit my current budget. I have received no calls while at Michael's home. Nevertheless, there is still hope. The day is not over yet.

My goal is two customers per day, but I am realistic because not every client will pay 150 euros. There also will be a day off now and then, days where I will not receive any calls and days where I might even be sick. If it turns out I earn an average of more than 4000 euros per month in Athens, I will be satisfied and can live well while putting money aside. That is my dream scenario.

I do not have to wait long before boarding bus E 22 going to Syntagma Square. Unfortunately, once again, the bus is crowded with no available seats. Although I am only carrying one bag today, the ride is still horrible. This bus has straps hanging from the ceiling for standing passengers to grab. I grasp one with one hand and stand with my feet slightly apart for better balance.

I could have fun and regard it as exercise, but in view of the deplorable circumstances, I do not feel up for it. – Traveling by bus is definitely not a permanent solution. If everything works out as well as I expect and I establish a small customer base by the end of August, I will fly to Germany and drive my car back to Athens stuffed with more clothes, especially autumn and winter clothes. At that moment, when it is most inconvenient, my phone rings. With great difficulty, I retrieve my phone from the side pocket of my handbag, wedge it between my shoulder and chin, and answer the call while trying to maintain my balance.

"Hello!"

"Hi! This is Ed. Am I speaking with the German lady from *Athens World*?"

"Yes, that's me."

The caller speaks in German with a Bavarian or Austrian dialect.

"Can you hear me?" I ask. "Right now, I'm on a crowded bus and can't hear you very well."

"Yes, I can tell. I'm having difficulty understanding you as well."

"Could you call me back, let's say, in about 15 minutes? By that time, I'll be off the bus and it'll be quieter."

Ed agrees and I end the conversation. I place my phone back in my handbag and close the zipper. This little undertaking in the horribly rocking bus triggers perspiration on my forehead and armpits. Since the bus is full and I have no seat, it really is no place to conduct a business call. I hope Ed will actually call back!

Thankfully, it is a short ride. After another ten minutes, the bus stops at Syntagma Square. I am glad to be off that bus. While walking, I listen for my phone. It remains silent. On Ermou Street, I head for the nearest café to use the restroom to freshen up. In case I get a little sweaty, I always carry deodorizing body wipes in my purse. I hope they are as refreshing as the packaging promised!

Somewhat refreshed, I visit the next big clothing store, pleased it has air-conditioning. The cool air feels fantastic! It is the right spot to stroll around for a while instead of burning in the Greek sun. Still waiting for my phone to ring, I wander around looking for sun hats. I am in luck. There is a white fabric hat with a wide brim. Considering the clothes I brought from Germany, the hat will go with almost everything. Trying it on in front of a mirror, I find it suits me well. Standing in line at the cash register, my phone rings. I quickly step aside and answer.

"Hello?"

"Hi, it's Ed again. I called earlier. Can you talk now?"

"Yes, I can, Ed! By the way, I'm Anika. Would you like more information?"

"Please! Say, how old are you and what color hair do you have?"

"I'm 35 and blonde. I charge 150 euros for one hour of steamy sex."

Speaking in my mother tongue is nice for a change. It is easier than speaking English.

"Okay, 35 is good. Are you slim?"

"Yes, I'm slim. I have a good figure. – I don't think you will be disappointed. —Are you at a hotel? Or do you live in Athens?"

"I'm here on business and staying at the Hilton. Can you come here?"

"Certainly. Do you want to make an appointment?"

"Yes. How about 6:00 p.m.?"

"That's fine."

"Great! I'll see you!"

"Ed, I need your last name and room number."

"My room number is 728 and my name is Ed Rosch."

"Thank you. I'll call you after 5:00 p.m., okay?"

"Great. Until then, Anika. I'm already looking forward to the steamy sex you've promised!"

"Thank you. I'm looking forward meeting you too! Talk to you later, Ed!"

Yippee! An appointment at the Hilton! And, he did not even say anything about my rate. And, he is German or Austrian. Super!

Paying for my hat, I walk outside and search for a café on one of the side streets off the Ermou pedestrian only zone. – Did I actually promise him steamy sex? God, I am an idiot!

At 5:30 p.m., before hailing a cab, I call Ed:

"Hi, Ed? It's Anika. I wanted to let you know that I'm on my way. I'll be there at 6:00 p.m."

"Great! See you soon, Anika!"

Fantastic. – It went smoother than I hoped. He will be my first customer I meet in one of Athens' grand and luxurious hotels.

Once again, I am in luck, the cab is air-conditioned. This way I will not get sticky shortly before my appointment. Slipping back into my gold high heels, I lean back and relax. The ride from Syntagma Square to the Hilton Hotel is much shorter than I thought. At 5:45 p.m., the taxi stops at the hotel entrance and I have to get out. Bummer! What am I going to do for 20 minutes? Approaching the revolving glass door, insecurity washes over me. What can I do so I do not stand out? Maybe grab a drink at the hotel bar. Entering the lobby with its leather-seating group, small boutique, and long reception desk, I take in the entire room with a single glance and discover the elevators off to the side. On the way to the hotel bar, I see a magazine and tobacco shop. How fortunate for me. Now I can browse until my appointment. I like that much better than sitting alone at the bar with nothing to do but feel tense and anxious. I am the only customer in the store. After inspecting the front pages of some German and English magazines, I scan through several. At 4:50 p.m. I buy a *Bunte* magazine and walk back into the grandiose lobby. I do not believe my purpose there is obvious to anyone who saw me.

I worried for nothing, especially considering the conservative floral dress I am wearing. Confident again, I cross the lobby and head for the elevators. When I get out on the seventh floor, I am anxious once more. Full of stage fright, I knock on room door 728.

20

Ed opens the door. The room is bathed in sunlight. Oh, my God! I need to change that immediately or Ed will see every little wrinkle on my face. Direct sunlight is the biggest enemy in my profession, especially at my age. I have to act quickly. With a smile on my face, I softly say meaningless drivel like, 'hi baby, nice to meet you', as I walk over to the large front window and draw the curtains closed.

"Let's make it a bit more comfortable in here!" I say, finishing off my superficial chatter as I turn to face Ed. Obviously surprised, he is still standing near the door wrapped in a Hilton bathrobe. Placing my new hat on a chair, I walk toward Ed. Since he stands there quietly, I am forced to say something. I ask:

"Hi, baby! Did you have a nice day? I'm glad you speak German. Where exactly are you from?"

"Yes, I had a good day, Anika, thanks for asking. Work is work. — Actually, I'm from Salzburg. Now let's have a look at you, you whirl-wind!"

Flustered, I turn once around so my knee-length, loose floral dress flairs outward. What is wrong with me? The way I have behaved since entering his room, he must imagine I am a nut job. Time to pull it to-gether! Unfortunately, I cannot do that with a snap of a finger, so I will buy myself time. I say:

"Wait, darling, let me use the bathroom to slip into something a bit sexier for you. You can't see enough of me in this dress."

I wink at him.

"Is that the bathroom?" I point to a door.

"Yes, that's it. Feel free to use it!"

"Go ahead and get comfortable on the bed, darling, I'll be right there to spoil you!"

My God, so far my performance has been crap! Inside the bathroom, I change into my striped bodysuit that barely covers my breasts and pussy. I also slip on black strapless stockings. After putting on gold-colored jewelry on my ears, neck, and wrists, I glance at myself in the big bathroom mirror. I think Ed will be blown away when he sees me! And, – since I promised him hot sex, – I decide to insert a vaginal suppository. Not because I need it for pregnancy prevention, but my body heat will melt the suppository in about ten minutes and then my pussy will be nice and wet. It fools the customer into thinking I am turned on by what he is doing to me. The suppositories are relatively tasteless, which is why it is okay for a customer to lick me while it dissolves. I finish off with a spritz of my perfume and take a deep breath to calm myself. I am ready to go on stage!

With my small bag of work equipment, I open the bathroom door and slowly step into the bedroom. Ed – 50-ish, tan, tall, slender, good-looking, salt and pepper hair – has taken off the bathrobe, is sitting naked on the bed smoking a cigarette. I guess he needed it considering my initial behavior.

"Damn, you look fantastic! Do you mind?" He holds up his cigarette.

"No, darling. You just sit there and finish your smoke. — I'm going to spoil you a bit, okay?"

"Fantastic, you little minx. I can't wait to see what you do to me!"

After placing my bag at the head of the bed, I crawl on hands and knees toward him and begin my performance by licking his proud member. Oral sex is always a good way to start. I first check that his cock looks healthy. Since I stupidly promised steamy sex, I decide to blow him without a condom. I run my tongue up his still flaccid peter and circle the tip of his cock. I happily note an immediate reaction. Ed watches the entire time. I spread my knees a bit more and arch my back so my butt sticks up. I have assumed this seductive pose many times, so my movements are catlike. I am firmly convinced my figure looks its best when giving a blowjob in this position. This, in turn, fortifies my self-confidence when dealing with a customer, even if he is new or someone I know.

Ed's upper body rests on a pile of pillows. Having put out his cigarette, he runs his hand over my almost bare back. So he can also reach my butt and pussy, I adjust the angle of my body. Determining I have teased his hard rod long enough, I insert it deep in my mouth and suck on it. Ed immediately groans aloud and then wheezes:

"Oh, baby! What are you doing?"

Well, I have to make up for my earlier behavior. I do not want him remembering me as some crazy chick, more like a blonde sex goddess. Ed reaches for my crotch and slides the flimsy material of my bodysuit aside. In order to make it easier for him to slide his finger into my pussy, I spread my labia with two fingers.

"You like that?" Ed asks as he pokes around.

Taking a break from blowing him, I reply:

"Yes, very much! If you want, you can fuck me real good. I also have a little sex toy you can stick up my butt."

I am not that indulgent with everyone. Bottom line, I have to make it up to Ed. Reaching for my equipment bag at the head of the bed, I pull out a small vibrator. It is slightly larger and thicker than a lipstick. Handing it to him, I say:

"But please don't switch on the vibrator. I don't like that in my butt."

However, Ed is content just fingering me. As he feels the liquid of the dissolving vaginal suppository, he says:

"Man, you're pussy is dripping, Anika. I take it you like what I'm doing!"

Releasing Ed's cock, I answer:

"You bet! I'm horny for your cock. What do you say? You want to start fucking me?"

"Hold on a second. I want to stick the toy in your butt. You'd like that, right?"

"Yes, of course! But take it easy fucking me with it, I don't want to come just yet. I want to wait until your hard cock is deep inside my pussy!"

"Okay, then stop blowing me! Let me focus only on you and your awesome butt!" Ed says. He moves into kneeling position right behind my spread legs. Wetting my middle finger, I spread my anus so Ed has an easier time sticking the small vibrator in my ass.

"So, you insatiable slut, now you're going to get what you've been longing for! — You like that, don't you? Watch out, good ole Ed will give it to you good!"

He thrusts the little vibrator deep in my butt and starts fucking me with it. At the same time, he uses his other hand to rub my pussy and clit roughly. It does not feel good. To put an end to it, I say after a few minutes of loud moaning:

"Ed, I can't wait any longer. Please fuck me! Please, I want to come with your dick inside me!"

"Okay, you fucking slut, as you wish. Brace yourself! Uncle Ed will fuck you 'til you lose your mind!"

"Great, — but wait a sec, let me grab a condom!"

A normal size rubber is fine for Ed. I grab one from the bag and roll it over his erection.

Ed is so excited his face is bright red. His expression slightly resembles that of a man possessed. I do not think he will take long to reach climax. Of course, I could continue playing with him for a while longer, but I do not want to pretend any longer than necessary. As the saying goes, brevity is the soul of wit. The important thing is Ed will believe he had steamy sex.

With the condom in place, I assume my previous position and invitingly stick my wet open pussy in the air. Without wasting a second, he forcefully rams his cock into my pussy. One hand still grasps the vibrator in my butt and his other grabs my hips as if fucking me were his last performance. I clench the bed sheet so I do not slide further up every time he thrusts.

I say, "Oh, Ed, you're a great fuck!" to spur him on. I sense he is about to climax. I groan:

"Yes, baby! I'm coming! Oh, God, yes, I'm coming!"

I fake a great orgasm because I know Ed is one of those men who need it in order to reach the peak. What do you know... he cannot contain himself. Between guttural noises, he shoots his load. Once finished, he falls back onto the bed with his eyes closed, breathing heavily from the exertion of reaching an orgasm. I reach around and gently extract the small vibrator from my butt and the still intact rubber. I let both items fall to the floor next to the bed. Then I lie down next to him, propping myself up on one elbow.

"Wow, that was a great fuck, Anika! — Did you enjoy it too?"

"Yes! It was great! I like sex this way. It doesn't happen every day. But this made work particularly fun for me!"

It is actually true. The last half an hour went smoothly. Ed, obviously satisfied, sits up, and offers me a cigarette. Politely, I decline. Naturally, he has one and we talk for a while. Ed tells me he works for a lighting company that supplies theaters and that they currently are working on a project in Athens. He also tells me about his problems working with Greek subcontractors and that he usually does not get to eat dinner until late in the evening, which upsets his stomach. He does not turn down his colleagues' invitations so as not to appear rude. When Ed finishes his cigarette and stubs it out, I ask:

"Darling, is it okay if I hop in the shower?"

"Yes, of course!"

Ed lights up another cigarette. I pick up the vibrator and condom on my way to the bathroom. The shower is big and luxurious. I treat myself to an extra-long shower with the massage function on. After dressing, brushing my hair, and applying fresh eye makeup, I return to the room. Meanwhile, Ed has placed three 50-euro bills in plain view next to my hat. Pointing to them, he says:

"Thank you, Anika. You earned it! I might call you again. I'll definitely keep your number."

"Thank you, Ed. Yes, it certainly was nice chatting in German again."

"That's true, I liked that too. My English isn't very good and trying to make myself understood at work every day is exhausting. I only called you because your ad said you're German. I never expected to be such a lucky dog and end up with such an attractive lady!"

"Why thank you, darling! I'm glad to hear you're happy with me!"

"Oh, yes, Anika, I truly am."

I pocket the bills and grab my sun hat. Ed, still naked, walks me to the door and gives me a peck on both cheeks. And that is that. Riding the elevator down to the lobby, I see I missed three calls while I was working. All three are unknown numbers. Oh well, that is just the way it is. — Hm, what to do now? It is too early to go back to my hotel. Grab a bite to eat? — Yes, I must eat something for dinner! While doing that, let's see if anything happens.

21

By the time I leave the Hilton, the temperature has become more bearable than earlier. I should avoid unnecessary walking during a heat wave. It only drains me. Even my new sun hat cannot prevent it. About 300 meters down the road from the Hilton Hotel is a subway station. From there I can catch a ride all the way to Monastiraki Square. As I am about to descend the wide staircase, my phone rings — an unknown number.

"Hello!"

"Are you the German woman?"

"Yes. My name is Anika."

"What services do you provide? How much do you charge?"

"I provide all kinds of services. Is there anything in particular you're interested in?"

"Yes, I'm into anal sex. I want to fuck a German woman's ass real good."

Oh my god! I do not care for his tone at all! Breathing deeply, I calmly reply:

"I'm sorry, I don't do anal. You should call someone else. Thanks for the call, bye."

I hang up. I am indignant. It rings again. Another unknown number. Perhaps it is someone else.

"Hello?"

"Why did you hang up on me? — I want to know how much you charge!"

"My rate is of no importance. I told you I don't do anal."

I am trying to stay calm. Why is he so pushy?

"Maybe I want a blowjob from a German woman. Tell me, how much do I have to dish out to see you?"

"My price is 250 an hour."

Mistakenly, I hope the increased rate will put an end to his belligerence.

"250? That's a lot! I'm sure you know we're in a big economic crisis. How about you adjust your rate accordingly?"

"I'm not forcing anyone to pay my price. They either agree or they don't. I don't think we're in agreement. Please try someone else and don't call me back! Okay? And thanks for asking!"

I hang up hoping the creep has gotten the message. It is not long before my phone rings again. Letting it ring, I consider what I should say if it is the same man. — Without a word, I will simply hang up. Yes, that is best. Obviously, he could continue to terrorize me with his calls. Since he has no caller ID, the number will not appear and there is no way to tell if it is him or someone else. It continues to ring, so I decide to answer. Again, it is the boor. – I barely manage to say hello when he starts:

"I want to meet you! When do you have time?"

Contrary to my intention, I answer:

"I thought 250 was too much for you. Why are you calling me back?"

"I want to fuck a German woman, understand?"

"No, I don't get it. I don't need your business! The matter is settled. I will no longer talk to you."

Irritated, I shove the phone in my bag as if that would make a difference! A few seconds later another unknown number. This time I pick up and do not say a word:

"Hey!" a voice says.

I immediately recognize it and hang up. Once I told my family, friends, and acquaintances in Germany that I planned to go to Athens to find employment, a few of them shook their heads and informed me that many Greeks hate Germans. I certainly was, and still am, aware that the Germans are blamed for their economic crisis. Greeks hold the Germans responsible every time pensions or jobs are cut. There must be intelligent Greeks who understand their own country is responsible for the current situation. I am certain there are plenty of Greeks who still like Germans a lot. That is due to our punctuality, dependability, Mr. Rehhagel – the Greek soccer team's former coach – reliable German automobiles, discipline, and hard work. Besides, Greek men are known for having a thing for blonde German women, not because German women are prettier than Greek women, we are simply different, that is all. I would not think their desire for German women had diminished during this crisis. Since being in Athens, I have only had good experiences with Greeks. Except for this one rude man, everyone else has been nice and polite. He was one of those men that can be found anywhere. I will not let him discourage me!

As I stroll through the old town, I come upon the square in the Roman Agora where the Tower of Winds stands. It is a well-preserved octagonal tower with beautiful reliefs of wind gods running around the upper part. Directly across from it is a garden with several restaurants. In order to enjoy the old tower for a while longer, I grab a free table at the closest restaurant. My phone has not rung in the last few minutes. Hopefully, the man has finally given up. The waiter arrives and I order a large bottle of water and saganaki, pan-fried cheese. It is good to give my feet a break. Even though I only worked two hours today, it somehow feels longer. I call Violet and this time she actually answers.

"Hi, Violet, it is Anika. How are you?"

"Oh, darling! I'm sorry for not returning your call, but today all hell broke loose! Today is the hottest day yet. All the men are apparently going crazy, thinking only about sex! Sex, sex, sex! My phone hasn't stopped ringing all day. This morning it started with Christo. He came to my place at 11:00 a.m. Afterward, I took a taxi to the 6 X Hotel in Glyfada to meet Spiros. Then, I get back home and I get a call from a cardiac surgeon from Thessaloniki, asking if I can come to the President Hotel. Obviously, I went. You know, it is in the middle of the city, right behind the Hilton Hotel! Damn, that man was exhausting. He wanted everything, starting with a blowjob. Then, he was on top and after that, from behind. Later, he fingers me a little, grabs and fondles my tits, and then he wants to lick me. After all that, he jerks off at the end without a condom on my ass. I tell you, it must be the heat wave. It makes them randy! Even Christo couldn't get enough and was on me like a rabbit. Every time he was about to come he wanted to change positions to draw it out. — I mean, a few more thrusts and he would have been relieved! What's with the delay? Anyway, today it took over a half an hour! Usually, he only needs 20 minutes, tops. Oh well, there are those days. Also, Werner from Belgium called, but I had already agreed to see Thassos the heart surgeon and was on my way to the President Hotel. You might not believe me, but Nikos just left my place. He pays 150. He's an optician with his own shop in Piraeus. He became one of my regulars through my ad in *Athens World*. All in all, it was a great day. Obviously, I'm exhausted! Before you called, Jonathan phoned to see if I could come to the Metropolitan Hotel! Certainly I can. See how crazy this day has been! I haven't even eaten a proper meal yet, but I'm drinking like I'm dying of thirst! I can relax for another 30 minutes before I have to grab a cab to the hotel. And, God willing, that'll be it for today. I mean, don't get me wrong, I'm happy to make so much money! But, darling, it's so exhausting! So, how was your day? Have you been busy too?"

"Yes, this afternoon I had an appointment with a young Greek man with a foot fetish and just now I was with an Austrian at the Hilton. Both paid 150. So, I did okay!"

I also tell Violet about the persistent, ill-mannered man who wanted to fuck a German woman. She reports she has also encountered similar guys. Then I describe my meeting with Lucio.

"I told you, darling, he still dreams about his teacher! I guess he never called me back because I'm not too good at role-playing. I'm sure he'll call you back. — So, he only paid 100? That's not much. Next time, if he wants to touch you, tell him it costs extra! — And he wants his ass spanked? With the whip? I couldn't do that. Francis was a customer I saw on two occasions and he also wanted to be beaten. I put my leather outfit and leather thigh high boots on, but I knew that didn't make me a dominatrix. Francis brought his own whip and told me to whip him hard. I couldn't do it! I was afraid of hurting him! Maybe you'll receive a call from him. His name might be Francis, but he's a Brit. I think he's into blonde, leather-clad women. If he calls me, I'll give him your phone number. Likewise, if you have a customer who asks if you have a friend, you can put in a good word for me. I mean, I'm not talking about exchanging customers, just if one asks for a recommendation without wanting to see both of us. He's going to someone else anyway, so why shouldn't it be me? If someone calls and asks if I work as a dominatrix, I can say I have a colleague who's much better at it than I am. Okay?"

"Yes, we can do that. I don't have a problem chastising someone."

"You have no qualms about hitting somebody? I mean, really beat someone with a whip until there are red welts. — You can do that?"

"Yes, I can. Think about it. The customer is asking to be beaten. He even pays a great deal of money for it. Why should I have misgivings if it's his wish? —Naturally, I have my limits. I could never seriously hurt someone, even if requested. I think I have good judgment when it comes to realizing someone's limit."

"Oh, darling, just looking at you, it would never cross my mind that you had that in you. But that means nothing. No one believed I would make it as a prostitute. Yet here I am. — And please, don't misunderstand me, just because you can beat someone doesn't mean I think you're a bad person! I'm merely stating that I can't do it. Then again, I'm not good at role-playing either. Perhaps it requires a certain amount of acting talent, who knows?"

"Yes, maybe it does. – In any case, I can do all that and I'm not ashamed to earn money with it."

"That's what matters. Each according to his or her talents! I was a fairly good hairdresser, but I think I am a better prostitute. I can't even imagine doing any other job. What? A cashier or secretary? Or a sales clerk? Can you imagine working eight hours on an assembly line for peanuts? —I don't think there's anything out there I am better suited for or would like more than pleasuring men for a half hour. Of course, only if they pay well! — Anyway, darling, I have to get ready now. I told you Jonathan is waiting for me at the Metropolitan Hotel. I'm hoping you get more business today! Bye now. Kisses, darling, and don't forget to call me again!"

"Thanks, Violet, have a nice evening!"

I eat my salty grilled cheese that, unfortunately, has the consistency of rubber. Lots of water is required to get it down my throat. Apart from the deplorable food here, I feel great, as if I am a tourist out on a beautiful, hot summer night in the middle of the old town in Athens without anything to worry about.

My phone rings. A Greek cell phone number:

"Hello! I saw your ad in *Athens World*. That's your ad, right?"

"Yes, it's mine. Would you like more information?"

He says yes, so I tell him about my services and the hourly rate.

"Oh, 150 euros. What does that include for that price?"

"Only safe sex, including oral. Are you interested in something special?"

"Yes. How about kissing? Do you kiss?"

"That depends. Right now, over the phone, I can't promise anything. Please understand that I would have to see you first. Ordinarily, it's a possibility."

"That's good. Kissing is important to me. And oral sex. Is that with or without a rubber?"

"I also can't say yet. Normally, it's with a condom, but if you look healthy, I might make an exception. Just so you know, you can't come in my mouth!"

"Yes, of course, I understand. Thanks for the information, Anika. I'll get back in touch. By the way, my name is Arthur."

"Thanks for calling, Arthur!"

"Okay, until later then! Bye, Anika."

Once we disconnect I save his number under 'Arthur-kissing'. If he calls again, I'll immediately know who it is. He didn't sound Greek, more like Northern European. It's still early and I think about what to do. Maybe I'll take a walk through the Plaka. Yes, I'm in a mood for that! After paying for my food, I follow the throng of tourists that have been meandering by.

Down a busy narrow street, I encounter one small souvenir shop after another. I see cotton crepe shirts and dresses that remind me of the bygone hippie era along with leather sandals no Greek would wear nowadays. Also, there is pottery decorated with various scenes from ancient mythology and Greek history. In a shop selling Greek soccer team merchandise, my curiosity gets the better of me and I inquire about the colors. The Olympiacos Piraeus soccer team has a red and white emblem and the Panathinaikos Athens soccer team has a green shamrock for their emblem. Apparently, both teams fight for the top spot in the Superleague Greece. Granted, I have no personal interest in this, but for work, it is good to know a bit about the Greek soccer teams. After all, men are obsessed with soccer and my job is not only about sex, it also requires small talk.

Strolling through the alleys of the Plaka, I attempt to read the Greek street signs and names of shops. In order to become familiar with the language, it is a useful exercise. Once I can read a word, the more likely I know the translation. For example, with a bit of deduction, I detect the word dentist in *Odontiatos*. And I deduce the word *Ilektrologos* means electrician. It is like a guessing game that allows me to expand my vocabulary the easy way. My phone rings and I see its Adonis, the man I spent time with on the roof terrace of the Ammas Hotel, where we had ice cream before I took him to bed as a paying customer.

"Hi, Adonis!"

"Hello, Anika! How are you?"

"I'm fine, thanks for asking! I'm becoming more and more familiar with Athens. How are you?"

"I'm okay. Can we meet tomorrow?"

"Certainly! When and where?"

"I'd prefer we meet in Glyfada at the Lenny Blue Hotel. At 2:00 p.m. would be great. Does that fit into your schedule?"

"Sure does. Can you give me the hotel address?"

"No, unfortunately, I don't have it."

"Can you tell me how to get there?"

"Yes, listen up; take the tram leaving from Piraeus that runs along the coast to Glyfada. It runs right by the hotel. The stop is near the hotel. Wait — it's on Metaxa Street, the second or third stop after the shops. Yes, that's where it is! Can you remember all that?"

"Certainly. I'll find the place. How do you want to meet?"

"I could call once I have the room number. Is that okay?"

"Yes, that's fine! I'll be in the vicinity of the hotel."

"That's perfect because I won't have much time. As soon as we're done I have to get back to the office."

"Okay, Adonis, I'm looking forward to seeing you tomorrow!"

"Yes, I'm already excited! See you tomorrow, Anika. Oh, and please wear something short again, a dress or a skirt. Mini's looks great on you, you foxy lady!"

"No problem!"

"Bye, Anika!"

"Bye, Adonis!"

Fantastic! I already have an appointment for tomorrow. Although Adonis can only pay 80, I'm glad he called again. Shortly thereafter, I hear my phone beeping, announcing an incoming text. It reads:

Hi. Can I have more information?

I text back:

Please call for information.

It beeps again:

I'm still at the office. Can't talk here.

I answer:

Then call me later.

He writes:

Okay!

I've told myself to stop giving out information via text messages. I need to hear the voice of the interested party. At least then, I can evaluate who I am dealing with. Any child could send a text to have a little fun with me. Plus, texting back and forth is annoying. I save the Greek cell phone number under 'Text inquiry'. I will see if he actually calls back after office hours.

The lights in the Plaka have now come on, making this idyllic place even more magical. I feel like I am on vacation. Strolling through the shops, I find one with a wide assortment of bags. As I take my time browsing, I also see a few laptop bags. Some are rigid, made of a light material. Each has a removable padded case inside, presumably to protect a laptop. With such a lightweight laptop bag, I could try taking my dominatrix equipment with me again during the day. Considering the colors of my summer clothes, I decided on the silver bag. It does not stand out too much and it goes with everything I can think of. Once I pay for it, I stick my good high heels, my *Bunte* magazine, and the carefully folded together sun hat inside. Since I have had enough of the hustle and bustle of the Plaka for one day, I leave the old city and catch a ride to the coast, midway to home, to spend time there.

22

Shortly before 10:00 p.m., I board a tram running from Syntagma Square to Athens' coast. Luckily, I manage to grab a seat, which makes riding public transportation considerably more pleasant. I received a few more calls and each time gave out information. Also, I heard back from the guy who sent me the text message. His name is Christo, a local, who said he would get back in touch. I change the entry in my address book from 'text request' to 'Christo – office'. I am hoping my stored entries will help me get a better idea of who is calling.

When the tram reaches the big marina of Kalamaki at the coast, I disembark. There is a nightclub adjacent to a big restaurant. The place is teeming with people and booming music. Strolling along the pontoons, I examine the sailing boats. On a few decks, groups of sailors are having a good time talking and laughing while drinking wine or beer. Maybe they are just starting their vacation and will head out tomorrow to the Aegean Sea or perhaps they have finished a beautiful sailing trip and are enjoying their last evening on board. I might be alone, but I am used to it, even when I lived in Germany. Granted, in Germany, I was not alone during work hours. I sat with my coworkers in a room with the heater on full blast as we watched TV while waiting for customers. When the doorbell rang, our madam answered it and led the client into the anteroom. Through a peephole in the wall, we observed the customers. However, since the entrance was dimly lit, I was never one hundred percent sure if I knew the client privately. It always left me feeling uncertain. When the madam signaled us, me and my colleagues – most of the time, it was a group of six or seven women – entered the anteroom. Rosi, the madam, introduced us individually to the customer, who by then was sitting on the couch. When a client had chosen a lady, she would first show him the bathroom and then go to one of the rooms. She would put on a CD approximately forty-five minutes long of pre-recorded cuddle music. Once the music stopped, the session was over and the customer needed to decide if he wanted to pay for another hour.

Being self-employed is much different! Now, I am alone during work hours, which I knew and I am okay with, so far. I prefer running around Athens alone instead of sitting in a room watching TV for hours with a bunch of women with whom I am really not acquainted with and who, like me, are trying to keep their true identity a secret. I made it a habit of avoiding intimate relationships with any of these women, keeping my distance yet remaining friendly, collegial, and respectful.

As I stroll around the marina's landside, I discover a bar with a large patio and sit down to have a Diet Coke. I even eat a few of the complimentary nuts. Scented candles, supposedly to keep mosquitoes away, decorate the tables. I remove my German magazine from my new light chic laptop bag and skim the pages since it is too dark to read. When my phone rings, I get up and walk a few meters away, out of earshot of other guests.

"Good evening!"

"Good evening. Excuse me for calling so late. Am I talking to the German lady with the ad in *Athens World*? Could you tell me a little about yourself?"

"Of course!" I reply and relay the relevant information.

"Okay, Anika, that sounds good. I live on an island and will be in Athens for a week the day after tomorrow. I'll be staying at a hotel in Glyfada. I'd like you to come to my room on Wednesday afternoon at 6:00 p.m. Discreetly, of course! Would that work? Are you available at that time?"

"Yes, I can make it!"

"Great. And please, Anika, be punctual. I hate to wait!"

"I can sympathize. Say, darling, what's your name?"

"I apologize, Anika, my name is Vangelis. I'm a 61-year-old retired captain. I take care of myself and I'm healthy. I'm hoping you'll like me!"

"Thanks, Vangelis! How do we go about meeting each other? Will you call me on Wednesday to tell me the exact address and room number?"

"I will be staying at the Congo Palace Hotel in Glyfada. It's on Poseidonos Street. Once I've checked in, I'll call you with the room number. Please, dress and act discreetly. I only stress this because it's a small hotel."

"I understand, Vangelis! You don't have to worry. I'll make sure I don't attract attention."

"Great, Anika. I'm looking forward to your visit. See you Wednesday!"

"Okay, talk to you then! Have a nice evening, Vangelis!"

I hang up and save his cell phone number under 'Vangelis – Capt.'.

Fantastic, I have an appointment for Wednesday! I Google the Congo Palace Hotel and find it right away. I simply love all the things I can do on my phone and while in this unfamiliar big city, it is essential for my job as a call girl!

Back at my table, I order another Diet Coke and grab a handful of nuts. Since it is nearing midnight, I leave the bar and stroll through the marina in the direction of Poseidonos Street. Still wide-awake, I enjoy the evening walk without worrying about baking in the sun. Now I understand why in summer the Greeks wait until the evening to become active.

Along the marina's harbor runs a road lined with trees and park benches on one side. On the other, large yachts are moored in the glassy water that reflects the surrounding lights. – On a 20-25 meter yacht, people in deep conversation sit at a large dining table at the stern. Blue and white uniformed crew members see to the group's need.

I sit on one of the benches and start people watching. At a slight angle from me, I observe a man on the deck of a yacht tinkering with something. Next, he disappears inside, turns off the light, comes back out on deck, and stands at the railing. When he notices me, he nods in greeting. I nod back. He is not wearing a uniform. Not a crew member. Lighting a cigarette, he enjoys his smoke leaning against the railing. It seems he is the only one on board. Since it is night and dark, I openly stare at him. I would never do this during daylight hours. He is also not ashamed and keeps looking at me. Can I catch him? It cannot hurt to try. He tosses the cigarette butt into the water and lowers the gangway. With his hands in his pockets, he slowly saunters over to me. Okay! What am I going to do if he speaks to me? – What should I say? Nothing? It is best to wait and see what he says!

"*Kalispera!*"

"Good evening."

He says something I do not understand in Greek. So I inquire:

"Do you speak English? Or German? I don't speak Greek."

"Ah! English?"

"Yes!"

"Where are you from?"

"Germany."

"Ah! Merkel-land."

"No, not Merkel-land, – Germany!" I say, upset about the stupid response.

If he is one of those who blame Germany for the mess in Greece, I am ending this conversation immediately. I have heard enough of that for one day! I reach with my left hand for the two bags sitting next to me on the bench.

"Oh, sorry! Germans are good!"

I refrain from replying and place my bags on my lap, an indication I am ready to leave.

"Please! Don't go. – I'm sorry!" he says conciliatorily. It seems he really means it. How could he have thought I might find his comment in good taste? Idiot! I set the bags back on the bench and look him in the eyes. He appears to be around 45, average height and build, straight black hair, and dark eyes. He does not look sinister and his English is passable.

"I'm Dimitri, and you?"

"Anika. My name is Anika," I reply in a less than welcoming voice. Let's see how this progresses.

"This is my yacht."

He points to his boat.

"Nice." I keep my reply short, making it easier for him to understand. Then, I add *oreo*, meaning *beautiful* in Greek. Dimitri laughs, pleased at my attempt to communicate in his language.

"Do you want to see my boat?" he asks.

I shrug. Why not? I know it is the right move. Now I merely have to wait for the right moment to let him know I only have sex for money. Dimitri beams confidently as he beckons me to follow. Grabbing my two bags, I walk across the road and up the gangway. Before boarding, he removes his shoes and places them in a woven wicker basket on the wooden deck next to the gangway. Handing him my two bags, I also take off my shoes and deposit them in the basket.

"Is this bag for work?" Dimitri asks, pointing to the laptop bag.

"Yes, it's for work," I reply.

"What kind of work do you do?" he asks. — This is the moment I have been waiting for!

If he does not bite, I am done wasting time touring his boat. Under the cover of darkness, I come right out and say:

"I provide sex for money."

I look him directly in the eyes the entire time. He makes a face as if he did not understand.

"What do you do?" he asks again.

"I make a living providing sex. I'm a prostitute."

I give him an easygoing smile. Still perplexed, he stands motionless in front of me. I take my bags back from him and stick the laptop bag next to my shoes in the wicker basket and hang the other over my shoulder. It is obvious he is too stunned to say anything, so I ask him straight out:

"Do you want to have sex with me?"

He swallows, smiles awkwardly, and nods. I guess something like this has never happened to him. But it is also a first for me! I am only this courageous because it is dark.

"Sex for money?" he asks.

"Yes, sex for money. Do you want that?"

"How much will it cost?"

"150."

"Good! I want sex with you," he says.

I can hardly believe it. His reply is 'good'! Here I was worried my rate was too high, considering I am merely fishing. All for naught! Dimitri agrees and rewards my courage. Now I am his for the next hour.

"Okay, Dimitri, show me your boat!" I encourage him by smiling and touching his arm. Dimitri takes the lead and opens the salon door. Switching on the light, he shows me around. It holds a dining table for six and a sitting group comprised of a couch, armchairs, and a small coffee table. Then there is a mini bar with three stools as well as a library and entertainment area with a flat-screen TV and stereo system. Next, we go below deck and he shows me the sleeping quarters. As I sit on one of the beds, he says:

"No, not here."

I get up and brush the wrinkles from the comforter. Dimitri says:

"We'll have sex upstairs. Would you like a drink?"

"Please!" I answer and we climb the stairs to the salon. Dimitri opens the bar cabinet and inquires about my preference. Seeing a bottle of Campari, I say:

"A Campari and soda, please."

"Okay. I'll have a whiskey and soda!"

Cheerfully, he mixes our drinks. In the meantime, I look around. On one wall between windows, an artist's detailed charcoal drawings of Greek buildings from the last century catches my eye. When Dimitri finishes mixing our drinks, I take the Campari and soda and follow him through the tinted glass door to the aft deck. We clink glasses and toast. Dimitri motions me to follow him to the forward deck. The deck in front of the bridge has a large padded sun area. Wow! Until now, I have only seen something like this in photos or movies. We place our glasses on a small table. Dimitri points with one hand at the big playground at his feet. Setting my handbag down, I look around. No one can see us on the forward deck. The bridge protects us from prying eyes on shore, not to mention it is dark and no one can be seen on the boats on either side. I unzip my dress for the third time today and slip out of it. Before I have a chance to fold it neatly and place it somewhere, Dimitri is all over me. Brazenly, he kisses me while one hand gropes my breasts and the other my butt. Mumbling something in Greek that is lost on me, he slides one hand between my legs and pushes his body closer to mine. I feel his cock through his lightweight cotton pants. It is rock hard. Good! While attempting to maintain a clear head, I try to open his belt as he enthusiastically fondles me all over. Noticing I am not making much headway, he unbuttons his pants, leaving me with a few seconds of respite.

"Take off all your clothes!" I say. Dimitri seems to understand and rids himself of his pants, underpants, and polo shirt. This gives me time to neatly fold my dress and place it in one corner of the lounge area. Grabbing the small toiletry bag with the condoms from my handbag, I place it at one end of the playground. Now that I am prepared, I can focus properly on my client. Dimitri takes me in his arms and kisses me wildly while mumbling in Greek. Clumsily, he tries to undo the clasp of my bra. Before he ends up ripping it or whatnot, I lend him a hand. Dimitri pushes me onto the lounge area and removes my panties. Spreading my legs, he looks at my exposed crotch and brushes his fingers over my vulva. Again, he mumbles something in Greek. Frantically, he starts licking my pussy. Dimitri is quite inept! – He is

127

hurting me. I wiggle into a position where his tongue can no longer touch my clit. However, Dimitri regards my movements as ecstasy and continues the enthusiastic tongue play. Out of nowhere, he kneels between my legs with his cock in hand and starts squirting all over my stomach. No warning whatsoever! Our little tumble did not even last 10 minutes. Finished, he plops down onto his back next to me and again mumbles something in Greek that is lost on me.

"I don't understand a word you're saying, darling!" I say with a smile.

"Oh, I'm sorry. I said it was great. And, you're beautiful." He moans and smiles.

"Thank you!"

Dimitri gets up and fetches our drinks.

"*Jamass!*" he says, raising his glass. I sit up and take my Campari and soda from his hand.

"*Jamass!*" I toast back in Greek.

Although I am done with my work, it is still too early to leave. Maybe we can chat for a while in broken English. Dimitri lights a cigarette and takes a deep drag.

"Do you have family?" I ask.

"Yes! Mother, father, and sister. No wife. I'm not married."

Raising his left hand, the one on which Greeks wear a wedding band, he spreads his empty fingers.

"And you?" he asks me.

"No, I'm not married. No children either."

"That's good! Children are a lot of work. Children are no good," he says. I am amazed by his sentiment. I wonder if his parents know what he thinks of children. I have always thought all Greeks wanted kids and grandchildren... I guess Dimitri is not one of them. Since it seems that is all he is going to say on the subject, I take another stab at small talk.

"So, what's your occupation?" I ask.

"I'm an architect," he replies.

"What do you design, private homes or commercial buildings?"

"Houses. Vacation homes and small hotels. Throughout the Peloponnese and Attica."

Before I can think of another question on this topic, Dimitri speaks.

"And you, how long have you been in Athens?"

"For one week now."

Dimitri nods and takes a sip of his drink.

"How long are you going to stay?" he inquires.

"I don't know yet. Perhaps indefinitely."

"Good!" he says happily and gets up to throw his cigarette overboard. When he returns to the lounge area, his cock is standing at attention again.

"Another round?" I ask, taken aback.

"Well, yes, look at him!" he replies, pointing to his boner.

"Okay, but first we need to freshen up!" I state.

"Freshen up?" he asks, confused.

"Yes, wash! Look, I have your sperm all over my belly."

"Wait!" he replies. He quickly pulls on his pants and disappears into the boat's interior. – I hear the shower running and then suddenly he reappears. A big towel is wrapped around his waist and another is draped over one arm. In his other hand, he holds a box of tissues. He holds the box out to me and I pull out two tissues to wipe the cum from my belly. As he unwraps the towel from his waist, I see he has removed his pants again and his boner is still, or yet again, rock hard. I guess Dimitri is ready for round two. When he sits down next to me, he props his upper body against the bulwark. I smell the soap he used. I wriggle down a little and take his small cock in my mouth. As I blow him, Dimitri strokes my hair and shoulders. Remembering I have not told him the rules, I interrupt the blowjob and look him squarely in the eyes.

"Dimitri! I don't want you squirting in my mouth. — If you want to ejaculate while I blow you, you must wear a condom! Do you understand?"

I pull out a rubber from my small pouch and hold it in plain view. He remains silent. I am not sure he understood everything I said.

"Do you understand? No sperm into my mouth!"

"Ah! Katalava. Yes, now I understand! No semen in your mouth! Only in the condom!"

"Exactly!" I say, still holding the rubber.

"No! Don't worry I won't come in your mouth!"

It seems he understands. I set the condom aside and continue my work. First, I lick his balls and then the insides of his thighs before taking his cock in my mouth again. Dimitri moans aloud in Greek. Talking faster and louder, I presume he is about to climax. So he does not accidentally come in my mouth, I stop. Dimitri immediately takes matters into his own hands and squirts onto his own thighs. I prefer that! As his Greek mumblings decrease and with his eyes still closed, he slides down onto the lounge area until he is lying next to me. This time too, it took him less than 10 minutes to come. Quite unusual. Some customers would love to come a second time around, but they never make it in time. Some are adamant about it and try in vain for a long time before finally giving up. I always find such attempts annoying, especially for me. I have never really understood what a man is trying to prove. Once Dimitri recuperates from his second climax, he hands me my drink and reaches for his own before lighting a cigarette. He looks sated, which pleases me! Granted, I do not understand what he is saying, but looking at him, I know it is nothing bad. I do not think he is a bad guy. As he finishes his smoke and tosses the butt overboard, I ask if I can use the shower. Looking at me mischievously, he says:

"I'm going to shower and then fuck you again!"

I do not believe it. He is ready again! What can I do or say? I am still on the clock, not even 30 minutes have elapsed. Nevertheless, this third time will be his last — if he actually pulls it off! So, I agree. Dimitri knots the towel around his waist and leaves to shower. Soon after, he comes back and drops his towel in front of me. Standing there with his erection pointing at me, he looks quite happy and I am wondering what he will do next! Lying down beside me, he again starts caressing my breasts and stomach. Then, he reaches down between my legs. I hope he is more skillful with his hands than he was with his mouth! Compared to the first two times, Dimitri does not seem to be in a hurry. However, since I have no desire to prolong his third orgasm, I grab a rubber from the package, tear the wrapping open, and roll the rubber onto his penis.

"Come on!" I say invitingly while spreading my legs. Although I use a regular size condom, it is almost too big for his penis. I hope it does not accidentally come off while fucking me. I must pay close attention. Dimitri pushes his needle into me and then pulls it a bit out again. Maintaining a slow and even rhythm, he moves his hips back and forth while closely watching the action. Then again, I am also watching and happily note the rubber is still in place.

As Dimitri hastens his movements, I am hopeful he will reach climax as quickly as he did the previous two times. It seems his new speed is tiring. He indicates he wants to switch positions. Turning onto my right side, he takes me sideways from behind. As he fucks me like a rabbit and once again mumbles excitedly in Greek, I quickly reach down to inspect the condom. It is still in place.

"Come on baby!" I encourage him. "Come on!"

Just then, Dimitri pulls his cock out of my pussy, quickly rolls off the rubber and squirts all over my butt. His cum runs down my butt and ends up on the padding of the lounge area. I am certain the material is easy to clean. Dimitri will mostly like have a crew member take care of it before family or friends come on board, – otherwise, he would have made sure not to soil it. What do I care — it is not my problem! Dimitri's panting slows and he rolls over on his back exhausted. With all four limbs comfortably stretched out, he breathes heavily. I reckon he has had enough. I would not permit another round anyway. Grabbing a few paper tissues out of the box, I wipe his sperm off my backside. I sit up and look at him.

"Good. That was very good!" Dimitri says with a blissful expression. "It's been a long time since I had sex."

"It was nice for me too!" I make an attempt at flattery.

I would also like to compliment him on his stamina, but I cannot think of anything appropriate to say. Once again, Dimitri hands me my drink. Once he has smoked half of his postcoital cigarette, I say:

"Dimitri, darling, I'd like to take a shower now."

"We can shower together," he replies.

I am definitely not showering with him! He can continue dreaming about getting lucky a fourth time. Sipping my now warm Campari and soda, I take in the nocturnal scenery. The water is calm and his yacht lies motionless.

For the first time since my arrival in Athens, I am overcome with peace as I gaze out over the dark glassy surface at the silhouettes of sailboats berthed farther out along the floating dock.

Dimitri tosses the cigarette butt overboard and hands me a towel. As I rise, I grab the small toiletry bag containing the condoms and return it to my handbag. With my clothes draped over one arm, I follow Dimitri inside the ship. We go one deck below to where the sleeping berths are and enter a cabin with an adjacent small bathroom. Since the shower stall is not all that big, I manage to make myself understood that I will be showering alone. Although Dimitri looks disappointed, he remains sitting on the bed in the cabin. From the looks of it, I believe it is his quarters. When I am finished, Dimitri hops in the shower while I dress.

"This is a beautiful boat," I say when he emerges to put his clothes on.

"It's a family boat," he replies.

"I take it you're the captain, right?" Dimitri nods.

"Yes, I steer the ship. However, we also have a crew: a couple Filipinos, a steward, and a deck hand. They don't live on board."

"Katalava — I understand," I say, and Dimitri laughs again at my attempt to answer in Greek. We return to the aft deck and I walk over to the wicker basket to grab my laptop bag and shoes. I stand there waiting for him to hold up his end of the bargain. It seems Dimitri is absentminded, so I offer him a charming smile and say:

"Dimitri, darling, please pay me my money."

"Oh, yes, of course!"

Pulling out his wallet, he takes out a 50-euro note and makes a show of handing it to me, saying:

"Thank you!"

Regarding the bill in my hand, I look at Dimitri questioningly.

"Dimitri, I told you my rate is 150 euros!"

"150?"

"Yes! That's my hourly rate!"

"No! Fifty!"

"No, I said 150 and you agreed. — What the hell!"

"Oh, no! I didn't hear that. I thought you said 50! – 150 is way too much!"

This is not acceptable! What am I going to do? I understand he might have misunderstood me, considering his broken English. Maybe that was why he agreed so quickly, thinking he was getting a great bargain!

Still, I cannot leave it alone. Is he laying it on a bit thick? Let me see if I stand a chance.

"Dimitri, I'm sorry, but I did say 150. I believe you when you say you only heard 50, but that's quite a misunderstanding."

I do my best to look disappointed, which has the desired effect. He is embarrassed.

"Could we meet again, Anika?" he asks shyly, still visibly embarrassed.

"Not for 50, Dimitri, but I might be willing for 70."

"Okay, Anika!"

He pulls out his wallet again and with an awkward smile, hands me a 20. I take it and thank him with a look of forgiveness. Remembering that I caught him calms me somewhat because such customers always get a better rate. When it comes down to it, he was an easy client, even with three rounds.

"So, Anika, can I have your phone number now? — I'd also like to go with you to a hotel. Maybe in Piraeus. That would be convenient since my office is there."

"That's not a problem, Dimitri. Piraeus also suits me. Okay, get your cell phone and I'll give you my phone number."

While storing my number, I smile at him again. He immediately calls me and as my phone hums, he says:

"Now you have my number!"

"Great, Dimitri, thank you!"

I kiss him on the cheek. He smiles, relieved. I am terribly embarrassed by the entire incident, but something like this can happen, especially when there is a language barrier.

In the future, I should ensure customers do not get my rate wrong. Perhaps I will ask them to repeat the fee. Such misunderstandings must be avoided! I know I am solely to blame. As we step on land, he asks:

"Can I drive you somewhere? Maybe back to your place? My car is right over there!"

"That's sweet of you, Dimitri, but no thanks, not today."

I brush another kiss on his cheek.

"Take care of yourself! And thank you, Dimitri."

"Good night, Anika. I'll call you!"

"Okay. Until then, darling! It was nice meeting you," I say, giving my best to part on amicable terms. Then, I turn around and leave.

I walk to the marina's nearest exit and hail a taxi for the ride home. – My phone has not rung during the interim, but business was good today. Granted, I could have accepted Dimitri's offer, but considering the awkwardness between us regarding my fee, I prefer not to spend more time with him. I simply want to be alone.

23

The next morning, as I busily sort my lingerie, someone knocks on my door. It is Sophie the maid with my laundry bag.

"Here you go, Kiria Ilona, your laundered clothes. They just dropped them off. It comes to 32 euros."

"Oh! — Thank you, Sophie!"

I relieve her of my bag and say:

"Come on in and I'll get you the money."

With conspicuous curiosity, she looks around my room. I regret inviting her in. There is certainly an undergarment flying around that I do not want her to see.

I quickly grab my wallet and take out the money. For bringing up the bag, I give her a two-euro tip, hoping she takes that as a sign to leave, but I am mistaken. She remains rooted in place. So I say:

"Thank you, Sophie. Have a nice day!"

Hesitantly, she thanks me and departs. Shutting the door behind her, I wonder if I tipped her enough. Why else would she just stand there? Turning my attention back to my lingerie, I search for something suitable to carry in the handbag on a daily basis instead schlepping my elaborate dominatrix outfit in a second bag. That way, if I receive a short-notice request for domination, I have something appropriate to wear. Granted, my new silver laptop bag is much lighter than my old black one, but it does not change the fact that it is still cumbersome carrying two bags for any period of time. I think it is easier to carry one heavy bag than two light ones. Between my sexy underwear, I see a full-length bodysuit made of large mesh. Rolled together, it does not take any more space than a regular bra and panty set. – That is it! Together with my shiny black vinyl cat mask, it will make me look mysterious and irresistibly sexy. Thinking of a suitable punishment device to go with the outfit, I look around and notice the bullwhip and handcuffs I had hung over the back of my desk chair. To make matters worse, I also see three dildos of various sizes and colors that I left on my desk in plain view. Sophie must have seen everything and froze. Crap! What must she think? I hope she does not mention this to Spiros — then again, she might be the type. The idea of them making fun of me behind my back about my sexual tastes does not sit well with me. Oh well, what is done is done.

Once calm again, I continue packing my handbag. Since the bullwhip is rather flexible, I roll it up and place it in the handbag that I will take today. Next, I place the full-length large mesh bodysuit that is now in a clear plastic bag on top and then the folded cat mask. Today, I have decided to wear my rhinestone-studded, acid-green lingerie set that looks fresh and bewitching against my tanned skin. I also pack a black lace bra and panty set with two strings of pearls. This one is for when I meet Adonis. And, in reserve, I pack my new red body mesh suit with vinyl trim. Since all sets are individually bundled in clear plastic bags, nothing will get mixed up. My handbag is now heavier than it was yesterday, but at least everything I need is in one bag, even for a game of domination should the need arise.

All my other domination items and specialty clothing I place neatly and easily accessible on a shelf in the wardrobe. I have amassed a small collection. A few years ago, I started buying my own sex toys for work. I no longer wanted to use the ones at the club since other women working there used them too. And even if condoms were rolled over the toys and were properly cleaned and sanitized after use, I did not want to stick a dildo in my pussy that was used by others. Some items I bought for myself. I enjoy pleasuring myself with sex toys. Obviously, I do not use my favorites for work. I keep work and private life separate.

As I continue rummaging through my drawer of lingerie, I discover a short, oh-so sexy black mesh dress. It is light and goes nicely with black strapless stockings. After placing both items in a clear plastic bag, I write on a piece of paper 'Mesh dress/stockings' and lay it on top of the lingerie for easy identification. – I do that with all the combinations I create, which keeps me busy for a while.

I received two phone calls this morning. The first man did not like my rate; the other introduced himself as Paul from Glyfada who immediately wanted to make an appointment for Friday but could not decide on the time. So, I have to be patient...

At 2:00 p.m., I am meeting Adonis in Glyfada. Once again, I am faced with the difficult decision — what to wear? After brief contemplation, I choose a denim mini skirt, a red and white-striped top with spaghetti straps, red high heels, and nautical fashion jewelry with big gold hoop earrings. All of this complements my ponytail hair-extension. I am going to look ravishing and sexy for the man with the briefcase full of toys! While laying out these items, my phone rings. Checking the display, I see it is a Greek cell phone number.

"Hello!"

"Good afternoon, this is Bruce. I'm calling from Vouliagmeni. Do you make home visits in this area or is it too far away?"

Although I think Vouliagmeni is farther south than Glyfada, at the moment, I am almost willing to travel any distance.

"Hi, Bruce, I'm Anika. Yes, I'll come to Vouliagmeni. Would you like more information?"

"Yes, that would be nice, Anika!"

Once I finish telling Bruce the usual, he says:

"That sounds good, Anika. Can you be at my place today later this afternoon? Do you have time?"

"Yes, that works. What time exactly?"

"Six o'clock would be best."

"Okay, Bruce, but I need your full name, address, and landline number. Could you text that to me?"

"Of course, I'll do it right now!"

Yippee! – I have an appointment! I am ecstatic! Once I receive Bruce's text, I am going look up his address on Google maps. He sounded British, I think. Damn, I forgot to ask his nationality. After enjoying another cup of coffee, I straighten up my room. Right now, it looks as if a bomb went off. Bagged and loose pieces of underwear are strewn about. Handbags are piled on top of the shoe cabinet while my shoes lay haphazardly under the bed. When I finally finish tidying up, I open my laptop and go online. I receive a short email from my friend Lisa in Germany. She wants to know how I am doing and hopes to hear from me. Other friends that I used to hang out with also want to know how I am doing... Quickly, I write a short email in response:

'Dear Lisa, Thanks for your email. I took a job waitressing in a bar and currently live in an apartment I share with two other women. So, I am doing okay – I will send more details when I am not pressed for time. Promise! Right now, I have too much to do. – Greetings to all! Kisses, Ilona'.

Although I feel guilty about lying and being abrupt, for the life of me I cannot invent anything else at the moment. I must create a new and believable story for my friends and family that will serve me in the long run... Once I hit send, I Google escort services and check out the women's profiles. Most show their face. I certainly would not, but not because of my age. My concern would be that someone from my private life might recognize me. That would be devastating! When I arrive at a website I like, I pull up the 'Greece' page. It lists around twenty ads. Half of them are escort agencies. The rest are ads placed by private individuals. I bookmark the site. Maybe one day I will place an ad on the Internet, who knows? For the time being, I will wait to see how my ad in the *Athens World* performs. Since I am new in town, I would think in the beginning, I would receive lots of calls.

My announcement should stick out to all regular readers of the weekly escort column. Perhaps the men, who on occasion engage the services of prostitutes, would call out of sheer curiosity. At least that is what I am hoping.

I shut down my laptop and go out onto the balcony. On my cell phone, I search for the address Bruce texted me shortly after our conversation and store his number in my client address book under 'Bruce - Vouliagmeni'. Having completed my chores, I lean back and close my eyes. I am now accustomed to the street noise and it no longer bothers me. I barely perceive the incessant honking. I would say I have become acclimated to living and working in Athens. At the moment, I do not have to worry about anything. My finances are in order and I have the feeling things will only get better. Even though I give a client a more affordable rate than I deem ideal, I still earn more than I did in Germany. My phone rings again.

"Hello!"

"Hi! I got your number out of *Athens World*. Do you have big tits?"

"Hi, I'm Anika. And no, I don't have big tits."

"Oh, that's too bad. What do you look like?"

"I'm a blue-eyed blonde with a slim figure. My cup size is 34B."

"Oh, a blonde and you sound nice too. However, I'm looking for a woman with big tits."

"I understand, but I don't have those! Sorry, baby. Anyway, thanks for your call!"

"Yeah, no problem. Bye!"

It is time for me to go to the bathroom to get ready for work. As I dress, I think about my second appointment in a private residence. It would be inappropriate to show up in a mini skirt. – Then again, it is summer and most tourists wear light clothes as I do. Even at the Hilton, I would hardly stand out dressed in a mini skirt. And, – Bruce never expressly asked me to dress discreetly... Perhaps there is room in my handbag for my red knee-length pencil skirt. After brief consideration, I roll it up and try stuffing it into my bag. It is no use, I am afraid the seams might burst. I hang the garment back up and decide to run around in my denim mini skirt.

The tram runs alongside the beach promenade from Phaleron to Kalamaki and onto Alimos, then it runs by the old airport and finally to Glyfada. That is where the tram leaves the coast and runs parallel to Metaxa Street. As instructed, I get off after the commercial area at the second stop.

Now I am in a residential neighborhood with huge mansions and apartment buildings surrounded by narrow gardens. The gardens do not look all that invitingly. I guess their main function is to provide a privacy barrier to the neighboring houses. I do not walk far before noticing the neon sign of the Lenny Blue Hotel. Looking at my watch, I see it is only 12:30 p.m. Since I still have plenty of time, I decide to return to Metaxa Street to check out the stores.

Seeing a branch of my favorite clothing store I frequented in Germany, I go inside and examine their latest collection. Among the summer clothes, I find an agreeably priced stylish dress and try it on. – It is a sleeveless, knee-length, red and white horizontally striped, figure-accentuating dress made of elastic material that greatly emphasizes my figure. It will complement my red shoulder bag, sun hat, and shoes nicely. Thinking about how well I did over the last few days, I decide to treat myself and buy the dress. However, to justify spending money on myself, I regard it as a business investment.

While in the changing room, I consider putting on the lingerie for my appointment with Adonis. That way I will not have to change at the hotel. Slipping out of my red bra, I switch to the black delicate lace one with a tiny pearl heart dangling between the cups. I arrange my breasts in the soft see-through lace of the underwire bra so my nipples point upward and my cleavage is nice and plump. Quite inviting! Donning the matching pair of panties, the two strings of beads cut deep into my crotch. Glancing at my watch, I see there is still more than 30 minutes until my appointment at the hotel that is a mere 500 meters away. Walking such a distance with the stringed beads between my legs might be uncomfortable or even painful. Therefore, I decide to wear my regular tanga. I place the bead panties in the side pouch with my phone so I can quickly exchange them once I am in the hotel elevator.

Fully dressed again, I drape my new find over one arm, pick up my handbag, and stand in line at the cash register. Once I have paid, I am again carrying two items: my handbag and a mundane plastic bag containing my newest acquisition.

24

As 2:00 p.m. approaches, I head for the Lenny Blue Hotel. Although my phone does not ring, I receive a text message from Adonis:

Room 42. See you soon, sexy!

I text back:

I'll be right there!

I pay for the candy bar and eat it while walking to the hotel. A few minutes later, I enter the lobby of the Lenny Blue Hotel. A middle-aged woman behind the reception counter starts talking to me in Greek.

Looking at her questioningly, I say:

"Hello. How do I get to room 42?"

"Fourth floor," she briefly answers in English and dismisses me. I walk to the elevator and see it is stopped on the fourth floor. I push the button and wait for it to arrive on the ground floor. Stepping into the elevator, I can tell it is ancient. As it groans its way up, I swiftly exchange my panties for the black lace with stringed beads. Arriving on the fourth floor, the elevator comes to an abrupt stop and I quickly exit. When I knock on room 42, Adonis opens it wearing only a white towel wrapped around his waist and a cigarette in one hand. We exchange kisses on each cheek. I am glad the room is dimly lit. Such illumination complements me and makes me look 30 years young.

"Hey, sexy! I like that pony tail!" Adonis greets me and looks me up and down.

"Damn, you simply look stunning in a mini skirt! But I bet you know that, don't you?"

"Of course. I still have the legs for it," I say seductively.

"So, how's business? Is your ad a hit?

"Yes, thank you. I can't complain!"

"Great, I'm happy for you!"

I drop my purse on an armchair. The room contains a four-poster wooden bed with open curtains and many small black silk cushions. On the wall to the right of the bed hangs a large mirror. Red-framed erotica adorns the remaining three walls. The wall opposite the bed has a flat screen TV mounted on it. The entire room is decorated in black and brown with flecks of red mixed in here and there. Having discarded the towel, Adonis leans naked against a bedpost and ogles me with a smirk on his face. Grabbing my small pouch containing the condoms from my handbag, I place it on the big mattress next to his open briefcase of toys. Adonis stubs his cigarette out in the ashtray on the nightstand and walks over toward me.

"You are a feast for the eyes, Anika!"

He moves behind me and holds my arm with one hand while his other moves down and reaches under my short denim skirt.

"Hey!" he says as he feels the beads in my crotch. "This is awesome! You're stimulating yourself. I like that. I like horny women! — Come on, I also want to see your front!"

We move in front of the big mirror. I place my hands against the glass while brazenly sticking out my butt. He reaches under the light fabric of my red striped spaghetti strap top and fondles my breasts while rubbing his hard cock against the back of my thighs.

"Take off your top, baby, I want to see more of you," he says.

I do as he wishes and bend forward, letting it slide down my out-stretched arms onto the ground. Adonis whistles through his teeth as he gets a good look at my beautifully packaged bosoms.

"Take off your skirt too, Anika. I can't wait to touch you all over!"

He searches for eye contact in the mirror. I accommodate his request by slowly opening the zipper of my skirt and seductively inching it down my legs until it lands on the floor next to my top. Now, only dressed in the flimsy material of my lacy panties with strings of beads, I again place my hands against the mirror and provocatively stick out my butt. Adonis pushes the elastic material of my bra under my bosom and starts massaging my nipples. Punishingly, he grinds his hard boner against my buttocks. I am supposed to feel his throbbing manhood. His pulling and twisting of my nipples makes them quite hard. Adonis seems happy with his accomplishment. He removes his hand and pushes it from behind between my legs. Skillfully, he parts my lacy underwear's two beaded strings. Then he sticks a finger in his mouth and wets it before slowly pushing it deep into my pussy and leaving it there. Adonis is more adept than other customers. From his expression, I can tell how much he enjoys teasing me.

"You get me all hot, darling," I say. "My mouth is watering just thinking about your big cock!"

"That's it, sexy. – That's the way I want you! Fucking horny and wriggling around on the sheets ecstatically. — And when you think you're ready to explode from lust, I'll shoot my hot sperm on your desirous, twitching body! Should we do it that way? I get you all hot and once I have squirted all over you, you pleasure yourself with one of my toys!"

"Yes, darling, that sounds fantastic. I only hope I can wait until you climax!"

Adonis withdraws his fingers from my pussy and repositions himself on one side of me. – One of his hands fondles my nipples off and on while the other massages and gently slaps my buttocks now and then. Next, he rubs his moistened finger over my bead-imprisoned labia and then finally over my clit. His playful teasing is fantastic. Since I am working and it is not about me, I concentrate on my job. – Expertly, Adonis works my erogenous zones while repeatedly pressing his cock against the side of my upper leg. At some point, he moves behind me and sticks his big hard rod between my slightly spread legs.

"Hold onto it with your thighs!"

I squeeze my legs together and feel his boner press against the strings of beads. I like how he stimulates my clit. Adonis unhooks my bra and lets it drop to the floor with my other clothes.

He grabs my breasts firmly in both hands. I moan aloud as he lightly kneads my bosom while teasing the nipples with pulls and twists. He moves his hips leisurely back and forth, rubbing his cock between my thighs. I allow myself to be stimulated by his fondling. If I wanted, I could easily dismiss his touch. That is up to me. I am not defenseless against his will and sexual technique. Such a thing is preposterous.

Although, one time, I gave myself permission to enjoy good sex during an appointment. Why should I not have exhilarating orgasms every now and then? Certain things are merely better or possible when carried out with someone else. Or, is it written somewhere that prostitutes cannot express sexual desire during work or succumb to them when with a client?

It is my habit not to look for something else in a customer. I also do not want him to fall in love with me or vice versa. — That is taboo. I had my experience when I was younger. Nowadays, I know better. Adonis seems to sense my sexual tension and says:

"Shall we look for a sex toy you might enjoy using today?"

"Oh, yes!" I reply. "Show me your treasures!"

He releases me and we walk over to the bed. – While examining his splendid collection of toys, my eyes land on the big purple silicone dual mode vibrator again. In operational mode, it can move up and down or rotate its head. This multi-function toy also has a finger attachment that can be switched to vibrate to stimulate the clitoris.

I suspect it is Adonis' favorite piece. He might presume women are into this Jack-Of-All-Trades. I do not want to ruin the image he has of the female sex and certainly not the image he has of me! Therefore, before the day comes where Adonis beats me to it, I decide to use the purple silicone monster for today's session. That way I am in charge of the toy and not at the mercy of his play. Grabbing the deluxe vibrator from the briefcase, I say:

"I'm going with this gem today!"

"Oh, yes, I'm sure you'll love it. That thing does things even I can't do," Adonis says jokingly. "But first, I'm going to fuck you, sexy! Bend over the bed. I want to take you from behind!"

Hastily, I grab two extra-large rubbers from my pouch. Kneeling in front of him, I run my tongue over the tip of his cock and tear one condom wrapper open. Having rolled it over his erection, I turn around and kneel on the edge of the bed so I am at the right height for him to fuck me from behind. Adonis clutches my hips as he gently shoves his penis between the two strings of beads as far as it goes into my pussy. So far, I allowed myself be turned on by his advances, but from now on I must keep my *itchiness* in check and concentrate solely on work. All I have to do is anticipate his deep thrusts and move accordingly to soften the impact. I know it will not take long before he climaxes when he says:

"Turn around, sexy, lie down so I can kneel before your pussy!"

Lying there with my legs spread far apart, I grab the purple silicone monster and roll the other rubber over it. Since my pussy is stretched out from Adonis' fuck, there is no problem sliding the big vibrator deep into me. I make sure the stimulating finger attachment does not touch my clit! While kneeling between my legs, Adonis pulls the condom from his dick and tosses it on the floor. He grabs his cock and starts masturbating while staring intently at the penetrating vibrator parting the string of beads. Playing along, I lustfully wriggle around on the sheets, switch the vibrator to level one, and groan out loud. Level one is the rotating head feature and I really do not understand how that is stimulating. To me, it feels like a mood killer. However, Adonis does not need to know this. Who knows, maybe other women find this multipurpose feature fantastic. While Adonis squirts his cum on my belly, he closes his eyes and tilts his head back. He does not look at me until he manages to wring the last drop from his rod. As agreed upon, it is now my turn to perform. Continuing my seductive writhing on the sheet, I spread his sperm over my stomach while I push my pussy with the noisy head-rotating vibrator in it toward Adonis. I am beginning my main act where I pretend to have an overwhelming orgasm. Watching Adonis, I know he believes it is real. If he only knew how unpleasant this rotating monster feels in my pussy. After my pseudo climax has subsided, I turn off the vibrator and pull it out of my tormented pussy. Adonis is still kneeling between my legs, staring at me.

"That was amazing!" I lie.

"Yes," he says. "The sex we share is special to me too. We have the right chemistry! That doesn't happen often. And for me it's important, otherwise, I don't enjoy the sex."

As he lies down next to me, I rearrange the beaded strings so they lie loosely around my labia without pinching.

"I'd like to ask you something," he continues and turns on his side to look at me.

"Sure, go ahead!" I say openly.

"I know a Russian woman. – She might be your age, maybe a little younger. Anyway, she's been in Athens for a few years and works in your field. However, she doesn't place ads in the paper. Somehow, she finds customers and hopes for recommendations. I see her every now and then. She's nice. I mean, simpatico.

I was thinking the two of you, uh..." he hesitates for a moment, "might make a good team. Sometimes, men like two women at a time. I mean, oh, I don't know. But if you're up for it, I would arrange for both of you to come at the same time. – Afterward, you can decide whether you want to exchange phone numbers. That's entirely up to you girls. I'm not getting involved. So, what do you think? Should we try it out?"

Having listened carefully, I think about it. A Russian woman.

"How much does she charge an hour?"

"Less than you. — I would have to pay you so she doesn't see. Perhaps when she's in the bathroom."

"What's her rate?"

"I give her 60."

"That's not much. — Just so you know, if she asks, I won't lie and tell her I get the same, okay?"

"Okay." Adonis is grinning now. "I already thought as much, – but maybe she won't ask at all. I mean, I believe it's her regular rate. At least she always seems happy when I pay her. And I know she's glad for every job she can get. She won't complain or stop seeing me if she finds out I'm paying you more. So, I don't mind you telling her."

"Okay. I don't see a problem with it either. So, go ahead and arrange the meeting, providing, of course, she wants it too."

"Okay, I'll call her. Maybe sometime next week. We'll meet here again. It's convenient for her and me. She lives in Voula. How about you? Is this hotel okay with you?"

"Yes, it's fine! What's her name?"

"Natasha," he answers. — Of course, what else!

As he obviously does not have anything else to add, I ask:

"Do you want to use the bathroom first or can I use it?"

"Let me freshen up first. I have to get ready for a meeting."

He gets up, grabs the silicone monster off the bed, and disappears into the bathroom. When he returns, he hands me 80 euros. I wait until he is fully dressed before I stand up to say goodbye.

"Anika, the room is already paid for. – The minimum here is three hours. You don't have to hurry. Simply drop off the room key at reception."

Having said goodbye and pecks on the cheeks exchanged, he playfully slaps my ass before leaving the room.

25

Taking off the beaded panties, I pick up the used condom from the ground, toss it in the trash, and jump in the shower. There have been no calls during the time I was busy working. – Since I can use the room for almost another two hours, I stay for a while in the air-conditioned environment before facing the terrible heat outside.

My next appointment with Bruce is at 6:00 p.m. Since I was mistaken and Vouliagmeni is not that far away from Glyfada like I assumed, there is absolutely no reason to rush. I do not have to depart before 5:30 p.m. to make it to Bruce's in time.

Freshly showered, I wrap one of the big towels around me and sit down on the bed. – Turning on the TV, I find a porn flick. Switching channels shows me another adult movie. The next one is a Greek TV station and of no use to me since I do not understand a word. I quickly click through the channels in the hopes of discovering an English-speaking program. – But my search is in vain. At one point, I arrive at another station showing a pornographic film, which makes sense since this is an hourly hotel. Since it is in English, I watch for a bit. Thinking about Violet, I dial her number. She answers relatively quickly.

"Hello!"

"Hi, darling, it's Anika. How are you?"

"Oh, Anika! I'm great. I've been busy today. One of my regulars, Ilias, was already here this morning. – He always wants to shower afterward, which drives me nuts! I mean, why would he? – He gets undressed and directly pushes up the nightgown I wear especially for him. Then he fucks me from on top and from behind. That usually does it for him and he squirts into the rubber. – So, why does he need to shower afterward? — I don't see why he can't do what my other customers do and take some wet wipes to clean his Johnson. I always keep a box of wet wipes on the nightstand and a roll of plain paper towels. — Yet Ilias always insists on taking a shower. And he always takes his time! I swear, I don't get him! I always have to clean and dry the shower stall and put out a new bath mat. — Well, he does pay me 150 euros. And I've known him for seven or eight years. I guess I shouldn't complain. Still, it gets to me! Then I had a visit from Ioannis this afternoon. He didn't require a shower after sex. I handed him the wipes and that was that! Easy-peasy, as it always is with him. I start him off with a blowjob, then he pushes my bosom together and titty fucks me. Eventually, he comes and that is that. All in all, he's in and out of my place within 40 minutes and gives me 150. Anyway, how are you? Is business good?"

I tell Violet about my two recent clients and Violet cracks up when I share the payment mix up incident with Dimitri.

"Sorry, darling, but that's too funny. I have no problem imagining what that must have looked like. When I started here, I also couldn't speak Greek and I was often misunderstood, but something like what you experienced never happened to me! You really should learn more Greek. At least a bit so you can state your rate in Greek. That way, if a man can't speak English well, it won't occur again. I thought you knew Greek numbers! Next time, ask if he understood you. Make sure he confirms it! — Oh, darling, I'm sorry it happened to you, but just look at it from this perspective; he had a good time with you and I'm sure he'll call again. In our profession, cheap customers also bring in a good amount of dough. Think about it, back when I was paid in drachmas, what was I supposed to do with it? Exchange it into pounds? Or dollars? What for? The drachma wasn't worth anything. So I kept the money for living expenses and put the rest in my bank account. Nowadays, we're lucky to be paid in euros! And 70 euros is good money, even in a foreign country. — Sorry, darling, I hear my other phone ringing! I have to answer. Call me again, yes! Gotta go, talk to you later!"

"Okay, until later, Violet!"

Putting my phone away, I turn the TV back on and resume my search for an English-speaking program. Again, unsuccessful. Should I stay in this hotel room the entire time? No, I am already bored. Regardless of the heat outside, I would rather kill time strolling down Metaxa Street. I could follow it all the way to the coast and grab a bite to eat somewhere before heading to Vouliagmeni to see Bruce. Yes, that sounds better than staying here bored out of my mind.

Consequently, I dress and leave the hotel. – Walking along Metaxa Street, I pass a couple shoe stores. The temptation to spend money surfaces. Yes, I know, women and shoes! I am definitely a collector of these fashionable treasures. If I decide to stay in Athens, I will return in September to Germany to retrieve my collection of treasures that I have amassed so far.

In one store, I try on a pair of light-blue, silvery glittering high-heels and take them for a spin. I really have to restrain myself. Nevertheless, I stay resolute and return the little treasures back to the shelf. Before walking away, I throw one more longing look because I cannot stop thinking about what an elegant touch they would lend to a simple denim skirt.

There will come the day where I can afford such lovely treasures without my conscience berating me. Out on the street, I pass a Greek fast food chain I like and this time, give into temptation! They make great pizza with olives and feta cheese. I order a slice and attack it ravenously. Delicious! My phone rings, so I quickly force the bite of pizza down my throat and answer it.

"Hello!"

"Yes, hello! I'm Arnold. Do you come to hotels? I have a room at the Metropolitan Hotel."

Arnold speaks German. Fantastic!

"Hi, Arnold, I'm Anika. And yes, I visit hotels. Would you like to hear a little about me?"

"Yes, please!"

Once I have passed along my age, looks, and hourly rate, he says:

"Hey! Everything sounds fine. Is it possible to visit me this evening? Any chance you can come to my room at 9:00 p.m.?"

"Yes, that works for me."

"Great, then I would like to book you now! And please make sure nobody sees you knocking on my door. I'm on a business trip with some colleagues and they are staying on the same floor."

"Don't worry, I'll be discreet. Tell me your last name and your room number. That way I can call you shortly before I leave for the hotel."

"Yes, of course. My name is Arnold Bauer. I'm in room 351 at the Metropolitan Hotel."

I note everything, say goodbye to Arnold, and return the phone to my pocket. Yippee! Another appointment! The Metropolitan Hotel is on Syngrou Avenue. A taxi ride from Vouliagmeni to the hotel would get me there within 30 minutes. Happy and hungry, I wolf down the rest of the pizza slice. After paying my bill, I leave the restaurant and walk across the street to the sea.

Walking up to a café with a nice shaded patio, I grab a seat at an empty table and kill some time checking out the latest news on my phone. At 5:30 p.m., I call Bruce. He answers and tells me to call him back once I arrive at his home because the doorbell crapped out, so he will meet me at the garden gate. I ask:

"Is it all right if I show up in a mini skirt or should I wear something more conservative?"

"A mini skirt is fine. I don't care what my neighbors think if they see you."

"All right, Bruce, see you soon!"

"Okay, until then, Anika!"

26

After our phone conversation, I go to the nearby taxi stand and hold up the note with Bruce address so the driver can read it. He nods for me to get in and I take a seat on the back bench. I roll up the plastic bag with my new dress tightly and manage to stuff it into my already bulging handbag. The bag is now impossible to close. After about 15 minutes, the cab stops and the driver informs me we have arrived. Bruce lives on a mountain slope in a quiet residential area in Vouliagmeni. It is a three-story house with a large garden. As I slowly walk toward it, I dial his number. He immediately answers and I quietly say:

"Hi, Bruce, it's Anika. I'm in front of your house. Can you open the gate?"

"Yes, hold on, Anika, I'll come to the door!"

Next, I hear the buzzer of the garden gate and push it open. As I approach the front door of the house, it opens and an approximately 55-year-old, tall, slender man with a friendly face and strawberry blond short hair waits in the entrance. Bruce greets me with a firm handshake.

"Hello, Anika. Good day! Nice of you to come! Please come in. How are you?"

"Thank you, Bruce. I'm fine."

He releases my hand and beckons me into the hallway.

"Let me have a look at you, Anika!"

At that moment, my stomach flip-flops. Although I know I look good, I am uncomfortable when someone checks me out so carefully. It lowers my self-confidence and more so the brighter it is. Thankfully, we are not out in direct sunlight. – I manage to recuperate quickly. Instead of standing rooted in place, I take it upon myself to continue into the next room, a large split-level living room. The lower level of the living room is separated from a huge patio by a glass wall with sizeable sliding doors. The pulled out awning prevents the sunlight from entering the lower level. The view of the sea is breathtakingly beautiful. Looking down at a nicely curved bay, I see an unfamiliar marina with huge berthed ships. Impressed, I turn around to face Bruce and say:

"Wow! Your apartment has fantastic views. Congratulations!"

Bruce steps up next to me.

"Yes! Down there is Mariana Vouliagmeni," he says, pointing to the ships I just looked at in the bay.

"And yes, I'm also happy with the location."

Since I did not come here for a house tour and small talk, I come right out and ask:

"Well, darling, how can I be of service? Should I start by giving you a nice massage? And — which area are we going to use to enjoy ourselves? Here or in the bedroom? Oh, and, please, could I first use your bathroom?"

"Of course you can, Anika. Come on, I'll show you where it is."

Bruce escorts me to another wing of the modern and tastefully decorated house. Then he opens a door to a bathroom done in teak and black marble.

"Here you go, Anika, the bathroom! — I can do without a massage or normal sex. — I'd much rather go with you to my den to try something out on my desk. Is that okay with you?"

"That depends on what you have in mind!" I say curiously.

"Well come on, let me show you!" Bruce says and takes the lead.

I follow him into his den. In the center stands a large light-colored wooden desk. The window shutters are closed and a floor lamp in a corner casts the room in dim light. I like that. I see a monitor and keyboard on his desk and to the left of it, neatly aligned documents. I look at him questioningly.

"One moment, please!" Bruce says as he goes and grabs a hanger with a white shirt, a tie, and a leather belt from behind the open door of his den.

"I like your short skirt," he says, looking at me, "but I'd like you to exchange your top for this shirt and tie. Maybe you can stuff the shirt into your skirt, then you won't need the belt to hold the shirt together at your waist."

I cannot help but smile and say:

"Yes, that's not a problem, — but why the shirt and tie?"

"Anika, I don't know if it'll work, but I have a fantasy I'd like to act out with you."

He points to the desk chair and asks me to take a seat as he sits down on the edge of the desk and turns his upper body to face me.

"Okay, this is my fantasy: You're a schoolgirl and I'm your teacher."

"Okay... But why the shirt, tie, and belt?"

"They're supposed to represent an English schoolgirl uniform. Unfortunately, I don't have a blouse, nor do I have a red plaid or blue skirt and white socks for you. — I can overlook those details. However, if you wear the shirt and stuff it in your skirt, together with the tie it would definitely come close to a schoolgirl uniform. Of course, you can pull the belt through the loops of your skirt if you like, but I don't think the belt is all that important. — Anyway, back to my fantasy: You're my student and you have to sit here at my desk because you've earned detention. You can type away on the computer. — Is that okay so far, Anika? I want you to be honest and tell me if you don't like something or if you think you can't do it, okay!"

"So far, I don't have a problem, Bruce. Go ahead and continue your fantasy."

"Great. Okay, so then you do something naughty or filthy, something that'll provoke me. I mean, sexual provocation! — For example, you spread your legs so I can see your panties. Or put a hand between your legs and play with yourself. — Is that all right?"

"Yes, I'm fine with it. What else do you want me to do?"

"I'm going to ask you if you've ever made out with a boy and you can answer yes or no, I'll leave that up to you. You're welcome to spice up things with your imagination. — Anyway, I'm going to reprimand you, I mean the little schoolgirl from my class. Anyway, no matter how the game proceeds, I eventually want you to open my pants and give me a blowjob. That must be part of the little schoolgirl-teacher game. I'm sure I'll reach climax and then I'll instruct you not tell anybody, otherwise, I'll pay your mother a visit and tell her how unruly you are in the classroom and that you provoked me. — What do you say, Anika?"

Okay, so it is role-playing! I usually charge 200 — but now is not the time to talk money. I have missed my opportunity. I also do not see how I could get my point across without ruining the mood that has been established. As I want to focus on my job without thinking about it, I decide to leave it at the originally agreed upon 150. Perhaps an opportunity to broach the issue will arise at the end of our session. So, I answer:

"Yes, I think I can handle it, Bruce. – Okay, I'll disappear into the bathroom to change. I'll be your little schoolgirl when I come back, okay?"

"Wonderful, Anika!" — But wait. We both need names. What should my name be, given that I'm your teacher? You must always address me politely with Mr. so and so! So, pick a name for me."

"How about Mr. Smith?"

"Yes! That sounds good. I'm Mr. Smith. And you? Preferably a real German sounding name."

"Maybe Brigitte, Gaby, or Ulrike?"

"Ulrike. I like that name! I'll call you Ulrike."

"Great, I'll be right back."

"Good. — Oh, so you know, I'll have a condom in my pocket!"

"Good to know, Bruce. See you in a minute!"

"See you soon, Anika. My, my, you do have a great figure!"

"Thank you!" I say as I leave the den with the coat hanger. Once in the bathroom, I change into the white shirt, shove it into my denim skirt, and put on the already knotted dark-blue tie. However, I decide to forego the belt. It will simply get in the way. What else? So, he wants to seduce a little girl who is supposed to feel ashamed. A pedophile? Well, it is certainly better if he acts out his fantasy with prostitutes than actually assaulting little girls. My high heels do not fit the role of a little schoolgirl, so I remove my shoes and decide to walk barefoot into the study. I part my hair and braid it in two strands, one on each side like Pippi Longstocking. I believe the pigtails provide a cute touch. Inspecting myself in the short skirt, white shirt, tie, and my cute pigtails in the big mirror above the bathtub barefoot, I think I look girlish. Considering Bruce wants to seduce a naughty schoolgirl, I imagine he might appreciate my naked pussy, so I remove my panties. All that is left to play my role properly is to adopt the speech, gestures, and movements of a young girl. Everything is set for me to give a first-class performance as an English schoolgirl. Since Bruce's den door is closed, I knock like a good little girl.

"One moment, please!" he calls from inside. In a minute, he opens the door and looks at me with a friendly and dazzling smile.

"Oh, Ulrike, it's you. Come in!"

"Good morning, Mr. Smith. I was told to report to you after class."

Coyly, I step into his office and he immediately says:

"Yes, young girl, that's right. During class, I once again noticed you were inattentive. You were looking at your thighs with your hands under the desk. Every time I addressed you, you didn't even know what the question was that I asked... — So, Ulrike, what's going on with you?"

"I don't know, Mr. Smith. — At times, my mind just wanders."

"Okay. Where does it wander, Ulrike?"

"I don't want to say, Mr. Smith."

"I need to know, Ulrike! Come on, out with it!"

Slightly knock-kneed with my hands folded together in front of my midriff, I stand before him slightly swaying my hips back and forth while keeping my gaze directed at the ground. Towering over me now that I do not have shoes on, Bruce steps closer to me and looks disapprovingly down on me.

"I really can't tell you, Mr. Smith," I answer in a slightly tormented voice. "Please don't make me! I promise to pay closer attention in the classroom. And please, please don't tell my mom about it. Ever since dad left, she's especially strict!"

"Ah! Your father left?"

"Yes, a few weeks ago because Mommy was with another man."

"Oh, I didn't know. I feel sorry for you, my child! Nevertheless, I still want to know where your mind was during class. Perhaps it's easier for you to type it on the computer? — Come! Sit here!"

Bruce adjusts the big desk chair for me. The monitor displays a new Word file.

"Please, Ulrike, write down what you were thinking about. You don't have to be afraid. I want to understand what you're going through and I promise I won't let your mother know. – However, if you refuse to confide in me, you give me no choice and I'll have to punish you. — So, you decide. All I care about is your well-being, Ulrike!"

Bruce moves behind me and leans in close. His hot breath brushes my scalp. Sheepishly, I swing the chair left and right while wringing my still folded hands in my lap. This makes my skirt slide further up my thighs, but it still covers my smooth girlish shame.

"Okay, Mr. Smith, I'll write down my thoughts. But please, wait until I'm done before reading it. You make me nervous when you stand so close."

"Of course! Of course, Ulrike."

Bruce steps back and looks at me sternly before moving around to the front of the desk. I must say, he plays the role quite well. So far, our role-playing is good! Even I am amazed. – Using two fingers, I start pecking the keys:

'I'm so distracted in class because I can't stop thinking about my mommy's new boyfriend and his huge penis. Thinking about it makes me feel weird.'

When I finish, I put my hands back in my lap and squirm nervously in the chair. This makes my skirt slide up even further so that my shaven pussy can be seen at times. That is exactly what I want. I push the rolling desk chair a bit back and notice Bruce is throwing lustful, excited glances between my legs.

"I'm done," I say quietly, my head down.

"Good, Ulrike. I'm coming around now and we'll read it together. Don't be afraid, little one, I won't tell a soul, nor will I judge you! No matter what you've written, we'll simply talk about it."

Bruce appears next to me, squats down, and after a brief look at my thighs, he directs his gaze at the monitor.

"Do you want to read it out loud or shall I read it myself, Ulrike?"

"Please read it yourself, Mr. Smith!"

"As you wish, Ulrike. It says: 'I'm so distracted in class because I can't stop thinking about my mommy's new boyfriend and his huge penis. Thinking about it makes me feel weird.'"

I feel Bruce's eyes on me and, embarrassed, I raise my head and look shyly at him from the corner of my eye.

"You did well, Ulrike! You're a good girl! Your mommy can be proud of you. I'm proud of you! It's quite normal for something like that to make you feel weird."

"You really mean that, Mr. Smith?"

"Yes, of course, Ulrike! When did you see your mom's new boyfriend's penis?"

"When he came out of the bathroom and into my room to kiss me good night."

"I see! And, is he big? How do you know? Had you seen a penis before?"

I hold my two index fingers about 20 centimeters apart and say:

"About that big."

"Oh, that big! Was that the first or second time you saw a penis?"

"I saw Jimmy's before. He's Chantal's little brother. But his weenie is tiny. Nothing like the gigantic one!"

"Well, Ulrike, I can explain why that's the case. A little boy has a small weenie and adult man has a big weenie. My weenie is also bigger than Jimmy's."

"Oh, really! So it's like Rudi's, my mom's new boyfriend? Thinking about his huge penis makes me feel weird and all tingly down here."

I point one finger to my lap.

"Show me, Ulrike. Show me where it feels all tingly?"

"Well, down there!"

"That doesn't tell me anything, Ulrike. You need to show me what you are speaking about. And don't be afraid, I only want to see so I can understand!"

I spread my legs far apart so that my skirt rides up even further and exposes my pussy. – Now he has an unobstructed view of my clean-shaven, girlish-looking shame. Bruce suddenly inhales sharply through his teeth, letting me know he is utterly aroused.

"You're not wearing underwear!" he says, surprised.

"I always take them off when I get to school."

"Why do you take them off at school?"

"Because I can't do it at home. Somehow Mommy always knows and gets upset."

"Oh, okay. So you don't like wearing panties?"

"Not really. When I don't have them on, I have a nice tingly feeling down there and I like that."

"Well, that sensation is perfectly normal, little Ulrike! — I take it your mom has never talked about that with you?"

Shaking my head, I look at my crotch.

"I'm sure she will if you ask her! It's normal, little Ulrike!"

Bruce rises from his squatting position and sits down on the edge of the desktop with one butt cheek. Turning toward him, I ask:

"You're not mad at me now, are you, Mr. Smith? You really won't say anything to my mommy about it?"

"No, Ulrike, just like I promised! Now tell me, how old exactly are you?"

"I'm ten."

"Only 10 years old! Such a young little thing! — Okay, Ulrike, I'm going to show you my penis now. You can examine it for as long as you want. And, if you want, you can also touch it. A penis is a natural part of the male body. If you like it, little Ulrike, I'll let you see it more often. That way you can concentrate in class instead of thinking about the penis on your mom's boyfriend. But, it must stay our little secret! You understand? I can't help if you tell anyone! Then I would have to see your mom and tell her about it. Do you understand, little Ulrike?"

"Yes, Mr. Smith, I understand!"

Bruce gets up off the desk, opens his light summer trousers, and slowly lets them slide down his legs. – He is wearing no underwear. Stepping out of his pants, he comes back around the desk and squats down in front of me while resting his ass against the desk for support. His erect penis points at me like a finger. Startled, I shrink back into the rolling chair. Wide-eyed, I alternate my glances between his cock and eyes. His penis is circumcised.

"Please!" he says in the sweetest voice, "you don't have to be afraid! Go ahead and look. And touch it! — It won't hurt you. And neither will I, Ulrike, my cute little Ulrike!"

Moving myself and the chair closer, I run a fingertip over his penis' head.

"Your penis looks much different than Rudi's, Mr. Smith!" I say timidly.

"Is that so? In what way? Is it smaller? Tell me, Ulrike."

"Rudi's is a different color. His is black."

"Aha! Rudi has a black penis? Is Rudi a black man? Does he have dark skin?"

"Yes, kind of, but it's not black, more like dark brown."

"Okay, that is normal, Ulrike!"

"But I like yours better!" I say and give him a naïve smile.

Delighted, Bruce looks at me as I continue caressing the tip of his cock. – I gently stroke his swollen rod up and down while repeatedly watching him to see how aroused he is by my caresses.

"Can I grab it tightly?" I ask, feeling brave.

"Of course, Ulrike! You can touch it however you like! Experiment all you want."

I wrap my palm and fingers around his cock and squeeze my hand together. Bruce moans aloud.

Startled, I let go of his boner and timidly ask:

"Did I hurt you, Mr. Smith?"

"No, not at all, my little Ulrike! – Actually, it felt good. Do it again. Come on, my little pretty Ulrike! Do with it as you please! My God, Ulrike, and you're only 10 years old!"

"I'm getting all tingly again," I lie.

"We'll get to that at another time, Ulrike. Today is all about getting to know a penis. Wait, let me show you something! Hold on. You can also kiss it, you know!"

Bruce pulls the rubber from his pants pocket and tears open the wrapping.

"Okay. — Now I'm going to show you something, Ulrike. Pay close attention! That way you can do it next time, okay? I mean, you do want to learn, right, little Ulrike?"

"Yes, of course! You are my teacher, Mr. Smith. I always want to learn from you!"

"That's good, my little Ulrike. Now watch what I do! See this, it's a condom. It's like an elastic rubber bag that gets rolled on to a penis. See how I do it! Oh, my penis is also tingly, just like your little slit tingles. In a few minutes, my penis will be so tingly it will squirt fluid out of this small hole here on top. It'll burst from happiness, so to speak, Ulrike! And since we don't want the fluid, which is called semen, to make a mess on the floor, we roll this rubber over my penis. It will catch the fluid, the semen, which is also called sperm. — Did you understand all that, Ulrike?"

"Yes, Mr. Smith, I believe so. It sounds interesting, kind of exciting! Thank you for teaching me all this!"

After Bruce puts the condom on properly, he prompts me to lick the tip of his penis. The rubber is strawberry flavored. Although I know he wants me to take his entire cock in my mouth and suck on it, I am being coy and hesitant. And, since I am supposed to be a young inexperienced schoolgirl, I take my time.

"Hm, tastes good. Can I put it deeper into my mouth? Like a lollypop?" I ask shyly.

"Yes, of course, Ulrike! Go ahead and do that! Now, Ulrike! Stick it all the way in your mouth! As far as it'll go. And then, Ulrike, move your mouth all the way up and down my penis so you can experience the full flavor. You will feel it get all twitchy and then it will spit in the condom! Once we're done, I will show you what you've accomplished, my little one! So, move your mouth, stick it all the way in and then out again, and keep doing that, Ulrike! That's what you do to a tingling penis."

Having received proper instructions, I take his cock deep into my mouth and suck on it like a pro. And, just like he said, I feel the veins on his shaft sticking out and twitching. He seems close to climaxing. As I continue blowing him, he suddenly groans aloud and I feel him shooting off his load. Like an innocent young girl, I look up to see his reaction.

"Ulrike, that's enough now. Okay, my sweet little Ulrike! You've done great! See, I knew you were a good student. And so skilled! – Oh, Ulrike! I'm so proud of you! My little Ulrike! Tell me again how old you are!" he pants, struggling for air.

"I'm 10, Mr. Smith."

Like a good little girl, I close my legs and lean back in his desk chair with my hands primly folded in my lap. As Bruce pulls the rubber off his softening penis, he stops playing the role of Mr. Smith the teacher and is once again himself, a man who just ejaculated.

"Damn, Anika! That was fantastic!" he gasps.

He knots the top of the condom and holds it up.

"I don't think I have to explain this, do I?" he grins at me.

"That's correct, you don't. I believe I'm past that lesson," I reply. Bruce stands and pulls on his pants. Violet would like him — he does not even use a wipe after releasing his wad.

"May I use your facilities?" I ask.

"Yes, of course, Anika! You know the way."

I get up and leave the den. Forgoing a shower, I merely wash my hands and feet and gargle with my antiseptic mouthwash, which I always do after giving a blowjob, regardless if it was with or without a condom. Fully dressed, I leave the bathroom. Bruce shouts he is in the living room. As I enter, he hands me a glass of water.

"Thank you, Bruce. That's considerate of you!" I say as I accept the glass. Bruce raises his glass of water and toasts. I take a big gulp.

"Anika, you were simply marvelous! Thank you! – I'll definitely call you again. I've tried this several times with other prostitutes, but none of them really satisfied me. But you, you're a class act, Anika! Your imagination, appearance, movements – by the way, nice touch with the pigtails – just everything, simply amazing! I'm impressed!"

Although flattered, I keep my reply reserved:

"Thank you, Bruce. That makes me happy... May I ask you something?"

"Yes, of course, Anika!"

"Are there any other role-playing games you're interested in besides the schoolgirl and teacher scenario?"

Bruce laughs haltingly, obviously embarrassed.

"To be honest, that's the only fantasy I have. Why, is it a problem for you?"

"No, I merely thought you might be interested in playing an offender and I'm the police officer. Or, I could be your boss and you're my employee, or I could be a maid at the hotel where you're staying. There are many variations when it comes to role-playing games."

"No, those don't interest me. I simply get off on the idea of being a teacher who has an affair with one of his students."

"Are you a teacher?"

"No! I'm a real estate agent. – In my spare time, I'm a passionate musician. I play the violin. — And I'm a Brit, but I'm sure you picked up on that, right?"

"Yes, I did."

"I've had this dream of a teacher-schoolgirl scenario for quite some time. Maybe it comes from attending an English school and all the beautiful, unattainable girls in their sexy uniforms walked by without even noticing me. At the time, I was convinced they would notice me if I were a teacher. Who knows? – However, your performance was excellent, Anika! You have my utmost thanks!"

Now is my chance to mention that I specialize in role-playing and that my normal rate is 200 for that service. — But I will not because he might think I am making it up, trying to get more out of him due to his compliments and praise. Because I am a coward, I consider the matter closed and instead ask:

"So, how long have you lived in Athens?"

"Let's see... going on 12 years now. A lot has changed during that time. Back then, no one dreamt about an economic crisis. The Greeks literally threw handfuls of money out the window. Of all the Europeans, I think the Greeks lived the *sweet life* to the fullest. We had a good life here. It was nice! Everyone was always in a good mood, friendly, and outgoing. I never thought it would change. – Thankfully, the crisis doesn't affect my company. There are always plenty of rich people who'll buy real estate — and if the time should come where I start to hurt, then I'll go on tour as a fiddle player!" Bruce says and laughs. Then he asks:

"So, how about you? How long are you planning to stay in Greece?"

"Providing I establish a client base within two to three months that generates enough income, I'll stay for good. I like living by the sea!"

"Yes, me too. I mean, in England, I also lived by the sea, but it's not comparable. Here we have a better climate year-round."

I hand him my empty glass and he goes into the kitchen. When he comes back, he hands me one green and one brown bill and says:

"Thank you, Anika! I'll definitely call you again! Is it possible to ask for a favor?"

"Okay? What?"

"Next time you come, is there any chance you could bring clothes that would make a good schoolgirl uniform? I'm sure you have a white blouse and perhaps a dark blue or black short skirt, not that I have anything against your jeans skirt! That was fine for today. But it would be great if you could find an ensemble in your wardrobe that resembles a schoolgirl uniform. Perhaps you even have white knee stockings, that would be perfect, Anika! And if you have to buy a pair, I'll certainly reimburse you. — You know, that would really turn me on! Tell me, am I asking too much? Either way, I'll call you again, but it sure would be great if you had suitable clothing. It'll make our next session even better than today!"

"I'll see what I can come up with. I'm sure I'll find something. When you do call, give me enough time so I can get ready and pack."

"Of course, Anika! If I can, I'll call you a day ahead. Deal!"

"Okay. And thank you for the water, Bruce. Until next time! Have a nice evening!"

"Thank you, Anika! See you soon!"

Bruce escorts me to the front door and waves goodbye as I walk through the garden gate and out of sight.

27

Since I do not think I will find a taxi in this residential area of Vou-liagmeni, I decide to walk downhill toward the sea until I encounter a thoroughfare. Glancing at my phone, I see I missed two calls, each one an unknown number. Well, that is how it is. It only takes a few minutes to reach the coastal road with its restaurants, ice cream parlors, bars, and cafés. Since there is still time, I go into one of the bars for a drink and to change in the bathroom. My new dress is more appropriate for an evening visit at the Metropolitan Hotel than my denim mini skirt and striped top with spaghetti straps. In the bathroom, I am happy to find the toilets are clean. This is something that cannot be said of all Greek establishments. Using the bathroom's lounge area, I quickly change into my other clothes. My newly purchased summer dress looks stunning on me. Satisfied with my reflection, I return to the table and pass the time perusing online newspapers. A few minutes after 8:00 p.m., I call the Metropolitan Hotel. A woman rapidly answers in Greek and then English.

"Good evening. Please connect me with room 351. I'd like to speak with Mr. Bauer."

"One moment please!" she replies curtly as she connects me. I recognize Arnold's voice when he picks up after a couple of rings:

"Hello?"

"Hi, Arnold, it's Anika. I'm calling to let you know I'm on my way and will be there at 9:00 p.m. Okay?"

"Great, Anika. See you soon. I'm excited."

"See you, Arnold!"

After paying for my coke, I roll the plastic bag containing my denim skirt and top as small as possible and cram it in my handbag. The handbag's capacity is definitely exceeded. I should keep an eye out for a larger one. It does not need to be an expensive designer bag, but it should be stylish. Arriving on Athinas Street, I see plenty of taxis. I do not wait long by the curb before one stops and I hop into the back of the car.

"The Metropolitan Hotel, please!"

Hearing the taxi driver's grunt, I assume he understood me. He does not have the AC on because he is a smoker. Both front side windows are down. It is hot and stuffy in this taxi. And it stinks!

"Could you please close the windows and turn on the air-con-ditioning?" I ask politely. – He shoots me a grim look through the rear-view mirror and holds up his cigarette.

"I don't mind the smoke," I say graciously, "but please roll up the windows or keep them cracked and turn on the air-conditioning! It's awfully hot in here."

"I'm not turning on the air-conditioning!" he replies curtly and turns his attention back on the road. As there is no compromising with the man, I resign myself to my fate. If I could be certain of catching another taxi immediately, I would get out.

Between wallowing indecisively and my eagerness to arrive too early than too late, I stay put. Therefore, I allow myself to be driven along Athens' coast in a drafty, yet stinky taxi. Then again, I can imagine putting up with worse.

Approaching from the coast, the first hotel we encounter on Syngrou Avenue is the Metropolitan. The driver stops in front of the hotel entrance. The meter reveals my fare is 16.70 euros. Considering the driver's manners, I dispense with a tip and hand over the exact change!

It is 8:40 p.m. when I enter the Metropolitan Hotel. I take great delight in escaping the heat and into an air-conditioned building. As I inconspicuously glance around the lobby, I think about how to pass the remaining 20 minutes. I decide to visit the restroom to inspect my hair, given the drafty taxi ride. Crossing the grand lobby as if I belong, I make my way through a few seating areas with small side tables and follow a sign showing the direction of the restrooms. In front of the mirror, I see the breezy cab ride did not do much harm. After a few brush strokes, some hair spray, and quick lip touch up, I look presentable again. All that is needed now is a few drops of perfume and I am ready for my next performance. Once in Arnold's room, I will use the bathroom to change into my rhinestone-studded bra and panty set. It simply looks breathtaking with my tanned skin as the backdrop.

In the lobby, I sit on a couch and retrieve my phone. It is a great device for passing time. Shortly before 9:00 p.m., I ride the elevator to the third floor and walk down the corridor until I reach room 351. Since the corridor is deserted, I promptly knock on the door. I feel a little nervous, but before I can calm myself, the door opens and Arnold beckons me inside. Thankfully, the room lighting is muted and my beating heart immediately settles down. – Arnold closes the door and faces me, smiling:

"I love how Germans are always punctual! – Hi, Anika. Nice to meet you. How are you?"

"I'm fine, thank you. — No one saw me knocking on your door! The hall was deserted."

"Great. I appreciate that you remembered!"

Arnold, wearing round wire-rimmed glasses, a dark blue polo shirt, and blue jeans, is about 1.80 meters tall with thick blond hair.

"You look good," he says.

"Thank you, Arnold. So do you! May I use the bathroom to change? I'll be right back!"

"Yes, of course. Help yourself to whatever you need!"

"Thank you!" I reply and disappear into the bathroom. A large bathroom is always appreciated in my line of work. I like that it has a big mirror and a stool on which I can place my handbag. Now in my acid-green lingerie set, I feel extremely sexy. After switching my phone to silent mode, I grab my toiletry bag and return to the room. Arnold is still standing in the middle of the room, fully dressed.

"Hey, darling, how come you're still dressed?"

Walking up to him, I wrap my arms around his neck and then run them down his body. I immediately realize how tense he is.

"How about you get undressed and lie on the bed so I can start you off with a nice relaxing massage," I suggest.

"Yes, that sounds nice. Let's do that," he manages to say, sounding somewhat relieved.

"By the way, that green lingerie looks delicious on you. I like it."

"Thank you, darling," I say happily and release him. Arnold undresses as he walks over to the bed. In his navy blue underwear, he pulls the comforter back and lies down on his stomach. Kneeling beside him, I grab my massage oil and a normal and large condom from my cosmetic bag.

"Is this your first visit to Athens?" I ask, attempting to get a little small talk going.

"Yes, I'm here on business. When I was vacationing in Greece, I spent one day in the Plaka, but that was years ago."

Great, he can speak after all. After I warm a few drops of oil between my palms, I rub his back with even, circular hand movements and ask:

"So, how long will you be here?"

"I'm leaving tomorrow. You know, I've never hired a prostitute on any of my previous business trips. And I thought before I call a Greek, Romanian, or Russian girl, who might speak only passable English, it would be nicer to chat in German."

"Yes, – I also enjoy it when I get an opportunity to talk with my customers in German. – Since it's your last evening, are you and your colleagues going out later on?"

"Yes, at 11:00 p.m. we're meeting downstairs at the bar for a drink. Then we'll go out for a bite to eat and then to a club. A local we met through work and with whom we've become friends is taking us to one of the clubs on Syngrou Avenue. I'm sure we won't get back to the hotel before early morning. By the way, your massage feels great! It's very relaxing. Did you take a course?"

"No, not really. I taught myself. — I'm glad you're enjoying it. — May I?" I ask and before he replies, I tug his underwear below his ass cheeks. He does not resist. Again, I warm a few drops between my palms and gently massage his buttocks. However, for what I have in mind, his underpants will be in the way.

"Arnold, darling, do you mind if I completely remove your underwear?" This time I wait for a reply.

"Yes, of course, Anika. Do with me as you wish!"

Oh, I like his offer! I pull off his underwear and place it on the other bed. Now my oily hands can reach between his legs and continue massaging him. He jumps and says:

"Oh!"

"I hope you like that, baby!"

"Oh, yes! Keep going. I'm placing myself in your capable hands, Anika!"

"That's what I like to hear!" I reply happily.

Encouraged, I grasp his balls and massage them lightly. I slide my hand even further between his legs until I reach his penis. Wrapping my slippery hand around it, I knead it until he is rock hard. Arnold obviously enjoys it, for I hear:

"Oh! — Oh!"

I devised this technique for my more timid clients. This massage gives them a chance to relax. They slowly become properly aroused without having to do anything, minus the embarrassment because they do not look at me.

Arnold is getting to the point where he is nice and loose. I will be able to flip him over on his back soon. I kneel between his spread legs, take off my bra, and lower myself so my bare breasts brush over his oiled backside. Arnold utters:

"Oh my!"

Shortly thereafter, I tell him I want to continue the massage on his front and he immediately flips over. As he lies there with his hands crossed behind his head, smiling unconsciously, I know I can resume my performance. Kneeling on his right side, I let his cock slide through my left hand while my right gently kneads his balls. After a while, I change positions and squat over his thighs. Using one hand, I rhythmically rub his cock. Arnold remains passive, apart from uttering the occasional *oh*! With my other hand, I gently and erotically caress my breasts and seductively move my hips, hinting at a fuck. As it is obvious Arnold will not make a move, I take matters into my own hands to prepare for the finale. Since a rubber tears easily when encountering oil, I slide off him, bend over his cock, and take it entirely in my mouth, licking off as much oil as I can. Once again, Arnold rewards me:

"Oh — Oh my!"

Believing I have cleaned enough oil from his proud member, I rip open a normal size condom wrapper and roll it on. Now it is time for the conclusion of my performance. – I squat over him, push my thong aside, shove his cock all the way into my pussy, and ride him. Arnold loses his inhibition. He uncrosses his hands and brazenly grabs my breasts. While fondling my nipples, he repeatedly says:

"Oh, oh, yes — oh, yes!"

Now, his hips are matching my rhythm. Abruptly, he rears up and thrusts deep into me while uttering a prolonged *oh...yeah* during his climax. There you go! Everything worked out nicely. Now that the deed is done, Arnold becomes talkative. He tells me about his longtime girlfriend who broke it off. That he is still in pain about her leaving and that he is not ready to get involved with another woman. And having sex with me was important because he wanted to know how it felt to be with another woman after being in a loyal long-term relationship. I ask him how it felt. He answers — good, though it could have been reduced it to the fun of sex, but he did not know what to make of it, if that was good or bad. I reply that the only thing that matters is whether he regrets it. He responds:

"No, I don't regret it. I believe I'll do it again!"

We both laugh and he offers me a drink. I politely decline and ask if it is okay to use the bathroom.

"Of course!" he answers.

By the time I am fully dressed and back in the room, Arnold has turned on more lamps. Luckily, the subtle light is flattering, making me and the Metropolitan Hotel simpatico. Arnold walks over to his desk and grabs a few bills from his wallet. When he comes back, he hands me 170 euros.

"Here you go, Anika, thank you!" He smiles.

"Thank you, darling!" I reply, pleasantly surprised.

"And I hope you and your colleagues have a nice evening! Goodbye, Arnold!"

"Thank you, same to you. Bye, Anika!"

We exchange pecks on the cheeks. Arnold opens the door, peeks into the corridor to see if the coast is clear, and then beckons me to leave. As I walk with brisk steps to the elevator, I hear his door close. While waiting for the elevator to arrive, I think about my good fortune. Yippee, – I am 150 euros richer and I received a 20-euro tip. I simply love my job!

Riding down in the elevator, I check my phone. I missed one call, a Greek cell phone number. It happens! He will call back if he really wants to see me.

It is now dark outside. In front of me on Syngrou Avenue, cars and mopeds race by in both directions. Considering the early evening hour, I mull over my options for the rest of it... Although I have already made good money, it is definitely too early to knock off work.

As I stand there debating with myself, a taxi pulls up and the driver asks me something in Greek. I assume he is inquiring if I need a ride. So I merely say:

"No, thank you!"

He rolls up the front passenger window and drives off. I am thinking about grabbing a bite to eat, but of course, it should be a light meal. Yeah, that is what I will do! — It is best if I first go to the city center. If someone calls, I am in a central location, where I can easily reach every corner of Athens. Not far from the Metropolitan Hotel, I see a bus stop. Two minutes later, I am on an E22 bus that will take me directly to Syntagma Square.

28

I like Athens best at night. At that time, the scorching daytime temperature has turned comfortably warm. In the darkness, the dusty and, at times, muddy roads appear clean in the glow of lamps and headlights. Not seeing the city's trash and filth creates a more inviting atmosphere than during the day.

I walk across the illuminated Syntagma Square and stop next to the fountain. – The splashing of water drowns out the street noise. I feel completely at ease. I might be alone, but I am my own boss. I work in a trade I am familiar with and it comes easily to me. And, for being in Athens for only one week, I have already made good money, earning almost 1800 euros. I am extremely happy with my new life here! Whatever lucky stars might be watching over me, I would like to thank them all for smoothing the way!

As I prefer the pleasant sound of rushing water to the constant shrill noise of evening rush hour, I happily sit down on a bench and watch strolling locals and tourists. My phone rings. I answer:

"Good evening!"

"Hello, good evening. I'm Nikos. Do you speak Greek?"

"No, I'm sorry, but we can talk in English or German. I'm Anika, by the way."

"Hi, Anika. So, are you really a German?"

"Yes."

"Well — I want to make sure because many Serb, Bulgarian, and Russian woman state in their ads they are German just to get calls. — Anyway! This is great! — So, can you tell me a bit about yourself? Among other things, I'd like to know your rate."

"I'd love to, Nikos. I'm 35 with blonde hair, blue eyes, and a slim figure. I only do hotel and home visits. My hourly rate is 150 euros."

"That sounds good, Anika. I'm also 35, well groomed, and keep myself in shape. – Regrettably, I don't have much hair on my head." He laughs. "But when you say slim, you don't mean real skinny, do you?"

"No, I have curves. My cup size is 34 B."

"Okay. Just checking, I don't enjoy a stick in bed! — What are your hours, Anika? And, do you allow anal?"

"I always have my phone on. If I'm busy, you'll have to leave a message and if you want an appointment after midnight, I need enough prior notice. And yes, I provide anal sex, but I can't commit to it over the phone. I first have to see the size of your penis. Also, anal is an additional 50 euros."

"Oh, Anika, 50 more! — That's too much! I can't pay that. I'd really love to see you, and I'll even pay for the room, but — baby, I'm sorry,

I'm not willing to pay an extra 50 for anal intercourse. Come on, what do you say we leave it at 150 and give anal a try?"

What now? I want the work. However, I do not want to come down with my price either. My brain is in overdrive and I decide to agree to his terms. After all, he is Greek, probably lives in Athens, and is most likely familiar with others rates in *Athens World*. I am going to lose him if I insist on the extra 50. I am going to give him a break, hoping he will find me attractive and will be satisfied with my service, thus becoming a repeat customer! I need clients who want to hire me more than just once. As all this rushes through my mind, I realize he is waiting for an answer.

"Okay, Nikos. — I'm agreeing to 150."

"Finally! It's a deal, Anika. Unfortunately, this evening is no longer possible. How about tomorrow? – Do you know the Wicky Inn Hotel near the main train station?"

"No, I don't know that one."

"It's easy to find. It is near Victoria Subway Station. If you like, I can text you the address of the hotel. And please store my phone number!"

"Okay, Nikos, text me the address and I'll save your number. What time would you like to meet tomorrow?"

"Around 9:00 p.m. would be great. Maybe a little later... Are you free at that time?"

"Yes, the time is yours if you want. But call me as soon as you can to confirm the appointment and to let me know the exact time."

"Sure, Anika! You'll hear from me by tomorrow afternoon. Okay, until then, bye, baby!"

"Thanks for calling, Nikos. Talk to you tomorrow."

I made the right decision by agreeing to his terms. Although, I have to make sure I do not make it a habit. I must get better at reading people over the phone and then it will be easier for me to judge how much I can push my price. In Germany, I never had to worry about such decisions. I guess that is part of being self-employed. I look up Victoria Subway Station's address on my phone and see that it is not far from here. While stowing my phone, my grumbling stomach lets me know sustenance is required.

Without hesitation, I catch the next train traveling from Syntagma Square to Thiseio station. It is across from the ancient Archaia Agora in which the Temple of Hephaestus is located. There are numerous restaurants and cafés with beautiful views of the Acropolis, which is even more beautiful at night when illuminated. Incidentally, I am in the zone where I am allegedly working at a tourist bar through August. That reminds me, I still require a plausible story for my friends in Germany. But since I consider this matter unpleasant, I continue procrastinating. Too late, my bad conscience kicks in and reminds me I have only spoken to my father once and that I need to call him again. However, now is not the time!

I start walking among the tourists and immediately feel as if I am on vacation. What a great feeling it is! Noticing a restaurant with a free table and an incredible view, I walk over and sit down. Since it is late, I allow myself a glass of white wine with my chicken souvlaki and a side order of Kolokito Keftedes. – These are zucchini meatballs with feta cheese. Overhearing bits and pieces of the conversations from neighboring tables, I conclude I am surrounded by Germans, Dutch, and Americans.

Since the entire atmosphere is so beautiful, I take a few pictures of the passing throngs of people who are heading to the Acropolis. Depending on how the pictures turn out, I might email them to my friends. As three Americans next to me rise from their seats and are about to leave, I quickly get up and ask if they can take a picture of me. I always have a dumb look on my face when I take a selfie. One of the Americans thinks I should not be alone in the photo and stands next to me. He puts one arm around my shoulder and leans his head against mine.

"Let's say I'm your new boyfriend!" he says playfully in his American accent and I join in for the fun. Not being alone in a picture for a change is obviously nicer and livelier. Perhaps I can integrate him in my made-up story and use this picture to send to my friends.

"By the way, I'm Roger!" My photo partner introduces himself.

"Nice to meet you, I'm Anika!" I shake his hand.

"Hi, I'm Mike," the other American man says, the one who took the picture.

"And I'm Susan!" the third American, a young woman joins in.

"Are you on vacation too?" Roger asks and I say:

"Yes."

"So, where's your husband or boyfriend?"

Roger looks around carefully as if he is searching for someone.

"I'm here alone. Well, with a girlfriend. But tonight she's on a date with a Greek!"

"Hey, that doesn't mean you have to be alone. Why don't you join us?" Roger puts me on the spot.

"Yeah, come on. We're going to have fun. And it's good when there's another woman around, – that way Roger won't get on my nerves," Susan pipes in and starts laughing.

"What do you say, Anika. You want to be my date this evening! We'll have fun and turn Athens upside down!" Roger is persistent.

I like the young Americans outgoing nature. They seem to be in their mid-thirties, — like I am, I think. Although I am tempted to say *yes*, the spoilsport in me says *no*! Stick to the plan. Perhaps I will receive another call.

"I'm sorry, but I still haven't eaten!" I say evasively.

"No problem. We'll wait until you're done!" Roger is determined.

I shake my head, thank them for taking the picture, and their generous offer to keep me company. Then, I add:

"Besides, I have to get up early to catch the ferry to an island just off Athens."

Roger makes one final attempt to persuade me:

"Oh, Anika, who needs more than three hours of sleep when on vacation? Come on, join us!"

I dismiss him with a wave of my hand. Roger looks disappointed. Resigning himself to his fate, he kisses me goodbye as if we have known each other for years. He takes me into his strong muscular arms and hugs me so hard so that all air escapes me. Susan and Mike are holding hands and waving goodbye as they melt into the throng of passing tourists. Roger quickly follows and I sit back down at my table a little sad.

29

The next morning, I wake up to another glorious, sunny, hot day. I really enjoy not worrying about the weather. Every day seems like summer. It is rare for it to start raining unexpectedly or suddenly get cold. Back in Germany, I started each day watching the weather forecast to get an idea on how to dress. Here in Athens, I eat breakfast on the small table outside on my balcony while enjoying the morning heat, the gentle breeze coming from the sea, my breathtaking views of the Zea Marina with its many sailing boats, the view of the Saronic Gulf, and even further off in the distance, the dark silhouette of the island of Aegina.

From the Port of Piraeus, ferries run daily between the southern outlying islands of Athens. At the latest, after one month of non-stop work, I will allow myself a day off and take a day trip to Aegina.

Once breakfast is finished, I sit down at my makeshift desk, boot up my laptop, and open the file I use to keep track of work. I enter the weekday and date that I saw a customer, together with his name, telephone number, character, preferences, the amount paid, and, depending on whether I met him in a hotel or at home, I also note the hotel name or home address. This gives me a clear overview of my clientele and earnings. I walk to the closet that also contains a safe, remove the envelope with all the cash I have earned so far here in Athens, and add yesterday's earnings. I double check the total by recounting all the cash, check off the old amount, and write down the new sum on the envelope. Then I place the money back inside and lock it away in the safe. I love this ritual!

Since I only have one confirmed appointment today at 6:00 p.m. in Glyfada, I want to go to the tanning studio in a bit. If I do not receive more calls, I will spend the afternoon relaxing in my hotel room. As I enjoy one final cup of coffee on the balcony while looking at last night's photos and perusing my favorite online newspaper, my phone rings. It is an unknown number.

"Hello!"

"Anika?"

"Yes, who's this?"

"It's Richard. Can you come see me?"

Richard masked his number when he called. Great, he is ruining my plan for a quiet day in my hotel room. Unfortunately, I cannot afford to turn him down, even if he only pays 70. I reply:

"Of course, baby, I can do that. So, how are you?"

"I'm well, Anika, thanks for asking. When can you come?"

Since it is 11:30 a.m., I believe I can still treat myself to a visit to the tanning studio before seeing him. – Taking my subway commute to Syntagma Square into consideration, I answer:

"Richard, darling, I can be at your place at 1:30 p.m. Does that work for you?"

"1:30 p.m.? – Yes, that's fine. Meet me at the Rio Café. It's on Nikis Street, right around the corner from my home, okay?"

"Okay, Richard, I'll see you there. Until then, bye!"

"Bye, Anika, my sexy!"

I have to smile. I find it cute being called *my sexy* by this uncouth, clumsy, former Canadian boxing champion in his soft voice. Now I have to focus on getting ready. Do I want to return to my hotel room after my appointment with Richard or do I want to loiter in the city center and go directly from there to Glyfada to see Vangelis, the former captain? I decide on the latter. After my session with Vangelis at the Congo Palace, I will probably go back to Athens' city center so I will not have far to travel to see Nikos at the Wicky Inn hotel at 9:00 p.m. or so. Okay, I need to figure out what to wear. Without considering the weather, I think about my clients and the hotels I am going to visit. For Richard, it does not matter what I wear. Regrettably, I cannot dress slutty and enter the Congo Palace Hotel. And Nikos likes me dressed sexily. Therefore, I opt for my new red and white striped dress that I wore yesterday evening to the Metropolitan Hotel. It is sexy, but not to the point where I would attract attention. In the event I receive an earlier appointment unexpectedly, I have already readied myself first thing this morning. Meaning, I have shaved, showered, washed and styled my hair, moisturized my body from head to toe, and completed my makeup. Scrutinizing my nails, I can tell Maria did a great job. I might not have to see her until Saturday and then, probably only for a manicure. In the interim, I put on a red lingerie set. For my visit with Nikos, I pack another red set with two matching panties, one is crotchless. For my appointment with Vangelis, I am going with my white lace bustier set and matching white strapless stockings.

Selecting and packing all my work clothes took longer than expected. A glance at the clock and I immediately feel pressed for time. Telling myself Richard will wait if I am a few minutes late helps calm me down! If I run too late, he certainly will call. I will simply tell him I am on the way and everything will be fine. – So, Ilona, do not panic! Thankfully, the tanning studio has one bed available. Next time, I must call for an appointment that way I will not feel uncertain and I will get the tanning bed I prefer. Lying under the hot lights completely relaxes me. The intensive vitamin D bath gradually replaces the hurried feeling with an overall sense of well-being. I have worked up a sweat during my 12 minutes of tanning, so I use the provided towel to dry off, followed by deodorant wipes. Once I make Richard happy, I am going to take a shower at his place.

Emerging from the subway at Syntagma Square, I see I drove myself nuts for no reason. It is only 1:10 p.m. I am actually too early. When I find the café where I am supposed to meet Richard, he is already waiting at the counter with a Greek coffee and talking to the waitress. I guess I will join him!

"Hi, Anika, my love!" He greets me and gives me a peck on my cheek. "You look fabulous!"

The waitress does not hide her curious look. I immediately feel uncomfortable again, wishing we had not met here. Who knows what Richard told her about me? I need to calm down. It is not like he would tell her I am a prostitute he is about to bang in his apartment.

"Richard, darling." I greet him and remove my sun hat. As I sit on the bar stool next to him he asks me what I want to drink, but I tell him I would like to order myself. At some point, I must start speaking Greek, so why not now. The waitress has no problem understanding my order: a light Nescafé with plenty of milk. Richard is impressed, even the waitress praises my Greek. Although I know they are exaggerating, it is also encouraging. Richard continues chatting in Greek with the waitress. The few words I pick up as well as his gestures, I surmise he is raving about me. She also seems to think I am pretty. Oh well, the usual small talk. Ignoring their conversation, I drink my coffee. I hope Richard finishes soon so we can go to his place.

When I see he has drunk two-thirds of his coffee, I know it is time to leave. Greeks never empty their glasses completely like Germans do. I quickly down the last sip of my Nescafé and hop off the stool.

"Shall we?" I smile at Richard. He pays and we leave for his home.

"Anika, why don't we grab a bite to eat? I'm hungry."

"Richard, you know I'm not here to have lunch with you. Let's go to your place!"

"Yes, I know, Anika. But we could still go out to eat afterward. My treat, okay? I know a nice restaurant I'd like to show you."

"We'll see, Richard. Right now, I'm not committing myself. Let's go. I'm hot for you and I really need you to give it to me. Okay, baby?"

"Okay, Anika. I'm also hot for you!"

Once in his penthouse, the first thing I do is go out on the large roof terrace and look around. Richard follows and stands behind me as I lean against the railing to look down over Syntagma Square. Moving my hips, my butt chafes against his pants. As soon as I feel the swelling of his cock, I turn around and say:

"I think we better go inside. – Out here, people staying at Grand Bretagne Hotel can see us."

The thought obviously amuses Richard for he laughingly replies:

"So what? It beats looking at the parliament building!"

Naturally, he follows me inside. Taking off all my clothing apart from my shoes, I stand in front of him completely naked. It will not be a great feat getting him to climax. This is my third time with him and I feel completely at ease for I know exactly how to work him. Richard stands in front of me, seemingly indecisive. I give him time to get a good look at me. Since he is still not moving, I step toward him and rub my body against his clothes.

"Take off your clothes!" I quietly urge him. He unbuttons his short-sleeved shirt but does not take it off. Next, he undoes his pants and awkwardly removes them over his shoes while trying to maintain his balance. Now the former champ stands before me in only his under-wear, shoes, and unbuttoned shirt, and he is still clueless what to do next. I decide it is time to put him out of his misery. I pull his undies down and indicate he needs to take them off completely. Once again, he keeps his shoes on. I open the wrapper of a condom and roll it onto his erection. – I kneel, take it into my mouth, and Richard groans aloud. Wanting him to sit, I guide him to the desk chair and gently push him into it. Still kneeling in front of him, I continue sucking the champ's champion. He is enjoying it immensely, so I think why not just blow him. Let me see if he will come as quickly and without a fuss as when I fuck him. Sucking him vigorously, Richard groans again with his head thrown back and his big paws almost tenderly cradling the back of my head. It is amazing how gentle this brute of a man is! I feel his cock pulsating and a second later, he comes in the condom. This worked out great and it took less than five minutes. Just the way I like it! Releasing his cock and bracing myself with my lower arms on his thighs, I look at him and say:

"Darling, are you still hungry?"

"Yes, Anika. Will you join me? The restaurant is not far from here. It's Greek cuisine."

"Okay, but just this once, you hear? However, if I get a call from another customer, I'll leave immediately. You understand that, right?"

"Of course, Anika! Today, you are making an exception and if some-one calls, you have to go, no problem."

"Great! Okay then, let me clean up. Can I grab one of your fresh tow-els? I'd like to take a quick shower."

"Sure. You know where the towels are?"

"Yes, thanks!"

I wash thoroughly and dress. When I return, I pick up my handbag and Richard pulls his wallet from his back pocket and hands me 70 euros. I thank him with a peck on a cheek and pocket the money.

We leave his place and walk a couple hundred meters around the block to the restaurant. As we enter, the bartender chummily greets Richard. They speak Greek so fast that I do not get the gist of the con-

169

versation. Then Richard turns toward me, places an arm protectively a-round my shoulder, and continues in English:

"...and this is Anika, my German friend!"

"Pleasure to meet you!" the bartender says. He slightly inclines his head and smiles at me in an almost creepy way.

"Richard has been talking about you a lot. It's nice to finally meet you."

I do not believe it. He has been talking about me to this bartender. Is he for real? Richard does not notice my mood change and beams at me. Next, he lets go of my now stiff shoulder and gestures to a table by the window.

"This is where I always have lunch. Have a seat, Anika!"

Is Richard of sound mind? Perhaps all the blows to his head caused some damage after all. Now I know why he was so insistent I come to dinner with him, — he wanted to show off his trophy. If I continue meeting him in public places, it will not take long before the people living around Syntagma Square will know all about me. I cannot let that happen! I have to sit down with him and set him straight. And, I have to know what he has been saying about me. Breathing deeply and evenly, I calm myself. I wait for the bartender to take our orders and bring our drinks. After we clink glasses and toast, I lean over the table and quietly ask:

"Richard! What have you been telling people about me?"

"Only that you're my German friend and that we go out together."

"I hope you didn't tell them about our actual arrangement?"

"No! But if they think we're sleeping together that's fine with me!"

Amused, Richard laughs.

"It's what men and women do."

He is so naive! – I cannot believe he is bragging about me being his girlfriend and letting people think we are in a relationship.

"Richard, darling! People will start talking about me. That is some-thing I really don't want! – You can't tell everyone about our arrange-ment. You have to be discreet!"

"Anika! There is no reason to worry! Everyone knows me here. I've been living here since I gave up my boxing career and my mother is married to a Greek. We're a big family that owns lots of property in the city center. Everyone knows me. People have to talk about something. You're so pretty no one will say anything bad about you. So, please, don't worry!"

"No, Richard, it is you who doesn't understand! You know I'm a prostitute. What I do is illegal in Greece, at least the way I go about it. I'm breaking the law. So, having said this, I only want my clients to know and nobody else, otherwise, I could get in serious trouble!"

"Don't worry, Anika, I don't tell anyone you're a prostitute. All I say is you're my girlfriend from Germany. Everyone envies me. Please let me enjoy it."

I see I am not making any headway with him. Richard has no idea how people run their mouths. They are going to see through his story and figure out I am not his German girlfriend who sees him out of sheer sympathy. They will think he has a crush on his prostitute. If he is so well known around Syntagma Square, I am sure the people he confided in will eventually notice when his German girlfriend disappears for an hour into a hotel every now and then. And, as everyone knows, people like to gossip, even hotel staff and police officers. Considering my line of work, I certainly want to avoid drawing any attention! From now on, I am going to refuse to meet Richard in a public place and this will the first and last time I accompany him to a diner. I will only meet him in the building's foyer or, better yet, go directly to his apartment. It is best if the people he told do not see us together anymore so they forget about me.

The food is served. Richard ordered *stifado*, beef covered with some kind of tomato and onion sauce. – I am dining on grilled vegetables, slices of zucchini and eggplant fresh out of the oven. It is oily and filling, so I only manage to eat half. We are enjoying an excellent white wine with our meal. As other guests enter the restaurant and take a seat a few tables over, I happily note they are tourists and not one of Richard's Greek neighbors. After finishing our meal, Richard lights up a cigar. I find it incredible that some restaurants in Athens still allow smoking. I mean, nowadays it is illegal in Europe and Greece is part of it. Granted, there are no ashtrays on the tables, but as the bartender clears our dishes, he returns with an ashtray. Richard is in a talkative mood and tells me about his time as a boxer in Canada. Furtively, I look at my watch. It is almost 3:00 p.m. As soon as Richard is done smoking, I want to leave and get on my way. Regrettably, the waiter comes and serves us dessert, which he says is on the house. Richard quickly clues me in and tells me it is common for a traditional Greek restaurant to either provide a shot of booze or a small dessert free of charge. Our desserts are bowls of Greek yogurt with a halved pear and a generous dollop of some sweet sauce. I am a bit leery since this local dessert is unfamiliar to me.

I try a little spoonful. Surprisingly, it is quite delicious and I cannot stop raving about it. Richard is obviously pleased that I am praising this typical Greek dessert and offers me his bowl. Unable to resist, I take him up on his offer and finish his bowl.

30

An hour later on the tram heading toward Glyfada, my phone starts buzzing. It is a text from Nikos. He wants to meet tonight at 9:30 p.m. at the Wicky Inn Hotel. I send a reply back confirming our appointment. As I am about to place my phone back in my handbag, I see I have missed three calls. All three are from the same Greek cell phone number. Crap! I forgot to turn the ringer back on after my session with Richard. I am upset at my mistake. I really have to pay more attention and keep it together. Who knows, am I now to blame for letting an appointment slip through my fingers?

Considering this caller tried to reach me three times, I am sure he went to another working girl. Men usually call when they are horny. Meaning, they want sex right then and there. The majority of men are not like Vangelis, who plans for a sexual interlude. I am still waiting for him to call about the meeting later in Glyfada.

Then again, his is a different situation because he lives on an island. Perhaps there are no prostitutes, so he wanted to make sure a woman to his liking would come to see him when he is in town. At least it is the way I explain it to myself after one week of being a self-employed call girl.

Since it will not do any good to continue chastising myself, I relax by telling myself not to panic! Looking at the missed calls again, I see I received them around 2:40 p.m. That was when Richard and I were in the restaurant. So there, Ilona, you were with a client, give it a rest!

As I get much better reception traveling on a tram compared to the subway, I dial Violet's number. She immediately picks up with a cheerful:

"Hello, darling!"

"Hi, Violet! How are you?"

"Oh, I'm okay! Actually, I'm great! I've already had two customers today. First, Christos. No, not the Christos who only pays 60! This is a different guy, but he's also fast and likes it when I moan the entire time and call out his name," she says laughing like a teenager. "And he pays me 150 euros. Then, I received a call from Boris and had to get ready to meet him at the 6 X Hotel in Glyfada. I took a taxi because he didn't have much time and it was short notice. He took me in his arms as soon as I stepped into the room. Already showered, he stood there naked and took my clothes off lickety-split. He threw me on the bed and fucked me. Five minutes later, it was over. He even apologized for being so fast. — Like I mind when he doesn't take long! — He told me he had to get to the airport to catch a flight to Zurich but he was so horny he first had to see me. He had already laid out my fee on the nightstand before he went to take a shower. A 100-euro bill and three 20s.

Obviously, I held them up when he came back out of the bathroom and said: 'Darling, this is 160! This is too much. Don't you have a 50?' — 'No. Keep it. Anything for you, my lovely!' he told me. Then he kissed me goodbye and said: 'I'll call you in three weeks when I'm back in Athens and have more time.' — I always enjoy getting a tip! I mean, it represents a customer's satisfaction, right? — So, how are you doing? How's business?"

I tell Violet about yesterday's performance as Bruce's young school-girl, which makes her laugh.

"I could never do that! Don't you have to laugh when a customer requests such a crazy scenario?"

"No, I don't have a problem playing it cool and staying focused on my role. Naturally, it helps when I'm dressed accordingly. — I mean I couldn't play a schoolgirl if I was wearing a nurse uniform."

Violet is still cracking up. – She is in such an incredibly good mood that she perks me up too. I am glad I called. I ask if she knows any of my customers. But she has never heard of Bruce the realtor and part-time violinist, nor does she know Nikos, the anal sex fanatic.

"Darling, I don't do anal. At least not anymore! That was in the early days when it was included in the regular rate. Greek customers always stated that it's a Greek thing and that I, after all, am in their country! — They made it a principle not to pay one Drachma more for that service! The way they acted was like they invented anal sex. Simply incredible! And almost all Greek men are into it. It was always painful for me and after a few years, I said no more. And considering the way I live, I can easily survive without providing anal sex! I don't care that most women advertising in *Athens World* offer it at no additional charge. I mean, some even state *includes A-level*, which is only because we're in Greece! — Don't be surprised when a Greek complains about having to pay an extra 50 for anal. We're not in Germany or England! We simply have to adapt to our surroundings if we want to stay in business. — I'm sorry, darling, but that's the way it is! — You might want to think about eliminating such service to Greek men. They won't pay a dime more for it anyway. Offer it to foreigners, they're different, they appreciate such service and pay appropriately."

"I never looked at it that way, thanks for telling me. — So, Greeks are into anal, the French, oral. — How come I didn't see it?"

"That's because you have lots of other things to think about. I remember how it was when I started on my own. One is so intent on getting everything right and so ambitious to get as many customers as possible that one or another thing is overlooked. Don't sweat it! At least now you know. — Anyway, I really have to show you my place, darling! My apartment is only two kilometers from the 6 X Hotel. Sometimes I walk there. Only when pressed for time or during winter when it's cold and raining do I take a cab."

"Tell me, Violet, is the 6 X Hotel near the Lenny Blue Hotel?"

"Darling, it's one in the same! The one you were at with Adonis. For years, it was called the 6 X Hotel, so the name stuck. I've never gotten used to its new name. Anyway, I don't live all that far away. Maybe one day you'll come for a visit. By the way, every Thursday there is a big market in Glyfada. I often go there on my bicycle. We could meet there and then go to my place later for a cup of coffee! What do you think? Sometimes, there's a booth selling nice handbags and jewelry. Mainly, I go there for my weekly supply of fruits and vegetables. I guess you wouldn't be interested since you don't cook. Maybe we do it at a later time, once you have your own place. — In any case, the produce is fresh and reasonably priced. I might not cook every single day in summertime, but I at least have a salad almost every day. What do you usually eat, darling? Surely not fast food. You have to eat a good nutritious meal. That's important at our age! Your metabolism changes as you get older. - And smoking or too much alcohol, or whatever delicious sweet treats, all of that is not good for us. Greasy food is especially bad. It clogs arteries and goes directly to the hips! But you watch your diet, right?"

I use the brief pause to answer because if I wait too long she will simply continue talking without receiving an answer. Violet cannot help it; she has lots to say.

"Yes, I have the same problem. - Nowadays, I can't eat whatever I want. I really have to watch my figure, which I do. So, don't worry about me! — And you're wrong about the market, I am interested. What time do you usually go?"

"I usually get there by 10:00 a.m. Then I take my time browsing the entire market. Once I've seen all there is to see I do my fruit and vegetable shopping. I have two small baskets on my bicycle, one on the handlebars and one on the rack above the rear wheel. They usually hold all my groceries. Naturally, I have my phone on the entire time. Every morning at 9:00 a.m., I turn it on. That works for me. I don't really care if I miss a nighttime or early-morning call. You know, I only work during the day and early evening. I don't care for those late night work hours anymore, nor do I care for being woken up in the middle of the night or early morning. Shortly after midnight, when I go to bed, I turn my phone off. In the early days, I never turned it off! I was too afraid to miss even a single call. Kind of like you right now! I tell you, cell phones are a great invention. What would we do without them? Tell me, how would that work? How could we do our job? We'd have a landline for work and sit at home all day, waiting for it to ring. We wouldn't be able to shop or stroll through town without missing calls! Or, when you're at a hotel or someone's home, we'd also be unreachable. Imagine, you couldn't do your job while living in a hotel! — Or do you have some idea how that would work? I mean, I'm not that tech savvy when it comes to new technology, but I'm glad cell phones are around! I have so much more freedom since I bought one."

That's Violet, jumping from one subject to the next. But I leave it alone and simply say:

"Violet, tomorrow is Thursday! I wouldn't mind coming to Glyfada to meet you at 10:00 a.m. at the market. I mean, if you want my company."

"Of course, darling, that's a great idea! Call me once you get there and we'll arrange to meet somewhere. The market is near the town square. You know the one I'm talking about."

I have another call coming in, so I say to Violet:

"Sorry, darling, someone's calling, I have to hang up. — I'll call you back! Bye, Violet!"

"Yes, no problem, Anika! Kisses, and take care! Bye, darling!"

I answer the other call.

"Hello!"

"Hello, Anika. It's Vangelis. I'm sorry to be calling this late! Are we still on for 6:00 p.m.?"

"Yes, of course, Vangelis! I'll be there on time!"

"Great. I'm in room 21. And please remember not to draw any attention. Be discreet, Anika!"

"Yes, of course! Until later, Vangelis!"

"Yes, see you later, Anika. I look forward to seeing you!"

Grabbing my notebook from my handbag, I find the page where I wrote down the address of the Congo Palace Hotel, Vangelis' cell phone number, and the time of the appointment. Now I add the room number. The tram runs along the coast and I know it will not be long before it arrives in Glyfada. As I look out the window at the sea, I think about going to the market tomorrow in Glyfada. I am looking forward to it, as well as seeing Violet. The tram makes a turn onto Metaxa Street and I get off at the next stop. Now I am near the Congo Palace Hotel. There is still a half an hour before my meeting with Vangelis, so I stroll through now familiar back streets of the shopping district.

31

The Congo Palace Hotel is a multi-story building right in Glyfada on the coast. I hope the room Vangelis rented is not on the south side in direct sunlight. I walk through the lobby and one of the front desk staff watches me until I disappear into the elevator. Well, it does happen in small hotels such as this one. I quickly take off my sun hat and brush my hair while looking in the mirror inside the elevator. Perfect! I arrive on the second floor and walk along the corridor to door number 21. Inhaling deeply, I knock. Vangelis opens the door almost instantly. He is tall and slender with thick black-brown hair that is combed back. His dark eyes look friendly. He politely asks me inside. Thankfully, the lighting is in my favor. The windows are tinted and Vangelis has closed most of the drapes.

"Hello, Vangelis! Did you have a nice day?"

"Yes, Anika, thank you! I just arrived on the mainland. You know, I live on Paros, but every now and then, I have to come to the big city. That's when I see my doctor, shop, and visit friends and relatives — just for a change of scenery. So, how are you, Anika?"

"I'm fine, thanks. Okay then, I'll quickly disappear into the bathroom so I can get all sexy for you!"

"Sounds good! — Say, did someone notice you riding the elevator up to the second floor?"

"No, the lobby was empty and the clerk behind the front desk was busy on the phone. Don't worry, no one noticed me!"

"That's good because I've been coming here for years. Once in a while, I bring my wife along. I'm known here, so I don't want people to get the wrong impression, if you know what I mean?"

"Yes, of course, Vangelis. Don't worry!"

As soon as I am in the bathroom, I slip out of my dress and red underwear and put on my white lace bustier set. It is quite sexy with white strapless stockings. – Even I am turned on as I regard myself in the mirror. After applying a touch of perfume, I retrace the outline of my lips and I am done. Upon exiting the bathroom, I find that Vangelis has closed all the drapes and is sitting on the bed bare ass naked. He is a quite hairy dark skinned man. Glancing at his flaccid cock resting between his thighs, I can tell it will grow considerably once it is hard.

"Should I start you off with a little massage?" I ask as I open my small toiletry bag, grab two extra-large condoms, and place them on the nightstand.

"I'd love it, if you're up for it!"

That he has not complimented me on my appearance, especially standing there in front of him in my seductive lingerie, irritates me. Is white not his color? Would he have preferred me in black? Do not tell me he does not like my figure or thinks I am not pretty? — Although he looks me up and down, I do not hear anything like, *hey, you look sexy* or a simple *wow*! I am used to customers making some remark, but he simply stares at me without even saying so much as one word. Disappointed, I answer:

"Certainly. I'd love to give you a nice relaxing massage. — Please lie down on your stomach, darling."

Vangelis turns around and rests his head on his folded arms. Then he says:

"Oh, Anika, please be quiet! I don't want anyone to hear us. I have no idea how well this room is insulated."

"Don't worry, Vangelis, I'll be quiet."

Kneeling beside him, I start giving him a massage. I rub my hands in even circular motion over his hairy back all the way up to his shoulder blades, where I knead a bit harder. Vangelis utters not so much as a peep, no *oh that's good*, no *you're great, Anika*, he does not even grunt in delight. He simply lies quietly! Since I want to end the back massage, I quickly tie my hair together at the nape and move further down his body. I am about to move between his thighs. He does not resist and spreads his legs. With my tongue stretched out, I lick his perineal. Vangelis must not have anticipated it. He flinches. Slowly, I run my tongue over the area and up to his balls, which rest on the sheets, large and half-deflated.

Although this position is quite uncomfortable for me, experience has taught me that men become turned on when licked like this from behind. Thankfully, Vangelis is not the exception. Now, for the first time, he actually moans in delight. I just love it! As a prostitute, I somehow not only became accustomed to being paid in cash but also with praise. — And, Vangelis' moaning confirms I am doing a good job, which is important to me, otherwise I am miserable. Carefully, I move his balls aside and slide my head further down between his legs, licking the backside of his stiff member with my extended tongue. Once again, Vangelis moans aloud. That is it, baby! Tell me I am doing a great job. — Feeling his boner growing even more, I finish my prelude and say:

"Please flip over on your back, darling, I want to suck your cock!"

As Vangelis rolls onto his back, a huge, intimidating schlong confronts me. I immediately regret saying I want his cock in my mouth. Damn, I hope I can handle that monster. I am having a tough time putting on the extra-large condom. I might have a strong gag reflex, but my eyes tear up regardless. It seems Vangelis likes oral sex. He keeps pushing my head down so his cock goes deeper down my throat. I will not be able to bear this for long. There must be something else so this *deep-throating*, as it is commonly called, can come to an end. Then again, if he fucks me with that huge schlong I might also experience pain. I need a good alternative.

"Darling, the rubber is about to rip. I even put an extra-large on you. You're just too damn big. — Would you mind if I take it off and lick your cock without protection? Without a condom though, I can't take it all the way in my mouth."

"That's okay, Anika, I don't mind. I like that too. I'm also perfectly healthy, so don't worry. — So, you think my penis is large?"

As if he doesn't know!

"Yes, I do. Your wife is lucky. It's not often I see such a specimen."

He does not realize I feel sorry for his wife! A big schlong like that might be fun to play with, but getting it shoved down your throat or being roughly fucked with it is an entirely different ballgame. Giving my mouth a break, I use only my tongue and slowly lick the tip of his cock. Vangelis props himself up and watches enthusiastically as I teasingly lick his cock and balls all over. Although he has placed his hand again on my head, this time he only plays with my hair. I find this extremely unpleasant! So, I reposition myself so he can play with my pussy, not my hair. I would rather have him grope it than my hair! Finally, he opens my slit and sticks a finger deep inside me.

"Do you like that, Anika?"

"Oh, yes."

"Then you shall get more!" he replies and adds a second finger. He forcefully pushes them deep inside me, presumably the way he does with his cock. Needless to say, I pretend to enjoy it, moaning ecstatically every now and then. Nevertheless, I prefer him fucking me with two fingers than with his huge rod. Maybe with a massage and without a condom, I can get him to come. I prefer that over anything else.

"Darling, your cock is simply amazing! I can't stop looking at it. — May I continue or do you want to fuck me?"

"No, go ahead and enjoy my cock! But, can you reach an orgasm by playing with it? — It would be nice if you also climaxed, Anika. Just tell me what you like! I also want you to get something out of this. It's not only about satisfying me."

Oh my goodness! I always find it utterly ridiculous when a customer asks me what he can do so I have an orgasm. Not to offend him, I answer:

"With you, I could come easily. Let me rub your big cock against my pussy and I will come. Then I want to watch your big cock to explode all over. I'd really like that!"

"Yes, Anika, come for me. I want to hear you scream! — But not too loudly, okay?"

"Don't worry. I'm going to sit on you and then I'm giving your glorious boner a nice oil massage. — What do you say?"

"It sounds great. Go ahead. My cock is all yours! Do what you want to it, Anika!"

I remove my bustier and matching panties, drip a little oil in my hands, and sit on Vangelis' thighs.

"Damn, you're tits are fantastic, Anika! Can I touch them? Does this feel good?"

What do you know, I finally receive a compliment! Since he put me in a better mood and agreed to my oil massage proposal, I say:

"Yes, you can touch my breasts, it turns me on."

As I am yanking his boner and at the same time rubbing it against my pussy, I pretend to be aroused. Although Vangelis is busy fondling my breasts, he cannot help but watch the action between my legs. I think he loves viewing his pecker in action. It does not take long for him to reach a high state of arousal and so as not to come to an abrupt ending with this act, I take a break from massaging his cock and say:

"Lean back, darling, I want to titty fuck you."

Perhaps Vangelis thinks I am getting pleasure from this, which would not be off the mark. When I am in charge of determining the progress of intimate play, I am happy. With Vangelis lying prone on his back, I kneel over his legs and place his cock between my breasts. Vangelis obviously enjoys the view.

"Yeah, Anika, really use your tits and fuck it good! Oh, yeah, rub it real good. I'm almost there. It's going to explode at any moment now. Is that okay, Anika? Do you want it to come between your tits?"

"No, wait, baby! I want to come first. Hold on for another moment, I'm almost there!"

Since Vangelis has mentioned he is ready for the finale, there is no need to prolong it unnecessarily. I merely do not want him to come while I am in this position because I might end up with his cum squirting in my face. Therefore, I straddle him again so that his cock is aimed toward my pussy. Pretending to be wild with lust, I buff his big erection with my pussy. As I am about to fake an orgasm for him, he quietly speaks:

"Oh, God, I'm coming!"

And as he says the last words he explodes. However, he does not squirt his cum in a high arc, it merely erupts from his gland and slithers down the sides of his penis until the warm, milky-looking substance runs over my hand. Vangelis' hands tightly grab my thighs as he climaxes. The deed is done, so there is no longer the need to fake an orgasm, just a few moans will suffice. The idea of me coming drove him over the edge. It was what he wanted all along.

Once showered and dressed, I walk back into the room and find Vangelis sitting in his underwear at the desk surfing the Internet. He has placed three 50-euro bills next to my small toiletry bag.

"Anika, that's for you!" he says and points to the money. "And just so you know, next month I'll be back in Athens for a few days. Will you still be here?"

"Thanks, Vangelis! — And yes, I'll most likely still be here. I'm planning to stay at least through summer."

"Great, but I can't save your number. I'm hoping you'll keep your ad in the paper so I can look it up again."

"Of course, my ad will still be there."

After packing my things, I walk over to say goodbye.

"Wait, Anika, let me walk you to the door. Hopefully, no one will see you leaving my room. — Maybe it's better to meet at an hourly hotel next time. I mean, there are a few in this neighborhood, aren't there?"

"Yes, there's the Lenny Blue Hotel in Glyfada."

"That works, although I don't know it. I don't really care for carpeted hotel rooms. Maybe you can find a hotel like that and let me know the address. Next time, I definitely want to fuck you and then you can be as loud as you want! — Okay, Anika, until next time. And thank you very much!"

He gives me a kiss on the cheek before opening the door for me. Cautiously, he checks if the coast is clear and when he nods, I quickly depart and head for the elevator. Stepping into the lobby, a group of Americans returning from the beach provides excellent cover for me to walk across to the hotel's big glass door and out into the early evening heat of Glyfada without being noticed. Since my appointment with Nikos at the Wicky Inn Hotel isn't until 9:30 p.m., there is plenty of time to take public transportation to the city center. The illuminated display at the tram stop shows the next train to Syntagma Square is departing in six minutes. Perfect! I walk briskly to a kiosk, buy an ice cream, and enjoy it as I stroll back to the platform. Ice cream tastes much better than cock, I think. At least if you have no personal interest in a penis.

32

Around 9:00 p.m., I walk slowly by the Wicky Inn Hotel. It is located in a narrow, relatively dark alley not far from the main road, Patision Street. The hotel facade is also dark and the shutters on the upper floors are closed. It does not look all that inviting. I wonder why Nikos chose this place for our meeting. Is it the most affordable hotel in the area? I will definitely ask him. My phone rings. I take it out of the side pocket and answer:

"Hello!"

"Hi! This is Andreas. Am I speaking with the German lady with the ad in *Athens World*?"

"Yes, you are. My name is Anika. Good evening, Andreas."

"Good evening, Anika. Can you tell me more about yourself? How much do you charge an hour and what do you look like? Oh, and how old are you?"

"Sure. I'm 35, blonde with blue eyes, and a slim figure. I make hotel and home visits and my rate is 150 euros for one hour of safe sex."

"Wow! — Too pricey for me, Anika. Other women only charge 80 or 100. If you lower your price, we have a deal. I really would like to see you. So, the ball is in your court!"

Great! Another penny pincher! What shall I do now? Violet said I should be flexible in the beginning. I guess she is right. Listening to Andreas' accent, I determine he is definitely Greek. And he seems to be familiar with local escort service rates and he will not pay my price. So, do I take him up on his offer? I guess I must! Since I am establishing myself, I cannot afford to turn down a customer simply because he is unwilling to pay my standard fee.

"Andreas, it's your lucky day. Since I'm new in town, I'll lower my price. How about 100? However, anal is out of the question."

"It's a deal, Anika. I'm not into anal anyway. Okay, can you come to the Gordens Hotel in Glyfada?"

"That depends on when you want me there!"

"Right now."

"Sorry, Andreas, it's not enough notice. I'm on my way to an appointment in the city center. Perhaps later this evening I could be in Glyfada around 11:30 p.m."

"Oh, okay. Yeah, why not? So, 11:30 p.m. at the Gordens Hotel in Glyfada. It's a deal! Do you know the place?"

"No, but I'm sure a taxi driver knows the place.– Later, as soon as you're at the hotel and have the room number, please call or text me. I'm sure I can be there on time."

"Okay, I'll do that."

"Thanks, Andreas. See you later!"

Andreas hangs up and I save his number under 'Andreas - Gordens'. Yippee! — Another appointment! I might make a little less, but what the heck, 100 is still good money! Granted, by the time I am finished with Nikos, there will not be enough time to take public transportation to get to the Gordens Hotel on time.

I will have to dish out for a cab. When I am done with Andreas, it will be past midnight so there will be no other choice but to take a taxi again and then it will be the night tariff, which will cost even more. — At least I will keep most of the hundred, and if I am lucky, perhaps Andreas will book me again under circumstances that are more favorable. Right now, that is the most important thing!

My phone hums. It is a text message from Nikos. He is in room 32. I make a U-turn and return via Throma Street to the Wicky Inn Hotel. Its lobby is tiny and dimly illuminated, similar to the surrounding area outside. I ask the elderly gentleman sitting behind the front desk about room 32. He replies tersely:

"Third floor."

Although it is a small elevator, it has a mirror. I examine myself critically, run a brush through my hair, and once again, I am happy with my appearance. Nervous, I knock on number 32 and Nikos opens it only in underpants. He is tall and almost bald. He shaves the patches on his head where hair still grows. This is uncommon for Greek men because they are usually incredibly hairy, on their bodies and heads. Nikos seems friendly.

"Good evening, Anika! Come on in!"

"Good evening, Nikos!"

We exchange kisses and I walk by him into the room. Once again, I am in luck, the lights are dimmed.

"Nikos, I'll quickly freshen up in the bathroom and put on a sexy outfit for you, okay?"

Nikos thoroughly checks me out.

"You're already quite sexy, my little German lady — but hey, knock yourself out!"

I remove my sun hat and place it on the small bench across from the bed before disappearing into the bathroom. It is small but clean although I do not see a stool, which is always handy and is important to me. Oh well! Where can I place my bag? I guess the dry sink will do for now. I shed my clothes and hang them over the towel rack. I use the toilet to empty my bowels because I do not want any feces in my rectum for the upcoming anal sex and then hop in the shower and use a soapy finger to clean my anus. Once dry and dressed in my red lingerie, I switch my phone to silent mode, use my perfume decanter, grab my small toiletry bag stuffed with working equipment, and return to the main room.

Nikos is sitting on the bed with his back against the old bed's wooden headboard. I place my open bag on the nightstand and climb up on the bed.

"How would you like me to start, darling? Should I give you a little massage or would you rather have a blowjob?"

"How about you show me your beautiful tits and then go down on me and suck me real good? Once you have my cock nice and hard, we'll get you ready for a good ass fuck!"

"As you wish, baby. I'm fine with that."

By pushing the thin material of my bra underneath my breasts, they are completely exposed but still supported and perky. Nikos whistles through his teeth.

"Come here! I want to touch them."

I move next to him and stretch so he can grab my tits. He fondles and kneads my breasts and then plays with my nipples.

"Hey, they feel great! And they're real. Nowadays, you never know. — You have an awesome figure, Anika. You look great, considering you're 35!"

Pleased with his compliment, I jump for joy on the inside and kneel in front of him with my legs spread far apart while thrusting my tits toward him. The mirror across from the bed allows me to make sure I present him with my best poses. Nikos pushes his underpants under his balls and his cock pops out.

"And, how do you like this?"

"It looks marvelous! So, are you good to go?"

"Yes, but wait, let me sit on the edge of the bed and then you can properly do your thing!"

Nikos moves to the edge of the bed and places his feet on the floor while keeping his legs far apart. I take up a dog-style position between his thighs and since the wooden floor is quite hard on my knees, I ask Nikos to hand me a pillow. As I reach for a condom, Nikos says:

"Please, don't! — I am 100 percent healthy, Anika. Please take it in your mouth like it is, otherwise, I'll hardly feel a thing!"

Oral sex without a rubber is normal practice in all the clubs I worked. Even the escort service *Seven Heaven* here in Athens, advertises oral sex without protection. — Although I wanted to get away from this practice in my own business, I guess I can make an exception. Considering Nikos' words, and it is not like I have not done it before, I judge for myself whether his cock looks healthy or not. Nikos' member looks fine, so I set the condom aside and begin my oral sex performance. Nikos places a hand on the back of my head and gently pushes so his cock ends up deep in my mouth. Fortunately, his boner is not all that big and poses no problem for deep insertion. And, providing my anus gets a little foreplay, anal intercourse should be relatively painless too. Nikos is quite excited when he says:

"Spit on it! I'm into that, Anika! Spit on it and tell me what a filthy thing I have!"

Okay, that is easy. While sucking his cock, I repeatedly release it, give it a disapproving look, spit on it, swear at it, and slap it around:

"You filthy piece of shit! — You horny little bastard!"

Apparently, Nikos likes it. Every time I slap his cock, he moans in delight.

"You no good fucking rod!" I scream at it and immediately take it all the way into my mouth. Nikos moans continuously and then says:

"Oh, yes, Anika, that's it! Don't stop! Shout at it! It's a filthy thing. A fucking cheat! – Say it needs to be punished and that there will be no pussy! It's been a bad boy and is only allowed to fuck your ass. It deserves nothing better. Say it like that, Anika!"

I take my time dominating his cock while cussing at it using the most derogatory terms as well as slapping and biting it. As I want my rosette already nicely stretched out before the next act of my performance, I reach down with my right hand to part the crotch of my panties so I have access to both holes. I wet my middle finger and use it to massage my anus. As I stick my fingertip into my butthole, I spit on Nikos rod and abuse it some more. While biting and gently slapping it around from side to side, I gradually sink my finger deeper into my rectum. When my finger is inserted all the way, I move it around to prepare the orifice for something larger. Nikos notices my play and says:

"I like what you're doing there, baby! — Oh man, you have no idea how turned on I get just thinking about sticking it in your ass!"

Nikos is a man who likes to hold back so he gets the most out of it. However, in order to urge him on and not to prolong the act until who knows when, I tell him:

"Baby, my butt is aching for your bad boy. How about you stick it in? Or is it too soon for punishment?"

"Oh no, he's ready all right! Come and kneel on the bed. I want to take you from behind!" he immediately replies. He seems tense, but I hope he will not take long to come.

"Wait, let me grab a condom!" I say and quickly roll one over his cock. I snatch my personal lubricant out of my small pouch and rub it on his boner. Climbing back up on the bed, I assume a position on all fours and make a hollow back so my ass sticks up enticingly. As Nikos kneels behind me and looks in the mirror affixed above the bench where I discarded my sun hat, our eyes meet and I ask:

"Stick it in slowly!"

It seems he has not heard me because he immediately thrust his cock all the way into my keister.

"Slowly!" I say emphatically. – I might have stretched out my anus with one finger, but his cock is much thicker and I cannot help but cramp up as he penetrates me.

"Darling, this isn't working for me! You have to slow down and we need more lubricant!" I say determinedly as I move away from him.

"I'm sorry! I didn't mean to hurt you, Anika," Nikos says guiltily.

I reach for my personal lubricant again and squeeze enough on my hand to cover his entire dick.

"Okay, now do me nice and slow, baby!" I urge.

"Yes. My bad, bad Nicky will get the deserved punishment. He must look up your bottom. No pussy for him!"

Nikos is talking to his thankfully still rock hard pecker as he gradually pushes it into my butt. I feel my intestinal muscle relaxing and the pain subsiding. Nicely relaxed, I say to Nikos:

"Okay, darling, now everything's okay!"

Nikos immediately starts fucking me like a rabbit while lightly spanking my ass.

"There you go bad boy," he gasps. "See what you get for cheating!"

He thrusts forcefully into me and I have to grab the bed sheet so he does not push me forward. As his panting increases, he thrusts a few more times and finally reaches climax. I am happy the anal intercourse did not last long. Although I am glad it is over, I say:

"Darling, wait a little before you pull out your cock! — Let it become flaccid first. It deserves to be punished for a while longer. Otherwise, it'll be uncomfortable for me."

"Okay, baby, as you wish. I, for one, am finished. I'm exhausted! Damn, this was crazy! You have a fantastic ass, you know that? Such a great fuck!"

Breathing heavily, Nikos remains on his knees behind me, lightly holding onto my hips for support. If he abruptly removes his cock, it will feel as if I dropped a turd. In essence, it would be extremely unpleasant! When the bad boy finally softens, I move forward and let it slide out of me. Nikos gets up and rushes into the bathroom, but immediately returns with my handbag and clothes and discards them on the bed, saying:

"This way nothing gets wet when I shower."

I take the time to stretch out on the bed to relax. It is a 10:15 p.m. I actually must hurry to make my next appointment with Andreas, but I do not want to rush Nikos.

Taking my phone out of my handbag, I notice I have received two calls, so I switch the ringer back on. Grabbing my small toiletry bag, I stuff it and my phone back in the bag. As soon Nikos finishes in the bathroom, I hop into the shower. By the time I am done and come back into the room, Nikos is already dressed and smoking a cigarette. He holds out the pack to me, but I politely decline:

"Thanks, darling, but I don't smoke."

Nikos reaches into his pants pocket, pulls out a wad of bills, counts off three 50s, and says:

"This is for you, Anika! And, I'd like to call you again. — I'm hoping anal sex was okay for you too?"

"Yes, it was fine, once you slowed down. You know, you have to give me time to relax my anus, that way, I can also enjoy it."

"Great. So all I have to do is follow your lead, no problem, baby!"

"You want me to leave first?" I ask as I pick up my hat and handbag.

"Yes, you can go if you like. — But tell me, can I give you a ride somewhere? I drove my car. I know this hotel is a bit secluded and this dark neighborhood is no place for a pretty blonde to be running around late at night. — At least let me take you to a busier road. What direction are you going?"

"That's a great idea! I'd appreciate it if you could drop me off somewhere where I can grab a taxi! I have to be in Glyfada."

"Oh, yeah! I'm going to Palaio Faliro. I can give you a ride for most of the way. Hold on a moment! I'm almost ready to go."

He goes back into the bathroom and leaves the door open. I see him checking himself out in the mirror. He then pulls out a small bottle of aftershave from his blazer, covering up any womanly smell with some herbal male fragrance.

"You never know what the wife might smell!"

Grinning, he puts the bottle back and the two of us leave the room. When we are in the elevator, he playfully grabs my butt and says:

"Damn! You have a great ass!"

I wait nearby for Nikos to pay for the room at the reception desk and then we exit of the hotel together into the dark narrow street. We stroll along the road where one car after another is parked until Nikos stops at a white Mercedes Coupé S Class and opens the passenger door for me. The car has leather seats and the dashboard is made of fine wood. The young man must do okay for himself to be able to afford such a car. So why did he take me to such a dump, certainly not because of the cheap room rate.

"This is a fine car," I say as I buckle up.

"Yes, my work takes me on the road a lot. And this Mercedes is the right car for that. — And of course, I like it too!"

He grins again before driving off. I lean back in the plush leather seats and look out the window.

"So, tell me, why did you want to go to this hotel?" I cannot contain my curiosity.

"Because people who know me would never think I'd frequent such an establishment. In essence, I don't go to the popular hourly hotels for security reasons. — I thought you might not like that place, but I'm hoping you won't mind if we meet there again."

"No, it's okay. It might be old-fashioned, but at least it's clean. However, I don't care for its dark, deserted location!"

"Yes, you're right about that. I'm sure some questionable characters hang out in that neighborhood, which is why I'm glad you accepted my offer for a ride. — So, which part of Germany are you from, Anika?"

"Outside Cologne."

"Cologne, huh, I've never been to that city. I've been to Hamburg, Hannover, and Berlin. Nice cities. — But as a Greek, you Germans eat dinner way too early!"

"Yes, I know. Most restaurants close at midnight."

"Yeah, right, not the ones I frequented. It was only 10:00 p.m. and none of them would serve me a warm meal!"

Both of us laugh at his remark and spend the rest of the time talking about our different lifestyles. When we reach the coastal road, I say to Nikos:

"Just drop me off anywhere you can pull over. I'm sure I can catch a taxi here."

"Okay!"

When there is a break in traffic, Nikos pulls curbside and we quickly say goodbye before he drives off. As I search Poseidonos Street for a cab, I notice a tram stop across the road. Since Nikos has saved me time and it is only 10:50 p.m., I can save the cost of a taxi and ride the tram to Glyfada. I do not have to wait long before boarding one.

When the tram begins to move, I Google the Gordens Hotel and find the location right where Andreas described it to me, close to the beach. Reassured, I lean back and look out the window while thinking about my next customer.

33

During my ride to Glyfada, I receive a text from Andreas telling me his room number. I text back:

Thanks. I'm on my way!

By the time I hear the announcement for the upcoming stop at the Vergoti town square station, my destination, it is 11:20 p.m. Talk about good timing! I disembark and see the neon signs of several hotels. One is the Gordens Hotel. I enter a brightly lit lobby after climbing the few steps to the entrance. At the front desk is a young woman dressed in a drab gray suit. Walking up to her, I say:

"Good evening, room 510, please."

"Fifth floor," she replies pleasantly and nods her head at the elevator. This place does not seem to be a regular hourly hotel. From the looks of it, I would say it is a regular tourist hotel. In the elevator, I check my appearance in the mirror. After reapplying lipstick and perfume, I run my fingers through my hair and I am ready for my next client. When the elevator stops, I am confronted with a waiting couple far apart in age. He must be at least 60, whereas she looks 20, if that. His arm is tightly wrapped around her shoulder, giving the impression they are not father and daughter. We greet in passing and I head left to room 510. Not long after I knock, the door is opened by a man who reminds me of Obelix the Gaul. He is quite tall and large. And he wheezes, which means he has problems breathing. His slicked-back black hair is shiny as if he used a whole jar of mayonnaise on it. I feel insignificant next to this mountain of a man. Andreas offers his hand and greets me warmly.

"Come on in, Anika! Good evening."

"Good evening, Andreas," I reply in kind. His handshake is limp and damp. —Yuck! I do not care for damp hands, nor do I like big men. But it is not about what I like, I am here for him. Andreas closes the door and follows me into the room. The room furnishings are a simple modern style. The wall across from the large bed is one immense mirror. It makes the room appear more spacious. The entire seaward wall is glass and the sliding door to the balcony stands open.

"This is a nice room," I comment as I look around.

"Yes, I think so too. I like the Gordens Hotel for its cleanliness and proximity to the beach. — Would you like a drink, Anika?"

"Yes, please! A glass of water would be nice."

I set my handbag on the bed and walk out onto the balcony. The view of the tall palm trees, the dimly lit sandy beach, and the dark vast sea beyond is absolutely idyllic. The waning moon rising in the east illuminates part of the water's surface making it shimmer.

If it were up to me, we would sit out here and enjoy this beautiful nocturnal atmosphere while sipping drinks. At that moment, Andreas comes out on the balcony with his drink and a glass of water for me.

"Andreas, would you mind if I enjoyed the gorgeous view of the palm trees, sea, and moon for another minute. It's simply magical!"

"I'm glad you see it that way. I believe we Greeks sometimes forget that we're living in a magical place right on the coast. — So, Anika, how long have you been in Athens?"

"Just shy of two weeks."

"And, do you like the city?"

"It's okay. It's a bit too hot for me during the day and I find it too noisy and too trashy. I think the city's charm comes out when it gets dark, when it's no longer hot and I can't see all that trash flying around. — I simply adore the warm evenings. I only had a few of those back in Germany!"

We toast and silently stand for a while looking out over the railing at the vast sea. Since I came here to work, I snap out of it and say:

"Andreas, I'm going to the bathroom to freshen up and change, okay?"

"All right, Anika."

Andreas follows me back into the room. I hear his labored breathing with every step he takes. Although the bathroom is not all that big, it does have a stool for my handbag. I quickly switch my phone to silent mode before undressing. Andreas might be huge and looks like Obelix, but I do appreciate his good manners. All I need to do is ensure I stay on top. – Otherwise, I also might have problems breathing! I don the white lace bustier set and matching strapless stockings I wore this afternoon with Vangelis, believing Andreas will enjoy it too. I still do not have a clue how best to manage a man of his voluminous stature. But I feel certain he will not fuck me like a rabbit. At least I would not think so, considering his breathing problems! I grab my purse, drape my clothes over one arm, and return to the room. Andreas is naked with a towel wrapped around his waist and is heading for the now empty bathroom.

While he is in the shower, I try out different poses on the bed while watching myself in the mirror. Checking out the various light switches, I discover each lamp can be dimmed separately. The room has wooden flooring with no visible carpeting anywhere. I make a mental note of it, considering Vangelis, the retired captain, prefers non-carpeted hotel rooms. From my toiletry bag, I grab a couple condoms and a small bottle of massage oil and place them on the bedside table. I get comfortable on the bed and wait. When Andreas comes out of the bathroom, a big bath towel is wrapped around his waist again. He sits down next to me on the bed. I smile and ask:

"Okay, darling, how may I be of service? Would you like to start with a little erotic massage?"

"That sounds good. — You look sexy in that white lingerie, Anika."

"Thank you, Andreas! Please take off the towel and lie down on your belly. I'm going to start with a back massage."

When he removes the towel, he makes sure I cannot see his wiener. Strange! Taking into account why I am here, I am going to see it anyway. I kneel next to Andreas and warm some oil in my palms. His back is not hairy, but it is lightly tanned. Moving my hands in circular motion, I start massaging his back at his hips and move upward. I start kneading his shoulders and he groans.

"Am I hurting you?" I ask.

"A little bit. My shoulders seem to be tense. But please continue, Anika, it also feels good."

Using less pressure, I massage down his back. This time, I start rubbing his buttocks with circular hand movements. Slowly, I work my way back up along his spine and then on to his shoulders and upper arms before I repeat the process back down to his ass. As my fingers rub his buttocks, I slide one oiled hand deep between his thighs until I feel his testicles. Andreas winces slightly. I continue massaging his butt with alternating circular motions and work my way back up to his shoulders. Massaging his backside up and down a few more times, I decide it has received enough attention. Dripping more oil into my palms, I say:

"Turn around, darling, time to do your front."

Panting heavily, Andreas rolls onto his back. He crosses his arms behind his head and avoids eye contact. His wiener looks rather puny on his huge physique. Looking at his cock independently, it is really not that small. He has no reason to be shy. - Perhaps he has a different opinion because when he looks in the mirror all he sees is his disproportionate physique. That is fine with me; otherwise, he would a have a monstrous penis! Lying prone on his back, his gut prevents him from seeing his wiener and what I am about to do with it. I suggest:

"Andreas, don't you want to sit up a little? There's no need for you to lie flat, that was only for the back massage."

"I'd love to, Anika! Hold on."

Painstakingly, he raises his upper body and shoves a few pillows under his head.

"That's better. Now I can see what you're doing to me, sexy lady!"

I start rubbing his cock with my oiled hands. Andreas closes his eyes and moans repeatedly. He obviously enjoys my cock massage. I am sure I could get him off like this, but that would not be fair. I am certain he wants to fuck me. — I just wonder how? To prevent the condom from tearing easily, I must remove the oil from his cock. Having removed my bustier, I bend down and place his proud member between my boobs. By rubbing his stiff cock with my bare breasts, I transfer as much oil as possible to my skin. Now, Andreas has opened his eyes and is watching the action at his crotch intently. I believe my breasts have done all they can, so I lick the remaining oil off his boner. Andreas moans again and this time says:

"*Panajia Mou*! Maria Mother of God, this is fucking awesome!"

I roll a rubber over his clean shaft and perform oral sex before I start fucking him. Although I have had sex before with big men, Andreas tops them all. I mount him, although I am no longer able to reach the mattress with my knees.

His girth is simply enormous! I need to change positions, so I climb off him again. I take off my panties, slip out of my heels, and climb back aboard. This time I squat over him. In this position, I can balance myself on my feet. It might be more strenuous, but there is no other choice. Once his cock slides into my pussy, I start riding him. Using all my leg strength, I move up and down, up and down… I lean slightly forward, reach for his nipples with my fingertips and gently tweak them. Andreas moans again. I cannot tell whether it is due to shortness of breath or arousal. Perhaps both.

Since I do not sense any movement under me, it is up to me to set the speed and rhythm. I hope I am choosing correctly so he will climax. Up and down, up and down, all the while moving my hips and increasing speed.

Suddenly, I feel him trying to thrust his pelvis. It is obvious Andreas is mustering all his strength for a few thrusts to enjoy the final reward. The huge body beneath lifts me up as it spasms during climax. During this, I attempt to keep my weight on my knees while waiting for Andreas to calm down and find his breath. I slowly rise up a bit while holding the loaded condom in place so it does not slide of his softening penis. While disembarking, I grasp the rubber, pull it off, and place on the floor. Next, I kneel next to him and slowly caress his stomach and his chest. Andreas is a client who was easy to satisfy. Placing his great damp paw on mine, he squeezes it.

"That was pretty damn good, Anika! Thank you!"

"You're welcome, darling! — I'm glad you liked it. It's important to me."

"You're really pretty!"

"Thank you!" I smile charmingly, delighted to have made my customer happy.

"You know, Anika, I'm aware of how I look. I don't like when a girl I've called keeps looking at me in disgust while trying to get the job done as soon as possible. — I mean, I'm paying for it. — But you took your time and didn't make me feel like a huge lump of gross meat. I really appreciate that."

Moved by his honesty, I reply:

"You're not gross. You're simply a large man, like Obelix. — I know lots of women who are into men like you!"

Andreas shakes his head and says:

"You don't have to sweet talk me, Anika. As I said, I know how I look."

It's best we change the subject. At least, I find it uncomfortable.

"Andreas, are you an Athenian?"

"No, I'm not even a full-blooded Greek. My father is Moroccan. I was born and raised in Morocco. As a child, I spent each summer vacation in Greece with my mother's family. At that time, my parents worked in the fashion industry and founded their own company in Greece. Although the fashion label is rather unknown around the world, business is great and now I'm also part of it."

"That's interesting! Is it rude to ask the name of the label?"

"Yes, it is! – Let's just drop it, Anika!" he replies with a smile. "So, what about you? Why did you come to Athens? — I know lots of people who would give anything for a life in Germany."

"I was tired of lying about and hiding my profession. That's what I had to do in Germany. I grew up in an area that we refer to as a cow town. Actually, the entire region I used to live in was made up of cow towns, — yeah, and most people know each other. I constantly had to be vigilant and lie so no one would find out about my job as a prostitute. It was a heavy burden. — It was exhausting and I was tired of it! I chose to come to Athens because it's part of Europe, it's by the sea, and the climate is much better than in Germany."

Andreas laughs when I say cow town. Perhaps in English, the word does not exist. Nevertheless, I'm sure he knows the type of town I'm talking about.

"Did you work as a call girl in Germany?"

"No, I worked in clubs, similar to small brothels that operate out of private residences, mansions, or apartments. I worked at those places as a part-time prostitute. Here, far away from people who know me, I have the freedom to work full-time untroubled. I want to see how well I do here through the summer and if I make enough, I will move here permanently."

"Well, I certainly hope you stay!" Andreas is smoking a cigarette and sipping his drink. He fills a glass with water and hands it to me.

"To your success!" he says with a raised glass.

I shower and dress. – By the time I finish, Andreas is wrapped in a towel again, handing me a 100-euro bill. – Happily, I pocket the green note, kiss him on the cheek, and leave the hotel room.

34

Even though it is past midnight, I am wide-awake and energized. Standing at the intersection next to the Gordens Hotel, I search traffic for a car with an illuminated taxi sign on the roof. Waving my arm to attract attention to myself, a few cabs with passengers on board stop. When the drivers ask me where I want to go, I answer:

"Piraeus."

The majority nods in a dismissive way and drive on. Some stare at me before accelerating again. Luckily, I do not have a problem being patient; after all, there is no other appointment to rush to. — It is my time off and I feel completely at ease and happy. I mean, I have made 470 euros today! That is right, 470 big ones! I repeat the number a few times in my head because I am tickled pink.

This is by far the most I have made in one day. When I manage to hail a taxi, I will ask to be taken to Mikrolimano in Piraeus. It is a small harbor with colorful local fishing boats and a lively nightlife district with bars, restaurants, and cafés not far from my hotel. Today calls for a celebration, so I will treat myself to a pleasant late meal.

My phone rings. Unknown number. I step a few meters away from the curb and answer:

"Hello!"

"Hi! Are you free?"

The noise of passing traffic muffles the party on the other end.

"Yes, I am. My name is Anika. With whom am I speaking, please?"

"This is Ladis. — How much do you cost?"

"I charge 150 an hour. Anything else you'd like to know?"

"Yes. What do you look like?"

"I'm blonde with blue eyes and a slim figure."

"Okay. Can you come to my hotel room right now?"

Considering I am not tired and there is the possibility to make another 150, I decide to service one more client. I ask:

"What's the name of the hotel? Which district is it in?"

"I'm at the Emma Hotel in Piraeus. It's near the harbor. So, can you come?"

Piraeus is perfect! I might not know the Emma Hotel, but I am certain I can find it.

"Yes,– but it'll be another 45 minutes to an hour before I can get there."

"That's fine."

"Okay, but I need your name, the hotel address and phone number, and, obviously, your room number. I'll call you back to re-confirm and be there at the agreed upon time, okay?"

"Yes, okay. Hold on. – The number of the Emma Hotel is 210 45117000. It's on Notara Street 141. I'm in room 22."

Awkwardly, I stand there and search my handbag for a notepad and pen and say:

"Okay. Can you repeat it?"

Ladis relays the information again and I quickly scribble it down.

"Thanks. All right, I'll call you right back. What's your last name?"

"Ladis will do just fine."

"Of course! Talk to you soon."

I hang up and immediately dial the number of the Emma Hotel. A man answers and says something in Greek that I do not understand. In English, I ask:

"Please connect me with Mr. Ladis in room 22."

The man remains silent and connects me. Ladis answers after the second ring.

"Is that you, Ladis?"

"Yes. — So, are you on your way?"

"As soon as I hang up. See you in a bit, Ladis!"

"Great and hurry up."

Hurry up – how am I supposed to hurry up? The commute will take as long as it takes. I suspect Ladis has had a few too many drinks. But as long as he is not too inebriated, I do not have a problem seeing him. I do not like appointments with men who are completely toasted. Walking back to the curb, I look and wave at cabs again. By the time I finally catch one, it is 12:45 a.m.

Although the taxi driver does not know where the Emma Hotel is, he knows Notara Street. I am positive he will be able to find it. I reach into my handbag for my compact and check my appearance. Considering it is the middle of the night, I look fine. I spray a little *Must de Cartier* behind my ears. The cab driver quickly turns around and says:

"That smells good, miss."

"Thank you!"

I am hoping my next customer will have the same reaction. After a while, the taxi driver slows and pulls into a narrow road. Soon after, he points to the dim neon sign of the Emma Hotel. He stops, I pay, and get out. – The Emma Hotel is a three-story building that does not differ significantly from the neighboring homes. Light shines through a few windows on the first and second level. I push the ajar entrance door all the way and step into the foyer. On my left is a small reception desk with an elderly gentleman sitting behind it, who is busy watching a talk show on TV.

"Good evening," I quietly say in passing. Ladis did not tell me to be discreet, but considering the hour, I do not need to attract unnecessary attention. So, I simply behave as if I belong, continue on and walk up the staircase. On the second-floor, I hear soft music coming from one of the rooms. After finding room 22, I quickly smooth out my dress before knocking. Ladis opens the door and asks me in. He is tall with thick brown hair and dark eyes. His jeans have holes and his sleeveless T-Shirt shows off the tattoos on his upper arms. – I estimate he is in his early 30s.

"Hi, sweetie!" I say and offer my cheek for a welcome kiss.

"Hi," he says, giving me a cursory peck. He closes the door and we walk through a short, narrow hallway passing the open bathroom door on the left and into the small main room. It has one single bed pushed into a corner. The other furnishings are a wardrobe, a small table with two chairs, and a shelf holding a TV and a few personal items. – That is it. Attached to the ceiling is a spotlight, its beam directed at the pillow on the bed. I am definitely not lying there with my face under that bright light. It might make me look even older than I already am. The light next to the table is much softer and dimmer and it will absolutely suffice for my work. Ladis comes up behind me and grabs my butt. I place my hat on the table before turning to face him.

"Darling, I need to briefly use the bathroom. May I?"

"Sure, go ahead," he says, "but hurry back, I want to fuck!"

Although I smell alcohol on him, he does not seem drunk. The bathroom is also small. There is no stool nor does it have a free hook to hang my dress on. Placing my handbag in the dry sink, I undress and slip on my sexy red lingerie set. I am satisfied with my reflection after inspecting myself in the mirror. Grabbing my dress and handbag, I walk back into the room to find Ladis bare-chested, sitting on the edge of the bed smoking a cigarette.

Discarding my things on one of the chairs, I approach Ladis. He immediately extinguishes his cigarette and pulls me toward him. The light! The light over the bed must be off!

"Baby, can you do me a favor and turn the ceiling light off? It shines right in my eyes. And we want it cozy, don't we?"

"I don't care about cozy! I just want to fuck you!" Ladis says curtly and makes no move to switch off the light.

"Oh, come on! It bothers me. Please turn it off!" I try sweet-talking him. If I knew where the light switch was, I would turn it off myself. I do not care much for Ladis' manners. As if reading my mind, he asks:

"What's wrong? You don't like it here? Are you used to better accommodations? You're charging 150, that's a hell of a lot of dough. — And you have to perform accordingly! I make the rules, not you, is that clear?"

"What do you mean by that?"

"I mean, the light stays on! And I'm going to tell you how this goes down. So, do you want to stop complaining and make some money or what?"

I really do not like the sound of this, but I think it is best not to argue with him. Calmly, I answer pleasantly:

"Yes, of course! Come on, baby, let's forget about it and have some fun. It's why you wanted me here, right? Leave the light on if it's that important to you!"

"All right. So, entertain me!" he says and pulls me onto his lap.

I slide the thin material underneath my breasts and thrust them out toward him while I grab one of his hands and place it between my spread legs. Thankfully, he stops talking and busies himself with my genitals. I am still not happy about the unflattering spotlight, but it is what it is. Perhaps I will eventually locate the elusive switch and turn it off myself! Ladis pushes my panties aside and rather roughly inserts his middle finger into my pussy. Since it is dry, it hurts. Although I am really unhappy and experiencing a great deal of discomfort, I clamp my teeth together and remain quiet so as to not upset him again. Ladis vigorously sucks and bites one of my nipples. This hurts too, and since I cannot tolerate the pain any longer, I say imploringly:

"Not so hard, baby! That hurts. My nipples are incredibly sensitive!"

Thankfully, he abides by my wish without complaint and immediately sucks my nipple more gently. Reaching for his cock, I find his erection straining against the jeans, so I start rubbing my hand over the denim. While he is still raping my pussy with his middle finger, I open his fly and say:

"Sweetie, let me get to your cock. I'm so turned on by how hard it is. I want to suck it. Come on, let me have it!"

"You'll get it all right," he replies in his usual curt and rude manner. I do not let it bother me and slide off his legs. He quickly yanks his jeans off and tosses them passed the bed onto the floor. Ladis wears tight-fitting black underwear, which he also removes and carelessly throws onto the floor. Ladis is quite an unpleasant customer, but I guess I can stomach him for another 30 minutes until my time is up! And, he is not the first client to be rough with me. I take a condom out of the pouch and as I am about to roll it over his penis, he grabs my hand and gruffly says:

"Hey! — I want to have fun! We're not using that thing."

Whoa! Could he be any ruder? I can oblige him while performing oral sex, but definitely not during actual intercourse!

"Look, sexy, – I don't mind sucking your dick without a rubber, but I won't have you come in my mouth! Understand? And, if you want to fuck me, you better get used to the idea of wearing that thing! If not, you can forget about it. I'm serious. If you're not happy with that, I can dress and leave. We will simply forget about the entire affair. So, what do you say?"

"All right, you can put that thing on before we fuck. So, continue and really get me going!"

What a prick! I am never seeing him again! I could not execute this job if every customer was like him! Thankfully, clients like him do not come around often. I ignore my dislike for the man and continue doing my job so I can leave! Kneeling on the hard floor in front of him, I take his damn rod in my mouth and start blowing him. Considering I have run my tongue over his cock and balls for a while, I look at him and humbly ask:

"Do you want to fuck me now, baby?"

"Yes, lie down on the bed. I'm going to fuck you real good, you little slut!"

Once again, I ignore him and the remark because this is the first and last time he is going to put his hands on me. I simply want it over with and to get the hell out of here! Removing my underwear, I set it on the chair along with the rest of my clothes. I approach the narrow bed stark naked and lie down. What do you know, right next to the headboard is the light switch for the ceiling spotlight, which I immediately turn off. Ha! I get my way after all!

"Spread your legs wide!" Ladis orders rudely. He does not even comment about the light. Perhaps he did not notice. Holding the condom up for him to see, I say:

"Should I put it on or do you want to do it yourself?"

"Just give me that damn thing!" he hisses. He rips open the wrapper with his teeth and quickly rolls the rubber over his cock. At least he did not protest. Hopefully, he will not take long for the finale. This guy is such a boor! Ladis pushes himself between my legs and shoves his cock into me with one forceful move. He is hurting me!

"Put your hands behind your head. I want to grab hold of them," he growls after a few thrusts in the missionary position. Although I do not like it, I yield to avoid another argument and to get it over with now that we are in the final act. When I cross my hands above my head, he pulls them apart and grabs each wrist. Pressing me firmly against the mattress so I cannot move, he starts slamming his cock into me as if trying to reach my throat. Like a man possessed, he quickly and forcefully continues thrusting. With each drive, his loins slam against my pubic bone. My wrists also hurt from his tight grip. Ladis is strong and I cannot move my arms whatsoever. Right now, I am completely at his mercy. I only hope this session is soon over! With a reddened head and veins on his forehead clearly visible, he maintains his gaze on where the action takes place. Tense and in pain, I put up with his rough rabbit number. I hope the condom remains intact. It seems like an eternity has passed when he suddenly stops moving. He twitches and jerks, then muffles his cries as he starts ejaculating. At once, all the strength he possessed a few moments ago evaporates. His arms tremble but maintain their grip on my wrists as his midriff collapses onto me. He lays motionless. Finally, he releases my wrists and gets off! My shoulders, neck, arms, pussy, and pubic bone... — everything hurts! Although I am furious and want to scream at him now that it is over, I breathe a sigh of relief. Since my arms feel numb, I rotate my wrists and wiggle my fingers to get the circulation flowing again. Ladis sits on the edge of the bed smoking a cigarette. Charming as ever, he does not even look at me when he says:

"Okay, now make yourself scarce."

At the moment, I cannot imagine anything I would enjoy more! I get up and grab my lingerie before disappearing into the bathroom. Examining my wrists, I notice they are still red and tender from his tight hold. What a fucking degenerate asshole! Nevertheless, I will not say anything and will remain cordial, for my intuition tells me not to criticize this man for the way he treated me. I quickly freshen up and forego the shower. All I want is to get out of here as soon as possible. Nothing else matters! Back in the room, I quickly slip on my dress and pack my things. Ladis is still sitting in the same place smoking, but now he is in his underwear looking at his phone. Once again, he simply ignores me, which is fine with me. When I am ready to leave, I stand between him and the door and say:

"Okay, please pay me my money and I'm out of here."

"What money?"

He raises his head and gives me a dark look.

"My fee of 150."

"Ha, you want money? What for? Because I fucked you?"

Ladis offers a dismissive and evil-sounding laugh. I remain calm and say:

"We discussed this on the phone and you agreed, — so please hold up your end of the bargain. I came here and let you fuck me. I've done my job!"

I can tell he did not expect me to talk back and he immediately becomes angry. Should I have just left?

"Fine," he says grumpily and then adds, "but I don't have enough cash on me. I am going to call my friend and he'll bring it. — Sit down over there for the time being!"

His voice has an underlying threatening intonation. I think it is better if I leave! Suddenly I have a bad feeling in the pit of my stomach. Ladis gets up and stands in front of me, pointing at the chair beside the table.

"I told you to sit over there!" he orders again.

Damn, I should not have insisted on being paid! In an appeasing tone, I say:

"Okay, okay. — Don't worry about it! I'm just going to leave now! Don't bother your friend. I wouldn't want to put you in an awkward position. Sorry!"

As I am about to leave, he rushes over, grabs an upper arm tightly, and hisses at me:

"I told you to sit your ass down over there! I'm calling my friend now. — So don't worry, he'll pay you all right!"

He drags me back to the table and forcefully pushes me into the chair. God, I am such an idiot! What have I gotten myself into? Ladis is talking to someone on the phone, but not in Greek. I am not familiar with the language. Is it Russian? He might be Russian or Albanian, I have no idea, but that he is not speaking Greek worries me! He never takes his eyes off me while on the phone. Now and then, he laughs sardonically. My hearts starts pounding as I sit there in the chair. All kinds of thoughts flash through my mind. I am scared. What type of friend can he have? I am sure he will not be coming here to pay me. Maybe they are going to rape me! My God, I have more than 600 euros on me. Perhaps they are going to steal my money, passport, credit card, and phone! Who knows what men like this are capable of? I am in danger! — I must escape! As soon as possible! — But how? It is obvious Ladis will not let me go. Blood rushes from my head and I feel dizzy. My heart feels as if it is about to burst and my lips start to tremble. Should I try to talk to him again? Better not. It is what enraged Ladis to begin with. Since he has been talking to his friend, he is in a much better mood. That is not a good sign! What can I do? Ladis lights up another cigarette.

"Where are you from?" I break the silence from sheer embarrassment while trying to keep the concern in my voice in check. Intuition tells me I should not show any fear!

"I'm from Albania," he replies curtly.

"Ah," I murmur, aware of how difficult it is to hide my fear. Anxiously I wait on the edge of the wooden chair with my sun hat firmly clutched in my hands. – After a while, when nothing happens, my fear intensifies. Watching Ladis out of the corner of my eye, I see him fiddling around with his phone before making another call. I presume it is the friend he called earlier. From the sound of it, it seems he asked a question and did not get the answer he wanted for he immediately becomes angry again. Perhaps his buddy cannot get here soon enough for him?

Who knows, I am merely guessing. Once again, he rarely takes his eyes off me while on the phone. He is visibly upset when he hangs up and snuffs out his cigarette in the ashtray. Walking toward the bathroom, he stops, turns around, and shoots me a nasty look. With an underlying threat in his voice, he says:

"Stay put, don't move! I'm merely taking a piss. And so you know, I'm leaving the bathroom door open, so don't get any stupid ideas or you'll regret it!"

As he says this, he menacingly shakes a finger at me. I swallow the lump in my throat. — This is my chance to escape! – As soon as he disappears into the bathroom, I lean down and with trembling fingers hastily remove my shoes. My heart beats so fiercely that I hear it echoing in my head. Although my legs feel numb, instinct takes over as soon as I hear Ladis flipping up the toilet seat.

With my shoes and purse in hand, I take off at lightning speed and run barefoot to the door. All I can think about is getting out of here. Now! I make it to the door without Ladis noticing my escape attempt. Thankfully, the toilet is positioned so that his back is facing the threshold of the open bathroom door. As I fling open the door, he hears me. I start running for my life, heading toward the staircase.

My head pounds like it is going to explode. I move on autopilot and literally fly down the staircase. I make it one floor down, then another. I cannot hear myself think or if Ladis is following me. It does not matter; fear motivates my legs and I continue running as fast as I can! – Not paying any attention to the old man at the reception desk and not knowing whether he even noticed me, I sprint out of the hotel and run barefoot down the dark road at full speed. Holding my handbag close with my right arm so it does not swing around on its shoulder strap, I clutch my shoes in my left hand and keep running. Without caring if I am traveling in the right direction, I haul ass away from that hellhole. All that matters is getting as far away as possible.

The constant pounding in my head is giving me a headache. My heart is still beating fiercely and I cannot judge how much distance I have placed between myself and the hotel by the time I feel the first signs of exhaustion. There is no other choice but to slow down and, for the first time, I turn around to see if I am being pursued. Ladis is nowhere in sight! This realization makes me breathe a little easier! All I see are a few pedestrians I did not perceive as I rushed by. Further ahead, I notice a busy street much brighter than the dark side street I am currently on. Still acting on instinct, I keep walking and look nervously behind me repeatedly.

At that moment, I become aware that I am still barefoot, so I quickly set my shoes down and wipe the soles of my feet with a tissue before slipping them on. It seems I have managed to escape unscathed from that man and his plans for me. – Although my heart is still beating rapidly, I am able to think clearly again. Taking a few slow and even breaths, I feel myself calming down. Holding out my arm and looking at my hand, it shakes as if I had Parkinson's disease. Arriving at the brightly lit wide street, I realize it is the coastal road. Across the street, separated by a fence, large cruise ships are berthed. Pedestrians walk by me and cars blast their horns as they cross an intersection where the traffic light has turned green. I have often seen this practice and yet, I do not have an explanation for it. With each passing minute, I become calmer. Thank you! — Thank you, thank you, thank you, I whisper, thanking my lucky stars. Thank you!

35

Considering the horrible ordeal I just experienced, it is no wonder my appetite has disappeared. The mood to celebrate my successful day at Mikrolimano has passed.

As I am quite familiar with the area surrounding the Port of Piraeus, I continue walking until I reach the town square close to Dimotiko Theatro. – I am in luck, the bars are still open so I can get off my feet. Exhausted and still rattled, I am in desperate need of a drink. Seeing an empty table on one of the bar patios, I walk over and plop down in the padded wicker chair. For a moment, I close my eyes and try to make sense of what just happened. My mouth is dry and my tongue sticks to the roof of my mouth. I am terribly thirsty. The waiter approaches and I order a bottle of water and a split of white wine. It is not long before he returns and places two glasses, the wine, a bottle of water, and a bowl of peanuts on the table. Despite the late hour, many people are still out and about. That is fine with me. It gives me a sense of security. Right now, I need to feel a part of this strange city and its people. Granted, I might be sitting here alone, but being in the company of other people makes me feel safe! The idea of being in my hotel room paralyzes me. I am afraid of the ghosts that might come and haunt me when I am alone in the dark. – I am better off here, surrounded by lights, the carefree people occupying the neighboring tables, and pedestrians.

I unscrew the bottle of water, fill my glass, take a big sip and then fill my wine glass and start sipping it. I want to be tipsy by the time I go to bed. Hopefully, I will not have nightmares then. As all kinds of horrific scenarios of what could have happened play out in my mind, I continue sipping my water and wine and watch the action while constantly giving thanks for having made it out of the hotel in one piece! — I am so glad I managed to escape! Checking my phone, I see I have received numerous calls and text messages. Three calls are from an unknown number, one is from a Greek cell phone, and then there are two text messages. When I read the first one, my stomach sours immediately. It is from Ladis:

Come back or you'll regret it!

The second text is also from him, threatening me:

I'm going to find you, you fucking bitch!

Oh my God, he seems serious! And yes, all he would need to do is call me from a different number and perhaps disguise his voice to make an appointment. Or have his buddy do it and I would not be the wiser. Maybe his friend finally showed up and Ladis could not follow through with whatever he promised him on the phone. So now he feels like a fool and is out for revenge. He wants to show off for his friend and deliver on his promise for some fun with a prostitute. My hands shake again and I feel sick to my stomach. I must remain calm! – I need to maintain my composure! I am safe here! And no, going to the police is out of the question. The way I run my business is illegal here in Greece. I am a criminal, so to speak! Then again, the German police would also do nothing until after a crime was committed. They do not care about threats! So, I might as well forget about calling the police for help. I got involved with the wrong man and I stupidly insisted on payment. That is what I get for being greedy! So, no need to panic! It will not help anyway.

After a few deep breaths, I set my phone aside and think about the consequences his threats will have on my business. Should I give up on establishing my own business in Athens because of security reasons? Has my dream of being self-employed and making lots of money while living by the sea come to an abrupt halt? — No! I will not allow this incident to discourage me! Reading the short text messages once more, I store his number under 'Beware - Ladis'. He will not intimidate me that easily. From now on, I have to be more careful. As the sayings go, *better safe than sorry!* or *some things aren't worth all the money in the world*, or something like that.

Anyway, I must abide by these sayings! Granted, I will always face certain danger in my profession, but it is not like I have to run blindly toward them. As I mentioned before, I must get better at reading people over the phone and perhaps say no more often instead of regretting my decision to see a customer.

When I see the waiter at a neighboring table, I signal for another split of white wine. I turn off my phone and force myself to relax. After the waiter returns, I fill my glass and toast myself — I was incredibly lucky! The alcohol takes effect and I feel mellow and sleepy. I pay for my drinks and treat myself to a taxi ride home.

When I wake up the next morning, it is after 9:00 a.m. – The soles of my feet burn and sport abrasions. I was too distraught to notice last night, even after climbing into bed. Obviously all the wine I consumed numbed my brain and put me into a deep, dreamless sleep. I swing my legs out of bed and place my feet on the ground. I am rewarded with great pain. Stepping as lightly as I can, I shower, shave, brush my hair, and lotion my body from head to toe. I dab an antiseptic salve atop the scratches on my soles. It is an anti-inflammatory propolis ointment I always carry in my little travel pharmacy. Thankfully, I can treat my wounds instead walking on them to find a pharmacy.

I leave the bathroom on my tiptoes and prepare my breakfast. As I enjoy my breakfast outside on the balcony, my feet rest on the second chair cushioned by a towel. Ladis and his threats will not spoil my nice new life! After eating and enjoying another cup of coffee, I dial Violet's number. She answers immediately with a chirpy:

"Hello!"

"Hi, Violet, it's Anika. Good morning!"

"Hi, sweetie. Good morning! I'm getting ready to go to the market. So, are you joining me? Are we going to meet up there? How was business yesterday? Men are so much crazier about sex in the summer than winter. What do you think? During wintertime, I might not receive a single call for days. And that really drives me crazy! That usually never happens during the summer. Well, okay, maybe August, when most Greeks are on vacation and businessmen don't come to Athens. Sometimes I have two days off. However, during June and July, I'm usually swamped – Yesterday, I had to turn down two appointments because I was already booked at those times. Can you imagine! God, I was so annoyed. I mean, why couldn't they wait until the next day? But no, they're all itchy and want sex immediately. That's men for you, I tell you! I'm also convinced that some of my regulars look up a colleague or whoever when I'm not available at the time they want me. I don't care as long as they come back. I'm sure you know what I'm talking about."

Violet laughs youthfully and I take the opportunity to tell her about last night's unpleasant encounter.

"Honey, you must be careful! You can't just meet anyone. If you get a weird vibe about a man or, perhaps, he sounds drunk — or he's already unfriendly on the phone, then you should tell him no! I've had my share of bad experiences too when I was starting out here. Oh God, I don't even want to think about that! One guy tried to blackmail me, saying he was a police officer. He demanded to fuck me for free or else he'd arrest me for illegal prostitution and have me thrown in jail! I believed him. – I saw him for half a year and went to the hotels he ordered me to before I courageously told him off, saying I wouldn't service him anymore and he might as well arrest me. I also told him I would make his life a living hell and have him brought up on charges! — Yeah, and the next time he called I didn't go and that was that. I never heard from the man again! – Thinking back, I should have immediately asked to see his badge, but I was simply too scared and too naïve at the time! So, darling, always proceed with caution. Better safe than sorry! It's better to have a little less money in our wallets than ending up raped, beaten, robbed, or who-knows-what. We still make enough money! Always! – There's no need to service every guy who calls!"

"Yes, I'm hoping next time I'll be smarter. In any case, from now on, I'll be more vigilant. Believe me, I've learned my lesson. I never want to put myself in such a situation again. — You know, I had such a great day. I made 470 euros, so I thought I'd take on that customer and make it a super duper day! God, I was so stupid."

"Yes, you were. — Next time you have a great day, turn off the phone and treat yourself a little, enjoy your success! I'm sorry, here I am giving advice when, who knows, perhaps I would have done the same. Anyway, what's done is done. Just be sure to be careful from now on! He might try to lure you to another hotel. Or maybe that friend of his or some other buddies will call you. Pay attention when someone calls. Listen to the dialect. I'm sure his friends are also Albanians. If you're not sure, ask the man for his nationality. And whenever you're asked to come to a hotel near Piraeus, I'd be especially cautious. Next time someone wants you in the middle of the night, don't go to a small, unknown hotel. Go to the Hilton or the Grand Bretagne, those hotels are safer. — Never go to a dump like the one you were in. Understand! Stay away from those places!"

"Yes, I will, I promise! You're absolutely right. – It's good to have a friend I can talk to about things like this and other issues, of course!"

"You can talk to me about anything, darling! Be extra attentive during the next few weeks! – Okay, now stop thinking about everything that could have happened and instead, think about your future and remain positive! Don't give the man the power to destroy your new life. Keep your head up and continue your work. You are on your way to making good money. — So, I guess you're not up for meeting me at the market in Glyfada today, are you?"

"No, not really. I'll take a rain check. Let's do it next Thursday. My soles still hurt after running for my life on bare feet. I simply want to stay off them as much as possible. A quiet day will do me good right now. – Okay, that's enough of that. There's something else I've been meaning to ask you. Do you know someone who specializes in Botox? I'd like to get my forehead done as soon as possible. You know, I'm seeing the first signs of frown lines between my eyebrows. It makes me look old. I read somewhere Botox can get rid of wrinkles. — Any chance you know someone who performs such treatments?"

"Oh, darling, I've often thought of it. Listen up, I know a good dermatologist. Her name is Eleni. She used a laser on me when some small veins popped. They're so visible on my light skin compared to someone with a tanned complexion. – Maybe you have small veins that popped, but with your tan, they don't stand out. I'll call Eleni and ask if she does Botox. — You know, I'm scared of needles, but if you have it done and it looks good, then I'll have some work done too! Maybe that way I won't need a facelift. So, what do you say, should I call her?"

"Yes, please, call her! And also ask her about the cost of such a treatment."

"All right, sweetie. I'll call you as soon as I know something."

"Fantastic. Okay, Violet, I'll talk to you later. Have fun at the market!"

"I will. Take care of yourself, darling. Kisses! — Oh, don't forget, you're joining me next Thursday at the market!"

Once again, I am incredibly happy I have Violet to talk to. I would probably feel much different about my new home if I did not have her to confide in. That would be very sad. I know many prostitutes have no one to talk openly with about their professional concerns. For a long time, I was one of those women. Anyway, I should busy myself with something I enjoy or else my mind will wander back to last night and contemplate the scary question of how I can avoid running into Ladis again. — In case I get an appointment, I grab my handbag and pack it with freshly laundered lingerie, replenish my supply of condoms, top off the massage oil, etc. while I mull over what I should wear today. Seeing as my packed lingerie is black and I will be wearing black pumps, the dress should match. After some consideration, I opt for a black and white outfit: A white dress with laces in the back. I lay out coordinating fashion jewelry and think, perfect! Since there is no reason to dress yet, I neatly place the items conveniently on the bed. In a better mood again, I treat myself to another cup of coffee on the balcony. Again, I set my freshly salved feet on the chair with the towel while I lean back and read an online newspaper.

Around noon, my phone rings. My heart immediately skips a beat when I see the call is from an unknown number. Taking a deep breath, I pick up:

"Hello?"

"Yes, hello! Do you have an ad in *Athens World*?"

"Yes, I do. My name is Anika."

"Hi, Anika! My name is Petros. I'm a student. — Can I ask you a few questions?"

"Of course. What do you want to know?"

"How old are you? How much do you charge for an hour? And is it possible for you to come to my home? I live on Mesogeion Street."

Relieved, my heartbeat returns to normal because I am convinced Petros has no dealings with Ladis. So, I answer all his questions.

"Okay. That sounds good. Are you free tonight?"

"Yes, I am. However, in order for me to come to your home, I need your full name, address, and your landline number. – I see you've masked your phone number."

"Yes, I'm calling from my cell phone. Naturally, I'll give you all the information you need."

"Great. Any chance you can text it? I'll call you on your home phone to verify the number and to confirm the appointment, okay?"

"Yes, that's not a problem, but I'm not at home at the moment. I'm still at the university. I won't be home until after 8:00 p.m."

"Petros, what time do you want me to come?"

"Um, 10:00 p.m. would be great."

"Okay, that works for me."

"Anika, – I have one more question: do you have black leather clothes?"

"Yes, I do."

"Could you wear it for me?"

"Well, I won't come to your home dressed in black leather, but I can bring a few items along and change there. Do you have any other questions or wishes?"

"Yes — well, actually, no. I'm sorry. It's the first time for me with a prostitute."

"Okay, so what else did you want to ask me? Is it about the leather outfit? Do you want me to act out a certain scenario with you?"

"No, it's okay."

"You're sure?"

"Yes, really. Maybe I'm just nervous and excited at the same time."

"That can happen, Petros. Well, if there's nothing else, I'll be waiting for your text and then I'll call you at home after 8:00 p.m., okay?"

"All right. Ring the bell with the nametag Papadopoulou on it. That's my last name. I'll buzz you in. And you'll bring your leather clothing, right, Anika?"

"Yes, I will! Okay, Petros, until later. Have a nice day."

"Thanks, Anika, same to you!"

Thank God this was a normal phone conversation. A minute later, my Phone beeps and displays the information. – I save both his phone numbers under 'Petros - leather'.

While I'm busy deciding and putting together my leather outfit for this evening, I receive a call. Answering, my heart immediately starts racing:

"Hello?"

"Hello! I'm sure you understand me if you're the German lady from *Athens World*."

Phew! I am relieved. It is a man who speaks fluent German! My pulse is still rapid when I answer:

"Yes, of course. Are you German?"

"No, I'm Greek. When I was five my parents moved to Hanover, so I went to school in Germany. I also did my studies there and got a job. I returned to Athens a few years ago. — So, tell me, how long have you been in Athens?"

"I've been here for less than two weeks."

"That's what I thought. – I have a subscription to *Athens World* and I haven't seen your ad before. – Not that I know all the escort ads by heart! — So, could you describe yourself and tell me about your conditions?"

"Yes, of course. First off, my name is Anika..."

"Oh, where are my manners. My name is Janis!"

"Hi, Janis! Okay, I'm 35-years-old, blonde with blue eyes, and a slim figure. I make home and hotel visits and my fee is 150 for an hour of safe sex."

"That sounds good. When can we meet, Anika?"

"You tell me! What time and where would you like to meet?"

"Do you work throughout Athens?"

"Yes."

"For me, it's best to meet in Alimos. Do you know Alimos? It's along the coast."

"Yes, I know where it is. Alimos is fine."

"Great. Let's meet at the Novotta Hotel. It's on a small side road off Poseidonos Street. Do you think you can find it?"

"I'm sure I can. Can you perhaps give me the hotel address or phone number?"

"Unfortunately, I can't. I don't have either. But once you're in Alimos, search for the Alpha Bank and you'll see the little road where the hotel is located."

"Will do! Maybe the taxi driver has an idea where it is."

"Yes, that's highly likely. — So, tell me, do you have time this afternoon?"

"Yes, I do. What time exactly do you have in mind?"

"3:00 p.m. Can you make it by then?"

"Yes, that's not a problem. Are we in agreement?"

"Yes, we are! We can meet in front of the hotel and go in together. I, obviously, will pay for the room. I'll be in my parked car. When I see a slender blonde, I'll get out and meet you near the hotel. Okay, Anika?"

"Janis, I prefer if you get a room before hand and then call or text me the room number. Then I'll arrive within a few minutes. Would that work for you?"

"Hm... no, Anika. I don't like your way at all! I think it's best if we enter the hotel together. I am more comfortable with that."

So what, does he intend to check me out from the privacy of his car and take off if he does not like what he sees?

What other reason is there for not renting a room ahead of time? Maybe he does not trust that I will show up. Then he would be out the money for the room. I simply must ask. I am not meeting him in this manner. I am warier now.

"Janis, that's not the way I do business. I don't want to be seen in public with a client. Who knows, maybe someone you know will see us entering the hotel together and then you're faced with an awkward situation. Why aren't you willing to do it the usual way and wait for me in the room?"

"Well, Anika, here it goes, I'm too embarrassed to walk up alone to the front desk to ask for a room for a few hours. If we enter the hotel together, it looks like you're my girlfriend or mistress, not an ordered prostitute. That's my reason. Please, can we do it my way! I promise to be there and I won't keep you waiting. Scouts honor!"

I have to laugh, which feels great. It is the first time since yesterday's horrendous experience.

"All right, Janis. We'll do it your way! I'll you see at 3:00 p.m. at the Novotta Hotel in Alimos, okay?"

"That's great, Anika, I can't wait to see you!"

"Thanks. I'm also looking forward to meeting you, Janis."

Honestly, I could not care less if someone sees us. My concern is that he is going to see me in broad daylight, which might give my real age away. Then again, I will be wearing my sun hat and sunglasses. As long as I do not put my face directly in the sun, I will be fine for the few minutes it will take to enter the hotel lobby. Before I continue putting together my leather outfit for Petros, I Google the Novotta Hotel in Alimos.

36

To give my sore soles a break, I am taking a taxi today to the tram stop in Phaleron. Luckily, when I arrive, I can immediately board the waiting tram. Watching the Athenians and tourists get on at each stop, I easily identify the foreigners by their casual summer clothes and their big bags of beach gear. I notice how much thicker and longer the Greek women's hair is compared to Northern European women. I am a bit jealous. Being German my hair is rather thin. Thankfully, my natural curls provide at least a little volume. I am also glad I have slow hair growth for I do not have to shave my lower arms often. My phone rings. A Greek home phone number. In essence, it could be anybody, even Ladis or one of his buddies. Although I hope it is someone calling in regard to my ad, I cannot help but feel anxious. My heart starts racing as I answer:

"Hello?"

"Hello! Am I speaking with the German lady?"

"Yes, you are. Hi, my name is Anika!"

"Hello, Anika. I'm staying at the Sofitel Hotel across from the airport. Any chance you could see me this afternoon?"

"That depends. What time do you have in mind? Let me see … I could be there around 5:00 p.m."

"That's fine. But first, I'd like to know what you look like, your hair color, and so on. Can you describe yourself a little? Oh, and I'd like to know what it'll cost to have some fun with you."

"Certainly!"

I tell the nameless caller everything he wants to know.

"Blonde, perfect! So, are we on for this afternoon at 5:00 p.m. at my hotel?"

"Hm, I think I can make it. I might run a few minutes late, but I'll be there no later than 5:30 p.m. Is that okay with you?"

"Yes, that's fine. – I have no other plans today except for getting spoiled by a pretty blonde, followed by a nice dinner out."

"Fantastic. — I still need your name and room number, darling. I'll call you back to confirm, as well as later on, about 10 minutes before I arrive for our appointment. Is that okay?"

"Of course. And excuse me for not introducing myself, Anika, my name is Pierre Lotsen. I'm in room 718. Have you ever been to the Sofitel Hotel?"

"No, why?"

"Because you need a keycard for the elevator. You just can't come up to my room. So, it's good you are going to call me before you arrive, that way I know when to go down to the lobby to meet you. Which reminds me, how will I recognize you? What will you be wearing?"

"I'll be wearing a snug white dress, a white sun hat, black pumps, and a black handbag with shoulder straps. – I'm sure you'll recognize me. How will I recognize you?"

I cannot help imagining that this is another scenario where he can check me out and then skedaddle if he does not like what he sees… Pierre responds:

"I'm 1.90 meters tall, slim, blond hair, and I'll be wearing dark blue pants and a white shirt. — And just so you know, as soon as I see you, I'll approach you and greet you like we're good friends. No one will be the wiser."

"Great, that's the way I like it."

"Anika, does the hotel number show up on your phone?"

"Yes, I have it."

"Great, so you'll call me right back, correct?"

"Yes, Pierre."

I hang up, wait a few seconds, and then dial the hotel.

Fantastic! Another appointment. – Once again I am sure he is not Ladis' frontman. — Now all I have to do is repack and adjust my schedule. I had planned to return to my hotel room for the rest of the afternoon after my session with Janis. Then I could grab my already packed bag with the leather gear for my appointment with Petros. Now there is no time, but I have thought of a solution that will eliminate the need to schlepp the leather outfit around all afternoon. After my meeting with Pierre, I will take the airport bus to the city center and visit the big sex shop in Omonoia Square.

I will buy the seductive leather outfit I spied earlier. Hopefully, it is still there. If it has been sold, I will simply look around for something else that is sexy and leather. There is nothing wrong with expanding my work wardrobe. Happy about my fast and easy solution to my dilemma, I relax in my seat and stare at the big blue sea through the tram window.

I disembarked in Alimos and look around. The Alpha Bank is a few meters away. According to Janis, the Novotta Hotel is located on a nearby side street. Since I have a good 20 minutes before my appointment, I sit down at a sidewalk café table and order a Diet Coke. At 1:50 p.m., I leave and walk down Von Falk Street. I immediately see two hotels right next to each other. The first one is the Novotta Hotel. As is common on most of Athens' streets, parked cars line both sides. My gaze wanders over the parked vehicles until an opening silver car door about 50 meters down catches my attention. A tall, black-haired man wearing dark sunglasses gets out and locks the door. He looks in my direction, then slowly circles his car, and stands on a spot on the sidewalk. It could be Janis. As I stroll over to him, the man says:

"Is that you, Anika?"

"Yes, and you must be Janis, right?"

"Yes, I am! And as promised, I didn't make you wait. Okay ... shall we? — And if I may, you do look good!"

He leans down slightly to look under the brim of my sun hat at my sunglasses. He has a friendly face, so I offer a smile and say:

"Why, thank you. And thanks for not making me wait! It's quite hot out here in the sun."

"You can say that again! Not like in Germany. Do you like the Greek climate or is the heat too much for you?"

"No, I like it. It's just that I prefer to stay in the shade during the day."

"Yes, don't we all! Here we are. Up these stairs is the hotel entrance."

We open the door and enter the lobby. A cool air-conditioned breeze rushes out. I remove my sun hat and glasses, shake my hair, and use my fingers to fluff it up. Janis speaks softly to the receptionist and receives a room keycard.

"Fourth floor," Janis whispers as we walk toward the elevators. Janis is damn good-looking. I estimate he is in his mid-forties. He is wearing lightweight, sand-colored pants and a turquoise striped linen shirt. When he notices me checking him out, he asks:

"Everything okay?"

"Oh, yes, everything's fine."

We enter the elevator and face each other.

"Now I can finally see your blue eyes. You know, I love blue eyes! — I've only become aware of it since returning to Greece. There are hardly any. — So, are you a real blonde or do you dye your hair?"

"It's a dye job. My natural hair is darker, like my eyebrows."

Janis leans in close to inspect my eyebrows and frowns.

"Huh, they look real blonde to me. So, you're a natural blonde, just not a peroxide blonde," he says with a wink.

We exit the elevator on the fourth floor and search for our room. It is a common modern hotel room. Thankfully, someone left the drapes closed and the sun is not flooding the room. Janis slides his keycard through the slot of a box that acts as a switch to supply the room with electricity. The air conditioner kicks in immediately.

"I'm going into the bathroom to freshen up," I say, and disappear without waiting for a reply. It is fairly roomy with a stool. After hastily washing my hands, I slip out of my black lingerie and don a lacy bustier and matching panties. The panties accentuate my butt. This set makes me look damn sexy. I apply a touch of *Must de Cartier*, switch my phone to silent mode, grab my little pouch, and walk back into the room to the sound of Janis whistling through his teeth.

"Damn! You look ravishing! — I'm going to visit the bathroom briefly. Don't disappear on me now, baby!"

In the meantime, I pull the comforter back, grab my small oil bottle, a hairband, a regular and an extra-large condom from my toiletry bag, and assume a seductive pose. I inspect my image in the mirror. In a little while, Janis returns from the bathroom with a towel wrapped around his waist.

"Should I start spoiling you with a little massage? It's good for your skin, especially after a shower."

"I'd like to, but my wife might smell the oil on my skin. And what would I tell her?"

"I'm sure you'll shower thoroughly afterward! At least, it's what you should be doing if you don't want your wife to smell anything."

"You're probably right. Okay, but later you have to scrub my back! I can't reach it. — So, you want me on my stomach here?" Janis points to the spot on the bed to my left.

"Yes, here is fine. Lie down and relax and leave the rest to me!"

"Oh, I'm happy to do so. But first, let me see your blue eyes again."

He moves closer and holds my head between both hands.

"Beautiful! Your blue eyes are simply beautiful and your makeup emphasizes them perfectly! I like it! If I weren't so horny, I'd rather invite you out for a coffee and gaze into your eyes as we get to know each other."

Although I am flattered, I refrain from saying anything. Janis discards his towel on the bedside table and stretches out bare ass naked on his belly. There is hardly any hair on his body, which is preferable when giving a massage for my hands slide easier over the skin.

I kneel next to him, warm some oil in my hands, and start massaging his back from butt to shoulders with circular movements. This man feels like he only has muscles. No fat, no loose skin. I increase the pressure slightly as I repeatedly knead his back from butt to shoulders.

"That feels good, Anika," he whispers. Looking at his profile, his eyes are closed. When my hands arrive back at his buttocks, I slide one further down and between his thighs. Janis twitches briefly and then parts his legs a bit. An obvious invitation. I work my way up again and then back down to his butt, but this time one travels even further between his thighs and makes first contact with his tight scrotum. Another obvious invitation follows. Janis immediately raises his pelvis. Grabbing my hairband, I tie my hair into a ponytail so it will not get in the way when I go from behind between his legs to lick his genitals. The moment my tongue touches his perineum, Janis groans:

"Oh, my God, what are you doing? It's driving me insane!"

Ignoring him, I continue my delightful tongue play and slowly lick his testicles all over. He is the only one getting pleasure from this for I do not find it all that erotic to have a wet-licked ball sack right in front of my face, quite the opposite actually. I know how much a man is turned on by this act.

A long time ago, I incorporated this tongue massage as part of my service since I wanted to make my customers happy. Janis raises his buttocks even higher in an attempt to receive oral sex. Using my hands, I spread his butt cheeks for easier access and start licking around his anus and up over his balls and penis. Like a contortionist, I bend this way and that in order to lick between his spread legs. Every time I close in on his anus, I can tell how excited he gets. I roll a rubber over my right middle finger, spit on his anus, and spread the saliva around with light finger pressure while my other hand reaches from below and massages his cock. Gently, I stick my fingertip into his butt. Without further movement, half of my finger disappears as Janis pushes backward. So that is what he desires! As Janis moans and gyrates his pelvis, his anus eats up my finger. It is obvious he enjoys anal sex. Not a problem.

However, today I will only use one finger. The small silicone vibrator I like to use for such occasions stays in the pouch. Janis should not experience everything during our first appointment. Every now and then, I lean in and spit on his anus so the area stays wet and slippery. Janis is extremely excited. Right now, it would not take much for him reach an orgasm. But since the session is not even half over, I do not him want to come just yet. So, I continue for a little while longer before asking:

"How about it, sexy, you want to turn around so we can fuck?"

"I won't say no to that!" he replies and rolls onto his back. I quickly pull the condom off my middle finger and drop it on the floor next to the bed.

"I could have easily come during your massage, but it's also nice to be able to look at you again. — Damn, you look so hot in that outfit!"

"Thank you, darling! How do you want to take me? – Should I lie down or sit on you?"

"Sit on me and take off your top. I want to see your tits bounce up and down."

I reach for a new rubber, lick the remaining oil off his cock, and roll the rubber over his erection. After lowering myself onto his cock, I remove my bustier and set it aside. – I start stroking the curves of my breasts and playing with my nipples.

Watching me, Janis lies motionless with his hands crossed behind his head. I start moving up and down in a slow, steady rhythm while gyrating my hips. For my breasts to bounce, I must move faster. However, there is plenty of time for that. Once I feel Janis moving and actually participating, I lean further back and increase my speed so my puppies bounce. Before long, Janis' thrusts become more urgent. As if frenzied, Janis fucks to reach climax. As he finishes coming, I let his cock slowly slide out of my pussy while monitoring the condom. Once his penis is in the clear, I remove the rubber and toss it on the floor next to the other one. Janis is lying prone on his back with his eyes closed, catching his breath. I dismount him and wait patiently for his breathing to return to normal.

"Darling, I'm going to disappear into the bathroom," I whisper as I get out of bed. I retrieve the rubbers and toss them in the bathroom trash can. I reposition my panties and return to the main room. Janis is sitting up in bed with his back against the headboard while one of his hands pats the mattress beside him, beckoning me.

"Come over here and sit or are you in a hurry?"

"No."

"That was absolutely great, Anika!"

"Good, that makes me happy!"

"No, I really mean it! This was the first time a woman put her finger in my butt."

He laughs, shaking his head.

"I mean, it's the first time I had a finger in my butt. I thought only men did it. — But that doesn't mean I'm gay!"

"Okay, but you liked anal action."

"Yes, — because a woman did it! I wouldn't let a man do that to me. You believe me, don't you?"

"Yes, of course. And let me tell you something, you're not the only man who likes it."

"Why, you know a lot of guys who enjoy it? — I mean, I know there are toys for couples, like strap-on dildos for the woman to fuck the man..."

"Don't worry, you're definitely not the only guy who has discovered he enjoys anal pleasures. I'd say at least 70 percent of all men like it — and they're not gay, mind you."

We sit a while longer on the bed and chitchat. Janis tells me he misses life in Germany, but his wife and three small children are not willing to start over in a foreign country. When I glance at my watch, Janis interprets it as a sign that our session is over. He gets up, grabs his wallet, and hands me 150 euros. I pocket the money and we go into the bathroom to shower. – I thoroughly scrub his back with soap. After dressing, we leave the room and walk to the elevator. Janis says:

"I like it when the hotel staff thinks we're lovers!" Before walking through the big, tinted entrance door of the hotel together, he kisses me on the lips.

37

Once Janis and I part ways, I check my phone and see that Violet called. Before I can return her call, I have to catch a cab to the Sofitel Hotel. After crossing Poseidonos Street, I walk to a bus stop and stand at the bus pull-in lane waving at yellow taxis. Luckily, I only have to wait a minute. I lean back in the cool taxi and call Violet:

"Hello?"

"Hi Violet, it's Anika. I'm returning your call."

"Yes! I called because I talked to Eleni, the dermatologist in Vouliagmeni. And yes, she offers Botox treatments!"

"Oh, that's great. — Did she say how much a treatment costs?"

"Yes. For the whole forehead and around the eyes it's 300 euros. – What do you think, too expensive? I don't know what the usual cost is for such treatment."

"I think her price is average. I asked around a little in Germany. Hospitals charge the most, up to 600, and the cheapest treatments are at so-called Botox parties. But I would never attend such an event. Considering Eleni will also do around the eyes, I think her price is acceptable. I'd rather go to someone you know than look around for a better price and end up with a doctor we know nothing about. — I'd feel more confident with a smoother forehead given the fact that I pass myself off as 35-years-old."

"Yeah, I understand that only too well. — Okay, let's see how the Botox procedure looks on you and then I'll also get some areas done! At our age, it's okay to give your self-confidence a boost. And 300 is not a huge investment. We're talking about two customers!"

"Yes, that's the way I look at it. Can you text me Eleni's phone number and address? Then I can call her for an appointment."

"Of course, no problem. And tell her I sent you!"

"Naturally! Do you want to come along when I go for my appointment?"

"I don't know yet … maybe. It all depends on whether I have to see any clients."

"Yes, of course. We'll play it by ear, okay?"

"We will! Do you have another customer lined up for today? I have to get ready for James now. For years, he's been seeing me every other month or so. He's an easy customer. No oral sex. We merely do some petting and then fuck. It never takes him more than 20 minutes. He cleans up with a wet wipe, dresses, places 150 on my pillow, then gives me a kiss, and pinches my butt to say goodbye."

Violet's brief description of her customer makes me laugh before I can answer her:

"Yes, I'm on my way to the Sofitel. At 10:00 p.m., I'm meeting a student in the inner city. He wants to see me in leather. — Everything's going well! I just saw Janis at the Novotta Hotel. He speaks fluent German. Do you know him?"

"A guy named Janis who speaks fluent German? No, I don't think so. I also don't know a student living in the city center. Who are you meeting at the Sofitel?"

"His name is Pierre Lotsen."

"Nope, haven't heard of him either. — Anyway, good luck, darling, and take good care of yourself! Remember, better safe than sorry!"

"Yes, I will. Have a nice day, Violet!"

Shortly after our conversation, Violet texts me Elenis' address and phone number. I call her office immediately and make an appointment for tomorrow morning at 11:00 a.m. I am curious how it will turn out! Will the injections hurt? What will I look like? How long will the treatment last? I really do not know much about it. Nevertheless, I am sure Eleni will tell me everything I need to know.

The cab driver interrupts my reverie and announces we are about 10 minutes away from the airport. I thank him and pull my compact out to give myself a once over. — I could not look better! I dab a splash of perfume behind my ears, then grab my phone and call Pierre's room at the hotel. He answers on the first ring and tells me he is on his way to the lobby. The taxi fare is quite expensive – 28.50 – and I did not even travel from Piraeus. I am sure that would be an additional 10 euros. Meaning, taking a cab back and forth to see a client at the Sofitel Hotel leaves me with a little more than half my earnings. I do not like that at all! — I will have to think about a new rate for visits to this hotel, but that can wait.

Now it is Pierre's time. When I enter the lobby, I recognize him immediately because there is only one tall, blond man and he is wearing a white shirt and dark blue pants. As he approaches, his left thumb is casually hooked on his pants' pocket, He says:

"Hi, Anika, nice to meet you!"

"Hi, Pierre!" I reply as he gives me a peck on the cheek. We take our time strolling through the lobby toward the elevator while making idle chitchat. Pierre glances at his watch and says:

"You're punctual. That's a German trait, correct?"

"So they say. In any case, it's important to me to be on time. Obviously, light traffic always helps."

Pierre slides his keycard through the slot next to the elevator and the door opens to a bell-like ding. Once inside, I remove my sun hat, shake out my hair, and quickly style it with my hand as Pierre watches my every move. – Although I cannot read his mind, he does not seem disappointed with me. It reassures and calms me, as well as provides me with more confidence. I smile at him and ask:

"Where are you from, Pierre?"

"Denmark."

The elevator stops on the seventh floor and we walk side by side to the room. Actually, it is a modern and elegantly furnished suite. I put my hat down and turn to face him. The party abruptly starts! Pierre relieves me of my handbag, places it on the desk, takes me in his arms, and kisses me so passionately that there is no time to catch my breath. He never mentioned kissing when we made our arrangement over the phone. However, I play along since his breath is not unpleasant. All I have to do is adapt to his kissing technique so he does not hurt me.

"Man, you, your blonde mane, and that white dress turn me on!" he manages to say between frantic French kisses. One hand holds me in an embrace, the other reaches down and slides up my dress. Although I would like to say something, there is no opportunity with his tongue constantly in my mouth. When he takes a break from his initial lustful assault, I quickly speak up:

"Wow, you're a wild one! What do you say; can I go to the bathroom and change into the pretty lingerie I brought along for you?"

Pierre pulls me close again and starts kissing me with his tongue playing deep in my mouth. He mumbles in between:

"Yes. Go! — Don't be long. I'm crazy about you."

I try to push him gently away since he is not loosening his grip on me. After a few more attempts to steal kisses, he finally releases me. Quickly grabbing my bag, I disappear into the bathroom. Phew! Pierre is obviously starving for attention. Now dressed in a black push-up bra with matching lace panties and strapless stockings, I walk back into the room in my high-heel pumps. – Pierre has undressed and draped his clothes neatly over a chair. He has a slight tan and a nice body.

"Wow!" he says. "Come and lie down on the bed and spread your legs wide! I want to lick you until you come! — Tell me, can you stay longer? Perhaps for another hour? Looking at you now, I'm dreaming of a few more things I'd like to do with you!"

I am conflicted. I could stay the extra hour and make more money, but then I might not be able to purchase the sexy leather outfit at the sex shop in Omonoia Square. I still have to travel an hour by bus to get to the city center and then it might take another half an hour to get to the store, by which time it is questionable if they will still be open. Moreover, I cannot show up at Petros' place without a leather outfit. Pierre is from Denmark, only passing through Athens, whereas Petros lives here. Perhaps he will enjoy what I am going to do to him and become a regular customer. Yes, I am dreaming, but it is a possibility. The chances of seeing Pierre again are slim, so I say:

"No, unfortunately, I can't, baby. I have another appointment afterward. Here's what we can do! Should you still want me to stay longer once the hour is up, I might be able to postpone my other appointment for 30 minutes. —Okay?"

I have compromised so as not to rob Pierre of his dreams.

"Yeah, okay. We'll see, sexy lady. Man, you have a terrific figure and such a hot snatch!"

I pulled off my black lace panties and lie on the bed with my upper body supported by several pillows and my legs spread far apart. Pierre kneels between my stocking-clad legs and lustfully leers at my exposed pussy. I believe he is just thinking about extending our session because of his current sexual tension. Once he has an orgasm and the pressure is relieved, he might be glad he did not commit to a longer session. — I have experienced this before. Some clients are so horny they think hours or even days are needed to fulfill all their sexual needs. Needless to say, for the majority, this does not ring true. Once they have an orgasm, they can think with their big brain. Pierre bows down and shoves his tongue deep into my pussy. This is much more pleasant than having his tongue shoved in my mouth. I do not mind passing the time in this manner. Now and then, and without hurting me, he circles my clitoris. I moan a little to reassure him he is doing a good job. Wow! This is easy money. As I watch Pierre utterly devoting himself to my pussy, I consider how I am going to satisfy him. Maybe he has already thought of something and I am racking my gray brain matter for no reason. A good 20 minutes have passed since we entered the room. He seems perfectly content with what he is doing.

Maybe it is time I treat him to a little orgasm. As enthusiastically as he has been licking me, I am sure he would enjoy that. I start gyrating my hips while increasing the urgency of my moans.

Pierre immediately responds in kind and starts darting his tongue in and out of me. That is it, baby. Soon, I will reward you! I hold him in suspense for a little longer and fake an orgasm. Unable to hold still, I wriggle around on the bed and snap my legs shut, trapping his head. Pierre simply continues undeterred. He is a real pussy connoisseur! To end my fake climax, I start relaxing my limbs and let my body sink into the pillows from exhaustion. Pierre is proud as a peacock. He runs his tongue over my vulva again, which tickles a bit, so I groan:

"Oh, baby, it's obvious you know what you're doing. I don't experience that often. But now she needs a two-minute break before she's ready for action again."

"So you liked it, Anika?"

"You can say that again, darling. Where did you learn to do it like that?"

"Oh, I once had a girlfriend who really enjoyed getting licked. Fucking wasn't her thing. I liked her a lot, so I tried pleasing her. — But, I also like fucking pussy. Maybe I'm not so good at it. You be the judge because I want to fuck you now, Anika, my sweet little blonde German whore!"

He leans in close as he talks and suddenly I have his tongue in my mouth again, which now tastes of my pussy. Even though I find it disconcerting that my pussy leaves such strong taste on a client's tongue, actually tasting it does not disgust me. My pussy tastes healthy. We smooch for a while and when I sneak a peek at his cock, I see it is standing at attention. I blindly reach for my toiletry bag, remove a rubber, and as Pierre briefly pauses to catch his breath, I quickly speak up:

"Look what I have. Why don't I put it on? Then you're ready to go for a nice fuck! — You do want to fuck me, right?"

"I'm not sure. Oh, what the heck. Give me the condom! I don't want to wait any longer."

Pierre does the deed himself. I get down on my knees and hands and raise my butt up in the air so it looks enticing. Basically, it is an invitation. Pierre has no qualms about accepting my offer and moves behind me. He shoves his cock between my thighs, bends over my back, and starts covering it with kisses. Straightening up, he searches for the entrance of my pussy. Using his finger, he parts my slit and pushes his Danish boner deep into me. He fucks me slowly and evenly by moving his pelvis back and forth until he is close to reaching climax. His movements become faster and more urgent, and then he comes while crying out in relief. That went smoothly! I am certain he is happy and exhausted and no longer interested in more time with me.

"Thanks, Anika! — I simply love blonde women," he says, laughs, and then continues:

"I was glad when I heard you were a blonde. I don't think I would have gone for a brunette German no matter how incredibly attractive I find your age. No, I think your blonde hair was the deciding factor. I'm into Nordic women! — You were just what I needed. I enjoyed it, baby. Thank you!"

"Thank you, Pierre. Do you mind if use the bathroom?"

"No, of course not! Go right ahead."

As I slide off the bed, Pierre joyfully stretches out and crosses his arms behind his head. I quickly hop in the shower, towel off, and dress. A swift glimpse in the mirror reveals that all I have to do is reapply my eye makeup, brush my hair, and use a little hair spray to hold it in place. All done! It is 5:50 p.m. when I turn on my phone's ringer and notice a missed call. I will look at it in a bit. Presently, I need to finish up with Pierre so I can depart for the city center as soon as possible. Pierre is standing in his underwear now.

"Too bad I'm leaving tomorrow morning, otherwise, I would have taken you again. — Here's your money. Keep the change! Bye, Anika!"

He hands me 170 euros and leans in to kiss me on the cheek. I am flattered by his compliment and happy about the tip. I thank him for his generosity.

Pierre remembers I cannot enter the elevator without his keycard and quickly puts on a shirt, pants, and shoes. When I enter the elevator and turn around, the last thing I see is his beaming face before the door closes.

38

I think about how great my meeting with Pierre went as I cross the street in front of the Sofitel to get to the airport building from where buses run to all areas of Athens. Sitting in the bus waiting for it to depart, I reflect on recent events. I have been so busy I have not had any gloomy thoughts about Ladis. And, although the soles of my feet burn a little, I have no problem walking. — It is important for me and my new business to meet nice customers who respect me as a prostitute even if they cannot pay my desired fee. I simply must listen to my gut instinct every now and then instead of overthinking it. – Certainly easier said than done.

Now, if I come again to the Sofitel Hotel, I will either ride the bus or raise my fee. If I charge 180, at least I will recoup one cab fare. It is a start.

The bus fills up with passengers with their bags stacked in the aisle in the rear. Finally, the bus gets under way. I grab my phone and check out the missed call. A Greek cell phone number. – Maybe I will be lucky and he will call back. As we reach Athens' city center, I exit at a stop adjacent to a subway station for a ride to Omonoia Square.

It is 7:40 p.m. when I set foot in the sex shop. I am greeted by the same staff: the grumpy man and bored woman. Perhaps they are an old married couple. Who knows, who cares. – This time I am not the only customer. There are two more. A young man is looking at porn and a middle-aged man is hanging around the corner featuring sex toys. I immediately head for the clothes section and instantly find the black leather outfit I want. I breathe a sigh of relief. Now, I am all set for this evening's appointment with Petros! Unfortunately, it costs 149 euros. Quite expensive. Maybe I can negotiate the price...let's see what the staff says. Who knows how long this outfit has been hanging there? Perhaps it is my lucky day and Mr. and Mrs. Personality will be happy to be rid of it for less. Let's see … who am I most likely to make headway with? I opt for the woman.

"Excuse me, I have a question."

"Yes?"

"I'm interested in this leather outfit, but I find the price too steep. If there's any chance you'll let it go for 100, I'll buy it!"

The woman looks at the price tag and then at her partner. He is in his own little world, staring straight ahead, looking at whatever with that gloomy expression of his.

"Spiros!" she yells.

Spiros jumps at his name and turns toward her. The woman gestures for him to come over. He approaches, slowly shuffling his feet. His expression never changes. The two speak quietly in rapid Greek. Needless to say, all is lost on me. From their gestures, I can tell a discount is certainly possible. Finally, the lady looks at me and says:

"If you don't need a receipt, you can have it for 110."

Not a bad counter offer! But I will not let her see I am pleased. Instead, I nod my head sideways as I have often seen Greek women do when they agree with something and calmly say:

"Okay! — Wrap it up, please."

In my head, I am celebrating — yippee! I received a 40-euro discount because 1. I opened my mouth and 2. I am willing to purchase it without a receipt! My sudden joyous mood sours. I believe it is transactions like mine that began the Greek crisis. That is what happens when people do not pay their taxes. — Although it is the truth, I prefer to ignore it and get back to feeling good about my new sexy leather outfit.

However, my bad conscience prevails. I try to ease it by telling myself that my transaction involved only a tiny amount... It is people who avoid paying their large tax debts, not the owners of this little establishment. The thought grows — small sums also add up to a lot! — Trying to think about something else, I purposefully look through the sexy clothing. Here and there, I see an outfit I like and imagine how I would look in it. Regrettably, I am not buying anything else. Carrying my newfound happiness in a chic bag, I finally leave the store and head to the subway station at Omonoia Square. Since it is after 8:00 p.m. and time to call Petros, I dial his number and after a few rings, he answers and says something in Greek.

"Hi, Petros. Is that you?"

"Anika?"

"Yes! Are we still on for our date? – I can be at your place at 10:00 p.m., right on time."

"Perfect. You have leather clothes with you, correct?"

"Yes, I do. All right then, see you later!"

"Okay, Anika, see you later!"

Glancing at the time, I decide to wait another half hour before leaving for Petros' place. I walk to the nearest café and eat half a pita bread with spinach. It not only keeps my hunger in check, spinach is also healthy.

When the 30 minutes are up, I hail the next available taxi I see and show the driver the note with Petros' address. He nods, I get in, and off we go. Petros lives in a neighborhood with similar-looking six-story buildings. The intercom next to the large entrance door has at least 30 names on it. Finding the nametag with Papadopoulou, I ring the bell. The buzzer sounds a moment later and I step into a sizeable hallway with a staircase of light brown marble.

As usual, I check my appearance as I ride the elevator up. Stopping on the fourth floor, I get out and the hallway is completely dark. No light is on and I cannot see a switch. One apartment door opens a crack and a young black-haired man waves at me. When I am nearer, I say:

"Hello, Petros."

"Hi, Anika. Come into my room. Excuse the mess, my roommates and I are students and we don't really know how to keep a clean house."

"As long as your bed or wherever we're going to have fun is clean, it doesn't matter. Oh, and I'm a bit picky when it comes to the bathroom," I reveal honestly. I do not want to roll around on dirty sheets or shower in a filthy bathroom.

"No, that's all clean. We have a cleaning lady for that," Petros says as he shoves me into his room. His desk is constructed of two sawhorses with a sheet of plywood on top that holds two computer screens, keyboards, hard drives, papers, folders, pens, magazines, books, a glass, a coffee cup, and all sorts of other things. Everything is discarded in no particular order, at least, not that I notice. Against the wall across from the desk stands a sleeper sofa. The remaining walls of the room are occupied by tall shelves and posters. One is of a blonde beauty clad in tight leather clothes posing on a motorcycle. Another poster depicts motorcycles flying through space. Then, there is a poster of a woman dressed completely in leather wearing a cat mask.

"Cute," I say. "Please show me the bathroom so I can change into my outfit."

"Can't you change in here? I'd love to watch."

Oh, my God! No, that's definitely out of the question!

"Petros, I'm not comfortable with that. I always change in private, not to mention, I have to use the toilet..."

"Bummer! Could you at least leave the bathroom door ajar once you're done peeing, that way I can see a little bit when you change clothes? — I'm sorry; I didn't think you would mind!"

"All right! You can wait in front of the door and watch once I open it a crack, okay?"

"Great, Anika, thanks! – I promise, I'll be quiet and won't take any pictures."

"I don't want you to take photos of me! Don't tell me you have a hidden camera set up in here?" I ask, suddenly on alert.

"Uh, no, – but I was hoping you'd let me take a few shots of you in your leather outfit."

"Absolutely not, Petros!" I reply horrified. "I'm not a fashion model, I'm a call girl! I'm not letting myself be photographed in sexy lingerie. You called the wrong girl if you want a model! I came here to have sex with you, that's it! Do you understand? — I don't mind talking about your sexual preferences and perhaps accommodating you, but taking pictures is a no-no."

Petros' expression is a mixture of surprise and disappointment. He must have thought he could simply take pictures of me. Amazing!

"Sorry, I was wrong ... what a pity! Although, I also have something else in mind. Should I address it now?"

"Yes, please do! — I'm all ears!"

"Okay, I want to touch you and your leather clothes and then fuck you, wearing a condom of course. At the end, I would like to come on your face. Seeing that in porn movies always turns me on. I've been meaning to do that for quite a while now. Oh, yeah, and I thought about taking a few photos of you with my cum on your face."

I stand there shaking my head, not believing what I am hearing. Then again, why am I surprised? It is clear he wants to reenact a pornographic scene that titillated him. Once he had those pictures of me, he would look at them every time he jerks off. Who knows, perhaps he might show them to his closest friends or maybe post them on Facebook...

"Petros, I don't care for someone coming on my face. However, I'll make an exception for you! But, you have to let me know when you're about to come because I don't want cum ending up in my hair, nor do I want it in my mouth! And don't even think about having me lick your boner clean! I only practice safe sex and that is not part of it. If you tell me when you're about to come, I will pull my hair back so you can squirt in my face. As soon as you're done, I'll disappear into the bathroom to wash my face. You won't have much time to enjoy the sight; we're not making a porno! So ... do you agree to my terms?"

Petros pouts, reminiscent of a little boy who did not get his way.

"Yes, I do. I never thought it would be such a big deal. But then I told you this is my first time with a prostitute. How would I know what's allowed and what isn't? In movies, everything goes."

"Now you know. Those are my rules. — Anyway, why don't you show me the bathroom!"

"Okay, follow me. It's down the hallway to the left, the last door on the right. I hung a fresh towel on the hook behind the door. Let me know if there's anything else you need."

"How about soap?"

"There's a bar on the sink and in the shower."

"Great, thank you, Petros!"

After closing the bathroom door, I sit down on the toilet. I think about Petros and hope he is not so disheartened he cannot get a boner. Otherwise, his first time with a prostitute will be a disaster! Therefore, as agreed, I will crack the door so he can sneak peeks while I change. I will simply have to put on a good performance. Having laid out my new leather outfit, I tie my hair up. I open the door a crack and go about my business without paying attention to what is going on in the hallway.

Slowly, I brush the shoulder straps of my white stretch dress to the side. Normally, I would take the dress off by pulling it over my face, but since that is not sexy, I let it slide down my back with my backside facing the door. When it sticks on my hips, I move them slowly so the dress creeps down inch by inch until my butt and satin slip are exposed. Thrusting out my butt provocatively, I strip off the dress the rest of the way. Folding it neatly in half, I hang it on the towel rod next to the sink. In only a bra and panties, I spin around once while watching myself in the bathroom mirror and when I stop, I make sure I face the partly open door so Petros can get a good look at my front side.

Sliding the bra straps off my shoulders, I pull it down to my midriff and expose my breasts. Then I undo the clasp and casually drape it over my dress on the towel rod. Moving my hands to the sides of my panties, I slowly and suggestively remove them.

Standing there naked, I regard myself in the mirror over the sink. What should I put on first, the leather skirt or top? I opt for the skirt. It has front and back panels of leather with metal rings attached to the stretchy material holding the pieces together. Since the skirt gives, I can step into it and slide it up my legs and over my thighs. The metal rings on the side stand out nicely on my tanned skin and look sexy. The corset is held in place by two Velcro straps. One is around the neck and the other down along the back, making it easy to put on and adjust. It is designed to cup and push the breasts up while boldly leaving the nipples exposed. Once I have finished changing, I get rid of the hair clip and shake my head so my hair transforms into a wild mane. Now ready for my main performance, I grab my little toiletry bag with the condoms and whatnot and turn to face the slightly open door.

Petros watches from the dark hallway of the apartment half a meter away from the door. When he realizes I am ready to come out, he quickly turns on the hallway light which, thankfully, is not bright.

"Thanks for letting me watch you change! That was fucking awesome!" Petros says as I walk by him. I am glad to hear it! Back in his room, I ask for cozier lighting. Petros experiments with different light sources and finally decides to leave the floor lamp next to the hide-a-bed on and a lamp above the desk. Since he is not the type to take the initiative, it is up to me to get things rolling. I snuggle up to him and start stroking his hair, shoulders, and arms. Then, I touch the area of his pants that interests me the most. Thankfully, I feel something hard under the material. Petros is fascinated and watches my every move. He cups my leather-clad butt and starts caressing it tenderly. As I continue to wriggle around, tease, and seduce him, I feel his growing excitement. Since he is still wearing his polo shirt, I reach to remove it, but he quickly lends a hand and tosses it onto an armchair. While I lick his nipples, my hands are busy with his fly. Here too, he intervenes and takes off his jeans and underwear together. Rigid and taut, it bobs against me. I like that. Petros grabs my hips and pushes his crotch firmly against my leather skirt. I do not think it would be difficult to bring him to climax. Nevertheless, it is too soon. I must prolong our foreplay. He mentioned, among other things, wanting to fuck me, so I try to steer our foreplay slowly in that direction.

"Come on and take a look at my pussy before you fuck her!" I instruct him and sit down on the sofa bed with my legs spread apart. I part my labia with two fingers so he can look at my pink hole. As Petros kneels before me on the floor and stares at my pussy in rapt fascination, I use two fingers of my left hand to spread my lips even more while the fingers of my right hand massage my hole.

"Holy mother of god, this turns me on immensely!" he says with slightly reddened cheeks, then adds:

"Your pussy is fan-fucking-tastic. May I lick it?"

"Yes, by all means, knock yourself out!"

I spread my legs even further and thrust out my pussy so it is directly in front of his face. Timidly, he starts licking my labia. He is extremely gentle. I have no problem believing it is his first time, so I leave him alone to freely explore. Gaining courage, he properly licks and rubs his face against my wet pussy. I come right out and say:

"Come on, it's time for you to fuck me! Your tongue play has made my pussy all hot."

"Great! You have a condom?" Petros asks.

"Yes, hold on, I'll put it on."

"I can do that myself, no problem."

"All right, but make sure it's on properly!"

"Yes, I will!"

As Petros busily rolls the rubber over his cock, I ask:

"You want to fuck me here on your bed or at the desk?"

"Would my desk be all right?"

"Yes, I'll lean over it and you can take me from behind. Is that okay with you?"

"Yes! I like that."

We move to the desk and I positioned myself in front of his desk. Petros pushes his cock deep into me and groans. After a few thrusts, he says:

"I believe I'm done fucking you. I'd rather come now!"

Before he finishes speaking, I feel his cock sliding out of me. By the time I turn around, he has already removed the rubber and his right hand is holding his unprotected penis.

"Do you want to sit back down on the sofa bed? That way I can kneel over you and come on your face without difficulty," he asks.

"Yes, that's fine, but don't forget to warn me!"

Sliding the scrunchy from my wrist, I tie my hair back. I lean back on the sleeper sofa. Petros kneels and yanks on his wiener in front of my face. All I have to do is wait for him to warn me. Watching him closely, I see his face contorting. The entire time he is jerking off, he stares at my breasts.

"Now!" he suddenly gasps. "I'm coming!"

With a feeling of disgust, I quickly close my eyes before his warm cum lands on my eyelids, nose, and lips. Petros' groans sound tormented. I keep my eyes and mouth tightly closed until I hear his panting subside and he gets up off the hide-a-bed. I hastily reach for the tissue I had tucked under the hem of my skirt for wiping the sticky goo from my face. Without a word, because I am afraid some residue might enter my mouth, I hurry into the bathroom to wash my face. Okay, that is over and done with! I really find that practice disgusting. Granted, I could refuse this service, but right now, I need every cent I can earn. I appreciate every customer who treats me decently and pays me well. However, every profession comes with tasks that are not particularly pleasant. It is not only a dilemma faced by prostitutes. Walking back into Petros' room, I find him seemingly exhausted on his sleeper sofa.

"Are you okay? Was it what you expected?" I want to know.

"It was even more exciting. Absolutely fantastic! Thanks, Anika. I'm sorry you didn't like it all that much. Anyway, I have a question."

"Shoot!"

"Do you have other leather clothes, like boots and gloves?"

"Yes, I have those too."

"Would you come and see me again and wear the boots and gloves? I think it'll feel absolutely great when you touch my cock with leather gloves."

"Of course, no problem."

"Could we do it with me squatting over you, but this time, you give me a blowjob, with a condom obviously, and when I'm ready, I take my dick out of your mouth, pull off the condom, and squirt on your face?"

"Yes, Petros, we can do all that. Just make sure to make the appointment early in the morning. You know, I don't carry my leather outfit with me on a daily basis. The sooner I know the better."

"Sure, Anika. Where do you live?"

"In Piraeus."

"Okay, that's not just around the corner. — In any case, thank you for today, Anika."

"My pleasure. Can I take a quick shower?"

"Of course."

I vanish into the bathroom, shower, dry off, dress, and pack my things. Thankfully, I no longer feel repulsed. Instead, I am glad that despite my initial misgivings, everything worked out well and Petros wants to see me again. When I reenter his room, he hands me 150 euros and asks if I would care for a drink. I politely decline and Petros dons his underwear to escort me to the apartment door. Greatly satisfied, I step into the elevator 30 seconds later and walk out of this typical Athenian apartment building in good spirits.

39

Out on the road, it is dark, hot, and noisy. Although I am in a great mood, for some reason I feel tired, actually exhausted. Checking my phone, I see I received a text message:

Please send info.

It does not take long to make up my mind. I will not give out information via text, period! I text back:

Call me for information!

A moment later, my phone rings. I immediately answer:

"Hello?"

"Hi! You said to call for information."

"Yes, hi, I'm Anika. And you are?"

"George. Please tell me a little about yourself."

"I'm 35 years old, blonde with blue eyes, and a slim figure. I charge 150 euros for one hour of safe sex."

"Thank you."

He hangs up. That is okay, I am spent for the day anyway. I could not take on another client. I look for a bus running to Syntagma Square so I can ride the subway to Piraeus. While waiting at the bus stop, my phone rings.

"Hello!"

"Yeah, it's me, George. Sorry about hanging up on you, I had to. So, 150 you said?"

"That's correct."

"Would you lower your price? I mean, all I want is a blowjob."

"No, my rate is for one hour of sex, which includes oral sex."

"Oh, okay! I'm only interested in a good blowjob. Any chance you can make an exception? I'm quite young and not well off."

"No, baby, I'm sorry. I don't give discounts to young men. You'll have to try elsewhere. I'm sure you'll find a prostitute here in Athens who'll blow you for less — but it's not going to be me."

"Oh, that's too bad!"

"Good night, baby, and good luck!"

This time I am the one who hangs up. The right bus stops and I get in. Not many people travel by bus at this time of day, so there is no problem getting a seat. As the bus drives off, I close and rest my eyes for a few minutes. – I might be tired, but I am also thirsty and my stomach is growling. Huh? Not sated despite the half a pita bread with spinach? The rumblings are unmistakable. Not a problem because unlike the cow town I come from, here in Athens I can always find a place serving food at whatever time of day.

As I disembark the bus before Syntagma Square, I notice a fast food restaurant and head directly for the door. I am in the mood for a double burger and a large Coke, even if it is not a healthy or light meal. I better not tell Violet; otherwise, I will have to listen to a lecture about fast food and its effect on women of advanced age. Looking at my watch, I see it is just after 11:00 p.m. After receiving my order on a paper-lined tray, I carry it outside and sit at one of the establishment's small tables. I had forgotten how great a double burger tasted and savor each bite. How much did I make today? 450 and a 20-euro tip. Another good day's work!

Once finished with my late dinner, I lean back and watch passersby assemble on both sides of the road at a pedestrian crossing, where they wait for the light to change to green and cross in a wide stream. As soon as it switches to red, the flow of endless people stops only to continue as soon when it changes back to green. Having watched this play for a while, I grab my phone and call Violet. She does not answer. I send a short text message informing her of my Botox appointment with Eleni tomorrow at 11:00 a.m. Glancing at my watch, it is 11:40 p.m. and I decide to call it a day. Heading for the subway station, I catch a train to Piraeus.

Friday, I rise at 7:30 a.m. feeling rested and fit. The abrasions on my feet are barely noticeable. Nevertheless, I treat them again with my propolis ointment. Outside on the balcony it is still nice and cool. Granted, it depends on the person. As a German, if this were my first day here, I would find it quite warm. Looking down over the railing of my balcony, I see the thermometer at the pharmacy. Right now, it is in the shade displaying a temperature of 28 degrees Celsius. I am eating breakfast at my little table dressed only in panties and a bra. My appointment for Botox treatment is at 11:00 a.m. I cannot wait to see the result. I am hoping the injected areas will not be visible or swollen so I can still work today. – Granted, I might not have a scheduled appointment with a customer yet, but I am not worried about it as the day is still young. Critically inspecting my finger and toenails, I realize I could also do with at least a manicure. I am going to ask Maria in Glyfada if she can fit me in later, sometime early this afternoon.

After a long and substantial breakfast, I update my account book. In the eleven days I have been here, I have made 2730 euros. That is quite good! After finishing in the bathroom, I look through my closet and decide on a sand-colored, sleeveless, knee-length sheath dress. I grab my gold wedges, an ochre-colored, short-sleeved jacket, and my brown handbag. This outfit suits any occasion. My phone rings even before I am fully dressed. It is Dimitri!

"Hello?"

"Anika?"

"Yes, it's me!"

"This is Dimitri. Dimitri with the boat."

"Hi, Dimitri! How are you, darling?"

"Okay. Can we meet?"

"Yes, it's possible. When and where?"

"Right now – I'm in Piraeus. Do you have time?"

Crap! That will not work. I have to get to Vouliagmeni to see Eleni. What shall I do?

"Dimitri, it's too soon. How about later this afternoon, at 4:00 p.m.? I can come at that time. Does 4:00 p.m. work for you?"

"Uh — no. I have to be on a construction site this afternoon and I don't know if I have tonight time."

"All right! Call me back later when you know something."

"Okay, Anika, I'll call you later!"

"Great."

"Anika. — I can't stop dreaming about you! Kisses!"

"Kisses, Dimitri!"

As soon as I hang up, I receive another call. It is Violet.

"Hi, darling! Good morning. — So, are you excited yet about the Botox treatment? Unfortunately, I can't come along. Marko is coming at noon. Don't forget to call me later. I want to hear how it went!"

"Good morning to you too, Violet. Of course I'll tell you all about it, and yes, I'm a little excited. — Dimitri just called. You know, the man with the boat in Kalamaki. He wanted to see me this morning, but unfortunately I had to tell him no. He said he might call later. – We'll see, but right now, I have to be on my way to Vouliagmeni in a few minutes."

"Don't worry about Dimitri! I believe it's good if we're not always immediately available. It lets your client know he isn't the only one. Sometimes I purposely hesitate and pretend to rearrange a few meetings so it appears I am trying to accommodate whoever is calling. It usually flatters them. Marko, who'll be coming later, usually stays for almost a whole hour. God, it's annoying! Not that he wants to fuck the entire time. No, he wants to talk, lick, fuck, and then talk again. He deliberately prolongs it. He even sneaks peeks at the clock. – It's like he wants every cents' worth of his 150 euros. Then again, it's what he pays me for! What can I do? I really have to watch myself so I don't look bored! — I always make noises like oh, oh, or ah, ah, and when he licks me, which I absolutely can't stand, I always pretend to reach climax quickly and then tell him he can no longer touch my pussy because my clitoris is too sensitive after the orgasm. When we're done with that act, he lights up a cigarette. — That's another thing I can't deny him, but for the love of God, we're in my bedroom! – In my opinion, it isn't gentlemanly. A real gentleman would show consideration. – However, Marko is a boorish Greek and not a gentleman. Anyway, he always talks about his hotel on the Peloponnese and updates me on how it's doing. Like I care! I'm always glad when he's finally ready and pulls his cock out of me. He rips off the rubber and comes all over my stomach, tits, or ass, all depending on the position we're in. I always prefer my clients come in the rubber baggy and then dispose of it in the small pot I've placed especially for that purpose on my bedside table. — But don't think it is piling up with condoms! I always empty it after each session! The same goes for the bed sheets. – You really have to come and visit me! I have lovely satin sheets in pinks and reds. – I believe these colors are the most suitable for a sex bed. – I thought about buying a few black sheets, but even the smallest piece of lint stands out. I'll stick to my red, magenta, and pink colors."

Violet takes a breath and I use the opportunity to interrupt:

"Sorry, darling, I can't continue this conversation. I have to get to Vouliagmeni, but I'll call you as soon as my appointment with Eleni is over. I promise!"

"Yes, of course, darling! I'll be thinking of you. Oh, God, I'm so scared of needles. I don't know if I could do it. Let's see how you look. – As I said, if it turns out well, I might have to overcome my fear of needles and get some work done! I wonder if she can give me a sedative beforehand? Do me a favor and ask Eleni. Otherwise, I might pass out. Okay, darling, kisses! And don't forget to call me!"

"I will! Later, Violet!"

I really have to get going now. Hurrying, I finish dressing, grab my bag with my work equipment and lingerie, and head out the door to catch a bus to the southern area of Athens.

When I arrive at my destination on Planeromenis Street in Vouliagmeni, I stand at the side entrance of a mansion and ring the office bell of Dr. Eleni Karagiannis. The buzzer sounds and I push open the heavy front door and step directly into a large reception area. A young woman introduces herself as Angela. She asks my name, the time of my appointment, and the reason I am there. Showing me to an adjoining room, Angela asks me to take a seat. She leaves and returns with cream and crepe tape.

"I'm going to rub numbing cream on the areas to be treated. That way the injections are easier to bear," she says, and begins rubbing cream onto my forehead and around my eyes. Then she tears off strips of crepe tape and applies them over the creamed areas.

"There you go, all done! Someone will be with you in about half an hour."

I thank Angela and once she is out of the room, I take out my compact and inspect my taped face. Well, I certainly do not mind the numbing cream. I wait about 40 minutes before the door opens and a good-looking woman in her mid-forties walks in. Naturally, she introduces herself with her given name, Eleni. After we shake hands, she asks me to follow her into the treatment room and I sit sideways on the examination table.

"So, Anika. — Are you a Swede?"

"No, I'm German."

"Oh, how lovely. I love Germany. – I drive to Germany regularly to attend conferences. I definitely want my kids to study there when the time comes."

As she is talking, she pulls the tape off my face and uses a cotton swab to wipe away whatever cream residue is left. Reaching into her coat pocket, she pulls out a kohl stick and says:

"So! You don't have many wrinkles. Nevertheless, Botox will tighten your forehead skin nicely. Look at the ceiling without raising your head."

I do as told and feel my forehead wrinkling. Eleni uses the stick and marks a few dots on my forehead. Then she says:

"So, now smile as widely as you can. Yes. That's good. Keep smiling like that!"

As I smile broadly, I feel the wrinkles around my eyes turning into crow's feet. Again, Eleni marks a few dots around my eyes.

"Wonderful. So, now give me a nasty or serious look."

She shows me the expression. As I mimic her, I feel a frown line forming between my eyebrows. Again, she marks a few dots.

"Okay, you're all prepped," Eleni says, then gets up and walks over to the refrigerator. She uses a syringe to draw a little liquid from a small vial and comes back.

"Now lie down and relax. We applied numbing cream, but the injections can still hurt. However, the pain won't last long. So don't worry!"

I cross my hands the way I do when I have to see the dentist and expect pain. When Eleni makes the initial stick with the fine needle, I cringe. That is some numbing cream! I feel everything and the pain is excruciating!

"Don't worry, Anika, it doesn't last long. Do you think you can take it? If it gets to be too much for you, I can take a short break. Just let me know."

"No, Eleni, it'll be fine. Just do it, that way I'm done with it."

She continues with the injections. I lose count when the pain causes my eyes to tear. I cannot help thinking of Violet and her fear of needles. I do not think she would survive this. That brings the old saying to mind, *beauty is pain*, and I wonder who came up with it. That person certainly did not have Botox treatments, I know that much. Eleni goes back to the refrigerator and refills the syringe with miracle serum. Now she injects the liquid around my eyes. – Presently, I can handle the pain better because I know it stops as soon as Eleni withdraws the syringe.

"So, Anika, you're all done, you brave German woman!" She laughs and dabs the upper half of my face with an alcohol-soaked cotton swab. As she disposes of the swab, I notice blood on it.

Eleni grabs a big mirror and holds it in front of me.

"So," she says, "now you see where I made the injections. The little swelling you see will disappear in no time. Make sure you keep your head out of the heat for two days. After you wash your hair, do not use a hooded hair dryer or blow dryer. During the next four hours, do not lie down to rest or nap. For the rest of the day, do not lower your head. —Like this!"

She shows me.

"When you need to pick up something from the ground, don't lean over. Instead, lower yourself by bending your knees. In a few days, you'll notice your forehead tightening, but you won't see the full results for a week. — And I want to see you again in 10-14 days. I'll check if any area needs another injection. Most of the time, I have to add a little here or there. It's also important to see my customers again after their treatment so I can judge their reaction to Botox. So, ask Angela to give you an appointment. — So, how do you feel?"

"Good, now that it's over. You were right, the pain stopped as soon as the needle was out. Can I put on makeup to cover the reddened areas?"

"Of course! Oh, and wear a sun hat. — Any other questions?"

"Yes, how long does a Botox treatment last?"

"It differs from patient to patient. In my experience, when it's the first treatment, the effect will subside in approximately four months. Then it's time for new injections. – After the second treatment, the effect will last a bit longer. With a little luck, five months. If you do it regularly, it will usually last six months. But that's as long as it'll last. No reason to lie to you."

"Thanks, Eleni. Okay! I'll schedule an appointment for 10-14 days with Angela. I'll see you then."

"Great. Remember; don't lower your head for the rest of the day. Always keep it up! Bye, Anika. If you have any questions, call me!"

Once I have stepped out of the practice, I grab my compact and carefully inspect my forehead and the areas around my eyes in the magnifying mirror. As long as I have no customer appointments, there is no need to dab concealer on the reddened areas. It is too bad I thought my sun hat did not go well with my outfit. I left it at home. Now, I must deliberately avoid sun light. It is 1:15 p.m. Since there have been no calls or texts while I was in with the doctor, I call Maria in Glyfada to see if she can work me in on short notice for a manicure. She says I can come at 2:30 p.m., which works well for me. I go to the bus stop and take the E 22 bus to Glyfada. Since I am early, I grab a seat at a beach café and call Violet to tell her about my Botox experience.

"Oh my God! The numbing cream didn't really work? That's terrible! I don't think I could handle it, darling. And it actually requires a whole week for the Botox to take effect? Huh, and here I thought I'd see you tomorrow and examine the results. Are we still getting together tomorrow or do you already have an appointment? I don't have one until the afternoon. With Jeff at the Grand Bretagne Hotel. He's British, a banker. I met him a few months ago and he became one of my regulars. He's a real gentleman. Although he finishes within 30 minutes, he always gives me 170. And on Sunday at 6:00 p.m., Jack comes over. You know the Jack I'm talking about. The man who wants to have a relationship with me. He already asked if I want to accompany him to dinner after we're done. I definitely won't do that. That's out of the question! He can come over, have sex, put the money on the table, and then vamoose! — Although I know he's serious about having a real relationship with me, I don't see how it would work. I mean, how do you go about starting a relationship with someone who's been your customer for years. Okay, so we're familiar with and trust each other, but imagine how that would play out! I don't think it would work. — Anyway, tell me, what's on your schedule for tomorrow?"

"I have no appointments yet for today or tomorrow. I'm actually a bit worried, but I'm hoping someone will still call... — Anyway, as far as I'm concerned, we're still on for tomorrow. I'm looking forward to seeing you again!"

"Fantastic! I'll keep my fingers crossed that you get some calls. I'll call you tomorrow as soon as I'm done with Jeff. Bye, darling!"

"Great, thanks, Violet. See you tomorrow!"

40

While receiving a manicure from Maria, my phone rings. Unknown number. Since Maria understands English well, I cannot talk openly. Crap! – Perhaps if I choose my words carefully, she won't be any the wiser. I answer:

"Hello?"

"Hello, Anika?"

"Yes. Who am I speaking to, please?"

"This is Paul. I called a few days ago. I live in Glyfada. Do you remember?"

Although I cannot exactly recall, his name does ring a bell, which is why I say:

"Oh, yes, Paul. How are you?"

"Thanks, Anika, I'm well. I'm home for the weekend. Is there any chance you can come give me a massage today?"

"Yes, that's possible. What time do you have in mind?"

"6:00 p.m. Can you make it then?"

"6:00 p.m. is great. Text me your full name, address, and home phone, and I'll call back later, okay?"

"Not a problem, Anika. I'll do it right now. You will bring the massage oil, right?"

"Yes, of course."

"Great, talk to you later. Bye, Anika!"

"Bye, Paul!"

That was nondescript. As far as Maria is concerned, I made a date with a friend. Nothing to it! Since I am already in Glyfada with nothing else planned for the afternoon, sticking around until 6:00 p.m. to see Paul fits nicely. I now remember my previous phone conversation with him and his wish for a massage. He sounded English. I should have asked. Actually, I should ask every caller for his nationality. However, I forgot to... again! Maria has not finished my fingernails yet, when my phone rings again.

"Hello!"

"Yes, hi! Can you tell me something about yourself? Like how much you charge?"

"I'm sorry, but I'm indisposed right now and can't give out information. Can you call back in a bit, perhaps, 30 minutes?"

"Sure, no problem! Talk to you then."

"Great, thank you!"

That went well. I hope he actually calls back. Before saying goodbye to Maria, I make an appointment for next Saturday. It is 3:20 p.m. when I walk out of the nail salon and cross Metaxa Street toward the sea.

Since the sun is high in the sky and I am supposed to avoid it because of my recent Botox treatment, I stay on the side of the road shaded by buildings. I check Paul's text while walking. His last name is Ashton and he lives on Karman-Saki Street here in Glyfada. Given that I have lots of time and a need to avoid the sun, I head for a small, Greek grill near the town square. After ordering a grilled cheese sandwich and a Diet Coke, I pull up Paul's address on Google maps. He lives near a golf course not far from here. My phone rings. I answer:

"Hello?"

"Hi, again! You told me to call back for information. Can you tell me a little about yourself."

"Of course. My name is Anika and I'm 35-years-old, blonde with blue eyes, and a slim figure. I do home and hotel visits and my rate is 150 euros for one hour of safe sex."

"That sounds good. I'm at the Olympic Hotel. Can you come see me?"

"Sure. Can you tell me exactly where the Olympic Hotel is?"

"It's in the city center."

"That's okay. What time do you want me there?"

"At 10:00 p.m. tonight would be great."

"That's fine. Let me have your full name and room number. Oh, and the phone number of the hotel would be nice. That way I can call you back to confirm and then we're all set for this evening. — By the way, where are you from, darling?"

"Oh, I'm sorry, my name is Roberto Rodari. I'm Italian. I'm in room 403. Isn't the hotel's phone number on your display?"

I make a note of it and reply:

"Your right, I have the hotel's number. I'm all set. I'll call you back right now, okay, Roberto?"

"Yes, but don't wait too long, I'm about to leave, okay?"

"Of course!"

I hang up and quickly dial the number of the Olympic Hotel. A high-pitched female voice answers in rapid Greek.

"Good day. Do you speak English?"

"Yes. — How may I help you?"

"I'd like to speak to Mr. Roberto Rodari, room 403."

"One moment please."

I hear clicking and then ringing. Roberto immediately picks up.

"Hello?"

"Yes, it's me Anika. Okay, Roberto, we're all set for tonight!"

"Great! See you later!"

Happy about having another appointment for this evening, I store the phone number under 'Olympic Hotel'. Business is booming after all! I am also downright ecstatic I have not heard from Ladis or one of his friends. — Nevertheless, it does not mean I am in the clear. I still have to be on guard and careful about whom I make an appointment with!

Next, I Google the Olympic Hotel and see that it is close to the Arch of Hadrian near Athens' center. To pass the time, I read my favorite online newspaper. All of a sudden, I remember I had a Botox treatment this morning and that I have not checked myself out lately! I also remember I must not lower my head. That will pose a problem. If I have to give a blowjob, my head usually is down. Crap! When providing that little extra during a massage, like licking a guy's balls, I also have my head down. Today I will have to get creative. Taking out my compact, I study my face and notice the redness and swelling from the injections are gone. Using the magnifying mirror for a close-up, I still see one or more puncture marks. Other than that, I look quite normal, just like before the Botox treatment. At 5:40 p.m. I leave the restaurant, cross the street, and find the nearest taxi stand. Hopping into the first one in line, I show the driver the note with Paul's address.

He looks at it and asks me if I know where it is. That is exactly what you want to hear from your driver! Unfortunately, he has no GPS in the car, which makes me wonder how he finds an address in this metropolis. Although I find the situation incredulous, I answer:

"It's near the Glyfada golf course."

"Okay, we'll find the street," the driver says unperturbed. He closes the windows before taking off. Driving along the road adjacent to the golf course, my driver stops and asks for directions to Karman-Saki Street from a pedestrian. The man, presumably a local, points down the road and says something in Greek. My cab driver continues, pulls into the next road, and starts looking at house numbers. When we reach Paul's home, he beams and says:

"Here we are!"

I pay the fare and get out. Paul lives in a three-story apartment building surrounded by a wide garden. The iron garden gate stands open. I approach the entrance and ring the bell with his name. Paul buzzes me in, letting me know he lives on the second floor. He is tall, slender, straight, dark blond, wears glasses, and seems to be around 35 years old.

"Hi, Anika, I'm glad you made it. You look fabulous. Can I offer you a drink?"

"Hi, Paul. Thanks for asking, but no, I don't want a drink. You have a lovely place."

"Thank you! Regrettably, I'm not here often. My job takes me on the road a lot."

"What do you do, if I may ask?"

"I work for a company that sells ship navigation equipment. We have an office in Piraeus."

"Oh, I see! But traveling around the world must be interesting."

"Yes, it is. I enjoy my job."

Before we become sidetracked, I need to steer the conversation back to the reason for my visit. We are still in the hallway near the entrance, which transitions into a bright, spacious, yet sparsely furnished living room. One wall is entirely glass including the sliding doors and in the background, the golf course is visible. The doors are open and a slight breeze blows through the apartment.

"Please show me the bathroom and the room where you want to receive the massage."

"Of course. Follow me, Anika!"

Paul opens the door to a spacious bathroom. An enormous pile of clothes occupies the ground in front of the washing machine. He notices me staring at the pile of laundry. He says:

"Please excuse the mess. I just arrived today around noon. I don't have a housekeeper and I haven't gotten around to doing my laundry yet."

"That's okay. Your laundry doesn't bother me, darling!"

Paul shows me to the bedroom. He has a king size bed covered with a light brown sheet. Unfortunately, the rest of the bed is not made.

"Can you finish making the bed while I'm in the bathroom preparing? And you might as well undress and lie down on the bed — I'll be right back to pamper you."

"Oh, the bed. I'm sorry, Anika. I guess I'm a typical bachelor. I don't care if the bed isn't properly made. I'll place a large bath towel on the sheet so the oil won't stain it. Is that okay?"

"Yes, that's a good idea. Okay, I'll be right back. And Paul, could you close the curtains? It'll make it cozier."

"Certainly."

For today, I packed a champagne-colored satin and lace bodysuit, but since I do not want it sullied by the oil, I put on my other outfit — a summery, fresh orange-colored bra and panty set. I can always take off the bra. It does not matter if the panties connect with oil, it will wash out easily. By the time I walk back into the bedroom, the curtains are shut. Paul is wearing light blue underwear and lying on a big, white terry cloth towel. His glasses rest on the bedside table. Seeing his whole face, he looks damn good.

"If you don't mind, I'll massage your back first," I suggest. He replies:

"But then I can't see you. — And you look so sexy! I also want to touch you, Anika. Come on, sit on top of me!"

Well, he is the customer! I guess I will start on the front. I must remember not to lower my head! I constantly remind myself. After climbing on top of Paul's slim, toned body, I lower myself onto his underpants. Instantly, I feel his arousal growing against my pussy. It seems his baby-blue panties are filling out nicely. I like Paul and for some reason, it feels good to sit on him. Should I allow myself to get stimulated? Why not!

"Take off your bra. I want to touch your tits, Anika. My God, I'm already fucking horny!"

You can get me fucking horny, I think as I open my bra and toss it on the foot of the bed. But Paul does not grab my tits, he keeps his hands crossed behind his head and starts moving his hips instead, which feels good. I open the bottle of oil and pour plenty in my hands. I arch my back and lean forward only enough so that my hands touch his upper body and I can still hold my head up high. Unfortunately, I have no idea how to go about massaging a chest... I am used to starting with the back and by the time the customer turns around it is all about his cock.

I try to look sexy straddling Paul while rubbing oil over his chest with circular hand movements. Will he enjoy having his nipples played with? I lightly twist them with my thumbs and forefingers. – Happily, I note a positive response from Paul. Uncrossing his hands, he reaches for my boobs. He is quite talented. He lightly tweaks my nipples while moving his hips so his big boner massages my pussy. I give in to the sensation and take great delight in my increasing state of arousal. I can regain control now and switch back into work mode or enjoy the stimulation a while longer and simply climax. I like the latter option. – Since I usually only satisfy myself alone or with the help of sex toys, I allow myself this pleasure. Paul senses my arousal, which I do not hide.

"Oh, God, – I bet your cock is huge. It feels fantastic against my pussy."

"That's what I like to hear. I'm looking forward to sticking my huge cock in your pussy!"

"Yes, later. Don't stop rubbing it against my pussy. It's driving me wild!"

"I'm only too happy to oblige! After all, I know exactly what makes you whores tick. You're all sluts who can't think of anything else other than sucking and fucking cocks. But that's why I love you!"

Ignoring his insult, I decide to get my fair share of pleasure as quickly as possible because I do not want to climax when his cock is inside me. I do not allow such intimacy between a client and myself. I have my own rules. Feeling the sensation of an upcoming beautiful orgasm, I give in to Paul's tweaking and twisting of my nipples and at the same time, enjoy his huge cock rubbing my pussy until I finally lose my senses. My climax intensifies Paul's arousal, which is good.

"Anika, raise up a little, – but otherwise stay exactly the position you're in," he urges excitedly. Creating some space between us, I straddle him with my legs spread far apart. He immediately frees his dick from his underpants and start yanking on it hard and fast. He releases a big load. Lying there exhausted, we finally look at each other. I ask:

"How about a little back massage?"

"Oh, yes! That would be great. Earlier I was too hot for you. — I'm sorry I didn't fuck you. — But it seems you had fun too."

"That's right! — Okay, you might as well turn around now, darling!"

Ten minutes into the relaxing back and shoulder massage, I quietly say:

"Stay put and relax, darling. I'm going to quickly disappear into the bathroom."

"Okay," he hums sleepily, not moving a muscle. It is 6:45 p.m., so I quickly shower and dress. As I walk back into the bedroom, Paul rolls on his back, puts his underpants and glasses back on, and lights a cigarette. Grabbing his wallet from the nightstand, he pulls out three brown bills.

"Hold on, Anika, I'll walk you to the door. And thank you! You really turned me on. Tell me was your orgasm real?"

Paul gets up and hands me the bills. After I pocket them, I say:

"Thank you, darling! And yes, it was real. Sitting on you with your big boner rubbing my pussy really got me going. Despite my profession, I'm also a woman with desires. — And you have a wonderful specimen!" I say honestly.

A little embarrassed, he laughs and we say goodbye at his apartment door with kisses to the cheeks.

"Sometime in the future, I'll call you again, Anika. Until then, take care of yourself!"

"Okay, Paul, you too. It was nice meeting you."

41

Not far from Paul's apartment in Glyfada's town square, is a department store with a large cosmetic section. It occurs to me that my supply of rubbers needs to be replenish, which is why I am heading there. Luckily for me, condoms are on sale – two four packs for the price of one. I might as well stock up! With forty packages of normal and extra-large sizes in my basket, I stand in the checkout line. Unfortunately, rubbers do not come in size *small*. Oftentimes, I could use those. I guess men of the world would be embarrassed to wear a small condom. Instead, their weenie gets lost in a normal size rubber. It is not until the cashier scans each pack individually that I become aware of another female customer blatantly staring at me. Although I smile, I cannot help wondering what she might be thinking.

Glancing at my phone, I see Dimitri tried to reach me several times. Should I call him back? – I mean, he is not a customer who contacted me through my ad. I caught the fish myself and he is not married or in a relationship.

Having paid for my purchase, I walk over to a quiet corner of the cosmetic section and dial his number.

"Anika?"

"Yes, hi, Dimitri. I saw you tried to reach me a few times."

"Yes! Can you come to my boat at 10:00 p.m.?"

"Oh, darling, 10:00 p.m. is not good for me."

"Please, Anika, come see me!"

"Darling, I really can't! I already have an appointment at that time. I'm sorry, Dimitri. Let's do it another day."

"That's a pity, Anika. But yes, I'll definitely call you again. I would very much like to see you."

"I'd like to see you too, Dimitri. Take care of yourself, darling, bye!"

Finishing the conversation, I see I have missed another call. Oh well, it is what it is! I now know better than to get upset about missed calls. It is simply part of my profession as a call girl. Locating the department store rest rooms, I take the condoms out of their cardboard packaging so they do not occupy so much space and fit in my handbag. In case I am checked by security, I stick the receipt in my wallet and throw the empty boxes in the trashcan next to the sink. I ride the elevator to the ground floor and step out into the warm evening air of Athens.

I really like Glyfada with its long, wide shopping street, numerous taxi stands, good bus and tram connections, and its location near the sea. I have no problem imagining living in this neighborhood. I might as well begin searching for a suitable hotel for September is approaching faster than I like. And I definitely do not want to stay in Piraeus.

I take my time strolling through the shops, enjoying the coolness of the air conditioners. In my favorite clothing store, I check out the new merchandise. In a store selling accessories, I see a simple, light-brown sun hat with a wide brim. The same model is also available in pink. Trying it on, I find it creates a sassy look. Although the light-brown hat does not make much of a statement, it goes better with my sand-colored dress, short-sleeved jacket, and blonde hair. Without giving it much thought and without a guilty conscience, I simply go ahead and buy both hats. I immediately put on the light-brown hat and place the pink one in a bag. It might not look professional, but I am going to see my next customer carrying a shopping bag. Fortunately, it is a beautifully designed paper bag that will not embarrass me.

With plenty of time on my hands, I consider taking a tram to the city center and waiting near the hotel. Unfortunately, I would not know what to do there and I am not in the mood to walk around tiring myself or worse, end up lost in an unfamiliar area. Therefore, I decide to stay here in Glyfada. – I will make an exception and pay for a cab to the Olympic Hotel later on. Strolling to the nearby beach promenade, I sit down on a bench and watch the approaching sunset. At 9:30 p.m., I walk over to one of the taxi stands and grab a ride to the city center.

Although I have only been in Athens just short of two weeks, – it seems as if I have been here much longer. Nowadays, I am quite familiar with a few neighborhoods and I no longer feel so nervous or self-conscious when I walk into an unfamiliar hotel. Now, my heartbeat stays steady when I smile at the hotel staff and confidently cross the lobby toward the elevators. Nevertheless, before I knock on the door of a new customer, I do feel a twinge of stage fright. Today's door is that of Roberto Rodari, who opens it shortly after my knock.

"Ciao la mia, Anika, my, you look gorgeous! Come in, sweetie, so I can eat you!"

"Hi, Roberto! You're in good mood."

"Yes, because I know I'm about to nibble on a beautiful lady. And I really need to, mia Cara!"

I estimate Roberto, who is not much taller than me, is around 40. He is wearing a white hotel bathrobe and smells of freshly applied aftershave. Overall, he presents a pleasant appearance.

"I'd like to freshen up and change, baby. Is it okay if I quickly use your bathroom?"

"Oh! No, no, no! I want to undress you myself. Come to me, my angel. You look delightfully better than I expected."

Roberto leans against the desk as his hands reach for me. After removing my jacket and discarding it along with my two bags on an armchair, I approach him and let him hug me. I do not enjoy customers undressing me, nor do I care for being fondled while wearing my private, personal undergarments. For that, I have work clothes. Not to mention, the flesh-colored set I am currently wearing is not seductive, thus I do not feel sexy. But it is not like I can convey this to Roberto. Patting me on the butt, he starts kissing me. Although I am not okay with this, I cannot be too picky in my job, especially considering my hourly rate. So I simply put up with him sticking his tongue into my mouth and exploring it vigorously. One of his hands slides under and up my dress, lustfully grabbing my buttocks. I reach behind my back and try to open the zipper of my dress to speed this striptease along. Roberto's hand reemerges from under my dress to assist. He smiles self-assuredly as he opens the zipper in one swift move and lets my dress slide down my body so it ends up on the floor around my feet. I really do not like my clothes touching the floor. It is not like we are lovers overcome with passion.

"Hold on, darling, let me pick up my dress!" I grab it and throw it over the armrest of the chair. Some order must prevail! Roberto's hands roam over me as we continue smooching. I know my chance to go to the bathroom has passed. I will have to do without. I push the bathrobe off Roberto's shoulders. He removes it completely and stands naked in front of me. Concerned my personal lingerie might become stained with sweat or semen, I quickly say:

"Wait, darling, I want to be naked when I snuggle up against you."

I remove my underwear and place them on the armchair with the rest of my belongings. Roberto looks at me lustily and whispers something in Italian.

"Bella mia, you're nicely tanned! I guess you like sunbathing in the nude, my sweetie. No tan lines. — Spread your legs, I want to put a finger in your pussy!"

I sit on the edge of the desk and spread my legs wide. Roberto, the wild short Italian, urgently reaches for my crotch and starts fingering me while kissing me. I offer a few moans and groans so he believes he is turning me on. – Then again, it is not like Roberto needs encouragement. He is as hot as Tabasco sauce. Since his hard gigolo is already pressing against my pussy and the rubbers are still in my purse, I interrupt him.

"Darling, let me grab a condom, then I don't mind you fucking me here on the desktop. Then we'll move to the bed and you can take me from all angles."

Gently, I free myself from his tight hold. He does not resist. I promptly grab a couple rubbers with green wrappers, indicating normal size, from my toiletry bag, tear it open, and roll the rubber over the absolutely randy Italian cock. The wrappers of the extra-large condoms are dark blue, which makes distinguishing sizes easy for me. That is better than searching the small print. I wonder if that was the manufacturer's objective. Who knows? Folding Roberto's bathrobe twice, I use it as a cushion on the edge of the desk. I am barely in position when he rams his cock deep into my pussy and starts fucking like a rabbit. Bracing myself with my arms, I hold tightly to the far edge of the desk. Roberto steadies himself by holding on to my hips. The desk and I bounce in unison. Bang, bang, bang... A few minutes of these hectic thrusts and I have had enough. My hands are tired. Losing my grip, I slide backwards.

"Come on, Roberto, let's go to the bed. I want you to take me from behind."

Although he groans with displeasure, he consents and pulls his cock out of my pussy. I immediately slide off the desk. Despite a soft bathrobe to sit on, my butt hurts. The bed will be more comfortable. As soon as I assume the doggie position, my randy Italian customer is already pressing against my rear end. Making sure to keep my head always upright, I look over my shoulder and ask:

"Is the rubber still in place or should we exchange it?"

"I believe it's okay," he replies. I double check his assessment and see he is correct. Roberto thrusts his wild gigolo into my pussy.

"Mamma mia, you've got a great ass! I'm going to fuck you real good. You like getting fucked hard, don't you? You deserve it, my sweetie! I wouldn't want you leaving here thinking Roberto was a bore. Roberto is a stallion, a wild stallion, bella!"

I have forgotten how long he has been fucking me like this, but it is obvious he can go on without end. I guess it will be challenging to get him to climax. I am always at a loss with clients like him because I have no idea how they usually get themselves off. At least there would be some direction if I knew their methods. Anyway, it is what it is and I simply have to figure out what drives him nuts. I begin by suggesting we change positions.

"Come on, Roberto, let's switch to a different position. Do you want me to sit on you or shall I lie down?"

"Why don't you lie down, I don't really care to be on the bottom. Mamma Mia, you drive me insane with your sexy suntanned body and your clean-shaven pussy. I'm going to lick your snatch for a while and then I'll fuck you again. I want you to have fun too, bella!"

Aha! Perhaps if I fake an orgasm that will do the trick and make him come. Sadly, that is not so easy. Roberto alternates between licking and fucking me in various positions. Then he is on top, next he rolls me on my side and fucks me from behind, and so on and so on. Presently, I have exchanged the condom twice as well as faked three orgasms for him, but he does not tire of fucking me like a rabbit. I am wondering if he took Viagra. It does not matter how I encourage him, he just keeps fucking frantically without anything happening... Although he is doing all the work, I am weary and hopeful he will finish soon – somehow! I cannot help thinking I should say or do something so he will not be fucking me for another two hours!

"Roberto, darling, is there anything special I can do to help you come?"

"Why?"

"Well, I want you to have fun too."

"Don't worry, bella, I'm having fun, but I guess you want to see me squirt?"

"Yes, of course, baby!"

"Okay! Then I'll come for you now, my pretty little puttana!"

He pulls his cock out of me, removes the rubber, and takes hold of his rod. I am lying in front of him on my back with my legs and arms stretched out. Roberto's face has been tense and red for some time. Suddenly, he kneels between my legs and stares at my shaved pussy while seemingly trying to strangle his cock. Then again, that is probably exactly what his cock wants, to be emptied. With a muffled loud cry, he suddenly climaxes and squirts his load onto the sheet between him and my crotch. Finally!

In the bathroom, my watch tells me it is 11:10 p.m. In essence, he has fucked me for over an hour. Thankfully, I am not in pain. I am simply exhausted and decide right then to call it a day. Roberto pays me and tips me 10 euros. – This makes me happy and I thank him with a little peck on the cheek. As we say goodbye, he looks happy and calls me *Bella Signorina*. In hindsight, I have to admit he was not such a bad customer. He simply took much longer than most of my other clients.

42

After entering my room at the Lilo Hotel, I set air conditioning to 19 degrees Celsius and open the balcony door. On my way home from the bus stop I bought two cold beers at a periptero. Naked, I lay a towel over the balcony chair and plop down. I put my feet up on the other chair and pop off the cap of one bottle of Amstel Gold. The escaping carbonation hisses. I pour the golden liquid into a typical Greek glass-for-everything. Here is to you, Ilona! You deserve a cold beer after a good day's work! The first long gulp soothes my throat and tastes so delicious that I once again think beer is the most refreshing drink on earth. Funny part is I am usually not a beer drinker.

Checking my phone for the first time since visiting Roberto at the Olympic Hotel, I notice a missed call. Unknown number. Not giving it a second thought, I lean back and sip my beer while enjoying the warm, late night air of Athens. Feeling a cold draft coming from my room, I get up and set the air conditioning to 23 degrees Celsius, then go back outside and close the door as much as possible without locking myself out. There is no way to unlock the door from the balcony, so if it engages I am screwed. Sitting back down, I empty the beer bottle into my glass and relax. By the time I have finished my glass, I am overcome by fatigue. I quickly clean up and go to bed.

The soft ringing of my phone startles me. Switching on the light, I look at the display. An Athens landline with a Glyfada area code. I have memorized all the different codes I have received. The city code for Athens is 210, if area code 45 follows, then the call comes from Piraeus. If it shows 33, then the call originates in the city center, and if an 89 follows, well then, the call is from Glyfada. I quickly rub my eyes and answer.

"Hi! Are you the German woman?"

"Yes, my name is Anika. Who are you?"

"I'm René. Can you come and see me?"

"Where are you, René? And when do you want me there?"

"I'm at home and I'd like you to come right now. — I also need to know how much you charge."

René's French accent is unmistakable. Nevertheless, I have to proceed with caution.

"My rate is 150 an hour. And you want me to come right now? It's only 6:00 a.m."

"I know. I'm sorry. Can you or not? — I just got home! I was out all night with my colleagues at a music club and now I'm in the mood for sex. Is that possible? Can you come to my home? Right now?"

René seems a little tipsy, but not drunk. While making up my mind, I ask:

"Where do you live? I need your name, full address, and home phone number. — Tell me, are you calling me from home right now?"

"Yes, I am. I live at number 10 Pallodios Street in Glyfada. Call me when you get here. My name is René Bosquier. Don't use the doorbell or else the other people in the house might wake up. I'll come and open the door for you once you call. So, will you come to my home?"

I don't think I have anything to worry about with him. The only thing that is unusual is the requested time. As I quickly scribble down his name and address on the notepad on my nightstand, I think about how long it would take me to get there. I need five minutes in the bathroom, two minutes to walk downstairs and out to the road, another five minutes before I catch a cab, plus the 20 minutes to get to Glyfada.

"I can be at your place in 30-45 minutes. But first I'm going to call you at home to confirm and then I'll be on my way."

"Okay, I'm right here, waiting for you. I'm really horny."

"Great! And, baby, please don't fall asleep or I'll have to use the doorbell!" I say jokingly and René promises to stay awake. I hang up and immediately dial his number. René answers on the first ring and everything is set. I hop into the shower, dry, dress, and put makeup on, which I do in record time. Noticing the time, I see my five minutes have long since elapsed. Grabbing my bag and shoes, I fly down the stairs barefoot since I make better time and less noise. Reaching the lobby, I quickly slip into my shoes and walk outside. Now on the street in the early morning hours with my arm stretched out to hail a taxi, I am wide-awake. Although traffic is light, plenty of cars drive by, among them yellow cabs. The first one I wave at stops. I get in and tell the driver to head for Glyfada. Since there was no time to jot down the address, I quickly and clearly write it down on a piece of paper and hand it to the driver. Thankfully, the cab has GPS, and the driver enters the address. When the taxi stops in front of number 10 Pallodios Street, I ask the driver to pull a bit ahead. As I pay him, he is grinning. He seems to know why I am here.

René lives in a grand two-story house in an upscale area where only rich people reside. Violet told me that the locals in Glyfada are mostly well off Greeks and Northern Europeans. In essence, great clients. I grab my phone and call René. He answers immediately and tells me to walk through the garden gate and to wait at the front door. He will be right there. I do as I am told and as I step up to the front door, René opens it just far enough for me to slip inside. Closing the door softly, he faces me and holds an index finger in front of his mouth while nodding at me to follow. We walk down the ground floor hallway until we reach his ajar apartment door. The entire time I am trying to be as quiet as possible in my heels on the marble tiles. Once we are in his place, René shuts the door gently. Grinning, he turns to me and says:

"Hi!"

Although he seems a bit drunk, his smile looks harmless and sweet. René is an incredibly handsome man. I guess he is in his mid-forties. He is approximately 1.85 meters tall, has a mop of curly, short black hair, a three or four-day old beard, dark eyes, and tanned skin. Looking at his open bathrobe, I see he wears chic, tiny underwear. His abdomen does not resemble a six-pack, it is merely flat, which I find much more attractive than bulging muscles. Slowly, he leads the way into the bedroom. – All I see is a mattress on the floor, no other furnishings. French books and DVDs are piled on the floor on one side of the mattress and on the other side, a reading lamp and an ashtray. A flat screen TV is mounted on the wall facing the mattress. On the ground below are a receiver, a DVD player, and two big speakers. Since the ceiling light is pleasantly dimmed, I immediately feel at ease in his bedroom. With nowhere to put my handbag, I set it on the floor and remove my dress. Propped up by a few big pillows, René watches me from the mattress. He is smoking while I striptease. By the time I approach him, I am wearing only my black satin lingerie and pumps. He says:

"Take off your shoes and bra too. — Then come down here and blow me."

I slip off my shoes, take off my bra, and place it on the floor next to my dress. Thankfully, the floor looks clean. I grab a couple of rubbers from my bag and as I am about to open one, René says:

"Come here — we don't need a condom! I'm healthy. You don't have to be afraid. Honestly!"

Great, now what am I supposed to do? – Although I take his word for it to ease my conscience, I still take a scrutinizing look at his French wiener before I take it in my mouth.

"Okay, but don't come in my mouth, do you understand! Also, if you want to fuck me you must wear a rubber! Promise me!"

"Yes, I promise! Now come here. I'm so fucking horny. It seems like I've been waiting forever. And I didn't fall asleep! — I believe I deserve a nice blowjob now, right?"

He laughs and stubs out his cigarette in the ashtray. I move up to his side, bend over him, and maneuver his cock out of his tight designer underwear. Although it is hard, it is rather tiny compared to the rest of his body. There should not be a problem blowing him. René might seem drunk, but he is behaving decently. – I cannot help worrying though about him falling asleep or about him not being able to come at all, considering his alcohol level. Since he passed my thorough inspection, I put his rod in my mouth and lick and suck it until René says a short while later:

"Sorry, but I have to come now."

I quickly take his cock out of my mouth and start licking his balls while giving his twitching rod a hand job and making sure its head is pointed at his belly so he does not come in my face or in my hair.

René thrusts forcefully upward as he gives in to his orgasm and then slumps down, exhausted. I remain kneeling beside him and stroke his softening Frenchman. – This would be a short session if I left now, perhaps too short. I ask if he would like a little massage before falling asleep. René barely manages to open his eyes and replies: "That would be great!" He rolls over on his belly. After oiling my hands, I start rubbing his back gently. Glancing at his hands, I do not see a ring. I figure he is not married, so my next thought is if he is in a relationship. I guess once I use his bathroom I will know if a woman lives here too, although, I do not think so. I finish my short, relaxing massage by resting my hands lightly on his butt, followed by quietly saying:

"Okay, baby, that's it. May I use your bathroom?"

René answers sleepily:

"Yes, of course. It's across from the bedroom. Fresh towels are in the cabinet under the sink. Please help yourself!"

Since René has not fucked me or put his hands on me, I merely freshen up and rinse my mouth. Taking a quick look around confirms my suspicion that René lives alone. No womanly stuff whatsoever. Going back into the bedroom, I get dressed. Half asleep, René gets up, dons his robe, and hands me three 50-euro bills.

"Sorry I'm drunk — you look great. Maybe I'll call you again. What was your name again?"

"Anika. My name is Anika. Thank you, darling, now go on and get some sleep. It was nice meeting you."

"*Episis!*" he replies and notices my questioningly look. He explains:

"Sorry, it's one of the few Greek words I know. It means *likewise*."

Before I walk out his apartment door, he staggers slightly, smiles, and then brushes a kiss on each cheek. I quickly head for the main road to catch a taxi home. Presently, it is bright outside and the sun is already as hot as it is in the afternoon when it is high in the sky. I cannot help thinking about my early morning appointment with René. That guy should not have a problem getting laid for free! Maybe the ladies he meets want more than a simple tumble in the sack and he is not the committing type. That might be why he phoned a call girl, no complications! She simply disappears when the deed is done. No muss, no fuss. When the taxi stops in front of the Lilo Hotel, it is almost 8:00 a.m. Since it is too late to crawl back into bed, I decide to do some early shopping and then a visit to the tanning studio.

43

Shortly before noon, my phone rings. Unknown number.

"Hello!"

"Good day! Am I talking to the German lady with the ad in *Athens World?*"

"Yes, you are. My name is Anika. Would you like some information about me?"

"Yes, please!"

I tell the interested unknown party all the pertinent information about me and the services I provide. Since he speaks fluent English, I assume he is a Brit.

"Anika, I have a special request, but I don't know if you provide that service. I'd like you to be my sex slave for an hour. If you don't offer that, perhaps you'd recommend a colleague?"

I think about it quickly. Although I could easily assume the role, I am not keen on experiencing pain or ending up with bruises or welts. So, I inquire:

"What exactly do you have in mind? — Oh, and I still don't know who I'm speaking with."

"I'm sorry. My name is Kevin. I'll be in Athens on Tuesday. I'll be staying at the Kamazon Hotel. I'd like to meet you there so I can dominate and beat you a little. Don't worry, I won't hit hard. I'm merely into giving orders. I also insist you carry them out. I'm sure to insult you. I'm into that. So, what do you say?"

I know I can stand a little pain and for some reason, I can see myself playing this role. I answer resolutely:

"Yes, I can accommodate you, Kevin."

"And how much would something like that cost?"

"I charge 500 an hour for a little abuse, light beatings, and obeying sexual commands."

"Okay, that's reasonable. — What do you say? Do we have a date for 8:00 p.m. Tuesday at the Kamazon Hotel?"

"Yes, we do. I still need your full name. On Tuesday, once you know your room number, you need to call me back."

"Of course. My last name is Morgan. I expect I'll be checking in around 4:00 p.m."

"Okay,– I'll see you Tuesday!"

I Google the Kamazon Hotel and see it is a four-star hotel near Syntagma Square. I would have canceled Tuesday's appointment if it had been a dive in a shady area of Athens or Piraeus. Then again, it occurs to me that Kevin did not give me his phone number! His number was not displayed and I forgot to ask him about it. Oh well, it can happen. I think I will be safe in a four-star hotel in the center of Athens. – That alone gives me comfort. This will be my first time as the submissive party, so I regard it as an experiment. After making a note of it, I call Violet.

"Hi, Violet, it's Anika. How are you?"

"Oh, Anika, I can't talk long. I have to see Bertrand in Kifissia. He's a Frenchman that called me half an hour ago. He's staying at the Theodoro Hotel, which is quite far. I have to take a cab. I can't wait to see that bill; it'll cost me a fortune. But what's the alternative? If I say something, he might not call again! Usually, he stays at the Grand Bretagne Hotel, which is much closer. I even asked why he wasn't at the Grand Bretagne Hotel. He said it was because he was meeting friends in Ekali. This way he won't have such a long commute. Isn't that nice for him, meanwhile, my commute is now twice as long. Anyway, he wants me there at 1:00 p.m. So, darling, let's talk later. I have to call a cab to pick me up and I need to get ready before it gets here. It's the hottest time of the day and I'm not in the mood to stand on the street waiting to find a cab driver gracious enough to drive me to Kifissia! You know how it is with the taxi drivers here. They won't always drive you where you want to go. It's always a drama with them! Some don't have that GPS thing, others smoke like a chimney, and some won't turn on the air conditioning so they can save gas. With the windows down, the cab becomes a wind tunnel and my hairdo ends up a disaster! Moreover, I have a date with Jeff afterward. It would be less stressful if Bertrand were staying at his usual hotel. What can you do though! — I won't see him until tonight. Sorry, darling, but I have to go now. I'll call you later!"

I barely get out a *bye* when the line goes dead. In any case, considering my current appointments, there is a good chance we will spend a nice evening together. That would make me happy. I clean my room, hand wash a few panties and bras in the bathroom sink, and lay out new lingerie sets for the next few days. I fill my laundry bag that I will drop off later with Spiros at the reception desk and then restock my pouch with condoms and top off the massage oil. At last, I sit down and record recent appointments and earnings. Reviewing my ad in the newest edition of *Athens World* for the umpteenth time, I still find it engaging and it stands out because it is listed last in the column. My phone rings and the display tells me it is Adonis, the one who drives the Jeep.

"Hello, Adonis!"

"Hi, Anika! How are you?"

"I'm fine, Adonis, thank you, and you?"

"I'm great. Listen, I've spoken to Natasha and she'd like to meet you too. Do you have time Monday at 3:00 p.m.? It's best if we meet at the Lenny Blue Hotel in Glyfada again. Can you make it?"

"Yes, I can! Are you going to call me back to confirm or should I be at the hotel shortly before 3:00 p.m. and wait for you to call with the room number?"

"Just be at the hotel. In case something comes up, I will call you. — Sometimes, I go and pick up Natasha, so she might already be in the room with me. —I'm looking forward to you two! And please, wear a mini skirt again! God, I am already getting hard just thinking about you, sexy!"

I laugh and say goodbye to Adonis. Then, I call my father. Our conversation is short and sweet, the way I prefer it. He only asks about the weather and how much longer I plan to stay in Athens. I tell him the summer weather is nice and promise I will definitely come to Germany in September. Nevertheless, I still do not know whether I will stay or load up my car and drive back to Athens. Somehow, I sense he is glad I am gone. I guess he prefers having his divorced daughter living in a foreign country rather than in his house. Perhaps I am imagining it.

When my phone rings again that afternoon, I see the call is from the Hilton.

"Hi! This is Harry. Am I speaking with the charming lady with the ad in *Athens World*?"

"Yes, you are. I'm Anika. Hi, Harry!"

"Hello! Can you tell me a bit about yourself and your conditions?"

"Certainly! I'm 35-years-old, blonde with blue eyes, and a slim figure. My rate is 150 for a sexy hour."

"Sounds good. Are you free at 6:00 p.m.? Can you come see me? I'm staying at the Hilton."

"Yes, that's possible. What is your full name and room number?"

"My name is Harry Martin, I'm from Canada, and my room number is 556."

"Okay, Harry. Are you in your room right now?"

"Yes."

"Great, then I'll call back in a moment and we'll be on for 6:00 p.m., okay?"

"Why are you calling me back?"

"To make sure your information is correct so I won't have any problems visiting you in your room."

"Oh, okay! — Well, you'll see I gave you the correct information, but go ahead and call me back then, I'm here. "

"Okay, talk to you soon!"

The woman manning the front desk connects me to Harry's room. All right, we are all set for later. I record my new appointment.

Thinking about how best to go about it, I decide not to go back home after my appointment at the Hilton but instead, go directly from there to Glyfada. It would be a waste of time coming back to Piraeus just to change outfits for my night out at an English pub with Violet. Now, I have to figure out something suitable to wear for my appointment with

Harry and my date with Violet. I believe the red dress I wore to the interview with Elena from the escort service *Seven Heaven* seems appropriate for both occasions. Its design and length are suitable for visiting an establishment such as the Hilton and its color will attract attention when Violet and I go fishing. After placing matching lingerie in my bag, I grab my white sun hat. As I am about to leave my room for the subway station in Piraeus, my phone rings. It is Violet.

"Hi, darling, phew, Bertrand and Jeff wore me out! I'm going home now to lie down and rest a little. So, how's it looking? Are we still meeting at 8:00 p.m. at the town square? I'm looking forward to seeing you!"

"Hi, Violet! I'm on my way to the Hilton to see Harry, a Canadian. I have to be there at 6:00 p.m. Afterward, I'm coming directly to Glyfada. I'll call you once I'm at the town square, okay?"

"Sounds good, sweetie, until then, kisses!"

"Kisses, darling!"

Forty-five minutes later, I am standing outside the subway station at Syntagma Square, hailing a cab. As luck would have it, it is one of those taxi drivers Violet complained about. He is a smoker, so I ask him to put the cigarette out. Churlishly, he tells me to take another cab if his smoking bothers me. So, I get out, however, now I have to put up with the brutal afternoon heat until I can catch another cab. Although lots of yellow cabs rush by, every single one is occupied. Eventually, an empty cab pulls up next to me and I get in. Since the air conditioner is not on and I am in no mood for another smart retort, I simply pull my hair up off my neck believing I will survive the short ride to the hotel with the windows down. The taxi drops me off in front of the Hilton with only five minutes to spare before my appointment. Although this is pushing it, I am going to be on time. Briskly, I walk to the hotel restaurant and use the restroom to restore my hair to its usual lion's mane. Since my face is flush, I splash it with cold water, wondering how I got so quickly out of shape. In the past, my face never reddened after a little exertion. It must be due to my age and the heat. I must never meet a customer with such a discolored face. After a few minutes, my complexion returns to normal. I leave the restaurant and cross the grand lobby toward the elevators. Being a few minutes late is not the end of the world.

Standing in front of room 556, I smooth out my dress and put on a casual smile before knocking three times. Without the sound of approaching footsteps, it suddenly opens and I am confronted by a friendly looking, about 50 years old, rotund, Canadian with short hair. As far as I recall, I have never had a Canadian customer. But what does it matter, it is not like he will be much different than other Western men.

"Hello, Anika, come in!"

"Hi, Harry!"

"Well, look at you. You are quite stylish and good-looking as well!"

"Thank you, darling. How are you? Are you here in Athens for business or pleasure?"

"Business. Next week, I'm returning home to Canada. What about you? You're German, right?"

"Yes," I reply as I walk over to close the curtains.

"When did you arrive?" I ask.

"Almost a week ago. I accompanied a colleague to a pharmaceutical convention. We have a couple more meetings and then it's back to good old cold Canada. What about you? Have you been in Athens for a while?"

"No, I've only been here for two weeks. Although, I do like it and plan to stay for a while longer, at least through summer. Okay, why don't you get comfortable while I freshen up in the bathroom and change into something sexy for you, okay?"

"Of course. Help yourself to a fresh towel or whatever else you might need!"

"Thank you, darling!"

Once naked and my dress hangs on a hook, I slip on my red corset and matching strapless stockings. Although I find garter belts sexier, putting them on is a pain in the butt. When I walk back into the room, Harry is no longer wearing his bathrobe. Instead, he is sitting naked on the big bed with his legs crossed. I like what I see. The bed is nice and roomy and the mattress is not too soft or too hard. I would love to spend a night in this bed! Alone, of course!

"Wow, what a nice surprise! You are gorgeous, Anika. Come over here."

Harry motions for me to sit next to him. I set my equipment pouch on the bedside table and assume a seductive pose next to him. He runs one hand across my cheek, neck, cleavage, and then over my corset covered breasts and belly. As he approaches my crotch, I invitingly open my legs. He is watching intently as his hand strokes the insides of my thighs.

"You have beautiful legs, Anika. Nicely toned. It's important for a woman to have great legs. I mean, it doesn't matter how nice breasts and a figure are if the legs don't match."

He leans forward and runs his tongue over the inside of one thigh.

"May I lick you?"

"Yes. Take as much time as you want, baby!"

I remove my panties. Harry lies down with his face in front of my wide spread bent legs. Running a finger over my labia, he spreads my lips before his tongue touches my pussy. He is taking his time, which is fine by me. I do not have to think up anything as long as Harry knows what he needs to get aroused. He is quite committed. I am staring down at his thick blond hair and strong shoulders, contemplating the ancestry of Canadians. Most are either of British or French descent, right? I cannot tell. His left wrist sports a Breitling watch and his right pinkie, a flashy gold ring. While watching and thinking about him, I feel him growing urgent as he forcefully sticks his tongue in my pussy. I should respond, so I start gently moving my hips.

"Oh, baby, you really know how to use your tongue. It really turns me on!"

"I'm glad to hear it! I want you to be turned on, Anika. You should also get something out of our meeting. I like pleasuring women!"

"You're a real gentleman! You don't mind if I come while you lick me?"

"God, baby, come for me! I'll do whatever it takes."

I guess I have to work after all.

"Okay. I want you to lick my clit, but nice and slow. Be very, very gentle!"

"Yes, sweetie. I'll do my best to accommodate you."

And so it is. He really strives not to over stimulate my clitoris and instead, slowly and gently teases it from all angles. This is my cue to start my performance. I tense up and start breathing louder and faster. Without drawing it out too much, I fake an orgasm for him. Harry's looking at me, pleased with himself. As I let my climax slowly subside, I relax my muscles, slump down on the mattress, and look at Harry as if completely exhausted.

"Wow, that was amazing! How about for dessert, you give me a good fuck — or should I give you a nice blowjob? I'm in the mood for it!"

"Yeah! Why don't blow me now and then I'll fuck you!" Harry replies enthusiastically.

Grabbing a rubber, I roll it over his now obvious erection. He has reddish-blond pubic hair. Therefore, I believe he is British or Irish.

His cock is not very big, so I have no problem taking it deep into my mouth and sucking on it vigorously. Harry lies flat on his back while I squat over him so he has a good view of the pussy he just licked while I grab his balls with one hand and use the other to guide his cock into my mouth. After a few minutes, I stop my blowjob, turn around and slide his cock into my pussy, and then start riding him. Harry begs me:

"Show me your tits. I haven't seen your tits yet!"

Slowly, I untie the front laces of the corset and expose my breasts. Then I strip the bodice off and lay it aside. Harry moans as he massages and kneads my boobs. Soon, he is thrusting his pelvis more urgently. Knowing it is a sign of an impending orgasm, I reach with my right hand behind me and grab his balls. Applying light pressure, I knead his scrotum, hoping it will drive Harry over the edge. It seems to have the desired effect. Suddenly he arches his back and with a long, drawn out *aaaaaahhh* he starts climaxing.

That is a good boy, I think. As his spasms subside, my hand releases his balls and I rise up a bit. The condom remained properly in place, so I pull it off and discard it in the ashtray on the bedside table. – Once I go to the bathroom, I will dispose of it properly, as usual. As I lie next to Harry, he says:

"You have a gorgeous body, Anika. I've really enjoyed sex with you."

"Thank you, darling! — By the way, are you a French or British Canadian?"

"My ancestors are from Wales, but I don't have any relatives living there. That's actually sad. I like Wales. When I was a young man, I thought about moving there... I'm familiar with the area my family comes from, it's quite lovely. But that ship has sailed. I've established myself in Canada. I have a great job and a family. I'm also happy living there."

"I had a feeling you weren't of French descent. You seem more British. — Tell me, darling, do you mind if I use the bathroom?"

"No, of course not. Help yourself to whatever you need! The bathroom is fully stocked."

Feeling good about myself and my work, I take a long shower and cream my body from head to toe with the lotion provided by the hotel. Harry did say I could help myself to whatever! Now dressed and with my makeup applied, I return to the room.

"Would you like a drink, Anika? Excuse me for not asking you earlier. It was rude of me!"

"That's all right, darling — yes, a glass of water would be nice. But only if you don't mind me staying for a few more minutes."

"Not at all! Come and sit down. — Hey! Water is boring, let's have champagne!"

"Okay, champagne sounds good, but I still would like a glass of boring water. I'm thirsty."

"All right — here you go! One glass of boring water!" he says as he hands me the glass.

"Let's see what we have here? Ah, Moet!" Harry says as he opens the bottle from the minibar and fills two champagne flutes. We toast and drink. The champagne is simply delicious. Harry grabs his wallet and hands me my fee. I pocket the money and we fall silent. What is left to say other than thank you and goodbye, my job is done! — It is up to Harry to begin a conversation; he is after all the one who suggested we drink champagne. As I think about this, my gaze travels to the desk and I see an open copy of *Athens World*. So, I ask Harry:

"Where did you buy this paper? Downstairs in the hotel gift shop?"

"I didn't buy it. I believe it was here when I checked in along with some magazine about Athens. That's how I found you. — Say, do you also advertise on the Internet?"

257

"No, not yet. Right now I only have an ad in *Athens World*."

"The Internet is a bit confusing with all the available platforms for escort services and sex. Most of the time you can't even talk to the ladies in person. You are always referred to some agency. I like it much better the way we did it today. It's much more personal. Getting information about a person from a third party is so cold and impersonal. With you, at least we exchanged a few words over the phone and I was able to hear your voice and the way you talk. I find that important; it gives me some idea about the woman. – By the way, you were very friendly on the phone and your voice sounded quite charming!"

"Why thank you, Harry! It's imperative I hear a customer's voice. I would never agree to an appointment only by text. I want to talk to any potential customer. — Plus, I can't be sure if a texted request is real or a prank."

Harry agrees with me and we chat for a few minutes, sipping champagne. Then I say:

"Okay, darling, I have to leave now. Thanks for the bubbly and conversation. I hope you enjoy the remainder of your stay in Athens!"

"Thank you, Anika! It was wonderful to meet you. I'm going to keep your phone number. Who knows, perhaps one day I'll visit Athens again."

We exchange the usual kisses and say goodbye. A moment later, I am in the hotel elevator, 150 euros richer! Lately, I am always overcome with happiness every time I have performed my job well. The customer is happy and I was paid handsomely!

44

I walk toward Syntagma Square to catch a tram for Glyfada. Checking my phone, I see I have missed several calls while I was busy at the Hilton. Most calls I receive are from early afternoon until late evening. I know now I do not have to worry about the missed calls for I get plenty of work. What do you know, my phone rings. It is a Greek landline number with an Athens area code I am not yet familiar with. I answer hoping the woman next to me will not be able to overhear my conversation.

"Hello!"

"Yes, hi, this is George from Kifissia. Did you advertise in *Athens World*?"

"Yes. Would you like some information about me?" I ask softly.

"Definitely!"

In a subdued voice, I tell George what he needs to know.

"Okay, but I don't want to hire you today. Tell me, what do you all do for 150 euros?"

"Sex in various positions, including oral."

Although I am whispering, George seems to hear me fine.

"What about rimming?" he asks.

Oh my God, what is rimming? I have never heard of it! What am I going to do? – I could pretend I did not hear him, that way I buy my brain cells some time to come up with the answer.

"I'm sorry, George. I couldn't hear you. What were you saying?"

"Rimming. Do you also do rimming?"

It is of no use, I do not know what *rimming* is. I guess I have to come clean and ask.

"I'm sorry, George, can you repeat the word or perhaps explain it? I've never heard the expression before."

"Rimming! Would you lick my anus and stick your tongue in my butt?"

Oh my God! I have never done that... I do not even know what to say. – Nevertheless, I know I definitely do not want to do it! My silence stretches on so long that George asks:

"Are you still there? Can you hear me?"

"Um, yeah, I'm here. I'm sorry, but I don't provide such service. — I don't have a problem using a finger, but not my tongue. That doesn't sound like safe sex. I'm sure you understand, right?"

"Yeah, okay. If I told you I'm healthy and clean, would you do it?"

"No, as I said, a finger, no tongue!"

"Not even for a small incentive on top of your regular fee?"

"No, not for all the money in the world!"

"It's nothing dirty. I'll be completely cleansed. It would be like kissing and licking any other part of my body."

"George, honestly, I'm not squeamish! To be blunt, I just can't bring myself to lick a strange man's asshole!"

Although it is obvious the woman next to me does not understand English, I say this last sentence softly. – Thinking about the special massage I gave Janis yesterday, I might get close to the anus, but only close. That is a far cry from sticking my tongue in someone's butthole!

"Okay, Anika, why don't you think about it some more, it's not like I want to hire you today. I'll call you back sometime. Oh, and one more thing, would you come to my place? I live in Kifissia."

"That's not a problem, I just don't perform rimming. Honestly, I can pleasure you just as well with my finger! — For a home visit, I need your full name, address, and landline number. And, because you live in Kifissia, which is quite a distance for me to travel, I need at least two hours' notice."

"Of course, that's not a problem. I'd give you plenty of notice. Okay then, thanks for the information. Goodbye, Anika! I'm hoping you'll still change your mind. I'd really like to see you."

"Thanks for your call, George. Bye."

Phew! – That was a weird conversation! – I will have to Google *rimming*, I mean, I thought I had been in this profession long enough to hear it all... Well, to err is human.

The tram arrives at the town square in Glyfada. After exiting the tram, I find a seat at a little sidewalk café table on the corner of Metaxa Street and call Violet to tell her where to meet me. It is almost 8:00 p.m. Since it is Saturday, shops have been closed since late afternoon. Sipping the Diet Coke I ordered, I people watch until I see Violet walking down the sidewalk. I get up and we cheerfully greet each other with a big hug and sit down at our table.

"Hi, darling! Let's sit here for a while. It's still too early to go to the Klock House. We'll be the only ones there. Here we can talk undisturbed. What are you drinking? Coke? That's a lot of calories, darling!"

"No, it's Diet Coke. There aren't any calories."

"Oh! I guess I'll have one too," she says and gets up to buy her drink at the self-service counter. Violet is wearing a pink knee-length dress, silver high-heel sandals, and a turquoise clutch. With her pale complexion and long blonde hair, she looks quite elegant in that outfit. Her fingernails have French tips and the jewelry she is wearing consists of a matching set of a single-row pearl necklace and bracelet. She looks damn good for her age. When she returns with her Diet Coke, she puts her reading glasses on and studies my face.

"I don't see any change! What did Eleni do? You look like you did the last time I saw you. I can still see telltale signs of wrinkles on your forehead! Are you sure she injected you with Botox?" I laugh:

"I know she did. But she said the results will only become visible after a week. I told you that. Anyway, I believe my forehead will be wrinkle-free next week."

"Then let's hope the doctor knows what she's doing. Did it hurt a lot?"

"Oh yes, it hurt. But the pain was brief. It was gone as soon as Eleni pulled the needle out. I'm sure you could handle it!"

"Maybe. I guess Botox treatments are better than a face-lift. I've often thought about that. — I mean, I want to keep on working for years to come. So, I've already thought about that aspect. However, a face-lift is expensive. I'm also scared of that procedure, even more than needles! You have to call me as soon as you see a difference. I want to come right over and see you!"

"Okay, I'll inform you of any improvement."

"How did your appointment go at the Hilton? Was he nice?"

"Yes, he was a gentleman, just like I requested in my ad. I even had a glass of champagne with him after sex. He's attending a pharmaceutical convention here with some colleagues."

"I haven't received any calls from pharmacists, but then not everyone who comes to Athens on business wants sex."

"By the way, did you know the Hilton provides *Athens World* for their guests? Harry told me so. That's really great for us!"

"Of course I know! – So what, you didn't? That's how businessmen who stay in upper-class hotels like the Grand Bretagne, Hilton, or Metropolitan find us. Many big hotels throughout the city provide a complimentary copy of *Athens World*! I believe the hotels in Thessaloniki and Patras also provide it. I mean, at times, I get inquiries from luxury hotels in Thessaloniki. Obviously, I don't go there. I even get calls from the islands where I have two clients. One is Jerry, he lives on Ägina. He's quite old and can no longer visit me in Glyfada. Nowadays, when he comes, it almost seems he is going to croak on me. Ha, ha, ha! — But Ägina isn't far away. I simply consider it a day trip. The other man is Malcolm. He's a Brit and always come to Rhodes every August. So I have to fly to see him. Taking a boat would take far too long. But then he pays for everything. I even have my own private room at the same hotel Malcolm stays at, but we have sex in his room. We might go out to dinner together, but we each eat breakfast separately. I wish I hadn't been so stupid when we first reached an agreement for 300 a day. I should have asked for more. Oh well, that's okay. During the month of August, we don't see many businessmen in Athens and well-off Greek men are on vacation on one of the islands and business is always iffy. So, I'm lucky to have Malcolm. I mean, he always wants me for three days, so 900, but he gives me 1000 euros, so that's not bad! — Tell me, did you think all customers purchase *Athens World* at some periptero?"

"Yes — or in a drugstore."

"Oh God, you're so naïve," Violet says and we both chuckle.

As we sit there chatting, we both receive calls, but neither of us generates business. All the men only wanted more information. Hungry for a light meal, we leave the café and walk to a nearby barbecue joint. Violet feels it is not worth going to the pub yet because it will not get busy for at least another hour or so. After dinner, we stroll along Metaxa Street until we eventually turn into the side street and see the neon sign of the Klock House further down the road. The English pub occupies a two-story building. Inside, you can sit at a table or at the bar. Outside, there is a big patio with tables and benches separated by large planters, creating a cozy atmosphere. Violet says:

"Let's sit at the bar. No one is going to approach us if we are sitting at a table and men on the lookout for an adventure do not sit at tables either!"

"Well, you would know! I'm placing myself entirely in your hands!"

"Come on, let's find a spot at the bar!" she says and we commandeer two empty stools at the center of the bar. The establishment's ceiling fans provide a nicer temperature than most air conditioners.

45

We each order a Diet Coke simply because it has zero calories. The preferred entertainment of the Klock House is 80s music, with every fifth song a hit of the latest pop music. Most of the staff and guests speak English. Only here and there, do I hear a few Greek words being spoken. Violet and I visit the restrooms separately, not as girls usually do, and doll ourselves up as best we can. I am sitting on the barstool with my legs crossed and my dress pushed up so the majority of my upper thighs are exposed. We sit there dressed in pink and red, waiting to catch the attention of a fish. A young barman sporting cropped hair serves our drinks and a complimentary bowl of nuts. He and Violet greet each other like old acquaintances and then she introduces him as Johnny. He leaves us to tend to other guests. When he is out of earshot on the terrace, Violet leans over and quietly says:

"He's a client of mine. Don't let on that I've told you! He is 24 years old and I've been seeing him for two years. He's a nice guy and I let him come to my home. He can't afford a hotel and only pays 100. And even that is a lot of money for him. I mean, he manages only with bartending. It's not a well-paying job, so he mostly survives on tips. At least he's loosened up now. He was uptight in the beginning. Now he likes talking to me and seeks advice on how to deal with his girlfriends. Sometimes he tells me what one of his girlfriends said and then wants to know my opinion. I believe he thinks of me as a sex and relationship expert. Obviously, each time we see each other we also have sex. But he's always done quickly. He's an easy customer. Okay, enough of that, here he comes! Don't look at him funny. I don't want him to think we were talking about him. I also don't think any of his colleagues know about us. I'm his secret."

Now and then, while sipping our drinks, we look around the establishment. Two 60-year-old looking English-speaking men grab stools further down the bar and order Kilkenny Beer from the tap. Smoking cigars, they are in deep conversation not paying any attention to us. – So I tell Violet about my meeting with Kevin next Tuesday, where I will be his sex slave.

"What? — You really want to do that? What will you do if he starts hitting you hard? Don't let him bind or gag you! My God, I could never do that! You're too careless, Anika! Don't see that guy. What's he paying you, 500? — Okay, that's good money for one hour, but you don't know what you're getting yourself into. I find it dangerous! — I don't think I could allow somebody to beat me. A slap on the ass is one thing, we're used to that, but that's as far as I go. – I complain when someone grabs my boobs roughly. Unfortunately, too many men like doing it. It's terrible! — Darling, you have to cancel his appointment! I'll be worried sick about you!"

"Well... I want to try it out once. I want to experience it so I'll finally know if I want to make money being beaten. — Don't worry! He didn't sound like a psychopath, just an ordinary man. As soon as I hear from him and have the room number, I'll text it to you with the Kamazon Hotel's address. And if you don't hear from me within two hours, then you can notify the police, okay?"

"Oh, my God! – I don't know if I can do that. If something should really happen to you, they might think I had something to do with it. Or, at least, they'll know I'm a prostitute, which is illegal. – And I'm doing quite well here in Athens. I'm sure you understand that I would not want to jeopardize that."

"Obviously, I was pulling your chain. I could always leave a note behind in my hotel room. — But honestly, I'm not at all worried. If I was, I wouldn't do it."

"Okay, you do what you have to do! But be smart about it and listen to your womanly intuition! Don't only think about the five big ones — you know; better safe than sorry, darling!"

"Yes, I promise to be careful!"

We change the subject and talk about other experiences we've had during our professional lives. Then, out of nowhere, Violet knocks my leg with her knee and her eyes urge me to lean in close. As I turn my head so my ear is close to her mouth, she whispers:

"Don't turn around right now! A man sat down a couple of stools over and he greeted the bartender with a slap on the shoulder, like friends do. So it's not his first time here. And he's definitely a Brit. From London, I can tell. Right now, he's still alone. I don't think it's likely his wife or girlfriend will still show up. Couples go out together on the weekends. Maybe he's meeting a friend or a colleague. Who knows? Before anyone shows up, we should try to snag him. If a friend or an acquaintance of his shows up, he'll simply join us. Once men become absorbed in a conversation about cricket, tennis, golf, or whatever, it'll be much more difficult for us to get their attention."

"As I said; I'm placing myself entirely in your hands. Tell me, how do we go about it?"

"I'm going to ask him for a light. He's a smoker."

"But you don't smoke!"

"I know, but for our purpose, let's say I do. It's an easy way of making immediate contact. See what I have here!"

I hardly believe my eyes. Violet pulls out an open pack of cigarettes from her small handbag.

"Where did you get those from?"

"A customer forgot them at my place. And since it's been a while and

I haven't heard back from him, I confiscated them for this exact situation!"

She laughs mischievously and winks at me.

"I don't even know how to smoke. I'm hoping I don't have a coughing fit!"

Violet pulls a cigarette from the pack and rolls it in between her fingers before holding it with her left index and middle finger as smokers usually do.

"Well, so far you've convinced me. Let's see what happens when you take a drag," I say, poking fun at her. She takes a dry run on the unlit cigarette and looks at me questioningly.

"Bravo, just like a smoker. Don't inhale for too long though when he gives you a light. Be careful the smoke doesn't reach your lungs. Suck a little in your mouth and blow it back out."

Both of us stifle our laughter, even though we would rather burst out. My curiosity gets the better of me and I finally turn around to check out the fish Violet has chosen. Okay, a tall, slender blond man in his 30s. – He is dressed in a pastel, short-sleeve plaid shirt with brightly colored pants, a braided leather belt, and beige leather loafers. On the counter in front of him is a freshly tapped pilsner that he is reaching for while his other hand holds a cigarette. I hear Violet's bright voice:

"Oh no!"

Turning around, I see out of the corner of my eye that Violet has gotten our candidates attention. He stares at her.

"What's wrong?" I ask.

"I've misplaced my lighter! — I really would love to have a drag or two."

Playing the damsel in distress, Violet looks disappointedly at her cigarette and then at *our man*. Since first eye contact has been made and he is a gentleman, he quickly grabs his lighter from the top of his cigarette pack and looks back at Violet.

"May I?" he asks her before flicking his Bic.

"Oh! Darling, thank you! How observant," she says flirtatiously and leans in with her cigarette to the flame. With the first drag, she immediately coughs. It is quite embarrassing and I have a difficult time suppressing a laugh. Nevertheless, Violet is a master of the situation.

"Oh, — oh!" she says, coughing, "I thought I'd still enjoy it. I'm sorry, darling. It has been a while and these smokes are a bit stale. But thank you for lighting my cigarette! I'm Violet and this here is my friend, Anika. What's your name, darling?"

Somehow, Violet has a way of addressing people with *darling* or *baby* so it comes out sounding completely natural. Even with a strange man in a public bar. She does it in such a charming way it does not sound like a cheap come on. She sounds completely natural, which I admire.

"I'm Ethan, Ethan from England. Nice to meet you ladies!"

Feigning embarrassment, I pick at the hem of my dress. At the moment, I cannot come up with a good response, so I smile charmingly as I shake Ethan's offered hand.

"So, you're from England. Where exactly, Ethan? No, let me guess! London?"

"That's right. You can tell by my accent. – And you, where are you from?"

"Anika is from Germany. I'm also from the UK. —Birmingham, to be precise."

"Ah, Birmingham. Pretty area. So, what are you two doing here? Are you on vacation?"

"No, we live and work here. Ethan, darling, why don't you grab your stuff and join us! Or, are you waiting for your date?"

"No, I'm not. —I will join you as long as I'm not ruining your girls' night out."

"Great! Don't worry, you aren't ruining anything. A girls' night out is much more interesting in the company of a nice gentleman."

As Ethan walks over to retrieve his beer and smokes, Violet rolls her eyes as if to convey; the fish has taken the bait. About time. I have become a bit more outgoing, but still feel inhibited striking up a conversation with a strange man sitting next to me in a bar. Maybe I should have an alcoholic drink. It might help. – I lean in toward Violet and whisper:

"I'm going to order a real drink. Something alcoholic!"

When Johnny passes us at the bar, I ask for a glass of rum, which I mix with my Diet Coke. – Ethan places his beer and smokes next to our drinks, then excuses himself before heading to the restroom. – Now Violet leans slightly toward me and says:

"So, now we make idle chitchat with him until he has drunk his third beer. Did you see his wedding ring? If he's happily married, we might have a problem. Let's hope they have children because then we know the *honeymoon* phase is over."

I slightly tap her leg with my foot and nod toward the staircase leading up to the restrooms.

"I take it he's on his way back?"

"Yep."

Hoping the alcohol will help, I take a big swig of my rum and Diet Coke. Presently, the pub is jam-packed. Inside and out, all table and seats are occupied. – Naturally, the noise level is much louder with everyone talking at once and the music seems to have been turned up. Ethan scoots a stool nearer and we all squeeze closer. He orders drinks for us and a beer for himself, so I make myself a rum and Diet Coke again. The alcohol works, helping me to relax and loosen my lips. Now I have no problem with having a nice, normal chat with Ethan, after all, it is how we will get him into bed! Now we only have to figure out if he is willing to pay for it. Ethan tells us about himself and the group of students who have an apprenticeship for a week at the Saronic Hotel in Vouliagmeni. Evidently, he does it several times a year, but mainly during the summer. He also reveals he is married with three daughters. Then he inquires about what we are doing in Athens. Violet tells him we work in the entertainment industry.

"I'm afraid to ask what branch of the entertainment industry." Ethan laughs out loud. "Are you perhaps companions?"

"Yes, darling, you guessed it! I'm hoping you feel good in our company. As you can see, even in our free time we can't stop entertaining nice men. It's not just our profession, it's our calling, — isn't that right, Anika?"

"So true. We simply love it. You see, it doesn't matter that it's our girls' night out, we don't mind offering you intimate company."

Wow, I did not know I could be that brave. I hope I did not cross the line. I give Violet an insecure look, but she winks at me and adds:

"Yes, darling, and we can make you a great offer. Would you be interested in a little physical closeness? – Perhaps a nice relaxing massage? Or, can you think of a special wish we could make come true for you? Don't be shy, it's only us here, you're among friends."

Ethan downs his beer in one gulp and sets the empty glass on the bar counter. He is shaking his head, looking back and forth between Violet and me.

"Well, that was a surprise attack. So, you ladies really are... you know. And you do it for money?"

"Yes. Why, does that bother you, darling?" Violet is in her element.

"No, I wasn't born yesterday."

"I thought so. Up to now, it has only been harmless fun! It's entirely up to you how this evening proceeds. We can leave it at what we have now or we can have more fun. It's your call. We won't pressure you. After all, it's our girls' night out!"

"Sure, your girls' night out. — If I may inquire discreetly, if you were working, how much would your services cost?"

"On a regular workday, like tomorrow, it's 150 an hour for each, but tonight, as we're only out for fun and we want some more with you, you could get a great two for one deal. You've been a gentleman, you lit my cigarette, and you bought us drinks. That is something we know how to show appreciation for!"

"Oh boy, you two are crazy chicks! However, I find you both simpatico. —I'd be lying if I said I wasn't interested in taking the next step. But..."

"But what? What's on your mind! Would you like to know what an intimate hour with the two of us will cost?"

"Well, there's that, but I'd also like to know where this hour of fun would take place. — We can't go to my hotel, everybody knows me. Do you have an apartment or another solution?"

"There's a pretty no-tell hotel nearby. We'll even cover the cost of the room. And in regard to the first question, if you decide to have that sexy hour with us, it's a measly 200 euros"

"Oh boy, you really know how to drive a man crazy... – However, I don't know, to be honest. Don't be upset with me! — I'm really enjoying you girls' company, sitting here chatting. Perhaps we should leave it at that..."

"Certainly, baby, we accept your decision. If your reluctance isn't because of the price, then we'll forget about the subject. It's that simple. — *Jamás!*"

Violet raises her glass to toast with Ethan, but his beer glass is empty. He rapidly orders another one, clearly embarrassed. I have no idea how we will talk our way out of this awful situation.

"Other than the waiters, does anyone else know you here?" Violet asks Ethan.

"Not that I know of, why?"

"Follow me to the restroom in a minute. I want to show you something," she says as she gets up and heads up the staircase to the restrooms while leaving Ethan and me behind to wonder. I have no idea what she is up to. Ethan looks at me questioningly, but all I can do is shrug and say:

"I don't know what she has in mind. Just go after her and see what the surprise is."

Ethan gets up and follows her. – After a few minutes, Violet returns alone.

"What's going on? What did you do to him?" I ask, barely able to contain my curiosity.

"Quite simply, I dragged him into the unlocked staff toilet and that was that. He was immediately all over me and started kissing me and groping my tits. I reached down, touched his crotch, and started massaging his already hard cock. Ethan gasped with lust. I believe he needs a minute to calm himself before rejoining us. I don't imagine he stayed behind to finish the job. Our game would be over then. Anyway, I willingly took the risk. I even said that it was a taste of what he can expect. — I smoothed out my dress, used the ladies facilities, inspected myself in the mirror, and now I'm sitting here with you! — I tell you, he's as horny as a rabbit. Let's drink up and pay. When Ethan returns, we'll say we're leaving and that he's welcome to tag along. — Either he makes up his mind and we end up at the Lenny Blue Hotel or we'll say goodbye and go our separate ways. I'm betting he comes along or he might chase us down after a few minutes!" she whispers to me. Noticing Ethan approach, I nod to Violet and she signals Johnny to settle the bill.

46

Ethan decides to take us up on our offer. Violet and I leave the Klock House ahead of him and bide our time in front of a movie theater down the street.

A few minutes pass before he catches up. Violet leads the short walk to the Lenny Blue Hotel. Once inside, Violet takes care of the formalities at the front desk while Ethan and I wait at the elevator. Our room, number 10, is decorated in the usual erotic brothel theme and bathed in red light. Ethan is as horny for our bodies as a dog after a bitch in heat. I slip out of my dress and bra and place them neatly folded on a small table. Except for her lingerie, Violet also undresses. Her voluptuous boobs protrude nicely over the rim of her pink bra displaying an enticing cleavage. Sandwiched between us, Ethan starts fondling and kneading my breasts before leaning down to suck my nipples. He turns around and motorboats Violet's white breasts. The ensuing minutes are a frenzy of grabbing and smooching as Violet and I unbutton his shirt and remove his clothing one piece at a time. Finally, Violet sits on the edge of the bed with her legs spread apart. Ethan kneels down between Violet's thighs on the bedside mat, a plush flokati rug. I grab a rubber and roll it over his wiener.

"Lie down next to us so I can look at your pussy!" Ethan prompts me excitedly. After removing my panties, I lie down completely naked next to Violet and pull up my legs to present my pussy. Ethan slides a leg hole of Violet's panties aside and penetrates her. Steadily, he fucks Violet and fondles her breasts with his right hand while sticking two fingers from his left hand into my pussy. He sure has his hands full with us. All of a sudden, he pulls his cock out of Violet and slides over to me.

"Wait! You have to put a new condom on if you want to fuck me," I say.

"Why?"

"Because it's safer, we don't pass along germs."

"Okay, I'm going to go back to fucking you," he says, addressing Violet. "Turn around, I want to take you from behind now."

Violet kneels on the flokati rug and braces herself with her elbows on the bed. After finding the entrance to her pussy from behind, he thrusts into her. Hearing a loud *ooh* escape her lips, I know Ethan caused pain.

"Anika, I want you to assume the same position next to Violet. That way I can just slide over. You also want to get fucked, right?"

"Sure, darling. Go ahead and put your fingers back into my pussy!"

Ethan smacks my butt and says:

"No can do, you horny slut! I'm going to make you wait! But don't worry, you'll get yours!"

He is fucking Violet with slow thrusts while watching me twitch and moan, pretending to be turned on by the smacks to my butt. By the time he wants to do me, I have a new condom ready. I promptly pull off the used one, toss it on the ground next to the bed, and roll the new rubber over his penis. Violet makes brief eye contact with me to let me know she has had enough of him. Although in the position Ethan requested, he now wants me in the middle of the bed on all fours. He slaps his boner against my buttocks before sticking it all the way in and leaving it there. Turning my head to see what is going on, I see Violet kneeling behind him with a hand between his legs, stroking his balls.

"You do all the moving around!" Ethan addresses me. "I want to watch and feel your ass moving around!"

So his stick does not slip out of my pussy, I move my butt in a slow circular manner to get a feel for his penis. Having sized it up, I start repeatedly moving slightly back and forth while making sure to push my pussy firmly against his crotch so every centimeter enjoys the fun. Eventually, Ethan can no longer hold still and starts moving. It does not take long until he is wild with lust. Since I am on all fours, I arch my back and push my upper body backward so my ass sticks up. With force, Ethan immediately starts thrusting more urgently and I have to grab the bed sheets to stay in place. Ethan is in high gear. To drive him even wilder, Violet lies down next to me and presents her gorgeous alabaster body that is dressed in exquisite, lacy pink lingerie for his viewing pleasure. As Ethan is about to climax, he starts slapping my ass again. This always makes me think about cowboys since they spur their horses into a gallop that way. Finally, at last, he comes. Yippee ki-yay! It is over. – He has achieved his goal. Spent, Ethan falls onto the bed while I quickly inspect the rubber. All is well! I pull it off gently and go to discard it on the floor next to the other one when Violet says:

"Let me have it, I'm going to use the bathroom."

Picking up the other one, she disappears into the bathroom. Ethan gets up, grabs a pack of smokes from the back pocket of his pleated pants and lights up. Then he sits back down on the bed next to me.

"These hotels are found throughout Athens?" he inquires while scanning the plush room.

"Yes, and not only tourists or prostitutes and their suitors frequent them. Young Greek couples still living at home with their parents also use these hotels for sex."

"Interesting. It would have been great if such hotels had been around in London when I was in my prime. How much is the usual rate for a room and for how long can I book it?"

"As far as I know, it depends on the size and furnishings of a room. For two or three hours, it is anywhere between 25-60 euros."

"Can you stay overnight or is it only on an hourly basis?"

"I'm sure you could work out a deal to stay overnight. Usually these establishments rent by the hour. — Why? Are you planning on bringing your students here?" I ask, grinning. Ethan chuckles and replies:

"No, definitely not! They would only get stupid ideas in their heads."

When Violet returns, I excuse myself and hop in the shower. Once Violet and I are dressed, Ethan hands each of us a green 100-euro bill and asks if the room is already paid for. Violet shakes her head and Ethan says he will take care of it and that we can go. He is going to stay a bit longer.

"Thank you, darling, you're a real gentleman!" Violet says and gives him a kiss on the cheek. I say goodbye and before we leave the room, he calls after us:

"Thank you, ladies. I had an enjoyable evening with you!"

Once out on the road, Violet tells me Ethan asked whether she always uses this hotel when meeting clients.

"I told him I allow established clients to come to my apartment. He asked for my phone number, which I naturally gave him. Did he also ask for your number?"

"No, he didn't. I guess you're more his type."

"I don't know, perhaps it's because he can come to my home. Many men prefer visiting a private residence for their sexual fantasies. – Everybody knows why when they're seen entering a no-tell hotel. That's not the case with a private residence. – Anyway, we'll see. He might never call me. — So, what do we want to do now? Go home?"

"Let's see, what time is it. — Oh! It's already 1:25 a.m. Yes, I think it's time to head home."

"Okay. I only have a short walk home. I guess you're going to take a cab, right?"

"Yes, there's no other choice at this time of the night. I'll catch one at the nearest main road. — Okay, Violet, it was nice. I've enjoyed our time together."

"Yeah, me too. And next Thursday we'll meet at the market and go afterward to my place for coffee, all right?"

"Okay! I'm sure by then you'll see results of the Botox treatment. Take a good look at me now and put it to memory."

At that moment, a taxi pulls up next to us and the driver lowers the front passenger window and asks something in Greek. Violet talks to him and then turns to me:

"Hop on in, Anika, he'll drive you home. Have a good night, darling, we'll talk tomorrow! Okay?"

"Sounds good, bye."

I get in the cab and tell the driver:

"Piraeus, the Lilo Hotel, please."

"*Endaksi*, Piraeus!" he acknowledges, and off we go, driving through the lively and vibrant summer night in Athens.

Endaksi means *in order* or *okay*. One of the many Greek words I have learned. Checking my phone, I see I missed some calls. Before we arrived at the Klock House, I put the phone on silent mode so we would not be disturbed during our girls' night out. Jason from Kifissia called twice around 10:00 p.m. With him, I would have made 200... too late now. I will not let it ruin the pleasant evening. Violet and I had a beautiful and successful night! I lean back and close my eyes. Weariness envelops me.

It was quite a long day. I am going to sleep in.

47

While eating breakfast, my phone rings. It is Violet.

"Morning, darling! You won't believe what just happened! Ethan called! He wants to come over tonight. You know — not for a social visit. Something I would never allow. No way! He wanted an appointment for a sex session. He told me he can't get my red-haired pussy out of his brain. Just thinking of it gets him all hot and horny again. However, I don't feel too euphoric because he managed to get me to come down in my rate! He is only going to pay 100! His reason: There won't be any traveling or hotel costs if he comes to my home, and he can't afford more. If I insist on my usual rate, he'll have no choice but to turn me down. — Naturally, I tried to haggle with him and said I'd do it for 120, which still left him with a 30-euro discount. Then he brought up last night again, saying I was willing to do it for a 100 then, so why not now. He also asked for your telephone number, which I gave him. I don't know if he asked for it simply to put me on the spot, but I had other things on my mind. You know, over the years I've fine-tuned my ability to read men and I know Ethan won't pay me more than he's willing, red bush or not. So, I had a choice to make. Remain stubborn and make zero or give in and be 100 euros richer. Obviously, I gave in and told him he could come at 8:00 p.m. Jack will be gone by then. So, darling, I hope you're not upset with me. But now you know if he calls you: he'll only pay 100. Perhaps he'll justify it by saying he doesn't pay me more either. — Please forgive me, darling! Things like this can happen. I take it you made it home all right. Are you okay?"

"Yes, everything was fine. – The taxi driver knew the hotel and 40 minutes later, I was home. The traffic on Poseidonos Street was horrendous. In Alimos, we hit a traffic jam and it was stop-and-go for several kilometers. I was dead tired by the time I got to my room. Although, I've been seriously contemplating moving to Glyfada in August. –
I'm sure there are cheap hotels there too, right? I mean, so far, most of my appointments are in Glyfada. I only have a few in Piraeus. It would save me lots of travel time and cost. — First, though, I have to see how well business is going. And don't worry about Ethan! It's okay, I'm sure I would have done the same."

"Thank you, darling. – Hearing you say that means a lot to me! And I will make sure he's out once the hour is up. If he thinks he's going to get special treatment because I came onto him he has another thing coming. He already has a generous discount. — Darling, if you're serious about moving to Glyfada, I can show you a hotel near the town square where I stayed when I first started out. It might be outdated. I don't know when the last time it was renovated, but I should show it to you. Who knows, maybe you'll be okay with it. If you tell them you want to stay for more than a month, I'm sure it'll be inexpensive. All right, darling, Christo is coming tomorrow at 10:00 a.m. You know who I'm talking about — my elderly customer who pays 60, but is always done quickly. If I'm lucky, Socrates will visit on Wednesday. He already inquired if I have time early in the evening. I always make time for him! As I've said, I'm still waiting for confirmation. I'm curious how it'll be with Ethan this time. I haven't given him my address yet. I told him we'd meet in the parking lot near my home. — Do you already have clients booked for today?"

"No, nothing so far. Maybe Dimitri will call. He's the man I met at Marina Kalamaki. I'm going out for lunch, other than that, I will have to wait and see. Okay, Violet, I'll call you later. Have a nice day, bye!"

"Yes, bye, sweetie. Kisses!"

Dressed up in case I receive a business call, I walk down the street toward Mikrolimano to grab a bite to eat. This small harbor is a bit further away than Zeas Marina, but I do not mind because I need a change of scenery. Discovering a nice seafood restaurant along the sea, I sit down on the outside patio and enjoy shrimp saganaki.

By 7:00 p.m., I am becoming concerned since I still have not received any business calls, although I did receive two calls from local Greek men who wanted information. One found my rate too high and the other wanted a woman with voluptuous breasts and a big butt. At the most, my breasts are medium size. Only when I wear a push-up bra do they really shine. Thankfully, my butt is not large either — it is sexy.

Strolling around the harbor and marveling at the gorgeous boats, I fish my phone out of my handbag to check once more if I have received a call without noticing. Once again, zilch... Given that it is early Sunday evening, lots of people, families with children, couples, and groups of adolescent stroll along the marina's promenade. Not one soul is alone, except me of course. Although this fact does not sadden me, I am heading back to the Lilo Hotel because it is too crowded for me. After undressing, as soon as I boot up my laptop, my phone rings. Overjoyed that I finally am getting a call, I immediately answer it without bothering to check the display.

"Hello!"

"Hello! I'm David," says a soft male voice.

"Hi, David, I'm Anika. Would you like to know more about me?"

"Yes, please, Anika. You're German, right?"

I confirm his statement and tell him all he needs to know.

"Okay, that sounds promising, Anika. So, you're 35 years old. — That's an attractive age. I'm a few years older, 38. Tell me, Anika, are you also beautiful?"

"Yes, I am. – I wouldn't be successful in this business if I wasn't pretty."

"I meant no offense, okay! All I'd like to know is whether you're womanly?"

"Yes, I'd say I am womanly!"

"That's good. Because many women in your profession think they're beautiful, but I'm sorry to say, most lack charm and femininity. I include those characteristics when I speak of beauty. Okay, I believe it when you say you have all those womanly attributes, which is why I'd like to hire you. — So, Anika, would you have time tomorrow afternoon?"

"That depends on what time you have in mind. Also, where do you want to meet?"

"3:00 p.m. in Glyfada would be great. Do you know the Gordens Hotel on Poseidonos Street?"

"Yes, I do. Unfortunately, I'm already booked at 3:00 p.m. I can see you two hours earlier or later, say around 5:00 p.m."

"5:00 p.m. works too. So, are we on for tomorrow afternoon?"

"Yes, we are! Okay, when you have a room call or text me the room number and I'll be there shortly, all right?"

"Yes, I'll do that. I'm going to text you the room number as soon as I have it."

"Great! Until tomorrow afternoon then, David!"

"See you tomorrow, Anika. – I'm really looking forward to meeting you! Adieu!"

I save his number under 'David - Gordens' and immediately feel easier now that I finally have a new appointment. Today might have been a bust, but at least tomorrow, I already have two appointments!

So it will not seem like an eternity until bedtime, I decide to pass the time by taking an evening stroll. Walking down the staircase of the hotel, my phone rings. It is coming from the Hilton Hotel, a business call. Not wanting to talk out in the open, I answer:

"Hi, darling. Please call me back in a minute so we can talk in private. Thank you very much!"

Foolishly, I hang up abruptly and instantly regret it. It was rude not to even greet the caller. I hope he will call back! I fly back up the stairs and into my room and impatiently pace back and forth for five minutes until my phone finally rings again. Comforted, I see the number for the Hilton. I blurt out:

"Hi, darling! Sorry about earlier, but I wasn't alone. I'm so glad you called back. Hi, I'm Anika."

"Hello, Anika. — No problem! I'm Charlie. I'm calling about your rate and to find out if you have time to see me at the Hilton Hotel."

After telling Charlie the usual information, I also inform him I have time this evening.

"So, you say you're slim. — Slim is good, but I hope no bones are sticking out!" he says jokingly.

"No, don't worry. I'm not bony, darling."

"Great. Tell me, when could you be here?"

"In about an hour. — First, I need your full name and room number. Then I'll call you back shortly to confirm and then I'll be on my way."

"Outstanding. My name is Charlie Morin and I'm in room 921. Is that it?"

"Yes, darling. I'll call you right back."

Everything checks out and I literally hop into the shower, towel off, touch up my eye makeup, put on my white stretch dress, grab my purse, and leave my room and the hotel in an excellent mood.

48

To keep expenses as low as possible, I walk and catch the subway in Piraeus to Syntagma Square. From there, I will grab a taxi to the Hilton. Currently, in the evenings before and after sunset, I can make such a journey without exertion. As usual, I check my appearance in the hotel elevator mirror and smooth out my dress. Once on the floor, I confidently walk down the corridor. Passing a hotel employee pushing a tea cart laden with drinks, we greet each other cordially. No reason for her to suspect I am anything but a guest as I knock on door 921. Charlie opens it a moment later.

To my surprise, Charlie is a black man! – He did not mention this on the phone, but then why would he! He is a tall burly man wearing glasses and sporting a short beard.

"Hi, Charlie!"

"Hi, Anika. Come on in."

Walking into his room, I silently pray he did not notice my initial reaction to his skin color. So far, privately or at work, I have never had sex with a black man. This will be the first time. I never believed I would react so surprised. However, he will not see my embarrassment.

"Charlie, I haven't asked where you are from. America? Africa?"

"I'm from New York. Why do you ask? Because I'm black?"

"No, only curious. — Are you in Athens on vacation or business?"

"I came here for a convention. In two days, I'm flying back to the States. Today is my first day off, so to speak, so I wanted to treat myself to something especially; a charming German lady! — You should see your face, Anika. Are you sure you don't mind that I'm a black man?"

"No, that's not it. I don't mind at all. I merely didn't expect it. That's it. — Tell me, Charlie, may I use the bathroom? I'd like to freshen up and change."

"Certainly. — You're beautiful, Anika. I really hope my skin color doesn't bother you."

"It doesn't, Charlie, please don't worry about it!"

I abruptly disappear into the bathroom to escape the embarrassing situation. Breathing deeply, I compose myself. Whatever his skin color, it does not matter! I am not a racist. I once had an Indonesian boyfriend. Whether his skin is light or dark brown, it is all the same. I do not know why I reacted the way I did. I leisurely change into my sexy lingerie. When finished, I inspect myself in the mirror. Dressed in my chic, red mesh bodysuit trimmed in vinyl, I feel my old self again, ready to do my job. To improve my own well-being, I spritz *Must de Cartier* behind my ears and go back into the main room. Charlie is sitting on the sofa, still fully dressed. I immediately feel insecure, thinking Charlie saw my reaction to his skin color and now does not want to have sex. What am I going to do? It is difficult for me to be natural. Dressed in my beautiful mesh bodysuit and red patent leather shoes, I stop in the middle of the room and look at Charlie, expecting him to politely tell me why he does not want to have sex with me, given my reaction, and that we should just call it quits and he will reimburse me for my effort and travel cost... While I am thinking this, Charlie gets up and slowly approaches me. He stands before me, takes my bag, tosses it on the bed, and then takes me in his arms. My thoughts zigzag through my brain. What was I thinking? Then, I feel Charlie's hands on my hips and in my hair. They feel like ordinary hands; soft, warm and dry, nothing to be afraid of. Holding me close in one arm, Charlie's other hand grabs my hair at the nape forcing me to look into his eyes. Looking through his glasses at his eyes, I see warmness and compassion.

"I like you, Anika!" he says. "Make yourself comfortable on the bed! I'm going to hop in the shower. I'll be right back."

I manage to smile and say softly:

"Sure, darling."

Charlie releases me. Soon, I hear the shower running. Pulling the comforter back, I assume a seductive pose on the bed. When the sound of running water stops, I grab a condom in each size and set them next to the pillow. The scent of my perfume relaxes me. Charlie walks out of the bathroom naked and without glasses. Time to go to work.

"Take that outfit off; I want you completely naked when I take you," Charlie says, as he comes toward me.

"How do you want me, darling?" I ask as I kneel on the bed with my legs slightly apart. Teasingly, I slowly strip off my bodysuit so Charlie will not see my naked body all at once. He is sitting on the edge of the bed, watching me. His cock is still flaccid and appears to be somewhere between medium and large. Is that not the general census? Supposedly, black men have huge peckers. I hope Charlie is in the normal range.

"Lie on your stomach," he says. I push the pillow and rubbers aside and get into a prone position with my arms crossed above my head, curious to see what happens next. Charlie spreads my legs and starts roughly fondling my pussy. Finally, he parts my lips and puts a finger inside which, thankfully, is moistened. I move my pelvis, pretending to be turned on. He immediately takes it as an invitation to stick the finger even deeper and harder into my pussy.

"Let me have a condom. I want to fuck you now," he says gruffly. Since I am unable to see his cock, I reach and hand him an extra-large rubber to be on the safe side.

"Should I turn around?"

"No. Stay there! I'm going to take you from behind first," he replies curtly. I hear him tearing the wrapper. Shortly after, he is between my legs shoving his black wiener into my pink pussy. It does not take but a few hard thrusts before he moans out loud and comes. That was fast! What was I worried about? — Once Charlie is lying next to me, panting heavily, I quickly check out his cock. Choosing an extra-large condom was warranted. Even now, as it is softening, it is still larger than average.

"That was fast. Intentional?" I ask jokingly as I pull the rubber from his cock and toss it on the ground.

"I never do anything unintentionally, trust me, sweetie!" he manages to say, still breathing heavily. "We've only just begun. The rest of the hour is still ahead of us. This was simply to relieve the pressure. I'm going to take you again in a moment and then I can enjoy it."

I know without looking at my watch that I cannot protest. When we talked on the phone I said an hour of sex, not once he came.

"Come here and lie in my arm!" Charlie says holding his left arm out. I roll into it and snuggle up against him. Earlier, a strange smell perplexed me. Now I know it is coming from his skin. It is not body odor, aftershave, or whatever fragrance. Placing my hand on his chest, I play with his small dark curly hair. Some would say the hair feels somewhat scratchy, however, it is not unpleasantly so. Assuming Charlie would enjoy a blowjob and some cum is still on his cock, I get up to get another extra-large condom.

"What are you doing?" Charlie asks.

"I want to suck your cock, baby. — Why? You have something else in mind?"

"A blowjob would be great — but please without a rubber. Any chance of that happening?"

"Yes, as long as you wash it. I'm sure you understand."

"Naturally, Anika. — Give me a minute, I mean, we still have time, right?"

"Certainly. The hour isn't up yet."

"May I ask you something personal?"

"Sure, go ahead."

"Are you a natural blonde?"

"No, I dye my hair."

"It doesn't matter. I don't think I wouldn't have noticed the difference anyway. In any case, blonde hair looks good on you. I can't imagine you with different hair color. — As a black man, I naturally love blonde women and their pale skin. — Did it give you a thrill to have a black man in bed?"

I swallow and fib:

"Yes, such contrast during sex can be quite erotic."

"Glad to hear it. Earlier, I thought you had a problem with me being black. And I definitely didn't want you forcing yourself to have sex with me! — But once you came out of the bathroom, I set aside such silly notions. I wanted to eat you up. You really have a terrific figure. I know many young women in the States who starve themselves and have their breasts enlarged, thinking it'll make them oh-so sexy. — But that's not my taste, which is why I asked if you were bony." Charlie laughs and disappears into the bathroom!

So, those absurd thoughts I had when he was still dressed sitting on the sofa were for naught. Now relaxed, I know I will not act so stupid with the next black man I entertain!

Freshly showered, Charlie comes back and lies next to me on the bed. Now it is my turn to get his big schlong nice and hard again. Needless to say, I point out he is not to come in my mouth. It only takes a few minutes of oral sex before Charlie is extremely excited. He tells me to put a rubber on his penis and to stand up facing the balcony door. Puzzled, I get up, slip on my red heels, and walk over to the balcony door. Pushing the curtain aside, I happily note that it is already dark outside. It seems Charlie wants to fuck me while enjoying the view of the illuminated Acropolis. Standing with my legs slightly apart and bent, I lean forward and brace myself with my hands against the pane so my butt sticks out enticingly. Charlie has already put the rubber on his huge cock before stepping up behind me and shoving it deep into my pussy. A lot of time passes without Charlie approaching orgasm. I guess it takes him longer to come a second time.

"Turn around!" he says eventually.

Relieved from the uncomfortable position, I turn around. Wrapping my arms around his neck, I move my left leg around his hip, allowing him to penetrate me. – Charlie is not only a big man he is also very strong. As if I was light as a feather, he grabs my buttocks and lifts me up. I wrap my right leg around his hips and let Charlie do the all the work as I hang on like a monkey while his wiener slides in and out of my pussy.

Finally, his movements become uncoordinated and he comes with a loud *aaahhhh*. Hanging there, I let him ride out his orgasm. Afterward, he sets me down and buries his face in my hair. Although he did all the work, I am exhausted from keeping my legs around him. – My knees wobble and I need his help until the blood starts circulating in my legs again. Finally, I say:

"Okay, Charlie, you can let go of me now. May I use the bathroom?"

"Sure, go right ahead. I'll stay here and relax on the bed. Take all the time you need, sweetie."

When I am all done, I use my favorite perfume again. I still smell Charlie on me and it has now become unpleasant. When I walk back into the room, Charlie immediately jumps up and hands me a glass of water.

"I'm sure you're thirsty. Please, drink! — By the way, thanks for playing along. Sometimes I enjoy getting a workout during sex. My orgasm is the reward!"

Charlie laughs and I cannot tell if he means it or is pulling my leg. In one gulp, I almost finish the glass and set it on the coffee table.

"I can't say I like exhausting myself during sex. Your position was a nice change of pace," I comment carefully.

"Wait, let me get your money!" Charlie says and grabs his wallet from the desk. As he hands me some folded-up bills, he says:

"Keep the change!"

Without counting the money, I pocket it. Perhaps he included a tip, which is why I say:

"Thank you, darling! It was nice meeting you. — Tell me, what kind of convention did you attend last week?"

"Pharmaceutical," he says.

"I see! — Well, I wish you a safe flight home to New York," I reply with a smile, thinking he must be Harry's colleague, who also had me come to the Hilton. Charlie hugs me goodbye and escorts me to the door. Deeply satisfied that I had business today after all, I step outside into the warm evening air and start walking toward Thiseio. It is a part of Athens' old town that I am not quite yet familiar with. I will spend the rest of the evening here watching tourists. Perhaps I will receive another call, perhaps not, whichever is fine.

Checking what Charlie paid me, I notice I received a 20-euro tip. Fantastic! After all, money provides happiness!

49

The ringing of my phone rips me out of a deep sleep. I see it is a call from an Athens' landline. I answer with a *good morning* and hear a friendly-sounding Greek man. Unfortunately, I do not understand a word.

"Do you speak English, darling?"

"Yes. You don't speak Greek?"

"No, only English and German."

"Okay, that's no problem. — I'm staying at the Klaros Hotel on Syngrou Avenue and would like to know if you can come right now and how much you charge. Oh, and it would be nice to know a little bit more about you, what you look like and whatnot."

"Certainly. I'm slim-figured and blonde with blue eyes. I charge 150 for an hour of safe sex. I can be at your place in about 45 minutes."

"Wow, that's a lot! Would you do it for 100? Usually, I pay no more than 80 when I hire the service of ladies like you."

On one side, I know I could use the money, especially in the beginning, but on the other hand, I am tired of reducing my rate especially since it is the middle of the night. Taking a taxi there will cost at least 15 leaving me with only 70, not to mention the lost sleep. I reply:

"I'm sorry, darling, but my rate is 150. I don't work for less at night."

"Okay, I'm sorry, I'm not interested then. I would've liked to meet you, but I'm not willing to dish out almost twice what I usually pay. Good night!"

He hangs up. And I do not have his name. Who cares! I switch off the light and sink back into the mattress for 40 more winks.

Waking up the next morning, I feel a strange sensation on my forehead. It is tight. Grabbing the 5x magnification mirror, I finally see the results of my Botox treatment. My facial area is taut. Hooray! I am pleased and feel like calling Violet, but it is way too early. Instead, I am going out on the balcony while it is still nice and cool to enjoy the slightly salty breeze blowing in from the sea. It is a gorgeous summer morning in Piraeus and a fantastic morning in my new life. All in all, I am happy. My conscience is clear regarding last night's customer. I have earned more than 3000 in two weeks! — Yesterday, when I was walking around Mikrolimani, before I even had a prospective customer, I was already happy. Sometimes I wonder why I feel this way. Is it pure greed? Or, is it because I do not have a guaranteed income and I will soon have to pay for private health insurance? At my age, I must start setting aside money as nothing flows into my German pension fund. Had I stayed in Germany where I had a job with a fixed income along with hooking part-time, I could still have benefits like health insurance. At the time, I was fine if I had no clients, even for days. Now it is different. I will have to be patient and remain calm. No reason to start wallowing in self-pity! That is the price of being self-employed, sometimes you start sweating! Something will come up. In the meantime, I am enjoying my new life by the sea. – After breakfast, I call Violet.

"Good morning, darling! How are you?"

"Hello, sweetie! Christo's coming at 11:00 a.m. You know, the quick guy who only pays 60. Anyway, I'm all ready for him. The bed is made, windows are closed, and the air-conditioning is on. I'm wearing a black negligee he's so fond of. What's going on with you? Did you have any business yesterday?"

"Yes, I did. I was lucky to receive a call from the Hilton. – A black man from New York. It was my first time with a black man."

"Okay. You had a black man as a customer? Did you mind? I don't think I'm racist — I'm not, but I just can't service those men any longer. Obviously, I did in the beginning, but nowadays I can afford not to. I'm getting more sensitive the older I become. I've no idea why that is... but I also can't have sex with someone physically disabled. Oh God! When I see them, I change. Don't think I disapprove of these people, I don't! However, going to bed with one is so different compared to meeting them in public, at a friend's place, or wherever. — I'd feel sorry for the man and I wouldn't be my happy cheerful self who can get her suitor off without a hitch. I'd be too inhibited to perform my job. — And look, London is full of blacks. It's not like they're strangers to me. I had a fantastic doctor, my gynecologist, if you can believe it. I didn't mind. When he examined me, his hand felt and did what a white man's hand does. — But I don't want to have sex with a black man! — How was it for you?"

"Like I said, it was a first for me. At the beginning, I wasn't relaxed like I usually am with a white guy. — I don't know what I was expecting... somehow, I was able to do my job. Now I know I can be my usual relaxed self the next time I have a black man as a client. — I think it was only in my head. — In Germany, I once had a customer whose forearm was amputated and another time, I had guy who wasn't all there upstairs. However, my boss had known him for a long time and she said I didn't have to worry about being alone in a room with him. She was right. He was a kind soul, an easy customer. I gave him a blowjob with a condom and suddenly he came! — The other, the amputee, he never talked much. – I believe he had physiological problems. He never smiled and it didn't matter what I did, he remained closed off. He probably thought I was only interested in doing my job and getting out of there, although, that wasn't the case. I would have loved to see him happy. Happy customers have always been important to me! Maybe he thought of me as a cold, unfeeling prostitute, just there to be used and abused. Who knows?"

"Yes, who knows, darling! — Anyway, I feel better not doing certain things, like anal sex, BDSM, and servicing blacks and disabled people. — I simply can't relax and then I'm not happy either."

"Well, you don't have to. It's not like there's a law stating otherwise. We're self-employed and can choose whoever as clients. And that's that! – Don't worry, I won't look at you differently now. — Anyway, enough of this. Listen, this morning I saw the first results of the Botox injections! When I frown, you can only see a few signs of wrinkles, that's it. The frown lines between my eyes are gone. No matter how hard I try, my forehead remains nice and smooth."

"Fabulous! When can we meet? – Thursday, at the market? I'm already excited. I'm going to make an appointment with Eleni also."

"Yes, we'll get together on Thursday. But now, tell me, how was it with Ethan last night?"

"Oh, it was okay!" I told him we'd meet at the periptero next to a parking lot near my apartment. I told him to call once he arrived. It's not like I wanted to hang out on the street waiting for him to get there. How would that look? Everyone knows me. And what would old Panajota the periptero vendor think? Often, I buy something from her. — So, Ethan calls and two minutes later, I meet him. I'm wearing a knee-length, snug, floral summer dress with plunging neckline. So, quite normal. I greeted him and then we walked down the road to my garden gate. You know, I always tell my clients to use the stairs, never the elevator. The same I did with Ethan, in case he wants to come back. Anyway, it's more likely a customer will run into one of my neighbors when using the elevator and who needs that. I'm sure one of them would rope him into a conversation. You know old Greek women, all they want is gossip. — Now we're in my apartment and he tells me how nice and tasteful it is. Naturally, I thanked him. Then, I showed him the bathroom, instructing him to wash his hands and you know what! He looks skeptically at me, so I had to repeat myself. Anyway, I showed him the small guest towels I keep on the washing machine next to the sink. — You know, Anika, every visitor freshens up, at least their hands and cock. I mean, they touch me all over with their hands. They stick their fingers in me and want their balls licked. Who knows what they touched beforehand? He might have been surprised, but he did as I requested and I heard the faucet. You know what I mean, right?"

"Yes, obviously. I did that in the clubs back in Germany. – Once picked, I first took the customer into the bathroom, asked him to open his pants, freed his penis, and washed it under the running faucet with soap from a dispenser. Naturally, I made sure the water temperature was pleasant. – It was a good way to inspect the man's cock. Is it reddish? Are there pimples or eczema? Does he have cheese growing under the foreskin? — Yuck! God, I don't even want to think about it! Nevertheless, shit like that happens. — Depending on how it looked, I gave a blowjob with or without a rubber. Most customers hardened as I washed their proud members. They never complained about my erotic water massage. Regulars knew my procedure and usually fondled or fingered my ass as I washed them. Obviously, they had to wash their hands again before we went into a room. — But now, it's a different story when visiting hotel rooms. I still have to come up with something. I know some men wash themselves and their schlong beforehand, but you never know... I always examine a penis and pull the foreskin back before sucking it. The man is never the wiser because I do it playfully. What is your routine for hotels and home visits?"

"I always ask if they have already freshened up. If not, I ask them to take care of it. Nobody complains and why should they; we advertise we only provide safe sex. Personal hygiene is simply part of it."

"You're right. I'm just too chicken to ask my customers. I'll have to get over that. — Granted, it doesn't mean I won't perform a penis examination, but I sure as hell would feel easier about giving a blowjob without a condom. — Anyway, so how did it go with Ethan?"

"Okay. He came back out of the bathroom and I'm already in the bedroom, dressed only in a black camisole and crotchless panties. I'm posing seductively on the bed and point to the clothes valet. He looks around my bedroom and comments on how nice it is, much better than the red plush rooms of no-tell hotels. Once again, he mentions how crazy my red bush drives him, so I opened my legs and, I swear, I thought he'd never stop licking me. My God, he was like an animal, unable to get enough of it! He didn't even fuck me. Staring at my red bush, he whacked himself off and then came all over it. Quite disgusting! I immediately went to the bathroom. When I came back, Ethan was smoking, so I quickly opened the window and gave him a big glass of water with two ice cubes. I keep my windows closed during sex. You never know what noises a man might make and I certainly don't want others hearing it! — Yes, that's how it is when you service customers in your home. — Finally, he showered, dressed, and left. And he paid the 100 we agreed on. Let's see if he calls you. — Okay, sweetie, I have to go now! Christo could be here at any moment. We'll talk later! By the way, do you have business today?"

"Yes, I have two appointments in Glyfada. One guy is only paying 80, the other, my regular rate. Anyway, I'll tell you about them later! Bye, Violet, kisses."

"Yes, kisses, darling!"

Now I am faced with a difficult decision: what to wear today. Adonis, the guy with the Jeep, likes me in a mini. I wish I knew what David at the Gordens Hotel might like, but he is a new customer... I cannot go wrong with something feminine. Rifling through my closet, I decide on my short denim skirt for Adonis, which I go ahead and put on. For my appointment with David, I choose a white knee-length pencil skirt, which I pack in a plastic bag and stow in my silver shoulder bag. I slip into my pink pumps, which go with both skirts, don on a pink tank top with spaghetti straps, and my new pink sun hat. Examining myself in the mirror, I think I look cute, not slutty! So, that is taken care of.

I am looking forward to my meeting with Natasha and Adonis. I am simply unsure if I will give her my business number. Who knows if I want to remain in contact with her? I am sure I will not really be able to get to know her better this afternoon. I think it would be rash to give her my phone number already... I must think about it some more. In the meantime, I have to leave for Glyfada. My phone rings while I am on the bus. Since the windows are partially open and traffic noise is loud, I can barely hear the caller when I answer:

"Hi... question... where are you?"

I respond:

"Hi, darling. I'm sorry, I'm stuck in traffic and can barely hear you. Please call me back in 15 minutes or so, then I'll be somewhere quieter and we can talk, okay?"

While waiting for a reply, I realize the caller has long since hung up. Now I am upset that I took the bus instead of the tram. – No sense switching now, it will only be a waste of time. Arriving in Glyfada, I quickly head across the town square toward Metaxa Street and its many shops.

I am searching for a cell phone provider in order to purchase a SIM card with a Greek phone number. – I can give that number to Natasha!

Who knows, it might be good to be able to make contact with her, but I definitely do not want to give her my regular number. Too risky! Who knows, she might belong to the Russian mafia and then they would have my number. No way! After finding the store I am looking for, I select a Greek cell phone number. I am also buying a cheap cell phone. The friendly young Greek man helping me inserts the SIM card, activates it, and sets the language to German. Now, I have a new cell phone and SIM card for less than 40 euros, fantastic! I depart the store satisfied.

I continue strolling down the shopping street and visit my favorite clothing and shoe stores. As usual, I am tempted and cannot take my eyes off certain items. Repeatedly, I check my phone, but the man has not called back. – In a boutique, I see a lovely red handbag, a so-called bucket bag, which can be carried in the hand, at the elbow, or over the shoulder. Its size would be ideal as a workbag and it does not look clunky. On the inside, it has bright lining and several compartments to keep things tidy. Then, I see the price tag and I am immediately disinterested. 1200 euros! – What a shame! I will have to keep searching because I could really use one or two larger, stylish handbags.

Before 3:00 p.m., Adonis calls:

"Hi, Anika. We've just arrived at the hotel. Natasha's already here with me. We're in room 33. Will you be here soon, sexy?"

"Yes, I'll be there in a couple of minutes! Bye, Adonis."

Anxious to meet Natasha, I hurry to the Lenny Blue Hotel.

50

Adonis opens the door in his birthday suit. The furnishings of room 33 are green and gold. – Several erotic pictures and one large mirror adorn the walls. The round bed is covered with a white sheet and illuminated partially by an immense chandelier. Natasha is kneeling in the center, clad only in tiny panties. Adonis introduces us. Natasha slides over on her knees to the edge of the bed, offers me her hand, and says:

"Hello, Anika, nice to finally meet you. Adonis has had lots to say about you."

Although Natasha seems friendly, she is also hesitant, which immediately puts me on edge. – I might be used to working with other women in clubs, but this is different. I am an independent call girl and Natasha is, well, I do not really know what she is at this point! All I know is she is Russian and is passed from customer to customer. In a friendly manner, I answer:

"Hi, Natasha! Yes, Adonis has been raving about you too. —I guess it's time to have a sexy threesome!"

I address Adonis:

"I need two minutes in the bathroom and then I'll be ready to join you. I take it you both have already freshened up?"

"Yes, of course. Remember though, I want to take off your mini skirt! By the way, you look damn pretty. Pink is definitely your color."

"Thank you, darling. — Okay, I'll be right back!" I disappear into the bathroom.

Natasha has chin-length, straight blonde hair, and, if the lighting did not deceive me, blue eyes. Her skin is slightly tanned except where her bikini sits. Her breasts are quite large and unnatural looking. Her English is horrible, but at least I can understand her. Overall, my first impression of her is positive. Nevertheless, I will remain vigilant and learn as much as possible during the next hour. Perhaps I will learn a few things about her.

Since I am already wearing pink lingerie for Adonis, I only need to freshen up. I slip into a more provocative top, one in the same color, but with a plunging neckline. When I walk back into the room, Adonis is lying on his back while Natasha kneels next to him, sucking his cock. Seeing me, Adonis gently grabs Natasha by the hair and says:

"Our playmate is here. Come on, let's give her some attention!"

I place the bag with condoms on the nightstand as both get up. Adonis takes Natasha by the hand and holds out the other toward me. He guides the three of us to the large mirror. Looking at himself with a blonde on each side, he says:

"Could a man wish for more? Now I want to see how you girls caress each other. Come on, show me what you girls got!"

I do not recall Adonis saying anything about a lesbian show, but it does not seem to be a surprise for Natasha. She immediately approaches and snuggles against me without hesitation. Grabbing hold of her hips, I slowly start rubbing my crotch against hers. Adonis moves behind and pushes up my skirt. One of his hands travels between my legs and starts playing with my pussy. Sandwiched between Adonis and Natasha, I am left with not much to do. I simply let them grope me. Then Natasha slowly starts removing my top by pulling it over my head and letting it drop to the floor. – She opens the snap of my bra and mutters:

"Oh my, look what we have here! Gamotto, Babitschka, you have hot tits."

Without asking, she takes my nipple in her mouth and sucks on it and then switches to the other. In between, she repeatedly says something in a mixture of Greek, English, and Russian. Once she lets go of my breasts, she goes down on her knees and pushes my skirt further up. Adonis watches us in the mirror as Natasha takes off my underwear and presses her face against my cleanly shaven shame. Adonis has removed his hand and is now fondling my breasts. He cannot really see what Natasha is doing, who is doing nothing more than pressing her face against my vulva, pretending to lick me. Now and then, she moans out loud, so I join in, allowing Adonis to think we are really into it.– Natasha's pseudo licking becomes wilder.

"Do you like my pussy's smell, Natasha?" I ask. "You keep licking me like that, you're going to drive me wild and I'll come all over your tongue!"

"That's it, Anika, go ahead and come! Don't hold back. That's not what we're here for. Let Natasha go down on you. Then I'm going to fuck you," Adonis says encouragingly.

He is busy fondling my hard nipples, but he is doing it so roughly they are already sore. He pushes the hair away from my neck and kisses my nape. At least he is not trying to give me a hickey. I would have stopped him anyway. I cannot afford a hickey! But all is well, so I start stroking the back of Natasha's blonde head and get ready to fake a great orgasm for my two companions. When I start, Natasha plays along nicely. Adonis is obviously convinced it is actually real, but that is what counts. I slip out of my mini skirt and the three of us move onto the bed. – Adonis brought his briefcase of toys along and takes out a medium-size pink silicone dildo.

"Here, Anika, take it and stick it in Natasha's butt. Really fuck her with it. — That little Russian whore loves it!"

Natasha is already on all fours and sticks her ass in the air. I try to make eye contact to see if she is all right with it.

"Yes, Babitschka, it's okay. Just make it nice and moist. Not dry, you know! And slow, - *sigar, sigar...*!"

I understand only too well that moisture will make it more pleasant for her, but I do not see any lube, not in Adonis' toy case or anywhere else on the bed. I crawl over to the bedside table and grab one of my condoms and lubricant to put on the dildo. I am happy to see Adonis watching. I am sure it never occurred to him to have lubricant. With the dildo prepped, I slowly push it into Natasha's butt. Adonis is kneeling in front of her head with his cock in her mouth.

"Fuck her deeply!" he urges. I reply quietly:

"*Sigar, sigar!*" which is Greek, meaning *slow*. I can tell Natasha's sphincter is not yet relaxed and I do not want to hurt her. When I feel she is ready, I start shoving the dildo deeper as well as moving it in and out faster. I am surprised Natasha does not object to any of this.

After all, it is just like anal sex. – What is the difference between a cock in your butt or a dildo? A bit later, we switch positions. Now I assume the on-all-fours position because Adonis wants to fuck me from behind while I lick Natasha's pussy as she lies with her legs spread apart in front of me. Undeniably, this will not do! Pretending, I bend over and touch Natasha's vulva with only the tip of my nose. My long hair makes it hard to see what is actually taking place. Adonis seems happy seeing my head between Natasha's thighs. She plays along nicely and cheers me on in a mixture of Russian, Greek, and English:

"That's it, Babitschka, lick my muni, — yes, that's good! Bravo, Anika-mou! – *Dawai, dawai!*" she goes on until she fakes her climax. Now Adonis wants to assume new positions. This time he is lying on his back so we can spoil him with oral sex. Natasha is sitting on his right and I am on his left. Silently, we agree I will take care of his wiener while she plays with his balls. I say to Adonis:

"Remember, don't come in my mouth. – Warn me when you get close!"

"Okay, sexy. Natasha will take it when I'm ready. Don't worry."

Natasha will take it when I'm ready, meaning, she will swallow his sperm? My God. — I hope she does not! Then Adonis announces he is almost there and we switch positions. Now I lick his balls while Natasha takes his penis deep into her mouth. What do you know, when Adonis shows the first signs he is coming, Natasha sucks him even more eagerly and lets him come in her mouth. I am appalled! Adonis will never do that with me! Once finished, he lies back exhausted. Natasha quickly stands up and silently disappears into the bathroom. I hear her spit, cough, and rinse her mouth repeatedly. Okay, so she did not swallow the sperm, just held it in her mouth momentarily. A minute later, she is back on the bed with us. Although she is laughing and joking around with Adonis in Greek, I can still see disgust written on her face. As I kneel next to Adonis, he caresses my back and says:

"My compliments, you two blondes. You're a great team! I knew getting you girls together would be worth it. So, it's up to you whether you want to get something out of it for yourselves. I'll definitely want to see you two together more often."

Grabbing the dildo from the bed, he gets up, quickly kisses my forehead, and then turns to Natasha to kiss her too.

"Relax my beauties! I'll hop in the shower and get ready to head back to the office. You can stay and talk for a while. It's not like you had a chance earlier." He winks and laughs mischievously. Since I am getting comfortable on the bed, Natasha kneels next to me and asks:

"You're new here in Athens?"

"Yes. And you, for how long have you been here?"

"Three years now. But it's better here than in Russia. Greeks are good people. I have good customers. They always come back and some even connect me to friends of theirs. And you? Do you advertise online?"

Although I do not feel like revealing everything there is to tell, I am not going to lie because I sense Natasha and I could make a good team. Considering we were unrehearsed, today's performance went off without a hitch. But I am not willing to work for such little money, nor will I get a dildo shoved up my ass, or have someone come in my mouth. If I bring one of my clients to meet her, she cannot do such things. — Anyway, who knows what might happen, but I answer almost truthfully:

"Yes, I have an ad. And you? Do you advertise anywhere?"

"No! Too dangerous. Russians could find me and so could the police! The police will send me back to Russia and the Russians would take my money and make me work for them. — No, I don't advertise. All my business is through referrals. And only Greek men recommend me. — Anika, you're nice! If you like, we can exchange phone numbers. Maybe I'll come across a customer who wants two women."

"Let's talk money first. How much do you get from your customers?" Adonis reenters the room.

"Are you already collaborating? So, my sweeties, here's your money. I hope you girls have a nice day!"

He peels off the bills and holds in one hand three folded 20s for Natasha and in the other hand, four folded 20s for me. Bending over us to kiss us goodbye, he says:

"Stay put. You'll hear from me again. One more thing… would you see other guys? I have a friend I'd like to tell."

We both nod in the affirmative. – Satisfied, Adonis leaves the room looking conservative, dressed in a suit and tie with his briefcase of sex toys.

"Where were we? Oh yeah, we were talking money. I usually charge 150 an hour. However, since Adonis and I met on the road, we agreed on 80. And you? What's your rate?"

"Oh, Babitschka — you're German! You can ask that much. Not me! Adonis gives me 60, which is still good money for me. If I have two customers a day who each pay me 60 euros, that's a good day for me. In Russia, I'd never make that much. And I want to buy a car. A Volkswagen or a Mercedes. I'm saving up you know. — When you see one of my customers, I can't guarantee he'll pay your rate. But I can always say you're German. A pretty, smart, and sexy German! – Maybe then they'll be willing to pay more. I will call my clients and tell them about you."

I like Natasha and her simple, seemingly honest nature. She works for herself and is vigilant so she does not end up the property of a Russian pimp or fall into the hands of the police. Considering she has been here for three years and has not been caught, means she is taking precautions. And she is pursuing a goal, like Violet and I are doing. She is trying to better her life, although she is lax when it comes to her health. I would never take sperm in my mouth!

"Natasha, that's nice of you. But I'm sorry to say I can't make you such promises right now. If I come across a likely candidate, I'll contact you, but then you'd be making as much as my regular rate. And for a lesbian performance, I'd charge an even 200 for each of us! — That's one of the special services that many customers will gladly pay more for."

"200! Greeks don't pay that much! All they pay is between 60 and 120. I've never received more than that."

"May be so, – but I get many customers who are other nationalities. Some of them are businessmen who earn much more than the average Greek Joe and they don't mind paying for sexy entertainment. — As I said, I'm still new here and can't make any promises... Time will tell. And I'm okay with exchanging phone numbers. But you must never give it to somebody else, only with my consent. You must promise me! Don't save it under my name, make one up for me. I'll also save your number under a different name in case my cell phone ends up in the wrong hands. You know... what do you say?"

"Yes, using an alias is a good idea! — You are so smart, Anika!"

"And you should know, I make an extra 50 for anal sex or it's off the menu. Also, I don't take a dildo up the butt for the fun of it. In general, I mainly provide safe sex — meaning I don't let a guy come in my mouth and I prefer a rubber when giving oral sex."

"That's okay. I'm too chicken to refuse my customers. I also don't like that stuff in my mouth, which is why I immediately wash out my mouth and use mouthwash. — I know, it can still be dangerous..."

"That's your business. I'm just telling you, I never do that!"

Grabbing our phones, we exchange numbers. I save Natasha under 'Nectar' and she uses 'Andy' for me. While we chat, I can't help but repeatedly check out her breasts. Natasha notices and says:

"Yes, my operation didn't turn out well. Two years ago, I was fat, but then I became thin and my boobs collapsed. There was only skin, nothing inside. But I wanted to work and make lots of money, so I saved up for the operation. Now I have bigger breasts. They might not look nice, but it's okay! They look better in a bra and later in bed men usually don't care!" Natasha laughs, obviously carefree and over the fact that her breast surgery turned out badly.

Checking my watch, I see I should get going. My next appointment is at 5:00 p.m. Natasha lets me use the bathroom first. Showered, dressed, with freshly applied makeup, I bid Natasha goodbye with a peck on each cheek. I am glad I met her. I can see us working and benefitting from one another.

51

Once outside in front of the hotel, I notice two missed calls. This is part of my new professional life, but now I actually take it in stride. It is not far from the Lenny Blue Hotel to a tram stop. The Gordens Hotel where I am meeting David is only a few stops away.

Getting off at Vergoti town square with time to spare, I walk to the nearby beach and sit down at an outdoor café table. I call the tanning studio in Piraeus and a woman who only speaks Greek answers. Recalling a little Greek I have learned so far, I say:

"I'd like an appointment for tomorrow morning at ten on the strawberry tanning bed."

To my delight, she replies: "*Endaksi*," meaning *all right*.
I am quite proud I made myself understood. Next, I dial Violet's number.

"Hi, Violet, are you busy? There's something I'd like to tell you."

"Yes, darling. I'm expecting Vassili at 6:00 p.m. He lives in Thessaloniki and comes to Athens for business every month for a week. That's when he usually calls me. He's an easy guy. In a half an hour, more or less, he's finished. I start him off with oral sex, then we usually fuck a bit, him on top or from behind, and then he comes in his condom like a good little boy. He doesn't shower afterward nor does he smoke. He puts 120 on my nightstand, thanks me, and leaves! I wish all customers were that easy! You know how I like it. I want to make money without being fondled much. The older I get the pickier I become! Sometimes I wonder why my clients even come back. I guess most of them regard what they have with me as some kind of relationship and they aren't willing to end it. Familiarity plays a major part. What do you think?"

"Yes, I'm sure it does. I've also had regulars who saw me for years. And it's not like I constantly varied the service. Mostly, it was regular sex. – Men aren't as complex as we think. Perhaps they return simply because they're too lazy to look around for someone else. I believe most men are creatures of habit... Anyhow, I wanted to tell you something. I had an appointment with Adonis. You know the man I reeled in on the street in front of the Ammas Hotel. Today he introduced me to that Russian woman. Her name is Natasha. She's a few years younger than me but other than that, I don't know much about her except she's been in Athens for three years and her clients are mainly Greek men who pay her between 60 and 120 euros. She gets referrals from her customers. Anyway, we've exchanged phone numbers. I gave her the number for the second Greek cell phone I purchased. I think that was pretty clever because should she inadvertently give out my number, it's not the one I use on a regular basis or connected to my ad in *Athens World*."

"Yeah, it sounds like it was a really good idea! I would never have thought of it. Who knows, maybe she'll hook you up with one of her customers. Sixty is still better than nothing. It's nice pocket money. Be careful though about introducing her to your clients. Don't forget she's Russian… she might steal them away. Always watch out for yourself."

"Of course, I do! And I'll never talk about you, that's a promise! — Wait, my phone just beeped. It's David. He's a new customer I'm meeting at 5:00 p.m. at the Gordens Hotel. I have to go. Talk to you later, Violet. Have a nice evening!"

"Yes, same to you, my dear. Thanks for calling. Take care of yourself!"

"I will!"

David lets me know he is in room 501. – I text I am on my way. After paying for my cola, I cross the street and walk up the stairs to the Gordens Hotel. As I am about to knock on the door, I hear David talking on the phone and decide to wait until he is done. David's voice sounds calm and gentle. Once he hangs up, I knock and he immediately opens the door with a cell phone in his hand. David is dressed in light-colored trousers and a short-sleeve, sky-blue shirt. He is a tall, handsome man with slightly graying hair, clear blue eyes, and tanned skin.

"Come on in, Anika. Nice to meet you. You look great!"

He steps aside and I walk past him into the middle of the room.

"Hi, David, how are you?"

"I'm great, Anika, thanks for asking. Would you like a drink? A glass of water or I could send for coffee?"

"No, thanks, David."

"I'm sorry, Anika, but I haven't been in the bathroom yet. – Do you mind if I quickly hop in the shower? It's been a long drive and I'd like to freshen up before we get intimate."

"Of course, David, go right ahead. I'll use the bathroom once you're done."

"Great, I'll be back in a jiffy."

While David is busy freshening up, I remove my stretchy pink lace bodysuit and toiletry pouch with work stuff from my handbag and place them on the nightstand. This room reminds me of the one Andreas and I rented. One wall is entirely made of glass. The wall facing the bed is mirrored as well as a wall cabinet.

David walks back into the room wrapped in a big bath towel.

"Help yourself, Anika!" he motions to the bathroom. I look quite sexy in the pink lace bodysuit with its low-cut cleavage and with my long blonde hair, it looks great against my tanned skin. Perhaps I should say that this sexy bodysuit really accentuates my nice tan. Either way, I look great. Striking some poses in front of the large mirror, I enjoy my reflection.

In my pink high heels, I saunter deliberately back into the room. I might as well put on a little performance to flaunt my womanliness. David is lying in bed under a thin white sheet with it up around his chin. Strange! Watching me approach, he whispers gently:

"Anika, you look absolutely adorable. So much sex appeal! Very charming!"

"Thank you, darling. — Are you hiding from me or do you want me to join you under the sheet?"

"No! Wait, I have to tell you something, Anika. Sit next to me on the bed. Please!"

He nods to a spot on the bed beside him. Curious, I sit down with my legs crossed.

"Okay, darling, I'm all ears!"

"Anika, I'm also a girl, like you!"

"Okay!"

"Yes, I've been to the Netherlands several times for hormone injections. My breasts are already bigger and my nipples have become very sensitive. Would you like to see them?"

What am I dealing with, a transvestite, a gay man, or is he playing a game? David was dressed like a man. His voice might be gentle, but it is not effeminate. Curious as to what I am getting myself into, I say:

"Yeah, sure, let me see your boobs."

Pushing down the sheet, he exposes the hairless chest of a man. Looking at his nipples, I do not see anything out of the ordinary. His breasts certainly do not look feminine. However, since he mentioned he is a girl, I better play my part and treat him as such:

"Oh, what beautiful breasts and look at those nipples! They're downright begging for attention. And that's because of the hormone injections?"

"Yes, I've already been to the Netherlands four times. They already feel like those of a woman, very, very sensitive. – I feel like a girl, a very young girl. Like a virgin!"

"A virgin?"

"Yes, Anika! I'm a virgin. No one has ever touched me or my clitoris. Never!"

"How intriguing! – A woman's virginity is something special and it should only be lost when the moment is right. — Tell me, sweetie, what's your name?"

"My name is Sandra. Do you like my name?"

"Yes, it's a pretty and feminine name. It suits you well. I'll address you as Sandra from now on, okay?"

"Yes, please, Anika. You know, you're my girlfriend, my best friend who I can entrust everything with!"

It seems I am playing my part perfectly, although it would have been nice if he had mentioned it on the phone. I guess when he heard pretty, charming, and feminine, he forgot to mention role-playing, which I usually charge 50 euros more for... Oh well, it is too late to bring it up now. I will simply have to do my best.

"Sandra, darling, have you told anyone else about your injections?"

"Only the person I'm doing this for... is my boyfriend. However, he's been out of town on business for a while and I've been feeling so lonely... I'm a girl and I at least need a girlfriend to talk to!"

"Yes, of course. You know, you can talk to me about anything, Sandra. — Sweetie, may I touch your breasts?"

"Please do, Anika! Be careful though with my nipples, they're extremely sensitive!"

"Of course I'll be gentle; I know what a girl likes. I'm one myself."

Oh-so gently, I stroke David's chest. Either he really has no chest hairs whatsoever or he waxes his chest. In any case, his skin feels smooth and silky. This pleases him when I voice it aloud. Wetting an index finger, I carefully touch a nipple. Immediately, he starts moaning quietly and squirming under the sheet. I guess I need an even softer touch. Taking my time, I alternate between gently caressing his breasts and teasing his nipples with damp fingertips. I finally kneel down next to him so I can use both hands. Reassured by his lustful movements, I start to lightly pull, twist, and tweak his nipples. Feeling David is reaching his peak, I am unsure how this role-playing game should end. I decide to take a short break to see if he will offer me other parts of his body.

"Anika! Never in my life have I been touched in that way. I'm still a virgin! I'm inexperienced when it comes to love and sensual pleasures. All the feelings I'm experiencing are leaving me completely vulnerable. Please, Anika, don't stop caressing me!"

"I'm glad you enjoy it, Sandra. I'm curious though; may I touch your pussy with the sheet still covering it? I'll be careful. The sheet stays! — May I, Sandra, please?"

"Yes, Anika, you may touch it. Please touch my shame! Be as careful as you were with my breasts and nipples. Everything's so sensitive and tingly! I'm in a trance, Anika. Your caresses have placed me in a sensuous frenzy."

"I will provide you with relief, sweetie, but first I'd like to feel your shame!"

David moans pleasurably at my words and wriggles below the sheet in anticipation. I have my role down pat, the way it should be. Gently, I run my hand over the sheet where his crotch is. His penis is small and stiff. It is restrained by his underwear or the sheet would resemble a tent. – Since less material offers a greater response, I would prefer David's underwear off. I say:

"Sandra, sweetie, you're still wearing panties. Please take them off so it's easier for me to caress your shame. Isn't it longing for my touch!"

"Oh, yes, Anika. Wait a moment, please. I'll remove my underwear!"

David's hands move around under the sheet until they have accomplished their goal. I gently stroke his sheet-protected rod. Massaging it, I close my hand around it, and slightly push my hand between his legs and grab his sheeted balls.

"Sandra, does your pussy enjoy what I'm doing? Would it prefer that I tease it with my tongue?"

"With your tongue? — Just thinking of it makes me want to explode! You'd really enjoy licking my shame? My virgin shame? My clitoris? You know, it's insanely sensitive by now!"

"Yes, I would."

"Good, but wait a minute. I'm going to put my panties back on. Then you can tease my clitoris."

Taken aback by David's words, I patiently wait for what happens next. While David puts his undies back on, the sheet remains pulled up to his chin.

Abruptly, he pushes the sheet down to mid-thigh and for the first time I see his naked torso. The head of his penis pokes out from below the hem of his white, skimpy underwear. Ah, now I get it. His organ is the clit! Now I am supposed to lick it.

"Look at that! What a beautiful clitoris you have, Sandra! It's a nice pink and innocent looking. I'm afraid to touch it!"

"Don't be! You must touch it, Anika! My clitoris is longing for the touch of your tongue."

Taking it nice and easy, I first wet my index finger again and gently touch his penis. David twitches and groans. His legs are still crossed and his balls and the shaft of his cock are still hidden in his underpants. Only the head of his penis is sticking out. As I tease it with my finger, he presses his legs together and his abdomen spasms sporadically. – Then, when I am sure he is ready for salvation, I lean down, boldly stick my tongue out, and lick the tip.

"Sweetie, you have to warn me before your clitoris explodes! Make sure you don't forget. I want to watch as it twitches with excitement and becomes dark red before giving in to your desire. Promise me you'll warn me!"

"Yes, Anika, I promise. Please don't stop. Please! My shame aches for you. I'll tell you when it's time!"

I believe he understood the veiled message: he is not to come in my mouth. Since his cock is rather petite, I push his undies farther down and envelop it with my mouth. Swelling and throbbing, David sighs aloud and says:

"I'm coming soon, Anika! Oh my God, I'm coming!"

Swiftly, I pull his underwear down even further so I can lick his balls as I rub his cock with one hand until he squirts. All his cum lands on his belly. Atta-boy! The deed is done! Short of breath, David lies there with a faraway look while I sit on the edge of the bed and stroke his thighs.

"Anika, that was amazing! Thank you. If you like, go ahead and use the bathroom. I'm pressed for time and will be leaving soon."

"Thank you, David, I'll be right back."

Currently, he is talking in his normal voice with no sign whatsoever of little Sandra. Rising, I grab my small toiletry bag and disappear into the bathroom. Another satisfied customer. I believe I played my role well even if it was strange.

Showered and dried, I slip back into my comfortable denim mini skirt. Now that I am finished with David, there is no reason to wear my knee-length pencil skirt because I am heading home to my room at the Lilo Hotel for yogurt and to bide my time waiting for what else might happen this evening. Returning to the room, I find David already dressed. I wonder if he used the sheet to wipe the sperm off his belly or if he carries around wipes. Well, none of my business.

"Anika, it was a pleasure meeting you and I'll definitely call you again. You really do look extremely feminine. You really turned me on. You were very good. Thank you!"

With that, he hands me 150 euros. Pleased, I thank him and say goodbye to the man who supposedly received hormone injections in the Netherlands. For some reason, I am not entirely convinced his story rings true...

52

I cross the street in front of the Gordens Hotel and head for bus stop. Cars and mopeds fly down the road next to me, kicking up dust. It is hot and stuffy. I cannot wait for my bus to arrive. Standing there on the sidewalk, I contemplate the appointment I had with David. Suddenly a car pulls curbside and the passenger window rolls down. It is a cream-colored Mercedes. Leaning down to look inside, I see an elderly gentleman sitting behind the wheel who addresses me in English:

"Hello! I'm going to Piraeus. I can give you a lift if you're going that way."

How fortunate. Since the man is driving a new Mercedes and looks respectable, I remove my sun hat, open the passenger door, and get in:

"Yes, that's where I have to go. Thank you, sir, I'm so lucky!"

How nice it is to be sitting in an air-conditioned vehicle! The elderly driver looks visibly pleased, offers me his hand, and introduces himself as Nikos Protekos. Shaking his hand, I say:

"Nice to meet you, I'm Ilona Vertongen."

I am immediately angry with myself for giving this stranger my real name. Who knows, he could be a potential client. Naturally, Mr. Nikos is oblivious to my state of mind. Putting on the left turn signal, he waits for an opportunity to pull back into traffic. I wiggle my mini skirt down and cover the rest of my exposed thighs with my sun hat. After a few hundred meters, Mr. Nikos starts talking:

"So, where are you from, Ilona? I know you're not Greek, that's for sure. Are you from Russia or Bulgaria?"

"No, I'm from Germany."

"Oh! That's nice. What are you doing here? Are you on vacation?"

That's my opportunity to cast my net, which is why I am forthright with Mr. Nikos:

"No — I work here."

"Oh, I see! — What do you do, if I may ask?"

"I'm a self-employed call girl."

Although my voice sounds confident, I do not actually feel that way. Once again, I shot my mouth off prematurely. How will he react?

"Ah — A German prostitute. Don't get your hopes up about me. I have prostate cancer. Sex is basically out of the question."

Startled by his honesty, I look at him compassionately:

"I'm sorry. — Don't worry, I didn't take you up on your offer to put the moves on you. I'm merely glad to have caught a ride to Piraeus in such a fancy and air-conditioned car."

"I've made my peace with it. I might not have sex anymore, but I still enjoy the company of pretty women. Do you live in Piraeus or are you meeting someone?"

"I live there for the time being. And you? Do you also live in Piraeus? — By the way, my real name is Anika." I might as well correct my earlier mistake by giving out my alias.

"Anika! A much better name than Ilona. It has more oomph! — Ilona sounds somewhat lame, don't you agree? But hey, if you like it as your working name, so be it! — And to answer your question, no, I live in Vouliagmeni. I work in Piraeus. I'm the manager of a small shipping company. I have some work to do in the office. Truthfully, Anika, I think it's a shame you're a prostitute. I might not know you, but I definitely find you sympathetic. How long have you been working as a call girl here in Athens?"

"Just recently. But I like it here and I plan to stay for a while longer."

"That's nice. Maybe one day I can talk you into having a cup of coffee with me. No strings attached."

"Perhaps, I'm just not sure..."

"Why? Am I too old?"

"No!"

"I guess it's understandable that you're skeptical... Let me tell you a bit about myself. – My wife died four years ago and our two grown daughters live abroad. I'm here only for work. A year ago, I was diagnosed with prostate cancer. I don't really know what the future has in store for me, but I'm planning to enjoy every second of it. And that includes enjoying good company. Don't get me wrong, I have plenty of friends or colleagues, but I've known them for years and at times, they simply bore me. I'm in the mood for someone new. That's why I pulled over when I saw you at the bus stop. An old man like me would be honored to have a date with a pretty girl like you. But since there'd be no sex, I wouldn't pay you. However, I would make up for that with my generosity. I have a house on a nearby island. On weekends, I usually travel there by hydrofoil. I'd like to invite you to spend a weekend there with me. But as I said, I don't want sexual favors, simply a nice time by my swimming pool, followed by me taking you out for a nice dinner. I merely want to spoil you. It would make me happy. I enjoy treating beautiful woman well. So, Anika, please don't say no immediately and leave it at that. I'll give you my card and whenever you like, call me. — Maybe you'll find yourself in a position where you need help with the authorities. Whatever it is, you can always call me for help. — Okay?"

I watch Nikos' profile as he speaks. I believe I have good intuition for when somebody is spinning a yarn or is actually truthful. With him, I'm sure he means every word. Therefore, I decide to accept the situation for what it is. Nikos is definitely not the dangerous type, but I'm sure I will never accompany him to his island getaway. Perhaps one day I'll be happy to call him for assistance. Moreover, having a cup of coffee with him would surely be nice too.

"Thanks for your candor and kindness, Nikos. I truly appreciate it. I'll gladly accept your card, but other than that I make no promises!"

"That's all right, Anika."

Presently, we are near Piraeus and I ask Nikos if he can let me off at the Dimotiko Theatro.

"Sure, not a problem. If you don't mind, I'd like to show you where my office is located. It won't take long and that way you know how to get in touch with me personally. This way you'll see I'm not lying about my work."

"Okay, if it doesn't take long."

A few minutes later, we're cruising down the street along Piraeus' port and after another two turns, Nikos stops in front of a large modern building. A uniformed man walks up to the open driver's window and speaks with Nikos. After a brief conversation, the security guard returns to his post.

"That's Spiros. He wanted to know if I was going to park in the garage. If you ever come here, show him my business card and he will let you into the building. My office is on the seventh floor. — Okay, here is my card and now I'll take you to the square in front of Dimotiko Theatros."

"Thank you, Nikos."

"My pleasure. — By the way, tomorrow is a general strike day. Did you know that?"

"No, I didn't. I haven't read the local news yet. Thank you for letting me know. What will be affected?"

"As far as I know, all means of public transportation, including ferries, and any public service offices, for example, the post office. You might get lucky and find a cab. I'm guessing here and in Syntagma Square there will be demonstrations against austerity policies. If I were you, I'd stay away from the city center."

"Thanks for the information. It's good to know," I reply, and tomorrow evening's appointment with Kevin at the Kamazon Hotel immediately pops into my mind. I hope Kevin will not have a problem checking into the hotel in the afternoon and that all demonstrations will be over by the time I have to go there... With a bit of luck, I can catch a taxi to get to the city center! Having my car here from Germany would be great now, but there is one major drawback, my Golf has no air conditioning. Driving it in Athens' summer heat would be brutal. Therefore, I should sell my car and get one with air conditioning and GPS.

I must make sure to take care of that in time! Nikos stops at the bus stop at the town square. For some reason, I think it is rude to just hop out of the car, so I lean over and give Nikos a quick peck on the cheek. He immediately smiles, making me happy.

I am hungry, so I find a gyro joint for a pita. Sitting at a table in the shade, I wolf it down. While enjoying my shady spot with a view of the square, I also order a glass of white wine. Grabbing my phone, I check the latest news, which also mentions tomorrow's planned demonstration in front of the parliament building. It is approaching 8:00 p.m., so I start making my way to the Lilo Hotel. As soon as I am in my room, I strip off my clothes and dump the entire contents of my handbag on the bed. After separating the dirty laundry into two piles – one is for lingerie I plan to wash by hand – I stuff the remaining pile into the hotel laundry bag. At that moment, my phone rings. Unknown number.

"Good evening!"

"Good evening! I'm Harrison. Am I talking with the German lady?"

"Yes, you are. Would you like to hear more about me?"

Harrison confirms and I give him the pertinent information.

"Everything sounds good. — Do you have time this evening? Right now I'm in the inner city and I would like to meet you in a no-tell hotel."

"What time do you have in mind, Harrison and which hotel are you thinking about?"

"There's this place in Kolonaki, the Attokoi Hotel. I could text you the address, would that be okay?"

"That'll be great, Harrison. But I still need to know the time you have in mind."

"I could be there in half an hour. How about you?"

"I can make it in an hour. How about we meet at 9:30 p.m.?"

"That's fine. I'll call you as soon as I get there with the room number, okay?"

"Sounds good. Until then, Harrison!"

After receiving an appointment so unexpectedly, I am somewhat jumpy. Now it is time to freshen up and get ready. Not long after, I receive Harrison's text with the Attokoi Hotel address and jot it down. As it is not a call, his number is displayed. It is an English cell phone number. Now, I am left with the all too familiar question — what to wear. Inspecting my wardrobe, I opt for the sand-colored, sleeveless sheath dress. Harrison sounds like a true-blue Brit, which is why I assume he will appreciate a classic dress. Since it is nighttime, I will not need my sun hat. It is still quite hot outside and because I promptly perspire at the nape when my hair is down, I braid it into two pigtails, one on each side, held together with pink hair bands. They also look nice! Why have I not thought of this before? Compared to only one ponytail in the back, this style gives me a more youthful appearance.

Or am I mistaken? Is it only because of the Botox? — Who cares, I look great! I slip on my high heel, light-brown leather pumps, drape my ochre-colored short-sleeved jacket over one arm, and depart the Lilo Hotel in search of a cab.

53

After a short wait, a taxi pulls up, I get in the back and hand the driver the piece of paper with the name and address of the Attokoi Hotel. The man looks at it, starts grinning, and turns toward me:

"Ah, I see you have a date!"

"What gives you that idea?"

"I know the hotel. I've been there with a girlfriend."

He is still grinning as he puts the car into gear and heads for the hotel. I lean back and try to relax. Such short notice appointments always stress me more than when I have hours to prepare for my work. Needless to say, it makes a big difference when I already know the customer.

Closing my eyes in the hopes that it will help, I am startled by the harsh loud ringing of my new cell phone, whose settings I forgot to adjust! Only one person has that number.

"Hello, Natasha!" I answer.

"Hi, Babitschka! I spoke to Journalist. He's a good customer of mine. Actually, he goes by the name of Spiros, but I always address him by Journalist because that's his profession. Plus, lots of men have the name Spiros. Anyway, he's curious about you and wants to see us tomorrow! Can you come to Voula at 5:00 p.m.? We'll meet him at the Orion Hotel. It's close to the tram stop."

"Sounds good. How much does he usually pay?"

"He always pays me 100. You would have to talk to him. I told him you're German and that your rate is 150, but he didn't commit. Maybe he'll pay you 120, providing he's satisfied. I mean, you're pretty and smart... So, will you come tomorrow?"

"Yes, I'll be there. Where and what time exactly do you want to meet?"

"We can meet at a 4:45 p.m. at the tram station."

"Okay, Natasha. Thank you for thinking of me! — It makes me happy and I'll make sure to be punctual!"

"Good, Babitschka. And Journalist is okay. He's a good customer."

"Okay, until tomorrow then!"

"See you tomorrow, Babitschka!"

I hang up and change the setting to an agreeable ringtone and familiarize myself with my new device. When we reach the city center, I pay attention to which street the driver takes to get to the Attokoi Hotel. I have not Googled it yet, so I have no idea where it is located. My phone starts ringing. Harrison texts he is at the hotel and waiting for me in room number three. The street narrows and climbs toward Lykavittus, the highest hill of Athens, which is across from the Acropolis. I am going to visit the Acropolis someday. But that can wait.

It is not like theses attractions are only in town for a certain time.

The cab driver slows and pulls into an even narrower road. Shortly thereafter, he stops directly in front of a hotel entrance. The sign reveals in neon-green luminous paint: *Attokoi Hotel for beautiful hours.* I make the taxi fare an even 12 euros and get out. As soon as I walk up the few steps to the open entrance door, I am assaulted by the cold air of the air conditioner as I enter the lobby. They could save a bundle if they kept the door shut.

Actually, lobby is an overstatement. It is merely a narrow, brightly lit hallway with cream-colored walls. A young man stands behind what resembles a bar. He speaks to me and I ask where I can find room three.

"Follow the corridor and make a right turn at the end. Room three is the first door on the left," he relays the desired information in perfect English. Once I thank him, I follow his directions and knock on room three. Soft music is coming from inside. Harrison opens the door. He is tall, slender, and a redhead with lots of freckles. Pleased with his appearance, I enter the room and greet him:

"Hi, Harrison!"

"Hello, Anika! How nice that you could make it. — Those are cute pigtails!"

Since this hotel has no elevator and I could not check my appearance in the elevator mirror on my way up to the room, it completely escaped me that I had pulled my hair into pigtails!

"Sorry! I forgot about them," I quickly reply, pull off the hair bands and shake my head. Hopefully, the rest of my appearance is satisfactory.

"Don't be, Anika! I actually find them quite adorable. Please redo your hair. I like those pigtails! They instill a certain charm."

His statement makes me smile inwardly. I also like pigtails, but I do not believe they match the image of a sexy prostitute. However, apparently my customer thinks otherwise, so I do as he requests. Harrison walks over to a cabinet and adjusts the volume of an old-looking radio.

"Look at this, Anika, the radio is antique, but it still works!"

Finished putting my hair back into pigtails, I inspect the room. Basically, it is different from any hotel rooms I have ever seen. The walls are painted a light green and the furnishings are a mishmash of styles. It has two sturdy armchairs upholstered in a palm-patterned fabric, a small side table of solid dark wood, and an old refrigerator painted a shiny pink on which rests the '50s radio apparatus. There is also a gold-framed still life of fruits and wine grapes and one of a rearing stag. Then there is a large bed with a painted metal frame in silver aluminum. It reminds me of Grandma's living room, but also of cheap hotel rooms. What is most amazing is that I do not see a bathroom. – In one corner of the room, behind a carved, dark wood screen there is a shower stall. Harrison adjusts the bulky radio knobs until he finds a music station he likes.

"Harrison, where's the toilet?"

"Oh, that's across the hallway. There's one toilet for all three rooms on this floor. — That's a good station! Do you like this music, Anika?"

"Yes. I'm thinking about where it is best to freshen up and change. Have you already freshened up?"

"Yes, I showered at home. I own an apartment not far from here. I'm glad I did because I've never been here before. — Anyway, come on, I want to dance with you. This is a nice song," Harrison says and before I have a chance to reply, he pulls me into his arms and leads to a swing rhythm. Looking up at Harrison, he smiles at me and asks:

"May I kiss you?"

Not giving it much thought, I say:

"Yes, you may."

This buys me time as well as satisfies my client. I can always go to the bathroom to freshen up and change once the song is over. However, – I will have to put on my dress again because I do not want to walk across the hallway in my sexy lingerie. As soon as I am back, I will remove it and things will proceed in the usual manner. After sex, I can use the shower stall in this room. On the wall next to it hangs a little mirror. Harrison is kissing me gently. Obviously, he is not the stormy type, which is good, for it allows me to kiss and think at the same time. Having worked it out in my head, I give my customer all of my attention. He is still busy leading me to the beat of the music. For the next two minutes, I enjoy the extraordinary foreplay. When the song ends, I stop our kissing and say:

"Harrison, I'd like to go to the toilet to change."

"If you'd like, Anika, but you don't need to change for me. I'd prefer to open the zipper of your dress and strip it off. I'm not really into sexy lingerie. I like to get aroused by looking at a naked body. — Is it okay if you forego the sexy lingerie?"

"Yes, it's okay, but I still need to visit the toilet."

I disengage from his embrace, grab my handbag, and leave the room. The door across the hallway has two small brass plates, one of a little girl sitting on a pot and the other, a little boy peeing into a pot. A unisex toilet. The room is tiny. After washing my hands in a minuscule sink, I strip off my dress, put on a pink lace bra and matching panties, slip back into my dress, check my eye makeup, reline my lips, walk through a few spritzes of *Must de Cartier*, set both cell phones to silent mode, and then return to the room. I place my handbag on one of the sturdy armchairs and my work pouch at the head of the bed.

Harrison busily searches for a new station on the radio. He is a handsome and charming looking man, around 50 years old. His blue eyes sparkle as he approaches me and says:

"The way you look in those pigtails, you could be from the Netherlands or Denmark. At least it's the general image of the beautiful women there. — Come here, I'd like to undress you now."

"And what about you? Do you want to undress yourself or should I help you with that?"

"Whatever you want, Anika!"

He opens the zipper and pulls the dress over my head. Although he stated he did not care much for sexy lingerie, he whistles softly through his teeth when I stand before him in my pink lace underwear. He stares at my body as he unbuttons and slips out of his shirt. Then, he sheds his blue-checkered shorts. Once again, he takes me in his arms and starts kissing me. Snuggled up against him, I feel something stirring below. Harrison has a light tan and tiny, red chest hairs.

"You smell really good," he utters after kissing for a while. Then he starts stroking my back as we continue kissing. So far, he has not made any advances toward my bosom or pubic region. Obviously, he is taking his time. However, I want to be outside on the road without going past 60 minutes, so I try to speed things up and start touching his privates.

"Wait," he says. He takes me by the hand and leads me to the bed. I sit down on the edge of the bed and he kneels down before me.

"Please take off your bra."

Wordlessly, I obey and hang my bra at the foot of and over the silver aluminum railing of the old-fashioned bed.

"Lie down and relax. I want to spoil you a little with my tongue," he says as he removes my panties and shoves his head between my slightly spread legs. Leaning back on my elbows, I am pleased with the way things are progressing. My customer is happy without me having to come up with anything. Harrison is licking my pussy as tenderly as he kissed me. Sneaking a peek at my watch, I see we still have more than half an hour left. So to turn him on and to show him he is doing a good job, every now and then I moan quietly. Finally, Harrison stops to raise his head and asks me:

"Do you have a condom for me?"

"Yes, one moment. — Here you go. Should I roll it on or do you want to do it yourself?"

"I'll do it myself, thanks. Just get comfortable on the bed. I want to enter you now."

Gladly, I think and do as he says. A few seconds later, Harrison is on top of me in the missionary position. Less than five minutes later, he climaxes. He comes while contorting his face and making discreet noises. Done, he drops next to me on the bed and smiles at me. -What a charming and easy customer! Somehow, I like him. And not only because he is damn good looking. I like his entire persona.

"Anika, you're a godsend for me. Actually, I only wanted a roll in the sack, but somehow things happened differently and I felt like merging with you... — I've really enjoyed this simple sex. I'm hoping you had a good time too. It would mean a lot to me if you are at least not disappointed. I mean, I know this is your profession — and I might sound ridiculous, but for some reason, I'm hoping you had a few moments of pleasure too."

Oh God, what am I supposed to say now? Harrison would recognize a bold face lie. So, I say:

"Let me put it this way; you're damn nice and a handsome customer. My work couldn't have been pleasanter!"

"I'm glad to hear that, Anika! – Too bad I'm leaving tomorrow, I would like to have seen you again. Tomorrow morning I'm meeting my mother-in-law at the airport and flying to Thira. My wife, her sister, her brother-in-law, and their children are already there. It's an annual family gathering on the island. – But then the rest of the family won't do without at least coming for one visit a year to our house on Thira. — Naturally, we see each other regularly during wintertime in London, but that's not considered a family gathering. That's the way it is, not always fun, but you only have one family."

"May I ask what you do for a living, Harrison?"

"Of course. I own a gallery. My wife is an artist. Our house on Thira with the big studio and the grand light of the Aegean Sea is essential to her. She paints Greek motifs in pastels. Simply beautiful. – I love her paintings. She has the talent needed to capture the grand light of the Aegean Sea with a brush. — Unfortunately, things between us are no longer like they were in the beginning. I don't believe she's been unfaithful, but I can't help myself. And I don't feel ashamed. I don't know whether I'm cheating because of the sex or because of the feelings I no longer share with her. — Anika, I just thought of something! Could you come to Thira? At least for a day? — I would love to see you again. The whole family will be there until next week before we all fly back together to England without a stopover in Athens. I won't have an opportunity to meet you in Athens. What do you say? Will you come visit me on Thira? Obviously, I'll pay all your expenses!"

What a great offer! I know Thira by the name Santorini. It is an indescribably beautiful volcanic island that I have always wanted to visit. My brain goes into overdrive and comes up with all kinds of questions and figures. I need Harrison's help to clarify a few things.

"I've never done anything like that. I mean I've never visited a customer on an island. I've no idea how it works. Are there daily flights going back and forth between Athens and Santorini?"

"Yes, of course. A day will be much too short. I could only meet you in the early morning hours when the family thinks I'm playing tennis or

jogging. That means you would have to stay for at least one night. –
However, I would prefer if you stayed two nights. — You could arrive
in the afternoon and check into the hotel where I've already made arrangements. Obviously, it'll be a luxury hotel and I know it will be
along my route to the tennis courts. There are plenty to choose from. I
would see you the next morning, maybe even briefly in the evening,
and then you could take a mid-morning flight back to Athens. What do
you say? By the way, what's your daily rate, Anika?"

I am still busy calculating. My average daily income is 300-450. Violet charges 300 for her customer on Rhodes. I think 400 is fair. On the
other hand, Harrison might only see me once, briefly... Maybe too expensive? Since I am in the mood for such a work experience, I cautiously say:

"Well, for that long, I'd be okay with 800. What do you say? Are you
okay with that?"

"How many customers do you usually have in one day?"

"Two to three. Sometimes even four. It differs."

"Yes, in that case, 800 for two days is definitely okay. — You do
have to eat and Thira is not a cheap island."

"How does it work with the flight and hotel room? Like I said, I have
no experience with this."

"A good question. It's my first time too. — I can definitely book a
hotel room in your name, but you'll have to pay for it, either with cash
or credit card. If I do it, I might attract attention and get in trouble. The
same goes for the flights. You'd have to pay for them up front. When
we see each other, I'll reimburse you for your expenses and your rate.
I have no problem getting my hands on cash. — What do you say?"

"Let me get this straight: You'll call with the hotel information and
date and then I'll buy a round-trip ticket. Once we see each other,
you'll reimburse me for all my expenses plus pay me my fee, correct?"

"Correct! Let me summarize; there and back, flights will run about
200, plus taxi fares. A hotel room for two nights will cost at least 300.
I'm giving you 800. That works! For me, that is! How about you? Can
you pay for the round-trip flight up front?"

"Certainly. — Now it's only a question of when you want me there.
Tomorrow won't work because I already have two appointments.
Wednesday would be possible."

"Okay, let's say you take the Wednesday afternoon flight. Latest,
Wednesday morning, I'll send a text with the hotel information and
call you to make sure our arrangement is still on. What do you say?"

"Sounds good! So, is it a deal?"

"Great, we'll do it. Come here! Let's shake on it! You can definitely
count on me; you know that, don't you?"

"Yes, somehow I do. – If I didn't, I'd insist on an advance payment.
However, I believe I can trust you!"

"I'm glad. I won't disappoint you! — You know, Thira, or Santorini as you Germans called the island, is a special place. – It has a flair no other Greek island has."

"That would be great to experience. I've only seen photos of the island. — Do you mind if I quickly hop in the shower?"

"Of course not! Oh, and write down your full name for the hotel room."

"Sure!" I get up, grab a pen and notepad from my handbag, and write my real name on it: Ilona Vertongen. Harrison reads the note, grins, and says:

"Even your last name sounds Dutch, Anika."

Harrison places the piece of paper in his wallet for safekeeping, takes out my fee, and places the bills along with his business card on the small side table between the armchairs, and says:

"Here's your gift and my card, Anika. — Now you have my phone number, website address, email address, and my address in London. — A little reassurance for you."

"Thank you!" I reply and stick the money and business card in my wallet.

Once showered and dressed, I grab my bag. However, before I reach the door, Harrison grabs and kisses me again passionately using his tongue.

"See you in a couple of days!" I say smiling.

"I'll call you! I'm looking forward to Thursday morning! You can expect me as early as 8:00 a.m."

"Okay! Until then, darling!"

And I am out the door of the uniquely decorated Attokoi Hotel, happy about the prospect of a working trip to Santorini!

54

On the sidewalk, I switch my phones back on and see two missed calls. Both from Greek cell phones. That is okay! I could not take on another customer today anyway. The heat, the running and driving around, and, obviously, work have sapped my energy. Retracing the direction the cab took that brought me here, I turn left in front of the hotel and walk downhill until I reach Kolonaki town square.

Walking on these uneven sidewalks in high heels is arduous and I am longing to get off my feet. I am certain there is an available table at one of the many cafés surrounding the square. Finding a nice spot in a relatively quiet corner, I order a glass of water and a glass of white wine.

After spending a few minutes watching the never-ending flow of foot traffic in and around this lively square, my feet recover from the walk. I grab my city map and mark the location of the Attokoi Hotel on Arabovis Road. Now I know another no-tell hotel I can suggest to a customer. Even if the furnishings were thrown together, everything was clean and neat, that is what matters to me. Examining my map, I see the next subway station is quite a ways away.

Sighing, I think about treating myself to a taxi ride home. I have done well today. – Nevertheless, as soon as it crosses my mind, my conscience reminds me it is only 10:50 p.m. and early enough to walk to a subway station to catch a train to Piraeus. Do not be such a pansy, – there is no need for a cab!

Giving myself an inner kick, I down my drink, pay and start walking toward the Panepistimio Subway Station. Along the way, my phone rings. A Greek cell phone number. I answer:

"Good evening!"

"Hi! Are you the German lady with the ad in *Athens World*?"

"Yes, I am. My name is Anika. Do you want some more information about me?"

"Yes."

I politely tell the potential customer everything he needs to know and ask his name.

"My name is Tarek. Everything sounds good. I'd like an appointment! Can you come to my apartment in Piraeus?"

I swallow. A private apartment in Piraeus: I am not quite comfortable with that. I reply:

"I guess I could. However, I need your landline number, full name, and address. — Can you please send me a text, then I'll call you back on your house line."

"What do you want the landline number for? Why do you need to call me back? If you have something to ask me, do it now! — My landline number is none of your business."

His unfriendly tone triggers my alarm!

Tarek could be a friend of Ladis trying to lure me into the trap. My heart races and I am overcome with fear. Since I do not feel like explaining, I simply hang up. After few even breaths, I continue on my way to the subway station, wondering whether Tarek will call back. It does not take long before my phone rings again. Taking a deep breath, I pick up.

"Hey! Why did you hang up?"

"I'm sorry, I didn't hang up. Maybe we were disconnected. — Tarek, I refuse to come to your home if you don't give me your landline number. I won't do it. Perhaps you should call someone else. Thank you for your interest. — Good evening to you!"

With that, I end the conversation. Since I stopped to talk, I quickly save the cell phone number under 'Tarek - caution'. It provides me with a sense that I did something for my safety, although I perfectly know Ladis & Co. can always reach me with other phone numbers. The danger is not over yet. I have to remain vigilant. My brain flips between my unpleasant encounter with Ladis and my upcoming work trip to Santorini. Eventually, I reach the subway station and catch the train to Piraeus. Once there, I walk to the town square and treat myself to a glass of wine to celebrate a successful workday. While sitting here for the umpteenth time, I realize how familiar the Dimotiko Theatro square has become. It almost feels like home. What a nice feeling!

That night, my phone rings two more times. Both Greek men were not interested in sex. All they wanted was more information about me and my services. – Why would they need to call a prostitute for that in the middle of the night? They could've done it just as easily during the day! I cannot wrap my head around it! Thankfully, I manage to fall asleep quickly once both calls are finished. - My alarm clock goes off at 8:00 a.m. waking me from a peaceful slumber.

After breakfast, I hand wash a few bras and panties and then visit the tanning studio. Today is a general strike day. Sure enough, I do not see any public transportation in service. Returning to my room at the Lilo Hotel, I make myself comfortable on the balcony dressed only in underwear. While sipping a cup of coffee, I think about everything I need for my short trip to Santorini. Definitely a small suitcase, even better, a carry-on. Then I will not have to wait at baggage claim on Santorini and can immediately grab a taxi in front of the airport.

Such a small suitcase can be purchased right here in Piraeus. Near the harbor, I have seen several stores that sell travel bags, backpacks, and suitcases. But back to my original thought; which clothes should I take to wear on Santorini? Thinking about it is of no use, so I get up and go inside to look at my wardrobe. My denim mini skirt would be suitable for my trip there. I can easily store my phone or the boarding pass in the back pockets. With that skirt, I need three tops. One for the trip going, one for coming back, and one, no, two in reserve. I lay out the tops on the bed and think about what else to pack. Naturally, I need a bikini. Will one be enough? No! – Two is better. I do not like lying around in a wet bikini waiting for it to dry. I need a dry one to change into. Since I am going to spend two evenings in Santorini, I should pack two pretty summer dresses. Which ones? I like my turquoise, flowery, cotton stretch dress and the royal blue one in the same cut. My gold high heels go with both dresses and my denim mini skirt. However, I definitely cannot travel with only one pair of shoes. I need another pair, one I can also wear on the plane. Uncertain, I remember I have another day to make up my mind, my lingerie is much more important than street clothes. Harrison might have said sexy lingerie does not do anything for him, but it is not like I want to open the door for him completely naked. What should I wear for the morning he comes to see me?

Searching through my work clothes for more than half an hour, I final opt for a cream, almost translucent satin bodysuit with a deep-cut lace-insert in the back. My gold high heels go great with this outfit! If Harrison has time to visit me in the evening, then I am allowed to wear something sassier. I opt for my black fishnet dress with matching black fishnet stockings and black pumps. Satisfied with my preliminary selection of dresses and lingerie, I boot up my notebook and hunt for flights from Athens to Santorini. It is time to take care of the tickets. Looking at the schedule, I decide on the Wednesday flight at 3:20 p.m. It is supposed to land 45 minutes later and costs 65 euros. My return flight leaves Friday at 10:50 a.m. and it costs 73 euros. — My phone rings. A Greek cell phone number.

"Hello?"

"Hi! I'm William. I take it I'm speaking with the German lady from *Athens World*."

I reassure him and answer all his questions. He too wants to meet me at the Lenny Blue Hotel in Glyfada. This hotel seems to be popular. I really should find accommodation in Glyfada once my agreed upon time here is up. William tells me he is a former American soldier that has been living in Glyfada for 30 years. He likes playing tennis and loves traveling. He asks if I have a nice tan and if I have time tomorrow afternoon. I reply:

"Yes, I have an even tan. No tan lines. Unfortunately, I can't make it tomorrow afternoon, as a matter of fact, William, I'll be out of town until Friday afternoon."

"Oh, that's too bad! I don't yet have a time in mind, but I'd like to see you Friday afternoon, okay?"

"Yes, that's okay. Just call me when you've decided on the time."

"Will do, Anika! I'm really looking forward to meeting you. Until then!"

"Until then, William!"

Happy about a new client, I save his cell number under 'William'. Then, I dial Violet's number. She picks up rather quickly.

"Hi, Violet! How are you?"

"Oh, Anika, it's so hot. I just got back from shopping. I had to stand in front of the open refrigerator for a couple of minutes to cool off. I mean, the air-conditioning is on, but I was so hot I needed immediate cooling down and that was the only way I knew. – I could have undressed and taken a cold shower, but that was too much work. Then I would have to clean and dry the shower walls afterward, getting me hot and sweaty again. So, I'd rather stand in front of the open fridge for a while! What do you think? — How are you, darling? Do you have new customers? I still haven't gotten any appointments for today. Jorgos called and canceled because of the strike. Can you imagine? He has a car and he cancels! His argument was that the day of a general strike where public transportation isn't running, the streets would be crammed. He's afraid of being stuck in a traffic jam! What am I supposed to do? I'm losing 150 euros. That's what Jorgos pays. Who am I supposed to be angry at, Jorgos or the strike? I don't know. It's very upsetting! I'm glad cabs are at least still available. I mean, it would be stupid for them to strike at the same time as public transportation. Today is a great day for taxi drivers. If I get another appointment today and have to go somewhere, I'll call a cab to pick me up at home. It might be a little more expensive, but I won't have to stand in the heat, trying to wave down a cab, only to hear who knows how many times, I'm not going in that direction... — So, how are you? What are you up to?"

Violet seems to have vented enough, so I share the whole story regarding Harrison and my upcoming business trip to Santorini.

"Oh no, how can you be happy about that? All that work — packing, the long journey, not knowing if the hotel staff will be friendly, or if the room is clean. I only do that for Malcolm because I've known him for so long and because I always stay at the same hotel. — I wouldn't be happy to gain another island customer. Okay, I see Jerry on Aegina, but I never stay overnight. You know me by now, I prefer to stay at home. I don't like to go out of my way to meet a customer. That's me though, not you. I hope everything works out nicely and you have a great time and are paid really well! — Oh my God! We won't be able to get together at the market this Thursday! When will I see you? I want to see your forehead. Does it still feel tight?"

"A bit. Actually, I can hardly feel it. — Yes, I was thinking the same thing about market day, but that's how it is. However, I could come to Glyfada on Friday. We could arrange to meet somewhere."

"Yes, that would be great. Maybe I'll pick you up in the town square and we can go to my place for coffee. Let's do that."

"Okay!"

Violet tells me about last Sunday, when Jack came on strong again, trying to persuade her to go out with him. She ended up tossing him out because she had an appointment with Ethan. I told her about the enjoyable ride I took with Nikos Protekos, the gentleman who gave me his business card and who offered to be there for me should I need help.

"See, darling, that's how Greek men can be. You'd never see an Englishman do something like that! I don't think a German man would do something like that either, would he? I mean, offer that to a complete stranger, and give her his business card. You know, it's certainly good to know people who have influence, but believe me, many Greeks are merely show-offs. They like to hear themselves talk while assuming a persona of being rich and generous. You would do well to be wary of him!"

Looking at the clock, I remember all the things I still need to do for today's appointments. I say goodbye to Violet, quickly dress, grab my white sun hat and handbag, and head out the door. Hastily, I hurry to the port area to purchase a small suitcase. With the sun beating down, I am grateful for every speck of shade along my route. Although olive trees are planted here and there along the sidewalks, they are so low only dwarfs and children can walk beneath their branches without being scratched in the face. These trees are not shade providers, merely obstacles! Arriving at the first sidewalk vendor selling travel bags, suitcases, backpacks, and such, I find what I am looking for. It is a small red carry-on with wheels and a pullout handle. After paying 24 euros, I head back to the Lilo Hotel. – As soon as I am in my room, I hurriedly rid my body of my clothes and hop in the shower for two minutes. Fortunately, I do not see it the way Violet does, who would rather stand in front of an open refrigerator.

Once again refreshed and cool, I stretch out on the bed and close my eyes. I am beginning to understand why many Greeks take naps. This heat does not allow for much of anything other than breathing. Nevertheless, it is no use. I cannot sleep. Glancing at the clock, I remember I have to prepare for two consecutive appointments. The first is with Natasha and the second is with Kevin, who I am meeting at the Kamazon Hotel. Now, I am a bit anxious, thinking about being his submissive for one hour. However, I do want to try it! – Ignoring thoughts of doubt, I get up and walk over to my closet, where I am faced with the always-difficult question — what should I wear...

55

Violet's idea of calling a taxi to her address inspires me to do the same. It is more convenient than flagging one down on the road. I ask Spiros the receptionist to call a cab for a 4:15 p.m. pick up and to notify me when it arrives. A short while later, I am in an air-conditioned taxi being chauffeured along Athens' coast to Voula. I can also have a nice and comfortable journey to get to an appointment! Enjoying the ride, I think about my upcoming appointment with Natasha and Spiros, aka Journalist. I wonder how that will proceed. I am really not happy about the fact that I do not yet know how much I will be paid. It will be best for me to talk immediately with Journalist about my fee. Leaving it to his judgment as to what I receive once we are done is not acceptable! I have to make Natasha understand that this needs to be cleared up first. Maybe she does not mind not knowing and is happy when a client turns out to be generous, but she is also satisfied when she receives 60 euros. That does not work for me! My phone rings. A Greek cell phone number. I answer.

"Hello, Anika! It's Kevin. I just checked in the Kamazon Hotel. I am in room 332. I'll be here from 7:30 p.m. on."

"Perfect! I hope the demonstration is over by then. I have no idea how busy the city center is... Did you have any problems getting to the hotel?"

"I had a 45-minute delay because the police cordoned off Syntagma Square. They've just reopened it up to traffic. — Just give me a ring when you're nearby. And it's not a problem if you run late. I'll just spend the time enjoying a drink while I wait to meet you."

"Okay, I'll do that. I'll call as soon as I get to the city center. Until then, Kevin!"

I hang up and save his number under 'Kevin - slave girl'.

The taxi ride to Voula is also taking longer than I expected. At 4:40 p.m., I receive a call from Natasha.

"Babitschka, are you coming?"

"Yes, I'm on my way. I'm hoping the cab will get there, at the latest, in five or ten minutes. Traffic is horrendous."

"Yes, I know. It's because of the strike. It's always like this. The main thing is that you are on your way. If you cannot make it in time, I'll call Journalist and tell him we are running a few minutes behind. That's not bad. – He's Greek. He's also late at times. See you soon, Babitschka!"

"Yes, see you soon, Natasha!"

Shortly before 5:00 p.m., the cab pulls up in front of the tram station in Voula. Natasha is sitting in the shade waiting for me. She is wearing light blue shorts, a colorful patterned shirt, a baseball cap, and flip-flops. As I get out of the cab, Natasha removes her big sunglasses and walks over to me. After paying the taxi driver the 18-euro fare, the pedestrian light turns green and Natasha and I quickly cross the street. Once on the sidewalk, we greet each other by exchanging kisses.

"Come on! The hotel is right around the corner. Journalist is already there. He just called. You look chic, Anika-mou!"

"Thank you, you look good too, like a tourist! Did you have a nice day?"

"Yes, I came from the beach. — See, we're already here."

Following Natasha through the lobby, we are greeted by a friendly gentleman. At her request, we take the stairs. I am anxious as we stand in front of room number 28. Spiros opens the door. He is maybe in his mid-fifties to early sixties, a smoker, and wears thick horn-rimmed glasses. He is naked except for the towel wrapped around his waist. Natasha immediately strikes up a loud and lively conversation with him in Greek. As he repeatedly pinches her butt, he looks over at me. I have yet to be introduced. I really do not feel comfortable with the situation. Finally, they turn toward me and Natasha says in English:

"This is Anika, my German friend. Doesn't she look like a smart lady?"

"Yes, she certainly does," Journalist replies and then addresses me:

"Hello, Anika. How nice of Natasha to bring you along."

"Yes, it is. So, your name is Spiros, correct?"

"Yes, but I prefer to be called Journalist, like Natasha does. I like it. — Where are you from, Anika?"

"I'm from Germany. However, I need to discuss business briefly ... Journalist."

"Okay — if you must..." He laughs, pulls Natasha into his arms, and pinches her buttocks until she squeals.

"I'm sure Natasha told you that I charge 150 for an hour of safe sex. I want to know if you're okay with my rate."

"Hey, Anika! You must be a real German, talking first about money."

He laughs. Then Natasha says playfully:

"I told you, she's a smart German lady!"

"Yes! — Yes she is. And she's also sexy. — So, Anika, I always give Natasha 100, but if both of you make me happy and you're not picky about the time, then I'll pay each of you 120, but for that amount, I also want to see a lot! You know what I'm talking about, right?"

"You mean us touching each other like we're lesbians?"

"Correct. — And I want to fuck both of you. I want to come with each of you. That's necessary for that price. — What do you say?"

The terms are within an acceptable limit, but barely because Journalist did not contact me through the ad in *Athens World*. He is a referral.

Looking at Natasha, I see she has no qualms about anything. Actually, she is beaming.

"Okeydokey, let's get going, sweeties. I'll use the bathroom to freshen up," I reply nonchalantly, pretending to be the cool German.

"Wait, I'm coming with you, Babitschka!" Natasha says as I set my sun hat on the table. She hastily slips out of her clothes, throws them over the back of a chair, and accompanies me naked into the bathroom.

"You see, Anika-mou, Journalist is okay. He even is going to pay us each 120! He only does that to impress you. He was stunned to learn I have a German girlfriend. — Let me shower quickly. My skin is still very salty."

She climbs into the bathtub and turns on the faucet. I undress and hang my clothes neatly over the towel rack. Then, I freshen up and put on my black lace bra and panty set and high heel pumps. Looking at Natasha, I say:

"Natasha, there's something we need to discuss. If Journalist asks for my phone number, I won't give it to him! – And just so you know, I won't accept his number either if he tries to give it to me. He's your customer and it will remain that way. Just like my customers stay mine. — Don't you agree?"

"Oh, Babitschka, I'm glad you brought it up! I was thinking along the same lines. I even told Journalist that he couldn't ask for your phone number. After all, I know how men are. I agree with what you said and I won't give my number to any of your customers, I promise! — I believe I can trust you because you're German. I would never believe a Russian woman! She would try to steal all my customers away from me. — When Adonis told me about you, he said he felt sure you were an honest puttana. I don't think he would have brought us together otherwise."

Natasha has toweled off and we return to the main room together. I am confident again when I see Journalist standing naked at the open window smoking a cigarette. I am convinced it is best if I take control of the situation.

"Hey, baby! Make yourself comfortable on that armchair over there and watch Natasha and me as we play with each other!"

"That's a great idea! You look hot, Anika. Holy-moly! – Natasha didn't exaggerate."

Grabbing the small, black vibrator and a condom from my toiletry pouch, I place the items at the head of the bed.

"Lie down, sweetie!" I say to Natasha with a smile. She willingly follows suit and stretches out on the bed with her legs spread and her pussy in full view of Journalist. Kneeling next to her, I lean forward and pretend to lick Natasha's pussy behind a veil of loosely hanging hair. After this short demonstration, I sit upright and toss my head and hair back. I grab a condom and roll it onto the vibrator. – After one last eye contact with Natasha, I use it first to massage her pussy from the outside and then on the inside. I take my time so Journalist becomes properly turned on. Sure enough, it does not take long and he soon wants to join us. But I shake my head sternly and say with authority: "It's not your turn yet. Right now Natasha is mine!"

Standing there in obvious surprise, Journalist sits back down and slowly rubs his big boner while watching Natasha and me closely. Natasha's moaning sounds fake. Journalist does not seem to notice. How could he? It is not like he really knows her. And just like with Adonis, she continuously mumbles in Greek or Russian and a few things in English for my well-being. Since I am in charge, I want Journalist to fuck me first. So, I stop the vibrator performance, set it aside, take off my bra, stroke my breasts, and seductively say to Natasha:

"I'm so hot for you, baby! I'm going to do you and me at the same time. Raise your legs! I'm going to rub my pussy against yours until we both come!"

Natasha pulls her legs close to her belly and I move between them. This sight must drive Journalist wild. I move over Natasha's body as if we are fucking. I start faking an orgasm, quickly glance over my shoulder, and invitingly address Journalist:

"Come on over and fuck me! I am in real need of a big boner to massage my pussy from the inside."

Still moving over Natasha's body, I assume the on-all-fours position and wink at her. Journalist immediately springs into action and as he gets into position behind me, I hold out a condom for him to put on. Keeping an eye on him over my shoulder, I make sure he puts it on properly. When he is finished, I urge him on:

"Now give it to me, Journalist. Show me what a real thoroughbred you are and carry me to seventh heaven!"

While Journalist fucks me from behind, the doggie position easily supports me, so I groan as if I am nearing climax. I do not have to do this for long before Journalist comes. Natasha also groans with a twinkle in her eyes, which makes me smirk for I think I directed our performance nicely.

Once Journalist is done, he slumps next to Natasha on the bed, breathing heavily. I roll over and lay on her other side. What a stroke of luck that every hotel room is equipped with air conditioning! Nevertheless, I can still feel the outside heat creeping through the one open window. Thankfully, the AC is strong, otherwise, I do not know how I could have performed my job. Noticing Journalist's cigarettes, lighter, and an ashtray on the table across from the bed, I get up and place all three items on the bedside table next to him. I say:

"Here you go, darling, I'm sure you want to enjoy a smoke!"

After pulling the condom off his softening cock, I grab the vibrator and disappear into the bathroom. Once the sex toy is clean and my hands washed, I return to the room to find Natasha snuggled up in Journalist's arm, the two of them conversing lively in Greek. So I squat down next to them.

"Anika, you are a real professional, right?" Journalist asks.

"Yes, you can say that."

"How long have you been working in the industry?"

"For over ten years."

"And now you're staying here in Greece for a while?"

"That's the plan. — May I ask you something?"

"Yes, of course."

"What kind of journalist are you?"

"I'm a business columnist for a local newspaper. I also take pictures. I've already asked Natasha if she would like to be on film, but she isn't interested. Are you?"

"No, thanks, I'm not interested either."

"Suit yourselves. I would think an ad on the Internet together with professional photos could only help."

"Yes, it might. I'll let Natasha know if there comes a time when I need really good photos."

Was that an attempt to get my phone number? I do not know. It does not matter as I have declined his offer. We talk for a while about trivial things, such as today's strike and the impact on society. When Journalist finishes his second cigarette, I decide it is time for us girls to continue our performance.

It seems neither Natasha nor our customer has any idea on how to proceed, so I assume the role of director again.

"Darling, would you please go wash your proud member so the two of us can tease it with our tongues?" I urge Journalist and he immediately disappears into the bathroom.

"Anika-mou, you're doing well! I think Journalist likes you. You're probably the first German he's ever fucked and he's proud of that."

"Perhaps. At least so far, it's going well. Is there anything taboo for you when he joins you now?"

"No. — Most of the time he fucks me in the ass and once he's ready he pulls out, pulls the condom off, and jerks off in my mouth. I don't know if he has something else in mind today. But I believe that's the way he likes it best."

"And you're okay with his standard routine? I mean, him coming in your mouth has nothing to do with safe sex..."

"I know, Babitschka, but I think that's the only reason he calls me. I don't want to lose his business. Let him do it his way."

"Okay, it's your decision."

The door opens and Journalist stands before us freshly showered.

"Have another smoke, darling!" I say to him. "We're getting comfortable. Natasha is going to spoil me."

"Okay, but when I'm done I'll join you!"

"Of course, darling!"

Stacking several pillows against the headboard, I lie down with my upper body propped up so I can survey the room.

"Natasha, please put a new condom on our toy and spoil me with it."

Natasha placed a few condoms on the nightstand earlier, so she grabs one and rolls it over the vibrator. After removing my panties, I watch Natasha use the device on me. She is gentle and I am pleased to notice she is careful not to hurt me.

"Push it in, sweetie!" I say encouraging as I spread my labia. Considering the size of it, she really cannot hurt me. For a while, I am pretending to be the horny puttana and as soon as I see Journalist finishing his smoke, I roll onto my stomach and raise my butt teasingly in the air, telling Natasha to fuck me from behind. Kneeling beside me, she does as she is told. Journalist has a fantastic view of my pussy. This time when he comes over to the bed, I do not tell him no. Natasha and I stop our lesbian performance and I tell Journalist to lie down. As with Adonis, Natasha and I agree via eye contact that I will suck his cock first and she is in charge of his balls. Since his cock looks healthy, – I once again forego a condom during oral sex. Everything is running smoothly and I am in no mood for an argument. I only point out to him that he is not to come in my mouth. He promises to let me know in time. I want Journalist to enjoy our threesome so he will book us again. That is how I will establish my customer base! 120 is good money!

And Natasha also benefits. When I feel Journalist's growing excitement, I ask:

"Do you want to come now, darling, or would you like to come as you fuck Natasha? I believe she would like that."

"Yes, I will give it to her. She loves it when I make her squeal. Isn't that right, my little Russian slut?"

Natasha answers in the affirmative and assumes the on-all-fours position. I hand Journalist a condom and he quickly rolls it over his penis. Then, without warning, he penetrates Natasha's anus. She does not squeal, she actually screams in pain. Since I cannot sit there passively, I squat in front of Natasha's face and pretend she is licking me. Journalist is in his element and, at the moment, only interested in attaining an orgasm. He must not fail, that would be disgraceful. So he fucks Natasha right up until he is ready to ejaculate. When he pulls out of Natasha, she quickly turns around as he pulls off the condom, jerks himself off, and he comes in her mouth. Once again, I do not understand how she puts up with it. I really should talk to her about this again. As Journalist works the last few drops from his gland, he strokes the back of Natasha's head. While breathing hard he says:

"That's a good girl. That's my good little Russian whore!"

Natasha gets up. Her mouth is open and disgust is written on her face as she dashes into the bathroom. Spitting and choking sounds emanate from the bathroom. Water from the faucet flows, followed by gargling, and then the shower comes on. Journalist lights a cigarette and starts talking to me:

"You'll only do anal for more money but won't have anyone come in your mouth, correct? Not even if I pay a couple bucks more?"

"No, – not even for a ton of money. I only offer safe sex. Here and there, I make an exception where I don't insist on a condom during oral sex, but only when I think the customer's dick looks healthy."

"That's too bad, but you do have certain other qualities. Today's experience was quite different than when it's only Natasha. I bet Andreas would enjoy you two. Natasha knows him. I don't know if she's told him about you. He's a lobbyist. He also speaks German, among other languages. I could recommend you to him."

"Thanks, it's nice of you to offer, but I only work together with Natasha. You understand, right?"

"Yes, of course, I forgot," he lies, then takes his wallet out and places two 100 and two 20-euro bills in a pile on the table. When Natasha comes back out of the bathroom, Journalist announces:

"I'm showering next. I have to hurry."

Glancing at my watch, I think it is best if I immediately head to the inner city, considering the situation with traffic. Better safe than sorry. If I arrive too early at the Kamazon Hotel, I can always kill time strolling through the city center. While Natasha dresses, I ask her about Andreas.

"I haven't spoken to him yet. Sometimes he gives me 100, sometimes 120, but then he's a fat cat politician."

Whatever the case, politician or lobbyist, it does not matter as long as he is a nice client who pays well.

"See what you can do. As soon as I come across the right customer, you'll hear from me. — At the moment, I don't know anyone, but I also don't call my customers. That practice is rather unheard of in our profession... I'm surprised your customers haven't complained."

"They won't, they are Greek. Greek men don't care. Not one of my customers has ever told me not to call. Most men have a second phone, one only their girlfriends and puttanas know about. That's smart; the wife will never be the wiser. See, Greeks can be smart too!"

Smiling on the inside, I make a note of it. When Journalist vacates the bathroom, I get up to use the facility. As I finish showering, I hear the bathroom door open a crack and Journalist pokes his head in:

"Anika, thank you again. I just want to say goodbye! I have to go. I have to take care of things at the editorial office. — I'll see you again. Until then, take care!"

"Bye, Journalist! And thank you too!" I reply and step naked out of the bathtub, pleased about having another satisfied customer. A few minutes later, Natasha and I leave the Orion Hotel. She dons her big sunglasses, pulls her baseball cap low over her brows, and notices my questioning look. She says:

"This way no one recognizes me. I live here in Voula!"

As we say goodbye at the next street corner, I thank her again for a well-paid job. Natasha dismisses me and says:

"You don't have to thank me! I would not have made any money from Journalist if it weren't for you. He was only curious about you."

At a periptero, I buy a bottle of water and take a big swig before I start hunting for a taxi.

56

Only my white wide-brimmed sun hat protects my brain from melting into mush as I wait patiently curbside in the direct sun for a taxi to arrive. After what seems like an eternity, one finally stops and, completely exhausted, I flop onto the back seat.

"To the Plaka, please," I say.

"Are you sure? You know what's going on? It might take a while to get there."

"Yes, I know. Regardless, I have to go. Wait a moment, let me get the exact address."

"As you wish, madam," the taxi driver replies indifferently.

After removing the piece of paper with the Kamazon Hotel address from my wallet, I hand it to the driver. Looking at it, he says:

"The hotel is on a one-way street that's difficult to access from the direction we're coming from. If it's okay with you, I'll drop you off before we reach Syntagma Square. It isn't a long walk to the hotel."

"Okay, thank you."

At that moment, I remember I have not called Kevin back at the hotel. I dial the hotel number and a cheerful sounding woman answers. I ask to be connected with Kevin Morgan in room 338.

"One moment please," she replies.

I am on hold for quite a while before the receptionist comes back on the line and informs me:

"I'm sorry, madam, but there is no guest registered here under that name. Are you sure he's staying in our hotel?"

Flabbergasted, I do not know how to reply. Stammering, I respond:

"That is what I was told. Let me check again. — Thank you, goodbye."

What is going on? Did I make an appointment with a prankster? My heart is beating faster as I contemplate what to do. I guess I must call Kevin's cell phone number. After a few rings, a man answers in Greek, *Embros*, which means *come in*, a Greek way of answering the phone.

"Hello, this is Anika, who am I speaking with please?"

"Oh, hi, Anika, it's Kevin. So, how does it look, are you already in the city center?" he replies in fluent English.

"Not yet. I just tried to call you at the hotel and the woman at the front desk told me they do not have a guest by the name Kevin Morgan! — So, what is going on?"

"Yes, I know, Anika. — I didn't give you my real name. I didn't know you'd call me at the hotel. — Is it important? — I mean, I'm sure Anika is not your real name, is it?"

"No, of course it isn't. Nevertheless, when a customer wants to meet me at a hotel, – I'd like his name so I can verify he's actually booked a room. — What's going on? Why won't you give your real name? Are you a wanted man or something?"

"No, Anika, I'm not! Calm down for a moment, please! Let me explain. — My actual name is Evangelos Karmatis. I'm a banker from Cyprus. I used my real name to check into the Kamazon Hotel. I always stay there when I come to Athens. They know me. You're welcome to verify it! — I'm truly sorry, Anika. Please believe me, I didn't know my real name would be important. — I'll be heading back to the hotel now and you can call my room in five minutes, okay?"

Believing him, my anger slowly subsides. I reply:

"Okay, I will I call you in five minutes."

"Okay, Anika, talk to you soon. Since last week, I've been looking forward to our date!"

After ending the conversation, I glance at my watch and note the time. Looking out the window as we cruise along Vouliagmeni Avenue, a long and busy thoroughfare in Athens, I ask the driver how much longer he thinks we will need to get to Syntagma Square. He replies:

"We're making good time, so far. It seems the traffic jam in the city center is gone, so I believe we'll be there in a half an hour or so."

Since the five minutes have elapsed, I call the Kamazon Hotel. I immediately recognize the receptionist's friendly voice. I give her the new name and she puts me right through to room 338.

"Hello!" he says.

"Hi, it's Anika. I'll stick to calling you Kevin, it's easier for me, and you don't seem to care."

"That's okay, Anika. You see, everything is fine. And I'm not leaving my room anymore. Do you know when you might arrive?"

"Providing traffic stays the same, I should be there in a half an hour. Do you want me to call you again?"

"No, that's not necessary. I'm looking forward to our meeting!"

"Okay, Kevin, I'll see you in a bit!"

"Bye, Anika, see you soon!"

Before we reach the city center, my phone rings. It is Harrison. Since I was eagerly awaiting his call, I pick up with a cheerful:

"Hi, Harrison!"

"Hello, Anika! I hope you're okay and still coming tomorrow. I booked you a room at a fancy hotel. Do you have a pen and paper?"

"One moment, Harrison."

Grabbing a pen and paper, I jot down the address and phone number of El Torino Hotel on Santorini.

"The hotel is located on a busy road and only a ten-minute walk to Fira, the island capital. I can park my car there without it being seen from the street. The hotel is perfect for my needs. I'm hoping you'll like it too. The decor is simple, but suits the ambiance of an Aegean island."

After thanking Harrison, I inform him of my flight number and its arrival time. He promises to call me back no later than tomorrow, early evening. Pleased that my work trip to Santorini is going as planned, I lean against the back of the seat of the taxi and stare out the window for the remaining trip. – After paying the fare of 18 euros, I am glad we did not encounter a traffic jam. Who knows how much it would have cost then. Before reaching Syntagma Square, I walk along the shaded side of Mitropoleos Street for maybe a minute before suddenly arriving at the elegant-looking Kamazon Hotel. As always, during the elevator ride up, I take one last look at myself in the mirror. Reaching the floor and room, I am overcome with my usual stage fright. I knock on the door. Kevin opens it. He is a young, slender man with thick black hair and three-day stubble. I am happy to note the window curtains are closed and the room's lighting is nicely muted. Kevin wears a dark suit and tie.

"Come on in, Anika. I'm glad to finally meet you!"

"Hi, Kevin! — Well, your fictitious name caused me embarrassment! Also, I just noticed you don't even have a Cypriot cell phone number, but a Greek one. Are you still lying to me?"

Kevin shorty laughs and replies:

"My God, it's like talking to a detective! – Look, I'm not using my Cypriot cell phone number, which my relatives and business partners have, to call a prostitute. — Satisfied?"

"Yes, please forgive me for asking, it's simply that I was still a little skeptical!" I reply, believing he is being truthful. Why am I pestering him about his phone number? Who cares how many he has or which one he used to call me from.

"By the way, you look great, Anika! – You know, I already have a hard-on! For the past few days I've been imagining everything I'm going to do to you and that really turns me on."

"You remember we've talked about no hard abuse or anything similar that might damage or leave welts! — Only light slaps and verbal insults. Naturally, I'll be your humble servant and obey you."

The special emphasis I place on *humble* makes Kevin smile.

"Yes, I haven't forgotten what we discussed. But just in case, let's also agree on a safe word for you?"

"Okay, if I say *enough* you stop whatever it is you're doing. — And just to reiterate, I only provide safe sex. Meaning, you have to wear a condom if you want to stick your dick in my mouth. I'm not having you come in my mouth!"

"Oh! I thought oral sex was possible without a condom... I'm also sure I won't come in your mouth, I promise!"

„Okay, let me see your cock and I'll tell you if it's possible. I'm sorry about all this, but I need reassurances if you don't want to wear a condom."

"Unbelievable... — If you insist, have a look," Kevin says, opens his fly and digs out his semi-hard penis. I feel like a doctor about to examine a patient. I have never been this straight forward before.

"Thank you, your magnificent specimen looks fine," I say and smile conciliatorily.

"I'm glad to hear that!" he replies, smirking.

"And please, Anika, here's your money up front. This way you don't have to worry about it!" he says, and hands me five 100-euro bills. I thank him and pocket the money in my handbag.

"May I briefly use your bathroom? – I'd like to freshen up and change."

"Of course! Would you like a drink?"

"No thank you, I had something in the taxi."

Kevin makes a nice impression. Maybe he is from a wealthy, educated family. I put on the same bra I wore for my last appointment with Journalist, but the panties I slip on are fresh. Once again, I exchange my red heels for the black ones, a few spritzes of my favorite perfume and voila, I am a lovely slave. Stepping back in the spacious and modernly furnished hotel suite, I find Kevin sitting on the sofa with a drink in his hand. The only piece of clothing he has removed is his slacks. He is still wearing his undies, shirt, tie, jacket, even his socks and highly polished black shoes.

"Come here and kneel in front of me!"

Years ago, I often worked as a dominatrix's assistant, so I am familiar with such a command and, thus, have little fear or trepidation. I am merely here for role-playing. That is it! – Obeying him, I get down on my knees while keeping my face directed at the floor and my hands folded on my abdomen. The only unpleasantness is the hard floor, but I do not believe I am going to be in this position for long. Kevin sets down his glass of whiskey or whatever he is drinking, on a small side table and leans down. Lifting my chin with one hand, he says:

"I want you to look me in the eyes at all times! Do you hear? Constantly!"

"Yes, master!" I answer.

"Now, turn around!" he orders in an unfriendly tone.

I turn while rotating my head so I can look over my shoulder in order to maintain eye contact. Although it is not easy in this position, I manage. I am certain he thought I would forget, meaning, he could give me my first punishment. But I am familiar with games like this one as well as the rules of what can happen, although, this variant, receiving a command not to break eye contact is new to me. Admittedly, I do not care for it in this position. It is giving me a neck cramp.

"Get down on your hands!"

In the so-called doggie position, I keep my head turned as far as possible to maintain eye contact to Kevin, just at a different angle.

However, he is not paying attention to that; instead, he is watching one of his feet as the shoe tip lightly taps against my pussy. The pain is minimal and still within the framework of our agreement. Unexpectedly, he gives my butt a good hard kick so that my torso moves forward. I am happy my arms immediately lock, preventing movement. Kevin abruptly jumps into his role of disappointed master and yells:

"You better be looking back and in my eyes, you fucking bitch! Back on your knees! This time, lean back so you're near me. Come on now, you'll get it!"

His tone is nastier than it was a minute ago. Quickly, I do as I am told and back up close to him while maintaining eye contact.

Kevin loosens his tie and orders me:

"Turn around and put your hands behind on your back!"

I obey without hesitation. He ties my hands together.

"Master! Please do not bind them too tightly. Please leave enough room so I can free myself in an emergency!"

"Shut up!"

Responding in a tone that lets him know I have some say in this game, I reply:

"I mean it, Kevin! You never mentioned binding me. So, please respect my wish!"

"Of course. Now, shut up!" he says annoyed.

It seems he has to keep using that ugly tone, but at least I feel the knot loosening so I could slip out of it. Kevin stands up and moves in front of me. Now I have to look straight up to maintain eye contact. Since my knees are hurting, I secretly wish I could just get up. But now Kevin wants my face directly in front of his member. He is pulling his currently large, hard dick out of his underpants.

"Suck it!" he orders.

I stick my tongue out and lick the swollen tip of his cock. While doing this, I break eye contact for only a second. Kevin immediately slaps one of my cheeks and says harshly:

"I told you to never to break eye contact!"

I immediately resume eye contact and crane my neck to look up. It is not like I have to look at his dick while licking it, but I usually direct my gaze at whatever I am doing at any given time.

"Come now, open your mouth, and start sucking it properly!" he orders. Again, I break eye contact and he immediately slaps my face. It hurts, but not so much that it is unbearable. I am sucking his cock while looking him in the eyes. – It feels quite big and I am trying not to take it in all the way. Nevertheless, Kevin continues pushing his pecker all the way into my throat. Since I cannot help but cough and spit, I break eye contact.

"Look at me, you piece of shit!" he screams and then slaps me.

"You're a worthless slut! I want you to suck my stick properly now! You will take it all the way in your mouth while looking me in the eyes, you understand!"

Once again, I am trying my best but my gag reflex gets the better of me. My eyes tear up. This is uncomfortable. My nose is runny and I repeatedly have to spit. With my hands bound behind my back, I cannot even wipe my face. Tears run freely down my cheeks. Kevin really plunges into the role and repeatedly slaps my face while forcefully shoving his big hard cock against the back of my mouth. I cannot help but break eye contact when I choke, cough, spitting, sniffle, and tear up. This is what turns him on! It is exactly what he wanted. He can enjoy verbally abusing me while forcing his penis down my throat. While I am at his mercy, he holds my head in place by grabbing my hair tightly and pushing his dick deep inside my mouth. I am starting to choke continuously and an onslaught of rising bile is not far behind. Suddenly, he interrupts his game and walks over to his drink, leaving me alone on my knees sniffling, choking, and spitting. For me to think my torture is over is wishful thinking.

"Damn it, look me in the eyes!" he screams as he approaches quickly and throws his whiskey in my face. This also was not discussed, but it is not like he could plan every little detail of such a session and tell me about it beforehand. There is always room for spontaneity and as long as he keeps his promise to not leave any red marks or bruises, I really cannot use my safe word, *enough*! So far, he has stuck to the rules.

As I compose myself and think about what is in store for me next, Kevin pours himself a new drink and takes a big sip.

"Tell me, slut, are you ready for round two?"

"Of course, my master!" I reply submissively.

Again, Kevin steps up close and prompts me to lick his balls. Doing this without breaking eye contact is impossible so I end up with another slap in the face.

"You useless piece of crap! — Take my cock deep into your mouth and blow me properly. You're not here for your amusement, you fucking whore!"

Perfectly aware of that fact, I dread what comes next. Basically, I have to relive the torture I just overcame. The more I spit, sob, choke, groan, and suffer, the more excited Kevin becomes as he pushes his penis even deeper down my throat. Eventually, I cannot help it and I throw up while his cock is deep inside my mouth. I find it unbelievable, but honestly, Kevin actually enjoys it!

He keeps slapping my face as he pulls out of my mouth, then yells at me to look him in the eyes, which of course I am doing, while he jerks off his vomited-on and smelly cock until he comes and squirts his junk on my cleavage. — I am really not into this!

Nevertheless, I absolutely wanted to know how it is to sell your body as a sex slave. Now I can say with absolute certainty that it is not my thing, not even for the easily made 500 euros an hour. – Kevin is still standing in front of me with his semi-limp penis in his hand and his head thrown back. As it seems Kevin is oblivious to my presence, I quickly slide a bit away from him while I manage to free my loosely bound hands. They feel as numb as my legs as I try to get up. Kevin releases his dick and looks at me questioningly.

"Is everything okay?" he asks, still panting.

"Yes, everything's fine. My legs are asleep and my wrists are a bit sore, that's all. — Do you mind if I go to the bathroom?"

"Of course not, Anika, please go right ahead!"

Since I am not yet all that steady on my legs, I slip out of my high heels and walk barefoot into the bathroom. Undressed, I step under the shower's spray, let the water run over my face while repeatedly rinsing out my mouth, and wash myself. I wait for full feeling to return to my legs and wrists before getting out of the shower to look in the mirror. My face is flushed and the eyeliner around my eyes is smeared. Even my supposedly waterproof mascara lost its power as I now have black rivulets running down my cheeks. Grabbing the mouthwash from my handbag, I rinse thoroughly several times. Then I gently wash my face with cold water and look closely at the skin. It is merely flushed, which should go away within the next half hour. Thank God! I was not certain after all the slaps I received. I use the hotel-provided lotion to eliminate the black streaks from my ruined makeup. Taking my time dressing, I wash my face with soap, apply facial cream, and new makeup. Even with the Botox treatment and, considering what I just went through, I look horrible! Tired and exhausted, I walk back into the spacious room. Kevin asks me to wait until he is finished showering, so I walk over to a window, draw the curtain open, and watch the busy street in front of the hotel. Thinking of how loud Kevin was a few times, I wonder if he is concerned about some of the other hotel guests or passersby hearing him. Oh well, that is his problem. Maybe the hotel rooms are well insulated. If that is the case, I realize that no one could have heard me if it became necessary to yell for help. Kevin returns wrapped in a hotel bathrobe and picks up his drink.

"Anika, is everything all right? You don't seem all that happy."

"I'm merely worn-out. That's all. If that's all you wanted to know, I would like to get on my way."

"Sure, you can leave anytime you like, but I would still like to at least offer you something to drink! — I cannot help feeling bad about being a little rough with you."

"Perhaps, but don't worry about it. You stuck to what was agreed on and you paid my fee. So, everything is fine! I was under the impression I would have an easy time being a slave, but I'm afraid that isn't the case. Don't be angry with me, but I'm saying no to the drink. I'd rather get going now, okay?"

"Yes, of course. For what it's worth, you met all my expectations. Thank you, Anika! Perhaps I'll call you again. Have a nice evening!"

He has the audacity to give me a little kiss as we say goodbye. I quickly leave the room and head for the elevators, thinking I will definitely never again make an appointment with him. Obviously, I did not tell him that, after all, I would not want to ruin his evening.

57

Stepping out of the Kamazon Hotel, I head left in the direction of the city center. This evening, I will not be accepting any other customers, I know that much! It is not because I have already made enough today, it is because I must recuperate from the appointment I just had with Kevin. I never imagined he do something like that to me. Simply despicable! I am still feeling disgusted. Since I know Violet had her reservations about my appointment with Kevin, I decide to call her to let her know I am all right.

"Hi, Violet, it's Anika."

"Anika, darling, I'm so glad to hear from you. I've been worrying about you for the past two hours. I had no customers or anything else to do other than think about you! So, how was your session? Are you in one piece?"

"Yes, I'm fine. Kevin stuck to our agreement. However, I've realized I'm not cut out to be a slave. At least now I know, so that's good. Nevertheless, my new experience earned me 500 euros, so I'm not complaining. Anyway, how are you?"

"I didn't have one customer today! I've spent the day sitting on the couch watching TV with the air conditioner on. Did you see any of the demonstration in front of the parliament building?"

"Thankfully, no. It was over by early afternoon and by the time I got to the city center, traffic was almost back to normal."

"I really got angry watching the proceedings on television. Some of the demonstrators held up placards with pictures of your chancellor. You should have seen how they photo-shopped them! One was of her dressed in a military uniform with a swastika pinned to her chest and a Hitler mustache. — Be happy you didn't see it! And your minister, the one in a wheelchair, he was depicted as a torturer! — Tell me, darling, wouldn't it be better if your ad said you are a Dane or a Swede?"

"No, absolutely not! I'm not hiding my nationality. I am German, that's it. Why, what's wrong with that?"

"Yes, you're right. That was the coward in me speaking. Nowadays, I wouldn't want to be a German in Athens... I think you're quite brave."

"It has nothing to do with courage, Violet. I'm not intimidated by a few people carrying such signs. Or, do you think they'll succeed in stirring up the whole population?"

"No. — At least, I hope so. — I also hope there will be no demonstrations and strikes in the near future! That's when I lose financially. Can you imagine? Either a customer cancels, like Jorgos did or it is such a long commute that I end up paying steep taxi fares. — But enough about me, tell me in detail what Kevin did to you!"

Since I don't want to tell the entire terrible story to Violet, I simply say:

"Basically, I kneeled on the floor and gave him a blowjob while he verbally abused me and lightly slapped my face. That was it."

"That doesn't sound so bad. You were lucky! I guess he was a real gentleman. Maybe he'll call you again. What do you think? I mean, you already know the customer, so you could see him again. I don't understand why you say you're not cut out to be a slave."

"I didn't like being on my knees on the hard floor for that long. It really hurt."

"Oh! Yes, I can understand that. — So, what are you doing for rest of the evening? Do you have another appointment later?"

"No, I'm in the Plaka. I've called it a day and I am going to enjoy the evening."

"That's good, darling! You have to treat yourself every now and then! So then, call me again, perhaps from Santorini!"

"Yeah, sure! You have a nice evening too, Violet. Talk to you later!"

After hanging up, I notice Dimitri tried to call me. Since he is not married or in a relationship and because he is a fish I caught myself, I return his call.

"Hi, Dimitri, it's Anika. How are you? – I noticed you tried to call me."

"Oh, hi, Anika! Yes, I'd like to get together, but not tonight. Do you have time tomorrow morning? In Piraeus? I could pick you up somewhere and we'll drive to a hotel together. Please, don't say no again!"

"Tomorrow morning? Let me think... Yes, it's possible! However, I have to be back home no later than noon. I have things to do. So, do you think it's feasible?"

"Yes, Anika! I'm wide-open tomorrow morning. Just tell me when and where you want me to pick you up."

Thinking fast and considering I do not want to be out in the heat for long and because Dimitri only pays 70 euros, I ask:

"Do you know the Lilo Hotel? It's on the hill overlooking the Zeas Marina?"

"Yes, I know the place!"

"Good! Across the street, a little down the road, is a big store that sells porcelain. I'll be waiting for you there at 10:00 a.m. Is that okay with you?"

"Yes, that's great! I'm looking forward to seeing you, Anika. Have a good night!"

"Same to you, Dimitri. – I am also looking forward to seeing you again!"

Well, an easily earned 70 euros will be nice pocket change for Santorini. I am in the mood to spend at least a little money treating myself while there! Actually, why should I not start right now and look for a nice restaurant to have dinner! As I slowly walk down the Ermou pedestrian zone while on the phone, I find myself at Monastiraki square. It is full of musicians and groups of young people engaged in lively discussions about whatever, while others are showing off their break dancing skills. Tourists mingle with locals, take pictures, and spend a nice hot summer evening together in the heart of Athens.

Turning onto and walking down the Adrianou pedestrian zone that runs along the green area below the Acropolis, the Archaia Agora with the Temple of Hephaestus, I am back in the area where I allegedly work at a tourist bar. The sides of the pedestrian zone are lined with street vendors selling everything from handmade jewelry to pictures and all varieties of knick-knacks. Some vendors draw pencil sketches, others make necklaces or bracelets with silver wire working in the tourists' first names in Greek. For the first time, I notice among the street vendors, black people with colorful sheets displaying their wares. They are selling handbags, wallets, purses, DVDs, and Smartphone accessories. Some are small and brown-skinned and look as if they came from India, Bangladesh, or Pakistan. Others are tall and black-skinned and must come from Africa. Curious, I lean over a sheet with handbags. I like the large white braided faux leather handbag. It is the right size to hold all my daily items I use as a call girl. My apparent interest causes the black man step up next to me and rave about how beautiful the bag is. I ignore him and inspect it closely. Yes, it is the perfect bag! I wonder how much it costs since there is no price tag, so I look up at the black man and ask:

"How much for this bag?"

"40 euros, madam. A good price. The handbag is a good fit for you. Only 40 euros madam and it's yours!"

Thinking why not, after all, it is not like I am going to make it to this week's market in Glyfada and several new big handbags have been on my work accessories shopping list for quite a while.

"Okay, I'll take it!" I finally say, happy about my new find.

"Would you like a bag?" the street vendor asks as he removes the paper tissue stuffing.

"No thanks, it's fine like this."

Buying something nice for myself literally lifts me up and pushes the experience with Kevin temporarily into the background. Proud as a peacock, I sling the new bag over my shoulder along with my other bag and continue strolling slowly down the pedestrian zone.

As I arrive at another spread-out cloth with wares and bend over it, the two black vendors suddenly start arguing. Their eyes widen as each one grabs two corners of the cloth and pull it up, bringing them together so that the wares tumble into the middle of the sheet, which now resembles a sack.

One grabs the sack neck, heaves it over his shoulder, and starts running like he is being chased by a demon while his partner quickly grabs and squeezes a black trash bag filled with goods under his arm and takes up pursuit. Next, a jumble of angry people surround me with everyone yelling at the same time. A white street vendor pulls me aside next to his little jewelry stand as three armed policemen equipped with truncheons push through the angry mob and chase after the two black men. Standing there visibly scared and confused next to the young jewelry, I look at him questioningly.

"Where are you from?" he asks in English, yet with a clear German accent.

"I'm from Germany and I believe you are too, correct?"

"Yes! — And don't worry, this was nothing. The police won't catch them. Even if they do, they'll simply take the stuff for themselves and give it to their wives and daughters. That's all that's going to happen. Tomorrow, those black men will be back selling their wares and on it continues. What you've just witnessed happens almost every day."

"But why? I don't understand!"

"The blacks are illegal and they don't have a vendor license, like me, and others do. So, the police can always come and arrest them. But obviously they don't."

"Why not?"

"Because the prisons are already packed. Think about all the bureaucratic hassle it would cause to arrest illegals who illegally trade or sell illegally manufactured goods. The courts are already overburdened by trivial lawsuits, so I'm sure they're happy not having to deal with such cases. — What? Why do you look like that?"

"I don't know how I look. I simply find it incredible!"

"Not at all, it is quite normal."

"How long have you been in Athens?"

"Four years and you? Do you live in Athens?"

"Yes, but not long. Everything is still new to me!"

When two young girls stop and show interest in the friendly, young man's jewelry, he turns away from me and takes care of his customers. I nudge him gently and say:

"Thanks again and good luck on making a sale!"

"Not a problem! Hold on a moment, I want to give you my card. I also have a website. Perhaps you'll have a look at it. By the way, my name is Jakob."

And with that, he hands me his business card and winks at me.

"Thank you, I'm Anika," I reply, introducing myself.

"Bye, Anika! Come and see me anytime you're in the area."

Entering the flowing stream of passersby, it does not take long before I spot a restaurant that is to my liking. Once the waiter has listed today's specialties, I order vegetarian moussaka, a glass of white wine, and a bottle of water. I immediately feel better and it is the first time I have actually enjoyed the fact that I made 620 euros today. That is something! – And tomorrow I am off to Santorini. – What more could I ask for?

My meal is served and I am definitely delighted I ordered it. It is delicious. I store this restaurant on my list of good meals. Enjoying two more glasses of wine, I suddenly find myself getting tired. After taking care of the bill, I stroll along the nearest major road to catch a taxi home. It is great that there is no other option, so I do not have to feel guilty about taking a taxi! This must be the only good thing to come from today's strike day in Athens. Granted, it does cost more.

The next morning, my alarm clock goes off at 7:00 a.m. and I hit the snooze button and get comfortable in bed. I can treat myself to a two-minute period for waking up, but then I definitely have to get going. After breakfast, I grab my new roller-bag, place it open on the bed, and pack all the things I believe I need for my trip to Santorini.

Preparing for a little trip like mine or for a long vacation is basically the same. Unlike Violet, I have fun doing this. – At 9:45 a.m., I slip into my white stretch dress that laces up in the back, grab my handbag, and leave the Lilo Hotel to wait for Dimitri at the porcelain shop catty-corner across the road.

Shortly before 10:00 a.m., a gray Toyota SUV pulls up and Dimitri beckons to me.

"Good morning, darling," I say and lean over to peck his cheek.

"Anika, it's great to see you. You look fantastic."

Dimitri pulls back into traffic. When we stop at the next red traffic light, he looks at me and says:

"I know a hotel that rents rooms by the hour. I hope it'll be to your liking."

"It'll be fine as long as the room is clean."

"Yes, I certainly hope so. It's been quite a while since I last stayed there. It's called the Alonis Hotel."

A few minutes later, we are driving through the harbor area with its tall, dusty buildings. The streets are narrow and the sidewalks on either side are overflowing with parked cars and mopeds. Dimitri pulls into a lot in front of a dilapidated house that serves as a parking lot. We get out and Dimitri speaks with the parking attendant and hands him the car keys.

"Why did you give him the car keys?"

"So he can park it. That's the way it's done here. Isn't it the same in Germany?"

"Huh, I've never seen that before."

"Well, look at the size of this lot. All the cars you see parked in the back there, bumper to bumper, are long term. The parking attendant does that. Since we're only here for two hours, he might leave my car where it is, but if he needs to pull out one from the long-term area, he can move mine to make room for one of the other cars to get by. — Logical, right?"

"Okay, now I get it. Still, I find it strange, handing your car keys to a complete stranger. He could snoop through the trunk or glove compartment and take whatever he likes..."

"You mean stealing. — Your mistrust must be a German trait, right? We Greeks don't have that nature. In this regard, we think differently." Dimitri laughs as we continue walking by a few more houses on our way to the Alonis Hotel.

A middle-aged lady is sitting behind the front desk. Dimitri talks to her quietly and she hands him the key to number 414. Thankfully, I am used to the elevators now; it is quite ancient. As we ride up to the fourth floor, Dimitri is all over me. Kissing me, he holds me close and I can feel he already has a hard-on. Convenient, because I definitely do not want to prolong our session. The faster we are done the better. The room is a normal, simply furnished hotel room. I immediately go over to the window and close the curtains.

"Would you like to use the bathroom first?" I ask Dimitri.

"We could use it at the same time," he suggests, and I think that is not a bad idea! Maybe I can get him off in the shower.

"Yes, we could do that. Wait, let me quickly undress."

Dimitri also makes haste to get naked. I place my equipment pouch on the nightstand and take a condom along into the bathroom. – Today, I really do not care if my hair gets wet. Once I am done with Dimitri, the only thing I have to do is get to the airport for my flight to Santorini. Entering the bathroom, I note with disappointment that it only has a bathtub, no shower. — That is dangerous. It is too easy for two people to slip in a bathtub. I have to be extremely careful. After adjusting the cold and hot water so the temperature is pleasant, Dimitri climbs into the bathtub with me. Skillfully, I place soap in my hands and start washing Dimitri's boner. I have made the right decision to allow him to join me in the bathroom because while washing his shaft, he becomes even more excited. Supporting himself with his hands against the tiled wall, he suddenly starts ejaculating. I am delighted! Round one is finished. Once Dimitri's breathing returns to normal and I am finished bathing, both of us climb out of the tub. We each cover up in a towel and get comfortable on the bed. Dimitri lights up a cigarette and I try to start a conversation.

"So, have you been cruising around on your boat?"

"Yes, with the family. You know, Mom and Dad. We've been to the island Idra and to Ermioni. They are located in the Peloponnese. Do you know these places?"

"No. — Although I think I've heard of Idra. In Germany, we say Hydra. Is it the same one?"

"Yes, you spell all names differently. Let's see, Kerkyra you call Corfu, right?"

"Yes, we say Corfu. I've never heard the word Kerkyra."

"Well, it's Greek. — We also say Hellas, not Griechenland."

The weird and carefree way he announces the word Griechenland makes both of us laugh. Dimitri stubs his cigarette butt out in the ashtray, so I believe it is time to continue my work. Unwrapping my towel, I kneel beside him, open his towel, and lean down to his dick. It is still flaccid. I take it in my mouth and in no time, I feel the desired effect of it turning into another boner.

"Remember, don't come in my mouth!" I point out emphatically to Dimitri, who replies:

"Yes, I know! Don't worry, Anika!"

This time it takes a little longer for him to get there and as I feel his erection starting to throb, I cautiously stop sucking his cock and lick his balls. Dimitri is not the type to try to prolong his orgasm. He abruptly straightens up, takes hold of his twitching boner with one hand, and it does not take but a second before he starts ejaculating in a high arc. Shortly after, he slumps back down on the bed, panting heavily:

"Anika, I really needed you. I was so fucking horny! – I'm glad you had time this morning; otherwise, I would have had to take care of myself. This here was much nicer! Although I'm not sure if I can come a third time today, I'd love to go down on you so you also get a little out of our meeting. Would that be okay?"

I am thinking definitely not. I clearly remember how wild and roughly he licked me the first time we were together. How can I say no? At the moment, I have no idea! On the other hand, I am considering simply humoring him and after a short while, fake a climax and then this meeting will be finished in less than 40 minutes. As I like that outlook, I reply:

"I won't say no to that. — Come on, darling, get down between my legs and spoil me a little."

"Well, first I want another smoke..."

"Oh, come on, do me first. You got me all hot now!"

"All right!" he replies.

I support my upper body on pillows as Dimitri goes down on me and does all kinds of crazy things with his tongue in order to drive me wild. As my clitoris feels like crying out in pain, I ask him:

"Put your tongue in my pussy. There you go, baby, that's it, lick her inside, nice and deep."

Luckily, he does as I ask, thus no more pain and I can concentrate on faking an orgasm. As I am faking climax, I hold his head in place with my thighs while moaning loudly, and grinding my pelvis. – Dimitri is relentless and keeps flicking his tongue into my pussy as far as it goes.

"Dimitri!" I moan as I raise his head to look him in the eyes.

"Please stop now, you did great! But now I'm too sensitive down there. — Let me calm down a little why you enjoy your smoke, okay?"

"Yes, I'll do that. You taste good, Anika. Like a woman should, which really turns me on, just look at my cock!"

What do you know he has another boner. I do not believe it. I thought I was done with him and could concentrate on my upcoming flight to Santorini. Racking my brain for the best way to make his boner go away without actual sexual intercourse, Dimitri surprises me by going down on his knees right in front of me and starts jerking himself off. It seems his penis was not only hard it also needed relief! I remain where I am and give him a good view of the important part. Moistening a middle finger, I slowly stick it into my pussy while Dimitri watches in fascination. He starts babbling unintelligible stuff and finally shoots off his load, his third this time. I guess I can count myself lucky! I would much rather fake an orgasm for a client to get him off than actually be fucked by him or blowing him. I like making money this way! As Dimitri slumps back on to the bed, I know today's session is over! At the latest, in a half an hour, I am returning to my hotel room.

58

Having made one final check to see that I have packed everything I need for my work trip to Santorini, I turn off the air conditioner and close the curtains. Shouldering my handbag, I pick up my small roller suitcase with one hand and the laundry bag with the other hand and make my way down four floors of steps. Spiros is sitting behind the front desk. When he notices me, he looks at me questioningly.

"Hello, Spiros. Could you call a taxi, please? I'll be out of town until Friday. — Here is my room key and laundry bag."

"Of course, Kiria Ilona. Where are you off to, if I may ask?"

"I'm off to Santorini or Thira, as you Greeks call it."

"For business?"

"Yes, for business."

"Oh, how nice! I'm envious. I'll call a taxi right now. Do you have to go to the airport or are you taking a boat from Piraeus?"

"I need to go to the airport."

"*Amessos!*" he replies in Greek. It means *immediately*. My knowledge of Greek is definitely growing. At least as far as understanding goes. I sit on the couch in the lobby while Spiros is busy on the phone. Just then, my phone rings. Unknown number. Since I cannot talk freely here, I quickly step outside to answer the call. Luckily, the front of the hotel is still in the shade.

"Anika, this is Richard. Can you come over?"

"Hi, Richard! Sorry, darling, but I won't have time today. As a matter fact, I won't be in Athens until Friday."

"Too bad, Anika. I'm all horny for you."

"That's nice to hear, baby, but like I said, today is impossible. How about Saturday? – -Do you want to call me back or make an appointment?"

"Let's do it, Anika. Let's make an appointment for Saturday, but I don't know yet what time will be best... I'll call you back as soon as I know, my sweetie."

"Yes, do that, Richard. Okay, I'll see you in a few days!"

"Bye, Anika!" he says in that soft voice of his and hangs up. I hope he will still be horny for me on Saturday. I do not have to wait long before my cab arrives. Now I am actually starting my first working vacation! While enjoying the ride to the airport, I am overcome with travel fever, a feeling similar to being in love. While counting out the money to pay the 38-euro fare, I ask the taxi driver for a receipt. I usually never do this. This one is for Harrison, so I will be reimbursed. – The driver fiddles around with his taximeter and tells me it is not working properly and will not print a receipt. I stubbornly insist on some kind of receipt.

He opens the glove compartment and pulls out pre-printed receipt forms. After filling one out, he hands it to me. I am sure he will not declare this fare to the tax authority, but then, what do I care. The driver gets out and unloads my roller bag for me. Since I caused him additional trouble and he remained friendly, I hand him a two-euro tip. Proper service is worth my appreciation.

As I walk into the airport, I get all excited again because from here I can go anywhere in the world! Happiness overwhelms me as I think about being one of the many travelers who will soon be up in the air to be quickly transported to their destination.

It is only 2:00 p.m. and I still have plenty of time before my departure, so I stroll around the terminal and window shop while soaking in the airport atmosphere. Noticing an Italian fashion label boutique, I convince myself it would be prudent to buy a cardigan for the trip. It might be cold inside the plane. Merely standing here in my spaghetti strap top and denim mini skirt, I already feel a bit cold. The cardigan I try on looks adorable with the denim skirt. Without hesitating, I pay for my new treasure with my credit card. That is what it is there for! I see a bar, step up, and order a Diet Coke. While scanning the latest news on my phone, I come across an article about yesterday's demonstration in front of Syntagma Square and I see the placard of the German chancellor that Violet told me about.

Sometime later, onboard the plane, smiling happily as the acceleration of the aircraft pushes me against my seat back, I soon look out over the sparkling blue sea and the many little boats and Greek islands of the Aegean Sea until we arrive on Santorini. The landing approach is incredibly spectacular. Slowly, we almost circle the entire volcanic island. I get a view of its crater rim and the black abyss of the volcano, as well as a bird's eye view of the islands of Thirassia and of Nea Kameni, which almost takes my breath away. What an experience! Then I look down on the white houses of Fira, the island's capital. I see blue domes of churches, turquoise swimming pools, and big cruise ships that look like toys from up here. Then there is the deep, crystal clear water, black sand beaches, and an unbelievably bizarre coastline. Seeing everything, I cannot help thinking about the little German town I come from... This here is a completely different world! It is amazing how much my life has changed within a few weeks. I am happy and grateful to be here. I am so glad I had the courage to do this.

As the plane descends readying for landing, I feel I am the happiest person on board this machine. All the trouble and effort my work as a call girl requires has and will continue to pay off. As the saying goes, *no guts no glory*. That goes for any business. And the aspect of *easy money* is relative. – However, I am one of those people who are happy with their job and who do it with pride. Today, I am definitely pleased with my life! After landing, I do not have to wait long to exit the plane and a short time later, I am sitting in a taxi on my way to the El Torino Hotel.

I am relieved I left the sun hat behind. So far, there has been no reason for it, not to mention, holding onto it would have been cumbersome. As we pull into the grounds of the El Torino Hotel and I see it for the first time, it is even more impressive than the picture on the website. It consists of a white angular main building flanked on either side by many small, one to two-story cottages with rooms and suites. The garden and pool area is full of palm trees, bougainvillea, and oleander bushes. The overall color theme is white and turquoise. Still stunned by the beauty of it all, I pull my little roller suitcase up to the front desk. After checking in, a bellboy takes over and carries my bag to my reserved room. Although I have never stayed in such an exclusive luxury hotel, I am well aware the bellboy expects a tip. I have already thought ahead and pull out a five-euro bill from the pocket of my denim mini skirt.

Once alone, I inspect the room. The walls are creamy white, the furniture ivory, and the door and window frames are painted a delicate light blue. My quarters are spacious and the simple furnishings impart an atmosphere of coolness, which is welcome with these high summer temperatures. The four-poster bed has mosquito netting all around. — I hope it is merely decoration! The view from my patio door is of the beautiful swimming pool, which, given that I am a water rat, makes me want to jump in immediately. First, I quickly unpack my roller bag, drink a glass of water, slip into one of my bikinis, and grab one of the big towels provided especially for pool use before walking out the door. Dropping my towel, I jump into the cool water of the pool. I do not even care that I cannot hear my phone. The next half hour is mine alone. I swim until I am exhausted, get out, and sit on a lounge chair to dry off in the sun. At some point, my conscience bugs me, so I get up and retrieve my phone. I have received three calls during my trip. However, they were not from any of my regular clients. Since I do not have to worry about an appointment, I can do whatever I want for the entire afternoon. A waiter approaches and I order a shot of ouzo and continue relaxing poolside. Shortly before 8:00 p.m., I have showered and ready when my phone starts ringing.

"Hello!"

"Hey, Anika, it's Harrison. I cannot speak long. Did you have a good flight? Is the room to your liking?"

"Yes to both, Harrison, and thank you. Everything worked out well. I'm in room 16. Make a left after you go through reception and you'll find me."

"Okay! I'll be over tomorrow shortly after 8:00 a.m. I'm looking forward to seeing you. Have a nice evening!"

"Thanks, Harrison, until tomorrow morning then!"

Although Fira is only half a kilometer away, I call a cab because I am in no mood for unnecessary exertion, even if it is only walking. The taxi driver asks me where I want to go, so I say:

"As far downtown as possible."

"Are you going to watch the sunset?"

"I don't know, why?"

"Because here on Thira, sunsets are the most beautiful!"

"Oh, I didn't know."

"You have to see it! People come from far away to see our sunsets. Even from America."

I believe he may be exaggerating. I cannot see people traveling so far just to see a sunset, but then who am I to contradict his belief.

"Where would be a good spot to watch the sunset? Do you know a place? Also, I wouldn't mind grabbing a bite to eat at the same time."

"Yes, I know just the place, but it's not in Fira, it's in Ia. – It's a town a few kilometers north. There are several nice bars and restaurants."

Looking out the car's window at the sun, I see the big orange ball still hovering at a distance over the sea.

"Will we get there before the sun sets?"

"Yes, that's still about a half hour away. I can have you in Ia in 10 minutes."

"Okay, take me to Ia!"

The cab driver seems happy for he keeps blowing the horn enthusiastically as if to announce to the people he is on a mission and everyone should get out of the way! By the time we arrive, the sun's color is a dramatic blood orange and already nearing the horizon. As soon as I step out of the taxi, I do not know where to look first. I am standing in a picturesque village illuminated by the incredible sunset light, which creates such an atmosphere that I actually start to believe the taxi driver's story about people coming here from all over the world.

"You have to hurry! You have another 15 minutes to enjoy the sunset!" the driver says as he pulls away. Not knowing where to go, I follow the wide steps leading down between cube-like houses until I reach the first restaurant and ask for a table."

"Are you alone?"

"Yes."

"You are in luck. We still have a small table in a romantic spot available," the courteous waiter says and leads the way to the patio with views of the Nea Kameni crater, the silhouette of Thirassia, and a sky so illuminated by the setting sun that the color spectrum spans various tones of yellow and red. – At my table, the waiter is serving my pint of white wine when my phone rings... Crap! I have to answer. Quietly, I answer and say:

"Good evening."

"Hi! I'm calling in regard to your ad in *Athens World*. Could I get more information? My name is Panagiotis."

"Hello, Panagiotis, my name is Anika. I'm a 35-year-old blonde with blue eyes and I provide safe sex for 150 euros an hour."

"Okay! When can we meet? Do you have time now?"

"I'm sorry, Panagiotis, I'm out of town right now and won't be back in Athens until Friday."

"Too bad. I don't know if I can make it on Friday, but I know I cannot make it on the weekend. Maybe next week?"

"Yes, that's no problem. Where would you want to meet? Am I supposed to come to your home or are you staying in a hotel?"

"Neither! We would go to a no-tell motel. Do you know the Priamos Hotel?"

"No, I don't know that one. Do you have the address?"

"No. However, it's in the city center, 200 meters from Kallimarmaro Stadium. Wait, I'll describe it to you. If you come from the south and pass the ancient stadium in the city center, make a right at the next traffic light and then a left on the next street and you are there. You can't miss it."

"Okay, I'm fine with meeting you there next week. Do you want to make an appointment or do you want to call back?"

"I'll get in touch on Monday. Then I'll know exactly when I have time."

"Okay, Panagiotis, thank you for calling. Have a nice weekend!"

"You too, Anika."

By the time I hang up, half the sun has already dipped behind the sea. Luckily, I watched the sunset the entire time I was on the phone. After saving Panagiotis' cell number under 'Panagiotis - Priamos', I place it back in my handbag. Not long after, my meal is served, a dish called Pasticcio. Sitting here on my own, I think Violet can be glad that Malcom accompanies her to dinner when she goes to Rhodes to service him. At least she has entertainment. I might be in a beautiful place, but there is no one sharing my joy. A real shame... Pushing the gloomy thoughts quickly away, I enjoy my tasty wine and delicious Pasticcio. Signaling the waiter, I ask for the bill and ask him to call me a cab. It is time to stroll through the old town of Fira.

While waiting for the taxi, the west facing walls of the island's houses are no longer illuminated by the sun, but now, more and more lights come on in houses, courtyards, and streets. In a way, it looks as if the spots where the last rays of the sun hit the town have mysteriously turned into lanterns. The atmosphere is simply beautiful and romantic.

The waiter comes over and tells me my cab has arrived, so off I go, a few kilometers down the road to the touristy town of Fira.

Strolling along the narrow, dimly lit cobblestone streets of the old city, I enter several boutiques to try on clothes and shoes and buy a few postcards. Taking a break from my little shopping spree, I enjoy a shot of ouzo on the terrace of a nice bar on the edge of the caldera with a beautiful view of the houses below with their illuminated swimming pools, bougainvillea, and oleander bushes. Although it is already late, it is still balmy. I continue strolling and carefully check out every little shop. I see a bikini in one selling beachwear that I cannot resist. It is a pink push-up top with a cute bow at the cleavage and matching bottom. Even though it is expensive, I buy it. For some reason, my conscience is questioning when I will wear this bikini. It is not often I go swimming, I mostly work... but I am resolute and tell myself that when I go swimming, I want to do it in a beautiful bikini! — So, to really throw caution to the wind, I go ahead and buy a second bikini. It is turquoise with lots of decorative, silvery appliques. Leaving the shop highly satisfied, I am happy to note that my conscience has been silenced.

Since it is near midnight and I am uncertain if the taxi service here also doubles the fare once a new day starts, I hail a cab back to the El Torino Hotel. I might not be tired, but I have work to do in the morning so it is time for bed.

59

As there were no mosquitoes in my room last night, there was no reason to close the netting around the four-poster bed. I slept well. I am freshly shaved and showered with my hair washed and blow-dried. Naturally, I also creamed myself from head to toe. Standing in front of the bathroom mirror, I apply light eye makeup and outline my lips with a pink pencil. It is nearly 8:00 a.m. and I am ready for Harrison. I have made the bed, pulled the sheets tight, and the pillows are fluffed. I have also made sure to air out the room. Condoms, massage oil, and sex lube are on the nearby nightstand next to the four-poster bed. In the drawer, I have placed a small vibrator in case I need it. The window and patio door curtains are made of light, pale blue fabric, so they only darken the room slightly. I am wearing my cream-colored satin bodysuit with the seductive lace insert in the back as well as my good, gold high heels. Although I know Harrison, I am still a bit nervous. Last night, I wrote down all my expenses on a piece of paper and folded it around the receipts. For the taxi fares, round-trip ticket, and two nights at the hotel, Harrison must reimburse me 574 euros. Together with my fee for two working days, it comes to a total of 1374 euros. Nevertheless, I will not bring up my expenses just yet. I am positive Harrison is gallant enough to ask me about them. While thinking about this and that, my phone rings. It is Harrison. Although I am convinced he will not stand me up, my heart still starts to beat a little faster.

"Harrison, good morning!" I answer.

"Good morning, Anika. I can be in your room in two minutes. Is it okay or is it still too early for you?"

"No, that's fine. I'm ready for you."

"Good! Room 16, right? I'll be there shortly!"

"Okay!"

While looking out the window at the grounds behind the pool area, I see Harrison dressed in white tennis togs walking out the rear entrance of the main building of the El Torino Hotel heading for my room. – Should I find a music station on TV? Should I start by offering him a drink? This appointment requires more of me than when I meet a customer at his home or hotel room. Although I watch Harrison arrive at my door, I wait for him to knock and take a deep breath before opening it. He looks damn good!

"Hi, darling!" I utter warmly and we exchange obligatory kisses on both cheeks.

"Anika, you look absolutely adorable. I'm hoping you had a good journey and evening and that you're satisfied with the room."

"Yes, everything went smoothly. I had a good time and I like the room. Thank you, Harrison. Would you like a glass of water?"

"No, Anika, I'm fine. — First, I'd like to get something out of the way."

He pulls a wad of money from the pocket of his tennis shorts and counts off three purple bills, holding them up, asking:

"Will 1500 cover everything? I'm just estimating."

"Actually, that's too much. — Wait, let me show you the receipts."

"No, there's no need for that. All that's important is that you're happy with everything," he says, then walks over to the desk and places the money on it.

"You're too kind. Thank you, Harrison."

"Okay, now to us!" He smiles as he approaches me. Before I know it, he pulls and holds me close in his arms and starts kissing me. However, it is not eagerly, rather, passionately, as one hand runs down my back and over my bottom.

"Let's go to bed. I want to take off my tennis outfit. That bodysuit fabric feels fantastic, but please don't take it off yet, I'd like to do that myself in a bit."

Happy about having chosen the right lingerie for Harrison, I slip out of my high heels and assume a seductive pose on the bed. Soon after, Harrison settles down next to me in his boring white underpants and props his torso up with an elbow. His free hand starts brushing over my breasts while he studies me intently. Considering how bright the room is, I am not that comfortable. I would prefer he immediately attack and eat me up, but he is not doing that. I also do not see any stirring in his undies...

"Anika, I'm glad you trusted me and came to Thira. This is an extremely exciting experience for me. I told you already that I'm married and that I cheat on my wife every now and then. — I need to revive certain feelings. — And while anticipating our get-together, I became inspired!"

If that is the case, I wonder why nothing is moving in his underwear. But now, his hand has moved to my crotch and remains there motionless.

"May I ask you something personal, Anika?"

"Of course."

"Are you or have you been married?"

"I was married, I'm divorced now."

"How long did it last?"

"12 years, why?"

"Perhaps you have a better understanding of why I'm doing this. I've been married for 18 years. Happily so! And I love my wife. — But I no longer look forward to seeing her when she returns home after being gone a week. – During the first few years, I missed her after only a few hours. In later years, it took a few days until I longed for her. Nowadays, – she can be gone for a month visiting friends in the United States and when she returns, it feels to me as if she'd only gone shopping. — Can you sympathize? Did you also lose feelings for your spouse over the course of your marriage?"

"Yes, I know exactly what you're talking about."

"That's good. Then you know what I'm missing. Although it's not a tragedy for a long-time couple to lose these feelings of happiness, it's just nature's ironic way, yet it still pains me! At times, I don't see any other way other than finding those feelings with someone else. — But I'm not always successful. Oftentimes, it's merely plain old sex."

By now, his hand is massaging my pussy while applying varying pressure. It seems he wants to stimulate me. I commend his effort by rotating my pelvis and say:

"I can barely understand what you're saying, considering what you're doing to me. You really turn me on, Harrison."

"I'm glad! I'm aroused too. – May I open these snaps in the instep of your bodysuit?"

" Yes, of course, darling."

Remaining on one elbow, his other hand skillfully unfastens the snaps and exposes my cleanly shaven pussy. Carefully, he runs one finger through my moist slit. I let him do as he pleases, happy to see a bulge finally in his pants. Apparently, talking and fondling a woman is what gets him going.

"These feelings of desire are somehow connected to feelings of longing, don't you think, Anika? I cannot separate the two. As little as I miss my wife when she's on the road, I desire her just as much when she's back at home and we're in bed together."

"Harrison, could you please stop talking about your wife and focus fully on my body. Don't you feel my inner spasms every time you touch me that way?"

Harrison must have been waiting for such a reaction because suddenly he kneels beside me, spreads my legs even further apart, and stares at my pussy. It is impossible not to notice the pronounced bulge in his undies. I am glad, so I fake being aroused and seductively raise my hips slightly.

"Please do something with me, darling, anything," I beg him. His bright blue eyes sparkle as he leans down over me. Propped up on both hands, he moves over me, lowers his hips, and lightly pushes his privates against my pussy while watching me and grinning. He really is a damn good-looking man and I am comfortable with him. When Harrison's attractive, freckled face is close to mine, I grind my hips in a circular fashion. It feels incredibly good. However, before my sympathy for Harrison gets the better of me, I quickly focus on the job and repress any sexual desires I might have for him.

"Darling, don't you want to stick it in me and see what happens?"

"Yes, we can do that. Do you have a condom?"

"On the nightstand, help yourself! — I cannot wait to feel you inside me."

"That's good. Isn't this the desire we live for? I'm so glad you feel the way I do, Anika. — Wait, I'll be right inside you!"

Athletically, he moves off me and reaches for the condom. Taking off his underwear, he rolls it onto his dick. I watch to make sure he does it properly. I am happy with his work. Not all men have the skill to put on a condom easily. It takes practice, which many men require. Harrison swings back into position above me and supports himself on only one arm while the other hand takes hold of his cock and skillfully guides it into my pussy. He is quite a strong man! I wonder if he plays other sports, apart from tennis and jogging. I can easily imagine. — It is time to focus on work again, Ilona! A dick is inside you! — Composed again, I groan aloud and say:

"Don't move, darling. Just let me enjoy you inside me like this for a minute."

"Gladly, my little beauty. Tell me what you like. I will do whatever I can to make you happy."

Basically, I am in charge! At least I think so. Okay then, what do I want? I can see him tying me to the bedpost and letting him fuck me wildly while I remain completely passive. Unfortunately, I do not have ropes with me... Maybe the mosquito netting will be sufficient to tie my hands and feet to the posts. Should I suggest it? Will he like it? It is like I would passionately devote myself to him. Harrison might be a man who likes someone like that. Yet I do not want him to think I am into it! Who knows what he might come up with for our next encounter? I should be careful playing a submissive playmate. Harrison might like position 69. Considering how passionately he licked me the first time, it is an appropriate variant that provides great potential for reaching success.

"Since you've asked so nicely, I'd like you to fuck me slowly and thrust into me deeply several times. In and out, in and out, just to warm up. Then, we'll assume the 69 position and go down on each other. I remember only too well what you can do with your tongue, darling! — Do you like that too?"

"Yes, of course. That's exactly what we'll do, baby!"

I moan with each of his slow and deep thrusts.

"Let's switch, Harrison. I want to feel your tongue now. Come on; lie down on your back. I want your dick standing, not hanging," I say playfully.

I prefer to be on top in this position or else balls end up pressing on my eyes, which is something I do not care for, no matter how great the testicles! I also use this as an opportunity to strip out of my bodysuit. It is only getting in the way! – Not that I am keeping track of the time, but purely emotionally, we have had enough sex in 5-10 minutes, so Harrison might as well climax. – Without changing the hardly used condom, I stuff his proud member in my mouth and taste my pussy. It is much more pleasant to lick my own cum off a rubber-covered cock instead of tasting it on a stranger's tongue. Harrison is licking me gently. Holding his testicles, I let my tongue run over his fuzzy, big red balls. While working his cock with my tongue, I also move my backside properly so Harrison gets the best view possible. When I get the feeling Harrison is approaching his peak, I start faking an orgasm as well. Everything goes like clockwork.

As Harrison starts ejaculating, I keep his cock deep in my mouth. Only when it starts to soften, do I remove it and pull off the condom. Getting off Harrison, I say:

"I'll quickly disappear into the bathroom. Be right back, darling. Would you like a glass of water now?"

"Yes, please," Harrison says breathlessly and stretches out on the bed.

I toss the condom into a trashcan in the bathroom, rinse out my mouth, inspect my makeup, and then slip into the pink bra and panty set I specifically laid out for after sex. I have no idea how much longer Harrison plans on staying. Considering the relatively bright hotel room, I feel more comfortable with a few clothes on than being completely naked. On the way back to bed, I pick up two glasses and a bottle of water from the minibar.

"Harrison, darling, would you like to have breakfast with me? We could use room service."

"No thanks, Anika, I can't. I have to go soon. My family thinks I'm playing tennis. – Luckily, a buddy is covering for me. Otherwise, I wouldn't be able to have time for myself. My mother-in-law keeps her eyes on the whole family. She's a real witch!" he says jokingly. "Maybe I can sneak away tonight and come over. I haven't come up with anything yet, but I'm sure I'll think of something. I really want to spend at least another half an hour with you today. —Is that okay with you, Anika?"

"Yes, of course! Do you have any idea at what time I might expect you? Since I'm here on this extraordinary beautiful island, I'd like to go out and explore."

"Yes, of course, you have to, absolutely! — But I have no idea when I can sneak away, Anika. Let's do it like this; as soon as I know I'll call and then it'll take me at least half an hour to get here. — Is that okay?"

"Yes, that works. I'm planning to spend the late afternoon in Fira and that isn't far from the hotel. I would like to see you again this evening, Harrison!"

"That's nice to hear, Anika. But now it's time to freshen up. I should at least play one match with my buddy so I'm seen."

"Certainly! And if you can't make it this evening, call and let me know."

"I'll do that, Anika," he promises and disappears into the bathroom.

60

As soon as Harrison leaves, I hop in the shower and slip into my new pink bikini. Walking out the patio door and a bit further, I jump into the pool and swim for five minutes. – Oh, I really could get used to this! Laying down on one of the lounge chairs to dry in the sun, I think about how happy I am. After a hearty breakfast in the shady area of my poolside patio, I return to the room and call Violet.

"Hi, darling, it's Anika, how are you?"

"Oh, Anika, it's nice to hear from you. You wouldn't believe it, but Jack just showed up unannounced yesterday evening and knocked on my door. I looked through the peephole and saw it was him, so I opened the door and said: *Jack, what are you doing here? We don't have an appointment! You can't just show up at my door! — Do you have a customer inside or are you expecting one?* he asked. And when I said no, he says: *Then let me in, I have to talk to you! —* What else could I do but let him in. I've known him for more than 12 years. He's a regular who's also interested in dating me. We sat in the living room and I gave him a glass of water with ice cubes. He undid his tie and a few of the top buttons of his shirt and ran his hand through his thick black hair, but he didn't come on to me! Naturally, I was curious what he had to say. *Do you also have whiskey?* he asked. Of course, I have whiskey. I might not drink it and I never offer it to a customer, but it's something you simply have in the house. I placed a bottle and an empty glass with ice cubes on the coffee table. *I want you to quit your job and date me,* he said seriously. And as I'm about to respond, he said: *Let me finish, Violet! I have a proposition for you.–* Oh, darling, you won't believe the offer he made. For giving up my job and dating him, he'd pay my rent and give me a 2000-euro allowance per month! He actually used the word allowance! — All I have to do is be there for him at all times, go out with him, or on vacation, and make an effort to befriend his daughter. And, providing everything goes well, in one year I'm supposed to move in with him. Marriage is not excluded. Darling, I'm asking you, what's going on in that man's head? He's a successful real estate agent. I mean, he's been seeing me once a week for 12 years now and I know he could afford to see me twice a week. Why not leave it at that? Why does he want more? He said he cannot handle me sleeping with other men and he wants me all to himself. Then he said he likes me a lot and he wants to be together with me more often, but he doesn't want to make appointments or pay me every single time. — His proposal is definitely no solution. I mean, come on! And you know what, I think he thought I might consider his proposal, really! 2000-euro allowance. – I'd be dependent on the charity of one man! – Like I would give up my independence like that! I took my time and I was very understanding when I told him no, but that I was flattered by his offer. — I mean, you know, oftentimes we have to be sensitive and tactful with our customers, it's not like I want to lose Jack as a client! We talked for almost two hours, during which he drank five whiskeys. That's when the phone interrupted us. Walter called. He's coming to Athens tomorrow and wants to meet me at noon at the Grand Bretagne Hotel. He pays me 150 plus a 20-euro tip. When I hung up, Jack stood up abruptly, placed 120 euros on the sofa table and said: *thanks for the consultation and the whiskey. I'm going now!* — Imagine, he gave me money even though there was no sex. Then I felt uncomfortable. I called after him before he had a chance to open the door. He turned around and I opened the belt of my white kimono and stood there naked, wiggling my boobs invitingly, but he just turned around, walked out the door, and was gone! — Can you believe it? Isn't that horrible? It affected me deeply, but what could I do, give him false hope? I cannot do that. It simply doesn't work! So, worst case scenario, he won't see me anymore and I'm out 400 euros a month!"

"Oh, darling, I'm so sorry. I can imagine how you must feel! However, in my opinion, you reacted correctly. Maybe he'll calm down and look at it all a little less emotionally."

"Yes, Anika, — it was a terrible experience! Even watching TV afterward, I couldn't really follow the show. I was continuously thinking about Jack and his proposal. — I mean, I'm not all that young anymore and a few years down the road I might be glad to receive an offer like his — who knows?"

"But you do not love him one bit! And it seems he only wants to possess you... I'm convinced it's better the way it is, darling."

"Yes, my intuition is telling me the same thing. Anyway, I can't stop thinking about it. It's nice to be able to talk to you about it. — Christo is coming soon. You know, the guy who only pays 60. And Jorgos, who canceled on Wednesday because of the strike, will come later this afternoon. — I'm sure keeping busy will distract me. — So, how are you, darling? Is everything working out so far? Is the hotel all right? Have you seen Harrison yet?"

I tell Violet about my trip and Harrison's early morning visit. Promising we will talk again later tonight, we exchange kisses and say goodbye. Like I do every morning, I check my German phone and am surprised to see I actually received a text message from Lisa, my German friend. It reads: *Hello, Ilona. Are you all right? You promised to stay in touch. — So far I have not received a text or an email. The others say they haven't heard from you either... Get in touch with us, please! Greetings Lisa.*

Just then I remember the promise I made her ten days ago. I have not written to any of my friends yet... It is about time I do! — Obviously, I could send a little email right now from my phone and ask her to greet the others for me, but I am on Santorini and I want to savor every minute on this island instead of having to think about something I can write to Lisa and the others. Even though Lisa is one of my best friends who I love dearly, she will have to wait until the weekend. — I am confident by then I will come up with a good story that will make sense as to why I am not returning to Germany in the near future. To keep from feeling guilty, I send her a quick text:

Sorry, Lisa! I haven't gotten around to writing anyone. I'm so busy. And now I feel guilty... Everything is so different here and I'm still acclimating. I'm sure I'll write you this weekend. That's when I have my next day off! Love, Ilona.'

It might not appease her, but at least I can enjoy the next few days without guilt. The same goes for my father, I also should contact him again... However, that can also wait until this weekend!

An hour later, I arrive in Fira in a taxi. Of course, I could have gone on foot, but without a sun hat and shade on the sidewalk, 500 meters is a quite a distance and would be tiring. Walking along the narrow winding streets of the island's capital is no problem because there is lots of shade. I have my phone camera on and take pictures of a couple of green lizards sunning higher up on a whitewashed house wall, cats sleeping in the shade of flower pots and wall niches, and mosaics in different-colored pebbles, which can be seen in small squares and patios. I also shoot pictures of a group of mules loaded with colorful blankets as they trot past me with their heads held low, lush flowering bougainvillea, house-high cacti, and various art objects. Sitting down on the patio of a small café offering views overlooking the caldera, its islands, and the shimmering sea of the Aegean, I enjoy a drink, a Bellini, while reading up on Santorini's history. The island's volcano last erupted some 3600 years ago.

As the day is still young, I am thinking about what on Santorini I want to see. I could take a trip across the island, go to various museums, look at churches, or take a boat trip to the island of Nea Kameni. I think a little boat cruise will be the most pleasant way to spend the afternoon. The way to the old port of Fira is 250 meters down wide steps that zigzag all the way down to the sea. Some people ride mules down the steep mountain, but that is not my thing because I feel sorry for the poor animals and the way they struggle. As I repeatedly stop to look around in amazement or to answer a call, it takes me over an hour to reach the harbor. A wide two-masted motorized sailing ship is docked at the pier, also called a gulet, seemingly loaded with passengers. A crewmember standing at the gangway announces that the ship is ready to set sail. – I am told there is still a place for me, but I have to make up my mind right now... – Without further thought and without knowing where the ship is going, I quickly buy a ticket and hop on board. The gulet's engines are already running and I have just taken a seat when the ship starts moving. I am sitting on a wooden bench, protected from the sun by a canopy covering a good part of the deck. English tourists are on both sides of me. I ask the lady on my left where we are heading and she answers in best Oxford English:

"To the island of Nea Kameni. That's where we'll make port and then we can go swimming or if you want, you can explore the volcanic landscape of the island and hike from the hot springs all the way to the crater. We have two hours there before the ship heads back."

I thank her for the detailed account. The friendly lady is wearing shorts, a short-sleeved T-Shirt, light sneakers, and a small sun hat. In her lap rests a bag with a beach towel sticking out. Looking around at the other passengers, – I see they are also casually dressed and have beachwear with them, either in bags or backpacks. Yet I have only my small woven straw bag because it goes with all the clothes I brought along to Santorini. I did not bring a bikini or towel... And my gold high sandals with cork sole are not suitable for climbing a volcano. — I notice the nice lady on the left scrutinizing me from head to toe. She is right; I am certainly not properly attired for this type of trip. Full of doubt, I am happy for the distraction when my phone rings. I get up and walk over to the wind protected area behind the pilothouse and answer. Having quietly provided the caller with all relevant information, I walk over, lean against the railing, and take pleasure in the wind blowing through my hair. — At least that is something I can enjoy, even dressed the way I am. Once the ship anchors along the coast of Nea Kameni, I am the only passenger staying on board. In the distance, I see other tourists having fun, playing in the water, or readying for a guided hiking tour across the island. My phone rings and once more I am delighted with the distraction since I am stuck onboard for two hours.

It is late afternoon when I finally return to Fira and no longer feel out of place, or better yet, inappropriately clothed.

While sitting in a restaurant at the edge of the crater, I am about to order moussaka when my phone rings again. It is Harrison, telling me he has time around 7:00 p.m. to come to my room. Although I am famished and unhappy about the timing, work takes priority. Apologizing to the waiter, I get up, leave the establishment, and head for the El Torino Hotel. I hop in the shower and then try to deflate my hair by braiding it into two pigtails. Finished with my makeup and the room prepped for Harrison's visit, I wait for my client dressed in my little black mesh dress, fishnet stockings, and black patent leather pumps. Just before 7:00 p.m., there is a knock on my door. When I open it this time, he immediately flings himself at me.

"Take that off. I want you naked!"

"Yes, Harrison, give me a second!" I reply and try to disrobe as quickly as possible.

"I don't have much time, Anika — but I want to take you again."

"Of course, darling!"

Even Harrison undresses hastily and as soon as I am naked before him, he pulls me onto the bed and kneels down between my legs. Handing him a condom, I see he does not even have a stiffy yet.

I am stumped, which causes Harrison embarrassment. He might be horny in his head, but his penis is not playing along. – What do I do now?

"Harrison, lie down and relax. I'm going to spoil you a little with my tongue. You cannot let time pressure you. Whatever time you have will be enough for us. You'll see! Try to relax and enjoy what I'm going to do to you."

Harrison is slightly flushed. I see he is stressed. I hope I can remedy it. Leaning over, I engulf his limp dick with my mouth. However, even after careful sucking, licking, and good scenery, his member does not stir. Now I am really at a loss... Harrison groans, but not with desire, more out of desperation because his best friend is leaving him hanging. It makes no sense to continue my oral play. If Harrison cannot relax, there will not be any sex. I stop licking him and lie down on my side next to him on one elbow. As he looks seriously at me, I am unable to give him an encouraging smile. It is best to start a conversation about trivial things as a distraction.

"I'm sorry, Anika, I don't know what's going on."

"It's not a problem, Harrison. This happens more frequently than you might think. It's just that nobody wants to talk about it. Let's lie here next to each other and we'll think about something else."

"Okay, come a little closer, I want to hold you."

Snuggling up in his arms, I place my hand on his limp friend. Harrison has closed his eyes, which is good. I lie still to see what happens. It takes several minutes lying there motionless and silent before I feel his penis twitching. I am still not moving. As I feel his penis slowly growing in size, I apply gentle pressure. I cannot rush! The danger is not over yet. His best friend can still withdraw back into itself. Harrison keeps his eyes closed. He too is sensitive to his moving penis. Slowly and always in response to how it affects his growing erection, I change the pressure and style of how I grab and rub it. Harrison moans. This time it speaks of desire and not despair! I am still rather passive and wait for Harrison to show me what he wants. He says:

"Anika, give me the condom!" I am hoping the procedure of putting on the condom will not ruin things. For men who are unaccustomed to wearing rubbers, be it because they are married, stuck in a relationship, or because they mainly masturbate, this act can cause problems. However, I am lucky. Harrison remains in the prone position and skillfully rolls the condom over his erection. I ask:

"Should I ride you?"

"No. Lie down on your back. I want to get between your legs."

Okay, he prefers the missionary position. When I am comfortable, Harrison starts with push-ups.

As his movements become swifter, more urgent, and his head increasingly reddens, I know he will climax soon. And what do you know, suddenly his face contorts into a grimace and with a drawn out loud groan, he comes. Without putting much weight on me, he lies on top of me, breathing contently. Stroking his back, I cannot help think how damn good it feels. When he opens his eyes, he smiles at me. I am happy we have managed a successful quickie. If it had not occurred, it would have ruined my work trip. But now, I have another positive experience and I can feel good about the money I am earning, which he already paid me, plus some.

A short time later, I am strolling toward Fira with the incredibly gorgeous colors of the setting sun all around me. I return to the restaurant on the crater rim where I was not too long ago and finally order my longed for moussaka and a house wine. I have finished my work and can enjoy the rest of the evening on Santorini. Later, I wander through the narrow streets in old town Fira and as a reminder of this impressive volcanic island, I buy a heart-shaped pumice stone.

61

After landing at Athens' El Venizelos Airport the next morning, I exit the plane and immediately feel drained by the unbearable heat. Last night, I called Violet and she warned me about the expected heat wave. I had no idea it would feel this brutal on the mainland. It is like stepping into an oven. Not far from the airport is a Swedish furniture store where I am going to buy proper bedding and leisurely look around. I am still not used to only a sheet and bedspread on my hotel bed.

Taking my time in the linen department, I search for a summer blanket and two matching covers in blue with matching pillowcases. Happy about finally finding bedding I like, I enjoy a soft ice cream in the furniture store's food court. – Now carrying a second bag, I trudge through the sweltering heat of Athens until I reach the bus stop. Thankfully, I find a seat for the ride to Piraeus.

While on the bus, William calls to inquire if we can meet at 6:00 p.m. at the Lenny Blue Hotel. Although I have not even arrived home yet nor even given any thought about work – more like taking a day off to remember my stay on Santorini – I snap out of it and say:

"Okay, darling, I'll see you then."

"That's great, Anika. I'm looking forward to seeing you and I'll try to be on time."

After noting our appointment, I switch on my other phone and see that Natasha tried to get in touch with me this morning. I call her back and she excitedly tells me about a new job for us.

"Babitschka, I already told you about him, about Andreas. He lives in Kolonaki and is somehow involved in politics. He speaks German and I know him well. When I told him about you, he said he wanted to meet you! – We would go to his home. He has a nice apartment and a real butler and cook. Naturally, whenever I was there, most of the time they weren't around. So, what do you say?"

"Fantastic, Natasha. Thank you! But tell me, how much will he be paying us?"

"I usually get between 100-120. I told him you charge 150. His reply was that he wants to see us. So, will we?"

"Sounds good. When exactly does he want to see us?"

"Tomorrow at 7:00 p.m."

"That works for me. What about his staff? I don't want them to see or hear us!"

"Don't worry, Babitschka, the staff won't be there. The cook will be long gone by then and the butler is busy walking the dog. It's a big dog that needs plenty of exercise. I've seen the dog when the butler had his day off. Should we meet a half an hour earlier in Kolonaki at the town square?"

"That's fine. I know the town square, but where exactly?"

"We can meet at the café next to the big periptero."

"Great, Natasha! — It's really great that you are offering me work again. I'm hoping I can return the favor one day soon!"

"Think nothing of it, Anika-mou. Andreas is only seeing me because I'm bringing you along."

After our conversation, I note that appointment. A short while later, the bus from the airport to the Port of Piraeus arrives at its last stop. I hop into a waiting cab and enjoy the chauffeured ride to the Lilo Hotel. At the reception desk, Spiros is his usual friendly self. He inquires about my trip while handing me a package of my laundered clothes and empty laundry bag. Luckily, I can add the items to the bag containing my new bedding. I am glad when I finally make it all the way up to the fourth floor and into my room, where I relieve myself of the heavy bags. Next, I turn on the air conditioning, strip out of my clothes, and throw them and whatever else I wore on my trip into the laundry bag – except for the short mesh dress and strapless stockings, which I hang on a hanger for airing. Just because I have worn those items for ten minutes does not mean they need to be washed. I can wear them for another customer. – I put away my clean clothes, unpack my new bedding, and make my bed. Actually, I should wash it first, but I cannot wait that long as I want to sleep in it immediately. The material feels so cozy; I am looking forward to tonight. That is that! Finished cleaning up, I take a short rest on the bed. The ringing of my phone rouses me; I must have dozed off. The display shows it is Jason from Kifissia. I pick up:

"Hello, darling!"

"Hey, Anika, this is Jason. It's good to talk to you. – Are you in Athens? I tried reaching you last week, but you never answered."

"I'm sorry, Jason, I must have been busy. How are you?"

"Thanks to the air conditioner, I'm doing okay. Can we meet?"

"Sure, when and where, Jason? At your home?"

"Yes, at my home. Can you make it this evening? Around 10:00 p.m. at my place? — You see, I'm thinking about you so your journey home will be before midnight. — Do you still have my address, Anika?"

"Yes, I do. I'm all set and will be at your home tonight at 10:00 p.m!"

"Great! I look forward to seeing you again!"

"The same goes for me. See you later, Jason!"

I make a note of yet another new appointment. I am glad Jason called again. Our conversation chased away my fatigue. An hour later, after I hopped in the shower and ate toast with cheese, I feel in great in shape and ready to meet my new client in Glyfada – William. For the meeting, I am taking my new, white braided handbag I purchased from the black street vendor in the city center. It is fantastic how much stuff I can put in it.

In a knee-length front-buttoned puffy little black dress with white dots and black heels, I am off to work. Dressed in this manner, I can also show up at Jason's tonight. The question of whether I am going to wear a sun hat or not took some consideration, but given the fact I am going to be in vehicles and buildings most of the time, I decided to forego one even though the white hat would go great with my dress. As I am about to leave my room, I receive a call from Harrison.

"Hi, darling, how are you?"

"I'm fine, Anika. I'm calling to check on you. Did you make it home all right?"

"Yes, thank you. Everything went well."

"I wanted to thank you again for the wonderful time. Tell me, could I have your email address? I might write to you from London."

Uh, what am I supposed to say? I am not inclined to start a correspondence with a client. It would be too intimate, but how do I say noto to Harrison without hurting his feelings, which I am also not inclined to do. On the spot, I promise to text him my email address.

"No text please, Anika! You still have my business card, right?"

"Yes, of course."

"You have my address. Just send me a short email with *June* in the subject line that way I know it's from you. Would you do this?"

"Yes, I will. However, I won't be able to do it until tomorrow."

"That's okay. All right, I have to finish this call. Until I hear from you, Anika!"

"Okay, Harrison, thanks for calling!"

That was not too bad. Now I have time to open a new email account solely for work. I really would dislike giving him my private email address. It makes me wonder why I have never thought of it before. Since it is too late now to make it to Glyfada on public transportation, I hail a taxi around 5:30 p.m. in front of the Lilo Hotel.

During the ride, I receive a call from Violet:

"Hi, Violet, how are you?"

"Anika, are you back in town?"

"Yes, I arrived early this afternoon. I haven't called you because I've been quite busy. You know, it's been a week to the day since Eleni gave me the Botox injections. The effect is awesome! Since yesterday, my forehead has no worry lines, my crow's feet aren't as pronounced, and I look incredibly relaxed. It always perks me up when I look in the mirror!"

"Oh, darling! That's wonderful. I'll make an appointment too. Tell me, when can we get together? I also have to tell you something!"

"Right now I'm on my to the Lenny Blue Hotel in Glyfada to meet a guy called William. Afterward, I have a little time. I'm not scheduled to see my next customer, Jason in Kifissia, until 10:00 p.m. What do you think? Can we meet somewhere in Glyfada after 7:00 p.m?"

"Yes! Look, you have my address. Why don't you come to my place after you're done with William? Considering the heat, I don't want to go outside unless absolutely necessary. I have time until about 8:00 p.m. Then I have to get ready for Ilias. You know, the guy who always takes an extremely long shower after sex."

"That's a great idea. Let's do it! I'll see you at your place, darling. I'll call you when I grab a cab. Okay?"

"Okay, Anika, I'm glad you're finally coming to visit me at home!"

When we reach Glyfada, the taxi driver pulls onto Metaxa Street and asks me where I want to be dropped off. I tell him to continue driving until I say stop. A few meters behind the Lenny Blue Hotel, I tell him to stop and pay the 16-euro fare.

Although it is quite expensive, I cannot deny how much more convenient and relaxing a cab is compared to a bus, tram, or subway. Nowadays, I have a better understanding of Violet's great aversion for public transportation. – Since I have another 10 minutes to kill, I consider the best place to wait for William's text. Then again, I might as well go inside already and wait in the hotel lobby's adjoining room, which is furnished like a dining room. As I walk by the front desk, the familiar lady greets me like we are old friends. I am sure she knows what line of work I am in. I ask if it is okay to wait for my friend in the adjacent room and she replies warmly:

"*Sigura!*", meaning *sure*. It is good to be inside and out of the scorching sun. After switching my phone to silent, I look at my photos of Santorini while waiting to hear from William. My phone vibrates shortly before 6:00 p.m. I answer:

"Hi, Anika, I'm at the hotel. I'm in room 12. Are you nearby?"

"Yes, I'll be with you momentarily."

"Good, then I'll quickly hop in the shower. See you soon!"

"Yes, see you soon, William!"

Checking the time, I wait a few minutes before making my way to the elevator.

62

My heart flutters lightly as I enter room 12. William is a tall, strongly built man around 60 with black hair and blue eyes. He has a nice tan, a hairy chest, and wears nice smelling aftershave. He greets me dressed only in tight red briefs:

"Hello, Anika! You look great."

"Thank you, William. Do you mind if I quickly visit the bathroom before we enjoy ourselves?"

"No, of course not!" he replies in an American accent as he strolls to the corner of the room where a small round black-painted metal table stands. Grabbing two small bottles of sparkling wine from a supermarket cooler bag, he holds them up and says:

"When you're done, we'll first enjoy a glass while we get to know each other!"

"Sounds good, William. I'll be back in a flash."

The bathroom is big bright and equipped with a stool. Just the way I like it. For William, I brought along the black mesh dress and matching strapless stockings that I aired out for the entire afternoon. Finished dressing, I look in the mirror and see that my outfit looks great in this dark little African-themed room. Grabbing my bag, I join William. Sitting there on a chair next to the small table in the corner of the room, he welcomes me back with:

"My, my, aren't you damn sexy!"

I put my tool pouch on the mattress near the headboard and discard my handbag on a chair upholstered in zebra stripes. William takes off the screw caps of the sparkling wine bottles and hands me one.

"I'm sorry, but it seems these rooms don't come with glasses. We'll have to toast and drink out of the bottle. Cheers, Anika! Come, sit over here."

This is the first time I am drinking sparkling wine directly out of the bottle. I immediately have to burp and quickly apologize to William. However, he merely laughs and says:

"Don't worry about it, Anika. It's only us."

Sitting on a padded chair in front of William, I keep my back straight, my chest and breasts thrust out, and my legs crossed. As he takes a long sip, he eyes me up and down. I try to start a conversation.

"It's nice to meet you, William. — You mentioned you are a former American soldier. After your military service, did you first go back to the United States or did you simply remain here?"

"Anika, during my tour of duty here in Athens, I met a Greek beauty, fell in love, and married. Once I retired, my wife would have loved to live with me in the States... but I didn't want that! — I'm mean, just think; I'm from Nebraska, of all places! My wife had no idea what it was like to live there. I wasn't going back willingly. Now and then, we fly to the States, but not often. I love the Greek lifestyle. They are so laid back and know how to enjoy the sweet life. In America, that wouldn't be possible. It's all about working and surviving. — So, you're from Germany, right, Anika?"

"Yes."

"From the East or West?"

"The West. In fact, I'm from Rhineland."

"What brought you to Athens? – Have you fallen in love with a Greek?"

"No. — One of the main reasons is the climate. I definitely prefer this weather to the weather in Germany. And, living near the sea is nice."

"Yes, I understand only too well. Once you have a taste of the sun and sea you no longer want to do without. — But now to us. You look incredibly sexy. What a nice tan! I'm into that as you might have already guessed. I am a child of the sun and happiness."

William raises his bottle again. We toast and sip. To put an end to this conversation and to get his mind back to the actual purpose of my being here, I discard my bottle of sparkling wine on the table and say:

"That bulge in your underwear makes me curious. Why don't I take a closer look at your impressive piece while you continue to talk?"

Without waiting for a reply, I squat between his spread legs and pull his cock from his underpants. It is semi-stiff. He has to have a proper hard-on before I can roll a rubber over it. I pull his undies below his balls and run my tongue over his bulging shaved scrotum. William winces and says:

"Oh! Anika, you're doing exactly what I love. Bite them a little. It turns me on tremendously."

"No problem," I reply and carefully nibble on his testicles. – William is completely shaved. There is no pubic hair on his cock or balls, which I personally find unattractive. Nevertheless, in my line of work it can be beneficial for there is a guarantee no pubic hair becomes stuck between my teeth during oral sex. Having pubic hair stuck between my teeth or in my mouth is something I find quite disgusting, but it is part of my job. Unfortunately, not all men maintain their pubic area with the same diligence as they do their beards, so I am always happy to meet a customer with a nicely trimmed pubic region. As William's cock looks healthy, I have no objection to sucking on it without a condom.

"Anika, please remove your dress. You may keep the stockings and pumps on, but I want to see more of your beautifully tanned skin."

"Of course." I interrupt my scrotum nibbling to shimmy out of my fishnet dress. Discarding it on the chair next to my purse, I grab a rubber from the bed. Crouched between his legs again, I tear open the packaging and immediately hear William loudly protest:

"Oh please, Anika! Leave the rubber off. It's such a fun killer! I'm healthy. Honestly!"

"I believe you, darling. – I don't mind doing without during oral sex as long as you don't squirt in my mouth or else you have to wear it!"

"I understand and I want to come in your mouth — but that's later! Let's do without for now. Please!"

"Okay, — as long as you keep your promise."

"I will!"

Because I trust him, I set the condom aside and continue nibbling lustfully on William's scrotum. He groans aloud in obvious delight. I will never fully understand, but some men love experiencing pain in their testicles whereas others almost faint. After taking his suntanned dick all the way in my mouth and giving it my best, he says a few minutes later:

"Let's go to bed!"

I take another sip of sparkling wine, grab the rubber off the table, and walk over to the big, round bed.

"Lie down with your butt on the edge. First, I want to lick you," says William.

Although he still wears undies, his hard cock bounces up and down above his tight scrotum as he walks toward me. He kneels on the soft carpet in front of the bed and sticks his tongue in my pussy.

Thankfully, William is one of those men who know how to pleasure a woman. He does it without hurting me. This way, I could lie for hours while making easy money. But, I am not paid to have my pussy licked. More is expected of me. And so, I moan softly for William and move my hips slightly.

"I want to fuck you now or are you not ready yet?" he asks after a few minutes.

I assure him I am ready and slide further up on the bed, grab the condom and part my legs. William stands up, bends over to his sneakers, and removes a shoelace. He removes his underpants and uses the shoelace to wrap his scrotum tightly together above his balls. I have never seen a man do this. — I mean, a man tying his testicles together so tightly, even I become a bit anxious! William sees the look of shock in my eyes and reassures me:

"Don't worry, Anika! It turns me on."

He puts the rubber on, gets down between my legs, and sticks his penis in my pussy. His tied together scrotum bangs hard against my perineum every time he thrusts. He seems to love punishing his balls. Time goes by as he fucks me in a quick and steady rhythm. Either William has problems reaching climax or he has no problem restraining himself. Maybe he is waiting for me to reach climax. So, I might as well accommodate him.

Thrusting my pelvis toward him, I convincingly declare:

"Yeah, baby, I'm almost there! Fuck me deep and let me feel your balls!"

William increases his momentum as I busily fake a passionate climax. Even before my simulated orgasm fully subsides, William plops down next to me, obviously exhausted. Panting, he says:

"Now blow him until I come!"

His cock is standing straight out and his bound testicles are shriveled. Leaning over him, I take his penis deep in my mouth and work my magic. Before I know it, William arches his back and starts ejaculating. All the while I keep his rod in my mouth and firmly grab his balls with one hand.

"Oh my God!" William moans aloud over and over again while grimacing and only when all of his movements stop, do I release his privates. Great, that is done and over with.

"Should I loosen the lace?" I ask.

"No, wait. I've used a particular knot that you won't know how to open. A navy seal showed it to me. — But, of course, not on my balls." He laughs as he loosens the lace. "But then it's a perfect knot."

When his testicles are freed from their bonds, they really do not look abused. I mean, they were tied up for a good 15 minutes, plus what I did to them. Looking around the room, I see a comfortable light coming from three tubular rice paper lamps of varying heights standing in front of a light brown painted wall. Another rice paper lamp, a round one, hangs above a small table in the corner of the room where we sipped sparkling wine and each nightstand holds a little lamp made of the same material. All the lights reflect in the large wall mirror across the room. The wall to the right of the bed, which also has the bathroom and entrance door, is adorned with dark, wooden masks and long spears. William stands up and replaces the lace in his sports shoe. Grabbing the two sparkling wine bottles, he comes back to the bed.

"This would certainly taste better if it was chilled, but, unfortunately, there's no fridge in the room. Shame! – Next time I'll have to ask for a room with one. How do you like the room, Anika?"

"I like it. I like the large wall mirror. It makes the room appear much bigger. And I like the discreet lighting. The room seems to have an African theme. All in all, it's very romantic."

"Yes, I like it too. At the reception desk, they have a catalog containing photos of all the rooms. I chose this one because it doesn't have the usual pink, red, and gold colors. It doesn't look so kitschy, to be blunt. — Cheers, Anika!"

"Cheers, William!" I say as we clink our small bottles. The sparkling wine is warm so I only take a tiny sip.

"William, is it okay for me to use the bathroom to freshen up and dress?"

"Of course, Anika. — I hope we'll see each other again!"

"Me too. You have my phone number and I'm definitely here in Athens for the next two months."

"And after that? Are you going back to Germany?"

"Only for a couple weeks. I need to get a few things and drive my car back."

"Great, because I don't know exactly when I'm going to call you a-gain. Next week, I'm taking the misses on vacation for a month. Athens is unbearable in July. We're going on a Mediterranean Cruise. It's what we do every year. We love it."

"I hope you have lots of fun and get lots of rest! — I'd also like to see you again."

After I have finished showering and dressing, I walk out of the bathroom and find William has already placed my fee on the little table, plus a 10-euro tip. I am happy! I thank him and he says:

"Don't neglect your tan. It looks great on you, Anika!"

"You can count on it," I promise and leave the room.

Once out on Metaxa Street, I search for a taxi. I have been walking for about 300 meters when one pulls up next to me and the driver asks where I want to go. After I show him Violet's address, he rolls up the window and simply drives off.

I really have no idea why some of these drivers react like that! For-tunately, I do not have to wait long for the next cab. This driver lets me get in and has no problem taking me to my desired location. Thank God! As promised, I give Violet a call to announce my imminent arri-val. She says she is looking forward to my visit.

63

As I exit the taxi outside the five-story apartment building Violet lives in, I see her standing on a second-floor terrace waving at me. Of course, I have to walk up to the second level. I see three apartment doors. – The one on my right is open and Violet is standing in the doorway wearing a pink kimono. Once inside, she closes the door, we hug each other and exchange kisses.

"Now let me take a closer look at your face. Yes, I can see the difference on your forehead. It is incredible! Even the smallest wrinkle is invisible. I'll have to call for an appointment with Eleni soon. You look at least five years younger. Come, sit. We have little over a half an hour and then I have to get ready for Ilias. Where are you going again? Kifissia? You better take a cab to the Elliniko Subway Station. From there you can catch the train to Kifissia, which takes about 40 minutes. Every so often, I have to go that way. All right, now come and take a look around my apartment!"

"I already am. Your living room is huge! I would never have imagined it looking at the building from the outside. You've done a great job decorating, it's very tasteful!"

"Yes, it is 36 square meters. Moreover, there is not only a terrace facing out front, there is a balcony outside my kitchen and bedroom. On the balcony, I feed stray cats from the neighborhood. Come on, let me show you."

We walk into the kitchen and she opens the glass sliding door to a narrow, but long balcony with lots of potted rubber plants. Directly against the house wall stands several pots with water and one big bowl with dry cat food.

"The cats use the tree to climb up to my balcony. Wait, let me call Jenny, she's usually nearby. — Jenny, Jenny, come to mommy!"

What do you know, a sleek black and white cat climbs slowly up the tree and out on a limb that reaches the balcony.

"She doesn't know you. Just remain silent and still. Jenny, Pavlo, Rudi, Mavro, Harry, and Babette may also show up. Each is sterilized. I made sure of that. — They are my children. Oh, look at her, isn't my little Jenny a cutie? — Let's go back inside now. It's too hot out here."

Her kitchen is equipped with all kinds of fancy electrical appliances. The kitchen furnishings are chic and Violet asks me if I would like a cup of coffee. I decline because I only drink coffee in the morning. So instead, she grabs two glasses and a crystal carafe with water before we return to the living room. Before we actually sit down, she excitedly proposes:

"Come on, I want to show you my bedroom first!"

We go back out into the hallway and enter the second door on the right. Her bedroom is also spacious and furnished in an ultra-modern style. The room is bright and emits a welcoming atmosphere. Her bed is a king-size covered with a pink sheet and various sizes and shapes of satin pillows in pink, orange, and red tones on top. A white porcelain bowl with condoms stands on a rectangular long nightstand and next to it a matching pot for the used ones, and of course, cosmetics and wet wipes. The wall across from the bed is made up entirely of a mirrored wardrobe. The free wall holds a large print by Andy Warhol showing Marilyn Monroe's portrait in six different colors. I am impressed. Violet pushes a button and the window and balcony door blinds lower themselves. Now that the bedroom is dark, she demonstrates all her lighting options. Each lamp can be dimmed individually.

"Manolis, one of my long term clients, is an electrician. He gave my place the once over and installed everything like lamps, the television and stereo system, even the coffee machine. I had agreed to give him a generous discount when he comes to see me. That debt has long since been paid. That was two years ago when I got a new kitchen. Back then, I couldn't offer him much sex in exchange. Ha, ha, ha. — But he's a sweetie. He always comes over immediately when I need him. It makes me think he is just waiting for me to call and say: *Manolis, a bathroom lamp doesn't work. Could you come and look at it?* Soon after he's here, fixes what needs fixing, and then I give him a quickie for a fair price."

Violet pushes a button and all blinds retract back into the ceiling:

"Oftentimes, I merely close the curtains. They do the job just as well. But enough of this, come on, let's go into the living room and have a drink!"

Her living room also has marble flooring like the kitchen and hallway. Its furnishings are bright elegant oak, like her bedroom. On the floor in front of the large corner sofa is a thick natural Berber carpet. The decoration is simple, giving the room a classy atmosphere. I can tell Violet has spent a good portion of her income on high-quality furniture and now I understand why she feels so comfortable in her chic apartment. – I am still a long way away from being able to afford such a home.

"Okay, now I must tell you something! You'll never believe it, but Jack came by this afternoon. Not 30 minutes after I returned from the Bretagne Hotel, the doorbell rings and there he is. I open the door and I am about to let him have it when he asks: *Is someone here or do you expect someone soon?* When I shake my head, he simply lifts me up and carries me off into the bedroom saying: *I think you still owe me, darling!* — What was I supposed to say? I was so perplexed, I only managed to stammer: *Jack, Jack, what are you doing?* But he just threw me on the bed, pulled off my kimono, slipped out of his shoes,

pulled off his pants, took a condom out of the bowl, and fucked me. –
He kept his shirt and tie on! — You know, he took me as if he had the
right to do so. Don't get me wrong, I like Jack! I even like the way he
just takes me. Sometimes I feel like I'm losing my mind. However,
that's not a reason to start a relationship. It just wouldn't work out in
the long run. We have a great business relationship. That's it! I cannot
deny it. So, why should our arrangement change? I mean, it stands for
something! Maybe I got through to him now. I'm not sure. Anyway, at
least afterward, we lay next to each other exhausted and he kept looking at me without saying so much as one word. When I offered him a
glass of water, he quickly got up, threw the condom in the porcelain
pot, slipped back into his pants, and said: *I have to get back to the
office. What do you think, are we even now?* and I quietly said: *Yes,
darling. I'm glad you came. I'd miss you terribly if you were to leave
me.* — I could see it pleased him, even if he tried to hide it. Then he
kissed me goodbye and left without even turning around once. What do
you think?"

"Well, congratulations. He came back! It seems to me that he cannot
do without you or the sex. And that's the important thing, isn't it?"

"As long as he pays the next time he visits! Although I don't doubt he
will. He will never give me more than 150, – maybe just 100 and a
bouquet of flowers, or 120 and no flowers, which I like best. I mean,
fresh flowers are nice, but not as payment. — You know, this situation
with Jack got me thinking. What happens to us when we're old? Will
we live alone? In our industry, it's not easy to get to know a man. What
do you think?"

"I don't know, Violet. And to tell you the truth, I have others things
on my mind. For me, it's important I make it here in Athens so I can
live well and save lots of money. That's as far into the future as I'm
looking. — Sure, it would be nice not to be alone when I'm old and to
have a partner, which goes without saying! — But as to how that would
come about is a mystery to me and I'm not willing to deal with it
presently. I'm happy being here and establishing my business. That's
all I care about right now."

"Yes, I understand. Maybe I have these thoughts because I've started
menopause. Who knows?"

As we both sip our water, we are lost in thought. I decide to change
the subject:

"Tell me, when you sleep at night, is it on the sheet you had sex with
a customer?"

"Hell no! Every morning, I air out my bedding and stow it for the day
in the big dresser drawer between the clothes valet and balcony door.
When it's time for me to go to bed, nothing in my bedroom reminds me
of my clients."

"I thought you'd do something like that. There have to be certain limits when working at home. On Santorini, I slept on the same sheet Harrison and I had sex on. There was no way around it. It felt strange. Also, I've realized all that's involved with receiving a customer at home! It's certainly not like walking into a hotel room. You have to keep everything neat yourself."

"So true, darling. I have to keep my apartment immaculate at all times. And I have no help. Can you imagine how much work it is keeping this apartment clean? That's why I can't stand it when Ilias takes a shower after sex and then runs around soaking wet, making a mess, and my bath mat needs to dry. So of course, I have to clean and dry the shower stall and put a dry mat out while the wet one dries. — Yeah, that's additional work for me and it is included in the price! — Which reminds me, you haven't seen my bathroom yet or my workroom. — Come on!"

We get up again and Violet leads the way into a bright bathroom. Considering the other rooms of her apartment, this one is not proportionate. It is rather small. However, Violet made the most of the space and arranged everything efficiently. Next to the bathroom is another small room, her so-called workroom, which holds an ironing board, vacuum cleaner, basically all the stuff needed to clean an apartment.

"That was the tour!" she says. "Now you know my kingdom. Maybe you have a better idea why I won't even think about moving out of here in a year only to move in with Jack. — Ha! He has some funny ideas!"

"You have a beautiful apartment. You can be proud of what you've accomplished here. Forget Jack and his offer. I'm sure he'll remain a faithful client of yours. And that's all you want from him."

"Yes, you're right."

Looking at my watch, I'm stunned and say:

"It's already after 8:00 p.m.! – You have to get ready for Ilias. And I should get on my way to Kifissia. Where is the fastest place for me to catch a cab?"

"Head down the street for about 100 meters and you'll come to a major road. Luckily, the sidewalk is in the shade by now; otherwise, I would advise you to call a cab to pick you up here. However, home pick up costs three euros more. You can save that money."

Since we are on the subject, I tell Violet about the taxi driver who left me standing on the road.

"Yes, I know that! Some drivers don't believe short distances are worth their time. Of course, they would never admit it. He's obliged to drive a passenger to where they want to go and that includes short distances. But that's how drivers are here. They do what they want. — Okay, darling, I'm glad you came by! – Don't forget to call me!

Depending on how things look, maybe we can get together this weekend and go out. What do you say?"

"Yes, I'd love that. — Thank you for having me and showing me your apartment. You really have a nice place. It's so stylish, like you!" — Until next time, Violet!"

Hugging, we exchange kisses and then I am on my way to find a cab. Fortunately, I am able to catch one on my way to the main road. The driver drops me off at Elliniko Subway Station in less than five minutes. As I reach the city center, I switch trains and arrive in Kifissia around 9:00 p.m. This time, I am not going all the way to the town square and instead, sit down at an outdoor cafe at a nearby park.

I am famished, so I order a spinach pita with feta cheese and eat half. At 9:50 p.m., I hail a taxi for the journey to Jason's home. By now it is dark and the gruesome heat is a bit more bearable. – I walk straight through the unlocked garden gate and up to the front door. I ring his bell. I hear noise coming from inside and the door opens. It is Jason.

"Hi, Anika, come in, quickly! You know, this is the first time today I've stuck my head out the door. It really is unbearably hot."

I wait for Jason to close the door and then offer my cheek for the obligatory welcoming kiss.

"You look chic, Anika! I like your dress!"

"Thank you, Jason. It's nice to see you again. So what, you haven't been outside all day?"

"Nope. I've kept busy indoors all day. I'll tell you everything, but let's go into the living room first. By the way, just so I get it out of the way, I will drive you to the subway station later! So don't worry about your trip back to Piraeus."

Like my first visit, a glass of red wine is on the coffee table. I am afraid Jason is once again in a talkative mood, so I try to think of something to stop him.

"Jason, could I use the bathroom?"

"Of course, Anika. You remember where it is, right?"

"Yes, thank you!"

Once dressed in sexy lingerie, it might be easier to keep him from talking and focused on the actual purpose of my visit. For Jason, I have brought along my black satin bodysuit with white lace at the neck and leg openings. It resembles a maid's uniform and comes in handy for role-playing. This time I dispense with the strapless stockings. With my black pumps, this outfit is complete. As I walk back into the living room, Jason is sitting with his red wine in one hand and a cigarette in the other.

"Anika, once again you're a sight for sore eyes. May I offer you a glass of red wine? It came from the wine fridge and has had time to breathe. Or, would you like something else?– Perhaps a glass of champagne?"

"Thank you, Jason. I'm fine right now, maybe later after we've amused ourselves. I'd rather sit next to you and listen to why you haven't been out all day."

"Of course. Come sit here with me while I finish my smoke. Then we'll go upstairs to the bedroom. Okay, so this morning I went directly into the garage and got in my car. Once I arrived in Piraeus, I parked my car in the underground garage of the office building. Then, I took the elevator up to the office on the eighth floor. I had lunch at a shopping center and again, I parked in the underground garage. Yeah, and after lunch, I went back to the office and later, back home. Not once did I set foot outside. I usually have lunch in Piraeus. At Zea Marina and Mikrolimani, there are good restaurants that serve freshly caught fish. I love fresh grilled fish. Today, however, I didn't feel like putting up with this scorching heat. So, when I opened the door for you, it was the first time I had fresh air. Although, the air here isn't all that fresh. I wouldn't survive a Greek summer without air-conditioning. I cannot imagine how I did it as a kid. Or my parents and grandparents... — I still remember how old people died like flies during the summers. Summers were the seasons for funeral homes. That was when they sold the most coffins."

Jason takes a hit from his cigarette and then a gulp of wine. Kneeling before him, I start unbuttoning his shirt.

"I cannot imagine living here in Athens without air-conditioning either. – What do you say; shall we go upstairs to your bedroom? It's much more comfortable for me on the bed than down here on the ground."

"Of course, Anika, I'm sorry!"

Jason stubs out his cigarette, finishes his wine, and stands up. At the stairway, he waits for me to take the lead. Walking into his bedroom, I now know why. He has already prepared the room to my liking. The photos on the nightstand are gone, the bedspread on his side is folded back, and only one lamp next to the bed provides pleasant soft light. While I place my little bottle of massage oil and two condoms from my work pouch on the bed, Jason undresses.

"Darling, how about a little massage?"

"Oh yes, Anika, that would be great."

"Come over here and lie down on your stomach and relax!"

It is obvious Jason is not the type to lie in the sun. He has the so-called farmer's tan, which is just on the neck, face, lower arms, and calves. Basically, the places that are almost always exposed to the sun. I have already slipped out of my heels and am now kneeling next to Jason. Slowly, I add a few drops of massage oil to my palms and then distribute it over his back before beginning a gentle massage. It is nice to feel Jason relax under my gentle touch. He is breathing heavily, which does not surprise me, considering all those cigarettes he smokes.

372

I mean, I have seen him smoke one cigarette after another and I am sure he is doing that all day long. I also run my oily hands between Jason's thighs and massage his buttocks. However, I will not lick his privates from this position because I think it is too much for Jason and I am in no mood for acrobatics either. I finish the massage by slightly pressing my palms against his lumbar region.

"Did you enjoy it, darling?" I ask.

"Oh yes, Anika. I wouldn't mind if you did this to me every night. It feels incredibly good."

"I'm glad to hear it. Okay, turn on your back so I can make you feel even more incredible."

"Oh, yes, I cannot wait, Anika!"

Jason rolls over onto his back. His cock is not yet hard enough for fucking. Therefore, I lick his balls and semi-erection until I see a proper boner.

Next, I quickly I get up, step out of my bodysuit, and climb back onto the bed. Since Jason does not move, I take it upon myself to put the rubber on his best piece. I straddle him, lower myself onto his penis, and start riding him slowly. He cups my bare breasts and starts to caress them. As I feel his cock inside me growing, I start riding him a bit faster and harder. Apparently, I have found the right rhythm because Jason joins in and raises his pelvis only to come straightaway.

Wow, that was incredibly fast! But I am not complaining. I hope Jason had his fun. As his climax subsides, his panting eases, and his dick becomes flaccid, I hold onto the condom as I climb off him.

"I'm surprised you came so quickly, darling!" I say.

"I didn't see the need to prolong it unnecessarily, Anika. It's exactly what I needed. And you were simply wonderful, thank you!"

I do not know what I did that was so wonderful, but I will not bring it up and instead enjoy his compliment. Since we have finished with sex so quickly, I still have time for that glass of wine and some more of Jason's stories. It is easy with Jason after sex and I enjoy listening to his voice. Five minutes later, when I am back in the living room, I am freshly showered and fully dressed. Jason is also clothed, sitting in shorts and a short-sleeve plaid shirt with a cigarette in his hand.

"Anika, what can I offer you? Anything in particular?"

"I'll take that glass of wine, darling."

While he is getting me a glass and pouring the wine, I sneak a peek at my watch. It's 10:35 p.m. When I was in the bathroom, I glanced at my phone and saw only one missed call. So given the late hour and how tired I am, this is good. And the red wine will also have its toll, thus I will call it a day. Jason makes a sweeping hand gesture and says:

"You know, Anika, I'm the boss at the store and I sure as hell have my hands full with work. But one thing is important to me; I have to make sure my staff is well provided for. That's why twice a day I go and check all the water coolers in each department. And if one needs replacing or is about to need replacing, I take care of it. Sometimes I even have to switch out the carbon dioxide cylinder for a new one. A water bottle like that weighs 19 kilos. I really don't want my employees having to deal with that. That's why I do it. It's not beneath me as the boss to do this kind of work. On the few occasions I'm not at the office, my assistant takes care of the task. — You know, the way I'm dressed right now is the way I run around the office. Loose fitting, casual clothes are my thing. If I have a short-notice important meeting or have to go away on business, I have a storage room in my office where I store my so-called business attire. — Today, when I was in accounting removing the empty water bottle from the dispenser, a young staff member called me over to her desk. Naturally, I don't know all of my employees by heart! Apparently, the young lady didn't know who I was and told me in a bossy tone: *When you're done with the water cooler come back here and I'll give you money so you can go buy me and my colleague two frappes and pitas at the café across the road.* — That was a first for me! The young woman, believing I was her colleague, thought she could order me around and treat me like an errand boy. Obviously, on the inside, I was smiling, so I replied: *No, my dear, when it's break time you can go and get the frappes and pitas yourself!* Outraged, she said: *How can you say no? You are hired to do things for us.* So, I had to set her straight and told her calmly that I was not hired to do things for her, no one was, and that I was her superior, as a matter of fact, the top dog because I was the owner of the shipping company. — Oh, Anika, you should've seen her face. It drained of all color as if the guillotine was about to come down."

Jason is laughing so hard his body shakes. Even I have to chuckle at his little amusing story. – Considering Jason's casual clothes, I can understand how someone who does not know him might make the mistake of thinking he is an errand boy.

"It seems quite a memorable story! I'm sure it'll make the rounds at your office."

Since Jason has smoked three cigarettes and drank two glasses of red wine, I sneak another peek at my watch and decide I have given him plenty of my time.

"Darling, what do you say, can we get going to the subway station?"

"Of course, Anika. Wait, let me put the wine in the fridge and grab a new pack of smokes, then we can go!"

I finish my glass of wine and when Jason comes back from the kitchen, he is holding two 100-euro bills in his hand. He presents them to me and says:

"Here is your gift, Anika. Thank you so much for visiting me. It was lots of fun!"

After thanking him for his generosity, he drives me to the subway station and a half an hour later I am sitting on a train to Piraeus. I spend the time contemplating my eventful day and can hardly believe that just this morning I was still on Santorini...

64

From the subway station in Piraeus, I grab a cab to the Lilo Hotel. – I still have a little bottle of Mostra white wine in the refrigerator, which amounts to a regular wine glass. Now sipping my drink, I sit naked on the balcony and look out over the roofs of the buildings in Piraeus all the way to Zea Marina and the dark sea beyond. The burning heat of the day has developed into sweltering humidity. The chilled wine tastes delicious and helps relieve the tension this long day brought about. Since I have not received any calls, I switch my phone to silent mode. Once the air-conditioner has cooled the room enough for me to sleep, I go into the bathroom, brush my teeth, and hop into bed and snuggle up under my new bedding.

The quiet humming of my phone awakens me. Having been deep asleep, it takes a moment before I fully grasp what is happening. – Switching on the lamp, I check the display. My vision is blurry and I cannot make out the digits, but I can make out the name. René Bosquier is calling from Glyfada. Delighted, I answer the call:
"Good morning!"
"Hi! It's me René. Can you come to my home?"
Looking at the clock and seeing it is only 7:05 a.m., I reply:
"Yes, it's possible, René!"
"Good! When can you be at my place?"
"I'd say in about 40 minutes."
"Okay, I'll see you then. And remember, don't ring the bell! Call me when you get here and I'll come and open the door for you, baby."
"Sure, see you in a bit, René!"
Our brief conversation really woke me up and I already have one leg out of bed. First, I open the heavy balcony door curtains and turn off the air conditioner.
Even though he has once again called at a strange hour of the day, I am happy! René Bosquier remembered me. I dash into the bathroom and ready myself unusually quick. I am already wearing red lace underwear and grab another pair of red panties to take along. Picking up red high heels, at the last second, I also reach for my white sun hat. The sun will be out by the time I am done with René and it will most likely be another hot day. I run barefoot downstairs into the lobby before slipping on my heels to walk outside to hail a cab. Thankfully, there is no problem catching one this early on a Saturday morning. The first one I see stops and the taxi driver has no objection driving me to Glyfada. – He might not be driving with the air-conditioning on, but it is not a tragedy given the early hour of the morning. – While I am showing the driver my note with Rene's address on it, he asks me if I

know where it is, meaning, he has no GPS! I reassure him by saying:

"Yes, I know how to get there. When we're in Glyfada at the Church of Agios Konstantinos, I'll give you directions."

Glancing at my wristwatch it seems my travel time estimate of 40 minutes is not far off. Traffic is light and the cab driver flies along the coastal road at 120 kilometers an hour.

Once we arrive at 10 Pallodios Street, I pay 15 euros for the fare and get out. I call René and he promptly opens the door for me to enter. Like the first time, he seems tipsy, not drunk, at least not that I can tell. And once again, he looks fantastic. Quietly, he closes the door behind us and leads the way to his apartment. He looks at me, grins, and says:

"I'm glad you were able to make it. Me and a few people went to a bar and had an all-nighter again. Business partners, that is. Every once in a while I have to sacrifice a good night's sleep. Perhaps one day you'll be lucky and I'll call you during daytime hours. However, I'm not making any promises. — Go on into the bedroom and undress. I only want you to blow me."

"Sure, darling. How about a little massage to get things going?"

"That sounds good."

René lets his robe slide off his shoulders right where he is standing and lies down on his belly on the mattress on the floor. After removing my dress, bra, panties, and shoes, I grab the massage oil and two rubbers and kneel beside him. With a few drops of oil in my palms, I briefly rub them together before I start massaging his shoulders and down his back, using circular hand movements. René grunts in delight. As his legs are slightly apart and since this is not a massage to make him feel relaxed and sleepy but instead to arouse him, I slide one of my hands between his thighs and touch his balls. René responds by spreading his legs further as well as raising his butt. The last time, he came pretty fast during oral sex. Maybe this time I should start with anal pleasure. – Let's see how far I can go with him. Spreading his buttocks, I spit on his rosette. While applying a little pressure, I spread the gooey saliva, exciting him. To continue my anal experiment, I pull a condom over my right middle finger, spit again on his anus, and then carefully drill my protected finger into his butthole. My left hand comes in low and reaches for his tower that has now reached its maximum size and hardness. This type of massage turns René on so much he announces in a subdued voice:

"I'm going to come any moment now, baby. — What you're doing is driving me crazy!"

I am glad René likes this anal massage, but if he comes this quickly, he might want another round. That is something I would like to avoid! Slowly, I pull the finger out of his butt and say:

"Hold on, baby, I want to take him in my mouth. Just pull yourself together for a moment!"

"Okay, but I really could come right now. That is fucking awesome!"

"That's nice, but now it's time to turn around, baby! I'm sure your best friend will love a little spoiling with my tongue!"

"You might be right," he says and obeys me. Removing the condom from my finger, I place it on the ground next to the mattress, which I believe is a futon. Somehow, it feels different than the ordinary mattresses I am used to. However, I am sure regular mattresses are not supposed to be lying directly on the floor. Later, I will ask René about it. First, I bend down, lick his balls, and take his lightly oiled rod deep in my mouth and go to work on it. Sensing he is about to explode, I stop sucking and jerk him off with my hand while licking his balls.

"I'm coming!" René groans. Lift off! Semen squirts onto his belly. As long as he is moaning, I hold his softening buddy and his balls in my mouth. René got lucky this morning for he received anal and oral sex. He should be satisfied. Sneaking a peek at my wristwatch, I see the whole procedure did not even take 20 minutes. Perfect. René reaches for his pack of smokes lying on the ground next to the futon and lights one.

"Darling, tell me, is this a futon?"

"Yes, I love the texture of these things. I've been sleeping on one since childhood and I'm highly satisfied. — Why? Do you care that it lies directly on the floor?"

"No, not at all."

"I like being close to the ground. Don't ask me why! Maybe it is a matter of habit."

"Perhaps. Anyway, I'll quickly use the bathroom and then I'm gone so you can sleep. You must be dead tired, right?"

"Yes, sex has that effect on me. Luckily, I have the rest of the day off. — Thank you for coming. Now, go to the bathroom. I'll get your money ready and then walk you to the door."

As I step from the darkened bedroom into the wide hallway, I have a clear view of the daylight-illuminated living room. The entire wall facing the garden is made of glass. Curious, I take a few steps to get a better look and see a patio, swimming pool, and lawn. Nice! I would love to live like this. In the bathroom, I wash my hands and rinse my mouth thoroughly. I can dispense with a shower because once again René did not touch me. – When I exit the bathroom fully dressed, René is standing in the hallway in his bathrobe, holding out three brown bills.

"Thank you! And I'm sorry, but I've forgotten your name. What it is again?"

"Anika. — My name is Anika. Thank you and have a nice weekend, darling!"

René says goodbye and pecks both of my cheeks. He places an index finger over his lips before opening the door and leading me out of the house.

Now, I am ready to eat breakfast. So, I start strolling through the chic residential area while staying on sidewalks that lie in the shade until I reach a town square with cafés and shops. I am amazed how many people are out and about at this early morning hour. I sit down at a table on the shady patio of a self-serve café. The noise around me is quite loud. Greek women and men are busy talking loudly all at once. I wonder if anyone is listening to the others. It does not appear that way. I select my favorite pastry, bougatsa, and a mild Nescafé and pay for it at the sales counter. Since I am finished with my breakfast and already in Glyfada at this early hour of the day, I might as well give Maria at the beauty salon a call.

"Good morning, Maria. This is Anika from Piraeus. I have an appointment at 1:00 p.m. Would it be possible to reschedule for an earlier time? I'm already in Glyfada, so it would be better this morning."

"Good morning, Anika. Let me look at today's appointments. Uh, I can see you at 11:00 a.m. Would that work for you?"

"Yes, that's fine. Thank you, Maria!"

"See you then, Anika."

Okay, I still have two hours to wait. After buying another cup of coffee, I change my phone settings to hide my number and call my father's number. Now he cannot tell who is calling. I wonder if he will pick up. It rings for a while before I finally hear his voice:

"Vertongen here."

"Good morning, Dad. It's Ilona."

"Ah, Ilona, my child, it's nice to finally hear from you again! I was wondering if you were working so much that you had no spare time to call your old father."

Although he says this jokingly, I know there is a little truth behind it.

"Yes, Dad, I'm sorry. I was really busy. Besides, you know I don't like talking on the phone. So, tell me, how are you?"

"For the most part, I'm okay. It's raining today, so I have a good excuse not to do any gardening. But enough about me; how are you? When are you coming back? — You know, last week at the grocery store I ran into your former boss, Ms. Jansen. She asked about you. Obviously, I didn't have much to report. However, she said you could have your old job back if you wanted it. They haven't hired a new office assistant yet and they would be happy to take you back. Ms. Jansen said a few candidates were sent by the unemployment office, but they haven't decided yet because a new employee must be trained and cannot be immediately trusted. — Ilona, you know that business inside and out. You've never had problems doing the work and you seemed happy. So, what do you say? – Do you want to come back sooner? Ms. Jansen also said that if you quit because you didn't have enough vacation time, it could be remedied. They would find a way so you can go on vacation more often. Anyway, I'm supposed to give you her best and tell you that she would like to hear from you!"

"Oh, Dad. It's nice of Ms. Jansen, but I'm doing great here in Athens and I enjoy the nice weather, the sun, and the sea. I really don't want to come back just yet..."

"And what about your babysitting gigs? Don't you miss those little ones? You've been working for that family for years!"

"No, I don't miss it and I don't miss those two children either. They have a new babysitter by now. Most likely a young girl from the neighborhood and she is happy to make a little extra money. The children are old enough to be looked after by a young girl. It's not like they need their diapers changed, cooked for, or put to bed in the evenings. Nowadays, they watch TV, play computer games, brush their own teeth, and they even go to bed themselves. They don't need me anymore! And, I'm tired of babysitting. — Everything is fine the way it is right now, Dad!"

"Well, I don't know. Obviously, it's your life, but that you had to go to Greece, of all places! I mean, what's being reported in the news and what I read in the newspaper doesn't sound all that good. That country has no perspective. — But I don't want to talk politics with you! By the way, Ms. Becker, our cleaning lady, complained to me. She says that ever since you left she cannot get everything done in four hours a week. She said you maintained the house better than I do. — What do you think? Should I let her work two additional hours per week?"

"Yes, I think that's only fair."

"Well, if you say so. I can't judge stuff like that. — So, my child! It's fine that you want to stay in Greece a while longer, just make sure to say hello a bit more often. Take care of yourself, you hear!"

"Yes, Dad, I promise! Don't worry about me. Make sure you take care of yourself also, you hear. Hugs and kisses, Dad!"

"Hugs and kisses to you too, Ilona. Goodbye, my child!"

Although it is nice to hear the Jansen's want me back and would arrange for more vacation time, it would not be paid time off and I would not even dream of returning back to my old life. I know now there is no going back! And it does not matter that my father does not sympathize, he simply cannot.

I finish my coffee, don my sun hat, get up, and start walking in the merciless scorching sun while window-shopping along Metaxa Street. The wind blowing inland is hot and even though the temperature is anything but bearable, I cannot help but be incredibly happy. – I am checking out boutiques and looking at the pretty dresses on display until it is time for my appointment with Maria. While she is busy with my toenails, I receive a text message from Bruce in Vouliagmeni:

Hello, Anika, can you come to my place tomorrow at 5:00 p.m.? Greetings, Bruce.

I type:

Hi, Bruce. You bet! See you tomorrow!

Bruce replies:

Can you please bring clothing reminiscent of a schoolgirl uniform? — Perhaps you have white socks, that would be great.

I type back:

Yes, I'll put something together!

Perfect! Bruce replies and I say goodbye, typing:

See you tomorrow, Bruce. Kisses!

Yet Bruce sends another text:

Kisses! and our texting is over.

After Maria is finished and I have beautiful red feet and fingernails, I ask if she knows a store in Glyfada that sells socks. Frowning, perhaps because it is the wrong time of year to ask for socks, she replies after brief consideration:

"There's a shop that sells seasonal clothes. They sell socks during autumn and winter. Perhaps you can try them. Otherwise, I can't think of anyone selling socks this time of year."

She jots down the business name, hands it to me, and gives me directions. It is not far away and worth checking out.

On the way there, I inspect each fashion boutique I encounter. I am not doing this only because of my penchant for beautiful clothes, no; it also provides me with an opportunity to cool down. This is the only way I can stroll down Metaxa Street during a heat wave. When I find Maria's recommended store and ask the sales clerk for white socks that go above the knee, she gives me a funny look.

"No, at the moment, we don't have such items," is her verbatim response.

After thanking her, I think about how else I can fulfill Bruce's fervent wish. I cannot come up with anything. In my mind, I go through my wardrobe and select the items I am going to wear tomorrow in my role as Bruce's student. – I have a plain black mini skirt and a white blouse. I am sure Bruce has a black tie I can borrow for my performance. Maybe I can find something to substitute for the white over the knee socks.

In an accessory shop, I see a flat black and white peaked cap. I am sure this would be perfect for my role as a schoolgirl. Considering it is a business investment, I buy it. For some reason, I keep thinking about Richard, the former boxing champion. I hope to hear from him again. But as of today, he has not called. To continue using my time sensibly, I call the tanning studio in Piraeus to reserve a booth for 3:00 p.m. Then I head back to Glyfada town square to catch a bus to Piraeus. Nearing the bus stop, I see a fancy boutique that I must have overlooked when I came this way. Browsing through it, I come across a dress that would make another great business investment because it is plain cut with an unusual pattern. – At least that is what I tell my conscience, which does not bother me. Full of joy, I buy the sleeveless knee-length dress. The principal color is black, but large colorful jungle motifs are peppered throughout. – The variety of colors allows any number of shoes to go with the dress and I can grab whatever handbag of mine without selecting wrong.

I feel rather dazzled when I leave the boutique. I memorize the name and head straight for the bus stop to catch the next one to Piraeus.

Thankfully, on weekends, buses are not crowded and I have no problem getting a seat. At the Dimotiko Theatro town square, I get out and head for the tanning studio. My phone rings. I stop in a doorway and answer the call.

"Hello!"

"Hello! This is Mitso. Are you the German lady from *Athens World*?"

"Yes, that's me. Do you want more information about me and my services?"

"Yes, please. That would be nice."

I relay the relevant information Mitso needs to know. He asks: "And how does your schedule look? Do you have time today at 6:00 p.m. to come to Marousi? I can text you my address."

"Oh, Mitso, I'm sorry, but I can't make it at that time. I have an appointment at 7:00 p.m."

"Too bad, 6:00 p.m. is the only time that works for me. But I might call you again some other time. Adieu, Anika."

"Adieu, Mitso."

It happens. I save his cell phone number, place my phone in my handbag, and continue through the searing heat until I reach the tanning studio. After a short, intense artificial sunbathing session under the oh-so-hot fluorescent tubes, I am looking forward to my air-conditioned room. Now it is time to rest because before long it will be 5:00 p.m., at which time, at the latest, I have to get going again to arrive at Kolonaki town square on time to meet Natasha. As soon as I am in my room, my stomach grumbles. Looking inside the fridge, I see the selection is sparse. My choices are yogurt or a sandwich. Maybe I should visit a grocery store for proper grocery shopping instead of only looking in clothing and shoe stores... Grabbing two slices of toasted bread with cheese, I sit at my desk and boot up my laptop because I just remembered I promised to send Harrison an email. Before I can do that, I have to set-up a new account. – While eating, I write down all kinds of possible names for my business email address on a piece of paper. Afterward, I check online whether any are already taken and then I have my new email account and name — *Anika.Nissandra*. The name points to me but not to the industry I work in. Taking Harrison's business card from the little box I keep for such items, I start composing the email by writing in the subject line, *June*.

Thank you for your information! I will contact you again. Warm greetings, A. Nissandra.

Now I do not care who might read this email. It is definitely uncontroversial. For some reason, time flies by today. I meant to write Lisa and other good friends of mine a detailed email about my stay here in Athens. But now that I am pressed for time and unable to con-centrate, it will have to wait until tomorrow.

I add my last three appointments to my business Excel file and tally up my new earnings. I am at 5490 euros. Fantastic! Obviously, I do not have the entire sum of cash on hand in the safe. Some has been used for my hotel room, taxis, food and drinks, dresses, bikinis, hats, and bags. Regardless, I have made great money. I have never made that much in only a month. After powering down my notebook, I lie down for 15 minutes and read the news online. Once the time is up, I go into the bathroom and get ready for my appointment with Andreas. Obviously, I am going to wear my new dress!

65

Around 6:30 p.m., I arrive at Kolonaki town square in central Athens. Standing next to a periptero with a view of the café Natasha and I agreed to meet at, I search for her. A taxi pulls up. Natasha gets out and looks around. Once we make eye contact, I walk over to her.

"Hello, Natasha!"

"Anika-mou! You're already here. Have you been waiting long? I would have been here 10 minutes ago if it hadn't been for the heavy traffic on Vouliagmeni Avenue. But, we still have plenty of time. Andreas' apartment isn't far from here, only a few minutes' walk. Why don't we sit down and order a drink?"

"Yes, that's sounds good. What would you like?"

"I'll have a frappè with sugar and milk. Come on let's take this table. That's a fancy dress you're wearing. Andreas will like it. He has good taste."

Natasha tries her best to speak passable English. Once the waiter walks up to our table, Natasha orders a frappè and a Coke Zero for me. I read online that Coke Zero also has no calories. That is important to me. In addition to her three-quarter length jeans, Natasha is wearing a pink T-shirt bearing the logo *I love Greece* and colorful high heel sandals. Together with her baseball cap, she once again looks like a casually dressed tourist. When our drinks arrive, we toast each other. Natasha opens her purse and removes a paper bag.

"Look what I bought earlier. In case we need a toy for Andreas."

The bag holds a medium-size flexible silicone dildo. I smile and say:

"It's just the right size. Perfect! I also brought a small vibrator along for us to use, but I prefer your fancy dildo. — How is Andreas? What's he like? Can you tell me something about him? I'm a little nervous, you know."

"Babitschka, you don't have to worry. Andreas is quite normal. I've known him for more than two years. He's smart, always treats me nicely, and pays well, at least 100. I see him about once a month. He's my best customer! I'm sure you'll like him."

"Okay. — I'm not used to seeing a customer at his home when I've had no prior contact with him."

"You simply have to get used to it," Natasha replies as if there's nothing to it. She glances at her watch.

"If you like, we can stroll slowly in his direction. Andreas will already be there."

I pay for the drinks and Natasha thanks me. We start walking around a few street corners and continue along a busy, two-lane street where the sidewalks are protected from drivers parking their cars by metal posts set in the ground every few meters. I like that. – Greeks have no qualms about using sidewalks as parking spots for their cars or scooters. As a pedestrian, you are repeatedly forced to step onto the road to pass the parked vehicle. That is dangerous! On Salamas Street we approach an intersection,

Natasha stops in front of an old but newly renovated house located on the corner and says:

"Here we are. He lives on the fifth floor. He owns the whole house, but he only inhabits the upper floor."

She rings his bell. I have a hard time keeping my eyes off the nameplate. A minute later, Andreas' voice comes through the intercom:

"Come on up you two beauties!"

"You see, he can see us. He has a monitor next to his apartment door and he can see who's ringing his bell. Come on, let's take the elevator."

Checking myself out on the ride up in the elevator's mirror, I do not see how I could improve my appearance. Still, I am nervous and my heart beats faster than usual because once again I am apprehensive. Natasha winks at me, takes off her baseball cap, and shakes out her long hair. She seems completely relaxed and cheerful. She opens the elevator door and there is a short corridor with only one door at the end. The door is open and Andreas is standing in the doorway with a cell phone to his ear while holding a cigarette in the other hand. Gesturing to us to enter, we walk as quietly as possible so as not to disturb his conversation.

"Hello, my pretties!" he welcomes us and then kisses Natasha on the mouth while giving her butt a friendly slap.

"So, this is your German friend. What's your name, sweetie?"

"My name is Anika," I answer rather tensely.

"It's nice to meet you, Anika. I'm Andreas. — Natasha says you're German?"

He speaks the last sentence in proper German, so I answer in my mother tongue:

"Correct. — Your German is very good!"

"Thank you. My father always said I was a child with a knack for languages. Besides Greek, I also speak Spanish, English, French, and German fluently. — Unfortunately, I cannot speak to our little Russian girl in her native tongue. I've never bothered to learn that language and now I don't have time. Pity, I actually like Russian and it would come in handy at work. But, like I said, I lack the time. — Anyway, come on, let's go into the bedroom and get comfortable. By the way, you look ravishing, Anika! — Don't be afraid of me, I won't bite! Unless you want me to," he says jokingly and chuckles.

I am sure he can see how tense I am. I wish I could do something to loosen up. Maybe I will relax once I know how much I will be paid. Taking a deep breath, I ask:

"Andreas! Has Natasha mentioned my fee? I usually charge 150 for an hour of safe sex. Is that okay with you?"

"I don't believe it! Are you worrying about money? Believe me, if I had a problem with it I wouldn't have told Natasha to bring you along. — You really are a typical German. — Just relax and join us in having a little fun. I do hope you are able to relax now," Andreas says, and slightly shakes his head while smiling. As if on autopilot, I follow them into his bedchamber. As it slowly sinks in that he has no objections to my regular fee, I finally start to relax. That is all I wanted to know. I remember now that Natasha could not have understood us because we spoke in German. However, it is not like she cares, she is already busy undressing. — I tell myself to snap out of it and to get to work! — Fortunately, Natasha is in a great mood and says:

"Come on, Babitschka, I'm going to show you where the bathroom is. I want to take a quick shower, how about you?"

"I'm coming," I say, glad to have a few more minutes to compose myself. Looking over at Andreas who is standing there in his elegant housecoat, I walk toward him and give him a peck on the cheek and say:

"See you in a bit, darling. Please forgive my initial uncertainty. It had nothing to do with you. I'm sure we'll have lots of fun."

Andreas grabs me by the waist, pulls me close and says:
"I certainly hope so, my sweet! I like what I see. - Especially that you're not a youngster. I like real women. - You're an age I find utterly intriguing. — So, go to the bathroom, I'll be here waiting for you."

I am happy I managed to speak a few sentences while at ease. I follow the cheerful Natasha into a bathroom that takes my breath away.

"Incredible, isn't it? It's the biggest and most beautiful bathroom I've ever seen! Look at the illuminated pool and adjacent Jacuzzi. It easily accommodates six people. Andreas told me he plays with his dog in the water every now and then. Can you imagine? Look at these steps, built especially so the dog can go in and out easily. Andreas is crazy about his dog. Maybe you'll get to see it later. Right now, since we're here, the butler is walking it. I believe once we're gone, Andreas calls his butler to tell him he can come back. Look at the shower! You wouldn't believe all the features it has. Andreas showed them to me once, but I cannot remember all the settings..."

Natasha keeps on babbling while I marvel at the all-inclusive bathroom with its built-in swimming pool, Jacuzzi, sauna, and massage shower. It is incredibly luxurious and quite tasteful. Even I have never laid eyes on a place like this. A lot of natural stone was used for the walls and floor. The illuminated large tropical plants can make you forget you are in a house in the middle of Athens. Behind a partition partially made of rough natural stones that conforms to the oval swimming pool, are the toilet, a bidet, and a hand basin. I discard my bag on a bench below a huge tinted mirror and change into my work togs. For Andreas, I brought along my pink lace bodysuit with the low-cut décolleté, which I last wore when I was together with David. I looked damn sexy in it. Once Natasha finishes showering and toweling off, she puts on her skimpy black thong again.

"Babitschka! You look hot in pink! That outfit is perfect on you. So, what do you think of Andreas? He's nice, isn't he?"

"Yes, he seems to be."

"And he's good looking, right?"

"Yes he is. He really is."

"He has to look good, be charming, and smell good because he's into politics. He has class as they say. — Are you ready?"

"Yes, we can go. I'm going to take my stuff along and set it next to your clothes, okay?"

"Yes, that's fine."

Andreas stands in a doorway that leads from the bedroom to another room. He turns toward us when he hears us.

"Hey, Anika. Looking at your magnificent outfit, I'm scared to touch you. Even your shoes match. Unbelievable!"

"Don't worry, you may touch me wherever you want," I say and with my self-confidence back on track, I approach Andreas and sling my arms around his neck for an embrace. Andreas is around 50, slim, and a bit taller than I am in my high heels. He has curly brown hair, brown eyes, and he keeps himself clean-shaven. Placing his arms around me, he pulls me in for a kiss. Without asking permission, he sticks his tongue in my mouth, but I do not object. Unlike Adonis or Journalist, Andreas is not into starting things off with a lesbian show. For a while, we stand there in front of his bed kissing. Natasha snuggles up close to Andreas' back and starts to moan, but what exactly she is doing I cannot tell because I keep my attention focused on Andreas. One hand grabs one of my breasts and starts caressing and kneading it before continuing further down between my legs. Sliding the instep of my bodysuit aside, one finger searches for the opening of my pussy. As he is taller than me, he has to squat a little in order to manage this, so I whisper in his ear:

"Why don't we go to bed? It would be much more comfortable for all of us."

I speak English so Natasha does not feel left out.

"You're right. Let's all get on the bed," Andreas replies in German.

When he lies down in the middle, I kneel on his right side. I do not have an actual plan, so I simply start by removing his underwear. That is when Natasha lies down between his legs and starts licking his balls. I also think it is best to start off our sex session with oral sex. As I am about to lean down to his genitals, Andreas grabs my upper arm and whispers in German:

"No, come here and lie down next to me. Natasha has it under control. I want you up here."

Addressing Natasha and saying something in Greek I do not understand, she answers him with "*Sigura, Agapi-mou*", which means *sure, my sweet*, and leans back down to take his medium-size cock back in her mouth. Lying next to him with my upper body supported on my elbows, Andreas whispers to me:

"Come, kiss me. I want to feel your tongue. I like kissing and you're a good kisser. I also want to talk German with you. I love the German language. It has certain clarity and it fits so well with your character."

To put an end to his talking, I lean over and cover his mouth with mine. For a while, we are busy smooching. In between, I manage to look at Natasha, who seems quite happy being in charge of Andreas' penis and balls. As soon as we take a break from kissing, Andreas immediately starts conversing in German:

"Tell me, where does a pretty little whore like you come from? I want to know everything about you. Where were you born?"

"I was born in Rhineland. What about you? Athens?"

"No, I was born in the Peloponnese region. Our neighbors were Germans. That was when I was first exposed to that foreign language. I was only four years old. Other than messing up men's heads with your beautiful body, what else do you do? Have you learned a trade? All you Germans usually do, that much I know. So, what's your trade?"

"I trained to be an office administrator and I've worked as a secretary."

"That's good. Whenever I fly to Berlin, I could use an experienced secretary. I'm in Berlin quite often. Would you like to accompany me to Berlin on Monday? We would stay at the Sofitel Hotel in downtown Berlin until Thursday. – The flight and hotel are on me. You are my guest. In the evenings, when you play my secretary, I'm going to give you good pocket money. I'd like having my own German secretary waiting for me in my bed at night! So, what do you say? Do you want to come?"

Still snuggled up next to him, I stroke his cheek and kiss his forehead. One of his hands is between my legs again fondling my pussy. He seems to get off on alternately kissing, petting, and talking. That is all that matters.

"Thank you for your offer, darling, but I won't be going with you to Berlin. I'm staying here in Athens. But if you want, we and Natasha can meet at any time. I like hearing you speak German."

Again, I cover his mouth with mine and we kiss. It seems Natasha is getting bored with whatever she is doing and asks:

"When are you going to fuck me, Andreas? My snatch is hot for your cock. Come on and fuck me, *Agapi-mou*!"

"Wait a little, Natasha. Don't be so rude. We have a visitor today. I'm taking care of her. I'll fuck you soon enough, don't worry."

It seems Natasha is already out of ideas, so it is up to me to determine the course of our threesome. Right now is as good a time as any. I suggest to Andreas:

"Darling, all this kissing and grabbing also got me hot for your rod. Come on, stick your cock in my pussy. I want to feel you inside me. I want to be fucked! — We can continue smooching and grabbing each other when Natasha gets her chance at your cock. Okay?"

"Your wish is my command. So, how you want me to take you?"

"I'll go down on all fours and you take me from behind. I love that."

"Okay, let's do it."

Addressing Natasha, he says in English:

"Natasha, let go of my dick. I'm going to fuck Anika first and then you can ride me. Come on, baby, let go of it already!"

Reaching for one of the condoms I placed on the nightstand next to a basket full of men's wristwatches, I roll it over his saliva-moistened penis. Although I do not know much about men's wristwatches, I did notice a Rolex and a watch completely made of gold. To expose my breasts, I roll the upper part of my bodysuit down to my midriff. On all fours, I make sure the instep of my bodysuit is pushed aside. Andreas is already kneeling behind me and I feel his dick enter me deeply. Natasha is now lying next to us.

She is pleasuring herself with her new toy while moaning loudly. She is faking masturbation and keeps stammering words in Greek, Russian, and English. Andreas does not take long to find his rhythm and is now smoothly thrusting into me while holding my hips for support. Natasha's right, he really is a nice customer. With him, I am actually able to relax and to let my mind and eyes wander around a little. So far, I have only seen his bedchamber and bathroom, but I can easily imagine the rest of the house is just as breathtaking. Getting a better look now, I see that Andreas had been standing in the doorway of a walk-in closet when Natasha and I returned from the bathroom. I notice now that Andreas must have switched off the light inside. To get my mind back on work, I softly moan and say:

"Damn, you feel so good, baby. I love the way you're fucking me. Don't stop!"

"Yes, my sweet little German. I hope I'm giving it to you good. After all, I want you to come visit me again and I don't only want you to look forward to the money."

"Come on, speed it up a bit, Andreas, and lightly spank my ass. That'll drive me insane!"

"As you wish, my little puttana! I want you to come!"

Now Andreas fucks me faster and starts groaning with each thrust. My moaning gets louder and I fake an orgasm for his pleasure.

"Oh, baby, that was great. – Now let me enjoy the last waves of ecstasy. My God, you were great, Andreas!" I say while repeatedly gasping for air.

"And now I'm hot, my ladies! Come on, Natasha, put that toy away! Now you may ride me as wildly as you want. — And Anika, come back in my arms like you were earlier," Andreas says excitedly in English so both of us can understand. Then he lies on his back.

Natasha immediately removes the used condom, tosses it on the ground, and rolls a new one over his boner. I shed my bodysuit and lie next to Andreas as I did earlier. Only when Natasha has his dick deep inside her pussy, do I look at him and whisper:

"You are a true gentleman, Andreas. I really appreciate it. Natasha certainly didn't exaggerate when she raved about you."

"What can I say, I adore women. I know they need to be treated well to have fun with them. Come on, kiss me!"

Again, I spoil him by French kissing him while Natasha does her best at riding his cock. This time, he is not in a talkative mood. When I hear him start to moan, I slide up so he can reach my breast with his mouth. Grabbing them and sucking on one nipple, he suddenly spasms, starts groaning and then ejaculates. And so, our performance comes to an end. – Natasha is waiting for Andreas to open his eyes again before climbing off him. I snuggle up against his side and run my fingers through his curly chest hair. Natasha's right again, he sure smells good.

"Come here, Natasha. Lie on my other side. I want to hold both of you for a few minutes. You girls are fantastic!"

For Natasha's sake, Andreas speaks English. She asks about his dog. I learn it is a giant black Schnauzer that Andreas always takes along every time he goes to visit his parents in the Peloponnese. The dog's name is Apollo.

After listening to Natasha for a few minutes talking about cars she is interested in and getting Andreas' opinion on them, I make eye contact with her and signal it is time to go.

"*Agapi-mou*, didn't I tell you Anika was a smart, sexy German?"

"Yes, you did and you were right, Natasha. I'm glad you brought her along."

"So, what do you say, did we do a good job and is it okay for us to leave?"

"Yes, of course. You girls wore me out. — So, if you like, off you go into the bathroom! I'll call you again for an appointment in the near future, okay?"

"Sure, *Agapi-mou*! — Come on, Anika, let's hop into that fancy shower. I know where the fresh towels are. I'll show you."

We rise out of his arms and Andreas reaches for a cigarette, looking quite emotionally. Once we are in the bathroom, Natasha shows me where the towels are and I grab a big fluffy soft terrycloth one. When we have both showered and stand in front of the big mirror putting on our makeup, Natasha winks at me and says:

"Did you hear, he wants to see us again! He's seen how smart you are. In our profession, being smart seems to be beneficial. I like working with you, Babitschka."

"I also enjoy working with you, Natasha. And thanks again for this job!"

When we walk back into the bedroom, Andreas has taken out his wallet.

"Natasha!" he says and hands her a wad of folded bills. Then he looks at me and says:

"Anika, here's your fee. I hope to see you again!"

"Of course. Thank you, darling, I would be happy to see you again."

Not bothering to count it, I simply stash the money in the side pocket of my handbag. Once we are dressed, Andreas accompanies us to the door in his bathrobe and we say goodbye. As soon as the elevator door closes, Natasha asks me:

"Did you count the money? I believe he gave me more today. Come on, let's each have a look!"

She is visibly excited. What do you know; Andreas gave us each 150!

"Look at this, Babitschka! I didn't even say anything and he just gave me what he gave you. You are my lucky charm!"

"That's great! See, Andreas is a gentleman; he knows proper etiquette. Now I find him even more likable. Thank you for introducing him to me, Natasha!"

Outside on the street, we briefly exchange kisses on each cheek, promise to stay in touch, and go our separate ways. Walking down the street, my stomach starts growling. I mean, really growling. Apparently, it is time for a proper meal! I continue through the narrow alleyways of Athens heading for the old town that, according to my map, is not far.

66

On the way to the Plaka, the old town, my phone rings and I simply answer without looking at the display. Since traffic is so loud that I can barely hear the caller, I ask if he can hold on a moment and seek shelter. Finding a deeply recessed doorway, I try again:

"Hello! I'm Anika. I'm sorry, but the street noise was too loud and I had to find a quiet spot. How can I help you?"

"Hello, Anika, that's not a problem! I know how loud Athens can get. By the way, I'm Arthur. Perhaps you remember me. I talked to you about two weeks ago. I was wondering if you have time this Monday during the afternoon?"

"Okay, so you know my conditions and I don't have to repeat them, right?"

"Correct. You asked if I was interested in something special and I said I love to kiss. You couldn't say yet whether you could blow me with or without a condom."

Somehow it rings familiar, but I still cannot recall our previous conversation exactly. Since I am wide open Monday afternoon, I reply:

"Yes, Monday afternoon works. What time do you have in mind? Am I coming to your home or am I meeting you at a hotel?"

"In a hotel in Piraeus. – It's called X-Dream Hotel. It's close to the port. Perhaps you know it?"

Now the name of the hotel immediately rings a bell. – It is the one where I went to see George. George, the man who ordered my dominatrix service.

"Yes, I know the hotel. At what time do you want to meet me?"

"At 2:00 p.m. That's when I'm on break. You know, I work in Piraeus and I would you like to eat you for lunch," Arthur says jokingly.

"That's fine! — Tell me, Arthur, what's your nationality? I can tell you're not Greek."

"I'm Norwegian. So, naturally, I'm into blondes. – You're a blonde with blue eyes, correct?"

"Yes, that's right."

"Great, both features are equally important to me. So, on Monday, how do we hook up? Should I rent a room at the X-Dream Hotel and text you the number?"

"Yes, that's best. If anything changes, please call and let me know."

"Of course I would. So, everything's set?"

"Yes."

"Okay, Anika, have a nice weekend!"

"Same to you. See you Monday!"

Arthur hangs up. That is when I notice I already saved his cell phone number under 'Arthur-kissing'. Pleased that I also have an appointment for the day after tomorrow, not only tomorrow, I continue at a fast pace through the old town. Eventually, my phone rings again. This time it is Violet. In the narrow streets of the Plaka where the noise level is not so high, I immediately answer:

"Hi, Violet! I'm walking through the city center, looking for a restaurant. I'll call you back as soon as I've found a place to sit comfortably, okay?"

"Yes, of course! But preferably before 9:00 p.m. That's when I have to get going to the Metropolitan Hotel. I received a call from an Italian. He's a new guy. His name is Giovanni. I'm meeting him at 9:30 p.m. I've already ordered a taxi to pick me up. Okay, darling, talk to you soon!"

"Until then, Violet!"

As I pass the first restaurants, I check out their menus, which are displayed on what looks like easels. I am in the mood for greens. As all the establishments pretty much have the same selection of dishes, I grab a table at the next place with a nice view of the Acropolis. Looking at my watch, I see I have 10 minutes left to talk to Violet. Dialing her number, I say:

"Hi, Violet, it's Anika. I'm sorry it took so long!"

"That's okay, darling! Sometimes time just gets away from us and suddenly the day is over. Then there are days where time seems to stand still and we sit there twiddling our thumbs waiting because the phone doesn't ring and we have no clients... Anyone who thinks we make our money lying down has no idea what our job entails. — Listen, I've made an appointment with Eleni for a Botox treatment. I have to be there Monday at 11:00 a.m. Do you want to come with me?"

"Unfortunately, I can't, Violet, I have an appointment in Piraeus at 2:00 p.m. It's too stressful to ride down to Vouliagmeni and then to come rushing back to Piraeus. — I'm sure you will do fine without me. Remember, all she's doing is pricking you with a needle. That's it. It'll help you. Also, remember the pain is gone as soon as Eleni pulls out the syringe. A week later, you won't find any wrinkles on your forehead!"

"Yes, I'm looking forward to that! You definitely look fantastic. — So, who are you seeing Monday? Is it someone you know?"

"No, his name is Arthur. He's Norwegian and works in Piraeus."

"Oh my God, Arthur? — I know Arthur, darling... He has a terrible dick. I call it a curved righty. I know he pays 150, but you sure as hell are going to earn it. You'll be exhausted when he's done with you. He's a stallion and it takes him forever to come with a condom on his cock. Nevertheless, he knows he has to wear one. Just be careful. The extreme curvature of his wiener is rough on a rubber and tears it easily. Oh, darling, I don't envy you getting Arthur's business! I had to see him quite often at the X-Dream Hotel in Piraeus. He could have come to my home, I was fine with it, you know. He always wears suits and makes a neat impression. However, he didn't want to. He said Glyfada is too far away for him. One day he asked if I had a girlfriend I could bring along, but of course, at that time I didn't have one. Yeah and then his calls became fewer and fewer until eventually, I didn't hear from him at all. But I expected it when he asked me to bring a friend. Nothing to be sad about, it's business. As I said, his righty is terribly unpleasant. A banana doesn't compare to it!"

"Thanks for the heads up. I've never had a righty. Then again, I've never had a lefty either. So far, I've only heard about them. I guess I'm not going to be spared this experience after all... I will manage his crooked boner somehow. He says he likes to kiss and, if possible, he wants a blowjob without condom. What do you say?"

"You can do without a rubber during oral sex, no problem. At least I thought he was healthy and careful. He's married to a Greek woman and married people usually pay more attention to their health than single people. As far as I know, he doesn't constantly switch playmates. I'm sure he got tired of his girl and saw your ad in *Athens World*. Depending on how you see it, luck or damnation, you might end up seeing him for a while. — Darling, I have to go. My other phone is ringing. The cab is waiting outside my door. Take care! Kisses, darling!"

"Kisses, Violet. Talk to you tomorrow."

As the waiter has already served my salad with chicken breast, I quickly put my phone away and dig in while sipping white wine between bites. Although I am enjoying my dinner, Violet's account of Arthur's righty makes me pensive. What is the best way to deal with such a banana? Unfortunately, it is not like I can do anything about it, be it while fucking or giving a blowjob. I guess it is best to give him a nice oily hand massage. However, that is probably what his wife prefers, which is why Arthur will not be into it... He is into kissing, so at least for a bit, I will know what to do. Somehow, I will manage his thing! After I have finished my meal, I feel completely at ease. Since it is still early evening, I decide to stroll along the illuminated footpath of the Acropolis. Now, I am familiar with the area and whenever I want, I know where to go to catch a taxi. After about an hour, I have gone as far as the path will take me. I have had a long day, made 300 euros, and bought a nice dress. So, what else can I expect from an already good day? On the northern slope of the great rock on which the Acropolis is enthroned, small houses sit at odd angles next to and above each other. In between, a type of labyrinth-like staircases and alleys lead all the way to the Plaka.

While walking along these passages locals and tourists have been walking on for centuries, I stop at one of the many bars to celebrate my free time with another glass of white wine. Before midnight, I walk to the Acropolis Station and take the subway to Piraeus. After walking the final few steps to my hotel and up four floors, I fall exhausted into bed.

Last Chapter

The next morning, after I have enjoyed my breakfast, I boot up my laptop to check if I have received any emails. After Lisa's last text message, I receive an email from another friend, Carina, asking me to let her know how I am doing. Yes, it is about time to tell my friends about my time in Athens. They should not think just because they are out of sight they are out of my mind. Because that is not really true! It is simply that I am sick to my stomach about having to come up with another story, at having to lie again. It is not like I have another choice. These lies have been part of my life since the age of 26. During the first years, it was easier because I was not actually lying; I was merely withholding information about myself and not making up an entirely new life. When Manfred was away on weekday business trips, two nights during those trips I worked as a bar girl in a nightclub. It was not exactly my thing because drinking alcohol was required. That is why I did not stay there long and instead started working as a prostitute at a so-called nudist club. When Manfred was home on weekends or we were together with friends or relatives, the question of how I spent my evenings never came up. Everyone assumed I kept busy doing housework or watching television.

After my divorce from Manfred, when I moved back into my father's house, that is when withholding information turned into lying. So, I made up the story about babysitting for a wealthy business family in town. To this day, my father and all of my friends still think it is true.

Now I have to come up with another story that sounds believable. — I am really having a hard time with it! — Coming up with a story is not the issue, my issue is with having to be deceitful to the people I hold close to my heart and who I trust and who trust me — and who I call my friends... Gazing at my keyboard, I dream about how nice it would be if I did not have to lie and the others would regard my profession as a prostitute like any other job. Then I would come home from my part-time office job in the afternoon with Chinese take-out food and my father would be waiting at the set table and eventually inquire:

"So, tell me, how was it at the club last night? Did it go until the wee morning hours? I didn't hear you come home."

"I'd say; it went well. I had three customers, so I made 90 euros. I knew two of them. They came after work as usual. The third one was a new customer. He came in around 11:00 p.m. He was from Belgium. Everything was fine. I left the club around 1:00 a.m., and 20 minutes later, I walked in the door here at home. — Anyway, let's eat, Dad, and enjoy the meal!"

"Thanks, same to you! How was the office this morning, everything okay there too?"

"Yep, just a normal day. — How was your morning?"

"I kept busy gardening. At 11:00 a.m. I took a break and had a drink. Once we finish our meal, I'm taking a nap. – Tonight, I'm going to Jakob's Bar to watch the soccer game."

"Okay. — I guess the club will be empty tonight considering a soccer game is on. Maybe they'll let me take the night off and I can get together with Lisa... Let me call them!"

Yes, I can imagine having a conversation like that with my father. And if I were to have a girls' night out with Lisa at our favorite bar, sitting there dolled-up sipping Prosecco, the conversation might go as follows:

"How was your day at the store, Lisa?"

"It was okay. The new fall merchandise came in. There are some nice pieces of clothing. By the way, the cozy cashmere sweaters in different colors would go well with your leather pants. You really should come see us again! We might be a bit more expensive than your favorite clothing stores in the big city — but our beautiful pieces are one of a kind and not comparable to the line of manufactured fashion items you're so fond of!"

"Yes, I know, you keep telling me! I promise, the next time I'm in town during the day I will come see you at the store. Count on it! I really could do with one or two pretty sweaters that'll go with my leather pants for wintertime. And I love cashmere."

"And, how was it at the office and the club?"

"It was a usual day at the office: writing invoices, making blueprints, photocopies, brewing coffee, answering the phone, etc... — At the club, I met a male virgin. — Can you believe a dad brought his son? The boy had not yet experienced a woman and the father thought it was about time. From the five girls he could choose from, the boy picked me. Granted, it's not the first time I had relations with such a young man, a virgin, if you will, but at least the previous ones came on their own or with a buddy. They weren't coerced into it by their father! I found it strange. The boy hardly opened his mouth in his father's presence. When we were in the room, I was about to introduce him to sexual intercourse, but it turned out the boy knew more than his father thought. I started blowing him and he almost came prematurely. I had to take it down a notch and proceed more carefully. We were in the missionary position when he came and his head was so red I thought it might burst. Once the deed was done, the boy lost his inhibition and started talking to me. – He didn't care for his meddlesome father's intent to hire a hooker for him for an hour, but he didn't know how to refuse without angering his father. His father is apparently one of those guys who likes hanging out in bars, drinking, and bragging. And the boy was worried that soon all his drinking buddies will know how he lost his virginity. — Once it was finished and father and son left, Betty, my colleague, told me that as soon as the boy and I disappeared into the room, the father picked her for himself. She said the old man fucked her like a hungry wolf. Betty believed he was merely using the boy as an excuse to come to the club in order to get his own freak on. In any case, the father had to hurry in order to be done before his son, so he wouldn't be the wiser. — I tell you, there are all types of guys!"

"Bullcrap! The father didn't use the boy as an excuse. He simply got horny as soon as he saw you sexy ladies. That's when it occurred to him to satisfy his own needs!"

"Yes, that makes sense."

Yeah, that could have been a chat with Lisa. I sigh. Everything could be so beautiful! — Also, with my other friends, the old clique from the equestrian club, I imagine having a relaxed conversation in which my work is socially acceptable. For example, at the barbecue Rolf and Carina give for their friends. That is where the following could take place: Jasmine tells us anecdotes about the elementary school where she teaches first graders. It is always funny to hear what the little ones all come up with and it has become part of our regular entertainment at get-togethers. We cannot help burst out laughing when Jasmine shows us the jumping-dachshund-dance she taught her students last week. Each of us tells a story out of their personal life or work. Trivial things that happen in everyday life and which make us chuckle.

Or, perhaps, we talk about experiences we have learned from doing the wrong things because that is also part of our lives. Harry might ask me:

"So, how have you been doing lately? – Did anything out of the ordinary happen with a customer? Did you make good money?"

"Yeah, I made good money. — And I had a customer who's into certain role-playing games. He wanted to be a prisoner so I played his prison guard. – Unfortunately, all I could find in the club was a policewoman's uniform to slip on. We really have to get a better selection of costumes. — Speaking of, since you work for the correctional institution, don't you have an old uniform shirt for me, one with those epaulettes and state insignia on the sleeves and chest? — It would come in really handy! Maybe you also have an official tie and cap, something authentic. I could wear a belt over the shirt and bunch it up at the waist, together with thigh-high leather boots. I think it would make me look strict and sexy at the same time. What do you think?"

"Well, Ilona, you'd swim in my service shirt! Also, I don't think it's such a good idea for me to give you part of the original correctional state uniform. It might get me in trouble!"

"Wear a regular blue shirt, find a bunch of old keys, and put them on a large metal ring attached to your belt. You should also wear leather gloves. I think leather gloves are a must!" Carina might throw into the conversation...

As I sit here daydreaming, I am becoming aware of the fact that it would only take one small step to make it a reality. All it would take is for me to be courageous enough to come out and tell the truth. Well, at least with my friends. – They are open-minded tolerant people. I can easily imagine their utterly amazed faces if they heard about my second career as a prostitute — I do not think they would condemn it or end our friendship. As far as my father is concerned, he is a different story. I do not think he would look at me the same way if he knew I am a prostitute. I might as well look at it objectively!

Getting up, I make myself a cup of coffee and go out onto the balcony. My next appointment is not until 5:00 p.m., when I will meet Bruce in Vouliagmeni. — It is only 12:30 p.m., giving me plenty of time to get my correspondence out of the way. The decision is made! Grabbing my coffee, I sit back down at my laptop and open my email account. I am going to send a general email to all five of my friends and write in the subject line, *Life in Athens.* Taking a deep breath, I start typing:

Hello my friends,

I'm finally taking the time to write you about my time in Athens and to tell you how I'm doing. I've already written you, Lisa, and told you I've found a job in a bar and that I'm living in a residential community...
What I'm going to write next is one of the hardest things I've had to do, but I believe the time has come to reveal what I've been keeping secret from you all. We've known each other for almost half our lives. We've always been there for each other. Friendship is what unites us. I'm hoping our friendship is strong enough to survive what I'm confessing now: Lisa, I lied to you. I'm not working in a bar and I'm not sharing an apartment with two other women. Here's the truth:
I came to Athens to establish myself as a self-employed call girl.
I'm renting a room in a small hotel and I have placed an ad in a Greek weekly newspaper. It states I'm an attractive, charming German lady who is interested in meeting generous gentlemen. — The meaning behind it is clear: I make home and hotel visits — selling sex.
Perhaps you're wondering what made me do this. Well, here it goes: You don't know this, but I've been a part-time prostitute since I was 26. When I was married to Manfred, I secretly went to local clubs to earn extra pocket money. After our divorce, I was never a babysitter for a wealthy family in the city. — No, in the evenings, I worked as a prostitute in one club or another. Moving here hasn't changed me. I am the way you've known me for over 20 years.
Let me tell you my reasons for coming here to Athens to try to start another life. First, ever since my teenage years, I have been dreaming

about living by the sea and in a warm climate. Second, I'm making more money here working as a self-employed call girl than I was making in Germany working two part-time jobs. Third, which is most important, I was sick and tired of always having to hide my work!

Here in Athens, nobody knows me. Here, I don't have to watch what I say, nor do I have to watch what I'm wearing. Here, I'm not constantly reminded that I'm a liar! Lying doesn't come easily to me. In all these years, I've never gotten used to it, even though lying about my secret work as a prostitute comes easily to me now. That's only because I've rehearsed them over and over so I'll never slip-up.

Having to lie about something I like to do is weighing heavily on me.

Lying to the people you love the most is anything but nice, believe me, it eats you up... That's why I'm telling you the truth about me now.

Right now, I don't really know what else to say other than I'm hoping this will not affect our friendships, even if you're disappointed in me now for lying to you for all these years. Maybe I needed this time and this distance between us to muster up the courage to come clean and to let you into my whole life.

Take your time, but please send me a reply!

Sincerely, as always, your Ilona

Having finished writing my confession, I feel exposed and vulnerable. Relief should not feel this way. Something is not right. If only I knew what. I still have a lump in my throat. Rereading the entire email, I think, yes, that is it. I could tell my friends in this way and I am certain they would show understanding. Maybe they would say:

We understand you couldn't come clean 10 years ago. Friendship and trust take time to develop. Our mutual trust has a history.

As I read the email over and over again, something dawns on me; I am not feeling relief because there is one thing I cannot foresee. – Granted, I can see myself confessing to my friends about my real life, but can they keep it to themselves or will they unwittingly divulge my secret? If that is the case, and even though I do not know these other people or care for them, I would not like being despised, discriminated, ostracized, and insulted by them! That is inevitable! In essence, I would have to ask my friends to handle my confession confidentially. Basically, make them complicit by telling them about my real life. That would be unfair. It is better to continue lying and keep them in the dark... As long as prostitution is not fully socially accepted, I cannot tell anyone the truth of my real profession for they might suffer repercussions! — Melancholic, I delete my confession email and compose a new one:

Hello my friends,

As you might have heard from Lisa, I'm doing well. It didn't take me a week before I found a job as counter help at a tourist bar in the middle of the old town in Athens. My German, English, Dutch, and the few words of French I know come in handy. I'm practicing my Greek daily. Now that it's high season, I'm working 10-hour shifts. Pay and tips together amount to more money than I made in Germany working two jobs as a secretary and babysitter.

My shift starts at 2:00 p.m. and usually goes until around midnight. Often, I go for a one or two-hour stroll through the old town after work. Thursday or Sunday is my day off. I'm enjoying playing tourist and going to the beach.

Come mid-September, I'm going to start working full-time at an English pub located in a southern district of Athens. The owner of the pub, obviously an Englishman, is a friend of my current boss. For now, I'm sharing an apartment with two other women in the inner city. In mid-September, when I switch jobs, I'm going to rent a room or small apartment in Glyfada or in the nearby surrounding area. Come the beginning of that month, I'm planning on coming to Germany for two weeks to pack up my car with fall and winter clothes and then I'm going to drive back to Athens. I'm looking forward to seeing you all!

Until then, I'm going to continue enjoying my free mornings sitting on the balcony dressed in only a bikini and marveling at the view over the rooftops of the Plaka toward the Acropolis. I love knowing the sun is out every day and the evenings are warm. Everyone has a relaxed attitude, the Greeks, my colleagues, and guests... I feel charged with energy. Life is good to me and I'm enjoying it!

Yes, of course, I miss you all, but then I'm still on the planet. Once I'm all settled, you all should come and vacation here with me in Athens. Or perhaps we will all go and stay on any one of the beautiful Greek Islands. Please write to me! I want to know what's going on in your lives. Are you still getting together for barbecues? Who's burning the sausages this time? I promise I'll write more often!

I might be far away, but you're always close to my heart,
Hugs and kisses,
Ilona

I click on *attachments* and upload three nice photos I keep on my laptop. One is of Roger, the American man who put his arm around my shoulder. Another is of the Plaka with a view of the Acropolis and one is a selfie I took at the beach with the sea in the background. As I calmly and carefully read this email again, I am quite certain I came to the right decision. – Moving the mouse over the *Send* button, I click it.

Okay, that is over with... Now for the continuation of my life as an independent call girl in Athens!

An hour later, I stand on the street outside my hotel and hail a taxi for the trip to Vouliagmeni for my next appointment with Bruce.

Note of thanks

I'm thanking my husband for always being there for me with advice and deeds, as well as criticism and praise. Thank you, darling!
And special thanks to my dear friend Gaby! She always looked out for me and constantly motivated me. She was my reader, critic, and editor. — Her excellent German and English language skills were indispensable when it came to the translation! — Thank you, Gaby!
Holger (Holli) Flock and his wife Lori translated the German text into English. Holli quickly worked himself into the spicy novel and managed to interpret my narrative style very well into English.
Working with them was easy and fun! Thanks, Lori and Holli!

About the author

Maria van Daarten was born and grew up in the Rhineland/Germany. For many years she has travelled through Southern Europe. She took on a variety of jobs in order to support herself and a lifestyle that gave her plenty of free time.
Today she is married and lives in Berlin. However, she continues to spend a large part of every year in Southern Europe enjoying the sunny climate.